READER'S DIGEST CONDENSED BOOKS

Gladiolus
by Charlene Tarbox

READER'S DIGEST® CONDENSED BOOKS

Volume 3
1986

THE READER'S DIGEST ASSOCIATION
Pleasantville, New York

READER'S DIGEST CONDENSED BOOKS
Editor-in-Chief: John S. Zinsser, Jr.
Executive Editor: Barbara J. Morgan
Managing Editors: Anne H. Atwater, Ann Berryman, Tanis H. Erdmann,
Thomas Froncek, Marjorie Palmer
Senior Staff Editors: Jean E. Aptakin, Virginia Rice (Rights), Ray Sipherd, Angela Weldon
Senior Editors: M. Tracy Brigden, Linn Carl, Margery D. Thorndike
Associate Editors: Thomas S. Clemmons, Alice Jones-Miller,
Joseph P. McGrath, Maureen A. Mackey, James J. Menick
Senior Copy Editors: Claire A. Bedolis, Jeane Garment
Associate Copy Editors: Maxine Bartow, Rosalind H. Campbell, Jean G. Cornell,
Jean S. Friedman, Jane F. Neighbors
Assistant Copy Editors: Ainslie Gilligan, Jeanette Gingold
Art Director: William Gregory
Executive Art Editors: Soren Noring, Angelo Perrone
Associate Art Editors, Research: George Calas, Jr., Katherine Kelleher

CB PROJECTS
Executive Editor: Herbert H. Lieberman
Senior Editors: Catherine T. Brown, John R. Roberson
Associate Editor: Dana Adkins

CB INTERNATIONAL EDITIONS
Executive Editor: Francis Schell
Senior Staff Editor: Sigrid MacRae
Senior Editor: Istar H. Dole
Associate Editor: Gary Q. Arpin

Reader's Digest Condensed Books are published every two to three months at Pleasantville, N.Y.

CONTENTS

7

LIE DOWN WITH LIONS
by Ken Follett
PUBLISHED BY WILLIAM MORROW & COMPANY

177

TREE OF GOLD
by Rosalind Laker
PUBLISHED BY DOUBLEDAY & COMPANY

343

THE DEEP END
by Joy Fielding
PUBLISHED BY DOUBLEDAY & COMPANY

495

CRY WILD
by R. D. Lawrence
PUBLISHED BY SOUVENIR PRESS

LIE DOWN WITH LIONS

A condensation of the novel by

Ken Follett

Illustrated by John Raynes

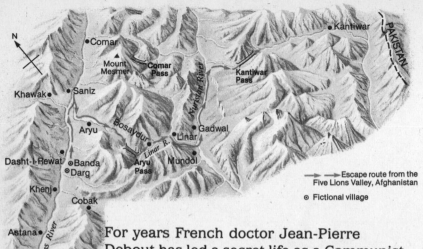

N

● Kantiwar

PAKISTAN

● Comar

Mount
Mesmer

Comar
Pass

Kantiwar
Pass

Kurstan River

Khawak ● ● Saniz

Bosaydur

Aryu

Linar R.

● Gadwal

● Linar

Dasht-i-Rewat

◎ Banda
◎ Darg

Aryu
Pass

Mundol

➤ ➤ Escape route from the
Five Lions Valley, Afghanistan

Khenj ●

Cobak

◎ Fictional village

Astana ●

Five Lions River

Rokha

0   5   10
▮▮▮▮▮▮▮
Miles

For years French doctor Jean-Pierre
Debout has led a secret life as a Communist,
patiently waiting for a chance to serve
the cause. Now, at last, that chance
has come. His Russian masters have sent
him on a spying mission deep into
war-torn Afghanistan, to Banda, a remote
village in the Five Lions Valley.

Everything seems perfect until
events in the tiny village take a very
unexpected turn. Ellis Thaler, an old rival of
Jean-Pierre's, turns up on an important
mission of his own, and the two men find
themselves pitted against one another
as never before. Both of them are in love with
the same woman; both of them have crucial,
but conflicting, tasks to carry out—and
only one of them can succeed.

Intrigue, romance, and heart-stopping
suspense in the best Ken Follett tradition.

PART ONE: 1981

CHAPTER 1

THE men who wanted to kill Ahmet Yilmaz were serious people. They were exiled Turkish students living in Paris, and they had already murdered an attaché at the Turkish embassy and fire-bombed the home of a senior executive of Turkish Airlines. They chose Yilmaz as their next target because he was a wealthy supporter of the military dictatorship and because he lived, conveniently, in Paris.

His home and office were well guarded and his Mercedes limousine was armored, but every man has a weakness. Yilmaz would leave his house two or three evenings each week, driving a Renault station wagon, and go to a side street in the 15th district to visit a beautiful young Turkish woman who was in love with him. The students decided to put a bomb in the Renault while Yilmaz was at her apartment.

They knew where to get the explosives: from Pepe Gozzi, one of the many sons of the Corsican godfather Mémé Gozzi. Pepe was a weapons dealer. He would sell to anyone and had helped the Turkish students with their previous outrages. But there was a snag in the car-bomb plan. Usually Yilmaz would leave the girl's place alone in the Renault—but not always. Sometimes he took her out to dinner. Occasionally he would go home in a taxi, and the girl would borrow the car for a day or two. The students were romantic, like all terrorists, and they were reluctant to risk

9

killing a beautiful woman whose only crime was the readily pardonable one of loving a man unworthy of her.

They discussed this problem. Rahmi Coskun, a handsome, passionate young man with a bushy mustache, proposed consulting a bomb expert. He suggested Ellis Thaler. An American who called himself a poet but in fact made a living giving English lessons, Thaler had learned about explosives as a conscript in Vietnam. Rahmi had known him for a year or so. They had both worked on a short-lived revolutionary newspaper called *Chaos*, and Ellis seemed to understand Rahmi's rage at what the barbarians were doing to Turkey. The other students were reluctant to bring in a non-Turk, but Rahmi was insistent, and in the end they consented.

Ellis came up with the solution to their problem immediately. The bomb would have a radio-controlled arming device. Rahmi would sit at a window opposite the girl's apartment, watching the Renault. In his hand he would have a small radio transmitter the size of a pack of cigarettes. If Yilmaz got into the car alone, Rahmi would press the button on the transmitter, and a radio signal would activate a switch in the bomb, which would then explode as soon as Yilmaz started the engine. But if it should be the girl who got into the car, Rahmi would not press the button, and she could drive away in blissful ignorance. "No button, no bang," said Ellis.

Rahmi liked the idea and asked Ellis if he would collaborate with Pepe Gozzi on making the bomb. "Sure," said Ellis.

Then there was one more snag. "I've got a friend," Rahmi said to the two of them, "who wants to meet you both. This is the friend who gives us the money for explosives and cars and bribes and guns and everything. He needs to be sure the bomb will work, and he wants to feel he can trust you. All you have to do is bring the bomb to him, explain to him how it will work, and let him look you in the eye."

"It's all right with me," said Ellis. Pepe agreed, and Rahmi set up a rendezvous for the four of them on the following Sunday.

THAT Sunday morning Ellis woke up suddenly, feeling frightened. A moment later he remembered the reason why he was so tense. In his mind he ran over his plan. If all went well, today would be the triumphant conclusion to more than a year of careful work. And he would be able to share that triumph with Jane, if he was still alive at the end of the day.

He turned his head to look at her. His heart leaped, as it did every time he saw her face. She lay flat on her back, with her turned-up nose pointing at the ceiling and her dark hair spread across the pillow like a bird's unfolded wing.

It was a rare delight to see her like this, in repose. Normally she was animated—laughing, frowning, registering surprise or compassion. Her commonest expression was a wicked grin. Only when she was sleeping or thinking very hard was she like this. Yet this was how he loved her most, for, unguarded, her appearance hinted at the sensuality that burned just beneath her surface like a slow, hot underground fire. When he saw her like this, his hands itched to touch her as passionately as when they had first become lovers, almost a year ago.

This had surprised him. When he had first met her, soon after he came to Paris, she had struck him as typical of the young and the radical in capital cities, organizing campaigns against apartheid and for nuclear disarmament, leading protest marches about El Salvador and water pollution, raising money for starving people in Chad. People were drawn to her by her striking good looks, captivated by her British charm, and energized by her enthusiasm. He had dated her a couple of times, and then—he could never remember exactly how it happened—he had fallen in love.

His gaze wandered around her little studio flat. When he had first seen it, she had just moved here from the suburbs, and it had been rather bare. Gradually she had transformed it into a cheerful nest. She earned a good salary as an interpreter, translating French and Russian into English, but her rent was high—the apartment was near the Boulevard St.-Michel—so she had bought patiently, saving her money for just the right mahogany table, antique bedstead, and Tabriz rug.

He rolled onto his side, facing her, and the movement woke her. Her large blue eyes stared at the ceiling for a second; then she looked at him, smiled, and rolled over into his arms. "Hello," she whispered, and he kissed her.

After a while she mumbled, "Do you know what day it is?"

"Sunday."

"It's your Sunday to make lunch."

"I hadn't forgotten."

"Good. What are you going to give me?"

"Steak, potatoes, snow peas, goat's cheese, strawberries and Chantilly cream."

She lifted her head, laughing. "That's what you always make! How about some variety in your cooking?"

"Hey, the deal was, each of us would make lunch on alternate Sundays. Nobody said anything about making a *different* lunch each time."

She sighed, feigning defeat.

His day's work had been at the back of his mind all along. He was going to need her unwitting help, and this was the moment to enlist it. "I have to see Rahmi this morning," he began.

"All right. I'll meet you at your place later."

"There's something you could do for me, if you wouldn't mind getting there early. I need help with a little conspiracy."

"Go on," she said.

"Today is Rahmi's birthday, and his brother Mustafa is in town, but Rahmi doesn't know." If this works out, Ellis thought, I'll never lie to you again. "I want Mustafa to turn up at Rahmi's lunch party as a surprise. But I need an accomplice."

"I'm game," she said. She sat upright. "What do I have to do?"

"The problem is simple. I have to tell Mustafa where to go, but Rahmi hasn't yet made up his mind where he wants to eat. So I have to get the message to Mustafa at the last minute. And Rahmi will probably be beside me when I make the call."

"And the solution?"

"I'll call *you*. I'll talk nonsense. Ignore everything except the address. Call Mustafa, give him the address, and tell him how to get there." All this had sounded okay when Ellis dreamed it up, but now it seemed wildly implausible.

However, Jane did not seem suspicious. "It sounds simple enough," she said.

"Good," Ellis said briskly, concealing his relief. "I'll want to wait and see the surprise, but I'll get out of having lunch there."

Jane looked thoughtful. "They invited you but not me."

Ellis shrugged. "I presume it's a masculine celebration." He reached for the notepad on the bedside table and wrote Mustafa's name and phone number.

Jane got off the bed and crossed the room to the shower closet. Her mood had changed. She was not smiling. Ellis said, "What are you mad about?"

"I'm not mad," she said. "Sometimes I dislike the way your friends treat me. And I suppose I'm saying I don't like my status. I'm committed to you, everyone knows that, but you're not committed to me. We don't live together, I don't know where you go or what you do a lot of the time . . . and people know all this, so they treat me like a fool."

"I think you're exaggerating."

"You always say that." She stepped into the shower and banged the door. Ellis began to shave at the kitchen sink. They had had this argument before, and he knew what was at the bottom of it. Jane wanted them to live together.

He wanted it too, of course. He wanted to marry her and live with her for the rest of his life. But he had to wait until this assignment was over, and he could not tell her that, so he had said such things as, "I'm not ready," and, "All I need is time," and these vague evasions had infuriated her. It seemed to her that a year was a long time to love a man without getting any kind of commitment from him. It was true, of course. But if all went well today, he could make everything right.

He finished shaving and dressed quickly in faded denim jeans and a black T-shirt. After her shower Jane made coffee, and he sat opposite her at the little mahogany table. She poured his coffee and said, "I want to have a serious talk with you."

"Okay," he said quickly. "Let's do it at lunchtime."

"Why not now?"

"I don't have time."

"Is Rahmi's birthday more important than our relationship?"

"Of course not." Ellis heard irritation in his tone, and a warning voice told him, Be gentle, you could lose her. "But I promised, and it's important that I keep my promises; whereas it's not important whether we have this conversation now or later."

Jane's face took on a set, stubborn look that he knew. She wore it when she had made a decision and someone tried to deflect her from her path. "It's important to *me* that we talk *now*."

For a moment he was tempted to tell her the whole truth right away. But he was short of time, and he was not prepared. So he said, "I think you're being silly, and I won't be bullied. Please let's talk later. I have to go now." He stood up.

As he walked to the door she said, "Jean-Pierre has asked me to go to Afghanistan with him."

This was completely unexpected. "Are you serious?" he said.

"I'm serious."

Ellis knew Jean-Pierre was in love with Jane. So were half a dozen other men. That kind of thing was inevitable with such a woman. None of the men were serious rivals, though; at least he had thought not, until this moment. He shook his head in disbelief. "You can't go to Afghanistan."

"Why not?"

"Because you love me."

"That doesn't put me at your disposal. I won't wait forever."

"I'm not asking you to wait forever, only a few hours." He touched her cheek. "You won't go to Afghanistan, will you?"

"I don't know," she said levelly.

He tried a grin. "At least not before lunch."

She smiled back and nodded. "Not before lunch."

He looked at her for a moment longer; then he went out.

THE broad boulevards of the Champs Élysées were thronged with tourists and Parisians out for a morning stroll under the warm spring sun. Ellis stood near the appointed café, carrying a backpack he had bought in a cheap luggage store. He looked like an American on a hitchhiking tour of Europe.

There were two possibilities as to the identity of Rahmi's "friend" who financed the little terrorist group. The first was that he was a wealthy, freedom-loving Turk who had decided, for political or personal reasons, that violence was justified against the military dictatorship and its supporters. If this was the case, Ellis would be disappointed.

The second possibility was that he was Boris.

Boris was a legendary figure in the militant circles within which Ellis moved. He was said to be a Russian, a KGB man willing to fund any leftist act of violence in the West. It was certain that the Russians gave money to such groups as the Turkish dissidents. They could hardly resist such a cheap and low-risk way of causing trouble. And since in this line of work money was not kept in bank accounts or moved around by telex, somebody had to hand over the actual bank notes, so it followed that there had to be a Boris figure. Ellis wanted very badly to meet him.

Rahmi walked by at exactly ten thirty, wearing a pink Lacoste shirt and immaculately pressed tan pants, looking edgy. Ellis followed him, staying ten yards behind, as they had arranged. At the next sidewalk café sat the muscular, overweight form of Pepe Gozzi in a black silk suit, as if he had been to church, which he probably had. He held a briefcase in his lap. He got up and fell in alongside Ellis in such a way that a casual observer would have been unsure whether they were together or not.

Rahmi headed up the hill toward the Arc de Triomphe. Three blocks east he turned into a side street and across the road into the Hotel Lancaster.

So this was the rendezvous, thought Ellis. The marbled entrance hall was cool after the heat of the street. Rahmi was getting into a tiny elevator at the far end of the lobby. Ellis and Pepe squeezed in behind. Ellis' nerves were drawn wire-tight as they went up. They got off at the fourth floor, and Rahmi led them to room 41 and knocked.

The door opened slowly.

It was Boris. Ellis knew it as soon as he saw the man, and he felt a thrill of triumph and at the same time a shiver of fear. Moscow was written all over him, from his cheap haircut to his solidly practical shoes, and there was the unmistakable style of the KGB in his hard-eyed look of appraisal and the brutal set of his mouth.

He held the door half open for a moment while he studied them; then he stepped back and said in French, "Come in."

They walked into the sitting room of a suite. A carton of cigarettes and a liter of brandy stood on a delicate bowlegged side
table. In the far corner a half-open door led to a bedroom.

Rahmi's introductions were nervous. "Pepe. Ellis. My friend."

Ellis put his backpack on the rug and sat down.

Boris gestured at the brandy bottle. "A drink?"

Ellis did not want brandy at eleven o'clock in the morning. He
said, "Yes, please. Coffee."

Boris gave him a hard, hostile look, then said, "We'll all have
coffee," and went to the phone to call room service. After he had
hung up, he addressed Pepe. "I'm glad to meet you," he said in
French. "I think we can help each other. Show me the bomb."

Pepe opened his briefcase. It was packed with blocks of a
yellowish substance. Boris poked one of the blocks with a forefinger. The substance yielded like putty. He sniffed it. "I presume
this is C_3," he said. Pepe nodded. "Where is the mechanism?"

Rahmi said, "Ellis has it in his backpack."

"No, I don't," Ellis said.

The room went very quiet. A look of panic came over Rahmi's
handsome young face. "What do you mean? You said . . . I told
him you would—"

"Shut up," Boris said harshly. Rahmi fell silent.

Ellis spoke with a casual indifference he did not feel. "I was
afraid this might be a trap, so I left the mechanism at home. It can
be here in a few minutes. I just have to call my girl."

Boris stared at him for several seconds. Ellis returned his look
as coolly as he could. Then Boris said, "Why did you think this
might be a trap?"

Ellis shot him an arrogant look, shrugged, and said nothing.

Boris continued to look searchingly at him. Finally the Russian
said, "I shall make the call."

Ellis choked back a protest. This was a development he had not
expected. How would Jane react to the voice of a stranger? He
regretted using her like this, but it was too late now.

He told Boris the phone number, and Boris began to dial. The
others waited in silence.

Boris said, "Hello? I am calling on behalf of Ellis."

Perhaps the unknown voice would not throw her, Ellis thought. She had been expecting a somewhat wacky call anyway. "Ignore everything except the address," he had told her.

"What?" Boris said irritably. "Yes, I am, but never mind that. Ellis wants you to bring the mechanism to room 41 at the Hotel Lancaster in the Rue de Berri."

There was another pause. Play the game, Jane, thought Ellis.

"Thank you," Boris said, and hung up. To Ellis he said, "She knew I was Russian. How did she find out?"

Ellis was puzzled for a moment, then realized. "She's a linguist," he replied. "She knows accents."

Pepe spoke for the first time. "While we're waiting for her to arrive, let's see the money."

"All right." Boris went into the bedroom and came back in with a large brown envelope. He handed it to Pepe. Pepe opened it and began counting hundred-franc notes.

Ellis thought, I hope Jane doesn't wait before making the call to Mustafa. I should have told her it was important to pass the message on immediately.

After a while Pepe said, "It's all there," and put the money back into the envelope.

The four men sat in silence for several minutes.

Boris asked Ellis, "How far away is your place?"

"Fifteen minutes on a motor scooter."

There was a knock at the door. Ellis tensed.

"She drove fast," Boris said. He opened it. "Coffee," he said disgustedly, and returned to his seat.

Two white-jacketed waiters wheeled a trolley into the room. They straightened up and turned around, each holding an MAB pistol, standard issue for French detectives. One of them said, "Nobody move."

Boris gathered himself to spring; then the bedroom door flew open, and two more men in waiters' uniforms stood there, armed like their colleagues. Boris looked resigned. Ellis let out a long sigh. It was all over.

A uniformed police officer walked into the room.

"A trap!" Rahmi burst out. "This *is* a trap!"

17

"Shut up," said Boris, and once again his harsh voice silenced Rahmi. He addressed the police officer. "I object most strongly to this outrage," he began. "Please take note that—"

The policeman punched him in the mouth with his fist.

Boris reeled back, then touched his lips. He looked at the blood on his hand. "Remember my face," he told the police officer in a voice as cold as the grave. "You will see it again."

"But who betrayed us?" cried Rahmi.

"Him," said Boris, pointing at Ellis.

"Ellis?" Rahmi said incredulously.

"The phone call," said Boris. "The address."

Rahmi stared at Ellis. He looked wounded to the quick.

Several more uniformed policemen came in, and the three prisoners were handcuffed and taken down in the elevator and outside one at a time. The officer turned to Ellis. "There is a black Citroën DS parked in front of the hotel for you." Hesitantly he added, "Sir."

I'm back on the side of the law, Ellis thought. He went down in the elevator, through the hotel lobby, and out into the sunshine. The police were loading the three prisoners into squad cars. On the other side of the street was the black Citroën. There was a driver in the front and a passenger in the back. Ellis got into the back. The car pulled away fast.

The passenger turned to Ellis and said, "Hello, John."

Ellis smiled. The use of his real name was strange after more than a year under cover. He said, "How are you, Bill?"

"Relieved!" replied Bill. "For thirteen months we hear nothing from you but demands for money. Then we get a phone call telling us we've got twenty-four hours to arrange an arrest squad to be ready in the vicinity of the Champs Élysées. But to get the exact address we have to wait for a phone call from an unknown woman asking for Mustafa. And that's all we know!"

"It was the only way," Ellis said apologetically.

"Well, it took some doing. Especially the last-minute room-service act! So tell me whether it was worth it. Who have we got in the bag?"

"The Russian you just saw is Boris," said Ellis.

Bill's face broke into a broad grin. "No kidding."

"No kidding. But nobody's going to get much information out of him. He's the dedicated type. The important thing is we've taken him out of circulation and really slowed the operation down. The Corsican is Pepe Gozzi, a weapons dealer," Ellis went on. "He supplied the hardware for just about every terrorist action in France in the last couple of years, and a lot more in other countries. He's the one to interrogate. If you offer him immunity, Pepe will testify against all the political people he sold stuff to."

"Unbelievable." Bill looked dazed. "In one day you've nailed probably the two biggest instigators of terrorism in the world."

"One day?" Ellis smiled. "It took a year. The young guy is Rahmi Coskun. He and his group did the Turkish Airlines fire-bombing a couple of months ago. If you round up the whole group, you're sure to find some forensic evidence. Give me a pencil and I'll write down the names and addresses."

"Save it," said Bill. "I'm going to debrief you completely back at the embassy."

"I'm not going back to the embassy. I'll give you some essential names; then I'll meet you tomorrow morning and give you the detail stuff. I have a lunch date."

Bill rolled his eyes up. "Who's your date?"

"Jane Lambert. Hers was one of the names you gave me when you originally briefed me."

"I remember. I told you that if you wormed your way into her affections, she would introduce you to every mad leftist, Arab terrorist, and avant-garde poet in Paris."

"That's how it worked, except I fell in love with her."

Bill looked appalled. "Uh, what's she really like?"

"She's not crazy, although she has some crazy friends. What can I tell you? She's pretty as a picture and bright as a pin. She's wonderful. She's the woman I've been looking for all my life."

"Well, I can see why you'd rather celebrate with her than with me. What are you going to do?"

Ellis smiled. "I'm going to open a bottle of wine, fry a couple of steaks, tell her I catch terrorists for a living, and then ask her to marry me."

CHAPTER 2

JEAN-PIERRE Debout leaned across the hospital-canteen table and fixed the brunette with a compassionate gaze. "I know how you feel," he said warmly. "I remember being very depressed toward the end of my first year in medical school. It seems as if you've been given more information than one brain can absorb, and you don't know how you will master it in time for the exams."

"That's *exactly* it," she said, looking adoringly at him as she forked a piece of meat into her mouth. As she began to chew, Jean-Pierre lost interest. He hated to watch people eat. And lately he had no enthusiasm for casual conquests, even though she was very pretty. The only girl who fascinated him for more than a few minutes was Jane Lambert—and she would not even kiss him.

It was six months now since he had first seen Jane's stunningly pretty face across a crowded room at a cocktail party. They had become friends, but she seemed to be committed to Ellis, the American, even though he was ten years older than she. If only Ellis would drop out of the picture—get run over by a bus or something. Although lately Jane's resistance had seemed to be weakening—or was that wishful thinking?

The brunette said, "I hear you're going to Afghanistan for two years to work for the rebels. Why two years? People who do this usually go for three to six months, a year at the most. Two years seems like forever."

"Does it?" Jean-Pierre gave a wry smile. "It's difficult, you see, to achieve anything of real value in a shorter period. The idea of sending doctors there for a brief visit is highly inefficient. What the rebels need is some kind of permanent medical setup, a hospital that stays in the same place and has at least some of the same staff from one year to the next. And the cost of transporting the volunteers to the country and bringing them back makes their 'free' services rather expensive." Jean-Pierre put so much effort into speaking this lie that he almost believed it himself, and he had to remind himself of his true motive for going to Afghanistan.

Just then he saw Raoul Clermont, the editor of *La Révolte*, coming across the canteen. What the devil was the fat journalist doing in the hospital canteen?

"I need to have a word with you," said Raoul without preamble.

Jean-Pierre gestured to a chair. "Raoul—"

"It's urgent," Raoul cut in.

Jean-Pierre saw pleading in his eyes and heard a note of panic in the fat man's voice. Surprised, he stood up. "Okay." He excused himself to the brunette and took Raoul's arm, and they walked out of the canteen.

"Monsieur Leblond sent me," Raoul said.

"I was beginning to think he must be behind this," said Jean-Pierre. It was a month ago that Raoul had taken him to meet Leblond, who had asked him to go to Afghanistan, ostensibly to help the rebels, as many young French doctors did, but actually to spy for their enemy, the Russians. Jean-Pierre had felt proud, apprehensive, and most of all thrilled at the opportunity to do something really spectacular for the cause. His only fear had been that the organizations that sent doctors to Afghanistan would turn him down because he was a Communist. But they had no way of knowing he was actually a party member, and it had not happened. Jean-Pierre had been accepted immediately by Médecins pour la Liberté. He had told Raoul the good news, and Raoul had said there would be another meeting with Leblond. Perhaps this was to do with that. "But why the panic?"

"He wants to see you now."

"*Now?*" Jean-Pierre was annoyed. "I'm on duty. I have to see patients—I can't just walk out of here."

"Surely someone else will take care of them."

"But what is the urgency? I can't leave for two months."

"It's not about Afghanistan. Monsieur Leblond will explain."

Jean-Pierre threw up his hands. "I can't just walk out."

"What would happen if you were taken ill?" said Raoul.

"I would tell the nursing officer, and she would call in a replacement. But—"

"So call her."

They had reached the entrance of the hospital, and there was a bank of internal phones on the wall. This may be a test, thought

Jean-Pierre; a loyalty test, to see whether I am serious enough to be given this Afghanistan mission. He picked up a phone.

"I have been called away by a sudden family emergency," he said when he got through to the nursing officer. "You must get in touch with Dr. Roche immediately to cover for me."

"Yes, Dr. Debout," the nurse replied calmly.

Jean-Pierre hung up. "All right," he said to Raoul. "Let's go."

They walked to the car park and got into Raoul's Renault 5. He drove fast through back streets. Jean-Pierre felt nervous. He did not know exactly who Leblond was, but he assumed he was high up in the KGB. Had he done anything to offend that much feared organization? Surely they could not have found out about Jane.

His asking her to go to Afghanistan with him was no business of theirs. She was not a nurse, but she could take an intensive crash course, and her great advantage was that she could speak Farsi, the Persian language, a form of which—Dari—was spoken in the area where Jean-Pierre was going. He hoped Jane would go with him out of idealism and a sense of adventure; she would forget about Ellis while she was there, and would fall in love with the nearest European, who would of course be Jean-Pierre.

Raoul parked the car outside an expensive apartment building in the Rue de l'Université. It was the place where Jean-Pierre had met Leblond the last time. They went inside, climbed to the first floor, and Raoul rang a bell. Monsieur Leblond opened the door. He was a short, slight, balding man with spectacles, and in his charcoal-gray suit and silver tie he looked like a butler. He led them to the room at the back of the building, where Jean-Pierre had been interviewed. The tall windows and the elaborate moldings indicated that it had once been an elegant drawing room, but now it had a nylon carpet, a cheap office desk, and plastic chairs.

"Wait here for a moment," said Leblond. His voice was dry as dust. He went out through a different door.

Jean-Pierre sat on one of the plastic chairs. Raoul remained standing. In this room, thought Jean-Pierre, that dry voice had said to me, "You have been a quietly loyal member of the party since childhood. Your character and your family background suggest that you would serve the party well in a covert role." I hope

I haven't ruined everything because of Jane, he now thought.

Leblond came back in with another man. The two of them stood in the doorway, and Leblond pointed at Jean-Pierre. The second man looked hard at him, as if committing his face to memory. He was big, with broad shoulders and a droopy mustache. He wore a green corduroy jacket with a rip in the sleeve. After a few seconds he nodded and went out.

Leblond closed the door behind him and sat at the desk. "There has been a disaster," he said. "There is a CIA agent among your circle of friends."

"No!" Jean-Pierre exclaimed intensely.

"Someone called Ellis Thaler."

Jean-Pierre was so shocked he stood up. *"Ellis?"*

"You *do* know him. Good."

"Ellis is a CIA spy?"

"Sit down," Leblond said levelly. "Our problem is not who he is, but what he has done."

Jean-Pierre was thinking, If Jane finds out about this, she will drop Ellis like a hot brick.

Leblond was speaking. Jean-Pierre forced himself to concentrate. "The disaster is that Ellis set a trap, and in it he caught someone important to us, who has been arrested. Raoul and I have never met your friend Ellis, of course. Therefore neither of us knows what he looks like. But you do. That is why I have brought you here. Do you also know where Ellis lives?"

"Yes. He has a room in the Rue de l'Ancienne-Comédie."

"Does the room overlook the street?"

Jean-Pierre frowned. He had been there only once. Ellis did not invite people home much. "I think it does. Let me think. Yes. The window faces the street. Why is it important?"

Leblond hesitated; then he spoke. "I regret having to use you in an . . . action . . . such as this, when you have never done anything for us before. But we don't have anyone else who knows Ellis. So. Listen carefully. You are to go to his room. If he is there, go inside—think of some pretext. Go to the window, lean out, and make sure you are seen by Raoul, who will be in the street."

Jean-Pierre asked, "And if Ellis is not there?"

23

"Speak to his neighbors. Try to find out where he has gone and when he will be back. If it seems he has left only for a few minutes, or even an hour or so, wait for him. When he returns, proceed as before. Go inside, go to the window, and make sure you are seen by Raoul. Your appearance at the window is the sign that Ellis is inside. Have you understood?"

"I know you want me to identify him," said Jean-Pierre. "And when I have done it?"

Leblond gave the answer Jean-Pierre had hardly dared to hope for. "We are going to kill him, of course."

JANE spread a patched white cloth on Ellis' tiny table and laid two places with an assortment of battered cutlery. She found a bottle of Fleurie in the cupboard under the sink, and opened it. She was tempted to taste it, then decided to wait for Ellis.

She did not like his room. It was bare, cramped, and impersonal. Jane had been quite shocked when she first saw it. She had expected this warm, relaxed, mature man to live in a place that expressed his personality—an attractive, comfortable apartment containing mementos of a past rich in experience. But you would never guess that the man who lived here had been married and had fought in the Vietnam War. The cold white walls were decorated with posters. The china came from junkshops, and the volumes of poetry on the bookshelf were only paperbacks.

It was the room of a withdrawn man, a secretive man, a man who would never share his innermost thoughts with anyone. Gradually, and with terrible sadness, Jane had come to realize that Ellis *was* like that, like his room, cold and secretive.

It was incredible. He was utterly uninhibited and would do anything and say anything without anxiety or hesitation or shame. But there had been too many times when she had been laughing with him, or listening to him talk, or watching the skin around his blue eyes crinkle as he thought, only to find that he had suddenly turned off. In those switched-off moods he was no longer loving, no longer amusing, no longer thoughtful or considerate or gentlemanly or compassionate. He made her feel excluded, an intruder into his private world. It was like the sun going behind a cloud.

She thought she was going to have to leave him. She loved him to distraction, but it seemed he could not love her the same way. He was thirty-three years old, and if he had not learned the art of intimacy by now, he never would.

She sat on the sofa and began to read *The Observer*. There was a report from Afghanistan on the front page. It sounded like a good place to go to forget Ellis.

The idea had appealed to her immediately. Although she loved Paris, and her job was at least varied, she wanted more: experience, adventure, and a chance to strike a blow for freedom. She was not afraid. Jean-Pierre said the doctors were considered too valuable to be sent into the combat zone. She was intensely curious about the life-style of the Afghan rebels. "What do they eat there?" she had asked Jean-Pierre. "What do they wear? Do they live in tents? Do they have toilets?"

"No toilets," he had replied. "No electricity. No roads. No wine. No cars. No central heating. No dentists. No phones. No restaurants. No Coca-Cola. No weather forecasts, no social workers, no lipstick, no fashions, no dinner parties, no taxi ranks—"

"Stop!" she had interrupted him. He could go on like that for hours. "They must have buses and taxis."

"Not in the countryside. I'm going to a region called Five Lions Valley, a rebel stronghold in the foothills of the Himalayas. It was primitive even before the Russians bombed it."

Jane was quite sure she could live happily without plumbing or weather forecasts. Her father, if he were still alive, would have said, "Good luck, Janey." He had been a doctor and understood the importance of doing something *worthwhile* with one's life.

Her reverie was disturbed by a footfall on the stairs. It did not sound like Ellis' step. Then there was a tap at the door.

Jane put down her paper and opened it. There stood Jean-Pierre. He was almost as surprised as she was. They stared at one another for a moment. Jane said, "You look guilty. Do I?"

"Yes," he said, and he grinned.

"I was just thinking about you. Come in."

He stepped inside and glanced around. "Ellis not here?"

"I'm expecting him soon. Have a seat."

Jean-Pierre lowered his long body onto the sofa. Jane thought, not for the first time, that he was probably the most beautiful man she had ever met. His face was perfectly regular in shape, with a high forehead, a strong, rather aristocratic nose, liquid brown eyes, and a sensual mouth partly hidden by a full dark brown beard, with stray flashes of auburn in the mustache.

She liked him a lot. She liked his idealism and his dedication to medicine. He had enormous charm. He also had a manic imagination, which could sometimes be very funny. People said that his gaiety had its reverse side, in moods of black depression, but Jane had never seen any evidence of that.

"Have some of Ellis' wine," she said.

"No, thanks." He was looking very solemn. "I need to have a serious talk with you."

"We had it three days ago, don't you remember?" she said flippantly. "You asked me to leave my boyfriend and go to Afghanistan with you—an offer few girls could resist."

"Be serious."

"All right. I still haven't made up my mind."

"Jane. I've discovered something terrible about Ellis. He's not what he pretends to be."

Jane thought he was being melodramatic. "There's no need to speak in a voice like an undertaker. What do you mean?"

"He's not a penniless poet. He works for the U.S. government."

Jane frowned. "The U.S. government? He gives English lessons to French people who work for the American government—"

"I don't mean that. He spies on radical groups. He's an agent. He works for the CIA."

Jane burst out laughing. "You're absurd! Did you think you could make me leave him by telling me that?"

"It's true, Jane."

"It's not true. Ellis couldn't be a spy. Don't you think I'd know? I've been practically living with him for a year." Even while she spoke Jane was thinking, It could explain a lot. She did not *really* know Ellis. But she knew him well enough to be sure that he was not base, mean, treacherous, or just plain *evil*.

"It's all over town," Jean-Pierre was saying. "Someone important was arrested this morning, and everyone says Ellis was responsible."

"Oh, Jean-Pierre, it's laughable," said Jane. She suddenly felt very warm. She went to the window and threw it open. As she glanced down she saw Ellis' blond head ducking into the front door. "Well," she said to Jean-Pierre, "here he comes. Now you're going to have to repeat this ludicrous story in front of him."

"I intend to," said Jean-Pierre. "Why do you think I am here? I came to warn him that they're after him. Somebody wants revenge."

Jane realized Jean-Pierre was sincere. He really believed this story. Well, Ellis would soon set him straight.

The door opened and Ellis walked in. He looked very happy, as if he were bursting with good news. He stopped, surprised to see Jean-Pierre. His smile faded a little. "Hello, you two," he said. Closing the door behind him, he locked it, as was his habit. Jane had always thought that an eccentricity, but now it occurred to her that it was what a spy would do. She pushed the thought away.

Jean-Pierre spoke first. "They're on to you, Ellis. They know. They're coming after you."

Jane looked from one to the other, then put her arms around Ellis, kissed him, and said, "Jean-Pierre has been told some absurd story about your being a CIA spy."

Jean-Pierre was leaning out of the window, scanning the street below. Now he turned back to face them. "Tell her, Ellis."

"Where did you get this idea?" Ellis asked him.

"It's all around town."

"And who, exactly, did *you* hear it from?" asked Ellis in a steely voice.

"Raoul Clermont."

Ellis nodded. Switching into English, he said, "Jane, would you sit down? I have something to tell you."

It *couldn't* be true. Jane felt panic rise in her throat.

Ellis glanced at Jean-Pierre. "Would you leave us?" he said in French, but Jean-Pierre didn't move.

Jane embraced Ellis again and pleaded, "What are you going to tell me? Why won't you simply say that Jean-Pierre is wrong? Tell me you're not a spy, Ellis, before I go crazy!"

27

"It's not that simple," said Ellis.

"It *is* simple!" She could no longer keep the hysterical note out of her voice. "Jean-Pierre says you're a spy, that you work for the American government, and that you've been lying to me, continuously and shamelessly, ever since I met you. Is it true or not?"

Ellis sighed. "I guess it's true."

Jane felt she would explode. "It can't be!" she screamed.

Ellis' face was set like stone. "I was going to tell you today."

There was a knock at the door. They both ignored it. "You've been spying on me and all my friends!" Jane yelled. "I feel so *ashamed.*"

"My work here is finished," Ellis said. "I don't need to lie to you anymore."

"You won't get the chance. I never want to see you again."

The knocking came again, and Jean-Pierre said, "Open the door, for heaven's sake!"

Jane unlocked it and opened it. There stood a big, broad-shouldered man in a green corduroy jacket with a rip in the sleeve. "What do you want?" she said. Then she saw the gun.

The next few seconds seemed to pass very slowly.

Jane opened her mouth to scream; then, instead of screaming, she tried to slam the door. As she swung it toward the gunman, he stuck his foot in the way. The door bounced back. He's going to kill Ellis, Jane thought. She threw herself at the gunman, beating his face with her fists, for suddenly, although she hated Ellis, she did not want him to die.

The man was distracted for a fraction of a second. With one arm he hurled Jane aside. She fell heavily. The arm that had shoved her came back and flung the door wide. As the man swung his gun hand around, Ellis came at him from behind the door with a wine bottle raised high. The gun went off as the bottle came down, and the shot coincided with the sound of glass breaking.

Jane stared, horrified, at the two men. The gunman slumped, Ellis remained standing, and she realized the shot had missed.

Ellis bent down and snatched the gun from the man's hand.

Jane got to her feet with an effort.

"Are you all right?" Ellis asked her.

"Alive," she said.

He turned to Jean-Pierre. "How many on the street?"

Jean-Pierre glanced out the window. "None."

"They must be concealed." Ellis pocketed the gun and went to his bookcase. "Stand back," he said, and hurled it to the floor.

Behind the bookcase was a door. He opened it, looked at Jane for a long moment, as if he had something to say but could not find the words. Then he stepped through the door and was gone.

Jane walked slowly over to the secret door and looked through. There was another studio flat, sparsely furnished and dreadfully dusty, as if it had not been occupied for a year. There was an open door and, beyond it, a staircase.

She turned back. The gunman lay on the floor, out cold in a puddle of wine. It all seemed unreal: Ellis' being a spy, Jean-Pierre's knowing about it, and Ellis' escape route.

She looked at Jean-Pierre. He too seemed stunned. After a moment he crossed the room to her and put his arms around her. She slumped onto his shoulder and burst into tears.

PART TWO: 1982

CHAPTER 3

THE river came down from the ice line, cold and clear, and it filled the valley with its noise as it boiled through the ravines and flashed past the wheat fields in a headlong dash for the lowlands. For almost a year that sound had been in Jane's ears: sometimes loud, when she went to bathe or when she took the winding cliffside paths between villages; and sometimes soft, as now, when she was high on the hillside and the Five Lions River was just a glint and a murmur in the distance. Listening, she heard something else, and she realized that the new sound was the baritone of a propeller-driven aircraft.

Jane opened her eyes. It was an Antonov, the slow-moving reconnaissance plane that was the herald of jet aircraft on a bombing run. She sat up and looked anxiously across the valley.

She was in her secret refuge, a broad, flat shelf halfway up a cliff. Above her, the overhang hid her from view without blocking the sun. Below, the approach was steep and bare of vegetation. No one could climb it without being heard and seen by Jane. The privacy of the place was important, because she came here to take off her clothes and lie in the sun, and the Afghans were as modest as nuns. If she were seen naked, she would be lynched.

To her right the dusty hillside fell away rapidly. Toward its foot was the village of Banda, fifty or sixty houses clinging to a patch of uneven, rocky ground that no one could farm. The houses were made of gray stones and mud bricks, and each one had a flat roof of pressed earth laid over mats. Next to the little mosque was a small group of wrecked houses. One of the Russian bombers had scored a direct hit a couple of months back. Jane could see the village clearly—it was deserted under the hot blue sky.

To her left the valley broadened out. The small stony fields were dotted with bomb craters, and on the lower slopes of the mountainside several of the ancient terrace walls had collapsed. The wheat was ripe, but no one was reaping.

Beyond the fields, at the far side of the valley, ran the Five Lions River. Jane scrutinized its length. There were no women bathing or washing clothes, no children playing in the shallows, no men leading horses or donkeys across the ford.

Farther up the mountainside were the caves. That was where the villagers were, the men sleeping after a night of working in their fields, the women cooking and trying to stop the children's wandering, the cows penned and the goats tethered and the dogs fighting. The Russians bombed the villages, not the bare hillsides; a cave would protect her from everything but a direct hit.

The roar of the jets now filled the valley as they passed over Jane, heading northeast. She squinted to look at them—four silver killers, the summit of mankind's ingenuity, deployed to maim illiterate farmers and knock down mud-brick houses.

In a minute they were gone. Banda was to be spared, for today. Slowly Jane relaxed. Banda had escaped bombing last summer, and the whole of the valley got a respite during the winter; but it had started again in earnest this spring, and Banda had been hit several times, once in the center of the village.

The courage of the villagers was amazing. Each family had made a second home up in the caves, and they climbed the hill every morning to spend the day there, returning at dusk, for there was no bombing at night. Since it was unsafe to work in the fields by day, the men did it at night—or rather the older ones did, for the young men were away most of the time, shooting at Russians down at the southern end of the valley or farther afield. This summer the bombing was more intensive than ever in all the rebel areas, according to what Jean-Pierre heard. If Afghans in other parts of the country were like these here in the valley, they were able to adapt and survive: salvaging a few precious possessions from the rubble of a bombed house, tirelessly replanting a ruined vegetable garden, nursing the wounded and burying the dead, and sending ever younger teenage boys to join the guerrilla leaders. The Russians could never defeat these people, Jane felt, unless they turned the whole country into a radioactive desert.

As to whether the rebels could ever defeat the Russians, that was another question. The Afghans were brave and irrepressible, and they controlled the countryside, but rival tribes hated one another almost as much as they hated the invaders, and their rifles were useless against jet bombers and armored helicopters.

She pushed thoughts of war out of her mind. This was the heat of the day, the siesta time, when she liked to be alone and relax. She put her hand into a goatskin bag of clarified butter and began to oil the skin of her big belly, wondering how she could possibly have been so foolish as to get pregnant in Afghanistan.

"How could you make such a mistake?" Jean-Pierre had yelled, and she had had no answer.

But now, lying in the sun, cheerfully pregnant, she could see that it had been a deliberate mistake. She had wanted a baby, and she knew Jean-Pierre did not, so she had started one by accident.

Why did I want a baby so badly? she asked herself, and the answer came to her out of nowhere. Because I was lonely.

It seemed ironic. She had never felt lonely in Paris, living on her own; but when she was married, and spent every night with her husband and worked alongside him most of every day, she had felt isolated, frightened, and alone.

They had married in Paris just before coming here. It had seemed a part of the adventure somehow: another challenge, another risk, another thrill. Everyone had said how happy and beautiful and brave and in love they were, and it had been true.

No doubt she had expected too much. She had looked forward to ever growing love and intimacy with Jean-Pierre. But he seemed to think their relationship after marriage should be just what it had been before. He behaved in every way like a courteous boyfriend rather than a natural, loving husband. Then his furious reaction to her pregnancy made him suddenly seem a stranger. She had never been so miserable in her life.

Finally, one morning he had put his arm around her and apologized. He had explained that he was already afraid of losing her, and that if she were to be the mother of his son, he would be absolutely terrified, for then he would lose them both. This confession had moved her to tears, and she had realized that in getting pregnant she had made the ultimate commitment to Jean-Pierre. She made up her mind that this marriage would work, come what may.

He had been closer to her after that. He had taken an interest in the growing baby, and had become anxious about Jane's health and safety, the way expectant fathers were supposed to.

Jane touched her tummy, feeling the shape of the baby. According to Rabia Gul, the old village midwife, it would be a girl, for it could be felt on the left side, whereas boys grew on the right side. Rabia had accordingly prescribed a diet of vegetables. For a boy she would have recommended plenty of meat. In Afghanistan the males were better fed even before they were born.

Jane's thoughts were interrupted by a loud bang. For a moment she was confused, associating the explosion with the jets that had passed overhead several minutes before on their way to bomb some other village. Then she heard, quite close by, the scream of a child in pain and panicking.

She realized instantly what had happened. The Russians had littered the countryside with antipersonnel mines. Their ostensible aim was to block guerrilla supply lines, but since the guerrilla supply lines were the mountain pathways used daily by old men, women, children, and animals, the real purpose was straightforward terror. That scream meant a child had detonated a mine.

Jane jumped to her feet. The sound seemed to be coming from somewhere near the mullah's house, which was about half a mile outside the village on the hillside footpath. Jane quickly put on her clothes and ran that way. Rushing through the coarse undergrowth, she realized that the first long scream had become a series of short, terrified yells that were coming from a clump of camel grass and juniper bushes. She pushed through the shrubbery and glimpsed part of a bright blue coat. The child must be Mousa, the nine-year-old son of Mohammed Khan, one of the leading guerrillas. A moment later she was beside him.

He was kneeling on the dusty ground. He had evidently tried to pick up the mine, for it had blown off his hand, and now he was staring wild-eyed at the bloody stump and screaming in terror.

"Oh, dear God. You poor child." She knelt in front of him, hugged him, and murmured soothing noises. After a minute he stopped screaming, too shocked now to cry. She found the pressure point in his armpit and stopped the gush of blood.

She was going to need his help. She must make him speak. "Mousa, what was it?" she said in Dari.

He made no reply. She asked him again.

"I thought . . ." His eyes opened wide as he remembered. "I thought it was a ball! I picked it up!"

She held him tight, soothing him. "And what happened?"

"It went bang," he said. He was becoming somewhat calmer now. She kissed his forehead. It was damp and cold.

Jane looked down at her clothes, which were what the Afghan women wore: a sack-shaped dress over cotton trousers. She tore at the dress's thin material, ripping off several wide strips. With these she began to make a tourniquet. Mousa watched her, wide-eyed and silent. She snapped a dry twig from a juniper bush and used it to finish the tourniquet.

Now he needed a dressing, a sedative, an antibiotic to prevent infection, and his mother to prevent trauma. Jane wished she had been less hasty about tearing up her dress. With much of her upper half exposed, she would just have to hope she did not meet any men on the way to the caves. She picked up the child, and cradling him on the rise of her belly, she began to walk slowly up the hill. She could manage it only because he was half starved. A nine-year-old European child would have been too heavy.

After forty or fifty yards she became exhausted. She set Mousa down, hugging him gently while she rested near the top of the hill. Suddenly a man appeared on the path ahead. Jane recognized him. Oh, no. It's the mullah! Of all people.

Abdullah was a short man of about fifty-five, rather tubby, despite the local shortage of food. With his tan turban and billowing black trousers he wore an argyle sweater and a blue pin-striped suit coat that looked as if it had once been worn by a London stockbroker. His luxuriant beard was dyed red. He was Banda's mullah.

Abdullah mistrusted foreigners, despised women, and hated all practitioners of foreign medicine. Jane, being all three, had never had the least chance of winning his affection. To make matters worse, many people in the valley had realized that taking Jane's antibiotics was a more effective treatment for infections than inhaling the smoke from a burning slip of paper on which Abdullah had written with saffron ink, and consequently the mullah was losing money. His reaction was to refer to Jane as "the Western whore," but it was difficult for him to do more, for she and Jean-Pierre were under the protection of Ahmed Shah Masud, the guerrilla leader, and even a mullah hesitated to cross swords with such a great hero.

When he saw her, he stopped dead in his tracks, an expression of utter incredulity transforming his face into a comic mask. He was the worst possible person to meet. Any other village man would have been embarrassed to see her with her dress half torn off; Abdullah would be enraged. He began a high-pitched shout of abuse. His face empurpled with fury, he walked toward her and raised his stick.

Jane pointed at Mousa, who was dazed by pain and weak from loss of blood. "Look!" she yelled at Abdullah. "Can't you see—"

But he was blinded by rage, and he brought down his stick on her head with a whack.

Jane cried out in pain and anger. She stumbled backward, and he raised his stick again. Suddenly inspired, she leaped at him and poked her fingers into his eyes. He roared like a wounded bull. While he was blinded, Jane grabbed his beard with both hands and tugged. He stumbled forward, tripped, rolled a couple of yards downhill, and came to rest in a dwarf willow bush.

Jane thought, Oh, Lord. What have I done? Looking at that malevolent priest, she knew he would never forget his humiliation. He might complain to the village elders. He might even go to Masud and demand that the foreign doctors be sent home. But then it struck her that, in order to make any kind of complaint, he would have to tell his story in all its ignominious details, and the villagers would ridicule him forever afterward. So perhaps she would get away with it.

She turned around. She had something more important to worry about. Mousa was standing where she had set him down, too shocked to understand what had been happening. Jane took a deep breath, picked him up, and walked on.

She reached the crest of the hill, crossed the stony plateau, and began to descend the far side of the ridge. A moment later she passed a group of children playing. They stared at Mousa's wound, and then they all ran ahead of Jane, shouting the news.

The daytime hideout of the villagers of Banda looked like the desert encampment of a tribe of nomads: the dusty ground, the blazing midday sun, the remains of cooking fires, the hooded women, the dirty children. Jane crossed the small square of level ground in front of the caves. The women were already converging on the largest cave, which Jane and Jean-Pierre had made their clinic. Jean-Pierre heard the commotion and came out. Gratefully Jane handed Mousa to him, saying in French, "It was a mine. He's lost his hand."

Jean-Pierre took Mousa inside, laid him down on the rug that served as an examination table, and began attending to the child. Jane felt a little light-headed and sat down. Mousa's mother, Halima, came running into the cave and began screaming when she saw her son. I should calm her, Jane thought, but why can't I get up? I think I'll close my eyes. Just for a minute.

By nightfall Jane knew her baby was coming.

When she came around after fainting in the cave, she had what she thought was a backache—caused, she assumed, by carrying Mousa. Jean-Pierre agreed with her diagnosis, gave her an aspirin, and told her to lie still. Then he cleaned and dressed Mousa's stump, gave him penicillin, and injected him against tetanus.

Late in the afternoon Jean-Pierre prepared to leave. He was scheduled to hold a clinic tomorrow in a village several miles away. By the time he kissed Jane good-bye, she was beginning to wonder whether her backache might be the beginning of labor, brought on early by her ordeal with Mousa. She asked him.

"Don't worry," he said briskly. "You've got another six weeks to wait." So she let him go.

When the sun began to set behind the western cliff wall, Jane walked with the women and children down the mountainside to the darkening village, and the men headed for their fields, to reap their crops while the bombers slept.

The house in which Jane and Jean-Pierre lived actually belonged to the village shopkeeper, who had gone with his family to Pakistan. The front room, formerly the shop, had been Jean-Pierre's clinic until the intensity of the summer bombing had driven the villagers to the caves during the day. The house had two back rooms, bedroom and living room. At the side of the house was a mud-walled courtyard, containing the cooking fire and a small pool for washing clothes, dishes, and children. The shopkeeper had left some homemade wooden furniture, and the villagers had lent Jane several beautiful rugs for the floors. Jane and Jean-Pierre slept on a mattress, like the Afghans, but they had a down sleeping bag instead of blankets. Like the Afghans, they rolled the mattress up during the day or put it on the flat roof to air in fine weather. In the summer everyone slept on the roofs.

Walking from the cave to the house had a peculiar effect on Jane. Her backache got much worse, and when she reached home she was ready to collapse with pain and exhaustion. She did not have the energy to climb up the outside ladder onto the roof to fetch the mattress, so she lay on a rug in the bedroom. The backache came in waves, and soon she was in no doubt that she was having contractions. She was frightened. She closed her eyes and tried to take slow, deep, regular breaths, as Jean-Pierre had explained, but it was difficult to be so controlled when all she wanted to do was cry out in fear and pain.

Another contraction began, and this one *really* hurt. As soon as she felt strong enough, she realized, she would have to go to the nearest house and ask the women to fetch Rabia, the midwife.

As soon as the spasm passed, she forced herself to get up. She hobbled from the bedroom into the living room. She felt a little stronger with each step. But a new contraction began, and she sank to the ground, thinking, I'm going to have to do this alone.

Next time she opened her eyes, there was a man's face close to her own. He looked like an Arab sheik. He had brown skin, black eyes, and a black mustache, and his features were aristocratic— high cheekbones, a Roman nose, white teeth, and a long jaw. It was Mohammed Khan, the father of the wounded boy, Mousa.

"I came to thank you for saving the life of my son," Mohammed said in Dari. "Are you sick?"

"I'm having a baby."

"Now?" he said, startled.

"Soon. Help me into the bedroom."

He hesitated. Childbirth, like all things uniquely feminine, was considered unclean. But to his credit the hesitation was only momentary. He lifted her to her feet and supported her as she walked into the bedroom. She lay down on the rug again. "Get help," she told him.

He frowned. "Where is Jean-Pierre?"

"Gone to Khawak. I need the midwife."

"Yes," he said. "I'll send my wife, Halima, to fetch her."

"Thank you," said Jane. "Tell her to hurry."

Mohammed left. Jane was lucky it was he and not one of the other men. The others would have refused to touch a sick woman, but Mohammed was different. He was one of the most important guerrillas, and in practice was the local representative of the rebel leader, Masud. Mohammed was only twenty-four, but in this country that was not too young to be a guerrilla leader or to have a nine-year-old son. He had studied in Kabul, he spoke a little French, and he knew that the customs of the valley were not the only forms of polite behavior in the world. His main responsibility was to organize the convoys to and from Pakistan, with their vital supplies of arms and ammunition for the rebels. It was one such convoy that had brought Jane and Jean-Pierre to the valley.

Because of the Russian attacks, Mohammed changed his routes constantly. In Paris Jean-Pierre had got hold of American maps of Afghanistan, and they were better than anything the rebels had, so Mohammed often came to the house to look at them before sending off a new convoy. Perhaps it was this familiarity that had emboldened Mohammed to come in and to help her, when other men would have refused. Or perhaps it was indebtedness for her rescue of Mousa, his only son. I made a friend and an enemy today, she thought: Mohammed and Abdullah.

The pain began again, the worst so far, and it left her feeling shivery and nauseated. When another contraction began, she burst into tears. "Help me," she sobbed.

Suddenly there was a strong arm around her shoulders, and a woman's voice in her ear murmuring soothing words in Dari. Without opening her eyes, Jane held on to the other woman, weeping and crying out as the contraction grew more intense and then at last began to fade.

She looked up and saw the serene brown eyes and nutshell cheeks of old Rabia, the midwife. "May God be with you, Jane Debout," she said in the usual formal greeting.

"And with you, Rabia Gul," Jane whispered gratefully.

"Are the pains coming fast?"

"Every minute or two."

Another woman's voice said, "The baby is coming early."

Jane turned and saw Zahara Gul, Rabia's daughter-in-law, a voluptuous girl of Jane's age, with wavy near-black hair and a wide, laughing mouth. Of all the women in the village, Zahara was the one to whom Jane felt close. "I'm glad you're here," she said.

Rabia said, "The birth has been brought on by carrying Mousa up the hillside. Shall I make everything ready for the baby?"

"Yes, please." Goodness knows what kind of primitive gynecology I'm letting myself in for, Jane thought; but I can't do this alone, I just can't.

The two women got busy. Rabia washed her hands ritually, calling on the prophets to make her red-faced—which meant successful—and then washed them again, thoroughly, with soap and lots of water. Zahara brought in a jar of wild rue, and Rabia lit a handful of the small dark seeds with some charcoal. Jane recalled that evil spirits were said to be frightened off by the smell of burning rue. She consoled herself with the thought that the acrid smoke would serve to keep flies out of the room.

Rabia was a little more than a midwife. Delivering babies was her main work, but she also had herbal and magical treatments to increase the fertility of women who were having difficulty getting pregnant. She was probably the oldest woman in the village, being somewhere around sixty. She was short—not much more than five feet tall—and very thin, like most of the people here. Her wrinkled brown face was surrounded by white hair. She moved quietly, her bony old hands precise and efficient.

Jane's relationship with her had begun in mistrust and hostility. When Jane had asked whom Rabia called upon in cases of difficult deliveries, Rabia had snapped, "May the devil be deaf, I've never had a difficult birth, and I've never lost a mother or a child." But later, when village women came to Jane with minor menstrual problems or routine pregnancies, she would send them to Rabia instead of prescribing placebos, and this was the beginning of a working relationship. Rabia began to turn up at the clinic once or twice a week to talk to Jane and watch her work. Jane took these opportunities to explain, rather casually, such things as why she washed her hands so often, why she put all her instruments in boiling water after using them, and why she gave lots of fluids to infants with diarrhea.

In turn, Rabia had told Jane some of her secrets. Mistrust had given way to wary mutual respect, and now Jane was glad to have the help of an old woman who had delivered hundreds of babies and had herself given birth to eleven.

There had been no pain for a while, but in the last few minutes, as she watched Rabia move quietly around the room, Jane had been aware of new sensations in her abdomen: a distinct feeling of pressure, accompanied by a growing urge to push. The urge became irresistible, and as she pushed, she groaned.

She heard Rabia say, "It begins. This is good."

After a while the urge went away. Zahara brought a cup of green tea. Jane sat upright and sipped gratefully. It was warm and very sweet. She watched Rabia spread a plastic sheet on the floor and cover it with a layer of sandy earth, which Zahara had brought from outside in a bucket. Rabia had laid out a few things on a cloth on the floor, and Jane was pleased to see clean cotton rags and a new razor blade still in its wrapping.

The need to push came again, and Jane closed her eyes to concentrate. In the next pause Rabia eased off Jane's trousers and began to massage her stomach with some kind of lubricant. "The head is down," she said after examining her. "All is well. The baby will come very soon. You should get up now."

Zahara and Rabia helped Jane stand and take two steps forward onto the earth-covered plastic sheet. Rabia got behind her and said, "Stand on my feet."

Jane did as she was told. Rabia eased her into a squat, crouching behind her. This was the local birthing position. "Sit on me," said Rabia. "I can hold you." Jane let her weight settle on the old woman's thighs. The position was surprisingly comfortable and reassuring.

Jane felt her muscles begin to tighten again. She gritted her teeth and bore down, groaning. Zahara squatted in front of her. At last the pressure eased, and Jane slumped, exhausted and half asleep, letting Rabia take her weight.

When it started again, Zahara suddenly said, "It comes."

"Don't push now," said Rabia. "Let the baby swim out."

The pressure eased once more. Rabia and Zahara changed places, and now Rabia squatted in front of Jane, watching intently. The pressure began again. Jane gritted her teeth and cried out with the pain—and suddenly it eased. Rabia reached down, calling out the names of the prophets. Through a haze of tears Jane saw something round and dark in the midwife's hands. The baby was born. Jane saw its tiny form cradled on Rabia's arm. Its

41

skin was wrinkled and wet, its head covered with damp dark hair.

"Is it all right?" she asked.

Rabia did not reply. She pursed her lips and blew on the baby's squashed, immobile face.

It can't be dead, thought Jane. Then Rabia blew again, and the baby opened its tiny mouth and cried.

Jane said, "Oh, thank God—it's alive."

Rabia picked up a clean cotton rag and wiped the baby's face.

"Is it normal?" asked Jane.

At last Rabia spoke. She smiled and said, "Yes. She is normal."

She's normal, Jane thought. She. I made a little girl. A girl.

Suddenly she felt drained. "I want to lie down," she said.

Zahara helped her step back to the mattress and put cushions behind her, while Rabia held the baby and the cord was cut.

"Give her to me," said Jane.

Rabia handed the baby over. Jane put the baby's face to her breast. She was exhausted but blissfully happy. She looked down at the little girl. "Chantal," she said. "Her name is Chantal." Then she closed her eyes and slept.

CHAPTER 4

ELLIS Thaler took the Eastern Airlines shuttle from Washington to New York early in the morning. At La Guardia Airport he got a cab to the Plaza Hotel in New York City, and after satisfying himself that no one was following him, he hailed a cab on Central Park South, went to Pennsylvania Station, and took the train to Douglaston, Queens.

He continued to check for a tail, for this was one assignation his enemies must never learn about. He got off the train at a connecting stop and waited on the platform for another train. Because of his precautions, it was five o'clock when he reached Douglaston. From the station he walked briskly to a suburban street within sight of Long Island Sound and stopped outside a small house with mock-Tudor gables. As he walked up the path, the front door was opened by a blond girl of thirteen wearing a Michael Jackson T-shirt.

Ellis said, "Hello, Petal."

"Hi, Daddy," she replied.

He kissed her, feeling as always a glow of pride simultaneously with a stab of guilt.

He followed her into a small, neat living room. "Won't you sit down?" said Petal.

Ellis sat down.

"Can I get you something?" she asked.

"Relax. You don't have to be so polite. I'm your daddy."

She looked uncertain. After a moment she said, "I have to brush my hair. Then we can go. Excuse me."

"Sure," said Ellis. She went out. He found her courtesy painful. It was a sign that he was still a stranger. He had been seeing her at least once a month for the past year, ever since coming back from Paris. Sometimes they would spend a day together, but more often he would just take her out to dinner, as he was going to do today. His aim was a modest one: he wanted to take a small but permanent place in his daughter's life.

It had meant giving up fieldwork. His superiors had been highly displeased. There were too few good undercover agents. He too had been reluctant, but he could not win his daughter's affection if he had to disappear every year or so to some remote corner of the world, unable to tell her where he was going or why or even for how long.

He missed the excitement, the danger, the thrill of the chase, and the feeling that he was doing an important job that nobody else could do quite as well. But for too long his only emotional attachments had been fleeting ones, and after he lost Jane, he felt the need of at least one person whose love was permanent.

While he was waiting, Gill, his ex-wife, came into the room, cool and composed in a white summer dress. He kissed her proffered cheek. "How are you?" she asked.

"The same as ever. You?"

"I'm incredibly busy." She started to tell him, in some detail, how much she had to do, and as always, Ellis tuned out. He was fond of her, although she bored him to death. It was odd to think he had once been married to her. But she had been the prettiest girl in the English department, and he was the cleverest boy, and it had been 1967, when anything could happen, especially in California. They were married at the end of their first year. Then Ellis flunked his exams and got thrown out of college and therefore was drafted. Gill had known by then that the marriage was not going to work, and she was just waiting for Ellis to make his escape.

He was in the hospital in Saigon with a bullet wound in his calf—the helicopter pilot's commonest injury, because his seat is armored but the floor is not—when the divorce became final.

She had not told him about the baby. He found out a few years later, when he became a spy, tracked Gill down as an exercise, and learned that she had a child with the late '6os name of Petal and a new husband called Bernard. Not telling him about Petal was the only mean thing Gill had ever done to him, he thought, although she still maintained it had been for his own good. He had insisted on seeing Petal from time to time, and he had stopped her calling Bernard "Daddy." But he had not sought to become part of their family life, not until last year.

Borrowing Gill's car, Ellis drove Petal to a Chinese restaurant in Little Neck. She liked Chinese food. She relaxed a little once she was away from the house, and they talked about her friends and schoolwork. Then he asked her if she wanted to go to Washington and stay at his place one weekend. "It's only an hour on the plane," he said, "and we could have a good time. And you've never seen my apartment. I have a spare bedroom. . . ." He trailed off. He could see she was not interested.

"Oh, Daddy, I don't know," she said. "I have so much to do on weekends—homework, and parties, and shopping. . . ."

Ellis hid his disappointment. "Don't worry," he said. "Maybe sometime when you're not so busy you could come."

She was visibly relieved. In the car on the way home she asked him whether she was too young to have a boyfriend.

Ellis wanted to say yes, but he couldn't stop her growing up. "You're old enough to date, but not to go steady," he said. He glanced at her to catch her reaction. She looked amused. Maybe they don't talk about going steady anymore, he thought.

When they reached the house, Bernard's car was in the driveway. He was in the living room, a small, good-natured man with very short hair. Petal greeted him enthusiastically, hugging and kissing him. He seemed a little embarrassed. He shook Ellis' hand firmly, saying, "Government still ticking okay back in D.C.?"

"Same as always," Ellis said. They thought that he worked for the State Department and that his job was to read French newspapers and magazines and prepare a daily digest for the France Desk.

"How about a beer?"

Ellis did not really want one, but he accepted just to be friendly. Bernard went into the kitchen to get it. He was credit manager for a department store in New York City. Petal seemed to like and respect him, and he was gently affectionate with her. He and Gill had no other children.

He came back with two glasses of beer and handed one to Ellis. "Go and do your homework now," he said to Petal. "Daddy will say good-bye before he leaves."

She kissed him again and ran off. When she was out of earshot, Bernard said, "She isn't normally so affectionate. She seems to overdo it when you're around. I don't understand it."

"Don't worry about it," Ellis said. "How's business?"

"Not bad. High interest rates haven't hit us too badly."

They talked about the economy for a few minutes; then Ellis got up to leave. He went to the foot of the staircase and called, "Bye, Petal."

She came to the top of the stairs. "Bye," she said.

Gill drove him to the airport. When they were on the road, she said, "Petal told me she didn't want to spend a weekend with you. You must be upset. I'm sorry."

"It's my fault. I didn't think it through. Before I came along, she had a mommy and a daddy and a home—all that any child wants. But I'm not *just* superfluous. By being around, I threaten her happiness. I'm an intruder. That's why she hugs Bernard in front of me. She doesn't mean to hurt me. She does it because she's afraid of losing *him*. And it's me who makes her afraid."

"She'll get over it," Gill said. "America is full of kids with two daddies." She patted his knee. "Don't be too hard on yourself. You just weren't made for this. You don't want a house, a job, the suburbs, children. I loved you because you were different, crazy, exciting. You would do *anything*. But you're no family man."

He sat in silence, thinking. Is it true? I don't want a house in the suburbs, he thought, but I'd like a home: maybe a villa in Morocco or a loft in Greenwich Village or a penthouse in Rome. I don't want a wife to be my housekeeper, cooking and cleaning and taking the minutes at the PTA, but I'd like a companion, someone to share movies and poetry with, someone to talk to at night. I'd even like to have kids, and raise them to know about something more than Michael Jackson.

Gill stopped the car, and he realized they were outside the Eastern Airlines terminal. "Thanks for the ride," he said.

"You need a woman like you, one of your kind," Gill said.

Ellis thought of Jane. "I met one, once. She married a handsome doctor."

"Is the doctor crazy like you?"

"I don't think so."

"Then it won't last. When did she get married?"

"About a year ago."

"Ah." Gill was probably figuring that that was when Ellis had come back into Petal's life in a big way. "Take my advice," she said. "Check her out."

ON THE plane Ellis found a newsmagazine in the seat pocket, and it had an analysis of the situation in Afghanistan. There was a buildup of Russian troops and arms going on, it said, in preparation for a major summer offensive. The rebel leader, Masud, was mentioned, and among the crucial target areas the article listed the Panjshir Valley.

Ellis remembered Jean-Pierre talking about the Five Lions Valley. Ellis had picked up a little Farsi in Iran, and he knew that *panjshir* meant "five lions." He looked out the window, watching the sun set. There was no doubt Jane would be in grave danger this summer. But it was none of his business. She was married to someone else now.

ALLEN WINDERMAN TOOK ELLIS Thaler to lunch at a seafood restaurant overlooking the Potomac River. As the White House was paying, Ellis ordered lobster and a glass of white wine. Winderman asked for Perrier and a salad.

He was a typical Washington operator. Everything about him was tight: his tie, his shoes, his schedule, and his self-control.

Ellis was on guard. He could not refuse an invitation from a presidential aide, but he did not like Allen Winderman.

Winderman got right down to business. "I want your advice," he began. "What do you know about Afghanistan?"

Ellis felt suddenly cold. Sooner or later this is going to involve Jane, he thought. They know about her, of course. I made no secret of it. I told Bill in Paris I was going to ask her to marry me. I called Bill subsequently to find out whether she really did go to Afghanistan. All that went down in my file.

"I know a little," Ellis said cautiously. "The Afghans are wild, ragged, fierce mountain tribesmen, hardly out of the Middle Ages. They're said to be elaborately polite, brave as lions, and pitilessly cruel. Their country is harsh and arid and barren. But they're all poets, the way all Frenchmen are gourmets and all Welshmen are singers. What do *you* know about them?"

"There's no such thing as an Afghan," Winderman said. "There are six million Pushtuns in the south, three million Tajiks in the west, a million Uzbeks in the north, and another dozen or so nationalities with fewer than a million. They're like the American Indians, who never thought of themselves as one people, but as Apache or Crow or Sioux. The Afghan tribes would just as soon fight one another as fight the Russians. Our problem is to get them to unite against the Russians."

Ellis nodded, wondering, When does Jane come into all this? He said, "So the main question is: Who will be the big chief?"

"That's easy. The most promising of the guerrilla leaders, by far, is Ahmed Shah Masud, in the Panjshir Valley."

The Five Lions Valley! What is Winderman up to? thought Ellis. He asked, "What makes Masud so special?"

"Most of the rebel leaders are content to control their tribes, collect taxes, and deny the government access to their territory.

Masud does more than that. He comes out of his mountain strong-hold and attacks. He's within striking distance of three strategic targets: the capital city, Kabul; the Salang Tunnel, on the only highway from Kabul to the Soviet Union; and Bagram, the principal military air base. He's in a position to inflict major damage, and he does. He has studied the art of guerrilla warfare. He's easily the best military brain in the country. And he has finances. Emeralds are mined in his valley and sold in Pakistan. Masud takes a ten percent tax on all sales and uses the money to fund his army. He's twenty-eight years old, and charismatic. The people worship him. Finally, he's a Tajik. The largest Afghan tribe is the Pushtuns, and all the others hate *them*, so the leader can't be a Pushtun. Tajiks are the next biggest nation. There's a chance they might unite under a Tajik."

"And we want to facilitate this?"

"That's right. The stronger the rebels, the more damage they do to their enemies, the Russians."

"What do you want from me?" Ellis asked.

"I want to pick your brains. Is there any way an undercover agent could promote an alliance between the Afghan tribes?"

"I expect so," said Ellis. The food came, giving him a few moments to think. When the waiter had gone away, he said, "It should be possible, provided there is something they want from us—and I imagine that would be weapons."

"Right." Winderman started to eat. Between mouthfuls he said, "At the moment, they buy their weapons across the border in Pakistan. All they can get there are copies of Victorian British rifles—or, if not copies, the genuine article, a hundred years old and still firing. They also steal Kalashnikovs from dead Russian soldiers. But they're desperate for small artillery—antiaircraft guns and hand-launched ground-to-air missiles—so they can shoot down planes and helicopters."

"Are we willing to give them these weapons?"

"Yes. Not directly—we would want to conceal our involvement by sending them through intermediaries. But that's no problem. We could use the Saudis."

"Okay." Ellis swallowed some lobster. It was good. "Let me

48

say what I think is the first step. I'd have Masud run a training scheme in the Five Lions Valley. Each rebel group would send a few young men to fight alongside Masud for a while and learn the methods that make him so successful. They would also learn to respect him and trust him, if he is as good a leader as you say."

Winderman nodded thoughtfully. "That's the kind of proposal that might be acceptable to tribal leaders who would reject any plan that committed them to take orders from Masud."

"Is there one rival leader in particular whose cooperation is essential to any alliance?" asked Ellis.

"There are two: Jahan Kamil and Amal Azizi, both Pushtuns."

"Then I would send in an undercover agent, with the objective of getting the two of them around a table with Masud. When he came back with all three signatures on a piece of paper, we would send the first load of rocket launchers. Further consignments would depend on how well the training program was going."

Winderman lit a cigarette. "This is exactly the kind of thing I had in mind. What's the downside risk?"

Ellis considered. "If the Russians caught the agent, they could get considerable propaganda value out of the whole thing. At the moment they have what the White House would call an image problem in Afghanistan. Their allies in the Third World don't enjoy watching them overrun a small, primitive country. Their Muslim friends in particular tend to sympathize with the Afghan rebels. Now, the Russians' line is that the so-called rebels are just bandits, financed and armed by the CIA. They would love to be able to prove that—by catching a real, live CIA spook right there in the country and putting him on trial. In terms of global politics, I imagine that could do us a lot a damage."

"What are the chances that the Russians would catch our man?"

"Slender. If they haven't been able to catch Masud, why would they be able to catch an undercover agent sent to meet Masud?"

"Good." Winderman stubbed out his cigarette. "I want you to be that agent."

Ellis was taken by surprise. "I don't do that stuff anymore," he said, but he could not help thinking, I would see Jane!

"I talked to your boss on the phone," Winderman said. "His

opinion was that an assignment in Afghanistan might tempt you back into fieldwork."

So it was a setup. Ellis hated to be manipulated. But he wanted to go to the Five Lions Valley.

There was a long silence. "Will you do it?"

"I'll think about it," Ellis replied.

CHAPTER 5

THE Five Lions River was never warm, but it seemed a little less cold now, in the balmy evening air, when the women came down to their own stretch of the bank to bathe. Jane waded into the water with the others, lifting her dress inch by inch until the water was up to her waist. Then she began to wash. After long practice she had mastered the peculiar Afghan skill of getting clean all over without undressing.

She came out of the river, shivering, and stood near her friend Zahara, who was washing her hair in a pool, with much splashing and spluttering. Jane was now accepted by the village women as one of them. The last vestiges of reserve had vanished after the birth of Chantal, which seemed to have confirmed that Jane was a woman like any other. The talk at the riverside was surprisingly frank—perhaps because the children were left behind in the care of older sisters and grandmothers. Consequently, during the past six weeks Jane had sometimes been able to turn the evening bathing session into an impromptu health education class. Birth control was the most popular topic, although the women of Banda were more interested in how to ensure pregnancy than in how to prevent it. But there was some sympathy for Jane's idea that a woman was better able to care for her children if they were born two years apart rather than every twelve months.

Today there was an air of excitement. The latest Pakistan convoy was due back. The men would bring small luxuries—a shawl, some oranges, plastic bangles—as well as the all-important guns and ammunition for the war. Zahara's husband, Ahmed Gul, a son of the midwife, Rabia, was leader of the convoy, and Zahara was visibly excited at the prospect of seeing him again.

Jane's skin dried almost immediately in the warm, dusty air. It was now the height of summer, and every day was long, dry, and hot. The women began to drift back to the village. Jane walked with Zahara, half listening to her talk and thinking about Chantal. There had been conflicts over child care with the midwife, whose advice Jane had ignored. Rabia had said the baby should not be washed for the first forty days, but Jane bathed Chantal every day like any Western baby. Then Jane had caught Rabia giving Chantal butter mixed with sugar, feeding the stuff to the child on the end of her wrinkled old finger, and Jane had got cross. The next day Rabia had gone to attend another birth, and sent one of her many granddaughters, a thirteen-year-old called Fara, to help Jane with Chantal. This was a great improvement. Fara had no preconceptions about child care and simply did as she was told. She required no pay. She worked for her food and for the privilege of learning about babies in preparation for her own marriage. Her initial awe of Jane was gradually turning into something more like adoring loyalty.

Jean-Pierre had come into his own. He was gentle yet confident with Chantal, and considerate and loving with Jane. It was he who had suggested that Chantal could be given boiled goat's milk when she woke in the night, and he had improvised a feeding bottle from his medical supplies so that he could be the one to get up and Jane could sleep.

By now the group of women had reached the cluster of houses that formed the nucleus of the village, and one by one they disappeared behind the mud walls of their courtyards. Jane scared off a flurry of chickens and shoved aside a scrawny cow to get into her own house. She found Fara singing to Chantal, who was alert and wide-eyed. She's such a *pretty* baby, Jane thought, with her fat cheeks and her tiny nose and her blue, blue eyes.

She sent Fara to make tea. A few minutes later Jean-Pierre came in. His baggy cotton trousers and shirt were grimy and bloodstained, and there was dust in his long brown hair and his dark beard. He had been to Khenj, a village ten miles down the valley, to treat the survivors of a bombing raid. Jane stood on tiptoe to kiss him. "How was it?" she said in French.

"Bad." He gave her a squeeze, then went to lean over Chantal. "Hello, little one." He smiled, and Chantal gurgled.

Fara came in with hot green tea, some of the flatbread they called *nan*, and a stone jar of new butter. Jane and Jean-Pierre began to eat. The butter was a rare treat. Their evening *nan* was usually dipped into yogurt, curds, or oil. At midday they normally ate rice with a meat-flavored sauce that might or might not have meat in it. Once a week they had chicken or goat. Jane, still eating for two, indulged in the luxury of an egg every day. At this time of the year there was plenty of fresh fruit—apricots, plums, apples, and mulberries by the sackful—for dessert. Jane felt very healthy.

After they had finished their supper, Jean-Pierre went outside and returned with a bowl of mulberries. Jane picked up Chantal and began to nurse her. "I got another complaint about you today," Jean-Pierre said.

"From whom?" Jane said sharply.

"Mohammed Khan. He says you have been teaching the village women to be barren."

Jane sighed. It was not just the stupidity of the village menfolk that annoyed her, but also Jean-Pierre's deferring to her accusers. "Abdullah Karim is behind it, of course," she said. The mullah's wife was often at the riverside, and no doubt she reported to her husband everything she heard.

"You may have to stop telling them how to avoid pregnancy," said Jean-Pierre with a patient air that irritated Jane. "It's creating difficulties. If we offend them, it would give the Médecins pour la Liberté a bad name, and the rebels could decide to do without French doctors."

Jane said flatly, "We'll just have to take that risk."

"And why should we?" he said. He was getting angry.

"Because there is really only one thing of permanent value that we can give these people, and that is information. It's all very well to patch their wounds and give them antibiotics to kill germs, but they will never have enough surgeons or enough drugs. We can improve their health permanently by teaching them basic nutrition, hygiene, and health care. Better to offend Abdullah than to stop doing that."

"Still, I wish you hadn't made an enemy of that man."

"He hit me with a stick!" Jane shouted furiously. Chantal began to cry. Jane forced herself to be calm and rocked the baby for a moment. Before the argument could continue, they heard shouting, and a man's voice came from their courtyard.

Jean-Pierre called out in Dari, "Come in."

It was Mohammed Khan. "The convoy was ambushed," he said without preamble. "We lost twenty-seven men—and all the supplies."

Jane closed her eyes in pain. She could not help but picture it: the moonlit line of brown-skinned men and scrawny horses stretched out unevenly along a stony trail through a narrow, shadowy valley; the beat of the rotor blades in a sudden crescendo; the flares, the grenades, the machine-gun fire; the panic as the men tried to take cover on the bare hillside; the hopeless shots fired at the invulnerable helicopters; and then at last the shouts of the wounded and the screams of the dying.

She thought suddenly of her friend. Zahara's husband had been with the convoy. "What—what about Ahmed Gul?"

"He came back. But he's wounded."

"Who from this village died?"

"None. Banda was lucky. My brother Matullah is all right, and so is Alishan Karim, the brother of the mullah. There are three other survivors—two of them wounded."

Jean-Pierre said, "I'll come right away." He stepped into the front room of the house, now the medical storeroom, to get his bag. Jane put Chantal down in her makeshift cradle in the corner. Jean-Pierre would probably need help.

Mohammed said, "We have almost no ammunition."

Jane felt little regret about that. She hated the war and would shed no tears if the rebels were obliged for a while to stop killing poor homesick seventeen-year-old Russian soldier boys. But the convoy's loss of much needed medical supplies was a real waste.

Mohammed went on. "We have lost four convoys in a year. Only three got through."

"How are the Russians able to find them?" she asked.

Jean-Pierre spoke through the doorway. "They must have intensi-

54

fied their surveillance of the passes by low-flying helicopters—or perhaps even by satellite photography."

Mohammed shook his head. "The Pushtuns betray us."

The three of them went out into the courtyard. Jane paused to give Fara instructions about changing Chantal, then hurried after the two men.

It was dark as they approached the mosque, an open-sided building that looked like a glorified bus shelter. The villagers prayed there, but they also used it as a meeting hall, marketplace, schoolroom, and guesthouse. And tonight it would be a hospital.

Oil lamps suspended from hooks in the stone columns now lit the verandalike building. The six survivors of the ambush were huddled in a group on the beaten-earth floor. The three uninjured ones squatted on their haunches, still wearing their round Chitrali caps, looking dirty, dispirited, and exhausted. Jane recognized Matullah Khan, a younger version of his brother Mohammed; and Alishan Karim, thinner than his brother the mullah but just as mean-looking. Two of the wounded men sat on the floor with their backs to the wall, one with a filthy, bloodstained bandage around his head and the other with his arm in an improvised sling. At first glance their wounds appeared slight.

The third injured man, Ahmed Gul, was lying on a stretcher made from two sticks and a blanket. His eyes were closed and his skin was gray. His wife, Zahara, squatted behind him, cradling his head in her lap, stroking his hair, and weeping silently.

Jean-Pierre called for a table, hot water, and towels, then got down on his knees beside Ahmed. After a few seconds he looked up at Jane and said in French, "He's in a bad way."

Jane could see bloodstains on Ahmed's chin. He had been coughing blood, a sign that he had internal injuries.

Zahara looked pleadingly at Jane. "How is he?"

"I'm sorry, my friend," said Jane gently. "He's bad."

Zahara nodded resignedly. She had known it, but the confirmation brought fresh tears to her handsome face.

Jean-Pierre said to Jane, "Check the others for me—I don't want to lose a minute here."

It looked as if it might be a long night.

AHMED DIED A FEW MINUTES after midnight. Jean-Pierre felt like crying with sheer frustration, for he knew he could have saved the man's life, if only he had had an anesthetist and electricity and an operating theater.

He covered the dead man's face, then looked at the wife, who had been standing motionless, watching, for hours. "I'm sorry," he said to Zahara. She nodded. He turned away, weary to his bones. He had been working on mangled bodies all day, but this was the first patient he had lost.

He felt a hand on his shoulder, and turned to see Mohammed. He felt a stab of guilt.

Mohammed said, "It's the will of Allah."

Jean-Pierre nodded and packed his instruments into his bag. Without looking at Mohammed, he said, "What will you do now?"

"Send another convoy immediately," Mohammed replied. "We must have ammunition."

Jean-Pierre was suddenly alert, despite his fatigue. "Do you want to look at the maps?"

"Yes."

The two men walked through the village to the shopkeeper's house. In the living room, Fara was asleep on a rug beside Chantal's cradle. She awoke instantly and stood up. "You can go home now," Jean-Pierre told her, and to Mohammed, standing waiting, he said, "You know where they are."

Mohammed nodded and opened a painted wooden chest. He took out a thick bundle of folded maps, selected several, and spread them on the floor. Jean-Pierre looked over Mohammed's shoulder. "Where was the ambush?" he asked.

Mohammed pointed to a spot near the city of Jalalabad.

The trails followed by Mohammed's convoys were not shown on these or any other maps. However, Jean-Pierre's maps showed some of the valleys, plateaus, and seasonal streams where there *might* be trails. He now suggested, "You could swing more to the north, around Jalalabad." Above the plain in which the city stood, there was a maze of valleys, like a cobweb stretched between the Konar and Nuristan rivers.

Mohammed shook his head. "There have been too many ambushes there. No. The next convoy will swing *south* of Jalalabad."

Jean-Pierre frowned. "I don't see how that's possible. To the south there's nothing but open country all the way from the Khyber Pass. You'd be spotted."

"We won't use the Khyber Pass," said Mohammed. He put his finger on the map, then traced the Afghanistan-Pakistan border southward. "We will cross the border at Teremengal." His finger traced a route from there to the Five Lions Valley.

Jean-Pierre nodded, hiding his jubilation. "It makes a lot of sense. When will the new convoy leave here?"

Mohammed began to fold up the charts. "The day after tomorrow. There is no time to lose." He replaced the maps in the painted chest, then went to the door.

Jane came in just as he was leaving. Jean-Pierre's medical bag was on the floor where he had left it, and Jane bent to pick it up. His heart missed a beat. He took the bag from her quickly. "I'll put this away," he said. "You see to Chantal. She needs feeding."

The baby was awake and crying. As Jane settled down to feed her, Jean-Pierre carried the bag and a lamp into the front room. Boxes of medical supplies were arranged on the shopkeeper's crude wooden shelves. He put his bag on the blue-tiled counter and took out a black plastic object about the size and shape of a portable telephone. This he put in his pocket, then returned to the living room. "I'm going down to the river to bathe," he said to Jane. "I'm too dirty to go to bed."

She gave him the dreamy, contented smile she often wore when feeding the baby. "Be quick," she said.

He went out. Lamps still burned in a few houses, and he heard from one window the sound of a woman weeping bitterly, but most places were quiet and dark. He followed a stony path between two barley fields. In one he heard the hiss of scythes, and on a narrow terrace he saw two men weeding by lamplight. He did not speak to them.

He reached the river, crossed the ford, and climbed the winding path up the opposite cliff. After ten minutes he reached the high point he was seeking. He took the radio from his pocket and extended its telescopic antenna. It was the latest and most sophisticated small transmitter the KGB had. He pressed the talk button and spoke in English and in code. "This is Simplex. Come in, please.".

After the third try he got a crackly, accented reply. "Here is Butler. Go ahead, Simplex."

"Your party was a big success."

"I repeat. The party was a big success," came the reply.

"In preparation for the next one, I need three camels." In code that meant, "Meet me three days from today."

"I repeat. You need three camels."

"I will see you at the mosque." That too was code. "The mosque" was a place some miles away, where three valleys met.

"I repeat. At the mosque."

"Today is Sunday." That was not code; it was a precaution. The dullard who was taking all this down might not realize it was after midnight, with the consequence that Jean-Pierre's contact would arrive a day early at the rendezvous.

"I repeat. Today is Sunday."

"Over and out."

Jean-Pierre collapsed the antenna and returned the radio to his pocket; then he made his way down the cliff to the riverside.

He stripped off his clothes quickly, stepped gingerly into the Five Lions River, and began to scrub himself. Kneeling in the shallows, naked and shivering beneath the stars, he scrubbed and scrubbed as if he would never stop.

"THE child has measles, gastroenteritis, and ringworm," said Jean-Pierre. "He is also dirty and undernourished."

"Aren't they all," said Jane.

They were speaking French, as they normally did together, and the child's mother wondered what they were saying. Jean-Pierre spoke to her in Dari, saying simply, "Your son will get well."

He crossed to the other side of the cave and opened his drug case. All children brought to the clinic were automatically vaccinated against tuberculosis. As he prepared the injection he watched Jane soothe the frightened child with light, reassuring caresses. When she swabbed the skin of the boy's right arm with alcohol, her expression became serious, and she ground her teeth—a sign that she was concentrating. Jean-Pierre knew all of her expressions, and none of her thoughts.

He speculated often about what she was thinking, but he was afraid to ask her, for he had to be constantly on his guard for fear something he said—or even the expression on his face—might betray him. Any talk of truth and dishonesty, or trust and betrayal, or freedom and tyranny, was taboo; he was wary even of quite innocent topics. Consequently, there was a peculiar lack of intimacy in their marriage.

"Ready when you are," Jane said, and she smiled at him.

He took the child's arm and said in Dari, "How old are you?"

"Five."

As the boy spoke, Jean-Pierre stuck the needle in. The child immediately began to wail. Jean-Pierre released the child, who went to his mother. He counted out thirty 250-gram capsules of griseofulvin and handed them to the woman. "Make him take one every day until they are all gone," he said in simple Dari. That would deal with the ringworm. The measles and the gastroenteritis would take their own course. "Keep him in bed until the spots disappear, and make sure he drinks a lot."

The woman nodded.

"Does he have any brothers and sisters?" Jean-Pierre asked.

"Five brothers and two sisters," the woman said proudly.

"He should sleep alone, or they will get sick too." The woman looked dubious. She probably had only one bed for all her children. There was nothing Jean-Pierre could do about that. What the child really needed neither Jean-Pierre nor its mother could provide—plenty of good, nutritious food.

There was one more patient: the local *malang*. Half mad, he wandered the Five Lions Valley from Comar, twenty-five miles upstream of Banda, to Charikar, in the Russian-controlled plain sixty miles to the southwest. He spoke gibberish and saw visions. The Afghans believed *malangs* to be lucky, and not only tolerated their behavior but gave them food and clothing.

He came in, wearing rags around his loins and a Russian officer's cap. He held his stomach, miming pain. Jean-Pierre shook out a handful of diamorphine pills and gave them to him. The madman ran off, clutching his synthetic heroin tablets.

"He must be addicted to that stuff by now," Jane said. There was disapproval in her voice.

"He is," Jean-Pierre admitted.

"Why do you give it to him?"

Jean-Pierre had reasons of his own, but he said to Jane, "The man has an ulcer."

He began to pack his bags with equipment and drugs. In the morning he had to hold a clinic in Cobak—six or seven miles away across the mountains—and he had a rendezvous to keep on the way. He filled a flask with purified water to drink while he was away. He would be fed by the villagers there.

He took his bags outside and loaded them onto the bad-tempered old mare he used for such trips. This animal would walk all day in a straight line but was highly reluctant to turn corners, on account of which Jane had named it Maggie, after the British prime minister, Margaret Thatcher.

Jean-Pierre was ready. He went back inside and kissed Jane's soft mouth. Then he left the cave and led Maggie down the mountain to the deserted village. Heading southwest, he followed the riverbank, walking quickly and tirelessly under the hot sun. He was used to it.

As he left his doctor persona behind and thought ahead to his rendezvous, he began to feel a sense of the past. Looking at the khaki-colored rock walls of the gully through which he was striding, he saw scenes from his childhood. His earliest memory was of his papa's trial, and of the overwhelming sense of outrage and injustice he had felt when they had sentenced him to five years in jail. At that age—Jean-Pierre must have been four—he did not know what it meant to be a hero of the Resistance. He knew his father was a Communist, as were his father's friends.

It was not until Papa came out of prison, ill and dying, that Jean-Pierre talked to him at length and finally understood the injustice of it all. After the Germans invaded France, the French Communists, being already organized in cells, had played a leading role in the Resistance. But when the war was over, his father had carried on the fight against right-wing tyranny in Algeria, then a French colony. The Algerians were oppressed and exploited by their rulers but struggling courageously for their freedom in another cruel war. Because of Papa's work for their liberation, he had been convicted of treason.

As Jean-Pierre grew older he learned nothing to change his conviction that the Communist movement, guided from Moscow, was the only hope for the oppressed people of the world, and the only means of destroying the judges who had so brutally betrayed his papa, a hero who had risked his life for his fellowmen.

They'd regret it now, Papa, if they knew what revenge I'm taking, Jean-Pierre thought as he led his bony mare up the Afghan mountainside. Because of the intelligence I have provided, the Communists here have strangled Masud's supply lines. Single-handedly, Papa, I have almost destroyed the effectiveness of this barbarian who wants to take his country back to the dark ages of savagery, underdevelopment, and Islamic superstition.

Of course, strangling Masud's supply lines was not enough. The man was already a figure of national stature, with the brains and strength of character to graduate from rebel leader to legitimate president. He was a Tito, a de Gaulle, a Mugabe. He had to be not just neutralized, but destroyed—taken by the Russians, dead or alive.

The difficulty was that Masud moved about quickly and silently, like a deer in a forest. But there would come a time, sooner or later, when Jean-Pierre would know for certain exactly where Masud was going to be for the next twenty-four hours, and then Jean-Pierre would use his radio to transmit a special code, and the hawk would strike.

He wished he could tell Jane what he was really doing here. He might even convince her that it was right. However, he knew instinctively that she would not forgive him for deceiving her as he had. In fact she would be enraged. She would leave him immediately, the way she had left Ellis Thaler. So in his terror of losing her, he continued to deceive her.

Complete safety was not possible, but he took every precaution against discovery. When using the radio, he spoke in code, and his radio was small enough to be concealed in the false bottom of his medical bag, or in his pocket when he was not carrying the bag. Its disadvantage was that it was powerful enough only for very short conversations. In consequence, Jean-Pierre had to meet with Anatoly, his contact, to pass on his information.

He breasted a rise and looked down. He was at the head of a small valley bifurcated by a tumbling mountain stream. On its near side was a little stone hut. The region was dotted with such primitive buildings, put up by the nomads and traveling merchants who used them at night.

He set off down the hill, leading Maggie. Anatoly was probably there already. Jean-Pierre did not know his real name or rank, but assumed he was a colonel in the KGB. Despite his rank, Anatoly was no deskman. Between here and Bagram was fifty miles of mountain country, and he walked it alone, taking a day and a half. He was an Oriental Russian, with high cheekbones and yellow skin, and in Afghan clothes he passed as an Uzbek, a member of the Mongoloid ethnic group of north Afghanistan.

As Jean-Pierre neared the hut he whistled a tune, in case anyone other than Anatoly should be inside. He tied Maggie to a tree, then ducked his head and entered. The cool interior of the hut was empty. He sat down with his back to the stone wall and after a few minutes closed his eyes. He was tired, but too tense to sleep. This was the worst part of what he was doing: the combination of fear and boredom that overcame him during these long waits. He had learned to accept delays in this country without wristwatches, but he had never acquired the imperturbable patience of the Afghans.

He sensed the presence of someone else and opened his eyes to see Anatoly's Oriental face inches from his own.

"I could have robbed you," said Anatoly in fluent French.

"I wasn't asleep."

Anatoly sat down cross-legged on the dirt floor. He was a squat, muscular figure in baggy cotton shirt and trousers, with a turban, a checked scarf, and a mud-colored woolen blanket, called a pattu, around his shoulders. He let the scarf drop from his face and smiled, showing stained teeth. "How are you, my friend?"

"Well."

"And your wife?"

The Russians had been dead against the idea of his bringing Jane to Afghanistan, arguing that she would interfere with his work. Jean-Pierre had pointed out that he had to take a nurse with him anyway, and in the end they had agreed, but reluctantly. "Jane is fine," he said. "She had the baby six weeks ago. A girl."

"Congratulations!" Anatoly seemed pleased.

"You hit the convoy I told you about in our last meeting."

"Yes. Your information is very good. Congratulations again."

Jean-Pierre felt a glow of pride. "Our system seems to be working very well," he added modestly.

Anatoly nodded. "What was their reaction to the ambush?"

"Increasing desperation. They're running out of ammunition."

"And the next convoy—when will it depart?"

"It left yesterday."

"They *are* desperate. Good." Anatoly reached inside his shirt and brought out a map. He unfolded it on the floor. It showed the area between the Five Lions Valley and the Pakistan border.

Jean-Pierre concentrated hard, recalling the details he had memorized during his conversation with Mohammed, and began to trace for Anatoly the route the convoy would follow on its way back from Pakistan. Although he did not know exactly when they would return, Anatoly had people in Peshawar who would let him know when the Five Lions convoy had finished buying what they needed. From that he would be able to work out their timetable.

Anatoly made no notes, but memorized every word Jean-Pierre said. When they had finished, they went over the whole thing again, and then the Russian folded the map and put it back inside his shirt. "And what of Masud?" he said quietly.

"We haven't seen him since last I spoke to you."

"Masud is a fox," said Anatoly with a rare flash of emotion. "Oh, we will catch him. He cannot elude us forever—we are so many, and so strong, and our blood is up." Conscious that he was revealing his feelings, he became practical again. "Batteries," he said, and brought a battery pack out of his shirt.

63

Jean-Pierre extracted the old batteries from his radio and exchanged them for new ones. They did this every time they met, to be sure that Jean-Pierre would not lose contact simply by running out of power.

As Jean-Pierre was putting the radio back into his medical bag Anatoly said, "Have you got anything in there for blisters? My feet—" Then he stopped suddenly, frowned, and cocked his head, listening.

Jean-Pierre tensed. In the next instant he heard a footfall outside, and then a shadow darkened the sunlit entrance and Jane walked in.

"Jane!" he said.

Both men sprang to their feet.

Jean-Pierre said, "What is it? Why are you here?"

"Thank heavens I caught up with you," she said breathlessly.

Out of the corner of his eye Jean-Pierre saw Anatoly turn away, as an Afghan would turn away from a brazen woman. The gesture helped Jean-Pierre recover from the shock of seeing Jane. He looked around quickly. Anatoly had put away the maps several minutes earlier, fortunately. But the radio—the radio was sticking out an inch or two from the medical bag. However, Jane had not seen it—yet.

"Sit down," said Jean-Pierre. "Catch your breath." He sat down at the same time and shifted his bag so that the radio poked out from the side away from Jane. "What's the matter?" he said.

"A medical emergency I can't solve."

Jean-Pierre's tension eased a fraction. "Have some water," he said. He reached into his bag with one hand and with the other pushed the radio in while he rummaged for his flask of purified water. He handed her the flask. The evidence was now out of sight. What else was there to make her suspicious? She would assume Anatoly was a stranger sharing a resting place, but she might have heard him speaking French. Still, that was not uncommon. If an Afghan had a second language, it was often French, and an Uzbek might speak French better than he spoke Dari. What had Anatoly been saying when she walked in? Jean-Pierre remembered. He had been asking for blister ointment. That was perfect. Afghans always asked for medicine when they met a doctor.

Jane drank from the flask and began to speak. "A few minutes after you left, they brought in a boy of eighteen, with a very bad thigh wound. He was hurt in the fighting near Rokha, and his father had carried him all the way up the valley—it took him two days. The wound was badly gangrenous by the time they arrived. I gave him six hundred milligrams of crystalline penicillin, injected into the buttock. Then I cleaned out the wound."

"Exactly correct," said Jean-Pierre.

"A few minutes later he broke out in a cold sweat and became confused. I took his pulse. It was rapid but weak."

"Did he go pale or gray, and have difficulty breathing?"

"Yes. I treated him for shock—raised his feet, covered him with a blanket—and then I came to catch up with you." She was close to tears. "His father carried him for two days. I can't let him die this way."

"He needn't," said Jean-Pierre. "Allergic shock is a rare but quite well-known reaction to penicillin injections. The treatment is half a milliliter of Adrenalin, followed by an antihistamine— say, six milliliters of diphenhydramine—repeated every ten minutes if necessary. Would you like me to come back with you?"

Jane sighed. "No," she said. "There will be someone else dying on the far side of the hill. You go on to Cobak."

"If you're sure."

"Yes."

A match flared as Anatoly lit a cigarette. Jane glanced at him, then looked at Jean-Pierre again. "Half a milliliter of Adrenalin and then six milliliters of diphenhydramine." She stood up.

"Yes." Jean-Pierre stood up with her and kissed her. "You must hurry. Would you like to take Maggie?"

"I don't think so. On that path, walking is faster."

Jean-Pierre watched her go out. After a minute or two he went to the doorway. He could see her, two or three hundred yards away, a small, slight figure in a thin cotton dress, striding determinedly up the valley, alone in the dusty brown landscape.

He came back inside and sat down. He and Anatoly looked at one another. "That was close," said Jean-Pierre.

65

CHAPTER 6

THE boy died.

He had been dead almost an hour when Jane got back, hot and dusty and exhausted to the point of collapse. The father was waiting for her at the mouth of the cave, looking numb and reproachful. He said nothing. She went into the cave and looked at the boy. Too tired to feel angry, she was overwhelmed by disappointment, and wept later as she lay in her bed on the roof of the shopkeeper's house, with Chantal on a tiny mattress beside her. Her tears blurred the stars before she fell asleep.

The next day she walked up the mountainside with her medicine case and opened the cave clinic. As she dealt with the usual cases of malnutrition, malaria, infected wounds, and intestinal parasites, she thought over yesterday.

It was fortunate that Jean-Pierre had stopped on the way from Banda to Cobak—to rest, presumably—at the little stone hut, giving her a chance to catch up with him. She had been so relieved to see Maggie tethered outside, and to find Jean-Pierre in the hut with that funny little Uzbek man. The two of them had jumped out of their skins when she walked in. It had been almost comical. It was the first time she had ever seen an Afghan stand up when a woman came in. She recalled that he had been asking Jean-Pierre for blister ointment, and he had been speaking French. It was the first time Jane had heard French spoken with an Uzbek accent. It sounded the same as a Russian accent.

During the day her mind kept returning to the Uzbek. There had been something odd about him.

At noon she closed the clinic, fed and changed Chantal, then cooked a lunch of rice and meat sauce and shared it with Fara. In the heat of the day she went down to her secret place, the sunny ledge hidden below an overhang on the mountainside. There she did her postnatal exercises, determined to get her figure back. As she stretched, she kept visualizing the Uzbek man rising to his feet in the hut, and the expression of astonishment on his Oriental face. For some reason she felt a sense of impending tragedy.

66

When she realized the truth, it did not come in a sudden flash but was more like an avalanche, starting small but growing inexorably until it swamped everything.

No Afghan would complain of blisters on his feet. For, having walked long distances all their lives, Afghans had no knowledge of such things. It was as unlikely as a Gloucestershire farmer saying he had beriberi. And no Afghan, no matter how surprised, would react by standing up when a woman walked in. If he was not Afghan, what then was he? His accent told her, though only because she was a linguist, with a command of both Russian and French. He had been speaking French with a Russian accent.

So Jean-Pierre had met a Russian disguised as an Uzbek in a stone hut at a deserted location.

Was it an accident? That was possible, barely, but she pictured her husband's face when she had walked in, and now she could read the expression that she had not noticed then: a look of guilt.

No, it was no accidental encounter—it was a rendezvous. Perhaps not the first. Jean-Pierre was constantly traveling to outlying villages to hold clinics—indeed, he was unnecessarily scrupulous about keeping to his schedule of visits, a foolish insistence in a country without calendars and diaries, but not so foolish if there was another schedule, a series of secret meetings.

And *why* did he meet the Russian? Hot tears welled up in Jane's eyes as she realized that his purpose must be treachery. He gave them information, of course. He told them about the convoys. He always knew the routes, because Mohammed used his maps. He knew the approximate timing, because he saw the men leaving, from Banda and other villages in the Five Lions Valley. He gave this information to the Russians, obviously, and that was why the Russians had become so successful at ambushing convoys in the last year; that was why there were so many grieving widows and sad orphans in the valley now.

What's wrong with me? she thought in a sudden fit of self-pity, and fresh tears rolled down her cheeks. First Ellis, then Jean-Pierre. Was his love also faked? She buried her face in her hands. It was almost unthinkable.

Jane wiped her face on her sleeve and headed back up the

mountain, for it was time to feed Chantal. As she began to think more clearly, it seemed to her that she had felt a vague dissatisfaction throughout their year of marriage, and now she could understand. In a way she had all along *sensed* Jean-Pierre's deceit. Because of that barrier, they had failed to become intimate.

When she reached the cave, Jane told Fara to take her siesta, then sat down with the baby to feed her. Jean-Pierre's treachery came to seem less than cataclysmic. She felt sure his love for her was not faked. What would be the point? Why would he have brought her here? She was of no use to him in his spying. It must have been because he loved her.

And if he loved her, all other problems could be solved. He would have to stop working for the Russians, of course. Then he would have to take her and Chantal back to Europe.

Back to Europe. They would go back to Paris, where there were postmen and bookshops and tap water. Chantal would have pretty clothes and a pram and disposable diapers. They would live in a small apartment in an interesting neighborhood, where the only real danger to life would be the taxi drivers. They would start again, and this time they would really get to know one another. They would work to make the world a better place, by gradual and legitimate means, without intrigue or treachery.

Fara came in. Siesta time was over. She looked at Chantal; then, seeing that the baby had now fallen asleep, she sat cross-legged on the ground, waiting for instructions. She was the daughter of Rabia's eldest son, Ismael Gul, who was away at present, with the convoy. . . .

Jane gasped. Her father is with the convoy, she thought.

Jean-Pierre had betrayed that convoy to the Russians. Fara's father and thirty or so other men from the valley would die—unless Jane could do something to prevent it. But what? A runner could be sent to meet the convoy and divert it onto a new route. Mohammed could arrange that. But Jane would have to tell him how she knew the convoy was due to be ambushed—and then Mohammed would undoubtedly kill Jean-Pierre.

There had to be another way.

She went to the mouth of the cave and stood looking out. Now that the siesta was over, the children had come out of the caves and resumed their games among the rocks and thorny bushes. There was nine-year-old Mousa, son of Mohammed—even more spoiled now that he had only one hand—swaggering with the new knife that his doting father had given him. Mohammed would probably be with his family now in their cave, but Jane was reluctant to seek him out openly, for that would scandalize the community.

How shall I appeal to him for help? she wondered. She *had* saved his boy's life. Mohammed owed her a debt of honor. She could say, Do this for me because I saved your son. It might work.

But Mohammed would ask how the Russians had found out the route of the convoy.

What could she say to him? I can't tell you.

Then what makes you so sure? he might ask.

I overheard a conversation. I have a hunch. I saw it in the cards. I had a dream.

That was it: a dream.

Then she saw him. He stepped from his cave, tall and handsome, wearing traveling clothes: the round Chitrali cap; the mud-colored pattu that served as cloak, towel, blanket, and camouflage; and the leather boots he had taken from the corpse of a Russian soldier. He walked across the clearing and took the footpath down the mountainside toward the deserted village.

Jane watched him disappear. It's now or never, she thought, and she followed him. When she was out of sight of the caves, she broke into a run and called out. He turned.

"God be with you, Mohammed Khan," she said when she caught up with him.

"And with you, Jane Debout," he said politely.

She paused, catching her breath. "How is Mousa?" she asked.

"He is well and happy, and learning to use his left hand. He will kill Russians with it one day."

"I'm so glad we were able to save his life," she said.

"I am forever in your debt."

That was what she had been angling for. "There is something you could do for me," she said.

69

His expression was unreadable. "If it is within my power . . ."

"It is within your power," she said. "But it will cause you some small trouble."

"What is it?"

"You may think it the whim of a foolish woman. But I want you to send a runner to the convoy and order them to change their homeward route."

He was taken aback. "But why?"

"Do you believe in dreams, Mohammed Khan?"

He shrugged. "Dreams are dreams," he said evasively.

Perhaps that was the wrong approach, she thought; a vision might be better. "While I lay alone in my cave today in the heat of the day, I thought I saw a white pigeon."

He was suddenly attentive. Afghans believed that white pigeons were sometimes inhabited by spirits.

Jane went on. "But I must have been dreaming, for the bird tried to speak to me. I couldn't understand it, although I listened as hard as I could. I think it was speaking Pashto."

Mohammed was wide-eyed. "A messenger from Pushtun . . ."

"Then I saw Ismael Gul, the son of Rabia, the father of Fara, standing behind the pigeon. There was a knife in his heart, and he was weeping tears of blood. He pointed to the handle of the knife, as if he wanted me to pull it out of his chest. The handle was encrusted with jewels." Somewhere in the back of her mind she was thinking, Where did I *get* this stuff? "I got up from my bed and walked to him. I was afraid, but I had to save his life. Then, as I reached out to grasp the knife . . ."

"What?"

"He vanished. I think I woke up."

Mohammed frowned importantly, as if carefully considering the interpretation of the dream. "What kind of jewels were in the handle of the knife?" he asked.

Oh, Lord, she thought. What is the correct answer supposed to be? She thought to say emeralds, but they were associated with the Five Lions Valley, so it might imply that Ismael had been killed by a traitor in the valley. "Rubies," she said.

He nodded slowly. "Did Ismael not speak to you?"

"He seemed to be trying to speak, but unable to."

He nodded again. "The omen is clear. The convoy must be diverted. It will be done, I promise."

"I'm so relieved," Jane said truthfully. "I didn't know what to do. Now I can be sure Ismael will be saved." She wondered what she could do to make it impossible for Mohammed to change his mind. She could not make him swear an oath. She wondered whether to shake his hand. Finally she decided to seal his promise with an even older gesture. She leaned forward and kissed him. "Thank you!" she said. "I know you are a man of your word." Then she ran up the path toward the caves.

At the top of the rise she stopped and looked back. Mohammed was striding down the hill, his head high and his arms swinging. I should be ashamed, Jane thought; but it worked.

She walked on. Next she had to confront Jean-Pierre. He would be home around dusk. She would take him for a walk, she thought. She was not sure exactly what to say to him either, but at least she could tell the truth.

Down in the village, she still had not made up her mind when he arrived a few hours later. She wiped the dust from his face with a damp towel and gave him green tea in a china cup. She sat with him while he drank his tea, and then, when he had rested for a little while, she said, "Let's go out, like we used to."

He was a little surprised. "Where do you want to go?"

"Anywhere. Don't you remember last summer, how we used to go out just to enjoy the evening?"

He smiled, faintly bemused. "All right."

Jane told Fara to prepare their evening meal—tea, bread, and yogurt. Then she and Jean-Pierre left the house. The daylight was fading and the evening air was mild and fragrant. As they strolled through the fields to the river, Jane recalled how she had felt on this same pathway last summer: excited, and determined to succeed. She was proud that she had coped so well but glad the adventure was about to end.

She began to feel tense as the moment of confrontation drew nearer. They waded across the river at a place where it spread wide and shallow over a rock shelf; then they climbed a steep

71

path up the face of the cliff on the other side. At the top they sat on the ground and dangled their legs over the precipice. A hundred feet below them the Five Lions River hurried along, jostling boulders and foaming angrily through the rapids. Jane looked over the valley. The cultivated ground was crisscrossed with irrigation channels and stone terrace walls. The bright green and gold of ripening crops made the fields look like shards of colored glass from a smashed toy. On the far side of the valley the farmland struggled to climb the lower slopes of the mountain but soon surrendered to the dusty rock. From the cluster of houses off to the left, the smoke of a few cooking fires rose in straight lines until the light breeze untidied it. The same breeze brought snatches of conversation from the women bathing beyond a bend in the river upstream. Their voices were subdued, and Zahara's hearty laugh was no longer heard, for she was in mourning. And all because of Jean-Pierre . . .

The thought gave Jane courage. "I want you to take me home," she said abruptly.

At first he misunderstood her. "We've only just got here," he said irritably. Then he looked at her and his frown cleared. "Oh."

"Yes," she said firmly. "Home."

He put his arm around her. "This country gets one down at times." He was looking at the rushing river far below their feet. "You're especially vulnerable to depression now, just after the birth. In a few weeks' time you'll find—"

"Don't patronize me!" she snapped. "Save your bedside manner for your patients."

"All right." He took his arm away. "We decided, before we came, that we would stay here for two years. Short tours are inefficient, we agreed, because of the time and money wasted in training, traveling, and settling down. We were determined to make a real impact, so we *committed* ourselves to a two-year stint—"

"I've changed my mind."

"You're not *entitled* to change your mind."

"You don't own me!" she said angrily.

"It's out of the question. Let us stop discussing it."

"We've only just begun," she said. His attitude infuriated her.

72

The conversation had turned into an argument about her rights, and she did not want to win by telling him that she knew about his spying. Not yet anyway. She wanted him to admit that she was free to make her own decisions. "You have no right to ignore me or override my wishes," she said. "I want to leave this summer."

"The answer is no. We agreed on two years," he said stubbornly.

"That was a long time ago, and before we had Chantal."

"Then the two of you should go, and leave me here."

Jane considered that. It would mean Jean-Pierre would be able to continue betraying the convoys, and every few weeks more husbands and sons from the valley would die. And it would destroy their marriage. "No," she said. "I won't go alone."

"I will not go," he said angrily. "I will not!"

She took a deep breath. "You'll just have to—" she began.

"I don't have to," he interrupted. He pointed his forefinger at her, and she looked into his eyes and saw something there that frightened her. "You can't force me to. Don't try."

"But I *can*—"

"I advise you not to," he said, and his voice was terribly cold.

Suddenly he seemed a stranger to her. I don't know this man, she thought in a panic. After a whole year I still don't know who he is! "Do you love me?" she asked him.

"Loving you doesn't mean I have to do everything you want."

"Is that a yes?"

He stared at her. She met his gaze unflinchingly. Slowly the hard, manic light went out of his eyes, and he relaxed. At last he smiled. "It's a yes," he said. She leaned toward him, and he put his arm around her again. "Yes, I love you," he said softly. He kissed the top of her head.

She rested her cheek on his chest and looked down. A white pigeon, like the one in her invented vision, was floating effortlessly down toward the far bank of the river. Jane thought, Oh, God. What do I do now?

It was Mohammed's son, Mousa—now known as Left Hand—who was the first to spot the convoy when it returned. He came racing into the clearing in front of the caves, yelling, "They're

73

back! They're back!" Nobody needed to ask who *they* were.

It was midmorning, and Jane and Jean-Pierre were in the cave clinic. The faintest hint of a puzzled frown crossed Jean-Pierre's face. Jane turned away so that he should not see the triumph she felt. She had saved their lives! Rabia's son Yussuf, who sings so beautifully; and Sher Kador, the goat boy; and Ali Ghanim, who has fourteen children. All the mothers and daughters who would have been in mourning could now rejoice.

The patients melted away to go down to the village to welcome the travelers home. "Shall we go?" Jane said.

"You go," Jean-Pierre replied. "I'll finish up here, then follow."

"All right." Jane picked up Chantal and took the steep footpath toward the village. She could feel the heat of the rock through the thin soles of her sandals.

She still had not confronted Jean-Pierre. However, this could not go on indefinitely. Sooner or later he would learn that Mohammed had sent a runner to divert the convoy from its prearranged route. Naturally he would then ask Mohammed why this had been done, and Mohammed would tell him about Jane's "vision." But Jean-Pierre knew Jane did not believe in visions....

Why am I afraid? she asked herself. Perhaps it's the peculiar look in his eyes sometimes. . . .

As she reached the village she began to hear the random, exuberant gunfire that signified an Afghan celebration. She made her way to the mosque—everything happened at the mosque. The convoy was in the courtyard, men and horses and baggage surrounded by smiling women and squealing children. Jane stood watching. It was worth it, she thought. It was worth the worry and the fear, and it was worth manipulating Mohammed in that undignified way, in order to see this, the men safely reunited with their wives and mothers and sons and daughters.

What happened next was probably the greatest shock of her life. There among the caps and turbans appeared a head of curly blond hair. It emerged from the crowd, and she saw, hiding behind an incredibly bushy blond beard, the face of Ellis Thaler.

Jane's knees suddenly felt weak. He walked toward her. He was wearing the loose pajamalike cotton clothes of the Afghans, and a dirty blanket around his broad shoulders. The little of his face that was still visible above the beard was deeply tanned, so that his sky-blue eyes were even more striking than usual, like cornflowers in a field of ripe wheat. He stood in front of her, his face solemn. "Hello, Jane."

She realized she no longer hated him. A month ago she would have cursed him for deceiving her and spying on her friends, but now she could tolerate him. "Ellis," she said weakly. "What in heaven's name are you doing here?"

"The same as you," he said. "I'm here to help the rebels." He hefted his bag, a large sausage-shaped thing of khaki canvas. "Who does the baby belong to?" he asked.

"Me. And Jean-Pierre. Her name is Chantal." Jane saw that Ellis suddenly looked terribly sad. She realized he had been hoping to find her unhappy with her husband. I think he's still in love with me, she thought. She tried to change the subject. "But how will you help the rebels?"

"I'm going to teach them how to blow up roads and bridges. So you see, in this war I'm on the same side as you."

But not the same side as Jean-Pierre, she thought. What will happen now? The Afghans did not for one moment suspect Jean-Pierre, but Ellis was trained in the ways of deception. Sooner or later he would guess what was going on. "How long are you going to be here?" she asked him. If it was a short stay, he might not have time to develop suspicions.

"For the summer," he said imprecisely.

"Where will you live?"

"In this village."

"Oh."

He heard the disappointment in her voice and gave a wry smile. "I shouldn't have expected you to be *glad* to see me."

Jane's mind was racing ahead. Suddenly she felt able to confront Jean-Pierre. Why is that? she wondered. It's because I'm not afraid of him anymore. Why am I not afraid of him? Because Ellis is here.

"On the contrary," she said. "I'm happy you're here."

There was a silence. Ellis clearly did not know what to make of

Jane's reaction. After a moment he said, "Uh, I have a lot of explosives and stuff somewhere in this zoo. I'd better get to it."

Jane nodded. "Okay."

He disappeared into the melee, and Jane walked slowly out of the courtyard, feeling stunned. Ellis was *here*, in the Five Lions Valley, and possibly still in love with her.

As she reached the shopkeeper's house Jean-Pierre came out. He had stopped there on his way to the mosque, probably to put away his medical bag. Jane was not sure what to say to him. "The convoy brought someone you know," she began.

"A European?"

"Yes. Go and see. You'll be surprised."

He hurried off. Jane went inside and put Chantal into her cradle. What would Jean-Pierre do about Ellis? she wondered. Well, he would want to tell the Russians. And they would want to kill Ellis. So I have to stop his getting in touch with the Russians. But how?

Jean-Pierre must have some means of contacting them in an emergency. But there are no phones here, no mail, no carrier pigeons. . . .

He must have a radio. He needed one to arrange those urgent meetings in stone huts. He *must* have a radio.

She went into the front room of the house. There on the tiled counter was Jean-Pierre's medical bag.

It was the obvious place. She undid the clasp and went through the contents, taking them out one by one. There was no radio.

He *must* have one, she thought, and I *must* find it. If I don't, either Ellis will kill him or he will kill Ellis.

She decided to search the house. She checked through the medical supplies on the shelves, hurrying for fear that he would come back before she was finished. She found nothing.

She went into the bedroom and rummaged through his clothes, then the winter bedding, which was stored in a corner. Nothing. Moving faster, she went into the living room and looked around frantically. The map chest! She opened it. Only the maps were there. She lifted the rug in case there was a concealed hole in the floor. Nothing.

It had to be somewhere. She went back to the front room. His bag was so much the obvious place, for he took it with him wherever he went. She picked it up. It was heavy. She felt around inside it yet again. It had a thick base.

Suddenly she was inspired. The bag could have a false bottom. She probed the base with her fingers. It must be here, she thought. She pushed her fingers down beside the base and lifted. The false bottom came up easily.

With her heart in her mouth she looked inside. There, in the hidden compartment, was a black plastic box. She took it out.

Just then she heard the back door open. Terrified, she dropped the radio to the floor and spun around. It was only Fara. "Oh, Lord," Jane said aloud. She turned back, her heart racing.

She had to get rid of the radio before Jean-Pierre returned. But how? She could not throw it away—it would be found. She had to smash it. But she had no hammer. A stone, then.

She hurried into the courtyard. The courtyard wall was made of rough stones held together with sandy mortar. She reached up and tugged at one in the top row. A stone about the size of a can of beans came loose. Just right. She picked it up and hurried back into the front room. She placed the radio transmitter on the counter, then lifted the stone above her head and brought it down with all her might on the radio.

The plastic casing cracked. She lifted the stone and brought it down again. This time the casing broke, revealing a printed circuit, a loudspeaker cone, and a pair of batteries with Russian script on them. She threw the batteries onto the floor, then started to smash the mechanism.

Suddenly she was grabbed from behind, and Jean-Pierre's voice shouted, "What are you doing?"

She struggled against his grip, got free for a moment, and struck another blow at the little radio.

He grasped her shoulders and hurled her aside. She stumbled and fell to the floor. He stared at the radio. "It's ruined!" he said. He grabbed her by the shirt and hauled her to her feet. "You don't know what you've done!" he screamed. There was despair and hot rage in his eyes.

"Let me go," she shouted. "How dare you manhandle me!"

"How *dare* I?" He let go of her shirt and punched her hard in the stomach. For a split second she was paralyzed with shock; then she cried out and bent over, with her hands clutching her middle, so she did not see the second blow coming.

His punch landed full on her mouth. She screamed, and fell to her knees on the dirt floor and began to sob with shock and pain and misery. Her mouth hurt so much she could hardly speak. "Please don't hit me," she managed. "Don't hit me again."

He knelt down and thrust his face into hers. "How long have you known?" he hissed.

She licked her lips. They were swelling already. She said, "Since I saw you in the stone hut . . . on the way to Cobak."

"But you didn't see anything!"

"He spoke with a Russian accent and said he had blisters. I figured it out from there."

There was a pause while that sank in. "Why did you wait until now to tell me?" he asked.

"Ellis is here."

"So?"

Jane summoned up what little courage she had left. "If you don't stop this . . . spying . . . I'll tell Ellis, and he will stop you."

He took her by the throat. "And what if I strangle you, you little slut?"

"If any harm comes to me . . . Ellis will want to know why. He's still in love with me."

She stared at him. Hatred burned in his eyes. "Now I'll never get him!" he said. She wondered who he meant. Ellis? No. Masud? Could it be that Jean-Pierre's ultimate purpose was to kill Masud? His hands were still around her throat. She felt his grip tighten. She watched his face fearfully.

Then Chantal cried.

Jean-Pierre's expression changed dramatically. The hostility went from his eyes, and to Jane's amazement he put his hands over his eyes and began to cry. "I'm sorry," he said. "I'm sorry for what I did to you. My life's work . . . all for nothing."

She realized with astonishment and a trace of self-disgust that she felt pity for him. And she was no longer angry with him, despite the continuing pain in her stomach. She gave in to the sentiment and patted his back, as if comforting a child.

"Anatoly's accent," he mumbled. "Just because of that."

"Forget Anatoly," she said. "We'll leave Afghanistan and go back to Europe. We'll go with the next convoy."

He took his hands from his face and looked at her. "When we get back to Paris . . ."

"Yes?"

"When we're home . . . I still want us to be together. Can you forgive me? I love you. Truly, I always have. And we're married. And there's Chantal. Please, Jane. Promise you won't leave me."

To her surprise she felt no hesitation. Here was the man she loved, her husband, the father of her child. She smiled at him with her swollen lips. "I promise I won't leave you," she said.

CHAPTER 7

Ellis was frustrated and angry. He had been in the Five Lions Valley for seven days and still had not met Masud. He was angry because it was daily purgatory for him to see Jane and Jean-Pierre living and working together and sharing the pleasure of their happy little baby girl. And he had nobody to blame but himself for all this. He had volunteered for the mission in the foolish hope that he might win Jane back. It was unprofessional as well as immature. All he could do was get out of here as quickly as possible. And he could do nothing until he met Masud.

The guerrillas had said he would meet Masud today, but the great man had not shown up so far. Ellis had walked all day yesterday to get here. He was at the southwestern end of the Five Lions Valley, in Russian-controlled territory. He had left Banda accompanied by three rebels—Ali Ghanim, Matullah Khan, and Yussuf Gul—but they had accumulated two or three more at each village, and now they were thirty altogether. They sat in a circle underneath a fig tree near the top of a hill, eating figs and waiting.

At the foot of the hill on which they sat, a flattish plain stretched south—all the way to Kabul, fifty miles away. In the

79

same direction, but closer, was the Bagram air base. The plain was a fertile mosaic of fields and orchards crisscrossed with streams, all feeding into the Five Lions River as it flowed, wider and deeper now but just as fast, toward the capital city. A rough road ran past the foot of the hill and up the valley as far as the town of Rokha, which was the northernmost limit of Russian territory here. There was not much traffic on the road: a few peasant carts and an occasional armored car. Where the road crossed the river there was a new Russian-built bridge.

Ellis was going to blow up the bridge.

The lessons in explosives, which he was giving the guerrillas in order to mask for as long as possible his real mission, were hugely popular. This was despite his limited Dari. The idea of blowing things up appealed so much to the Afghan machismo that he always had an attentive audience.

Ellis stood up as the guerrillas suddenly went quiet. He looked around and saw another group of seven or eight men approaching over the hill. Their rifles and round Chitrali caps marked them as guerrillas. Ellis said, "Who is coming?"

"Masud," replied Ali Ghanim, the father of fourteen children.

"Which one is he?"

"The one in the middle."

Masud looked just like the others at first: a thin man of average height, dressed in khaki clothes and Russian boots. He was light-skinned, with a sparse mustache and a wispy beard. He had a long nose, and his alert dark eyes were surrounded by heavy lines that made him look at least five years older than his reputed age of twenty-eight. It was not a handsome face, but there was in it an air of lively intelligence and calm authority.

He came to Ellis with his hand outstretched. "I am Masud."

"Ellis Thaler." Ellis shook his hand.

"We're going to blow up this bridge," Masud said in French.

"You want to get started?"

"Yes."

After Masud went around and greeted each guerrilla, they went down the hill in a straggle, heading for the river. When they were about three hundred yards from the bridge, a small convoy of

Russian army trucks began to cross it, and they all hid while the vehicles rumbled by, heading for Rokha. Ellis lay beneath a willow tree and found Masud beside him. "If we destroy the bridge," Masud said, "we will cut their supply line to Rokha."

After the trucks had gone, they waited a few minutes, then walked the rest of the way to the bridge and clustered beneath it, invisible from the road. Ellis saw that it was a simple stringer bridge—two long steel girders, or stringers, supporting a flat slab of concrete road and stretching from one bank to the other without intermediate support. The concrete was dead load—the girders took the strain. Break them, and the bridge was ruined.

Ellis set about his preparations. His TNT was in one-pound yellow blocks. He made a stack of ten blocks and taped them together. Then he made three more stacks, using all his explosive. He was using TNT because that was the substance most often found in bombs, mines, and hand grenades. The guerrillas got most of their supplies from unexploded Russian ordnance.

The girders above him were I beams, spaced about eight feet apart. Indicating the space between the beams, Ellis said in Dari, "Somebody find me two sticks this long." One of the guerrillas walked along the riverbank and uprooted two young trees.

Ellis put a stack of TNT on the lower lip of one of the I beams and asked a guerrilla to hold it in place. He put another stack on the other I beam in a similar position and then forced one young tree between the two stacks so that it kept them both where they were. After that he waded through the river and did exactly the same at the other end of the bridge.

He described everything he did, in a mixture of Dari, French, and English, letting the guerrillas pick up what they could. He fused the charges with Primacord, the high-explosive detonating cord that burned at twenty-one thousand feet per second, and connected the four stacks so that they would explode simultaneously. He then made a ring main by looping the Primacord back on itself. The effect, he explained to Masud, would be that the cord would burn down to the TNT from both ends, so that if somehow the cable was severed in one place, the bomb would still go off. He recommended this as a routine precaution.

He felt oddly happy as he worked. There was something soothing about mechanical tasks and the dispassionate calculation of
poundage of explosive. He trailed the Primacord through the
water so that it was less visible—it would burn perfectly well
underwater—and brought it out onto the riverbank. He attached a
blasting cap to the end of the Primacord, then added a four-
minute length of ordinary, slow-burning blasting fuse wire.

"Ready?" he said to Masud.

Masud said, "Yes."

Ellis lit the fuse, and they all walked away briskly, heading
upstream along the riverbank. Ellis felt a certain secret boyish
glee about the enormous bang he was about to create. The others
seemed excited too, and suddenly they all became alert. Then he
heard it—the distant rumble of tank tracks.

The road was not visible from where they were, but one of the
guerrillas quickly shinned up a tree. "Two tanks," he reported.

Masud took Ellis' arm. "Can you destroy the bridge while the
tanks are on it?" he said.

Oh, damn, thought Ellis. This is a test. "Yes," he said rashly.

Ellis scrambled up the tree alongside the guerrilla and looked
across the fields. There were two black tanks trundling heavily
along the narrow stony road from Kabul. They were probably
being delivered to Rokha after being repaired at Bagram.

Ellis began calculating. The tanks were going at about ten
miles per hour, so they would reach the bridge in a minute and a
half. The fuse had been burning for less than a minute. It had at
least three minutes to go. At present the tanks would be across the
bridge and a safe distance away before the explosion. He had to
shorten the fuse.

He dropped from the tree and started to run, Ali and two more
men close on his heels. The others were taking cover along the
riverbank. A moment later he reached the bridge and dropped
beside his blasting fuse, slipping his kit bag off his shoulder. He
continued to calculate while he rooted around in the bag for his
pocketknife. He handed it to Ali, grabbed the fuse wire at a point
a foot from where it was joined to the blasting cap, and held it
with both hands for Ali to cut. When Ali had done so, Ellis held

the severed end in his left hand and the burning fuse in his right. He was not sure whether it was time yet to relight the severed end. He had to see how far away the tanks were.

He scrambled up the embankment, still holding both pieces of fuse wire, and poked his head up over the parapet of the bridge. The great black tanks rolled steadily closer. How soon? He was guessing wildly. He counted seconds, measuring their progress, and then, not calculating but hoping for the best, he put the burning end of the disconnected blasting fuse to the cut end that was still connected with the bombs.

He put the burning fuse down carefully on the ground and began to run. Ali and the other two guerrillas followed him. At first they were hidden from the tanks by the riverbank, but as the tanks came closer the four running men were clearly visible.

The gunners in the tanks hesitated only momentarily. Afghans running away could be presumed to be guerrillas, and therefore suitable for target practice. There was a double boom, and two shells flew over Ellis' head. He changed direction, dodged again, and a second later heard another boom. The shell landed close enough to spatter him with earth and stones. Then he heard a machine gun open up. He ran harder, his heart pounding and his breath coming in great gulps. I don't want to die, even if she loves him, he thought. He saw bullets chip a boulder almost in his path. He swerved suddenly, but the stream of fire followed him. He heard one of the guerrillas behind him cry out; then Ellis was hit twice in succession. He felt a burning pain across his hip, then an impact, like a heavy blow, in his right buttock. The second slug paralyzed his leg momentarily, and he stumbled and fell. He sat up, ignoring the pain. The two tanks had stopped on the bridge. Ali, who had been right behind him, now put his hands under Ellis' armpits and tried to lift him. The pair of them were sitting ducks. The gunners in the tanks could not miss.

Then the bomb went off.

It was beautiful.

The four simultaneous explosions sheared the bridge at both ends, leaving the midsection—with two tanks on it—totally unsupported. At first it fell slowly, its broken ends grinding; then it came free and dropped, spectacularly, into the rushing river, landing flat with a monster splash. The waters parted majestically, leaving the riverbed visible for a moment, then came together again with a sound like a thunderclap.

When the noise died away, Ellis heard the guerrillas cheering. Some of them emerged from cover and ran toward the half-submerged tanks. Ali lifted Ellis to his feet. "I'm not sure I can walk," he said. He heard shots. Looking up, he saw the surviving Russians trying to escape from the tanks, and the guerrillas picking them off as they emerged. They were cold-blooded, these Afghans. Looking down, Ellis saw that the right leg of his trousers was soaked with blood.

Masud came up to him, smiling broadly. "That was well done, the bridge," he said in French. "Magnificent!"

"Thanks," said Ellis. "But I didn't come here to blow up bridges." He felt weak and a little dizzy, but now was the time to state his business. "I came to make a deal."

Masud looked at him curiously. "Where are you from?"

"Washington. The White House. I represent the President of the United States."

Masud nodded, unsurprised. "Good. I'm glad."

At that moment Ellis fainted.

HE MADE his pitch to Masud that night.

The guerrillas had rigged up a stretcher and carried Ellis up the valley to Astana, where they stopped at dusk. Masud had already sent a runner to Banda to fetch Jean-Pierre, who would arrive sometime tomorrow to take the bullet out of Ellis' backside. Meanwhile, they all settled down in the courtyard of a farmhouse.

An hour or so after arrival Ellis was given hot, sweet green tea, which revived him somewhat, and later they all had mulberries and yogurt for supper. When they had eaten, the guerrillas casually moved off, leaving Masud and two of his lieutenants alone with Ellis. Feeble as he felt, Ellis knew he and Masud had to talk now, for there might not be another chance for a week.

Then Masud spoke. "Many years ago a foreign country asked the King of Afghanistan for five hundred warriors to help in a war.

The Afghan king sent five men from our valley, with a message saying that it is better to have five lions than five hundred foxes. This is how our valley came to be called the valley of the Five Lions." He smiled. "You were a lion today."

Ellis said, "I heard a legend saying there used to be five great warriors, known as the Five Lions, each of whom guarded one of the five ways into the valley. And I heard that this is why they call you the Sixth Lion."

"Enough of legends," Masud said with a smile. "What do you have to tell me?"

"I have first to ask you for your assessment of the war."

Masud nodded. "The Russians have twelve thousand troops in the town of Rokha, the gateway to the valley. Their dispositions are as always: first minefields, then Afghan troops, then Russian troops to stop the Afghans' running away. They are expecting another twelve hundred men as reinforcements. They plan to launch a major offensive up the valley within two weeks. Their aim is to destroy our forces."

"And will the offensive succeed?"

"No," said Masud with quiet confidence. "When they attack, we melt into the hills, so there is no one here for them to fight. When they stop, we harass them from the high ground and cut their communication lines. Gradually we wear them down. They find themselves spending vast resources to hold territory, with no military advantage. Finally they retreat. It is always so."

It was a textbook account of guerrilla war, Ellis reflected. There was no question that Masud could teach the other tribal leaders a lot. "How long do you think the Russians can go on making such futile attacks?" Ellis asked.

Masud shrugged. "It is in God's hands."

"Will you ever be able to drive them out of your country?"

"Only with supplies of the most modern weapons, especially portable surface-to-air missiles to fight against aircraft and helicopters."

"I agree," said Ellis, following the script he'd rehearsed for this conversation. "More important, the United States government agrees. We would like to help you get hold of better weapons and to see you make real progress against your enemy with those weapons. How soon do you think the Afghan Resistance will be able to launch unified countrywide assaults on the Russians?"

Masud shook his head dubiously. "The unification of the Resistance is at a very early stage."

"What are the main obstacles?"

"Mistrust between different fighting groups is the main obstacle. We are different tribes, different nations, and we have different commanders. Other guerrilla groups ambush my convoys and steal my supplies."

"Mistrust," Ellis repeated. "What else?"

"Communications. We need a network of messengers. Eventually we must have radio contact, but that is far in the future."

"Mistrust and inadequate communications." This was what Ellis had hoped to hear. "Let's talk about something else." He fought off the terrible fatigue he felt from great loss of blood. "You here in the valley have developed the art of guerrilla warfare more successfully than any other rebel leaders in Afghanistan. We would like you to train men from other parts of the country in modern guerrilla tactics. Would you consider that?"

"Yes—and I think I see where you're heading," said Masud. "After a year or so there would be in each zone of the Resistance a small cadre of men who had been trained in the Five Lions Valley. They could form a communications net. They would understand one another. They would trust me."

"All right," said Ellis. He had run out of energy, but he was almost done. "Here's the deal. If you can get the agreement of other commanders and set up that training program, the U.S. will supply you with RPG-7 rocket launchers, ground-to-air missiles, and radio equipment. But there are two other commanders in particular who *must* be part of the agreement. They are Jahan Kamil, in the Pich Valley, and Amal Azizi, of Faizabad."

Masud grinned ruefully. "You picked the toughest."

"I know," said Ellis. "Can you do it?"

"Let me think about it," said Masud.

"All right." Exhausted, Ellis lay back on the cold ground and shut his eyes. A moment later he was asleep.

JEAN-PIERRE WALKED THROUGH THE moonlit fields in the depths of depression. There was no way out. He had to leave Afghanistan. His usefulness as a spy was over. He had no means of contacting Anatoly, and even if Jane had not smashed the radio, he was unable to leave the village to meet Anatoly, for Jane would know what he was doing and would tell Ellis.

It all came down to Ellis. I'd like to kill Ellis, he thought, if I had the nerve. But how? I have no gun. What would I do, cut his throat with a scalpel? He's much stronger than I am.

Jean-Pierre decided to turn in. He was sleeping badly, but he had nothing else to do but go to bed. He headed for home.

Somehow the fact that he still had Jane was not much consolation. Her discovery of his secret seemed to have made them less intimate, not more. A new distance had grown up between them, even though they were now planning their return home and talking about their new life back in Europe.

He went into the shopkeeper's house. Jane was still up. She spoke as soon as he walked in. "A runner came for you from Masud. You have to go to Astana. Ellis is wounded."

Ellis wounded. Jean-Pierre's heart beat faster. "How?"

"Nothing serious. I gather he's got a bullet in his bottom."

"I'll go first thing in the morning," he said.

"The runner will go with you. You can be back by nightfall."

"I see." Jane was making sure he had no opportunity to meet Anatoly. But she was guarding against a minor peril and overlooking a major one: Ellis was *wounded*. That made him vulnerable. Which changed everything.

Now Jean-Pierre could kill him.

JEAN-PIERRE was awake all night thinking about it. Just before dawn he got up, lit the fire, and went to the river to bathe. When he came back, the runner was in his courtyard, drinking tea made by Fara. Jane was feeding Chantal on the roof. Jean-Pierre went up and kissed them both good-bye. Every time he touched Jane, he remembered how he had punched her, and he felt shame. She seemed to have forgiven him, but he could not forgive himself.

He led his old mare through the village and down to the

riverside; then, alongside the runner, he headed downstream.

The valley must have been an idyllic place once upon a time, he thought as he rode south in the bright morning sunshine. Watered by the Five Lions River, made secure by its high valley walls, organized according to ancient traditions, and undisturbed except by a few butter carriers from Nuristan and the occasional ribbon salesman from Kabul, it must have been a throwback to the Middle Ages. Now the twentieth century had overtaken it with a vengeance. Almost every village had suffered some bomb damage—and all this waste and destruction because men such as Masud tried to resist the tide of history. Jean-Pierre could imagine what his father would say about these rebels: They're bandits, bamboozling the ignorant peasants into supporting them. Feudal institutions have to be wiped out before socialism can come in.

With Masud, the strongest of the rebels, out of the way, all this fighting would end. And with Ellis out of the way, Jean-Pierre could deal with Masud.

They went through Sangana, with its cemetery and sandy beach, then followed the road around a bend in the river. There was a stretch of farmland in front of them and a cluster of houses up on the hillside. A minute or two later a young boy approached to lead them to a large house at the edge of the farmland.

Jean-Pierre felt no doubts, no hesitation about what he was planning to do. He just took his medical bag off the horse, gave the reins to the boy, and went into the courtyard of the farmhouse.

Twenty or more guerrillas were scattered around, squatting on their haunches and staring into space. Masud was not there, Jean-Pierre noticed, but two of his closest aides were. Ellis was in a shady corner, lying on a blanket and covered with a sheet.

Jean-Pierre knelt down beside him. He was evidently in some pain from the bullet. "It hurts, eh?" he said in English.

"It sure does," said Ellis through gritted teeth.

Jean-Pierre pulled the sheet off him. The guerrillas had put a makeshift dressing on the wound. Jean-Pierre removed it. He could see immediately that the injury was not grave. Ellis had bled a lot, but once the bullet was dislodged from his muscle, the wound would heal fast.

No, it won't, Jean-Pierre reminded himself. It won't heal at all.

"First I'll give you something to ease the pain," he said. Ellis had a huge scar, shaped like a cross, on his back, and Jean-Pierre wondered how he had got it. Probably a memento of the Vietnam War.

Jean-Pierre opened the medical bag, took out a large syringe, and began to fill it with digitoxin. The drug came in small vials, and he had to empty four of them to get a lethal dose. It would give Ellis a heart attack, and he would die. There would be no inquest, no postmortem, and no suspicions. In the West they would not doubt that Ellis had been wounded in action and had died of his wounds. Here in the valley everyone trusted Jean-Pierre and would accept his diagnosis.

The injection was ready. He bared Ellis' upper arm and, from sheer force of habit, swabbed a patch with alcohol.

At that moment Masud arrived. He seemed to come from nowhere, making Jean-Pierre jump. Masud put a hand on his arm. "I startled you, *Monsieur le docteur*," he said. He knelt down at Ellis' head and said in French to him, "I have considered the proposal of the American government."

Jean-Pierre knelt there, frozen, with the syringe in his hand. What proposal? What the hell *was* this?

"It is good," Masud was saying. "But I have been asking myself how I am going to fulfill my part of the bargain."

Of course! thought Jean-Pierre. The Americans have not sent a top CIA agent here just to teach a few guerrillas how to blow up bridges and tunnels. Ellis is here to make a deal!

Masud went on. "This plan to train cadres from other zones must be explained to the other commanders. This will be difficult. They will be suspicious—especially if I present the proposal. I think *you* must put it to them, and tell them what your government is offering them."

Ellis spoke with some difficulty. "I'd be glad to do that. You would have to bring them all together."

The shape of the deal was becoming clear to Jean-Pierre.

"Yes." Masud smiled. "I shall call a conference of all the Resistance leaders, to be held here in the Five Lions Valley, in the village of Darg in eight days' time. I will send runners today with the message that a representative of the United States government is here to discuss arms supplies."

"Will they come?" Ellis asked. "What about the two we particularly want—Kamil and Azizi?"

Masud shrugged. "It is in God's hands."

Jean-Pierre was trembling with excitement. This would be the most important event in the history of the Afghan Resistance.

Ellis was fumbling in his kit bag. "I may be able to help you persuade Kamil and Azizi," he was saying. He drew from the bag two small packages and opened one. It contained a flat, rectangular piece of yellow metal. "Gold," said Ellis. "Each of these is worth about five thousand dollars."

It was a fortune. Five thousand dollars was more than two years' income for the average Afghan. Masud took the piece of gold and hefted it in his hand. "What's that?" he said, pointing to an indented figure in the middle of the rectangle.

"The seal of the President of the United States," said Ellis. "Will that help to persuade Kamil and Azizi?"

Masud nodded. "I think they will come."

You bet your *life* they'll come, thought Jean-Pierre.

And suddenly he knew exactly what he had to do. The three great leaders of the Resistance would be together in the village of Darg in eight days' time. He had to tell Anatoly. This is the moment I've been waiting for, he thought. I'll have Masud where I want him—and two other rebel leaders too.

"A summit meeting," Masud was saying. He smiled rather proudly. "It will be a good start to the new unity of the Resistance, will it not?"

Either that, Jean-Pierre thought, or the beginning of the end. He pointed the needle at the ground and depressed the plunger, emptying the syringe. He watched the poison soak into the dusty earth. A new start, or the beginning of the end.

JEAN-PIERRE gave Ellis an anesthetic, took out the bullet, cleaned the wound, put a new dressing on it, and injected him with antibiotics to prevent infection. Around midafternoon he packed his bag and climbed onto Maggie for the journey home.

Ellis would stay behind for a few days—the wound would heal faster if he lay still and quiet. Jean-Pierre was anxious now that Ellis should remain in good health, for if he were to die, the conference would be canceled.

As he rode up the valley he racked his brains for a means of getting in touch with Anatoly. He knew he could not go to him himself. So somehow he had to send a letter. But who would be trustworthy enough to deliver it?

He had not resolved the problem when he reached home at dusk. It was when he was emptying the contents of his medical bag in the storeroom and saw the diamorphine pills that he realized there was one person he could trust with the letter to Anatoly.

He found a pencil, took the paper wrapping from a package of cotton swabs, and tore a rectangle out of it. There was no writing paper in the valley. He wrote in French.

To Colonel Anatoly of the KGB—

Masud has called a council of leaders of the rebellion. They meet eight days from today, on Thursday 27 August, at Darg. The conference has been called for them to talk with a CIA agent known to me as Ellis Thaler, who arrived in the valley a week ago.

This is our chance!

He added the date and signed it "Simplex."

He did not have an envelope. He had not seen one since he left Europe. He rolled his letter into a cylinder and put it into one of the containers for dispensing tablets. Writing "Anatoly—KGB" in European letters on the label, he put the container into an empty drug box marked POISON! and tied up the box with string. Finally he wrapped the box in a threadbare towel and left the house with a handful of diamorphine tablets in his shirt pocket. "I'm going to the river to wash," he called up to Jane, who was on the roof with Chantal, catching the evening breeze.

He headed out through the fields. A mile or so from the village, on a rocky outcrop of the mountain, was a solitary cottage that had been bombed. He walked slowly toward it, picking his way gingerly across the uneven ground. He stopped at the pile of rubble that had once been the front of the house and called out.

A shapeless form rose from the ground at his feet. The *malang*, the mad fellow, stood up.

Jean-Pierre had not seen him in a while. He said in Dari, "God be with you."

"And with you, Doctor."

Thank God he was in a coherent phase. "How is your belly?"

The man mimed a stomachache. As always, he wanted drugs. Jean-Pierre gave him one diamorphine pill, letting him see the others, then putting them back in his pocket. The *malang* ate his heroin and said, "I want more."

"You can have more," Jean-Pierre told him. "A lot more. But you have to do something for me."

The *malang* nodded eagerly.

"You have to go to Charikar and give this to a Russian soldier." Charikar was permanently in Russian territory. And Jean-Pierre, not knowing Anatoly's address, had decided on a soldier, rather than a post office, as the destination.

Now, was there any way Jean-Pierre could ensure that the *malang* actually followed these orders? He was inspired with an idea. "And buy a pack of Russian cigarettes," he said.

The *malang* held out empty hands. "No money."

Jean-Pierre gave him a hundred afghanis. That should ensure that he actually would go to Charikar. Was there a way to compel him to deliver the package?

Jean-Pierre said, "If you do this, I'll give you all the pills you want. But do not cheat me, for if you do, I shall know, and I will never give you pills again, and your bellyache will grow worse and worse and you will swell up and then your guts will burst like a grenade and you will die in agony. Do you understand?"

"Yes."

Jean-Pierre stared at him in the faint light. The whites of his mad eyes gleamed back. Jean-Pierre gave him the rest of the pills. "Eat one every morning until you come back to Banda."

He nodded vigorously, and turned away and began to run along the rough path with his odd, animallike gait. Watching him disappear into the gathering darkness, Jean-Pierre thought, The future of this country is in your filthy hands, you poor, mad wretch. May God go with you.

A WEEK later the *malang* had not returned.

By Wednesday, the day before the conference, Jean-Pierre was distraught. And as if to add to his worries, aircraft activity in the valley had increased. All week the jets had been howling overhead to bomb the villages. Banda had been lucky. Only one bomb had landed, in Abdullah's clover field, but the constant noise and danger made everyone irritable.

Jean-Pierre went through the morning's patients mechanically. The *malang* should have got back the day before yesterday. What had happened? Jean-Pierre looked at his wristwatch. It was ten thirty. Any minute now the *malang* might arrive, bearing a pack of Russian cigarettes as proof that he had been to Charikar.

Jean-Pierre was bandaging a small boy from the next valley who had burned his hand on a cooking fire, when there came from outside the flurry of footsteps and greetings that meant someone had arrived. Jean-Pierre contained his eagerness, but when he looked around, to his intense disappointment he saw that it was not the *malang* but two strangers.

The first of them said, "God be with you, Doctor."

"And with you," said Jean-Pierre. "What is the matter?"

"There has been a terrible bombing at Skabun. Many people are dead and many wounded."

Jean-Pierre looked at Jane. He could not leave Banda without her permission, for she still was afraid he would contact the Russians, but clearly he could not have contrived this summons. "Shall I go?" he said to her in French. "Or will you?"

Jane hesitated. She knew she could not deal with major traumatic wounds. "You go," she said.

"All right." Skabun was a couple of hours away. "I'll try to get back tonight." He finished bandaging the boy. He filled his bag with medical supplies, put a blanket over his shoulders, then said to the two messengers, "Let's go."

A couple of miles outside Banda they turned off the cliff path and headed north on a path unfamiliar to Jean-Pierre. "Is this the way to Skabun?" he asked.

"Yes," replied one of the messengers.

A few minutes later they saw one of the little stone huts in which travelers could rest or spend the night. To Jean-Pierre's surprise the messengers headed for it. "We haven't time to rest," he told them irritably. "Sick people are waiting for me."

Anatoly stepped out of the hut.

Jean-Pierre was dumbfounded. He did not know whether to be exultant, because now he could tell Anatoly about the conference, or terrified that the Afghans would kill Anatoly.

"Don't worry," Anatoly said, reading his expression. "They're soldiers of the Afghan regular army. I sent them to fetch you."

It was brilliant. There had been no bombing at Skabun—that had been a ruse, dreamed up by Anatoly for getting Jean-Pierre to come. "Tomorrow," Jean-Pierre said excitedly. "Tomorrow something terribly important is happening."

"I know, I know. I got your message. That's why I'm here. The *malang* arrived in Charikar yesterday. Lord knows what happened to him on the way. Why didn't you use your radio?"

"It broke," said Jean-Pierre. He did not want to explain about Jane right now. "The *malang* will do anything for me, because I supply him with heroin, to which he is addicted."

Anatoly looked at Jean-Pierre with something like admiration. "I'm glad you're on my side," he said. He put an arm around Jean-Pierre and led him into the hut, where they sat on the earth floor. "How do you know about this conference?" Anatoly began.

Jean-Pierre told him about Ellis, about the bullet wound, about Masud's talking to Ellis when Jean-Pierre was about to inject him, and about the training scheme and the promised weapons.

"This is fantastic," said Anatoly. "Where is Masud now?"

"I don't know. But he will arrive in Darg today, probably."

Anatoly nodded. "Describe the CIA man."

"Well, five feet ten, a hundred and fifty pounds, full beard, blond hair and blue eyes, age thirty-four but looks older, college educated."

"I'll put all that through the computer." Anatoly stood up. He went outside, and Jean-Pierre followed him.

Anatoly took from his pocket a small radio transmitter. He extended its telescopic aerial, pressed a button, and muttered into it in Russian. Then he turned back to Jean-Pierre. "My friend, you have succeeded in your mission," he said.

Jean-Pierre said, "When will you strike?"

"Tomorrow, of course."

Tomorrow. Jean-Pierre felt a wave of savage glee. Tomorrow.

The two Afghans were looking up. He followed their gaze and saw a helicopter descending, presumably summoned by Anatoly. It landed on a patch of ground a hundred yards away.

Jean-Pierre walked over to the chopper with the three men. He wondered where to go once they departed. He thought he'd better sit in the stone hut for a few hours before returning home.

He held out his hand to Anatoly. *"Au revoir."*

Anatoly did not take it. "Get in."

Jean-Pierre was flabbergasted. "What?"

"You're coming with us."

"Where? To Bagram? To Russian territory?"

"Yes."

"Why? I can't—"

"Stop blustering, and listen," Anatoly said patiently. "First, your work is done. Your assignment in Afghanistan is over. Tomorrow we will capture Masud. You can go home. Second, you are now a security risk. You know what we plan to do tomorrow, so you cannot remain in rebel territory."

"But I wouldn't tell anyone!"

"Suppose they tortured you? Suppose they tortured your wife or your baby daughter?"

"But what will happen to them if I go with you?"

"Tomorrow, after the raid, we will capture them and bring them to you."

"I can't believe this." The idea of not returning to Banda was so unexpected that it disoriented him. Would Jane and Chantal be safe? Would Anatoly let the three of them go back to Paris?

"Get in," Anatoly repeated.

The two Afghan messengers were standing on either side of Jean-Pierre, and he realized that he had no choice. He climbed into the helicopter. Anatoly and the Afghans jumped in after him, and the chopper lifted. Nobody closed the door.

As the helicopter rose, Jean-Pierre got his first aerial view of the Five Lions Valley: the white river zigzagging through the dun-colored land; the village of Banda, with its yellow-and-green patchwork fields. I spent a year of my life there, he thought, and now I'll never see it again. He identified the village of Darg, with its doomed mosque. This valley was the stronghold of the Resistance, he thought. By tomorrow it will be a memorial to a failed rebellion. And all because of me.

CHAPTER 8

JANE was becoming anxious about their journey home with the next convoy. This afternoon, while Jean-Pierre was at Skabun, she was trying to decide what supplies they would need. From the valley to the Khyber Pass was a one-hundred-and-fifty-mile trek. Coming in, it had taken fourteen days. Now they had to do the return journey carrying a two-month-old baby. There would be horses, but for much of the way it would not be safe to ride them, for the convoys traveled by the smallest and steepest of mountain paths, often at night.

She made a sort of hammock of cotton, to be slung around her neck, for carrying Chantal. Jean-Pierre would have to carry whatever supplies they would need during the day. There would be a basic medical kit—antibiotics, wound dressings, morphine. And food. Coming in, they had had a lot of high-energy Western rations—chocolate and packet soups and the explorers' perennial favorite, Kendal Mint Cake. Going out, they would have only what they could find in the valley: rice, dried fruit, dried cheese, hard bread, and anything they could buy on the road.

She would leave her Polaroid camera behind—it was a cheap one—but of course she wanted to take most of the photographs. She looked through them, wondering which to throw away.

Jane began packing clothes into a bag while Fara swept the

floor and Chantal slept in the next room. However, there was not much to pack: apart from Chantal's diapers, just one clean pair of knickers for herself and one for Jean-Pierre, and a spare pair of socks each. Neither of them would have a change of outer clothing. One pair of trousers, a shirt, a scarf, and a pattu-type blanket each would suffice for the whole trip and would probably be burned in a hotel in Peshawar in celebration of their return to civilization.

That thought would give her strength for the journey. "Civilization," she said aloud, and Fara looked at her inquiringly. Jane smiled and said in Dari, "I'm happy because I'm going back to the big town."

"I like the big town," Fara said. "I went to Rokha once." She continued sweeping. "Masud has sent my brother to Jalalabad," she added in a tone of envy.

"When will he be back?" Jane asked, but Fara had become dumb, and then Jane realized why.

The sounds of whistling and a man's footsteps came from the courtyard; there was a tap on the door, and Ellis Thaler's voice said, "Anyone at home?"

"Come in," Jane called. He walked in, limping. "How do you feel?" she asked him.

"Foolish," he said with a rueful grin. "It's an embarrassing place to get shot in."

"If embarrassed is all you feel, it must be getting better."

He nodded. "Is the doctor in?"

"He's gone to Skabun," Jane said. "There was a bad bombing raid, and they sent for him. Anything I can do?"

"I just wanted to tell him that my convalescence is over."

"He'll be back tonight or tomorrow morning." She was observing Ellis. With his mane of blond hair and curly golden beard he looked like a lion. "Why don't you cut your hair?"

"The guerrillas told me to grow it, and not to shave."

"They always say that. The object is to make Westerners less conspicuous. In your case it has the opposite effect."

"I'm going to look conspicuous in this country regardless of my haircut." He looked curiously at her packing. "What's that for?"

"For the journey home. We are leaving here."

He looked surprised. "How will you travel?"

"With a convoy, as we came."

"The Russians have launched their summer offensive," he said. "They've taken a lot of territory during the last few days. They've advanced over country through which the convoys ordinarily pass."

Jane felt a chill of apprehension. "Are you saying the route to Pakistan is closed?"

"The *regular* route is closed. You can't get from here to the Khyber Pass. There may be other routes."

Jane went to Jean-Pierre's chest and took out his American maps of Afghanistan. Kneeling on the floor, she began to shuffle through them. "Show me how far the Russians have advanced," she said.

Ellis knelt on the rug beside her and traced a line across the map with his finger.

Jane felt a surge of hope. "It doesn't look to me as if the Khyber Pass is cut off here," she said. "Why can't we go this way?" She pointed to a place on the map a little to the north of the Russian front.

"I don't know if that's open," Ellis replied. "It may be impassable. You'd have to ask the guerrillas."

"There's got to be more than one way out of this country," she said. She was angry now. She was *not* going to be defeated. She stood up, tucked the maps under her arm, and went out, leaving Ellis kneeling on the rug.

She headed for Mohammed's house. Mohammed himself might not be there—she had not seen him for a long time—but he lived with his brothers, in the usual Afghan extended family, and they too were guerrillas. If any of them were home, they might be able to give her information. She marched straight into the front room of the house—the men's parlor.

Three men were there: Mohammed's eighteen-year-old brother, Kahmir Khan; his brother-in-law Matullah; and Mohammed himself. They looked up at her, startled.

"God be with you, Mohammed Khan," Jane said. Without paus-

99

ing to let him reply, she squatted on her haunches like them. They were too astonished to say anything. She spread out her maps on the floor. The three men leaned forward reflexively to look at them. "Look," she said. "The Russians have advanced this far—am I right?" She retraced the line Ellis had shown her. Mohammed nodded in agreement. "So the regular convoy route is blocked. What is the best way out now?"

They all looked dubious and shook their heads.

"Why not this way?" she asked peremptorily, drawing a line parallel with the Russian front.

"Too close to the Russians," said Mohammed.

"Here, then." She traced a more careful route.

"No," he said again.

"Why not?"

"Over that mountain range there is no saddle." A saddle was a pass.

"There *must* be another way out!" Jane cried. She was frustrated and impatient. She decided to say something mildly offensive, to liven them up a bit. "Is this country a house with one door, cut off from the rest of the world because you cannot get to the Khyber Pass?" The phrase "the house with one door" was an Afghan euphemism for the privy.

"Of course not," said Mohammed stiffly. "In summer there is the Butter Trail."

"Show me."

Mohammed's finger traced a complex route that began due east of the valley, proceeded through a series of high passes and dried-up rivers, then turned north into the Himalayas, and finally crossed the border near the entrance to the uninhabited Wakhan Corridor before swinging southeast to the Pakistani town of Chitral. "This is how the people of Nuristan take their butter and yogurt and cheese to market in Pakistan." He smiled and touched his round cap. "That is where we get the hats." Jane recalled that they were called Chitrali caps.

"Good," said Jane. "We will go home that way."

Mohammed shook his head. "You cannot."

"And why not?"

"The first problem is the altitude. This route goes above the ice line. That means the snow never melts, and there is no running water, even in summer. Second is the landscape. The hills are very steep and the paths are narrow and treacherous. Even local guides get lost here. But the worst problem is the people of Nuristan. They rob and sometimes murder travelers. This route is no good for Europeans, impossible for women."

"Will you send convoys that way?"

"No. We will wait until the southerly route is reopened."

She stood up, bitterly disappointed. Her return home was postponed indefinitely. The strain of life in the valley suddenly seemed too much to bear, but she forced herself to be polite. "You have been away a long time," she said to Mohammed. "When did you get back?"

"Today. I went to Faizabad."

"A long trip. You must be tired." Faizabad was a large town in the far north. The Resistance was very strong there. The Afghan regular army had mutinied, and the Russians had never regained control. Jane rolled her maps, tucked them under her arm, and went out.

The guerrillas were doing a lot of traveling lately, she thought. Mohammed had been to Faizabad, Fara's brother had gone to Jalalabad. . . . Jane recalled that one of her patients had said that Masud had sent her husband to Paghman, near Kabul. And Zahara's brother-in-law Yussuf Gul had been sent to the Logar Valley, on the far side of Kabul. All four places were rebel strongholds.

Something was going on.

Jane forgot her disappointment for a while as she tried to figure out what was happening. Masud had sent messengers to some—perhaps all—of the other Resistance commanders. Was it a coincidence that this happened so soon after Ellis' arrival in the valley?

Jane went into her house, put away the maps, and told Fara she was going to the river to bathe.

She picked up a towel and headed for the women's beach. Eight or ten village women were bathing there. Zahara, Jane's friend, no longer in mourning for her husband, was splashing a lot as usual out in midstream.

Jane slowly waded into the water. She did not approach Zahara immediately, although of all the women in the village, Zahara was probably the most likely to know what was going on.

When the other women got out of the water, Jane followed a minute or two later and dried herself in silence. It was not until Zahara and a few other women began to drift back toward the village that Jane spoke. "How soon will Yussuf be back?" she asked Zahara in Dari.

"Today or tomorrow. He went to the Logar Valley."

"I know. Did he go alone?"

"Yes—but he said he may bring someone home with him."

"Who?"

Zahara shrugged. "A wife, perhaps."

Jane was momentarily diverted. There had been village rumors lately that Yussuf might marry Zahara. If these were true, her cool indifference would mean she was worried. She did not want Yussuf to bring home a wife.

"I don't think he has gone to get a wife," Jane said.

"Why?"

"Something important is happening. Masud has sent out many messengers. They can't all be after wives."

Night was falling as they made their way back to the village. From the mosque came a low chant: the eerie sound of the most warlike men in the world at prayer. As the women paused in front of the building Jane glanced in. The men were on their knees, with Abdullah, the mullah, leading them. Their weapons, the usual mixture of ancient rifles and modern submachine guns, were piled in a corner. The prayers were just finishing. As the men stood up, Jane saw that there were a number of strangers among them. She said to Zahara, "Who are they?"

"By their turbans,. they must be from the Pich Valley and Jalalabad," Zahara replied. "They are Pushtuns. Normally they are our enemies. Why are they here?" As she was speaking, a very tall man with an eye patch emerged from the crowd. "That must be Jahan Kamil—Masud's great enemy!"

"But there is Masud, talking to him," said Jane, and she added in English, "Just fancy that!"

Zahara imitated her. "Jass fencey hat!"

It was the first joke Zahara had made since her husband died.

The men began to come out, and the women scuttled away to their homes, all except Jane. She thought she was beginning to understand what was happening, and she wanted confirmation. When Mohammed emerged, she spoke to him in French. "I forgot to ask whether your trip to Faizabad was successful."

"It was," he said, without pausing in his stride. He did not want his comrades or the Pushtuns to see him answering a woman's questions.

Jane hurried alongside him. "So the commander of Faizabad is here?"

"Yes."

Jane had guessed right. Masud had invited all the rebel commanders to the Five Lions Valley. "What do you think of this idea?" she asked him. She was still fishing for details.

Mohammed looked thoughtful. "Everything depends on what Ellis does tomorrow," he said. "If he impresses them as a man of honor and wins their respect, I think they will agree to his plan."

"And you think his plan is good?"

"Obviously it will be a good thing if the Resistance is united and gets weapons from the United States."

So that was it! American weapons for the rebels, on condition they united against the Russians.

They reached Mohammed's house, and Jane turned away with a wave. She knew it was time for Chantal to be fed. At home, she dismissed Fara and went straight to the baby, who lay on a folded towel inside her cradle. The rebels and the war, Ellis and Mohammed and Masud, all receded into the background as Jane looked at her. She sat on a rug with her back to the wall and cradled Chantal in her right arm. Finally, nursing her baby, Jane relaxed.

A while later she was singing a lullaby to Chantal when she was interrupted by a voice from outside. "Come in," she called.

Mohammed entered. "Where is Jean-Pierre?" he asked.

"Gone to Skabun. Anything I can do?"

"When will he be back?"

"In the morning, I expect. Do you want to tell me what the problem is?"

"Alishan has arrived with Masud. He wants more pills."

Alishan Karim, the brother of the mullah, suffered from angina but would not give up his guerrilla activities, so Jean-Pierre had given him nitroglycerine to take. "I'll give you some," she said. She found the tablets on a shelf beneath the shopkeeper's counter, poured about a hundred into a container, and handed them over to Mohammed.

"Why did Jean-Pierre go to Skabun?" Mohammed asked.

"There was a bombing there this morning."

"No, there wasn't."

"Of course there wa—" Jane stopped suddenly.

Mohammed shrugged. "I was there all day with Masud. You must be mistaken."

She tried to stay composed. "Yes. I must have misheard."

"Thank you for the pills." He went out.

Jane sat down heavily on a stool. There had been no bombing at Skabun. Jean-Pierre must have gone to meet that Russian, Anatoly. She did not see how he had arranged it, but she had no doubt whatsoever.

What was she to do?

If Jean-Pierre knew about the gathering tomorrow and could tell the Russians about it, then the Russians would be able to attack. They could wipe out the entire leadership of the Afghan Resistance in a single day.

She had to see Ellis.

She wrapped a shawl around Chantal and carried her out of the house, heading for the mosque. Ellis was in the courtyard with the other men. "Ellis," she said. "I need to talk privately to you."

He got up, and they went out through the arch and stood in front of the mosque. "What is it?" he asked.

"Does Jean-Pierre know about this gathering you have arranged, of all the Resistance leaders?"

"Yes. When Masud and I first talked about it, he was right there, taking that slug out of me. Why?"

Jane's heart sank. Now she had no choice. "I have something to tell you," she said, "but I want your promise that no harm will come to him."

He stared at her for a moment; then realization dawned. "Oh, God," he said fervently. "He works for them. Of course! Why didn't I guess? In Paris he must have led them to my apartment! He's been telling them about the convoys—that's why they've been losing so many!" He stopped suddenly and spoke more gently. "It must have been terrible for you."

"Yes," she said. Her face crumpled, tears rushed to her eyes, and she began to sob. She felt weak and foolish for crying, but she also felt that a huge weight had been lifted from her.

Ellis put his arms around her and Chantal. "You poor thing," he said. "How long have you known?"

"A few weeks."

"Both of us," he said. "We both did it to you."

"Yes." She buried her face in his shirt and cried without restraint, for all the lies and betrayals and spent time and wasted love. Chantal cried too. Ellis held Jane close and stroked her hair until eventually she began to calm down. "I broke his radio, you see," she said, "and then I thought he had no way of getting in touch with them. Today he was called to Skabun to see to the bomb-wounded, but there was no bombing at Skabun today. . . ."

Mohammed came out of the mosque. Ellis let go of Jane and looked embarrassed. "What's happening?" he asked Mohammed.

"They're arguing," he said. "Some say this is a good plan and it will help us defeat the Russians. Others ask why Masud is considered the only good commander, and who is Ellis Thaler that he should judge Afghan leaders? You must talk to them some more."

"Wait," Ellis said. "There's been a new development. There has been a leak."

"What do you mean?" Mohammed said dangerously.

"The Russians may know about the conference."

"Who?" Mohammed demanded. "Who is the traitor?"

"Possibly the doctor, but—"

Mohammed rounded on Jane. "How long have you known this?"

"You'll speak to me politely or not at all," she snapped back. "I warned you, didn't I? I told you to change the route of the convoy after I'd had that vision. I saved your life, so don't point your finger at *me*."

Mohammed's anger evaporated, and he looked sheepish.

Ellis said, "So that's why the route was changed!" He looked at Jane with admiration.

Mohammed asked, "Where is he now?"

"We're not sure," Ellis replied. "But if he has contacted the Russians and told them about tomorrow's meeting, they will surely attack and try to take Masud."

"This is very bad," said Mohammed. "Masud must leave immediately. The conference will have to be called off."

"Not necessarily," Ellis said. "We could turn this to our advantage."

"How?"

Ellis said, "In fact the more I think about it, the more I like it. This may turn out to have been the best thing that could happen."

THEY evacuated the village of Darg at dawn. Masud's men went from house to house, gently waking the occupants and telling them that their village was to be attacked by the Russians today and they must go up the valley to Banda, taking with them their more precious possessions. By sunrise a ragged line of women, children, old people, and livestock was wending its way out of the village along the dirt road that ran beside the river.

Darg was different in shape from Banda. In Darg all the houses were crammed together on a thin shelf between the foot of the cliff and the bank of the river. There was a bridge just in front of the mosque, and a barley field was on the other side of the river. It was a good place for an ambush.

Masud had devised his plan during the night, and now Mohammed and Alishan Karim made the dispositions. Ellis wondered, as he laid his explosives, whether the Russians would come. Jean-Pierre had not reappeared, so it seemed certain that he had succeeded in contacting his masters, who would not resist the temptation to capture or kill Masud. But that was all circumstantial. And if they did not come, Ellis would look foolish, having caused Masud to set an elaborate trap for a no-show victim. The guerrillas would not make a pact with a fool. But if the Russians do come, Ellis thought, and if the ambush works, the boost to my prestige and Masud's could be enough to clinch the whole deal.

Ellis trailed his detonating cord in the river and brought its end out at what was to be his position, in a tiny one-room house on the riverbank, a couple of hundred yards upstream of the mosque. He used his crimper to attach a blasting cap to the cord, then finished the assembly with a simple army-issue pull-ring firing device.

By nine o'clock everything was ready, and the guerrillas made breakfast. Even that was part of the ambush. They could all get into position in minutes, and then the village seen from the air would look more natural, as if the villagers had all rushed to hide from the helicopters, leaving behind their bowls and rugs and cooking fires, so that the commander of the Russian force would have no reason to suspect a trap.

Ellis ate some bread and drank several cups of green tea, then settled down to wait as the sun rose high over the valley. He expected the Russian attack either this afternoon or at dawn tomorrow. If he were their commander, he would reason that the rebel leaders had assembled yesterday and would leave tomorrow, and he would want to attack late enough to catch any latecomers, but not so late that some of them might have left already.

At around midmorning the guerrillas' heavy weapons arrived, a pair of Dashokas—12.7-mm antiaircraft machine guns—each pulled along the road on its two-wheeled mounting by a rebel. A donkey followed, loaded down with cases of Chinese armor-piercing bullets.

Masud announced that one of the guns would be manned by Yussuf, one of Rabia's sons, who, according to village rumor, was likely to marry Jane's friend Zahara; the other by Abdur, a guerrilla from the Pich Valley, whom Ellis did not know. The guns were dismounted, then taken, each carried by two men, up the steep steps cut into the cliffside that towered over the village. The mounts and the ammunition followed.

Ellis watched from below as they reassembled the guns. At the top of the cliff was a shelf ten or fifteen feet wide; then the mountainside continued up at a gentler slope. The guerrillas set up the guns about ten yards apart on the shelf and camouflaged them. The helicopter pilots would soon find out where the guns were, of course, but they would find it very difficult to knock them out in that location.

Midday passed without lunch. That was because the guerrillas did not have any food. Ellis found it hard to get used to the rather simple idea that when there was no food, nobody ate. He sat in the doorway of the little house, trying to catch what breeze there was. He could see the fields, the river with its arched rubble-and-mortar bridge, the village with its mosque, and the overhanging cliff. The majority of the guerrillas were in houses close to the cliff, where it would be difficult for helicopters to strafe them, but inevitably some were in the more vulnerable forward positions nearer the river.

A series of shouts told Ellis that the sentries on the surrounding hillsides had spotted distant helicopters and had signaled to Yussuf on the cliff top, who had spread the word. There was a flurry of movement throughout the sunbaked village as guerrillas manned their posts, retreated farther into their cover, and checked their weapons. Three men armed with Kalashnikov rifles melted into the mosque's shadowy interior. Now the village, seen from the air, would appear deserted, as it normally would during the hottest part of the day, when most people rested.

Ellis listened hard and heard the menacing throb of approaching helicopter rotors. He nervously loosened the safety pins in the firing device. The helicopters roared closer, but he could not see them. He saw, however, a guerrilla dive into the river from the far bank and begin swimming across toward him. When the figure emerged, he could see that it was scarred old Shahazai Gul, the brother of the midwife. Shahazai's specialty was mines. He dashed past Ellis and took cover in a house.

For a few moments there was no sound but the heart-stopping throb of rotor blades, and then the first helicopter flashed into view over the cliff, going fast, and wheeled down toward the village. It hesitated over the bridge like a giant hummingbird.

It was an Mi-24, known in the West as a Hind. The gunner sat low in the nose, with the pilot behind and above him, like children playing piggyback; and the windows all around the flight deck looked like the multifaceted eye of a monstrous insect. The humpbacked helicopter had a three-wheeled undercarriage and short, stubby wings with underslung rocket pods.

Five more Hinds followed in rapid succession. They overflew the village and the ground all around it, scouting, Ellis presumed, for enemy positions. This was a routine precaution. The Russians had no reason to expect heavy resistance, for they believed their attack would be a surprise.

A second type of helicopter began to appear, and Ellis recognized the Mi-8, known as the Hip. Larger than the Hind but less fearsome, it could carry twenty or thirty men, and its purpose was troop transport rather than assault. It hesitated over the village, then dropped suddenly sideways and came down in the barley field. It was followed by five more. A hundred and fifty men, Ellis thought. As the Hips landed, the troops jumped out and lay flat, pointing their guns toward the village, but not shooting.

To take the village they had to cross the river, and to cross the river they had to take the bridge. But they did not know that. They were just being cautious.

Shahazai had laid mines in the barley field, Ellis recalled. Why had none of them exploded yet? A moment later he had the answer. One of the soldiers stood up—an officer presumably—and shouted an order. Twenty or thirty men scrambled to their feet and ran toward the bridge. Suddenly there was a deafening bang, loud even over the whirlwind of helicopter noise, then another and another as the ground seemed to explode under the soldiers' running feet. Ellis thought, Shahazai must have pepped up his mines with extra TNT. Clouds of brown earth and golden barley obscured the men—all but one, who was thrown high in the air and fell slowly, turning over and over like an acrobat until he hit the ground and crumpled in a heap. As the echoes died, there was another sound, a deep, stomach-thudding drumbeat that came from the cliff top as Yussuf and Abdur opened fire. The Russians retreated in disarray as the guerrillas in the village started firing their Kalashnikovs across the river.

One of the Hips in the barley field blew apart, and Ellis realized that Yussuf and Abdur must have hit it. The Hinds—the humpbacked gunships—were still circling. Now the Russian commander brought them into action. One of them swooped low over the river and shelled Shahazai's minefield. Yussuf and Abdur fired at it but missed. The mines exploded harmlessly, one after another. The Hind rose again, driven off by Yussuf, but another one descended and strafed the minefield again. Yussuf and Abdur poured a constant stream of fire at it. Then it lurched, part of a wing fell off, and it nose-dived into the river. Ellis thought, Nice shooting! But the approach to the bridge was clear, and the enemy still had more than a hundred men and ten helicopters.

The Russians took heart then, and most of them—eighty or more men, Ellis estimated—began moving toward the bridge on their bellies, firing constantly. Suddenly there was a lull. Ellis looked up. The Hinds in the air were going after Yussuf and Abdur on the cliff. The Russian commander had correctly identified the heavy machine guns as his main target.

As a Hind swooped toward the cliff-top gunners, Ellis had a moment of admiration for the pilot, for flying directly at the guns. He knew how much nerve that took. The aircraft veered away. They had missed one another. Another Hind descended toward the cliff like a hawk falling on a rabbit, but the guns drummed and the helicopter exploded in midair. Another Hind swooped. The gunners were a fraction wide this time, but they shot off the helicopter's tail, and the aircraft went out of control and crashed into the face of the cliff. But the note of the guns had changed. Only one was firing. The other had been knocked out. Ellis peered through the dust and saw Yussuf's form moving up there. So he was still alive. Abdur had been hit.

The three remaining Hinds circled and repositioned. One climbed high above the battle. The Russian commander must be in that one, Ellis thought. The other two descended on Yussuf in a pincer movement. When Yussuf aimed at one, the other swooped lower. Ellis noticed that the Russians flew with their doors open, just as the Americans had in Vietnam.

The Hinds pounced. One dived at Yussuf and veered away, but Yussuf scored a direct hit and the chopper burst into flames. Then the second was swooping, rocket pods and guns blazing away. It fell suddenly, going twenty or thirty feet straight down, and crashed on the ledge just a few yards from Yussuf. But its engine seemed to catch again, and to Ellis' surprise it began to lift. Its gunner had been firing all the time, but now he stopped. Ellis saw why, and his heart sank. A machine gun came tumbling over the edge of the cliff in a welter of camouflage, bushes, and branches, followed immediately by a limp mud-colored bundle that was Yussuf. As he fell down the face of the cliff he bounced off a jagged outcrop halfway, and his round Chitrali cap came off. A moment later he disappeared from Ellis' view. He had almost won the battle single-handed. There would be no medal for him, but his story would be told beside campfires in the cold Afghan mountains for a hundred years.

The Russians had lost four of their six Hinds, one Hip, and about twenty-five men, but the guerrillas had lost both their heavy guns, and now they had no defense as the two remaining Hinds began to strafe the village. Ellis huddled inside his hut, wishing it were not made of mud. The strafing was a softening-up tactic. After a minute or two, as if at a signal, the Russians in the barley field rose from the ground and rushed the bridge.

This is it, Ellis thought; this is the end, one way or another.

The guerrillas in the village fired on the charging troops, but they were inhibited by the air cover, and few Russians fell. Almost all the Russians were on their feet now, eighty or ninety men, firing blindly across the river as they ran. They were yelling enthusiastically, encouraged by the thinness of the defense. The guerrillas' shooting became a little more accurate as the Russians reached the bridge, and several more fell, but not enough to halt the charge. Seconds later the first of them had crossed the river and were diving for cover among the houses of the village.

There were about sixty men on or near the bridge when Ellis pulled the handle of the firing device.

The ancient stonework of the bridge blew up like a volcano.

Ellis had laid his charges to kill, not for a neat demolition, and the explosion sprayed lethal chunks of masonry like a burst from a giant machine gun, taking out all the men on the bridge and many still in the barley field. Ellis ducked back into his hut as rubble rained on the village. When it stopped, he looked out again.

Where the bridge had been, there was just a low pile of stones and bodies. Part of the mosque and two village houses had also collapsed. And the Russians were in full retreat.

As he watched, the twenty or thirty men still left alive scrambled into the open doors of the surviving Hips and took off from the field to join the two Hinds in the air. Then, without a parting shot, the aircraft soared over the cliff top and disappeared.

As the beat of their rotors faded, Ellis heard men cheering. We won, he thought. We won! And he started cheering too.

CHAPTER 9

"AND where have all the guerrillas gone?" Jane asked.

"They scattered," Ellis replied. "This is Masud's technique. He melts away into the hills before the Russians can catch their breath. They may come back with reinforcements—they could even be at Darg now—but they will find nobody to fight. The guerrillas have gone, all but these few."

There were seven wounded men in Jane's clinic. None would die. Twelve more had been treated for minor wounds and sent on their way. Only two men had died in the battle, but by heartbreaking bad luck one of them was Yussuf. Zahara would be in mourning again—and again it was because of Jean-Pierre.

Jane felt depressed, despite Ellis' euphoria. "What about your conference?" she asked him. "If all the guerrillas have gone . . ."

"They all agreed," Ellis said. "After the success of the ambush they were ready to say yes to anything. In a way, the ambush proved what some of them had doubted: that Masud is a brilliant leader and that by uniting under him they can achieve great victories. It also established my macho credentials, which helped."

"So you've succeeded."

"Yes. I even have a treaty, signed by all the rebel leaders and witnessed by the mullah."

"You must be proud." She reached out and squeezed his arm, then withdrew her hand quickly. She was so glad he was here to keep her from being alone that she felt guilty about having been angry with him for such a long time. But she was afraid she might accidentally give him the mistaken impression that she still cared for him in the old way, which would be awkward.

She looked around the cave. The wounded guerrillas were comfortable on rugs or blankets. They would stay in the cave all night. It was too difficult to move them down the hill. They had water and a little bread, and two of them were well enough to get up and make tea. Mousa, the one-handed son of Mohammed, was squatting in the mouth of the cave, playing a game in the dust with his knife. He would stay with the wounded men, and in the unlikely event that one of them should need medical attention during the night, he would run down to fetch Jane.

Everything was in order. She wished them good night, patted Mousa on the head, and went outside. Ellis followed. Jane felt a hint of cold in the evening breeze. It was the first sign of the end of summer. She looked up at the distant mountaintops of the Hindu Kush. The snowy peaks were pink with the reflection of the setting sun. This was a beautiful country. I'm glad I've seen it, she thought, even though I can't wait to go home.

She walked down the hill with Ellis, glancing at him now and again. The sunset made his face appear bronzed and craggy. "You look tired," she said.

"It's a long time since I was in a real war," he replied. "Peace makes you soft." He was very matter-of-fact about it.

Down in the village of Banda there was an air of celebration. Men and women stood talking animatedly, the children were playing noisily, and somewhere a man was singing. The thought of spending the evening alone seemed unbearably dreary to Jane, and on impulse she said to Ellis, "Come and have tea with me."

"I'd like that," he said.

JANE sat on the cushion with her back against the wall, her favorite position while she nursed Chantal. And she felt particularly comfortable with Ellis here. "As soon as the route to Pakistan is open and the convoys begin again," she said, "I'll go home. What about you?"

"The same. My work here is over. The agreement will have to be supervised, of course, but the Agency has people in Pakistan who can do that."

Fara brought in tea. As Jane sipped it she wondered about Ellis' next job. "So what will you do when you get home?" she asked. "Go back to devising cute ways of killing Castro?"

"The Agency is not supposed to do assassinations," he said.

"But it does."

"There's a lunatic element that gives us a bad name, but we need a central intelligence agency. We live in a hostile world, and we need information about our enemies."

Jane sighed. "But look what it leads to," she said. "You will send more and bigger guns to Masud so he can kill more people faster. That's what you people always end up doing."

"It's not just so that he can kill more people faster," Ellis protested. "The Afghans are fighting for their freedom, and they're fighting against a bunch of murderers—"

"They're *all* fighting for their freedom," Jane interrupted. "The PLO, the Cuban exiles, the IRA, the white South Africans, and the Free Wales Army."

"Some are right and some aren't."

"And the CIA knows the difference?"

"It ought to."

115

"But it doesn't. Whose freedom is Masud fighting for?"

"The freedom of all Afghans."

"Nonsense," Jane said fiercely. "He's a Muslim fundamentalist, and if he ever takes power, the first thing he'll do is clamp down on women. And how do you think he will treat his opponents, given that his political hero is the Ayatollah Khomeini?"

Ellis said, "Do you *seriously* think Masud's regime would be worse than that of the Russians?"

Jane thought for a moment. "I don't know. The only thing that's certain is that Masud's regime will be an Afghan tyranny instead of a Russian tyranny. And it's not worth killing people to exchange a foreign dictator for a local one."

"The Afghans seem to think it is."

"Most of them have never been asked."

"I think it's obvious. However, I don't normally do this sort of work anyway. Usually I'm more of a detective type. In Paris I hunted down and caught some very nasty terrorists."

For a moment Jane was seized by nostalgia as she thought of the time—was it only a year and a half ago?—when she and Ellis had been happy and none of *this* had happened. No CIA, no Jean-Pierre, no Afghanistan. "I suppose I ought to say that I seem to have misjudged you. But you can't wipe it out, can you?" she added. "Everything that has happened—your lies, my anger."

"No." He was sitting on a stool, studying her intently.

Suddenly she did not want him to leave. "Why don't you have supper with me?" she said. "It's only bread and curds, though."

"All right."

She had finished feeding Chantal and held her out to him. "Let me go and tell Fara." He took the baby, and she went out into the courtyard. "Make bread for two people, please," Jane said in Dari. Fara's eyes widened, and Jane realized it was shocking for a woman alone to invite a man to supper. So what? she thought, and went back into the house.

Ellis was sitting on the big cushion under the oil lamp, dandling Chantal on his knee. She was looking up at him, gurgling happily and kicking her fat feet. Jane stopped, and a thought came unbidden into her mind. Ellis should have been Chantal's father.

THEY WALKED UP THE mountainside at midnight, Jane leading the way, Ellis following with his big down sleeping bag under his arm. They had bathed Chantal, eaten their meager supper of bread and curds, and settled the baby down for the night on the roof, where she was now fast asleep beside Fara. Ellis had wanted to take Jane away from the house where she had been someone else's wife, and Jane had felt the same, so she had said, "I know a place where we can go."

Now she turned off the mountain path and led Ellis across the stony ground to her secret retreat, the ledge where she had sunbathed before Chantal was born. She found it easily in the moonlight. She looked down into the village, where the embers of cooking fires glowed in the courtyards and a few lamps still flickered. She could just make out the shape of her house. In a few hours, as soon as day began to break, she would be able to see the sleeping forms of Chantal and Fara on the roof. She would be glad. This was the first time she had left Chantal at night.

She turned around. Ellis had unzipped the sleeping bag and was spreading it on the ground like a blanket. Jane felt awkward.

"Come and sit down," he said.

She sat beside him on the sleeping bag. They both looked down at the darkened village. They were not touching. There was a moment of strained silence. "Nobody else has ever been here," Jane remarked, just for something to say.

"What did you use it for?"

"Oh, I just used to lie in the sun and think about nothing."

He put his arm around her and hugged her. She turned her face to him. He kissed her softly.

"Oh, Jane, I've missed you." He closed his eyes and spoke in a murmur. "Most of the time I didn't even realize it."

She kissed his face lightly. The awkward feeling was going rapidly. She thought, Last time I kissed him, he had no beard.

For a while they talked of their life together in Paris—the parties, the political arguments in cafés. He told her some of the terrible things about flying in Vietnam. Then they were quiet, the only sounds their breathing and the rushing river on the far side of the valley. Jane looked at the stars. They were very bright, and there were no clouds. The night air was becoming cooler. We'll have to get inside this sleeping bag before too long, she thought. She looked forward to falling asleep close to him.

The thought came to her that she had missed Ellis more than she had ever admitted to herself; indeed, the reason she had been so angry with him for so long was that she had continued to love him all along, and she loved him still. And as she admitted it, a terrible weight lifted from her mind. She turned to him, but he was asleep. So she said, "I love you, dear. Sleep well," and then she closed her eyes.

AFTER a year in the valley Jean-Pierre found the city of Kabul frightening. The buildings were too tall, the cars went too fast, and there were too many people. After twenty-four hours he was still jumpy. It was ironic. He was a Parisian!

He had been given a room in the unmarried officers' quarters. They had promised him an apartment as soon as Jane arrived with Chantal. Meanwhile, he felt as if he were living in a cheap hotel. He stood at his window, looking over Kabul at night. He could not smell the night air, for the window was nailed shut. His door was not locked, but there was a Russian sergeant with a pistol standing guard at the end of the corridor.

Where was Jane? The raid on Darg must have been over by nightfall. For a helicopter to go from Darg to Banda and pick up Jane and Chantal would be the work of a few minutes. The helicopter could get from Banda to Kabul in under an hour. She would be so glad to see her husband that she would be ready to forgive his deceit, see his point of view about Masud, and let bygones be bygones, Jean-Pierre thought. For a moment he wondered whether that was wishful thinking. No, he decided; he knew her quite well, and she was basically under his thumb.

He heard footsteps outside in the corridor. Would it be Anatoly, or Jane—or both? He opened the door and saw two rather large Russian soldiers and a third, smaller man in an officer's uniform. He was disappointed. The two soldiers stepped through the door rudely. Jean-Pierre went back a pace, a protest rising to his lips, but before he could say anything at all, the nearer of the two grabbed him by the shirt and smashed a huge fist into his face.

Jean-Pierre let out a howl of pain and fear. The other soldier kicked him in the groin with a heavy boot. The pain was excruciating, and Jean-Pierre sank to his knees, knowing that the most terrible moment of his life had arrived.

The two soldiers pulled him upright and held him standing, one at each arm, and the officer came in. Through a haze of tears Jean-Pierre saw a short, thickset young man with a wooden truncheon in his gloved hand.

For the next five minutes the two soldiers held Jean-Pierre's squirming, shuddering body while the officer smashed the truncheon repeatedly into his face, his shoulders, his knees, his shins, his belly, and his groin. Every blow made him scream in pain, and every pause made him scream in anticipation of the next blow. At last there was a longer pause, and Jean-Pierre began to babble. "Oh, please, don't hit me. Please, don't hit me again, sir; I'll do anything. What is it you want? Don't hit me—"

"Enough!" said a voice in French.

Jean-Pierre opened his eyes and tried to peer through the blood streaming down his face at this savior. It was Anatoly.

The two soldiers let Jean-Pierre sink to the ground. His body felt as if it were on fire. He opened his mouth and spoke through smashed lips. "Why . . . why have they done this?"

"You know why," said Anatoly.

Jean-Pierre shook his head from side to side. "I risked my life for you. . . . I gave everything. . . . Why?"

"You set a trap," Anatoly said. "Eighty-one men died today because of you."

The raid must have gone wrong, Jean-Pierre realized, and somehow he was being blamed. "No," he said, "not I—"

"You expected to be miles away when the trap was sprung," Anatoly went on. "But I surprised you by making you get into the helicopter and come with me. So you are here to take your punishment—which will be painful and very, very prolonged."

"No," said Jean-Pierre, fighting to think, despite the pain. "I came here. . . . I risked my life. . . . I gave you information on the convoys. . . . You attacked the convoys . . . did far more damage than the loss of eighty men." He gathered his strength for one coherent sentence. "If I had known of a trap, I could have warned you yesterday."

"Then how did they know we would attack the village?" Anatoly demanded.

Jean-Pierre racked his confused brain. "Was Skabun bombed?"

"I think not."

That was it, Jean-Pierre realized. Someone had found out that there had been no bombing at Skabun. "You should have bombed it," he said.

Anatoly's Oriental face looked thoughtful. "Somebody there is very good at making connections."

It was Jane, thought Jean-Pierre, and for a second he hated her.

Anatoly said, "Has Ellis Thaler got any distinguishing marks?"

"Yes," Jean-Pierre said miserably. "A big scar on his back shaped like a cross."

"Then it *is* he," said Anatoly in a near whisper.

"Who?"

"John Michael Raleigh, age thirty-four, born in New Jersey. He was a dropout from the University of California at Berkeley and a captain in the U.S. Marines. He has been a CIA agent since 1972. Marital status: divorced once, one child, whereabouts of the family a closely guarded secret." He waved his hand as if to brush such details aside. "There's no doubt it was he who outguessed me at Darg today. He's brilliant and very dangerous. If I could have my pick of all the agents of the Western imperialist nations to catch, I would choose him. In the last ten years he has done us irreparable damage. In Paris he destroyed a network that had taken seven years of patient work to develop. And now—now we have him here."

Jean-Pierre, kneeling on the floor and hugging his battered body, closed his eyes in despair. All along he had been far out of his depth, blithely pitting himself against the grand masters of this merciless game, a naked child in a den of lions. He had had such high hopes. Working alone, he was to have dealt the Afghan Resistance a blow from which it would never recover. And he would have taken his revenge on the smug rulers of the West, the establishment that had betrayed and killed his father. But instead of that triumph, he had been defeated. It had all been snatched from him at the last moment—by Ellis Thaler.

He heard Anatoly's voice like a background murmur. "We can be sure he achieved what he wanted with the rebels. We don't know the details, but the outline is enough: a unity pact among the bandit leaders in exchange for American arms. That kind of thing could keep the rebellion going for years. We've got to stop it before it gets started."

Jean-Pierre opened his eyes and looked up. "How?"

"We have to catch this man before he can return to the United States. That way nobody will know that he got them to agree to the treaty, the rebels will never get their arms, and the whole thing will fizzle out. And catching him would almost make up for losing Masud. We would have neutralized the single most dangerous agent the imperialists have. Think of it: a real, live CIA man caught here in Afghanistan. For three years the American propaganda machine has been saying that the Afghan bandits are freedom fighters waging a heroic David-and-Goliath struggle against the might of the Soviet Union. Now we could have *proof* that Masud and the others are mere lackeys of American imperialism. We can put Thaler on trial."

As he listened, Jean-Pierre realized it *was* possible to turn this into a triumph, and it would still be a triumph for him personally, because it was he who had alerted the Russians to the presence of a CIA agent in the Five Lions Valley.

"Now," said Anatoly, "where is Ellis tonight? Did he have a base in Banda?"

"Yes."

"Then that is obviously the place to begin."

Yes, of course, thought Jean-Pierre. If Ellis is not at Banda, somebody there may know where he has gone. Somebody like Jane. If Anatoly went to Banda looking for Ellis, he might at the same time find Jane. Jean-Pierre's pain seemed to ease as he realized that he might get his revenge on the Establishment, capture Ellis, who had stolen his triumph, *and* get Jane and Chantal back. "Will I go with you to Banda?" he asked.

Anatoly considered. "I think so. You know the village and the people—it may be useful to have you on hand."

Jean-Pierre struggled to his feet, gritting his teeth against the agony in his body. "When do we go?"

"Now," said Anatoly.

THERE was no sharp division between sleep and wakefulness. At some point during the short night, they had zipped up the bag, and now they lay very close together. Ellis liked it. They had always slept close together, he remembered.

It was obvious that he had never stopped loving Jane. Do I have her now? he wondered. She had not said much, except, "I love you, dear. Sleep well," just as he was falling asleep. He thought it the most delightful thing he had ever heard.

"What are you smiling about?"

He opened his eyes and looked at her. "I thought you were asleep," he replied.

"I've been watching you. You look so happy."

"Yes." He took a deep breath of the cool morning air and raised himself on his elbow to look across the valley. The fields were almost colorless in the dawn light, and the sky was pearl gray. He was on the point of telling her what he was happy about when he heard a buzzing noise. He cocked his head to listen.

"What is it?" she said. A moment later she heard the unmistakable sound of helicopters.

The aircraft came into view over their heads, emerging from behind the mountain: three hunchbacked Hinds bristling with armament, and one big troop-carrying Hip.

"Get your head in," Ellis snapped at Jane. The sleeping bag was brown and dusty, like the ground all around them. If they could stay under it, they might be invisible from the air. Jane burrowed down into the bag. Ellis held her tight and rolled over, and the bag's pillowcase cover flopped over their heads. Now they were practically invisible.

They lay on their stomachs and looked down at the village. The helicopters seemed to be descending.

Jane said, "They aren't going to land *here*, surely?"

Ellis said slowly, "I think they are."

Jane started to get up, saying, "I've got to go down—"

"No!" Ellis held her shoulders. "Wait—just wait a few seconds and see what will happen."

"But Chantal—"

"Wait!"

On the roofs of the houses sleepy people were sitting up and staring dazedly at the huge machines beating the air like giant birds above them. Ellis located Jane's house. He could see Fara standing up and wrapping a sheet around herself. There beside her was the tiny mattress on which Chantal lay hidden by bedding.

The helicopters circled cautiously. They're aiming to land here, Ellis thought, but they're wary after the ambush at Darg.

The villagers were galvanized. Some ran out of their houses while others ran in. Children and livestock were rounded up and herded indoors. Several people tried to flee, but a Hind flew low over the pathways out of the village and forced them back.

The scene convinced the Russian commander that there was no ambush here. The troop-carrying Hip and one of the three Hinds landed in a field. Seconds later soldiers emerged from the Hip, jumping out of its huge belly like insects.

"It's no good," Jane cried. "I'll have to go down now."

"Listen!" said Ellis. "She's in no danger. Whatever the Russians want, they're not after babies. But they might be after *you*."

"I must be with her!"

"Stop panicking," he shouted. "If you're with her, she *will* be in danger. If you stay here, she's safer."

"Oh, God! If I must." She closed her eyes. "Hold me tight."

The troops encircled the little village. Occasional shots could be heard, but the soldiers appeared to be firing into the air to subdue the villagers. They were entering houses, driving out the occupants, and herding them into the courtyard of the mosque.

Suddenly Jane cried, "Look at Fara! What's she doing?"

Fara was kneeling beside Chantal's tiny mattress, and Ellis could just see a little pink head peeping out. Chantal appeared still to be asleep. He saw Fara place a cushion beside Chantal's head, then pull the sheet up over the baby's face.

"She's hiding her," said Jane. "The cushion props open the cover to let air in."

"She's a clever girl."

Fara then draped another sheet untidily over Chantal's body. She paused, studying the effect. From a distance the baby looked like a hastily abandoned pile of bedding. Fara seemed satisfied, for she descended into the courtyard.

"She's leaving her," said Jane.

"Chantal is as safe as can be in the circumstances."

"I know, I know!"

Fara was pushed into the mosque with the others. She was one of the last to go in. "All the babies are with their mothers," said Jane. "I think Fara should have taken Chantal."

"No," said Ellis. "Wait. You'll see." He still did not know what would happen, but if, as he feared, there was going to be a reprisal massacre, Chantal was safest where she was.

When everyone seemed to be within the mosque, the soldiers began to search the village again, running in and out of the houses, firing into the air. The helicopter that had stayed in the air flew low and scanned the outskirts of the village in ever increasing circles, as if searching.

One of the soldiers entered Jane's house. A few seconds later he came out and quickly ran up the outside staircase. "Oh, God, save her," whispered Jane.

He stood on the roof, glanced at the rumpled bedding, looked around at nearby roofs, and poked Fara's mattress with his toe.

Suddenly he turned away and ran down the stairs.

Ellis breathed again and looked at Jane. She was ghastly white. He looked at the mosque. He could see only a part of the courtyard inside. The villagers appeared to be sitting down in rows, but there was some movement to and fro.

"Oh, look!" Jane gasped. "The man in front of the mosque!"

Ellis looked. "The Russian officer in the peaked hat?"

"Yes. I know who that is—I've seen him before. It's the man who was in the stone hut with Jean-Pierre. It's got to be Anatoly."

"His contact," Ellis breathed as another figure emerged from the mosque, a bearded man in an open-necked white shirt and dark Western-style trousers. "It's Jean-Pierre," he said. "Now what's going on?"

"Oh," Jane cried out. "I thought I'd never see him again."

Jean-Pierre was speaking to the Russian officer and gesticulating, pointing up the mountainside.

"Is he pointing toward us?" Ellis asked.

"He doesn't know about this place. Nobody does. He must be pointing toward the caves and telling the Russians to look there."

"Yes."

"But that's *awful*. How could he . . ." Her voice trailed off, and after a pause she said, "But of course that's what he's been doing ever since he got here—betraying people to the Russians."

Ellis noticed that Anatoly appeared to be speaking into a walkie-talkie. A moment later one of the circling Hinds roared over Ellis and Jane, to land, audible but out of sight, on the hilltop.

Jean-Pierre and Anatoly were walking toward Jane's house, where Chantal lay concealed on the roof. Jean-Pierre was limping. "He's hurt," said Ellis. It looked to him as if Jean-Pierre had been beaten up, but he did not say so.

Jane's expression was drawn and scared as the two men below entered the building. "Don't cry, little girl," she whispered.

The two men now came out of the house. They stood in the courtyard talking intently. Jean-Pierre limped across to the staircase that led to the roof. He mounted the first step with evident difficulty, then got down again. There was another short exchange of words, and the Russian alone mounted the stairs.

Ellis held his breath.

Anatoly stepped onto the roof. Like the soldier before him, he glanced at the scattered bedding, looked around at other houses, and then returned his attention to this one. Like the soldier, he poked at Fara's mattress with the toe of his boot. Then he knelt down beside Chantal. Gently he drew back the sheet.

Jane gave an inarticulate cry as Chantal's pink face came into view. If they're after Jane, Ellis thought, they will take Chantal, for they know she would give herself up in order to be reunited with her baby.

Anatoly stared at the tiny bundle for several seconds.

"Oh, God. I can't stand this. I can't stand it," Jane groaned.

Ellis held her tight and said, "Wait. Wait and see."

The Russian appeared to be thinking.

Suddenly he seemed to make up his mind. He dropped the sheet, tucked it in around the baby, stood up, and walked away.

Jane burst into tears.

From the roof Anatoly called down to Jean-Pierre, shaking his head in negation. Then he descended into the courtyard.

"Now, why did he do that?" Ellis mused, thinking aloud. The shake of the head meant that Anatoly was lying to Jean-Pierre, saying, "There is nobody on the roof." The implication was that Jean-Pierre would have wanted to take the baby, but Anatoly did not. That meant that Jean-Pierre wanted to find Jane, but the Russian was not interested in her.

So what *was* he interested in?

It was obvious. He was after Ellis. Anatoly wanted revenge for yesterday's humiliation.

I should have thought of that yesterday, Ellis reflected bitterly, but I was flushed with success and thinking only about Jane. Besides, Anatoly could not *know* I was here. I might have been in Darg, or Astana, or hiding out in the hills with Masud. So it must have been a long shot. But it had almost worked. Anatoly had good instincts. He was a formidable opponent—and the battle was not yet over.

Ellis watched Jean-Pierre and Anatoly walk back toward the helicopters, still standing in the fields. The Hind that had landed on the hilltop near the caves took off again and rose over their heads. Ellis wondered whether the seven wounded guerrillas in the cave clinic had been interrogated or taken prisoner, or both.

It ended very quickly. The soldiers came out of the mosque at the double and piled into the Hip as fast as they had emerged. Jean-Pierre and Anatoly boarded one of the Hinds. The ugly aircraft took off one by one, lifting giddily until they were higher than the hill and then speeding southward in a straight line.

The villagers began to trickle out of the mosque, looking scared. Jane scrambled out of the sleeping bag and ran off down the hillside, slipping and stumbling as she went. Ellis decided to leave her alone for her reunion with Chantal. Then, remembering the seven wounded guerrillas and the one-handed boy in the cave clinic, he thought he would check on them. He rolled up his sleeping bag and set off up the mountain path.

At the clearing, he went into the cave. They were all there, lying still and quiet. "Are you all right?" Ellis asked in Dari.

There was no reply. None of them moved.

"Oh, God," Ellis whispered. He knelt beside the nearest guerrilla and touched the bearded face. The man was lying in a pool of blood. He had been shot in the head at point-blank range.

Moving quickly, Ellis checked each of the guerrillas.

They were all dead. And so was the one-handed child.

CHAPTER 10

JANE dashed through the village in a blind panic, sobbing and panting and repeating like a litany, "She must be all right."

She stumbled into the courtyard of the shopkeeper's house and climbed the steps two at a time to the roof, to fall on her knees and pull the sheet off the little mattress. The baby's eyes opened, she looked at her mother, and—for the first time ever—she smiled.

Jane snatched her up and hugged her fiercely. Chantal cried at the sudden squeeze, and Jane cried too, awash with joy and relief because her little girl was still alive and warm and squalling, and because she had just smiled her first smile.

After a while Jane calmed down and with Chantal descended into her courtyard, and there she met Fara. She put her arm around the girl, hugging her. "You saved my baby!" she said. "Thank you! Thank you!"

Fara beamed with pleasure for a moment, then burst into tears.

Jane soothed her. "What happened in the mosque?" she said.

"They asked where the American was. But nobody knew. The doctor asked me where you and the baby were, and I said I didn't know. Then they picked out three of the men: first my old uncle Shahazai; then the mullah; then Alishan Karim, the mullah's brother. They asked them again, but it was no use, for the men did not know where the American had gone. So they beat them."

"Are they badly hurt?"

"Just beaten."

"I'll take a look at them." Alishan had a heart condition, Jane recalled anxiously. "Where are they now?"

"Still in the mosque."

"Come with me." Jane went into the house and found her nursing bag. She headed for the mosque, clutching Chantal tightly. As she entered the courtyard Abdullah's wife saw her, bustled over importantly, and led her to where the mullah lay on the ground. At first glance he looked all right, so Jane went to Alishan, who was lying nearby, breathing with difficulty. She gave him a tablet for his angina and, after handing Chantal to Fara, examined him quickly. He was badly bruised, but no bones were broken. "How did they beat you?" she asked him.

"With their rifles," he answered hoarsely.

She nodded and then went to Shahazai, the scarred old fighter. He had already been examined by his sister Rabia, the midwife, who was bathing his cuts. He was all right.

We were lucky, Jane thought. The Russians came, but we escaped with minor injuries. Thank God. Perhaps now we can hope they will leave us alone for a while. Maybe until the route to the Khyber Pass is open again.

"Is the doctor a Russian?" Rabia asked abruptly.

"No, Rabia, Jean-Pierre's not a Russian. But he seems to have joined their side."

"So he is a traitor."

"Yes, I suppose he is." What was in old Rabia's mind?

"Can a Christian divorce her husband for being a traitor?"

In Europe she can divorce him for a good deal less, thought Jane, so she said, "Yes."

"Is that why you have now married the American?"

Jane saw how Rabia was thinking. Long Jane's leading supporter in the village, Rabia was planning a defense, according to which Jane had been rapidly divorced from the traitor under strange Christian laws, and was now married to Ellis under those same laws. So be it, Jane thought. "Yes," she said, "that is why I have married the American."

Rabia nodded, satisfied.

Jane did not consider herself married to Ellis. However, she *did* feel that her obligations to Jean-Pierre had ended. After what he's done, she thought, I don't owe him anything.

Her musings were interrupted by a flurry of activity at the mosque entrance, and Jane turned around to see Ellis walk in carrying something in his arms. His face was a mask of rage. The bundle in his arms was a child, and the child was dead, and when Jane looked closely she saw that it was the one Afghan child who sometimes seemed like her own—one-handed Mousa, the boy whose life she had saved. Tears came to her eyes.

The villagers clustered around Ellis. "They are all dead," he said, speaking Dari. "Shot by the Russians, each one."

Suddenly a great wail was heard, and Halima, the child's mother, pushed through the crowd. She took her son from Ellis and sank to the ground with the body in her arms, screaming his name. The women gathered around her. Jane turned away.

Beckoning Fara to follow her with Chantal, Jane left the mosque and walked slowly home. A minute later Ellis came into the house. He kissed her, then said, "You seem suddenly angry with me."

Jane realized that she was. "Men are so bloody," she said bitterly. "And in a way it was your fault that that child died."

Ellis looked astonished. "Why mine?"

"They beat Abdullah, Alishan, and Shahazai in an attempt to make them tell where you were. They were looking for you."

"I know. Does that make it my fault that they shot the boy?"

"It happened because you're here, where you don't belong."

"Perhaps. Anyway, I have the solution to *that* problem. I'm leaving. My presence brings violence and bloodshed, as you are so quick to point out. If I stay, not only am I liable to get caught, but my fragile little scheme to start these tribes working together against their common enemy will fall apart."

"But you can't go. The route to the Khyber Pass is blocked."

"There's another way: the Butter Trail."

"Oh, Ellis. It's very hard—and dangerous." She was no longer angry with him. She realized she would lose him again, and she would be alone. The thought made her miserable. "I didn't think I'd lose you again so soon."

He took her hand. "You haven't thought this situation through," he said. "Don't you know Jean-Pierre wants you back?"

Jane considered that. "But what would he do with me?"

"He will want you and Chantal to live out the rest of your lives in some mining town in Siberia, while he spies in Europe and visits you every few years for a holiday between assignments."

"What could he do if I were to refuse?"

"He could make you. Or he could kill you."

Jane remembered Jean-Pierre punching her. "Will the Russians help him to find me?" she said.

"Yes. First, because they owe him. Second, because they figure you will keep him happy. Third, because you know too much. You know Jean-Pierre intimately, and you've seen Anatoly. You could provide good descriptions of both of them for the CIA's computer, if you were able to get back to Europe."

So there would be more bloodshed, Jane thought. The Russians would raid villages and beat and torture people to find out where she was. "That Russian officer . . . Anatoly. Didn't he realize that if he had taken Chantal from the rooftop, I would have given myself up to be with her?"

Ellis nodded. "That puzzled me at the time. But I think he has another use for you."

"What use? What could they want me to do?"

"Slow me down."

"By making you stay here?"

"No. By coming with me."

As soon as he said it she realized he was right. But she had to go with him, she and the baby. There was no alternative. If we die, we die, she thought fatalistically. So be it. "I suppose I have a better chance of escaping from here with you than of escaping from Siberia alone," she said.

Ellis nodded. "That's about it."

"I'll start packing," said Jane. "We'd better leave first thing tomorrow morning."

Ellis shook his head. "I want to be out of here in an hour."

JANE TOOK A DEEP BREATH and started to pack.

She had two saddlebags that could double as backpacks. Into one she put clothes: Chantal's diapers, a change of underwear for all of them, Ellis' quilted down coat from New York, and the fur-lined raincoat, complete with hood, that she had brought from Paris. She used the other bag for medical supplies and food—iron rations for emergencies. She had found a local cake made of dried mulberries and walnuts, almost indigestible but packed with concentrated energy. They also had a lot of rice and a lump of hard cheese. The only souvenir Jane took was her collection of Polaroid photographs of the villagers. They also took their sleeping bags, a saucepan, Jean-Pierre's maps, and Ellis' military kit bag, which contained some explosives and blasting equipment—their only weapon. Ellis lashed all the baggage to Maggie, the unidirectional mare.

Their hurried leave-taking was tearful. Jane hugged and kissed Fara. Then she was embraced by Zahara; old Rabia, the midwife; and even Halima, Mohammed's wife. Ellis was embraced by Ali-shan and Shahazai. Then they left to cries of "God go with you!"

The village children accompanied them to the bend in the river. Jane looked back at the little huddle of mud-colored houses that had been her home for more than a year. She knew she would never come back, but she had a feeling that if she survived, she would be telling stories of Banda to her grandchildren.

It took them less than an hour to reach Dasht-i-Rewat, a pleasant village where the cottages were dotted along the northern bank of the river. Here it was that the pitted, snaking cart track that passed for a road in the Five Lions Valley came to an end. It was midday, but neither of them wanted to stop and eat. They hoped to reach Saniz, ten miles away at the head of the valley, by nightfall, and although ten miles was no great distance on level ground, in this landscape it could take many hours.

Ellis led the horse, and Jane carried Chantal in the sling she had devised, which enabled her to feed Chantal without having to stop. The ground began to slope up, gradually at first and then more steeply. They climbed steadily under the hot sun. Jane covered her head with her pattu; Chantal was shaded by the sling. Ellis wore his Chitrali cap, a gift from Mohammed.

When they reached the summit of the pass, the track ran along the mountainside, high above the Five Lions River. The path was still climbing but more gently, so they made better speed. They were delayed every mile or two by the tributaries that came rushing in from the side valleys to join the main river. The track would dive down to a log bridge or a ford, and Ellis often had trouble dragging the unwilling Maggie into the water.

The gorge narrowed, and the river below was littered with granite boulders. The landscape became bleak, and a cold wind blew down the valley, making Jane shiver despite the sunshine. The rocky terrain and the sheer cliffs suited birds. There were scores of Asian magpies.

At last the gorge gave way to another plain. Far to the east Jane could see a range of hills, and above the hills were visible the white mountains of Nuristan. That's where we're going, Jane thought, and she was afraid.

In the plain stood a small cluster of poor houses. "I guess this is it," said Ellis. "Welcome to Saniz."

As they drew level with the first of the houses a figure stepped out of it, and Jane recognized Mohammed. He was as surprised as she. Her surprise gave way to horror when she realized she was going to have to tell him that his son had been killed.

Ellis gave her time to collect her thoughts by saying in Dari, "Why are you here?"

"Masud is here," Mohammed replied. "Why are *you* here?"

"We're going to Pakistan."

"This way?" His face became grave. "What happened?"

Jane knew she had to be the one to tell him. "We bring bad news, my friend Mohammed. The Russians came to Banda. They killed seven men . . . and a child. . . ." He guessed then what she was going to say, for a look of pain crossed his face. "Mousa was the child," she finished.

Mohammed composed himself rigidly. "How?" he asked. "How was Mousa killed?"

Ellis said, "Kalashnikov," using a word that needed no translation. He pointed to his heart to show where the bullet had struck, and struggled to find words. "He died . . . knife in hand, blood on knife."

Mohammed swelled with pride even as the tears came to his eyes. "He attacked them—grown men, armed with guns. He went for them with his knife! The knife his father gave him! The one-handed boy is now surely in the warrior's heaven."

To die in a holy war was the greatest possible honor for a Muslim, Jane recalled. Mousa would probably become a minor saint. Ellis embraced Mohammed solemnly, saying nothing.

Jane suddenly remembered her photographs. She opened one of the bags on Maggie's back and rummaged through the supplies until she found the box of Polaroids. She located a picture of Mousa, then handed it to Mohammed.

The man was so moved he could not speak. He turned away, and when he turned back, his face was composed. "Come," he said.

They followed him through the little village to the edge of the river, where Masud and a group of fifteen or twenty guerrillas were squatting around a cooking fire. Mohammed strode into the group and without preamble began to tell the story of Mousa's death, with tears and gesticulations.

Jane turned away. She had seen too much grief. She sat on the ground, grateful to rest her legs, and began to feed Chantal. Ellis tethered Maggie, unloaded the bags, and got out Jean-Pierre's maps. He sat beside Jane to study them in the rapidly fading evening light. Jane looked over his shoulder. Their planned route continued up the valley to a village called Comar, where they would turn southeast into a side valley that led to Nuristan. This valley was the first high pass they would encounter. "Fifteen thousand feet," said Ellis. "That's where it gets cold."

Jane shivered.

When Chantal was fed, Jane changed her diaper and washed the old one in the river. She returned to find Ellis deep in conversation with Masud. She squatted beside them.

"You have made the right decision," Masud was saying. "You must get out of Afghanistan with our treaty in your pocket. If the Russians catch you, all is lost." Ellis nodded agreement. Masud went on. "However, it is a journey of extraordinary difficulty.

Much of the trail is above the ice line. Sometimes the path is hard to find in the snow, and if you get lost there, you die. I can help you. But, like you, I want to make a deal."

"Go on," said Ellis.

"I will give you Mohammed as a guide, to take you through Nuristan and into Pakistan. But you go alone. The doctor's wife and the child stay here."

It was heartbreakingly clear to Jane that she must agree to this. It was foolhardy for the two of them to try to make it alone. They would probably both die. This way she could at least save Ellis' life. "You *must* say yes," she told him.

Ellis looked at Masud. "It's out of the question," he said.

Masud, visibly offended, walked back to the circle of guerrillas. Jane said, "Oh, Ellis, was that wise?"

"No," he said. "But I'm not going to let you go."

She squeezed his hand. "I . . . I've made you no promises."

"I know," he said. "When we get back to civilization, you're free to do whatever you like. Anyway, we may not live that long."

That was true. Why agonize over the future, she thought, when we probably don't have a future?

Masud came back, smiling again. "I'm not a good negotiator," he said. "I'll give you Mohammed anyway."

CHAPTER 11

FIVE hundred Russian helicopters took off from Bagram half an hour before dawn. One by one they disappeared into the night sky. In turn, the Hind that Jean-Pierre and Anatoly were in struggled into the air like an ungainly bird and joined the convoy. Soon the lights of the air base were lost from view, and once again Jean-Pierre and Anatoly were flying over the mountaintops toward the Five Lions Valley.

Anatoly, after consultation with Moscow, had mounted what was probably the largest operation in the history of the Afghan war. He had convinced his superiors in the KGB and then the military bigwigs that they must catch Ellis Thaler.

Although Ellis and Jane had not been in the village when Jean-

Pierre and Anatoly had gone to find them, it was almost certain they had heard about that raid and had now gone into hiding. They would not be in Banda, but Anatoly had all the other possibilities covered.

Helicopters would land at every village in the valley and every hamlet in every side valley. The pilots would overfly all the trails and footpaths. The troops—more than a thousand men—were instructed to search every building and look under large trees and inside caves. Anatoly was determined not to fail again. Today they would *find* Ellis. And Jane.

As they approached the valley, the helicopters began to divide into smaller groups. Jean-Pierre and Anatoly were with the flight to Comar, the northernmost village of the valley. For the last stretch of the journey they followed the river. The rapidly brightening morning light revealed tidy ranks of sheaves in the wheat fields. The bombing had not completely disrupted farming here.

The sun was in their eyes as they descended to Comar. The village was a cluster of houses peeping over a heavy wall on the hillside. It reminded Jean-Pierre of perched hill villages in the south of France, and he felt a pang of homesickness.

He shifted his weight in the hard seat. Right now it would be good just to get out of the helicopter. He had been in pain more or less constantly since the beating. But worse than the pain was the memory of the humiliation. Each time he thought of that, he wanted revenge. He wanted to see Ellis beaten, in the same way, by the same brute soldiers, until he sobbed and screamed and pleaded for mercy. With one refinement: Jane would be watching.

BY THE middle of the afternoon failure stared them in the face yet again. They had searched the village of Comar, all the hamlets around it, all the side valleys in the area, and each of the single farmhouses in the almost barren land to the north of the village. Anatoly was in constant touch with the commanders of the other squads by radio. They had conducted equally thorough searches throughout the entire valley, and still they had not found Ellis or Jane or Chantal.

Jean-Pierre and Anatoly finished up at a horse station in the hills above Comar. The only male inhabitant seemed to be the horse dealer, a barefoot old man wearing a long shirt with a voluminous hood to keep off flies. When they had finished searching the hamlet, Anatoly sat in the dust, with his back to a stone wall, looking thoughtful. Jean-Pierre sat down beside him.

Across the hills they could see the distant white peak of Mesmer, almost twenty thousand feet high. Anatoly said, "See if you can get some tea."

"Make tea," Jean-Pierre shouted at the old man in Dari. He scurried away. Anatoly's men, seeing that they were to stay here awhile, killed the engines of their helicopters and sat around in the dust, waiting patiently.

Anatoly stared into the distance. Weariness showed on his flat face. "We are in trouble," he said. "But let us not give up hope. People cannot vanish into thin air. Our fugitives are somewhere. Let's try a different approach. Think. Somebody must have helped them hide. That means somebody knows where they are."

Jean-Pierre considered. "If they had help, it was probably from the guerrillas—the people least likely to tell."

"Our fugitives must have *some* enemies," Anatoly persisted.

Jean-Pierre shook his head. "Ellis hasn't been here long enough to make enemies, and Jane is a heroine. They treat her like Florence Nightingale. Nobody dislikes her—Oh!" Even as he was speaking he realized it was not true.

"Well?"

"The mullah. Somehow she irritated him beyond reason."

"He probably called her a Western whore."

"How did you guess?"

"They always do. Where does this mullah live?"

"In Banda, in a house about half a mile outside the village."

"Will he talk?"

"He probably hates Jane enough to give her away to us," said Jean-Pierre reflectively. "But he couldn't be *seen* to do it. Everyone by now knows I've been a spy, and he would clam up. I'd have to meet him in secret somehow." Jean-Pierre thought of the danger, and then of the humiliation he had suffered. Revenge was worth any risk. "If you drop me near the village, I can hide on the path to his house and wait there until he comes along."

"What if he doesn't come along all day?" Anatoly frowned.
"To make sure he does, we'll round up all the villagers in the
mosque, as we did before, then just let them go. We let the
women go first, and order them to return to their homes. Then,
when the men are released, they will all want to check on
their wives. Does anyone else live near the mullah?"

"No."

"Then he *should* hurry along that footpath all alone. You step
out from behind a bush—"

"And he slits my throat from ear to ear."

Anatoly shrugged. "You can take my pistol."

Jean-Pierre was pleased to be trusted that much. "I suppose it
may serve as a threat," he said anxiously. "But I'll need some
native clothes in case I'm seen by someone other than Abdullah."

"That's easy," said Anatoly. He shouted something in Russian,
and three of the soldiers jumped to their feet. They disappeared
into one of the houses and emerged a few seconds later with the
old horse dealer. Anatoly shouted an abrupt command, and the
soldiers threw the man onto the ground and pulled off his shirt.
They all laughed uproariously to see his stick-thin legs poking
out of his ragged shorts. They let him go, and he scuttled away.
Jean-Pierre took off his own European-style shirt and trousers
and donned the old man's long hooded shirt.

Anatoly and Jean-Pierre now climbed into their helicopter.
Anatoly took the pilot's headset and spoke into the radio micro-
phone at length in Russian. A few minutes later they took off with
the other helicopters and followed the Five Lions River southwest, going down the valley. At Dasht-i-Rewat they turned southeast, following the tributary Rewat upstream into the hills, in
order to approach Banda from behind the mountain.

Anatoly used the pilot's headset again, then came to shout in
Jean-Pierre's ear. "It is all arranged. The villagers are in the
mosque already. Where do you want to be dropped off?"

"Drop me there," Jean-Pierre said, pointing below. "Give me
ten minutes; then release the women and children. Then wait
another ten minutes and release the men."

"Right."

The helicopter descended into the shadow of the mountain. The afternoon was waning, but there was still an hour or so before nightfall. They landed behind the ridge, not far from the caves.

"Go," said Anatoly.

Jean-Pierre opened the door and jumped out of the helicopter, holding Anatoly's pistol in his hand. He hurried away with his head bent. After crossing the familiar clearing in front of his old cave clinic, he hurried down the hill and past the mullah's house. The valley seemed oddly quiet despite the ever present noise of the river and the distant whisper of helicopter blades. It was the absence of children's voices, he realized.

He turned a corner and crouched behind a clump of camel grass and juniper bushes. He was well hidden, but he had a clear view of the path, and he settled down to wait for the mullah.

A sudden burst of high voices from far down in the village told him that Anatoly had given instructions for the women and children to be released from the mosque. The villagers would wonder what the whole exercise had been for, but they would attribute it to the notorious craziness of armies everywhere.

A few minutes later the mullah's wife came up the footpath, carrying her baby and followed by three older children. They went past and turned the corner toward their house.

Soon afterward the Russian helicopters began to take off from the wheat field. That meant the men had been released. Right on schedule, Abdullah came puffing up the hill, a tubby figure in a turban and a pin-striped English jacket. Jean-Pierre got to his feet and stepped out from the bushes.

The mullah gave a cry of shock. He looked at Jean-Pierre and recognized him. "You!" he said. His hand went to his belt. Jean-Pierre showed him the gun. Abdullah looked frightened.

"Don't be afraid," Jean-Pierre said in Dari. He made an effort to bring his voice under control. "No one knows I am here. Your wife and children passed without seeing me. They are safe."

Abdullah looked suspicious. "What do you want?"

"My wife is an adulteress," said Jean-Pierre. "She has taken my child and left me. She has gone whoring after the American."

"I know," said Abdullah.

"I have been searching for her in order to bring her back and punish her." Abdullah nodded enthusiastically. "But the wicked couple have gone into hiding." Jean-Pierre spoke carefully. "You are a man of God. Tell me where they are. No one will ever know how I found out, except you and me and God."

"They have gone." Abdullah spat. "They left the valley."

"But where did they go?"

"To Pakistan."

To Pakistan! What was the old fool talking about? "The routes are closed!"

"Not the Butter Trail."

"*Mon Dieu*," Jean-Pierre whispered. "The Butter Trail." He was awestruck by their courage and at the same time bitterly disappointed, for it would be impossible to find them now. "Did they take the baby?"

"Yes."

"Then I'll never see my daughter again."

"They will all die in Nuristan," Abdullah said with satisfaction. "A Western woman with a baby will never survive those high passes, and the American will die trying to save her. Thus God punishes those who escape man's justice."

Jean-Pierre realized he should get back to the helicopter as quickly as possible. "Go to your house now," he told Abdullah.

"The treaty will die with them, for Ellis has the paper," Abdullah added. "This is good. Although we need American weapons, it is dangerous to make pacts with infidels." He hurried away.

Jean-Pierre drew the hood over his face and set off disconsolately up the hill. Anatoly was waiting in the clearing in front of the caves. He held out his hand for the pistol and said, "Well?"

"They have escaped us. They've left the valley."

"They can't have *escaped* us," said Anatoly angrily. "Where have they gone?"

"To Nuristan. They're heading for Pakistan by a route known as the Butter Trail."

"If we know their route, we can find them."

"I don't think so. There is one route, but it has variations. You can't follow these paths from the air. You can hardly follow them from the ground without a native guide, and maps do not show these trails and passes."

Anatoly lowered his voice. "You're too easily discouraged, my friend. Think. If Ellis can find a native guide to show him the route, then I can do the same."

Is it possible? Jean-Pierre wondered. "But there is more than one way to go."

"Suppose there are ten variations. We need ten native guides to lead ten search parties."

Jean-Pierre's enthusiasm rose as he realized that he might yet get Jane and Chantal back and see Ellis captured. "It might not be that bad," he said. "We can simply inquire along the way. Once we are out of this godforsaken valley, people may be less tight-lipped. The Nuristanis aren't as involved in the war."

"Good," said Anatoly abruptly. "It is getting dark. We've got a lot to do tonight. We start early in the morning. Let's go!"

CHAPTER 12

THEY were not following the route to Nuristan that Ellis had originally planned. Instead of going north to Comar and then east along the Comar River, they turned back south from Saniz and went east along the Aryu Valley. Mohammed had suggested this because it would get them out of the Five Lions Valley more quickly.

They had left before dawn and walked uphill all day, Ellis and Jane taking turns carrying Chantal, Mohammed leading Maggie. At midday they had stopped in the mud-hut village of Aryu and bought bread from a suspicious old man with a snapping dog. Aryu village had been the limit of civilization. After that, there had been nothing for miles but the boulder-strewn river and the great, bare ivory-colored mountains on either side, until they had reached an upland meadow and a handful of stone houses and some cattle pens. The houses and pens were empty. This was a summer pasture, and the cowherds had taken the cattle to their winter quarters. Here the three of them had spent the night.

Now it was morning and they had to cross the mountain range that for centuries had kept Nuristan more or less isolated from the rest of the world. They would climb the Aryu Pass, fourteen thousand feet high. Much of the way they would have to struggle through snow and ice. They hoped to reach the Nuristan village of Linar. It was only ten miles away as the crow flies, but they would be doing well to get there by late afternoon.

The sunlight was bright when they set off, but the air was cold. Jane was wearing heavy socks and mittens and an oiled-wool sweater under her fur-lined coat. She carried Chantal in the sling, between her sweater and her coat, with the top buttons of the coat undone to let air in.

They left the meadow, following the Aryu River upstream, and immediately the landscape became harsh and hostile again. Once Jane saw, far in the distance, a huddle of nomads' tents on a bleak slope. The only other living thing was a bearded vulture floating in the bitter wind.

There was no visible path. Jane was immeasurably glad that Mohammed knew the way to guide them. Soon there was a thin layer of snow on the ground, and Jane's feet got cold despite her heavy socks and her boots. Amazingly, Chantal slept much of the time. Every couple of hours they stopped for a few minutes' rest, and Jane took the opportunity to feed her.

The approach to the Aryu Pass was daunting. Looking at that steep climb, which was slippery with snow, Jane lost heart. As she stumbled upward, panting and aching, she recalled saying to Ellis, "I suppose I have a better chance of escaping from here with you than of escaping from Siberia alone." Perhaps I can't manage either one, she thought now.

When they were almost at the summit, Jane leaned forward to take the incline, thinking, Just a little more, just a little more. She felt dizzy. In front of her, Maggie skidded on the rocks, forcing Mohammed to run alongside. Jane plodded after them, counting the steps. At last she reached the level ground. Her head was spinning. Ellis, just behind her, caught her and held her upright. She closed her eyes and felt a surge of love for him.

"From now on it's downhill all day," he said.

She opened her eyes. She could never have imagined such a cruel landscape: nothing but snow, wind, mountains, and loneliness. "What a godforsaken place this is," she said.

He looked at the view, then said, "We must keep going."

As they descended, the snow began to clear, and the track was visible. Soon they were walking alongside a brook, heading downstream now, and the endless gray-and-white rock was relieved by a little coarse grass and a few low bushes. Still the wind hurtled up the gorge and penetrated Jane's clothing like needles of ice.

After a couple of miles they reached the first village in Nuristan. The men there wore thick sleeveless sweaters with a striking black-and-white pattern, and spoke a language of their own, which Mohammed could barely understand. However, he managed to buy bread with some of Ellis' Afghan money.

Jane was tempted to plead with Ellis that they stop here for the night, for she felt desperately weary. But there were still several hours of daylight left, and they had agreed they would try to reach Linar today, so she forced her aching legs to walk on.

To her immense relief the remaining four or five miles were easier, and they arrived well before nightfall. Jane sank to the ground underneath an enormous mulberry tree and simply sat still for a while. Mohammed lit a fire and began to make tea.

He somehow let it be known that Jane was a Western nurse, and later, while she was feeding and changing Chantal, a little group of patients gathered, waiting at a respectful distance. Jane summoned her energy and saw them. As a result of this impromptu clinic, Mohammed got a chicken, which he boiled in their saucepan. It was stringy and tasteless, but they were hungry.

They were then given a room in one of the village houses. There were mattresses for them and a crude wooden crib for Chantal. Ellis fell asleep instantly. Jane lay awake for a few minutes, relaxing. We escaped from the Russians, she thought as she drifted off to sleep. Maybe we really will make it home.

JANE woke when Ellis did, hearing the sound of two dogs barking. Then Ellis slipped out of bed fast.

The room was pitch-dark. She heard a match scrape; then a

candle flickered in the corner. "What is it?" she asked Ellis.

"I don't know," he whispered. He stepped into his boots, put on his coat, and went out.

Jane got up and followed him. Up on the hill she could see, by the moonlight, a lone figure running toward them.

Suddenly another figure was beside them. Jane gave a start, then recognized Mohammed. The blade of a knife glinted in his hand.

The figure came closer. Mohammed let out a grunt and lowered the knife. "Ali Ghanim," he said, and waved. Ali waved back and ran to the hut where the three of them stood. He and Mohammed embraced.

Jane waited impatiently for Ali to catch his breath. At last he said, "The Russians are on your trail. Masud has sent me to warn you. The day you left, they searched the whole Five Lions Valley for you, with hundreds of helicopters and thousands of men. Today, having failed to find you, they sent search parties to follow each valley leading to Nuristan."

"How did they know we had gone to Nuristan?" Ellis asked.

Ali did not know.

"Is there a search party in this valley?" Jane asked Ali.

"Yes. I overtook them just before the Aryu Pass. They may have reached the last village by nightfall."

"Oh, no," said Jane despairingly. "What can we do?"

"Leave now," said Ellis. "Before they catch up with us."

Jane looked at her watch. It was two a.m. She felt bone-weary.

"I'll load the horse," Ellis said. "You feed Chantal." He switched to Dari and said to Mohammed, "Will you make some tea? And give Ali something to eat."

THEY set off in the moonlight, heading for the Kantiwar Pass. Mohammed set a fast pace and whipped the mare mercilessly when she hung back. Jane found the track scary by night. Sometimes they walked in the sparse grass beside the Linar River, which was all right; but then the trail would hairpin up the mountainside to continue on the cliff edge hundreds of feet above, where the ground was covered with snow, and Jane was terrified of slipping and falling with her baby in her arms. The starlight was not enough to illuminate the river below, so the gorge seemed like a bottomless black pit beside her. Maggie kept stopping, and Mohammed would have to pull on the reins to make her go again.

Sometimes they passed through a silent hamlet, just a handful of houses and a waterfall. In one of the cottages a dog barked hysterically until someone silenced it with a curse. Then they were in the wilderness again.

The sky was turning from black to gray, and the stars had gone. It was getting light. Jane wondered what the Russians were doing. She walked a little faster. The hours crept by, and the miles seemed longer as the three of them trekked along the bank and that narrow cliff edge. At one point they had to make a long detour around a landslide that blocked their path completely.

The air became milder as the sun climbed the morning sky. Jane opened her coat and Ellis took his off. Mohammed retained his Russian uniform greatcoat, with characteristic Afghan indifference to all but the most severe changes in the weather.

Toward noon they emerged from the narrow gorge of the Linar into the broad Nuristan Valley. Here the way was once again quite clearly marked, the path being almost as good as the cart track that ran up the Five Lions Valley. They turned north, going upstream and uphill.

Jane felt terribly tired and discouraged. After getting up at two a.m., she had walked for ten hours, but they had only covered four or five miles. It was her third consecutive day on the march, and she knew she could not continue until nightfall. Even Ellis was wearing the bad-tempered expression that, Jane knew, was a sign he was weary. Only Mohammed seemed tireless.

In the Linar Valley they had seen no one outside the villages, but here they saw a few travelers, most of them wearing white robes and turbans. The Nuristanis looked with curiosity at the two exhausted Westerners but greeted Mohammed with respect, no doubt because of the machine gun slung over his shoulder.

As they trudged uphill beside the Nuristan River they were overtaken by a black-bearded, bright-eyed young man carrying

ten fresh fish speared on a pole. He spoke to Mohammed in a mixture of languages, but they understood one another well enough for Mohammed to buy three of the fish. The young man, whose name was Halam, said he had caught the fish in Lake Mundol, farther down the valley. He then slowed his pace to walk with them, enjoying talking volubly, apparently not much concerned about whether they understood him or not.

Like the Five Lions Valley, the Nuristan was a rocky canyon that broadened every few miles into small cultivated plains with terraced fields. The most noticeable difference was the forest of holly oak that covered the mountainsides like the wool on a sheep's back.

They were making better time now, and when they turned the next bend they saw the village of Gadwal. It was a startling sight as well as a welcome one. The wooden houses scrambled up the steep mountainside like children clambering on one another's backs, giving the impression that if one house at the bottom were to collapse, the whole village would come tumbling down the hill and fall into the water.

As soon as they drew alongside the first house, Jane, near collapse, sat down on the riverbank. Every muscle in her body ached, and she hardly had the strength to take Chantal from Ellis, who had been carrying her for the last few hours. A woman looked out from the house, and Halam went to talk to her.

"We must buy bread," Mohammed said as he tethered Maggie.

Jane thought they all needed something more substantial. "What about the fish?" she said.

Ellis said, "It would take too long to clean and cook it. I don't want to spend more than half an hour here."

Halam was now calling to them. The woman had invited them into her house. Jane stood up, then bent to pick up the baby. Suddenly she lost her balance, sank to the ground, and everything went dark.

When she opened her eyes, she saw a circle of anxious faces above her: Ellis, Mohammed, Halam, and the woman. Ellis said, "How do you feel?"

"Foolish." She sat upright. "I'll be all right."

"No, you won't," said Ellis. "You can't go any farther today."

Jane knew he was right. Her body would not take any more. "But what are we going to do?" she said.

"The Russians won't catch up with us today," Ellis said. "We still have a lead—we got up so early this morning. We'll stay here tonight and start early again tomorrow."

"I have a suggestion," said Mohammed. "I will go back and divert the Russians."

Ellis said, "How?"

"I will offer to be their guide, and I will lead them south down the Nuristan Valley, away from you, to Lake Mundol."

"But they must have a guide already," Jane said.

"He may be a good man from the Five Lions Valley who has been forced to help the Russians against his will. In that case, I will speak with him and arrange things."

"What if he won't agree?"

Mohammed considered. "Then, he is not a good man who has been forced to help them, but a traitor who willingly collaborates with the enemy for personal gain, in which case I will kill him."

"I don't want anyone killed for my sake," she said quickly.

"The piece of paper bearing the signatures of the tribal leaders is more important than the life of any of us," Mohammed said. "It represents the future of Afghanistan, the freedom for which my son died."

Ellis was thinking about practicalities. He said to Mohammed, "But you're not dressed like a Nuristani."

"I will change clothes with Halam."

"You don't speak the local language well."

"There are many languages in Nuristan. I will pretend to come from a district where they use a different tongue. The Russians speak none of these languages anyway, so they will never know."

"What will you do with your gun?"

Mohammed thought for a moment. "Will you give me your bag? My gun has a folding butt."

"Sure," said Ellis.

Jane asked, "What will happen when the Russians finally realize they are on the wrong trail?"

"Before that happens, I will run away in the night, leaving them in the middle of nowhere."

Ellis said, "If they suspect you before that, they will torture you to find out which way we went."

Mohammed looked heroically unconcerned. "They will never take me alive," he said.

"But we will have no guide," Ellis said.

"I shall find you another one." Mohammed turned to Halam and began a rapid multilingual conversation. Jane gathered that Mohammed was proposing to hire Halam as a guide. He was obviously a natural choice. Most local people had never ventured outside their own valley.

"He says he knows the way," said Mohammed, reverting to French. "He will take you to Kantiwar, and there he will find another guide to take you across the next pass, and in this way you will proceed to Pakistan. He will charge five thousand afghanis."

Ellis said, "It sounds like a fair price, but how many more guides will we have to hire at that rate before we reach Chitral?"

"Maybe five or six," said Mohammed.

Ellis shook his head. "We don't have thirty thousand afghanis. And we have to buy food."

"You will have to get food by holding clinics," Mohammed said. "And the way becomes easier once you are in Pakistan."

Ellis looked dubious. "What do you think?" he asked Jane.

"There's an alternative. You could go on without me."

"No," he said. "That's not an alternative. We'll go on together."

CHAPTER 13

ALL the first day the Russian search parties found no trace of Ellis and Jane. Jean-Pierre and Anatoly sat in a spartan windowless office at the Bagram air base, monitoring the reports as they came in over the radio network. The search parties had left before dawn—again. There were six of them at the start: one for each of the five main side valleys leading east from the Five Lions, and one to follow the Five Lions River north to its source and beyond. They had landed their helicopters at six different villages, and half an hour later all six parties had reported that they had found local guides.

"That was quick," said Jean-Pierre. "How did they find them?"

"Simple," said Anatoly. "They ask someone to be a guide. He says no. They shoot him. They ask someone else. It doesn't take long to find a volunteer."

One of the search parties tried to follow its assigned trail from the air, but the experiment was a failure. So all the parties went on foot, some with commandeered horses to carry their baggage.

As the day wore on and they waited for news, Anatoly grew bored and Jean-Pierre became tense. The parties made camp at nightfall without reporting any signs of the fugitives. Jean-Pierre felt dispirited as he and Anatoly left the office and walked across the concrete to the canteen. They ate a vile dinner of canned sausages and reconstituted mashed potatoes; then Anatoly went off moodily to drink vodka with some brother officers, leaving Jean-Pierre to retire early and lie awake on a hard army mattress, visualizing Jane and Ellis together.

The next day was no better, but late in the afternoon Anatoly, his Oriental face wreathed in smiles, came to Jean-Pierre's room. "Tomorrow we will catch your wife," he said cheerfully. "We have just received reports that Ellis and Jane have been seen in the Linar Valley. The search party has not made contact with them, but we are hot on their trail."

"Wonderful. Do we know where they are now?"

"Not yet," Anatoly said briskly. "We'll get more details when we meet the search team at a village called Mundol. It's in the Nuristan Valley, downstream of the point where the Linar joins the Nuristan. We'll spend the night there and then supervise the search in the morning."

A few minutes later they were in the air.

NIGHT fell rapidly as they flew downstream. The landscape below disappeared into darkness. The pilot spoke constantly on the radio, and Jean-Pierre imagined that the people on the ground at Mundol were guiding him. After fifteen minutes powerful lights appeared below. A mile or so beyond the lights the moon glinted off the surface of a large lake. The helicopter landed in a field, and a waiting trooper led them across the grass to a village on a hillside. The silhouettes of the wooden houses were limned with moonlight. They followed the trooper into one of the houses, where an army colonel brought Anatoly up to date on the latest developments.

"Our fugitives definitely passed through the villages of Bosaydur and Linar today," Anatoly relayed to Jean-Pierre. "At some point this afternoon the search party lost its guide—he just disappeared." Anatoly frowned, as if bothered by that loose end. "But fortunately," he continued, "they found another guide almost immediately, a genuine volunteer. He's here in the village somewhere. He claims to have actually seen the fugitives today, before he joined us. They passed him at the point where the Linar flows into the Nuristan. He saw them turn south, heading this way."

"Good!"

"Tonight, after the search party arrived here in Mundol, our guide questioned some villagers and learned that two foreigners with a baby passed through this afternoon, going south."

"Then there's no doubt," said Jean-Pierre with satisfaction.

"None at all," Anatoly agreed. "We'll catch them tomorrow."

JEAN-PIERRE woke up on an inflatable mattress—a KGB luxury—on the dirt floor of the house. The fire had gone out during the night and the air was cold. He sat up and rubbed his eyes, then saw Anatoly standing in the doorway, looking at him speculatively. "Good morning," said Jean-Pierre.

"Have you ever been here before?" Anatoly asked abruptly.

Jean-Pierre's brain was still foggy with sleep. "Where?"

"Nuristan," Anatoly replied impatiently.

"No."

"Strange. I was talking to the new guide a few minutes ago."

"What's his name?"

"Mohammed, Muhammad, Mahomet, Mahmoud—one of those names a million other people have."

"What language did you use with a Nuristani?"

"French, Russian, Dari, and English—the usual mixture. He

asked me who arrived with me last night. I said, 'A Frenchman who can identify the fugitives,' or words to that effect. He asked your name, so I told him. I wanted to keep him going until I found out why he was so interested. But he didn't ask any more questions. It was almost as if he knew you."

"Impossible."

"I suppose so," Anatoly said, and went out.

Jean-Pierre got up, pulled on his trousers and boots, and stepped outside. He found himself on a rough wooden veranda overlooking the whole valley. Down below, the river coiled between the fields, broad and sluggish. Some way to the south it entered a long, narrow lake rimmed with mountains. He walked down to the meadow, washed in the river, and got a cup of coffee from a group of soldiers standing around a cooking fire.

The search party was ready to leave. Anatoly had decided last night that he would direct the search from here, remaining in constant radio contact with the searchers. The helicopters would stay ready to take him and Jean-Pierre to join the searchers as soon as they sighted their quarry.

While Jean-Pierre was sipping his coffee, Anatoly came across the field from the village. "Have you seen that guide?" he asked.

"No."

"He seems to have disappeared. These people are impossible. I'll have to ask the villagers. Come and translate. Maybe they'll understand your Dari."

As they walked back across the meadow to the village, somebody called to Anatoly in Russian. Ten or twelve men, some Nuristanis in white and some Russians in uniform, were crowded together on a veranda, looking at something on the ground. They parted to let Anatoly and Jean-Pierre through. The thing on the floor was a dead man. His throat had been cut.

"Is this Mohammed, the guide?" Jean-Pierre asked.

"No," said Anatoly. He questioned one of the soldiers, then said, "This is the *previous* guide, the one who disappeared."

The villagers were jabbering in outraged tones. Jean-Pierre addressed them slowly in Dari. "What is going on?"

After a pause a wrinkled old man replied in the same language.

151

"He has been murdered!" he said accusingly. The dead man was a villager from the Linar Valley who had been conscripted as a guide by the Russians. His body, concealed in a clump of bushes, had been found by a goatherd's dog. The man's family thought the Russians had murdered him, and they had brought the body here this morning in an attempt to find out why. Jean-Pierre explained this to Anatoly.

Anatoly spoke to the soldiers. Several of them answered together in animated tones, "We didn't kill him."

Anatoly translated to Jean-Pierre. Then he looked thoughtful and added, "Perhaps the disappearing Mohammed killed this man in order to get the job of guide."

"Are you paying much?" Jean-Pierre asked.

"I doubt it." Anatoly asked a sergeant and translated the answer. "Five hundred afghanis a day."

"It's a good wage to an Afghan, but hardly worth killing for."

"Ask them if they know where Mohammed is."

Jean-Pierre asked. There was some discussion. Most of the villagers were shaking their heads, but one man raised his voice and said he'd seen him go north this morning.

"Did he leave before or after this body was brought here?" asked Anatoly.

"Before," said Jean-Pierre, and added, "I wonder why he went away, then."

"He's acting like a man guilty of something."

"He must have left immediately after he spoke to you this morning. It's almost as if he went because I had arrived."

Anatoly nodded. "Whatever the explanation is, I think he knows something we don't. We'd better go after him." He turned away and gave a rapid series of orders to the soldiers. Then he took Jean-Pierre's arm, and they walked briskly to the field where two helicopters were cranking. They boarded one of them.

Their helicopter took off, and both Anatoly and Jean-Pierre stood near the open door and looked down. A well-beaten path, clearly visible, led from the village to the top of the hill, then disappeared into the trees. They flew parallel with the Linar for a mile or so, then reached its mouth. Had Mohammed continued up the valley into the cold heart of Nuristan, or had he turned west into the Linar Valley, heading for Five Lions? Anatoly directed the pilot to turn left and follow the Linar.

They spotted him a few minutes later.

His white robes and turban stood out clearly against the gray-brown ground. He was striding out along the cliff top with the steady, tireless pace of Afghan travelers, his possessions in a bag slung over his shoulder. When he heard the noise of the helicopters, he stopped and looked back at them, then continued walking.

"Is that him?" asked Jean-Pierre.

"We'll soon find out," said Anatoly. He took the pilot's headset and spoke to the other helicopter. It went on ahead, passing over the figure on the ground, and landed a hundred yards or so in front of him. The man walked toward it unconcernedly.

"Why don't we land too?" Jean-Pierre asked Anatoly.

"Just a precaution."

The side door of the other helicopter opened and six troopers got out. The man in white walked toward them, unslinging his bag. It was a long bag, like a military kit bag, and the sight of it rang a bell in Jean-Pierre's memory. But before he could figure out what it reminded him of, Mohammed hefted the bag and pointed it at the troopers. Jean-Pierre realized what he was about to do, and opened his mouth to shout. Before words could come, he saw the snout of a machine gun emerge from the bag.

The sound of shooting was drowned by the noise of the helicopters, which gave the weird impression that it all took place in dead silence. One of the Russian troopers clutched his belly and fell forward, another threw up his arms and fell back, and the face of a third exploded in blood and flesh. The other three got their weapons raised. One died before he could pull the trigger, but the other two unleashed a storm of bullets. The body of Mohammed was lifted off the ground and thrown backward to land in a heap on the cold earth.

As his helicopter touched down Anatoly said disgustedly, "Now we'll never know why that guide got his throat cut."

They jumped out and walked over to the dead Afghan. The front of his body and most of his face were torn and destroyed, but

Anatoly said, "It's that guide, I'm sure. The build is right, and I recognize the bag." He bent down and carefully picked up the machine gun. "But why is he carrying a machine gun?"

A photograph had fallen out of the bag and fluttered to the ground. Jean-Pierre picked it up and looked at it. "Now I understand this," he said. "I know the dead man. He is from the Five Lions Valley, one of Masud's top lieutenants. This is a photograph of his son, Mousa. It was taken by Jane. I also recognize the bag in which he concealed his gun. It used to belong to Ellis."

"So what?" said Anatoly impatiently.

Jean-Pierre's brain was in overdrive. "Mohammed killed your guide in order to take his place," he began. "You had no way of knowing he was not what he claimed to be. In fact there was only one person who could possibly find him out. . . ."

"You," said Anatoly. "Because you knew him."

"He was aware of that danger and he was on the lookout for me. That's why this morning he asked you who it was that arrived with you yesterday. You told him my name. He left immediately." Jean-Pierre frowned. Something was not quite right. "But why did he stay out in the open? He could have concealed himself in the woods or hidden in a cave. It would have taken us much longer to find him. It's as if he didn't expect to be pursued."

"Why should he?" said Anatoly. "When the first guide disappeared, we didn't send a search party after *him*. We just got another guide and carried on. What went wrong for Mohammed was that the local people found the body and accused us of murder. That made us suspicious of Mohammed. He was unlucky."

"But what was his motive in all this? Why did he go to so much trouble to substitute himself for the original guide?"

"Presumably, to mislead us," Anatoly replied. "Presumably, everything he told us was a lie. He did *not* see Ellis and Jane yesterday afternoon at the mouth of the Linar Valley. The villagers of Mundol did *not* confirm that two foreigners with a baby passed through yesterday, heading south. He *knew* where the fugitives were—"

"And he deliberately led us in the other direction, of course!" Jean-Pierre felt elated again. "The old guide disappeared just after the search party left the village of Linar, didn't he?"

"Yes. So we can assume that reports *up to* that point are true. Therefore Ellis and Jane *did* pass through that village. Afterward Mohammed took over and led us *south*—"

"Because Ellis and Jane went north!" exclaimed Jean-Pierre.

Anatoly nodded grimly. "Mohammed gained them a day, at most. For that he gave his life. Was it worth it?"

Jean-Pierre looked again at the photograph of Mousa. "I think," he said, "Mohammed would answer 'Yes. It was worth it.' "

CHAPTER 14

THEY left Gadwal in the deep darkness before dawn, hoping to steal a march on the Russians by setting out so early. Ahead of them was a long, slow climb up the Nuristan Valley for eight or nine miles and then up a side valley. Once they were out of the Nuristan Valley, it would be much more difficult to trail them, for the Russians would not know which side valley they had taken.

Halam led the way; Jane followed, carrying Chantal; and Ellis brought up the rear, leading Maggie. Ellis had left most of his blasting equipment in Gadwal, but he had kept some TNT, a length of Primacord, a few blasting caps, and the pull-ring firing device, and had them stowed in the pockets of his down coat.

Halam was carrying a candle lantern, which threw grotesque shadows on the cliff walls. He seemed disgruntled. Yesterday he had been all smiles, apparently pleased to be part of this bizarre expedition, but this morning he was grim-faced and taciturn. Ellis blamed the early start. The path, such as it was, snaked along the cliffside, rounding promontories that jutted out into the stream, sometimes hugging the water's edge and sometimes ascending to the cliff top. After less than a mile they came to a place where the track simply vanished. There was the cliff on the left and the river on the right.

Ellis waded into the ice-cold water. At its deepest it was only up to his waist, and he gained the far bank easily. He returned and led Maggie across, then came back for Jane and Chantal. Halam followed, his mood worsening.

When dawn cracked the eastern sky, Halam snuffed the candle. They had to ford the river several more times in places where the path was washed away or blocked by a landslide. At one of these crossings they met a traveler coming from the opposite direction, a small man leading a fat-tailed sheep, which he carried across the river in his arms. Halam conversed with him in some Nuristani language, and Ellis suspected, from the way they waved their arms, that they were talking about routes across the mountains.

After they parted from the traveler, Ellis said to Halam, "Don't tell people where we are going."

Halam appeared to understand, but he did exactly the same thing with the next traveler they met. During the conversation Ellis thought he heard Halam say "Kantiwar," the name of the pass for which they were heading. Ellis was angered. As soon as the stranger was out of sight he said emphatically, "I have said you are not to tell people where we are going."

"I told him nothing," Halam said indignantly.

"From now on you will not speak to any travelers." It was important to shut him up. Halam had not really grasped the fact that Ellis and Jane were running away from the Russians.

A little later they met a white-robed mullah with a red-dyed beard, and to Ellis' frustration Halam immediately opened a conversation with the man.

Ellis hesitated only a moment, then went up to Halam, grabbed him in a painful double armlock, and marched him off.

Halam struggled briefly as the mullah watched, openmouthed. Looking back, Ellis saw that Jane had taken the reins and was following with Maggie.

After a hundred yards or so Ellis released Halam, saying, "If the Russians find me, they will kill me. This is why you must not talk to anyone."

Halam went into a sulk.

After they had walked on awhile, Jane said, "I fear he'll make us suffer for that."

"I suppose he will," said Ellis. "But I had to shut him up."

Halam passed the next traveler with only the briefest greeting, and Ellis thought, At least my technique was effective.

At midday they stopped in a village, and Halam got them invited into a house and given tea. Jane gave the woman of the house medicine for her children's intestinal worms, and in return got pan-baked bread and delicious goat's-milk cheese. Ellis would have liked to let Jane rest after eating, but he dared not risk it, for he did not know how close behind the Russians might be. He asked her to lead the horse while he took Chantal, judging that carrying a ten-week-old baby was more tiring.

Coming upon an eastward-leading side valley where a chattering stream flowed into the Nuristan River, Halam announced that their route lay up this valley. Soon they were climbing through a forest of silver birch, and the main valley was lost to view behind them. By dusk they had emerged into a bare, bleak, uninhabited landscape. It seemed to Ellis that they might not find shelter in such territory, so he suggested they spend the night in an empty stone hut they had passed half an hour or so earlier. Jane and Halam agreed, and they turned back.

Halam built a fire inside the hut while Ellis gave the horse some grain. Jane fed and changed Chantal, then fell asleep immediately. Ellis roused her to zip her into the sleeping bag. He took Chantal's diaper down to the stream, washed it out, and put it by the fire to dry. He lay beside Jane for a while, looking at her face in the flickering firelight while Halam snored on the other side of the hut. She looked absolutely drained, her face thin and taut, her hair dirty, her cheeks smudged with earth. He wondered how much longer she could go on. He had found her and lost her and found her again—a piece of luck that still made him reel when he thought of it. To lose her a second time would be unbearable. He lay staring at her for a long time, trying not to go to sleep for fear she might not be there when he woke up.

JANE dreamed she was in the George V Hotel in Peshawar, Pakistan. She was about to step into a hot bath when she heard someone calling her name. It must be room service, she thought; how annoying. In fact it was Ellis, and he was shaking her by the shoulder; and with the most tragic sense of disappointment she realized that the hotel was a dream, and in reality she was in a

157

cold stone hut in Nuristan, a million miles from a hot bath.

"You have to wake up," he was saying.

Jane felt almost paralyzed by lethargy. "Is it morning already?"

"No, it's the middle of the night. Halam has gone."

"Gone?" She was still sleepy and confused. "Where?"

"He didn't tell me. I woke up to find he had gone."

"You think he's abandoned us?"

"Yes."

"Oh, Lord. How will we find our way without a guide?"

"I'm afraid it could be worse than that. You said he would make us suffer for humiliating him in front of that mullah. Perhaps abandoning us is sufficient revenge. I hope so. But he may run into the Russians. I don't think it will take them long to persuade him to tell them exactly where he left us."

"It's too much," said Jane. "I'm too tired. I'm going to lie here and sleep until the Russians come and take me prisoner."

Chantal had been stirring quietly, moving her head from side to side, and now she started to cry. Jane sat up and picked her up.

"If we leave now, we can still escape," Ellis said. "I'll load the horse while you feed and change the baby."

Jane sighed. "All right," she said. She felt confused and frightened—afraid of the snow and the mountains and the Russians. She had been tired and tense and cold for too long.

Automatically she changed Chantal, using the dry diaper from the fireside. She could not remember changing her last night. She frowned, doubting her memory; then it came to her that Ellis must have taken the soiled diaper down to the stream and washed it and hung it out to dry. Jane started to cry.

She felt very foolish, but she could not stop, so she carried on dressing Chantal, with tears streaming down her face. Ellis came in as she was making the baby comfortable in the carrying sling.

"Maggie didn't want to wake up either," he said. Then he saw her face and said, "What is it?"

"I don't know why I ever left you," she said. "You're the best man I've ever known, and I never stopped loving you."

He put his arms around her and Chantal. "Good. Let's go."

Ahead of them was the Kantiwar Pass, at fifteen thousand feet a good deal higher than the last pass, the Aryu. They set off uphill through the thinning woodland. The moon was out, and the air was so cold it hurt to breathe. They soon left the trees behind and started across a plateau, like a moonscape, with boulders and craters and odd patches of snow. The temperature dropped steadily, the white patches increasing until the ground was a crazy chessboard.

At some point on that sloping upland they crossed the ice line. Jane became aware of the new danger when the horse skidded, snorted with fear, and almost fell. Then she noticed that the moonlight was reflecting off the boulders, as if they were glazed. The rocks were like diamonds, cold and hard and glittering. From then on she was terrified she would fall and crush Chantal, and she trod ultracarefully, her nerves so taut she felt she might snap.

After a little more than two hours they reached the far side of the plateau and found themselves facing a steep path up a snow-covered mountainside. Ellis went first, pulling Maggie behind him. Jane followed at a safe distance in case the horse should slip backward. They went up the mountain in a zigzag, and later Jane gave Chantal to Ellis and took the horse's reins from him, to transfer the strain to a different set of muscles. The wretched horse stumbled constantly now.

Eventually the path led them onto a ledge that wound far up the side of the mountain. They were very high. The ledge was steep and icy and only a few feet wide, and beyond the edge was a precipitous drop. Despite her extra caution, Jane slipped. For a heart-stopping moment she thought she was going to fall over the edge, but she landed on her knees and steadied herself with both hands. From the corner of her eye she could see the snowy slopes hundreds of feet below.

She stood up slowly and turned around. She had let go of the reins, which now dangled over the precipice. The horse stood watching her, stiff-legged and trembling. When she reached for the bridle, the horse took a panicky step backward. "Stop!" Jane cried. Then she made her voice calm and began to murmur reassuringly as she stepped slowly toward the horse. It stared at her, wide-eyed, breath like smoke coming from its flared nostrils.

Jane got within arm's length and moved to reach for its bridle.

The horse jerked its head away, stepped backward, skidded, and lost its balance, and to her unspeakable horror slid slowly on its back to the lip of the ledge and fell over, neighing in terror.

Ellis shouted, "Stop!" at Jane, and she realized she was screaming. She closed her mouth with a snap. He knelt down and peered over the edge, still clutching Chantal beneath his coat.

The horse had landed on a shelf just five or six feet down, and it was lying on its side with its feet sticking out into the void. "It's still alive!" Jane cried. "Thank God!"

"And our supplies are intact," said Ellis unsentimentally.

"But how can we get the animal back up here?"

Ellis looked at her and said nothing.

"But we can't leave her behind to die in the cold!" Jane said.

"I'm sorry," said Ellis. He unslung Chantal. Jane took the baby and put her inside her own coat. "I'll get the food first," he said. He lay flat along the ledge and swung his feet over to lower himself slowly, feet searching for the shelf. Jane watched him, petrified. Between the horse's rump and the face of the cliff there was not room for both of Ellis' feet side by side. He had to stand with his feet one behind the other, like a figure in an ancient Egyptian wall painting. He slowly lowered himself into a crouch, then reached for the straps holding the canvas bag of rations.

At that moment the horse decided to get up.

It bent its front legs and somehow managed to get them under its forequarters; then, with a wriggle, it lifted its front end and tried to swing its rear legs back onto the ledge.

It almost succeeded.

Then its back feet slid away, it lost its balance, and its rear end fell sideways. Ellis grabbed the food bag. Inch by inch the horse slipped away, kicking and struggling, while Ellis held on to the food bag. So determined was he, that the horse pulled him to the brink. At the last second he let go, and the horse made a noise like a scream and dropped away, tumbling over and over as it fell into the void, taking with it all their food and supplies and their sleeping bag.

Jane burst into tears.

A few moments later Ellis scrambled up onto the ledge beside her. He put his arms around her while she cried for the horse and the supplies and her aching legs and her frozen feet. Then he gently helped her up and said, "We mustn't stop."

"But how can we go on?" she cried. "We've nothing to eat, we can't boil water, we've no sleeping bag, no medicines—"

"We've got each other," he said.

She hugged him tightly. If we live through this, she thought, and if we escape the Russians and get back to Europe together, I'll never let him out of my sight, I swear.

"You go first," he said, disentangling himself. "I want to be able to see you." He gave her a gentle shove, and automatically she began to walk on up the mountain. Sometime later—it might have been minutes or hours, for she had lost track of time—Ellis caught up with her. "Look," he said, pointing ahead.

The track led down into a vast bowl of hills rimmed by white-peaked mountains. At first Jane did not understand why Ellis had said "Look." Then she realized that the track was leading *down*.

"This is it," he said. "This is the Kantiwar Pass. We've done the worst part of this leg of the journey. For the next couple of days the route will lie downhill, and the weather will get warmer."

Jane sat on an icy boulder. I made it, she thought. I made it.

Day was breaking. As the light slowly stained the sky from pearl gray to dusty pink, so a little hope crept into Jane's heart again. Downhill, she thought, and warmer. Perhaps we will escape.

Chantal cried. Well, *her* food supply had not gone with Maggie. Jane fed her, sitting on that icy boulder on the roof of the world, while Ellis melted snow in his hands for Jane to drink.

The descent into the Kantiwar Valley was a relatively gentle slope. Ahead of them the morning sky turned flame red, as if the world beyond were on fire. Soon there was a little stream burbling alongside them. They were below the ice line again.

After another two hours they paused to rest at the head of a narrow gorge. Ellis was looking back up the valley. Suddenly he gave a start and said, "Oh, my."

"What on earth is the matter?" Jane turned and followed his gaze, and her heart sank. Behind them, about a mile up the valley, were half a dozen men in uniform and a horse: the search party.

After all that, thought Jane. After all we went through, they've caught us anyway. She was too miserable even to cry.

Ellis grabbed her arm. "Quick. Let's move," he said. "We've got one chance left." As they hurried down into the gorge Ellis was surveying its steep, rocky sides.

"What?"

"A rockfall."

"They'll find a way over or around it."

"Not if they're all buried underneath it."

He stopped at a place where the floor of the canyon was only a few feet wide and one wall was precipitously steep and high. "This is perfect," he said. He took from his pockets a block of TNT, a reel of detonating cable, a small metal object like the cap of a fountain pen, and something that looked like a metal syringe, with a pull ring instead of a plunger. He fixed the small metal object to one end of the Primacord by crimping it with his teeth; then he fixed the metal object to the sharp end of the syringe. He handed the whole assembly to Jane.

"This is what you have to do," he began. "Walk down the gorge, paying out the cable. When you reach the limit of the wire, pull out the safety pins, like this." He showed her how. "Then watch me. Wait for me to wave my arms above my head. Then pull the ring. If we time this just right, we can kill them all. Go!"

Jane followed orders like a robot, without thinking. She walked down the gorge, paying out the cable. After a minute she looked back. Ellis was wedging the TNT into a fissure in the rock. She walked on until the cable became taut in her hand; then she turned around again. Ellis was now scaling the canyon wall, presumably searching for the best position from which to observe the Russians as they stepped into the trap.

She sat down beside a stream. Chantal's tiny body rested in the sling, which now went slack, taking the weight off Jane's back. Ellis' words kept repeating in her mind: "If we time this just right, we can kill them all." Could it work? she wondered. Would they all be killed? What would the other Russians do then? Would they send out a search party to look for the missing search party? The new party certainly would not complete that trip today, and it would be impossible to search at night. By the time they found the bodies, Ellis and Jane would be at least a day and a half ahead. It might be enough, Jane thought. I wish the soldiers would hurry. I can't bear the waiting, I'm so afraid.

She could see Ellis clearly, crawling along the cliff top on his hands and knees. She could see the search party, too, as they marched down the valley. Even at this distance their slumped shoulders and dragging feet showed them to be tired. They had not seen her yet; she blended into the landscape.

Ellis crouched behind a bluff and peered around its edge at the approaching soldiers. He was visible to Jane but hidden from the Russians, and he had a clear view of the place where he had planted the explosives.

The soldiers reached the head of the gorge and began to descend. One of them was riding, and had a mustache. Presumably, he was the officer. Another wore a Chitrali cap. That's Halam, Jane thought; the traitor. There were five others, and they all had short hair and uniform caps and youthful, clean-shaven faces. Two men and five boys, she thought.

She watched Ellis. At last he turned and, slowly and deliberately, waved both his arms in the air above his head.

Jane looked back at the soldiers. She had the syringe device in her left hand, and the forefinger of her right hand was crooked inside the pull ring. One jerk would light the fuse and detonate the TNT and bring the cliff tumbling down on her pursuers. Five boys, she thought. Joined the army because they were poor or foolish, or because they were conscripted. Posted to a cold, inhospitable country where the people hate them. Marched through a mountainous, icy wilderness. Buried under a landslide, heads smashed and lungs choked with earth and backs broken and chests crushed, screaming and suffocating and bleeding to death in agony and terror. Five letters to be written to proud fathers and anxious mothers at home: regret to inform, died in action, act of heroism, posthumous medal, deepest sympathy. The mother's contempt for these fine words, and the mother's grief when she realized that everything she had done for the boy—the pain and the work and the worry—had been for nothing. This miracle, her man-child, had been destroyed by braggardly men in a stupid, vain war. The sense of loss. The sense of loss.

Jane heard Ellis shout. She looked up. He was on his feet, not caring now whether he was seen, waving at her and yelling, "Do it now! Do it now!"

Carefully she put the pull-ring device down on the ground beside the rushing stream.

The soldiers had seen both of them now. Two men began climbing up the side of the gorge toward Ellis. The others surrounded Jane, pointing their rifles at her and her baby, looking embarrassed and foolish. She ignored them and watched Ellis. He climbed down the side of the gorge and walked up to Jane. "Why?" he said. "Why didn't you do it?"

Because they are so young, she thought; because they are young and innocent, and they don't want to kill me. Because it would have been murder. But most of all . . .

"Because they have mothers," she said.

JEAN-PIERRE opened his eyes. The bulky figure of Anatoly was crouching beside the camp bed. Behind Anatoly bright sunlight streamed through the open flap of the tent. In a flash Jean-Pierre recalled the events of the night.

He and Anatoly were encamped in the approach to the Kantiwar Pass. They had been awakened at around two thirty a.m. by the captain commanding the search party. A young Afghan called Halam had stumbled into the encampment, said the captain. Halam told them that he had been guide to the fleeing Westerners, but they had insulted him, so he had abandoned them. Halam had offered to lead the Russians to the fugitives, and an advance party of soldiers and a horse had left with the guide immediately.

Now, in the morning light, Jean-Pierre asked Anatoly, "What's the time?"

"Eight o'clock. I've just received a radio report from the advance party. We've caught the runaways."

Jean-Pierre's heart leaped. "For sure?" he asked.

"We can go and check just as soon as you put your trousers on."

It was almost that quick. They took off in a helicopter a few minutes later to fly down the Kantiwar Valley, scanning the ground for the advance party. Eventually they saw smoke. Someone had lit a fire to guide them in. They touched down on a level area near the head of a gorge. Jean-Pierre jumped to the ground, feeling sick with tension. Anatoly jumped out beside him. The captain led them down into the gorge.

And there they were. Jane was sitting on the ground beside a little stream, with Chantal in her lap. Ellis stood behind her. They both looked exhausted, defeated and demoralized.

Jean-Pierre stopped. "Come here," he said to Jane.

She got to her feet and walked toward him. He saw that she was carrying Chantal in some kind of sling around her neck. Ellis started to follow her. "Not you," said Jean-Pierre. Ellis stopped.

Jane stood in front of Jean-Pierre. He raised his right hand and smacked the side of her face with all his might. It was the most satisfying blow he had ever struck. She reeled backward, staggering, so that he thought she would fall. But she kept her balance and stood staring at him defiantly, tears of pain running down her face. Jean-Pierre saw Ellis take a sudden step forward, then restrain himself. Jean-Pierre was disappointed. If Ellis had tried to do something, the soldiers would have jumped him and beaten him up. Never mind. He would get his beating soon enough.

Jean-Pierre raised his hand to slap Jane again. She flinched and covered Chantal protectively with her arms. Jean-Pierre changed his mind. "There will be plenty of time for that later," he said as he lowered his hand. "Plenty of time."

JEAN-PIERRE walked back toward the helicopter. Jane looked down at Chantal and hugged her, as if it were the baby who needed comforting. In a way she was glad Jean-Pierre had struck her. The blow was like the decree absolute in a divorce. It meant that her marriage was finally, officially, definitively over, and she had no further responsibility. It was ironic, she thought, that she should feel completely free of him at the moment when he had finally captured her.

Now Anatoly took control. He told a trooper to bind Ellis' hands. The soldier produced handcuffs. Ellis held his hands out in front of him cooperatively, and the soldier manacled him.

Ellis looked cowed and dejected as they were shepherded to the helicopter. His utter submissiveness made Jane angry, not with him but with everyone else for making him like this: Jean-Pierre and Anatoly and Halam and the Russians. She almost wished she had detonated the explosives.

Ellis jumped up into the helicopter, then reached down to help her. She held Chantal with her left arm and gave him her right hand. He pulled her up. At the moment she was closest to him, he murmured, "As soon as we take off, slap Jean-Pierre."

Nobody else seemed to have heard Ellis. The passenger cabin was small and bare, with a low ceiling, so that the men had to stoop. There was nothing in it but a small shelf for seating, opposite the door. Jane sat down on it gratefully. She could see the pilot. The rotors were turning, and the noise was very loud.

Ellis squatted beside Jane, between the bench and the cockpit.

Anatoly boarded with a trooper beside him. He spoke to the trooper and pointed at Ellis. Jane could not hear what was being said, but it was plain that the trooper had been told to guard Ellis. He unslung his rifle and held it loosely in his hands.

Jean-Pierre boarded last. He stood by the open door, looking out as the helicopter lifted. Jane felt panicky. It was all very well for Ellis to tell her to slap Jean-Pierre as they were taking off, but how was it to be done? If she tried to hit him, she would probably lose her balance and fall out the open door. She looked at Ellis, hoping for guidance, but there was only a set, tense expression on his face. He did not meet her eye.

The helicopter rose ten feet into the air, paused a moment, then did a swoop, gaining speed, and began to climb again.

Jean-Pierre turned away from the door and saw there was nowhere for him to sit. He hesitated. Jane knew she should stand up and slap him—although she had no idea why—but she was frozen to her seat, paralyzed by panic. Then Jean-Pierre jerked his thumb at her, indicating that she should get up to let him sit.

That enraged her. She stood up, with Chantal swinging from

her neck, and thrust her face into his, screaming, "I hate you!" Her words were lost in the roar of the engines and the rushing wind, but her facial expression apparently shocked him, for he took a startled step back. "I hate you!" Jane shrieked again. Then she rushed at him with her hands outstretched and violently pushed him backward out through the open door.

THE Russians had made a mistake. It had been in fastening Ellis' hands in front instead of behind his back.

He had been hoping they would not bind him at all. That was why, by a superhuman effort, he had done nothing when Jean-Pierre started slapping Jane. There had been a chance they might leave him unrestrained. After all, he was unarmed and outnumbered. But Anatoly was a cautious man, it seemed.

Fortunately, Anatoly had not been the one to put the handcuffs on; a trooper had. Soldiers knew that it was easier to deal with a prisoner whose arms were bound in front, for he was less likely to fall over and he could get in and out of trucks and helicopters unaided. So when Ellis had submissively held out his hands in front, the soldier had not given it a second thought.

Unaided, Ellis could not overpower three men. His only hope was to crash the helicopter, and in that moment he thought, We're only twelve or fifteen feet up.

There had been an instant of frozen time when Jane stood at the open doorway and stared with a horrified expression as Jean-Pierre fell into space. Then Anatoly had sprung up and grabbed her arms from behind, restraining her. Now Anatoly and Jane stood between Ellis and the trooper at the other end of the cabin.

Ellis whirled around, sprang up beside the pilot's raised seat, hooked his manacled arms over the pilot's head, drew the chain of the handcuffs into the flesh of the man's throat, and heaved.

The pilot did not panic. Keeping his feet on the pedals and his left hand on the collective pitch lever, he reached up with his right hand and clawed at Ellis' wrists.

Ellis had a flash of dread. This was his last chance before the trooper in the cabin might decide to take the risk of shooting Ellis, even if it meant hitting the pilot.

Someone grabbed Ellis' shoulders from behind. A glimpse of dark gray sleeve told him it was Anatoly. Down in the nose of the helicopter the gunner turned around, saw what was happening, and started to get out of his seat.

Now Ellis jerked savagely on the chain. The pain was too much for the pilot, who threw up both hands and rose from his seat.

As soon as the pilot's hands and feet left the controls, the helicopter began to buck and sway in the wind. Ellis was ready for that and braced himself against the pilot's seat, but Anatoly, behind him, lost his balance and released his grip.

Ellis hauled the pilot out of the seat and threw him to the floor, then reached over the controls and pushed the collective stick down. The helicopter dropped like a stone.

Ellis turned around and braced himself for the impact.

The pilot was on the cabin floor at his feet, clutching his throat. Anatoly had fallen full length in the middle of the cabin. Jane was crouched in a corner, with her arms enclosing Chantal protectively. The trooper too had fallen, but he had regained his balance and was now raising his Kalashnikov toward Ellis.

As he pulled the trigger the helicopter's wheels hit the ground.

The impact threw Ellis to his knees, and the trooper staggered sideways, his shots going through the fuselage a yard from Ellis' head. Then he fell forward, dropping the gun and throwing out his hands to break his fall.

Ellis snatched up the rifle and held it awkwardly in his manacled hands. It was a moment of pure joy.

He got his finger to the trigger as the helicopter's engine stalled and the rotors began to slow. Glancing into the flight deck, he saw the gunner jumping out through the pilot's side door. Ellis moved so that Anatoly, who was stretched out on the floor, was between him and the door; then he rested the muzzle of the rifle on Anatoly's cheek.

The trooper stared at him, looking frightened. "Get out," Ellis said with a jerk of his head. The trooper understood and jumped out through the door.

The pilot was still lying down, and apparently having trouble breathing. Ellis told him to get out too. The man struggled to his feet, still clutching his throat, and went out the same way.

Ellis said to Jane, "Tell this guy to get out of the helicopter and stand real close, with his back to me. Quick, quick!"

Jane shouted a stream of Russian at Anatoly. The man got to his feet, shot a glance of pure hatred at Ellis, and slowly climbed out of the helicopter.

Ellis rested the muzzle of the rifle on the back of Anatoly's neck and said, "Tell him to have the others freeze."

Jane spoke again and Anatoly shouted an order. Ellis looked around. The pilot, the gunner, and the trooper who had been in the helicopter were standing nearby. Just beyond them was Jean-Pierre, sitting on the ground and clutching his ankle. He must have fallen well, thought Ellis; there's nothing much wrong with him. Farther away were five more soldiers, the captain, the horse, and Halam.

Ellis said, "Tell Anatoly to unbutton his coat, slowly take out his pistol, and hand it to you."

Jane translated. Ellis pressed the rifle harder into Anatoly's flesh as he drew the pistol from its holster and reached behind him with it in his hand. Jane took it from him.

Ellis said, "Is it a Makarov? Yes. You'll see a safety catch on the left-hand side. Move it until it covers the red dot. To fire the gun, pull back the slide above the grip, then pull the trigger. Okay?"

"Okay," she said. She was white and trembling, but her mouth was set in a determined line.

Ellis said, "Tell him to have the soldiers bring their weapons here, one by one, and throw them into the helicopter."

Jane translated and Anatoly gave the order.

One by one the soldiers came up and disarmed.

"Five young men," said Jane, pointing the pistol at them. "There was a captain, Halam, and five young men. I only see four."

"Tell Anatoly he has to find the other one if he wants to live."

Jane shouted to Anatoly, and Ellis was surprised by the vehemence of her voice. Anatoly shouted an order. A moment later the fifth soldier came around the tail of the helicopter and surrendered his rifle as the others had.

"That was well done," Ellis said to Jane. "He just might have ruined everything here. Now, can you make them all lie down?"

A minute later they were all lying face down on the ground.

"You have to shoot off my handcuffs," Ellis said to Jane.

He put down his rifle and stood with his arms outstretched toward the doorway. Jane pulled back the slide of the pistol, then placed its muzzle against the chain. They positioned themselves so that the spent bullet would go through the doorway.

Jane closed her eyes and pulled the trigger.

Ellis roared. His wrists hurt like the blazes. Then, after a moment, he realized they were not broken—the chain was.

He picked up his rifle. "Now I want their radio," he said.

On Anatoly's order, the captain began to unstrap a large box from the horse's back.

Ellis wondered whether the helicopter would fly again. Its undercarriage would be destroyed, of course, but the engine and the main control lines were on top. He recalled how, during the battle of Darg, he had seen a Hind just like this one crash twenty or thirty feet, then lift off again. This one ought to fly if that one did, he thought. If not . . .

The captain brought the radio and put it into the helicopter.

Ellis allowed himself a moment of relief. As long as he had the radio, the Russians could not contact their base. That meant they could not alert anybody to what had happened. If Ellis could get the helicopter into the air, he would be safe from pursuit.

"Keep your gun aimed at Anatoly," he said to Jane. "I'm going to see whether this thing will fly."

JANE found the gun surprisingly heavy. She stood in the doorway, aiming at Anatoly; with her left hand she patted Chantal's back. Chantal had cried, off and on, during the last few minutes, but now she had stopped.

The helicopter's engine turned over, kicked, and hesitated. Oh, please start, she prayed; please go.

The engine roared into life, and she saw the blades turn.

Jean-Pierre got painfully to his feet. Don't you dare, she thought.

Jane pointed the pistol at him.

He started to walk toward the helicopter.

"Don't make me shoot you!" she screamed, but her voice was drowned by the roar of the engine. Jean-Pierre kept coming.

Jane felt the helicopter shudder and try to lift.

Jean-Pierre was close now. She could see his face clearly, and there was a mad light in his eyes. He's lost his mind, she thought; but perhaps that happened a long time ago.

"I will do it!" she yelled. "I will shoot you!"

The helicopter lifted off the ground.

Jean-Pierre broke into a run. As the aircraft went up, he jumped and landed on its deck. He looked at Jane with hate in his eyes and gathered himself to spring.

She closed her eyes and pulled the trigger.

The gun crashed and bucked in her hand.

She opened her eyes again. Jean-Pierre was still standing upright, with an expression of astonishment on his face. There was a spreading dark stain on the breast of his coat. He spun around, facing out, and fell forward through the doorway.

I killed him, she thought.

At first she felt a kind of wild elation. He had tried to capture her. He had hunted her like an animal. He had betrayed her and beaten her. Now she had killed him.

Then she was overcome by grief. She sat on the deck and sobbed. Chantal began to cry too, and Jane rocked her baby as they wept together.

She did not know how long she stayed there. Eventually she got to her feet and went forward to stand beside the pilot's seat.

"Are you all right?" Ellis shouted above the roar.

She nodded and tried a weak smile.

Ellis pointed to a gauge and yelled, "Look—full tanks!"

She kissed his cheek. One day she would tell him she had shot Jean-Pierre, but not now. "How far to the border?" she asked.

"Less than an hour. And they can't send anybody after us, because we have their radio."

Jane looked through the windscreen. Directly ahead she could see the white-peaked mountains she would have had to climb. I don't think I could have done it, she said to herself. I think I would have lain down in the snow and died.

Ellis had a wistful expression on his face.

"What are you thinking about?" she asked.

"I was thinking how much I'd like a roast beef sandwich with lettuce and tomato and mayonnaise on whole wheat bread," he said, and Jane smiled.

Chantal stirred and cried. Ellis took a hand off the controls and touched her pink cheek. "She's hungry," he said.

"I'll go back and take care of her," said Jane. She returned to the passenger cabin and sat on the bench. Then she nursed her baby as the helicopter flew on into the rising sun.

PART THREE: 1983

CHAPTER 15

JANE felt pleased as she walked down the suburban driveway and climbed into the passenger seat of Ellis' car. It had been a successful afternoon. Ellis had been tense about introducing his daughter to his girlfriend, but Petal had been thrilled by Chantal, and everything had been easy. Gill too had cooed over Chantal, so Jane had come to know his ex-wife, as well as his daughter, and all in one afternoon.

Ellis put Chantal into Jane's arms and got into the car beside them. "Well, what do you think?" he asked as they pulled away.

"You didn't tell me she was pretty," Jane said.

"Petal is pretty?"

"I meant Gill," said Jane with a laugh. "They're fine people, and they don't deserve to be mixed up with someone like you."

She was joking, but Ellis nodded somberly.

They drove on in silence for a while. It was six months since they had escaped from Afghanistan. Now and again Jane would burst into tears for no apparent reason, but she no longer had nightmares in which she shot Jean-Pierre. Nobody but she and Ellis knew what had happened—Ellis had even lied to his superiors about how Jean-Pierre died—and Jane had decided she would tell Chantal that her Daddy died in Afghanistan in the war: no more than that.

Instead of heading back to the city, Ellis took a series of side streets and eventually parked next to a vacant lot overlooking the water. "I want to talk," he said.

"Okay."

"It was a good day. Petal was more relaxed with me than she has ever been."

"I wonder why."

"I have a theory," said Ellis. "It's because of you and Chantal. Now that I'm part of a family, I'm no longer a threat to her home and her stability. I think that's it anyway."

"It makes sense to me. Is that what you wanted to talk about?"

"No." He hesitated. "I'm leaving the Agency."

Jane nodded. "I'm very glad," she said fervently.

"The Afghan assignment is over, basically," he went on. "Masud's training program is under way, and they've taken delivery of their first shipment. Masud is so strong now that he has negotiated a winter truce with the Russians."

"Good!" said Jane.

"While I was in Washington, I was offered another job. It's something I want to do, plus it pays well."

"What is it?" said Jane, intrigued.

"Working with a new task force on organized crime."

Fear stabbed Jane's heart. "Is it dangerous?"

"Not for me. I'm too old for undercover work now. It'll be my job to direct the undercover men."

Jane could tell he was not being completely honest with her. "Tell me the truth," she said.

"Well, it's less dangerous than what I've been doing. But not as safe as teaching kindergarten. I'll be based here in New York."

That took her by surprise. "Really?"

"Why are you so astonished?"

"Because I've applied for a job with the United Nations," she said. "Here in New York."

"You didn't tell me you were going to do that!" he said, sounding hurt.

"You didn't tell me about *your* plans," she said indignantly.

"I'm telling you now."

"And I'm telling *you* now."

There was a silence. Eventually Ellis said, "Well anyway, as we're both going to be living in New York . . ."

"We could share the housekeeping?"

"Yes," he said hesitantly.

Suddenly she regretted flying off the handle. "Okay," she said in a softer voice. "Let's share the housekeeping."

"Actually . . . I was thinking of making it official. If you want."

This was what she had been waiting for. "Official," she said, as if she did not understand.

"Yes," he said awkwardly. "I mean we could get married. If you want."

She laughed with pleasure. "Do it right, Ellis! Propose!"

He took her hand. "Jane, I love you. Will you marry me?"

"Yes! Yes!" she said. "As soon as possible! Tomorrow! Today!"

"Thank you," he said.

She leaned over and kissed him. "I love you too."

They sat in silence then, holding hands and watching the sun go down. It was funny, Jane thought, but Afghanistan seemed unreal now, like a bad dream, vivid but no longer frightening. She remembered the people well enough—Abdullah, the mullah, and Rabia, the midwife; handsome Mohammed and loyal Fara—but the bombs and the helicopters, the fear and the hardship were fading from her memory. This was the real adventure, she felt—getting married and bringing up Chantal and making the world a better place for her to live in.

"Shall we go?" said Ellis.

"Yes." She gave his hand a final squeeze, then let it go. "We've got a lot to do."

He started the car and they drove back into the city.

Best-selling author Ken Follett makes the art of writing a successful novel seem deceptively simple. He starts out, he explains, with the smallest seed of an idea. In the case of *Lie Down With Lions*, he'd decided to base his story around a Western European woman in danger from the Russians in Afghanistan.

Ken Follett.

"To make her more vulnerable," he says, "I gave her a baby to look after. And to add to the drama, it only made sense for her to have the baby in Afghanistan. So I then had to know something of tribal midwifery there." Since Follett believes that good research is vital to a good novel, he relies regularly on the skills of free-lance researchers, one of whom used a computer to locate just what was needed: a doctoral dissertation on midwifery in Afghanistan.

One of the other fruits of his research was the character of the charismatic rebel leader, Masud. "He actually exists," Follett says. "He's noted in press releases and books on the Afghan conflict."

As he reached the end of *Lie Down With Lions*, Follett found that the plot was "rewriting" itself. "My heroine, Jane, got away from me," he explains. "She was supposed to blow up the young Russians who were chasing her, but in the end, *she* decided she couldn't do it. I had to come up with a new ending to accommodate her."

The wild beauty of the Afghan landscape has not, he says, lured him into going there. "I would have liked to visit the country while I was writing the book, but I decided that it would be far too dangerous. And anyway, I'm too much of a lover of luxury to put up with such primitive conditions."

At the age of thirty-six, with five previous best sellers to his credit, Ken Follett does indeed live in luxury, in an elegant house in London's Chelsea. There, over a typewriter, he puts in the long hours that the creative process ultimately demands. Does it ever require a lot of self-discipline to sit down and write? "No," he answers firmly. "It's quite simply what I like to do."

Neither love nor war would shake
Gabrielle's devotion to her heritage.

TREE
OF GOLD

A condensation of the novel by

Rosalind Laker

Illustrated by John Thompson

Silk—soft, elegant, luxurious. The fabric of royalty. The fabric that Napoleon Bonaparte is restoring to fullest glory now that the Revolution is over.

Silk has ruled Gabrielle Roche's entire life, and thus she is joining Émile Valmont in marriage to link her family's mill with his silk farm. The perfect plan.

But that perfection is shaken on the morning of her wedding by a chance encounter with Nicolas Devaux, the son of her father's most bitter rival. With just one look her love for Nicolas is sealed, even as her carriage drives her away to the man she must marry. Now Gabrielle is left with an impossible dream: someday she and Nicolas will honor the promise exchanged in that one unforgettable look.

A rich historical drama set against the backdrop of Napoleonic France.

CHAPTER ONE

NOBODY could have foreseen the danger. Least of all Gabrielle Roche, who was being driven to her wedding through the narrow medieval streets of the Croix-Rousse, the silk weavers' district of Lyons. It was the first day of spring, 1804. The sky was a clear morning blue, with a few harmless white clouds drifting light as dandelion down. The sunshine highlighted the stone walls of the ancient buildings, gleaming across the worn slabs of dark alleyways leading to inner courtyards but leaving in shadow the deep-set black-timbered doorways.

The windows on the street-level floor of every house were wide and high, built that way to allow plenty of light to enter the weaving workshops and loom rooms. And now, as the wedding carriage passed, the square windowpanes reflected back the day's brilliance with prism colors. In its wake the carriage left the scent of the garlands, tied with love knots of satin ribbon, that bobbed on the horses' harnesses and swayed in loops around the domed roof.

Gabrielle, outwardly the traditional bride—young, composed and ethereal—put her bouquet down on the seat beside her. "We'll see our weavers soon now," she remarked eagerly to her elder brother, who was escorting her to the ceremony. "I must be ready to wave to them."

Henri Roche sat squarely opposite her. At thirty-six he was fifteen years her senior, an overweight, abrasive man, and at her words his mouth compressed into a line of irritability. The weavers were of no interest to him except when they were working. He disliked the fact that his sister had asked that the driver keep a moderate pace throughout this district in order that she might make her farewells without haste to a part of her life that had come to an end. In his opinion she should never have been allowed to visit the weavers' homes as a child and take instruction like a common apprentice. Left motherless from birth, she had become an undisciplined young girl with a mind of her own.

"I hope this won't take long," he commented impatiently.

"You need have no fear of that," Gabrielle replied. "Time is too valuable to these hardworking people. You should know that, after all your years in the silk trade."

Word of her approach had preceded her. The noise of the looms in these houses was stilled briefly as the weavers who served Maison Roche came out to cheer and wave as she went by. Gabrielle stood to call from the open window of the carriage, knowing each weaver by name. Silk was in her blood as it was in theirs, and they respected her for it.

"Oh, thank you so much!" Gabrielle caught several nosegays of wildflowers that were thrown to her, the petals scattering over the carriage floor.

"We're going to be late," Henri informed her sharply.

Unconcerned, she continued to wave back to the family group at each doorstep. The craft of weaving generally involved the whole household, from the grandparents down to the youngest child, with family life invariably centered around the loom that occupied a large section of their living space. Weavers were a stubborn, independent breed of people, and Gabrielle considered herself fortunate to have been accepted into their community.

She gave a final wave and resumed her seat in a rustle of oyster silk, the Chantilly lace of her wedding cap wafting light as a cobweb on her luxuriant chestnut hair, which she wore drawn into a topknot, with curls at her forehead and at the nape of her swanlike neck. Pearl eardrops danced from the lobes of her pretty ears. A smile hid the pang the partings had given her.

"We can proceed now at a faster rate," she said.

Henri grunted. He gave the ceiling of the carriage a sharp rap with his gold-headed cane, and a sudden burst of speed made Gabrielle clutch the seat to steady herself.

Although Henri viewed his sister as a nuisance that he wanted out of the family home as much for the sake of his wife, Yvonne, as for his own, he conceded that her looks, particularly on this day in her wedding garments, were pleasing. Slightly above average height, possessed of a provocatively beautiful figure and a clear, warm voice, she had long-lashed violet-blue eyes set attractively wide apart. She was also lively and vivacious. Now she was about to wed a solemn intellectual, the owner of a silk farm, who had no liking for the social pleasures of city life that she had always enjoyed. As far as Henri was concerned, she was getting exactly what she deserved. Consulting his watch, he gave another rap of his cane as a spur to greater speed.

Neither he nor Gabrielle heard the warning shout to their coachman from a bystander who was able to see beyond a Renaissance archway through which their carriage was about to pass.

"Look out, citizen!"

It was too late. Seconds later Gabrielle was tossed from her seat onto the floor as the wheels of the carriage collided and locked with those of another that had emerged ponderously from the archway. In the impact Henri was thrown into a corner, where he held his breath, his eyes tightly closed, as the carriage teetered precariously. It hung suspended at a sharp angle for timeless moments until the terrified horses, straining to bolt, jerked it free. As it crashed down again onto its wheels Henri fell across Gabrielle, half crushing her with his weight. Managing to get up again, he was concerned for his sister.

"Are you harmed?" he demanded, hoarse with anxiety.

"I'm perfectly all right," she answered breathlessly. "Make sure nobody else is hurt."

He helped her back onto the seat, and she accepted his support thankfully, more shaken than she had at first realized. In looking out the window then, she saw what he had already seen. She sat as though frozen, taking automatically with nerveless fingers the bruised nosegay that he had rescued from the floor.

They had collided with a carriage in a funeral cortege, its sides hung with bleak drapery, its black horses plunging their plumed heads in snorting agitation. The mourners had broken rank from the procession in the rear to swarm forward and view the situation, a crowd in sober clothes, some red-eyed from grief momentarily forgotten in current outrage at what had occurred. As Henri prepared to alight, already fuming about the damage to his carriage, Gabrielle put a white-gloved hand on his arm.

"Do apologize to the bereaved family," she urged. "It must have been our coachman's fault."

His face contorted with temper. "Indeed I shall not! I've just realized whose funeral this is. I had heard that Louis Devaux was being brought home from Paris by his only son for burial today."

An icy chill slid down her spine. The family feud between the Roche and Devaux silk merchants was of long standing. It had had its origin in a business quarrel, and succeeding generations had been virulent and bitter rivals for commissions in the city of Lyons. Then the Revolution had given the feud a new and deadly twist, dividing the moderate Roches from the extremist Devauxs along political lines. Gabrielle shivered. Now, on this of all days, the feud had reached out a macabre hand to touch her in her wedding finery.

Suddenly she stiffened; a rearing horse in the funeral cortege had been seized by its bridle, revealing to her gaze for the first time today the deceased's son. He was struggling to quiet the horse. She recognized Nicolas Devaux. She had seen him once before, although at the time he had not seen her, a frightened little girl watching from behind the draperies of an upstairs window. He had stood belligerently before her father's house, a lean boy of fifteen with curly black hair, yelling his defiance of the Roche family and all it represented of the old France. His father had dragged him away, afraid he would be killed by the pistol being aimed by Henri Roche from the window.

That had been in 1793, when Lyons had been besieged and then half demolished during Robespierre's Reign of Terror—the time when the Devauxs had closed their mill and fled to join the extremists.

Eleven years had gone by since then, and yet there was no mistaking the gaunt sculptured face, the bold straight nose, the well-shaped mouth and the strong jaw, all of which had made him, with the passing of time, into a man of arresting appearance. The wild revolutionary had tempered to a virile and forceful presence.

The horse he was handling settled down at last. In the same instant Nicolas Devaux's eyes met Gabrielle's. It was a penetrating stare that bore into her, as if he were drawing the very essence of her into himself. Her old fear of him resurfaced, but with a dimension of excitement that caused her pulse to race. She forgot completely that she was a bride on her way to her wedding, and he, for his part, had become equally oblivious of his surroundings and why he was there.

He moved to the front of the horses as if to come across to her. But Henri, stalking forward, grabbed Nicolas Devaux's sleeve and, catching him unawares, hauled him about. "You Devauxs have always caused trouble in this city!" he cried. "Living or dead, anyone bearing your detestable name is not wanted here! Do you see what damage your hearse has done to our carriage?"

Nicolas threw off Henri's grasp, his black brows drawing together ominously. "It seems the Roches have learned neither manners nor tolerance since I was last in Lyons!"

Henri made a bullying gesture. "Damnation to you! Your late father is already damned!" Turning his back, he retraced his steps to the carriage. It dipped under his weight as he stepped back inside and dropped heavily onto the seat. Before the coachman could close the door, it was wrenched wide again as Nicolas leaned in and seized the lapels of Henri's coat.

"No man shall insult my father's memory. You'll give me satisfaction over this!"

Gabrielle gave a cry of dismay, sick with shame over her brother's actions. "No, please," she implored. "The collision was our fault, and words were said in haste."

Nicolas neither looked at her nor eased his grip on her brother. "That doesn't excuse a lack of respect for the dead."

She continued her attempt to intercede. "I'm on my way to my wedding. For that reason alone, I beg you to forgive what has taken place and retract your demand for satisfaction."

He answered her fiercely, "You'd be well advised to leave this carriage and escape the marriage, mam'selle. You'll have no happiness in wedlock with this fellow."

"He's not my bridegroom! He's my elder brother and my escort. I'm Gabrielle Roche, and I apologize fully on his behalf." Her voice rang with appeal. "Surely on this day of days amends can be made."

To her relief Nicolas released her brother then, throwing him back in the seat and turning to regard her again. The look he gave her was much as before, awakening the same response in her of mingled pleasure and trepidation. He spoke with care.

"I accept your apology on your brother's behalf, Mademoiselle Roche. But I repeat the advice I gave about escaping your marriage today. Wait awhile. Mistakes are made all too easily."

Her one thought was to get Henri away from the confrontation as quickly as possible. "I shall do what is best, Monsieur Devaux. Don't let us delay you any longer. I'm thankful this has been resolved peacefully."

He raised a questioning eyebrow as he stepped down to the cobbles. The very air seemed charged between them. "Has it?"

"Good-bye," she heard herself say.

He bowed to her and turned away. The carriage door was shut. As the wheels rolled forward Henri exploded with rage. "What infernal impudence! What bad blood!"

Nicolas, meanwhile, returned to his position, heading the procession of mourners. He turned his head, and his mesmerizing gaze held Gabrielle's once more as the wheels of her carriage began to spin across the cobbles. Her face was framed for him, like a lovely portrait, in the carriage window. Then, abruptly, and with a sudden burst of speed, she was swept from his sight.

Gabrielle sank back against the velvet upholstery, dazed but stimulated, almost as though laughter and tears were high in her.

Opposite her, Henri splayed his hands across his heavy thighs, which strained the burgundy doeskin of his pantaloons.

"You're looking pale." He attempted to soften the blunt manner he usually used toward her, knowing that bridal nerves often did unpredictable things to women. "Try to forget the little contretemps that took place. Remember that Émile is waiting for you."

She gave a little nod, and turned her head to look unseeingly at the passing wineshops and small cafés. Her brother's advice was not easy to follow. The look Nicolas had given her was not what a bride should receive from a man other than the groom on the day of her wedding. She must forget the whole incident, concentrate on other things. There was a lot to think about as the last hour of her single state drew to a close.

Since the age of sixteen there had been men wanting to marry her, but she had always been determined to make her own choice when the time came, in spite of tyrannical pressure from her father. The battles to retain her independence had been hard. Henri and his self-centered wife, Yvonne, had ranged themselves with her father against her. Her only allies had been the younger of her two brothers, Jules, and his sweet-natured wife, Hélène. Unfortunately, Jules was in the army and rarely at home. As for Hélène, although she was the one who tried to fulfill the whims of her cantankerous father-in-law, Dominique Roche, she had no influence with him on his daughter's behalf.

Gabrielle's hope had always been that she might take some official part in the manufacture of Roche silk, and to this end she had learned every stage of the procedure. It was not surprising that she looked beyond docile domesticity, for at the most impressionable time of her life she had experienced the full turmoil of the Revolution. The cry of liberty had been an echo of her own demands for the right to decide her future.

Lyons had suffered more than most cities in the Revolution. Since medieval times the city had been a great international trading center in cloth, although it was not until the introduction of silkworms into France in the fifteenth century that silk weaving took hold and flourished. At that time royal privileges had given Lyons complete control over all the raw silk in the land,

and the city continued to rise until the Revolution brought disaster to its luxury-based trade.

With these long traditions of supplying the rich and the noble, the people of Lyons had revolted against the new revolutionary regime that wished to redistribute wealth. Government forces had then moved against the city with a siege that brought starvation to its people. After holding out for two months, Lyons raised the white flag of surrender in the hope of mercy.

It was not forthcoming. As punishment the city was condemned to demolition, an ignominious fate. Every day smoke and dust from fires and explosions drifted in dark clouds across the peninsula on which the city stood at the confluence of the Saône and the Rhone rivers. No area escaped the butchering of Frenchmen by Frenchmen. The destruction and slaughter went on for two months and took more than two thousand lives, until in Paris the tyrant Robespierre fell from power and the Reign of Terror came to an end.

By then there were no Devauxs of the silk world left in Lyons. Dominique Roche had seized the chance to rid himself of his old enemies by denouncing them as extremists who were in league with the government forces against the Lyonese. Louis Devaux had had to flee for his life, taking his wife and son, Nicolas, with him. No Devaux had returned to Lyons until this day, and Gabrielle hoped Nicolas would leave after the funeral as speedily as he had left last time. It would be best for her never to see him again. He was too disturbing, too disruptive a personality.

"We're here," Henri said, breaking into her thoughts. They had stopped by the stone steps of their destination, one of the many churches that had been turned into public assembly halls since the Revolution. Gabrielle smoothed the gathers of her gown carefully into place. For all its delicate appearance, silk was a hardy fabric, and it had suffered no harm through her fall to the carriage floor. The current fashion of the skirt flowing from a high waistline suited her well. On the steps Henri offered her his arm, and they disappeared into the entrance.

Inside, an orchestra was playing in what had once been a side chapel. All marriage ceremonies were civil ones now, but she and

Émile planned to receive a religious blessing at another time.

There was a stir of movement among those present at the bride's arrival, and she caught an affectionate grin from her brother Jules. Sandy-haired and freckled, still retaining his boyish looks in spite of extensive service on foreign battlefields, he was tall and dashing in his gray-and-red hussar's uniform, his plumed fur hat held military-fashion in the crook of his arm. By his side, Hélène was smiling, dimples playing, happy in the occasion and in having her husband home again, however short his leave might be. She wore a fashionable turban of amber gauze that echoed the color of her eyes and set off the raven black of her smoothly dressed hair. Gabrielle was heartened by the warm expressions of these two who meant the most to her.

She looked beyond them to the head of the aisle, where Émile waited. His dark brown hair was winged with gray and shining in the sun's rays that poured down on him through a stained-glass window. Behind him the Tricolor flamed blue, white and red.

She returned Émile's steady gaze as she advanced step by gliding step toward him, her gown whispering about her. From the first he had pleased her with his meditative gray eyes, his lean, sensitive face, his deep, attractive voice and his quiet demeanor. She felt that with this intelligent older man she would be able to forget once and for all the swift, sweet love she had shared with Philippe, a weaver's son—an affair crushed by her father. She had been seventeen, and it had taken her a long time to recover from that youthful anguish.

Love, as she had once expected to find it, did not enter into this union, but she did want her marriage to Émile to be a good one. Although divorce had become commonplace since the Revolution, she was resolved that there should be no broken vows for her, and she knew Émile felt the same way. Now he was coming forward to meet her.

"My dear Gabrielle." He seized her hand and linked his fingers with hers as they turned together to face the magistrate.

"Citizen Émile Valmont and Citizeness Gabrielle Roche, you have come before the law of France to be joined in wedlock."

The ceremony went well until she removed her glove to receive the ring. As Émile made to slip the gold band onto her finger, she jerked her hand back involuntarily. She was aghast at her own action. A fleeting look of surprise passed across Émile's face, but he remained in control, simply tightening his hold on her fingers. Nobody else, except the magistrate, was aware of the instinctive last bid she had made for freedom.

Émile now bent his head to kiss her lips with reassurance and promise. Her panic ebbed away as if it had never been.

Well-wishers surrounded them. Her first kiss on the cheek was from Hélène. "May you always be happy, dearest Gabrielle."

"I echo my wife's sentiments, little sister." Jules embraced Gabrielle affectionately. With an age gap of only four years between them, they had always been close.

"How I wish your leave could have begun sooner," she said to him. "I've hardly had a chance to talk to you."

"I'll bring Hélène out to visit you before I leave," he promised.

That cheered her immensely. Then she turned to receive the kisses and embraces from the rest of her family and friends. Yvonne, Henri's wife, was as usual the height of elegance, wearing a dress of yellow-striped silk, with a large diamond brooch at her throat, and a hat ornamented with tall plumes. She exuded a strong perfume as she leaned forward to kiss the bride. "My good wishes. Your bridal gown is quite charming." Her glance was uncertain. "Oyster is not a shade that is easy to wear, although with my complexion I could get away with it."

Gabrielle hid her amusement; even at another woman's wedding, Yvonne could not cease to be completely self-absorbed.

More people came forward, and it took a little while before the bride and groom were able to leave the assembly hall and enter the waiting carriage. Observing the old custom that the bridal couple must make a grand entrance at the wedding feast, they were to be driven by a long route to her father's house, giving everyone else the chance to arrive first.

After waving to those gathered on the steps of the assembly hall, Gabrielle turned her head to look at her bridegroom sitting at her side. He was gazing composedly out the window at the passing scene, his fine profile etched almost coinlike against the sun. She would have liked to talk, but guessed he was thankful for this quiet respite before facing the feast and chatter that lay ahead. There would be plenty of opportunity to discuss and even argue points of view with him in the future, particularly whenever she should praise Napoléon Bonaparte for all he and Madame Joséphine had done to stimulate the Lyons silk trade.

Émile did not share Gabrielle's enthusiasm for Napoléon, yet he was always ready to listen to her opinions. That was why over the past months Émile had gradually won her trust and respect. There were depths in him that she still had to plumb, for they had had almost no time on their own; Hélène had always been present as chaperon. Only on the evening when he had proposed to her had they been alone together.

There had been moments when she thought she glimpsed in Émile a deep passion. Yet never once had he mentioned the word love. She would have liked him to hold her hand now on this drive, as he had done during the marriage ceremony. To encourage him she placed her hand with its new gold band palm downward on the seat between them. He did not appear to notice.

They arrived at her father's house in the Rue Clémont. It was a spacious residence—as much a showpiece as a home, since business associates and buyers were received there. Two offices, used by Dominique and Henri respectively, as well as design and checking rooms, were situated to the rear of the house. Every one of the main salons and upper rooms was hung with panels of Roche silk; the designs ranged from spectacular in the grand salon to modest in the smaller salons. During the Revolution the house had escaped damage except for a few broken windows. Shortly afterward Henri had married Yvonne and brought her home to live. Later Hélène had been the second bride to take up residence in her father-in-law's house, since Jules was away on active service most of the time.

Dominique Roche had received his guests in the grand salon and was awaiting the arrival of the bride and groom. The walls of the handsome room blazed with richly hued silks depicting golden peacocks, their tails fully spread. The whole salon dazzled and beguiled the eye like a jewel.

Dominique was seated in his great carved chair, with its seat and back of peacock brocade. Since a fall three years before, when he had damaged his hip, lack of exercise and his enormous appetite had increased his already considerable weight. Yet, in spite of being confined to his chair, he missed nothing that went on in his house or in his business domain. He used his wits now as never before to ensure that his elder son, impatient for full control, did not take over on any pretext.

"Émile and Gabrielle have arrived," said Hélène, lowering her smiling face toward his.

"Good girl." He nodded, closing his hand paternally over hers. He could always rely upon Hélène to keep him notified of any social development, but it was her being the wife of his favorite son that had truly endeared her to him. Unlike Henri and himself, Jules never bore malice; he had his late mother's lighthearted temperament as well as her charm. For Dominique it had been a bitter disappointment when Jules had announced his intention to go into the army and not into the silk business. He accepted his son's decision but made his own secret plan to bring Jules into Maison Roche when his soldiering days were done.

"Monsieur and Madame Valmont." The bridal couple had been announced, and as they came through the doorway applause erupted. A belligerent expression dominated Dominique's loose-jowled face. He felt the old resentment of his daughter rise up in him, for no reason other than that she was alive and his beloved wife was long since gone—because of her. On the day of Gabrielle's birth he had not so much as glanced in her cradle.

Today, as through a veil of memory, Dominique could glimpse again Marguerite—the only woman he had ever loved—in Gabrielle's dramatic beauty, her chestnut curls, her movements and her grace. As she curtsied to him while her husband bowed, he ignored her. "So now you are my son-in-law," he declared heartily to Émile. "May good fortune go with you and your bride."

Émile bowed again. "I thank you for your kind words."

Dominique, shifting in his chair, signaled that he was ready to rise from it. Leaning heavily on a walking stick, he would let no one but Jules help him into the adjoining dining salon, where the wedding feast was set out against a glittering backdrop of damask, silver and crystal.

Gabrielle followed with Émile, the rest of the company falling in behind. Her father's deliberate slight on this day had struck deep. Yet the fact that she had a will to match his meant that he had never broken her. She sometimes wondered if her passion for silk had its origin in a childhood of yearning to break through Dominique's hostility. Whatever its beginnings, she loved silk now for its own sake, and she regarded it as the most beautiful fabric in existence. Her life in the future, she knew, would be spent at the Valmont silk farm, a successful business located at a charming country estate outside Lyons.

The feasting lasted several hours. It was early evening when Gabrielle finally went upstairs with Hélène, who helped her change out of her bridal attire into a lilac traveling dress and coat. The journey to her new home would take no more than an hour.

"Here are your gloves." Hélène held them out to her.

Gabrielle took them and then caught her sister-in-law's hands in a tight clasp. "I shall miss you so much. Please visit me often when Jules's leave is over. It will be lonely without your company."

"You're forgetting you'll have Émile now."

A shuttered look came over Gabrielle's face. She withdrew her hands and began to put on her gloves. "Yes, so I shall."

Hélène watched her. It was almost possible to believe that Gabrielle was experiencing qualms, which was in total contrast to her self-assurance that morning while dressing for the ceremony. It seemed to Hélène that something had happened to her sister-in-law between her leaving the house and her return; perhaps the accident with the funeral cortege had upset her more than she had realized when she mentioned it.

"Are you ready?" she prompted the bride gently.

Gabrielle embraced Hélène and, with a smile arranged on her lips, swept ahead out of the room and down the stairs to the hall, where Émile was waiting for her and where everyone was gathered to send them on their way. Even Dominique was there, leaning on his stick, and she and Émile departed in the usual noisy excitement that accompanies the going away of newlyweds.

IN ANOTHER PART OF THE CITY, Nicolas Devaux shook the hands of departing mourners. They all knew him as if the eleven years since he had left Lyons had been only as many days.

As the last carriage left from outside the hotel, he went back into the building to confirm that he would be staying overnight. Then, lantern in hand, he set off for an address he had not seen since his family had departed from it in haste. It was in the Croix-Rousse quarter, where earlier that day the Roche carriage had halted the cortege like a last dart thrown at his father's memory.

In the quarter he ascended a flight of steps to reach a narrow cobbled street, and followed its winding slope upward. As darkness fell, lamplight appeared from the windows of the familiar stone houses that lined either side. Unlike the Roches, who several generations before had moved in their prosperity from the crowded heights to an elegant district, the Devauxs had remained at the heart of the industry, in an ancient house whose black façade hid a treasure trove of silks within.

His old home came into sight. From his coat pocket Nicolas removed the key that was about to take him into the past. What would he find after all these years? Preparing himself for the worst, he turned the key and let the door swing wide.

The beam of his lantern showed him the checkered marble floor and the staircase rising beyond. He stepped inside and closed the door behind him. The house smelled musty and neglected. But paintings still hung on the walls, and none of the hall chairs were overturned. No sign of disorder yet. He opened one of the double doors leading to the main salon and entered.

The damage there was worse than anything he had envisioned. The silk panels that covered the walls had been slashed to pieces. Gilded chairs lay in splinters, the stuffing ripped out of the silk brocade. He was appalled at the wanton destruction, for the finest Devaux silk had gone into this room. Stepping over the debris, he went to another pair of doors that led into a long, narrow room known as the gallery; it contained many portraits and pictures, all woven in silk. Not one had escaped bludgeoning.

The gallery opened into his father's office, which, he was relieved to see, had been left untouched. So had the adjoining design room, with its brushes and paints and colored inks ranged neatly in rows, half-finished designs on the sloping desk boards.

He went through an inner courtyard, and unlocked a door that led to the mill. Holding the lantern high, he sent its glow over sixty looms that stood dark and skeletal in four rows. Axes had been used on the sturdy looms, which bore raw gashes like wounds in the timeworn wood.

Moving slowly down one of the aisles between the looms, he remembered how he had been put to every task in this place, for his father had been determined that there should be no gaps in his knowledge of weaving. In early boyhood he had taken his turn under a loom, retying the threads as they broke—a grueling and exhausting task allotted to children. Fingers became sore and limbs cramped, and it was not unusual to see children weeping as they worked.

He completed his tour of the workshop, sometimes stepping accidentally on one of the hundreds of bobbins and shuttles that had been thrown across the floor. He had no sooner returned to the house than a knock sounded on the front door. Opening it, he was met by the sight of a short, grizzled old man in the weaver's garb of belted loose tunic and trousers, and a cap topped with a full, soft crown. The visitor seized Nicolas's hand in a gnarled clasp to pump it heartily.

"It is you, then, Citizen Devaux. I thought I had seen you come home to your roots at last."

Nicolas grinned broadly. "Jean-Baptiste Rouband! After all these years! Come in, come in. If it hadn't been for your timely warning when my father and I were marked men, I shouldn't be here today." He threw an arm around the old man's shoulder and shut the door. "This calls for a bottle of wine."

"Have you looked in the cellar yet?"

"There's been no time." Nicolas flung a hand in the direction of the open door of the salon. His tone bitter, he said, "See the damage that was done here in the name of law and order. The workshop has also suffered."

Jean-Baptiste took a few paces into the salon. "It's bad, but nothing that can't be put right. In any case, the law didn't do it."

"Then who did?"

The old man turned. "It was Dominique Roche's men. They broke in after you escaped. They would have done more damage if some of your weavers hadn't moved in to drive them out."

Nicolas had turned white. "It wasn't enough to put our lives in jeopardy! He had to destroy our home and mill."

"How did your mother stand up to the escape?"

"Not at all, I'm sad to say. She had been sick previously for several weeks. Having to leave her home in those circumstances hastened her death. There is no doubt about that." Nicolas moved restlessly, pacing to and fro. "I tell you, I have a heavy score against the Roches, and today more has been added to it."

"If you wouldn't be offended," Jean-Baptiste ventured warily, "I'd like to ask whether Dominique Roche's charge that your family collaborated with the Reign of Terror could have been upheld if it had been taken into the Lyons courts."

"Very possibly!" Nicolas did not hedge. "Feelings were running high at the time, and it would have been hard to find an unbiased judge." He stopped pacing. "That's enough gloomy talk for today. Let's see what can be found in the wine cellar."

He led the way down to the cellar. They were in for a pleasant discovery. Nothing there had been looted. Armed with bottles and glasses, the two men came back upstairs and settled themselves in what had been the family salon.

"When shall you be starting up the looms again, Citizen Devaux?" the old man asked.

Nicolas, reclining in a comfortable chair, regarded the weaver over the rim of his glass. "What makes you think I should want to live here again? After serving four years in the army, I rejoined my father in Paris, where we went into silk negotiating together. Now I control a number of looms in the outskirts of Paris."

"Silk isn't silk if it isn't woven in Lyons. Parisian silk? Bah!" Jean-Baptiste's contempt needed the leavening of a refill of his glass; he took a gulp. Then he added, "You needn't fear that the mud slung at your good name will stick. Times have changed."

"If I decide to come back to Lyons," Nicolas said, "it would be to reestablish myself in my own right. As for Parisian silk, I recently fulfilled a commission that was part of the refurbishing of the Tuileries."

The old man grunted. "You'd still do better in your own city. Besides, Maison Roche is certain to secure good commissions from Napoléon Bonaparte before long."

Nicolas narrowed his eyes. "So the Roches are in the running, are they? Maybe it *is* time for Maison Devaux to reopen."

"Well said!" Jean-Baptiste slapped his knee in triumph. "You mean it. I can see that! It's the best news I've heard in a long while." Putting his glass aside, he seized a bottle by its neck to swallow its contents jubilantly. He remembered little after that, and had no recollection of Nicolas helping him home.

Returning to the hotel, Nicolas guessed that Jean-Baptiste would always boast of being instrumental in restoring Devaux silk to Lyons. The truth was, it had been in his mind to return, as a member of the manufacturers known collectively as the Grande Fabrique, to this place where his forebears had produced the best of Lyons silk.

Once in his room, his thoughts went to the bride he had met that day. In the aftermath of that clash of locking wheels he had looked at her and wanted her and thought himself demented that during his father's funeral he should be seized by desire. Never in his life had he been so enthralled on sight by any woman. And he had sensed a response in her, making the rapport between them complete.

At the funeral reception a local mourner had given him valuable information about her, including the name and occupation of her bridegroom. If ever the chance presented itself, Nicolas intended to see her again.

By CANDLELIGHT Gabrielle prepared for bed. She was being assisted by the maid Émile had employed to wait on her. She had never had a personal servant before, and it was a novelty having someone put away her clothes and brush her hair.

She had made only one visit to Émile's house prior to her marriage and had liked it at first sight. Built of mellow stone, sunbaked to a golden hue, it dated back a hundred years or more and had well-proportioned rooms. Now that she was upstairs for the first time, she could tell that extensive redecoration had been done for her benefit, for the white paintwork of the bedchamber smelled pristine and the wallpaper was patterned prettily with blossoms from her favorite tree, the mimosa. The bed, also new, had a circular canopy from which filmy draperies looped down over the head and the foot, creating a tentlike look.

She liked everything about her new home. She felt safe in it, although it had never been her policy to seek security.

"Is there anything more, madame?" the maid asked.

She shook her head. "No, thank you. You may go."

Left on her own, Gabrielle crossed to the window and looked out. The moon was bright, and she could see beyond the formal flower gardens to the copse of trees that hid the silk farm beyond. On the day she had visited, Émile showed her the white stone silksheds with terra-cotta tiles, where thousands of eggs were being stored in a cold cellar until the time of hatching. After the hatching, the whole cycle of sericulture—the raising of silkworms for the production of raw silk—would begin again.

As a child, Gabrielle's favorite story had been that of the origins of silk. One day, when the Chinese empress Hsi Ling-shi was taking tea in her garden in 2640 B.C., she noticed that a cocoon had dropped into her cup. Seeing a fine thread loosened from it, she pulled it gently and, surprised to find it continuous, began to reel it on a twig. It proved to be several thousand feet long. Realizing its potential, the empress introduced sericulture on a large scale. For Gabrielle it had always been easy to feel akin to the empress in her love of silk.

By holding back the curtain and looking westward, she could just see the mulberry plantation spread out under the stars, the trees kept to size as bushes. Since silkworms were entirely dependent on mulberry leaves for their sustenance, it was no wonder that the mulberry had become known worldwide as the tree of gold, a magical name that appealed to her.

Émile, having come up the stairs, passed the bedchamber door to go into his dressing room. As he made ready for bed he was clear as to how it should be between Gabrielle and himself on their wedding night. He accepted that she did not love him. If he had needed proof, he had had it during the marriage ceremony when she had momentarily pulled her hand away from his ring. The hurt of it had been like a dagger thrust, the pain made worse by his desire for her. He planned to win her love gradually. He would rush nothing.

She was in bed when he entered the room, her hair copper bright in the candlelight. Taking the silver candlesnuffer, he put out the flame, then turned back the bedcovers and got in beside her. Trembling with restraint, he leaned over to cup her face with his hand and kiss her gently.

"Good night, my dear Gabrielle. Sleep well." Then, as he was about to withdraw to the far side of the bed, she flung her arms around his neck, pressing herself to him.

"What's wrong?" she cried in bewilderment. "I'm glad to be your wife."

He uttered a groan of joy, taking her mouth in passion. He found her generous and responsive, and he believed he had awakened a need of him in her that boded well for their married life. That she lay awake after he slept, he did not know.

CHAPTER TWO

Ten days went by before Jules and Hélène made their promised visit. Gabrielle ran down the front steps of the house to meet them, her arms held wide, her muslin gown billowing behind her.

"Welcome! Both of you! I've been watching the road for you."

Jules, alighting from the carriage first, greeted Gabrielle exuberantly. "Then here's your reward!" He caught his sister by the waist to swing her around, she laughing in protest, as if they were still in their nursery days.

Émile, emerging from the house at a more sober pace, creased his brows at this buoyant display of affection. He did not feel ready yet to share his lovely young wife with others. But with inherent courtesy he went forward to receive his company. "I endorse my wife's welcome," he said to them. "We are privileged that you can spend some time with us."

As the servants carried in the baggage, Émile took Jules through to the salon to offer him wine after the journey, while Gabrielle showed Hélène upstairs to the guest room.

"We shall be most comfortable here," Hélène remarked as she glanced around at the blue-and-white-striped wallpaper and the bed with its gilded moldings.

Gabrielle took her coat and bonnet from her. "How is Father?"

Hélène's dimples appeared. "He's difficult," she admitted. "He doesn't like to lose sight of Jules when he is at home, so it was quite difficult to get away. But Jules insisted."

"I'm glad. Father wants to rule everybody's life." Gabrielle sighed. "You are now his housekeeper, companion, nurse and slave. His hold on you is getting tighter and tighter. But enough about family frictions. Let's rejoin the men. They'll be wondering what has happened to us."

Jules and Hélène stayed for three days, and the time went by all too quickly for Gabrielle. The opportunity for which she had been waiting did not come until the final evening, when Émile invited Hélène to view his collection of rare silk moths from India and the Far East.

"At last a chance to talk to you alone," Jules said to Gabrielle.

"And I to you," she replied. "I know you've never wanted Hélène to endure the hardships of following you on campaign, but now she should go with you or you should buy a home of your own for her. She really deserves to have time to herself instead of being the mainstay of a house where she is never left in peace. Her duties have doubled since I married Émile."

Jules took her by the elbow and led her to a sofa, where they sat down together. "Hélène and I have talked the matter over," he began. "She does not want to move into a place where she would have little more to do than worry about me. It does her good to be busy. She also believes that Father needs her, and it pleases me that my wife can be a comfort to him." He saw a shadow pass over his sister's face. "I didn't mean to hurt you. I'm probably the only one, with the exception of Hélène, who knows that, in spite of everything, you do care about Father."

She gave a little shrug of resignation. "The filial bond is not easily broken. He is an extraordinary man, and I admire the power he wields. I should like to have it myself."

"Henri is the one who will inherit the power one day, which brings me to something else. Father has deteriorated in health. We must face the possibility that his life might not last as long as we would wish. When he does go, Hélène must not remain in the house. I don't want my dear wife to spend the rest of her life in submission to Yvonne."

"Why should she?" Gabrielle exclaimed. "These wars will end one day, and you'll be home to stay." She saw how the boyish look had gone from his face to reveal the soldier beneath.

"There's no guarantee that I'll be among those to survive."

"Don't say that," she implored.

"I have to speak of it. You see, we believe Hélène may already have conceived a child. If it is so, it means she would be more vulnerable than ever, being left a widow with a baby." He reached out to grip his sister's hand. "Will you promise me that you'll get her away from our father's house if, when he dies, I'm no longer able to protect her?"

"You know I will!" The promise burst from her. "I just hope and pray that particular duty never comes my way."

Some of his usual cheerfulness returned, and he smiled broadly. "I'll do my best to ensure it doesn't."

All that had been said filled Gabrielle's thoughts as she stood with her husband to wave farewell to Jules and Hélène the next day. When the carriage was lost from sight, she sighed and turned to walk back into the house with Émile, only to find he had not waited for her. During the next few days Émile was cool and withdrawn, and she realized with dismay that he had felt neglected. He was the last person she would ever have suspected of being jealous for her attention, and it was a relief to her when he recovered from his moodiness by the end of the week.

The spring of 1804 gave way to summer. Their marriage followed a smooth path, so that a sudden and unexpected confrontation between them was something of a shock to her. It occurred not long after the thousands of silkworms had hatched, bringing a bustle of activity throughout the silk farm.

Émile came into one of the smaller silksheds, where Gabrielle was laying out a fresh supply of mulberry leaves over netting that had been fastened across each tray of larvae. Silkworms are voracious eaters; it takes a ton of leaves to feed the worms that come from just one ounce of eggs. That same ounce eventually produces more than seventeen thousand miles of silk. .

Émile watched Gabrielle for a moment, then informed her crisply, "You are spending far too much time in these buildings and not enough on domestic duties."

"That's an unjust accusation!" she protested indignantly. She stood facing him in the aisle between the shelves of trays. "I should have thought, Émile, that you'd be pleased that I'm taking such an interest in our means of livelihood."

"I am, but it's not fitting that my wife should be working in the sheds like a hired hand. By all means visit them now and again to see what is developing. That is different. It won't be long before the larvae begin to spin their cocoons. Until then nothing of any real consequence happens to compel your presence here."

Her eyes flashed dangerously. He was forbidding her access to the silksheds! "Are you condemning me to boredom?"

He kept his patience. He had been prepared for difficulties in his marriage, aware from his first meeting with her that she was quick and intelligent and independent. Yet, if anything, he was more in love with her than ever.

"You can find plenty to do. It's high time we returned some of the invitations we have accepted over the past weeks. We've had no one to the house since Jules and Hélène were here."

"I can arrange a supper party," she said stiffly. "With a hired orchestra, and there could be dancing on the lawn."

"A capital idea!" he declared with more enthusiasm than the suggestion warranted. Then he took her by the shoulders, choosing to ignore her rigid stance, and his voice softened in tone. "The time has come for you to fulfill your rightful role in life."

Her face became bleak with disappointment. Jerking away from him, she flung up her hands in exasperation. "I can't remember a time when men have not tried to thwart my interest in silk. Everything I have ever learned has been through my own efforts, and it was my dream that one day my father would relent and let me take my place with Henri in the business. If my father had only seen that I had talent to match my brother's, I could have put new life into Maison Roche."

"Did you have the same aims toward the Valmont silk farm when you decided to marry me?"

She regarded him frankly. "Surely you guessed that. You had shown me that you were an enlightened man, ready to accept that the Revolution had given women like me new freedom."

His gaze was cool. "Is that the only reason you married me?"

"No! I visualized a true partnership, my role a dual one of wife and business aide." Her expression relaxed and she came forward to rest her hands against his chest, looking up into his face. "More than that, I respected and admired you. I would never want any difference of opinion to come between us."

He cupped her chin in the palm of his hand. "Accept my ruling, my dear. It is for the best. I love you, and what I want above all else is that you should become completely mine, as I am yours."

She turned uneasily away from him. If it had been possible to wish herself in love with him, she would have done it, for he was a good man with much kindness in him. But so far, fondness and loyalty were all she could offer. She said in a quiet voice, "I'll go and draw up that guest list."

In the days that followed, she went ahead with arrangements for the party and even began to look forward to it. The invitations went out, and she was disappointed when Hélène declined for reasons of her now certain pregnancy. It mattered less when Henri and Yvonne were also unable to accept. As for her father, he never attended any social function outside his own home. Still, the expected friends and business acquaintances numbered over a hundred.

Despite Émile's restrictions on her visiting the silksheds, Gabrielle snatched a few minutes now and again from her very busy schedule to see for herself when the silkworms had stopped eating and were about to spin. The delicate process began three days before the eve of the party. She watched the silk from the silkworms' spinnerets harden when it came in contact with the air and envelop the worms in misty veils.

By the day of the party the majority of the silkworms were encased in small golden yellow cocoons of silk, rounded and feather light. Gabrielle thought more than ever that silk was the queen of fabrics—beautiful, warm and strong. As she and Émile stood looking at them, he said, "I'm sure of a good season this year, and at the end of it you shall have a gown of Valmont silk."

She flashed him a look of delighted surprise. "I'll weave it myself on the loom I brought from home." Swiftly she planted a kiss on his mouth, and he clasped her to him.

The evening of the party was warm and mild, the velvet sky full of stars. Paper lanterns had been hung in the trees, creating twinkling rainbow-colored lights between the branches. People arrived in open carriages, the women wearing jewels and pastel gowns. Gabrielle's gown was cream lace over peach silk, and it wafted gently against her body. Émile had picked her a cream rose, and she wore it fastened by a pearl brooch amid the lace.

They stood side by side in the hallway to receive their guests. When the dancing began, some chose the wide terrace to be near the orchestra, while the rest spread out across the lawn in the glow of the little lanterns. After partnering each other in the first quadrille, Émile and Gabrielle separated to dance with their guests. Shortly before supper he reclaimed her attention as she stood talking merrily to several young people from Lyons.

"Gabrielle, my dear, I should like to present a guest who was delayed in getting here. Here he is . . . Monsieur Devaux."

For a second or two she did not move. Then, abruptly, she turned her head and looked fully at Nicolas. The sight of him brought delicious shock waves to her heart, and she saw a muscle clench involuntarily in his jaw, as if seeing her again had been the same for him.

"We have already met, have we not, Monsieur Devaux?" She

felt weak, engulfed by pleasure. And dread. Out of the corner of her eye she caught Émile's glance of surprise.

"You know each other?"

"Only slightly."

"It was the briefest of meetings," Nicolas said, bowing.

A chord of warning struck in her, and she adopted a bland tone, saying, "I know I echo Émile's wishes in hoping that you have a pleasant evening at our home."

"I thank you. You are most kind."

Émile took charge of him again, presenting him to those in the group she was with. As soon as it was possible, she slipped away and went into the house, needing to adjust to the impact of this unexpected reunion. In her bedchamber, she sank down sideways onto a chair and reviewed the situation.

What she was feeling in her heart she had known when she was seventeen. Now it had returned a thousandfold, stirring her mind and her body toward a path that was full of danger. It would take every bit of her strength of character to withstand the attraction of a man who was, to all intents and purposes, an enemy of hers and her family's.

She braced herself to face the rest of the evening, and Émile met her when she came out onto the terrace. "I've been looking for you. Is anything the matter?"

She assumed a bright expression. "Nothing that can't be amended later. I think it's time for supper now."

There was a rising buzz of chatter as people strolled into the long salon, where the buffet awaited them. Warily she watched for Nicolas, and she soon saw that he was with a group of her friends. He was being well entertained, for the men were good conversationalists and the women pretty.

Resolutely smiling and gracious, she moved among her guests, ensuring that plates were full and glasses replenished. She deliberately avoided the corner where Nicolas and her friends had seated themselves and eventually found herself next to Émile. She realized she had instinctively come to him for protection.

By the time the dancing was once again in full swing, the weather had changed and a storm threatened. A curiously warm wind had come up to send clouds scudding across the sky, and it was having an exhilarating effect on the women, swirling their skirts and buffeting them into closer contact with their partners. The orchestra, caught up in the same spell, had switched to a lively contredanse. Everybody joined in, Gabrielle among them. Linking hands, the dancers formed a large circle, which changed shape as they made their way across the lawn, winding in and out of the trees of the copse, where the shadows were dark and secret. The chain broke at every twelfth step so that people could catch hands with new partners.

Then, just as thunder rumbled and clouds gathered still closer, Gabrielle whirled forward to find herself facing Nicolas. His face was highlighted, as was hers, by the swinging lanterns overhead, and he saw her sparkling expression as his outstretched hands seized hers. He laughed under his breath, totally triumphant. "I've been waiting all evening for this moment!"

She laughed with him, feeling completely reckless as he swept her into the steps of the dance. The thunder had caused several couples to look skyward uncertainly, and in breaking the chain, they had left Gabrielle free to dance on with him. "I must confess that you were quite the last person I had expected to see this evening," she said quietly.

He was thoroughly amused. "You must have known that sooner or later we would meet again."

She looked down and away from him, sensing danger. It was a long time since she had felt so buoyant and lighthearted. "I didn't expect it to be in my own home out in the country," she said.

"Should I not have come?" he asked.

"Oh, yes. Why not?" She tilted her head back challengingly, her eyes full of mischief, her windblown skirt whirling about.

He had slowed the pace of their dancing to a leisurely drifting in and out of the trees. Inevitably, they came to a standstill, she to lean back against a tree, he to stand facing her, resting one hand on the bark beside her. The rumbling of the thunder was nearer.

"Have you been living in Lyons since the day we met?" she asked him.

"No. I returned to Paris the following morning. That's where I

have my silk looms. I'm back in Lyons now on a few days' visit to see about the repair of the family house in the Croix-Rousse. It's going to take months to put it in order again."

"Why is that?"

He could see that she did not have the least idea what damage had been perpetrated at her father's instigation. "Damp and dust are hard on silk. There's some other damage too."

Around them, other couples had spread out to linger by themselves. For Gabrielle the erotic atmosphere created by the approaching storm was spiced by an awareness of stolen kisses and embraces out in the heavy darkness. Suddenly she felt she had to keep talking.

"Do you plan to return to Lyons when your house is habitable?"

"That is my intention. More than that, I hope to settle here. Nobody born in Lyons ever feels really at home anywhere else."

That completed her feeling of being in full harmony with him. "Would you like to know my most favorite part of Lyons?"

He could not take his eyes from her. "Tell me," he urged.

"It's on the slopes of Fourvière. I should like to build a house there. It would be away from all the houses, streets and mills of the city, and yet the view would make it more a part of Lyons than my childhood home on the Rue Clémont."

"Have you picked the exact site?"

She smiled reminiscently. "Once. Long ago. My brother Jules and I were children and went on a picnic there. We found some Roman pottery. I marked a special spot with one of the shards."

"I should like to see it." He was serious. The mood between them had changed to a deeper, more intimate level. She realized too late what had happened, and attempted a teasing note.

"Then you must search for it yourself. It is my secret."

It did not work. His gaze remained steadily fixed on her. "Do you feel cut off from Lyons out here in the country?"

"I miss being at the center of everything in the silk trade."

He smiled. "Not many women would have given such a reason. They would have said they missed the social life, the gossip, the dressmakers. But then you are not like any other woman I have ever met, Gabrielle."

At his first use of her Christian name she rolled her head slightly away from him, looking back toward the distant lights of the house. "Am I not?" Her voice was barely audible.

"If time could be turned back to the day we met, I wouldn't stand aside and let you go."

She turned her head to look at him again. The rich pleasure she was experiencing in being with him must be strictly confined to the time left to them tonight, never to be repeated. "I'm happy that we met this evening," she confessed gently, "even though I shall try to ensure that our paths don't cross in the future."

He moved closer, looking down into her eyes. "I came here this evening only to see you. You know that."

"Then let us both be content that we had the chance to finish wondering about what can never be."

A great stream of forked lightning suddenly split the sky. In the fleeting bluish glow each saw the other's face nakedly revealed, and any last doubts about the magnetism that had first drawn them together were swept aside. As a tremendous clap of thunder followed, he wrapped her in his arms and kissed her with such passion that she could only cling to him in frenzied response. She knew then that she had been made for this man alone.

With the thunder came the rain, in great heavy drops. Nicolas and Gabrielle defied the downpour. It was only when someone charged past quite near them that they finally broke apart.

"Come away with me!" he urged tautly, flinging out a desperate hand to her. The lightning showed the wrenched passion of his face. "Now! This minute!"

"No! You must be mad!" she shrieked, making herself heard as the thunder boomed like a cannonade.

"It's a second chance! Don't you see? We belong together!"

"Never! I'm not yours! I never will be!" She was almost beside herself with panic. "Go away! Go out of my life!"

She swung about and ran from him. He shouted, "Keep away from those tall trees! They're dangerous in this storm."

She stumbled to a halt. "The orangery is close by," she called out. "I'll lead the way."

He nodded to show he had heard her. As the people clustered

under the trees crowded after her, lightning showed the way, and when she opened the door of the orangery, an aromatic scent drifted out to those following her. Inside, the women began shivering in their dampened gowns, for the temperature had dropped sharply with the coming of the rain.

Each flash of lightning showed the activity going on outside. Émile had organized the servants, who were holding up tarpaulins to form canopies under which guests were hurried.

Eventually all who had gathered at the orangery left, Gabrielle with the women under the canopies, the men preferring to make a dash across the lawn to the house. Once indoors, the party drew automatically to a close. Gabrielle, upstairs with some of the women at the time, did not see Nicolas leave.

When the last carriage had gone, Émile went to pour himself a large cognac. He was chilled and shivering. "I think we can congratulate ourselves on a successful party," he said to Gabrielle, who had put a silk stole about her shoulders for warmth, "even though it did end in such inclement weather."

"I agree. But there's just one thing." Her throat tightened. "Monsieur Devaux must never be asked to this house again."

"Why not?"

Her answer came readily. "I should have thought it unnecessary for you to ask. He is a Devaux. Surely you have heard of the old enmity between his family and mine?"

Émile was unperturbed as he swallowed a gulp of cognac. "You should let bygones be bygones. No good comes of keeping up old hatreds. Dominique is a man who harbors totally unbalanced grudges. Maybe he let a grudge run away with him in those revolutionary days when he denounced his enemies."

"You're turning this talk away from my simple request."

"I'm trying to remove the reason for it." He weighed his words carefully. "Devaux strikes me as a man who will do much for the silk industry. I intend to do business with him."

"No!"

"We discussed the amount of raw silk he requires for his Paris looms, and when he places an order I shall fill it."

She took several paces toward him, her hands clasped in agitation. "I think it best there should be no further contact, in order to avoid any possible trouble in the future."

Wearily Émile loosened his rain-dampened cravat and ran a finger around his high collar. "Be logical, my dear. I can't turn aside good trade. When this man reopens the Devaux mill in Lyons, he is going to be in the market for still more raw silk."

It was as if there were nothing to stop her hurtling toward Nicolas, no matter how hard she fought against it. She made a final, desperate appeal. "Do business with him if you must, but I beg you to excuse me from meeting him socially."

"Very well," he conceded. Something he saw in her eyes disturbed him, for it revealed an inner torment that was totally out of proportion to the situation. Intending to reassure her, he touched her face with his fingertips, but involuntarily she recoiled from his ice-cold hand, then caught it within her own.

"You're frozen through!" she said. "I had no idea! Get out of those wet clothes at once." He went without protest.

In the morning the good weather returned as if the storm had never been. Keeping tiredness and a headache to himself, Émile announced to Gabrielle that he had suffered no ill effects from the storm of the night before. As she poured his coffee she was unsure. His complexion looked patchy and his eyes red-rimmed.

By midday her worst fears were confirmed. Émile returned to the house from his office in a state of high fever. His doctor was summoned at once, and Gabrielle helped him to bed, where he collapsed thankfully.

It did not take Dr. Jaunet long to arrive. A cheerful, rotund man of middle age, he leaned forward to put an ear to Émile's chest and then to his back. His face gave nothing away, but outside the door he spoke seriously to Gabrielle.

"Nurse your husband with great care, Madame Valmont. The danger of a fever like this is that it can cause permanent damage to the lungs, resulting in consumption. It will be a hard fight."

"I'll do everything I can."

It proved to be a fight for Émile's life, and it lasted many days. Hélène, hearing how ill he was, earned Dominique's displeasure by leaving him to help Gabrielle care for her husband. Hélène was showing her pregnancy now, her health radiant. It was a challenge to her that she should help get Émile well again, although she did accept Gabrielle's decree that for the sake of her baby she must refrain from night duty and from lifting the patient.

With Émile indisposed, it was inevitable that those working in the silksheds should request his wife's decision on certain matters. He was still in a state of crisis when the *maître ouvrier* consulted Gabrielle over the most important issue to date.

"I regret having to trouble you, madame. Could you tell me the approximate amount of cocoons that Monsieur Valmont intended to set aside this year for breeding purposes?"

Émile had never mentioned it. "I don't know, and my husband is too ill to be asked. At the first opportunity I shall find out."

For another few days she did not think of the cocoons. Émile was delirious, and there was nothing she could do but sponge him down with cool water. When finally the fever broke and he slipped into a peaceful sleep, Gabrielle gave way to helpless sobbing. Hélène put an arm around her and led her away.

The next day, refreshed by a sound sleep, Gabrielle returned to the sickroom to hear that Émile had waked, taken a few sips of egg wine and slept again. She decided to go now to Émile's office in the hope of finding the information that the *maître ouvrier* needed. Leaving Hélène in charge, she left the house. It seemed like months since she had felt sunshine on her face.

In the small outer office, the clerk greeted her. "I heard the good news that Monsieur Valmont is better. How soon before he can get back to work?"

"That will be a long time yet, I'm afraid."

"I have letters I can't send without his authorization," he said. "Let me have them."

At Émile's desk she unlocked a drawer with his key. There was a purse of gold coins, a number of official-looking documents and some private letters, as well as an almanac. She glanced through its pages, and there, entered only a few days before his illness, was the information about the cocoons to be set aside. The *maître ouvrier* would be relieved to be able to go ahead.

She began to go through the correspondence the clerk had

given her. There was nothing so complicated as to necessitate her putting it aside for Émile. Then she came to a letter sent from Paris. She felt her heart stop. It was from Nicolas—a confirmation in writing of the amount of raw silk he would require.

The sight of his name aroused the memory of the kiss they had shared on the night of the storm. She remembered the wildness of his mouth, the marvelous closeness of his embrace. The yearning within her was as fierce now as it had been then.

This letter called for a penned reply. She wrote that the Valmont silk farm would not be able to supply the Devaux mill with raw silk, now or at any time in the future. She signed the letter, folded it and sealed it with red wax. There would be serious trouble when Émile found out about it, but that was a risk she had to take. All that mattered was that by this letter she had eliminated almost any chance of meeting Nicolas again.

She went through the rest of the correspondence, certain that she could keep the business running smoothly until Émile was well enough to take over. By then she would have established proof that she was able to combine the roles of wife, housekeeper and manager without detriment to any of them. She felt herself to be a whole person again, independent in her own right once more.

CHAPTER THREE

ÉMILE'S recovery was slow. When he was able, he asked about the business. Hélène, who happened to be alone with him at the time, told him soothingly that he had nothing to worry about. "Gabrielle is looking after everything," she said with the best of intentions.

To her surprise he uttered a tortured groan. Gabrielle, forewarned by Hélène of this reaction, sent the *maître ouvrier* and the office clerk to his bedside as soon as the doctor permitted it, to tell him of the work in hand. They kept their reports brief and reassuring. Émile was left with the impression that his wife was only a temporary figurehead, while the business continued to run according to his rules.

One month from the day of the party the cocoons put aside for breeding purposes began to show signs of life. Gabrielle and Hélène were in the sheds to see the first of the silk moths emerge. Dark and damp, they would soon be creamy white, with wings that would flutter ceaselessly.

"Won't they fly away, then?" Hélène looked uncertainly at the open window.

Gabrielle shook her head. "Centuries of domesticity have deprived these little silk moths of the power of flight." Then she added wryly, almost to herself, "Like women given in marriage."

The clerk from the office had entered the sheds. "You have a gentleman waiting to see you, madame."

"Who is it?" she asked, already on her way to the door.

"I think he's a new customer. A Monsieur Devaux."

She blanched upon hearing the name. She felt such a powerful love-attraction for Nicolas that she doubted her strength of will if she should be alone with him again. Nevertheless, she left Hélène, hurried down the path that led to the office and entered by the side door, taking her place at Émile's desk.

She rang the handbell, and the clerk responded by opening the door from the outer office and showing Nicolas in. She saw at once that it was going to be a difficult interview. His expression and his whole stance boded trouble.

"Good day, Gabrielle. So you are in charge for the time being?"

"I am," she replied evenly, aware that his presence was making a powerful pull on her senses. "Please be seated."

He put his hat and cane aside before taking the chair in front of her desk. "I hope Monsieur Valmont is well on the way to recovery," he said genuinely enough. "Your letter was a puzzle to me."

"Émile is making good progress, I'm thankful to say." Her voice tightened defensively. "Why should my letter have puzzled you? It was perfectly clear."

"Not to me. Your husband agreed to sell me raw silk, and I can't believe he would have changed his mind unless—"

She gave an abrupt shake of her head. "No, I didn't tell him of what passed between us. I can't understand why you should even want to buy from the Valmont silk farm. I think it is in questionable taste to want both a man's wares *and* his wife."

He became rigid with anger. "It would be if the incident between us had not ended as it did. I will remind you that I'm honor-bound to keep my agreement with Monsieur Valmont."

"I rescind whatever agreement existed on his behalf and take full responsibility for it. You are a Devaux and I am a Roche. Our families have never done business together."

"You *were* a Roche," he emphasized crisply. "As a Valmont you are in another category altogether."

"I'm still a Roche at heart."

Unexpectedly, he launched himself up out of the chair to slam both hands flat on the desk in front of her. "I have to overcome old prejudices against my family in Lyons if I am to reenter the Grande Fabrique, and I won't have the ground cut from under me by having it known that I wasn't considered a reliable customer by the Valmont silk farm!"

She stared at him unflinchingly. "The matter is closed."

He grabbed her by the wrists, pulling her to her feet on the opposite side of the desk. "Raw-silk buying has nothing to do with what is between us! You can't change that!"

She wrenched herself away from him, drawing back by her chair. "There is nothing between us! And your order is canceled!"

In the heat of the moment neither heard the handle of the door turn. Émile spoke from the doorway. "I must ask you to leave, Monsieur Devaux. I uphold my wife's decision."

They both swung around toward him, equally startled. Émile stood leaning for support against the doorjamb, his face ashen, Hélène holding him by one arm. Gabrielle gave a cry of concern. "You should never have come this far! It's too soon."

He ignored her, continuing to address Nicolas. "You heard me. And you have my word that this will remain a private matter."

"Then I'll not dispute your decision." Nicolas's face was still dark with anger. He picked up his hat and cane. "I'll take no more of Madame Valmont's time or yours." He bowed formally to each of them, then left the office at a stride.

Émile sagged weakly, and both women helped him to a chair. Gabrielle snatched a shawl to put around his shoulders, terrified he might suffer a full relapse. "What made you come here?"

Hélène answered. "It was my fault. I told Émile that someone called Devaux had arrived."

Gabrielle crouched down to look into his exhausted face. "How did you know I had refused Monsieur Devaux's order?"

He answered haltingly, breathless with exertion. "I didn't know until I heard what you were saying as I opened the door."

"Are you angry with me?"

Émile replied dryly, not taking his eyes from his wife, "Turning away a new customer and new orders is hardly likely to aid my peace of mind, or my pocket. Hélène, leave us, please."

As Hélène closed the door Gabrielle did not move from where she was. "I know I went against your wishes, and yet I can't pretend that I didn't enjoy being in charge."

He liked her frankness and candor. "I suppose I can't blame you for trying to get rid of Devaux," he conceded.

She saw his eyes had softened. "You are very understanding."

"If Devaux had been Bonaparte himself, I would never stand with another against my wife."

Impulsively she pressed her cheek fondly against the back of his hand. He had shown her the same loyalty that all along she had vowed to show him. Why, then, was the misery of Nicolas's departure making her scream inside as if she were dying?

ÉMILE's effort in reaching the office proved to be a turning point in his convalescence. Hélène went back home to Lyons, and every day Émile and Gabrielle spent a few hours at his desk going over the work she had done during his illness. Apart from some minor criticism, which was more to enlighten her than to find fault, he approved everything.

Then, one morning at breakfast, he said what she had been half expecting to hear for over a week. "There is no need for you to go to the office today. I'm sure you have plenty to do here, and it's time you made some social calls again."

As if to compensate for her brave nod of acceptance, he brought her a long-promised gift later that day. Some raw silk had come back from the workers, and he had filled a muslin-lined wicker basket with hanks that were white and lustrous, almost weightless.

"Here's the Valmont silk for your gown, my dear. Choose a color that you like, and the dyers shall dye it for you."

Her radiant expression was balm to him, for he wanted nothing to destroy the new harmony between them. In Gabrielle he had entirely the woman he wanted, and he was determined never to lose her.

She chose a soft apricot shade for the silk. On the day it was dispatched to the dyers, she spotted a notice in the newssheet, which she brought to Émile's attention.

"It says here that Joseph Jacquard is to demonstrate his new loom in Lyons. Jacquard was a weaver's son, who went successfully into hat-making, then loom-making. I should like to see the demonstration. Do let's go."

"I can't leave the business just now, my dear." He smiled at her. "Why don't you go? You could spend a few days at your father's house. It would do you good to visit Lyons again."

She left for the city two days later. The coach made good progress, and the journey took less than the usual hour. They entered Lyons by way of the hilly Fourvière quarter, and she told the coachman to halt for a few minutes at a certain point. Shimmering mistily in the heat, Lyons lay spread out below and up the hillside beyond; the Rhone and the Saône rivers threaded through the city like satin ribbons. She thought it wonderful to be returning to the city's throbbing life once more.

At her father's house, Hélène met her at the door and they embraced affectionately. Gabrielle noticed at once that there were shadows under her eyes. "Did your helping me with Émile's convalescence take its toll on you?" she asked.

Hélène shook her head. "No, no. I did so little. It was as much a rest for me as it was for him."

"Is it Father, then? Is he showing you no consideration?"

Hélène waived the query aside. "Don't look so worried. I've been suffering from the heat since my return home."

Gabrielle settled into her old room, and later Dominique received her in his office. He sat at his desk and greeted her stonily as she took a seat. "So Émile's silk crop is good this year."

"Yes, it is."

"It's rumored that the Devaux silk mill may be opened up again." He leaned forward in his chair, his expression one of malicious satisfaction. "Hélène told me how you refused the Devaux order and sent the fellow packing. Give me the details."

She had no intention of discussing it with him. "I did what had to be done. The authority was mine and I used it."

He rubbed his chin thoughtfully. He was beginning to see there was much of himself in Gabrielle. By her action over the Devaux matter she had shown that she was a Roche through and through, ruthless when the need arose. In addition, she seemed to be applying herself well to the responsibility of her husband's business at a time of emergency. "What brings you to Lyons now?" he asked.

"I want to see the Jacquard loom demonstrated. It may be that Maison Roche could benefit from changing to that loom if it should prove to be all that is claimed for it."

Dominique raised his bushy eyebrows cynically. "I remember Joseph Jacquard. He was, like the Devaux family, a traitor when Lyons was besieged. All he wants is to line his pockets. There'll be no change of looms for Roche silk unless Henri brings me an extremely convincing report."

She was affronted by his remark. "Henri has never sought change in his life."

"I suppose you would consider your opinion superior to his."

"I've always been ready to listen to new ideas and to judge for myself. I'll go to the demonstration with Henri and give you my own report." At that she left his office.

On the day of the demonstration it seemed as if the whole of Lyons were converging on the Place Sathonay. Weavers had left their looms to see the new invention for themselves, and the silk merchants and negotiators had filled the section reserved for them on one side of the platform on which the loom had been erected. It was with difficulty that Henri pushed a way through to the enclosure, with Gabrielle close behind.

At first sight there did not appear to be much difference in the loom except for a curious rectangular contraption supporting a circle of perforated cards, laced together and mounted on the top. Gabrielle saw that many of the low-ceilinged rooms that housed looms could not accommodate this extra height.

Henri, conscious of his own importance in silk circles, made sure that he and his sister came right to the front, where they could view the loom at close quarters. As he secured their places a civic dignitary mounted the steps to the platform. In his wake came Joseph Jacquard, a middle-aged man with mild eyes and thinning gray hair that fell straight on either side of his face.

The dignitary cleared his throat. "Citizens of Lyons! A man of our city comes before you today after an absence of some years during which he received a place personally recommended by General Bonaparte in the Conservatoire National des Arts et Métiers in Paris. Citizen Joseph Marie Jacquard has captured a combination of all the principles of weaving in his machine. I will now ask him to clarify the workings of this new loom."

The dignitary left the platform. Jacquard bowed before he addressed the crowd. His voice was thin, but it carried well in the attentive silence that had fallen.

"Fellow Lyonese! It is my earnest hope that my machine will bring a new prosperity to our city. It converts into a speedy process the making of the most complicated of figured silks." He spoke in some detail, then went to the loom and began to weave.

Gabrielle watched carefully. The pressing down of the treadle operated the harness and transformed the information on each punched card into the selection of the correct pattern of warp thread. When the treadle was released, the needles sprang back into position in readiness for the next card. She was deeply impressed. If this mechanism was generally adopted, it would increase the production of Lyons silk a thousandfold. And it would abolish forever the need to have little children crouch hour after hour under the looms to retie the threads as they broke.

"What do you think of it?" she asked Henri eagerly.

He shrugged noncommittally. "Silk would lose by it. There's no substitute for handwork."

"The loom produces the end product in either case," she said. "This would merely speed the process and help to bring down the cost of production. More people would be able to afford silk."

"Silk has never belonged to the hoi polloi. It never will, either, if I have anything to do with it."

She fell silent. Reaction among the other merchants seemed mixed; some were in favor of the new loom, some vehemently against it, for the same reasons as Henri. The rumble of their voices grew, but it was being outweighed by loud and undisciplined dissent from the weavers in the other part of the crowd.

"Your loom would bring starvation to us, Jacquard!" "What of work for our children?" "You're a traitor!" It was a mood of fear that gripped them, for they saw their number being diminished by this mechanized loom. They began to shake their fists at their would-be benefactor, but he tried to calm them down.

"My friends, you are mistaken! My mechanism would not decrease your work. It would increase it beyond your wildest dreams. And your children can grow tall and straight without their present labor that deforms their limbs! With my loom your income will rise steadily, as people in all walks of life find they are able to afford the lower prices of silk!"

The tumult of shouting and abuse was fast turning the weavers' crowd into a furious mob. The mention of lower prices had been the last straw. A single cry was taken up.

"Down with him! Throw him into the Rhone!"

Jacquard went pale and backed a pace or two toward his loom as the first of the mob began to clamber up onto the platform. Henri tried to hustle Gabrielle away, but their path was blocked by fellow merchants. Gabrielle, buffeted and crushed, glimpsed Nicolas as he swung up onto the platform to charge against the hostile attackers, hurling them back.

Bedlam erupted. Men swarmed up onto the platform from all sides, howling and bawling for Jacquard's blood. Gabrielle turned cold with horror as Nicolas and the hapless inventor became caught in the midst of them.

"Help those two men!" she cried in appeal to the merchants, but Henri was trying to pull her away with him.

"Have you gone mad?" he shouted. "We'll be drawn into this!"

As he spoke, Nicolas and Jacquard reappeared out of the melee, their clothes torn, to leap down onto the cobbles within a few feet of her. The inventor stumbled, but Nicolas yanked him upright and pushed the exhausted man forward. Pursuers came after them. Gabrielle stuck out her foot, and the leader tripped and fell headlong, causing others to collide behind him. This brought about a brief delay, and Henri, fearing the mob's wrath, was able to bear Gabrielle away. She looked back over her shoulder and saw that Jacquard's loom was being knocked to pieces with axes and mallets by those who had come prepared to destroy.

Later she heard that Jacquard had escaped and left Lyons in haste, fleeing his fellow townspeople for the second time in his life. Whether Nicolas had gone with him, nobody seemed to know. From the general gossip she learned that the Devaux and Jacquard families had been long acquainted; mentally Gabrielle commended Nicolas for going to the rescue of Joseph Jacquard.

Dominique taunted her with the fiasco of the Jacquard demonstration. "A fine waste of time that was. Jacquard won't dare show his face in Lyons again for many a year, I can tell you that."

She feared he was right, and was saddened by it. By way of consoling herself she remembered that during the time she had managed the Valmont silk farm, she had had dealings with a Madame Hoinville, a stouthearted widow who owned several looms in Lyons. When Madame Hoinville had negotiated with her for raw silk, she had made it known that she appreciated Jacquard's innovations.

Now, soon after Joseph Jacquard's flight, Gabrielle went to inspect the widow's small mill in the weaving district. Within her ancient house Madame Hoinville had two workshops with two looms in each. From the establishment's street level a couple of stone steps led down to a floor that had been lowered in the distant past to accommodate the height of the looms, although not even these rooms would be able to hold the extra height of the Jacquard mechanism.

The talk between the widow and Gabrielle turned inevitably to the Jacquard demonstration. "It was a pity that loom was destroyed before I could get a closer look at it," Madame Hoinville said. "I should like to see my weavers' burdens lightened. Even the strongest of the women tire quickly at these looms, and their poor backs pay the price." She put a hand to her own spine. "Since I take my turn working with them, I know what a benefit Monsieur Jacquard's invention would be."

"I agree completely," said Gabrielle.

The work that the Hoinville looms produced was selective and exquisite. Gabrielle thought it no wonder that the enterprising widow had created her own niche in such a competitive market.

When she left the premises Gabrielle turned homeward in a direction that would take her past the Devaux property. As she came level with it on the opposite side of the street, she saw that the house was closed and shuttered.

HÉLÈNE'S baby was born in December of that year of 1804, the same month in which Napoléon Bonaparte became Emperor of France. Dominique did not hide his disgust that his daughter-in-law had given birth to a girl. A grandson would have been a hope for the future of the business, but a granddaughter was useless.

By the end of three months Dominique had developed a senile jealousy of healthy, bonny little Juliette, who deprived him of Hélène's undivided attention. The truth was that he felt himself abandoned in the midst of his own family. He thought it a bitter trick of fate that Jules, the only child who was dear to him, should always be far away. He knew that his older son, Henri, was in for a fine shock when his will was read, a joke Dominique would be enjoying from his grave. Jules was the one who, ending his soldiering days in the face of unexpected riches, would receive full inheritance of Maison Roche and carry on its tradition. Surely by that time Hélène should have borne him a son or two.

With this in mind Dominique made no objection when Hélène told him that she intended to visit Jules, who had been posted to the Channel coast in preparation for the emperor's planned invasion of England. Gabrielle accompanied Hélène and the baby on their journey to Boulogne. They traveled in a Roche carriage, attended by a coachman and two maids.

The journey went well. As they neared the seaport they could see the tents of those following the soldiers clustered untidily at the edge of the large army encampments. Here and there goats were tethered and hens clucked in coops, for there were only half rations for officially recognized wives and children, and none at all for those without a legitimate claim to support.

Jules had posted a lookout, and before the carriage reached the gates of Boulogne, he came riding at a gallop to meet them. As soon as the carriage stopped and the women got out, he joyously embraced his wife. When Juliette was put into his arms, she rewarded him with a smile, and he was filled with pride. Again he and his wife kissed, the baby nestled between them. As the journey continued he rode alongside the carriage, talking to Hélène and Gabrielle through the open window.

"I'm afraid the accommodations I found for you are far from luxurious; yet I was lucky to get them. Every room is in demand."

He had not exaggerated the congestion of the town. Boulogne had become one vast army camp, teeming with soldiers, cannon, wagons and other equipment. The Grande Armée had gathered its strength into two hundred thousand men for the onslaught across the Channel. Only one barrier was delaying them. England's Royal Navy still had mastery of the seas, and there was no point in putting barges of troops out into the Channel for them to be sunk halfway across.

The accommodations Jules had found were in a small inn, and Gabrielle had to share a room with Hélène and the baby. It was only when Gabrielle went out that husband and wife were able to be alone together. As a result, Gabrielle came to know Boulogne almost as well as she knew Lyons. She spent hours strolling by the seawalls, exploring the winding streets and the markets. In a shop in a narrow side street she found a rare silk moth in a carved box and bought it for Émile to add to his collection.

The time passed quickly, and the end of June came with no sign of any movement being launched across the Channel. Rumor had it that Jules's regiment might soon be moving out in an easterly direction, since Austria and Russia were massing forces in readiness for an attack. Soon an order came through that the hussars were to leave Boulogne for another destination. Hélène courageously accepted the imminence of Jules's departure.

Two days later she and Gabrielle stood by the seawall to watch Jules ride out of Boulogne with his regiment. With the standard flying and the pipers and drummers of the band leading the way, the hussars were a spectacular sight in their red-plumed helmets, fur-lined cloaks, and crimson boots. Hélène held Juliette high in her arms, and Jules saluted them both proudly. When she could no longer see him, Hélène broke down. Gabrielle took the baby from her and helped her into the waiting carriage.

It was not long after Gabrielle's return home that the emperor abandoned his plans to invade England, and the bulk of the Grande Armée left Boulogne to meet the growing threat of attack in southern Germany. Then, in October, the British fleet scored a tremendous victory at Trafalgar; many French and Spanish vessels were sunk. All chance of a French invasion of England in the foreseeable future had been effectively destroyed.

Meanwhile Gabrielle occupied herself with the business of selecting dyes for the new silk crop and visiting the dyers. Émile was busy all the time and happy with her, and so she was content.

As autumn turned to winter, the newssheets reported with triumph the victories of the Grande Armée at Ulm and Austerlitz. Never had France had such a brilliant leader. By mid-December the Austrians had surrendered unconditionally, and the czar's forces had retreated into their own country.

Early in the new year of 1806 Gabrielle came out of the house one morning to find Émile waiting for her at the foot of the steps. "Have you left your work to come for a walk with me?" she asked lightheartedly, drawing on her gloves. Then she saw the grave expression on his face. A sense of foreboding overcame her. Her question came shakily. "What is it?"

"I have bad news, I'm afraid," he said sadly. "A messenger from your father's house just came to the office. Word was received in Lyons that Jules died twelve days ago of wounds received on the battlefield at Austerlitz."

Every vestige of color drained from her face. Émile darted up the steps to her, and she threw herself into his comforting arms.

 It WAS due to the determination of a hussar sergeant that Jules's body was brought home for burial. Officers, unless of exceptionally high rank, were usually buried near the battlefield, but Jules had once said he would like his final resting place to be in Lyons. Sergeant Gaston Garcin had heard him and remembered.

Gaston had been through every campaign with Jules since he had joined the regiment. And Gaston was wounded in the leg at the same time Jules suffered his fatal wounds. As a result, he found himself invalided out of the army. With his left leg still swathed in bandages, he began the long journey with the coffin-wagon out of Austria and across France.

In his mid-thirties, he was a broadly built, hefty towhead with onyx eyes. Large ears flanked his rough-hewn face. He had been a good soldier, clearheaded in a crisis, and had been proud to serve his country as a cavalryman. Basically an optimist, he enjoyed the excitement of the campaigns and knew that he would feel lost without them. And he was going to miss the horses as much as he would miss his comrades.

During the journey, people in the towns, villages and hamlets stood in respect as he drove past with the flag-wrapped coffin. On the outskirts of Lyons he unfolded a fresh Tricolor and spread it over the coffin to complete Jules's final homecoming in full splendor.

Gaston was sighted as soon as he turned into the Rue Clémont. When he drew up in front of the house, the family, alerted to Gaston's imminent arrival in a letter from a commanding officer, had gathered on the steps. Hélène came toward him. He clambered down awkwardly from the driving seat, his leg cramped with pain, and she spoke to him gently. "I thank you with all my heart for bringing my husband home to me, Sergeant Garcin."

Gabrielle also thanked him with all sincerity for his kind action. The servants then came to shoulder the coffin and bear it inside.

After the funeral Hélène received Gaston on her own in her salon. For over an hour they were closeted together while he told her of Jules's last days, and recounted anything he could remember of happier times. When she gave way to tears, he sat patiently until she dried her eyes and was ready to talk again.

"What are your plans now?" she asked him. He had already told her that he had no family.

"To find work, madame. I'm strong, and good with my hands. My game leg is not going to stop me from getting around."

"I think I can help you. I shall speak to my brother-in-law. I'm sure he will be able to provide employment for you."

Gaston was appreciative. Unemployment was high in these times, for war had brought its own financial difficulties to commercial interests.

Henri, having no need of an extra hand himself, sent Gaston with a letter to a civic official of his acquaintance. As a result, he found himself employed, but in the city's foulest and lowest-paid work—clearing household cesspits during the night. Hélène, however, was told by Henri only that Gaston was working for the city, and thus pictured him secure in a post of responsibility.

SEVEN months later the Roche family gathered for another funeral. Dominique had been grief-stricken by the death of his favorite son and had never recovered. For three days he had allowed no one in the family to come near him, although servants were permitted to come and go. Then, on the evening of the third day, he had suffered a massive stroke that left him paralyzed.

Hélène had been with Dominique constantly. When he died, the family were all around his bedside, but it was she who held his hand. Gabrielle's grief was tearless, and the more harrowing for it. She was filled with sorrow for what had never been between her father and herself. She would not have attended the reading of Dominique's will if the lawyer had not insisted that every member of the family be present in the grand salon.

There were some small bequests, which included an income

for Hélène until such time as she should marry again. Then came the moment for which Henri and Yvonne had been waiting. The lawyer cleared his throat.

" 'The rest of my estate, my house and its contents together with Maison Roche,' " the lawyer read, " 'I bequeath to my daughter, Gabrielle Valmont, to be held in trust for any son, or grandson, of hers. In the event of her failing to have such issue, the estate shall pass to my granddaughter, Juliette Roche, and in turn be held in trust for her son. It is my earnest wish and belief that Gabrielle will bring to the business the initiative and imagination that once were mine.' " There was stunned silence as the lawyer looked up from the document. "That is all, mesdames and messieurs."

Gabrielle sat dazed. Maison Roche was hers! Her dream had come true.

Henri, meanwhile, leaped from his chair with a great roar. "Damn him! Damn him to hell! Maison Roche is my birthright! I'll contest the will. I'll prove he was senile when he signed it."

The lawyer shook his head. "I drew it up two days after he had heard of Jules's death, and Dominique requested that a doctor be present so that he be judged of sane mind."

"He changed it *after* Jules's death?" Henri glared, jowls shaking as comprehension dawned. "The old devil never meant me to have the business, did he? He left it to his golden boy until an enemy cannon put an end to that dream, then bequeathed everything to Gabrielle instead. A woman! Untrained and useless. The daughter he hated from the day of her birth!"

Émile rose abruptly from the sofa, where he had been sitting beside his wife. "I will hear no more of these insults, Henri. Gabrielle has come into this inheritance through her own determination to learn the silk trade as well as any man. I'm sure we all wish Jules had lived to receive this inheritance, but since it has come to Gabrielle, she deserves the full support of her family."

Gabrielle looked up at him gratefully.

Henri now rounded in exasperation on his wife, who was sobbing noisily. "Be silent, woman! Haven't I enough to endure without your caterwauling? Maybe if I'd taken my father's sound

225

advice to divorce you for your spendthrift ways, I wouldn't have found myself in this ignominious position!"

Yvonne was furious, her face flushed high. "Don't try to shift the blame onto me! You shouldn't have quarreled with him so much. But that's like you, always thinking you're right!"

With an exclamation of wrath he seized her by the arm, wrenching her to her feet, and thrust her out of the room before him. Their quarreling faded out of earshot.

Hélène, who still sat on one of the scroll-ended sofas, watched the lawyer bow over Gabrielle's hand, offering to be of assistance at any time. Of those who had listened to the will, Hélène had been the least surprised by its contents, recalling how highly Dominique had come to regard Gabrielle after her handling of the silk farm during Émile's illness. Getting up from her seat, she went across to her sister-in-law to embrace her in her good fortune.

During the night Émile awoke from sleep to find that Gabrielle was not there. For a while he did not stir, thinking over the change that had come about in their lives. She had made clear to him her determination to run Maison Roche in the discussion they had had after coming to bed. He had thought it prudent to say nothing of the private talk he had had with Henri in the library. His brother-in-law had calmed down by that time, and it was agreed that Gabrielle should be given the reins for a few weeks, long enough for her to believe she had everything running her way. Then Henri and Émile himself would both exert pressure to get her to relinquish her responsibilities and become head of Maison Roche in name only.

Now his brow creased in a thoughtful frown. He had heard in business circles that Devaux had put to rights the damage done to his property in Lyons and had made the old looms serviceable again. Émile recalled the unease he had experienced when he saw his wife and Devaux alone in his office. Yet his wife was not one to be led astray by any would-be seducer. No, it was not Devaux he need fear as far as Gabrielle was concerned, for it was not another man who would ever drive a wedge between them. It was her own good fortune in receiving a rich inheritance.

"Damnation to it all!" Thoroughly disgruntled, he flung back the bedclothes and put his feet on the floor. He slipped his dressing gown over his nightshirt as he went from the room and down the stairs. As he had expected, a chink of light showed under the door of his late father-in-law's office, which Gabrielle had already decided to make her own. He pushed the door open.

She looked up from a pile of documents that she was leafing through as she sat at her father's desk, her feet showing bare beneath the hem of her nightgown.

"This is madness!" he pronounced angrily. "There's no need for you to be working at this hour."

She sat back calmly in the chair. "I couldn't sleep, and there's so much to be done. I can't discuss anything with Henri until I'm up to date with every fact and figure."

"Come to bed!"

"I think not. I'll read for a while longer."

His temper snapped. All he could think of was the threat that Roche silk would take her away from him. He had never laid hands on her roughly before, but now he seized her, wrenching her to her feet. She struggled against him, resisting the urge to cry out for fear of waking the household. He overpowered her and carried her back through the hall, upstairs and into their room, where he threw her down on the bed.

She had endured it all without a sound. Now she rolled her head away from him, resisting his attempts to turn her face back toward him. Then, suddenly, he flung himself down beside her and began to sob—heavy, wrenching sobs that shook the bed. Half raising herself, she looked at him. He was lying flat on his stomach, face in the pillows, his arms outflung, his hands clenched in despair. A tender, considerate man, he had developed an ungovernable rage because he could not bear to share her, not even with Maison Roche.

Unable to withstand such grief in another human being, she put out her hand to stroke his hair. At her touch he raised his tortured face to look at her. Reading compassion in her eyes, he hesitated only briefly before putting an arm around her waist to draw her close to him. She cradled him, and eventually he slept.

It was then that her own silent tears flowed. In anguish she yearned to be able to turn the clock back to her wedding day. Fate had given her a last-minute chance to change the course of her life and direct it toward another man. For Émile's sake, as well as her own, she should have seized it.

HÉLÈNE listened attentively when Gabrielle told her of Jules's wish that his wife should not remain in the house after Dominique's death. It had been settled that Henri and Yvonne should continue to live there. "But Jules did not know you would be mistress of the family house," Hélène replied. "You will need someone to be in charge of your housekeeping arrangements."

"I'll appoint a housekeeper. You must be free now to make your own home with Juliette. That's what Jules wanted."

"But I like living here." Hélène glanced about her at the small salon that was hers. Circular in shape, its walls were covered in a fruit-and-flower-patterned damask. "It was in this house that Jules was born and grew up. I feel close to him here, now more than ever before." Her eyes were full of appeal. "Don't make me leave yet. I will in time. When I'm ready."

Gabrielle knew she must respect her sister-in-law's wishes, but she immediately appointed a capable housekeeper. Hélène was thereby able to devote time at last to Juliette, and she found consolation in being with her.

Next Gabrielle interviewed several designers, looking for artists with clever new ideas. Eventually she engaged a young man named Marcel Donnet, who had recently come to Lyons from Paris. His work was brilliant. She asked him if he had seen the Jacquard loom.

"Yes, madame." His face sharpened with interest. "Have you considered introducing this mechanism?"

She set her elbows on the desk. "I'm keeping an open mind. I must try weaving on one of them myself before I make a decision. Do you think the finished product loses by this loom?"

"Not at all. On the contrary. Many human errors are eradicated."

After he had left, Gabrielle found herself heartened, and she needed heartening at the present time. Her relationship with

Émile was considerably strained by her devotion to Maison Roche, for she was spending more and more time away from him to be in Lyons. As for Henri, she had the feeling he was watching her like a hawk. When she had explained this to Émile, he had merely shrugged and said it would be much better for her, and for him, if she allowed Henri to be her manager.

Late one Friday afternoon she decided to do no more work that day. She had promised Émile she would leave Lyons and go home to the silk farm to be with him until Monday. It was a bitter cold December. She was warmly dressed, and in the carriage she had a muff for her hands. She had been thinking of investing in some younger, faster horses and buying one of the new speedy calashes that would be able to make the journey between Lyons and the silk farm in less time. Then, perhaps, she could get home for an overnight stay once or twice during the week.

As she rode, her attention was drawn suddenly to a beggar who was slumped against a wall as if he no longer had the strength to stand alone. It was the military color of his ragged coat that caught her eye. The man was thin as a skeleton, his unshaven face stamped by hunger. She recognized him.

"Stop!" she ordered the coachman. Alighting quickly, she ran to the beggar. "Gaston Garcin! What has happened to you?"

"Madame Valmont." He was filled with shame and tried to stand up straight. "I've had a spell of misfortune. It will pass."

"But I heard you were employed by the city."

"I fell ill, madame. A contagion contracted through my work. Since my recovery I have been unable to get anything else."

"Your recovery! You still look far from well to me." She remembered how fine his military bearing had been at Jules's funeral in spite of his wounded leg. "You're coming home with me," she said to him. "I'm going to see that you get well and strong again."

He passed a hand across his eyes, embarrassed by the tears that were rolling down his face. "You have saved my life, madame."

At the silk farm, Gabrielle discussed Gaston's future with Émile. He was in full agreement that employment should be given to the man, but he disagreed strongly with the situation Gabrielle wanted to offer him.

"A new calash is an unwarranted extravagance, as is making Gaston your coachman. He can work on the silk farm."

"I've made up my mind," she replied firmly. "I've seen a calash at a coachbuilder's in the Place des Célestins and it's exactly what I want. If you would care to come help me purchase the horses, I should be grateful."

"My wishes are not important?" he asked bitterly.

"You know they are," she protested. "This whole idea came about because I want to get home to you as quickly as possible."

He was unimpressed, and retreated into one of his quiet, withdrawn moods. Yet, when the time came for her to buy new horses, he went with her to ensure that she received the best available. Gaston was fitted out with new clothes and drove the calash in a dark blue caped greatcoat while the cold weather lasted, and with the coming of spring he was able to display his black-and-white-striped waistcoat and his lightweight blue coat with brass buttons. A wide-brimmed black hat turned up in the front, with a military cockade from his old regiment, gave him a dashing appearance.

Almost from the first day she had taken over Maison Roche, Gabrielle had felt that too much bread-and-butter work was done in recent years. This was silk in traditional designs made for retail sales shops as well as for dressmaking and upholstery workshops. She did not belittle the importance of such work, for it kept the looms going, but with her new designer, Marcel Donnet, she was aiming for the attention of the Mobilier Impérial. This was the Paris-based committee that had the authority to restore the great palaces of France and to commission beautiful furnishings for them. Gabrielle was certain that Marcel's marvelous designs were worthy of a commission from the Mobilier Impérial, and she was having samples woven for presentation. When they were ready, Henri would leave for Paris with them.

She and Henri were examining some of the completed samples when he gave her the news she had long awaited. "Devaux is back in Lyons. To stay this time, I hear. He's taking on weavers for his mill in the Croix-Rousse."

Her heart leaped. How was it possible for her to have this reaction to hearing Nicolas's name spoken after such a long time?

"I thought his silk interests were in Paris," she said levelly.

"He has sold them. Held out for a high price, I was told." Henri indicated the samples on the table before him. "If he's thinking of competing with us, he's in for a surprise. In all my years in silk I've rarely seen anything better than what we have here."

When all of the samples for the Mobilier Impérial were ready, Gabrielle supervised the packing of them herself. On the morning that Henri departed for Paris, she went into the design room to tell Marcel that his work was on its way. He put the brush he was using back in its jar before getting up and bringing over another high stool for her to sit on.

"Let's hope Monsieur Roche secures the commissions we're looking for," he said, reseating himself.

"It would be a turning point for Maison Roche. Of course, we stand a good chance with your designs."

He leaned an arm on the sloping surface of his drawing desk. "Speaking of turning points, there's something I've heard about the Devaux mill."

"Yes?" She was immediately alert.

"I was told that the new Jacquard looms have been installed throughout by Monsieur Devaux."

She felt an odd burst of excitement. She welcomed the chance to compete with Nicolas in the manufacture of Lyons silks, to match her designs against his, to become his rival in the race to secure commissions. She truly believed that rivalry was the only way to dispel the yearning that had no place in her life.

"Isn't he expecting labor troubles after what happened at Joseph Jacquard's demonstration?" she wanted to know.

"Ah, it's a few years since that demonstration took place, and last year was the hardest the industry has experienced for a long time. Men who are desperate for work are not going to turn down this chance. There may be demonstrations, but if Monsieur Devaux has the workers he wants, it is not going to trouble him."

"How I should like to see inside that mill."

"Monsieur Devaux probably has design secrets that he'll be guarding closely. It's my guess he won't let strangers in."

She smiled to herself. Marcel had no way of guessing that she did not consider herself to be a stranger to Nicolas, but business was business and they were competitors now.

She proved to be right in her belief that Nicolas would meet strong opposition to his Jacquard looms. She heard a few days later that independent weavers had advanced on Maison Devaux with bludgeons, homemade pikes, and rocks to throw. It had taken a strong force of police to disperse them, and many arrests had been made. She also heard that Nicolas's carriage had been stoned.

Gabrielle's desire to see the interior of his mill persisted. She could not dismiss it. Late one evening she asked the housekeeper to bring Gaston to her. As soon as he appeared she outlined a plan she had made and explained the help she needed from him.

He looked at her steadily for a long, unblinking moment. "What you ask can be done," he said at last. "Leave everything to me."

"Thank you, Gaston," she said with feeling. "I was certain I could rely on you."

Henri returned from Paris a week later. He was cautiously optimistic. The Mobilier Impérial had informed him that he would be notified of their decision in the near future.

During the days that followed, Gabrielle had to learn patience. Gaston made no comment on whatever he was doing to further her secret plan. One morning when he came to see her in her office she knew that he had finally made the necessary arrangements. "You want some money for the bribes now?" she asked.

"The sum to be paid is almost negligible, madame." Amused self-satisfaction passed across his face. "I made it my business to strike up an acquaintance with a young woman named Hortense, who winds thread for the Devaux mill. When I asked a particular favor of her, she did not refuse me."

"Indeed?" Gabrielle observed.

He gave an oddly crooked grin. "The only money needed is for Hortense's sister, a fellow worker. You will take her place for a day. All the girl wants is compensation for her loss of pay."

"And how much is required?" Gabrielle took out her purse.

He told her. It was a modest amount, and she added extra.

The day came for Gabrielle to take the girl's place. Suitably attired in a cotton cap, plain print dress and sturdy shoes, she left the house with Gaston just before dawn. It was quite a long walk to their destination, but a Roche carriage or her own calash would be noticed in the early morning streets near the Devaux mill.

As the sky filled with rising gold, Gaston led her down a dank alleyway, where he knocked on a door. It opened, and Gaston's acquaintance, Hortense, admitted them; her sister lay curled up asleep on a wall bed. Hortense was a strong-looking girl, with fine dark eyes. She addressed Gabrielle.

"*Bonjour*, citizeness. My sister and I are doing this as a favor to Gaston. If you're nabbed, say you're just an outworker who heard that my sister was sick and you asked to take her place. Do you have a noon piece?"

Gabrielle patted her apron pocket, where she carried a packet of bread and cheese. "Yes, I have."

"Come along, then."

When the three of them reached the end of the alleyway, Hortense blew Gaston a kiss from her fingertips and turned up the street with Gabrielle.

"How do you like working at the Devaux mill?" Gabrielle asked her as they hurried along.

"It was frightening at first, when the mob gathered outside, but now Monsieur Devaux has his own force of law keepers."

"What about the working conditions for you and the others?"

"Good. Wages are fair, and we can earn bonuses. The hours are long, but that's the same as everywhere else. Did you know Monsieur Devaux was born in Lyons?" Hortense did not wait for a reply, but chattered on. "He's a handsome man, no doubt about it. There's a woman from Paris, a Madame Marache, staying at his house now. She's quite a beauty." She drew breath. "Here we are. Keep your head down and follow me."

Male and female workers entered by the same side entrance. In the hallway there was chatter among them as hats and coats were hung on pegs. Some were already in the workshops and had set their looms going. To Gabrielle the looms had a new and unfamiliar sound. Gone was the *thwack, thwack* of the old handloom. This loom had a voice of its own—*bistonclaque, bistonclaque*.

At Hortense's side, she went into the loom room that opened

out of the hall, careful not to draw the attention of the *maître ouvrier*. And with Hortense she fetched the rich yellow hanks she needed for winding. Sitting down at her wheel, Gabrielle began the work of winding the continuous fine and glossy thread of the hank onto a bobbin. It was quite a few years since she had learned to wind, but the old skill soon came back to her. As she worked she began to take note of her surroundings.

She saw that this loom room had been of normal height, but the whole of the floor above it had been removed, leaving plenty of space for the mechanism at the top of the Jacquard looms. Beyond the first loom room was another. Gabrielle estimated there were at least seventy looms in operation.

"Watch what you're doing!" Hortense hissed, leaning over from the neighboring winder. "You're overwinding."

With dismay Gabrielle saw she had put too much silk onto the bobbin, and she had to rewind it. Later, when she had done several, these bobbins would be collected by one of the few children now employed at the Devaux mill for similar tasks.

Gabrielle's confidence grew, her speed on the winding wheel increased, and by the noon break she had become quite proficient.

In midafternoon some trouble developed on one of the looms in the other workroom. She could see the *maître ouvrier* on a ladder beside a repairer, investigating the trouble. It gave her the chance she was waiting for. She had seen that the designer's workshop was adjacent to the storeroom where the hanks were kept. On the pretext of fetching another, she paused by his door, tapped on it and entered quickly, closing it behind her. The designer, a young man, sat on a stool before his sloping desk. He paused in his work to look over his shoulder. "Yes, mam'selle?"

"I'm sorry to interrupt you, but I'm new here and I want to learn everything. Could you tell me exactly what you are doing?"

He was struck by her well-spoken voice and lovely face. "Come and take a look," he invited good-naturedly. He explained how he was transferring the sketch, which was of a new pattern shortly to go into production. It was of bees woven in gold on a rich blue background. "A card cutter will use my draft to punch holes in the cards, which will then be laced together as you see over there." He indicated some cards already laced and hanging on a frame. "The holes will convey the pattern on the loom. Every time the circle of these punched cards goes around, the pattern is repeated along the length of the fabric."

She asked him a few more questions, then thanked him and left. Of the work being done on the Jacquard looms, she had seen more than she had bargained for. And she had seen more than enough to know that herein lay the whole future of Lyons silk; the work being turned out was perfection. And the pattern of the golden bees on the designer's desk told her that Nicolas had a commission from the Mobilier Impérial, for Bonaparte had taken the bee as his imperial emblem. Nobody could weave the bee except by the emperor's express demand. Nicolas was much farther ahead of her than she had expected.

It was near the end of the working day when events took an unexpected turn. "Monsieur Devaux has just come in," Hortense said, giving her a prod. "He's looking at that faulty loom."

Overcome by curiosity, Gabrielle rose from her seat to get a better view and saw that Nicolas stood beside the repairer. Then she caught sight of a fashionable woman, tallish with feline looks, wandering along and glancing at the looms. This must be his guest and present companion, Madame Marache.

Abruptly Gabrielle sat down again and bent her head industriously over her work. Out of the corner of her eye she saw the woman approach; her long-sleeved gown of carnation velvet was worn with satin shoes to match. At the sight of the winders Madame Marache raised her eyebrows.

"What is going on here?" Her voice was attractive, her tone half amused. Hortense answered her, explaining the task in hand and its purpose. A ringed forefinger tapped Gabrielle patronizingly on the shoulder. "Let me take your seat, girl. I should like to try this bobbin winding with your tulip-yellow thread."

Dismayed, Gabrielle gave up her seat. The last thing she wanted was to be standing up conspicuously if Nicolas should come this way. Fortunately, Hortense rose to instruct Madame Marache, and Gabrielle took Hortense's place.

The woman proved to be surprisingly deft, but what was a

game to her was a loss of earnings to Hortense, who glowered. Gabrielle, glancing across the room, was alarmed to see Nicolas approaching the winders' section. Her heart began to hammer against her ribs, and she bent her head still farther over her work to avoid any chance of his recognizing her. Worst of all was the bittersweetness of being near him again.

"Is this where you are, Suzanne?" he exclaimed with a chuckle, sighting Madame Marache at the winding wheel.

"Come and look, Nicolas. I'm doing well, am I not?"

Gabrielle did not dare to look up, and so she was only able to see as far as the middle buttons on his cream silk waistcoat. He moved around to stand behind Madame Marache, taking both her shoulders into the curved palms of his hands. "Splendid! Who would have thought that I'd gain a new winder in my mill today?"

"Have you mended the faulty loom?" she asked.

"It was nothing more than a simple adjustment. Shall we go?"

She stood up then, sliding a hand into the crook of his arm, heedless of the disruption to work she had caused. It was he who thanked Hortense for showing Madame Marache how to use the winding wheel. As the two of them strolled back along the aisle, Hortense swore savagely over her loss of time and money. Gabrielle, changing places to sit at her wheel again, stood briefly to look after Nicolas and the woman in his life. She saw him pause to have a word with the *maître ouvrier*, Suzanne Marache going ahead of him through a doorway. The *maître ouvrier* glanced back at the winding section, and Gabrielle took her seat quickly, out of sight.

When a handbell rang at six o'clock, the winders sighed with relief, halting their wheels. The looms fell silent and the weavers took brooms to sweep up their scraps of silk and thread. Gabrielle took her shawl from its peg and wrapped it around her. She was leaving with Hortense but not going back home with her. Gaston would be waiting a short distance away.

There was quite a crush of people in the doorway. As Gabrielle reached the threshold and felt the cool evening air on her face, a heavy hand fell on her shoulder and gripped her hard.

"Not you! You're not leaving yet."

It was the *maître ouvrier*. At the last minute he had noticed she was a stranger. She reacted swiftly, wrenching around to loosen his grip, but it was in vain. The man seized her with powerful hands then, holding her in the hallway. When the last workers had hustled out, he said to Gabrielle, "What are you doing here? That has to be explained."

"It's simple," she answered. "I needed work, and one of the winders was sick. I took her place."

"I'll do my investigations among the workers tomorrow. For the moment the matter is out of my hands. Monsieur Devaux wants to see you in his study. I'm to take you there."

When she made no attempt to follow him, her face drained of color, he beckoned impatiently. "It's no good thinking you can persuade me to let you go. Now come along."

He led the way through both loom rooms to a small inner courtyard dividing the mill from the house. As she crossed the threshold into Nicolas's home, he himself stood by an open doorway leading off the hallway. "This way, Gabrielle," he said in a hard voice. She lifted her chin, summoning her courage. With even steps she walked past him into his study and went to stand by the fire. He closed the door, and they were alone together.

CHAPTER FIVE

"WHY?" Nicolas demanded harshly. "Of all people, why should you become what I can only term a spy?"

She swung around to face him. He was only a few feet from her, and he had so much anger in his eyes that she almost flinched. "I didn't think of it as spying. All I wanted was to see how you had adapted your building to take the height of the Jacquard looms."

"You could've asked me to show you."

"I was in no position to ask favors. We are now rivals in business. I admit I was in the wrong by coming here today, but in some ways it was an irresistible adventure."

He took a step toward her, as if he wanted to shake her in rage. "Adventure is not the word I would have chosen for tricking my designer into showing you our most secret pattern. It never occurred to him that an ordinary mill girl would understand the significance of the imperial bee. But you did!" He gave a sigh and rested his weight on the edge of his desk. "And now that you know how I've fitted in the Jacquard looms, do you intend to do the same?"

"Yes, if I'm not sent to prison."

"I'll not press charges." He still sounded grim. "I'm just thoroughly out of temper with you."

She moved with relief to take a chair. "If you mean what you say, I'm thankful for it."

"I mean it. As a matter of fact, I welcome you as a rival in the silk trade." He studied her from where he sat. "I hear you have been through the affairs of Maison Roche like the proverbial new broom and have changed almost everything."

She stiffened warily. "How could you know about that?"

"I've heard all I need to know from general talk. Your name is on everyone's lips as a new force to contend with in Lyons."

She sensed that the atmosphere was changing swiftly between them. Until now a degree of hostility had kept all else at bay, but their yearning for each other was coming to the fore again. He had moved his hands to grip the edges of the desk, almost as though he thought they might reach for her by their own volition, and she felt her insides melt at the thought of being held by him. It was time to leave. "I must go now."

He led her through the house to the front door. He opened it for her, then barred her way with his arm. "We're two of a kind," he said intently. "I look forward to competing with you for commissions from the Mobilier Impérial in the future."

"I shall welcome the competition." Then she was unable to resist asking him a question. "How did you know it was I in the winders' section this afternoon?"

He brought his face nearer hers. "I would know you anywhere."

She saw he was going to kiss her, and she was powerless to move, exulting in the prospect, her lids lowering as his mouth came closer. Then a step on the stairs shattered the moment, and Suzanne Marache's voice cut through to them.

"*Là, là!* There you are, Nicolas. Our food is getting cold."

His arm fell away from the door, and Gabrielle darted through it, escaping into the evening air, the return of sanity like a physical shock. But that night she lay awake, unable to stop wondering how it would have been between them.

In the morning she was back in her office working with renewed energy, taking the only course of escape from hopeless dreams that was open to her. When she heard not long afterward that Suzanne Marache had returned to Paris, she told herself that it was of no significance. Nicolas would soon take somebody else into his life. Even so, he would be no farther from her than he was already, for Émile would always stand between them.

HENRI received with dismay and disbelief the news that his sister intended to install Jacquard looms for the weaving of Roche silk. "You're out of your mind! The weavers would never tolerate them. You saw that for yourself. In any case, their houses aren't built to accommodate the height of those looms."

"I've considered every point you could possibly raise and I'm going ahead," she said. "There's an old convent that was abandoned when the revolutionary Convention outlawed Christianity. I've offered a fair price and believe it will be mine."

"You would turn it into a mill?" Henri could scarcely believe what he had heard. He glared at her belligerently. "I'll not let you do this. I'll query it with the lawyers."

"Calm yourself," she advised. "The lawyers are on my side, and the looms have already been ordered."

"This will ruin the business. I'll oppose you all the way!"

Her face grew stern. "Then you'll be the loser, Henri. Are you with me or against me? Make your choice."

After spluttering in exasperation, he gave a reluctant nod. "I can see I must stay with you for your own good."

When she was alone, she thought how her life had become a series of battles. She had to contend with Henri every day in Lyons, and whenever she was at home in the country, Émile tried to persuade her not to go into Lyons more than once a week.

"I'm not being unreasonable," he said patiently during her very next visit. "I miss you, my dear. It's lonely in the house when you're not here."

She had given up arguing that if she spent only one day in Lyons she would be reduced to a figurehead, with Henri in charge, because she had soon grasped that this was exactly what Émile wanted. Instead, she implored, "Please don't feel neglected." He had taken her onto his knees where he sat in his chair, and she had her hands linked behind his neck. Always when she was at home she demonstrated very deep affection for him.

"I love you, Gabrielle," he said gently. "If I did not, it would be a different matter. Why—"

She interrupted him. "Why am I not like other wives?"

He gave a laugh. "I wouldn't have you be any different, even if you do have a brain that is more suited to a man than a woman." His gaze on her softened. "I was about to say, Why is it, I wonder, that you have not yet given me a child?"

She turned her head away. Certainly she wanted a son to inherit Maison Roche. "The time will come," she said huskily.

"I believe the same. Your body is too perfect for there to be the flaw of barrenness in you."

· Later, lying in his arms, she pondered her failure to conceive. Always after their lovemaking she felt that something indefinable had eluded her, some spark left unignited. Maybe if her fondness for Émile could develop a little more, just to tip the scales to love, conception would follow. Then reason took over, causing her anguish. How could she ever hope to love Émile when another man kept her heart from him?

WHEN Gabrielle approached her weavers about coming to work the new looms she had ordered, they were suspicious and dubious; she even received threats and warnings, such as rocks hurled through the windows of the new mill. But by the time the final papers were signed and the convent became hers, she had hired almost a full complement of weavers for the number of looms about to be installed.

She supervised the positioning of the looms herself, having worked out exactly where they should be erected for maximum space and ease of access. And after the work started, a police watch was kept on the building in case there should be disturbances. When nothing occurred to disrupt the peace, the police were withdrawn to other duties.

It was the Saturday afternoon at the end of the first full working week and Gabrielle was sitting at her desk, finishing off some work before Gaston was to arrive to drive her home to Émile. Nobody else was in the building except the caretaker. Concentrating on her work, Gabrielle did not notice a rumble somewhere in the distance until suddenly her office door was flung open and the gray-haired caretaker stood there shaking with alarm and shouting, "Rioters, madame! On their way here! Flee while there is time!"

He himself sped away. Hastening around the desk, Gabrielle went out into the hall to the entrance doors, which had been left open by the caretaker. She stood at the threshold and looked up and down the street; then she felt herself quail. The rioters were advancing from both directions, armed with spikes and staves and carrying banners that read DOWN WITH JACQUARD! SAVE OUR LIVELIHOOD! PRESERVE OUR LOOMS!

She was not going to see everything she had worked for destroyed by a mindless mob. Darting back inside, she slammed the heavy doors closed and shot the bolts home. Then she ran into the first of the loom rooms. Although all the windows were covered with grillwork, for added protection she closed the interior shutters. The roar of voices in the street was now reaching a new dimension. Fearful of being attacked at the rear of the building, she raced to check that the doors were barred, and found all secure except the one leading out into what had been an herb garden. She was just in time. As she bolted the door she saw through the grille that the garden gate was giving way under the pressure of the men behind it.

Breathless through all the running about, she paused to think if there was anything she had overlooked. But she started violently as a rock thudded against one of the high shutters, smashing the glass outside. Next came a positive barrage as window after window disintegrated. Then an even more ominous sound followed. It was the rhythmic thudding of a battering ram against the entrance doors. Each thud seemed to shake the whole building, and she doubted that the ancient timbers of the convent could take the strain much longer.

She made a lightning decision. In her office there was a silk sample freshly made up from one of Marcel's latest designs. It was a spectacular blaze of sunflowers on cream satin. She ran to get it and draped it around herself hastily, like a giant stole. Then she returned to the archway of the first loom room and summoned up her courage as she waited in readiness.

With a resounding crash the entrance doors gave at last, and the rioters with the battering ram spilled into the hall, some falling in the melee. It gave her the chance she'd been hoping for. She stood in the archway in a silken dazzle of orange, yellow and gold. The brilliant effect was further enhanced by the sun's slanting in through the smashed doors to touch her from head to foot. Her chestnut hair was bright as flame.

"Weavers!" she cried in a tone of authority. "Stay where you are! Most of you know that I learned to weave in some of your homes and loom rooms. Would I betray my own apprenticeship? Trust me as you used to trust me! Let me show some of you the new life that the Jacquard loom has brought to Lyons!"

Those already inside the building were gaping at her. The suddenness of her appearance, the splendor of her silk drapery and her courage in standing up to them caused each man to stay where he was. "Give me a chance to save what I have achieved here," she added. "I even have work for those who want it."

She would have succeeded if it had been left to the ringleaders in the forefront. But there came a great surge of movement from the crowd outside, and those on the threshold were helplessly thrust forward. Nobody knew who threw the stone. It could have been aimed deliberately, or perhaps it had ricocheted off the doorway. But it struck Gabrielle on the side of her head, and she went reeling back, stunned by the pain. As she collapsed in a tangle of the satin stole, blood staining it, she felt herself heaved

to one side by someone coming from the loom room behind. The mob swarmed in from the street, shouting and yelling. She heard a pistol shot; then Nicolas's voice roared forth. "Get out! All of you! That was only a warning. I'll shoot the first man who takes another step forward!"

Gasping, she managed to look up. Nicolas stood with feet apart under the archway, a pistol in each hand. There was nobody in the loom room, which meant somebody else must be holding the herb-garden mob at bay. She let her head sink back again. There was a click as he cocked the second pistol, and it was enough to cause an immediate withdrawal of the intruders.

She could no longer concentrate. There was more shouting, the banging of a door somewhere, Gaston's exuberant laugh, and then Nicolas was lifting her up and carrying her to the sofa in the office.

"Is she badly hurt?" asked Gaston, serious and concerned.

"Just stunned. But it's quite a deep cut." Nicolas was stemming the flow of blood with a linen handkerchief. He drew away to remove his coat, then draped it over her. "Is the street cleared yet?"

Gaston went across to the window. "Yes, your men and the police have done their work."

"Then bring the carriage to the door from wherever you left it. We must get Madame Valmont home to her sister-in-law."

Gabrielle wanted to thank him for all his help, but she could only lie there, dizzy with pain. Suddenly Nicolas was carrying her again. Her head was against his shoulder, and he continued to hold her cradled to him as Gaston drove them to the Rue Clémont.

At the house, a manservant opened the door and Hélène's startled cry came from the hall. An explanation from Nicolas followed as Hélène led the way upstairs. They had reached the landing when Henri appeared.

"You!" he bellowed, spotting Nicolas. "How dare you enter this house! What have you done to my sister? Give her to me!"

Gabrielle felt Nicolas's arms tighten about her. Now it was Hélène who took command.

"Out of our way, Henri! This is no time for quarreling. You should be thanking Monsieur Devaux instead of shouting your head off at him." She thrust him aside, sweeping forward to open wide a bedchamber door, and Nicolas carried Gabrielle through.

Hélène folded the bedclothes back, and Gabrielle felt herself being lowered onto the bed. She moaned a soft protest as Hélène slipped Nicolas's coat off her and returned it to him. This was the only way Gabrielle was able to convey that she wanted him to stay. Somehow he must have understood that.

He took her hand in his and pressed it lovingly. "I must go," he said quietly. Then he went from the room.

Gabrielle learned from Hélène the missing details. Gaston had been on the alert for trouble. He had decided that in the event of an emergency a small loft window of the Roche mill could be entered from a neighboring roof. It was by this route that he and Nicolas—who had heard of the uprising from a guard—had gotten into the building, he to face the mob in the herb garden and Nicolas to take the main entrance.

As soon as she was able to travel, Gabrielle was taken back to the silk farm. The doctor, who had put four stitches in her wound, had advised complete rest for three weeks, a period that Émile was determined to extend. All his suspicions about Devaux, which had been dormant for a long time, had erupted again.

It was at an exhibition of silks that Gabrielle was to see Nicolas again. Some months had passed, and her mill was thriving. This exposition of 1808 was a chance to show that her silks were among the best.

In the exhibition hall a space was allotted to each member of the Grande Fabrique. Although Maison Roche, as a prestigious member, had received a place in the coveted main hall, it was in a far corner, away from the doorway.

When she had exclaimed in indignation that Maison Roche did not have a prominent stand, Henri shrugged. "What can you expect?" he said. "Roche silk is in a woman's hands now. Think yourself lucky you have a place at all in the exposition."

Her face had flashed her defiance of both him and the organizers. "I'll see that our silk is not overlooked. I promise you."

Now Henri took an enameled snuffbox from his pocket, inhaled a pinch of the contents and blew his nose ferociously. "What designs have you finally decided to show?"

When she told him, he glared at her in disbelief. "You can't show those. I forbid it. Keep to flowers, vine branches and rosettes. That's what buyers will be looking for. I know."

She answered him with firmness. "The day when anyone has the power to forbid me to do anything has passed, Henri. Marcel did the designs months ago, and all the fabrics are ready. That I was given such a poor position in the hall makes me even more determined to ensure that Roche silk never gets relegated to inferior status again."

The day before the exposition she arrived at the hall with Marcel and Henri. Émile was also with her. A room had been set aside for raw silk dealers, and he parted company with her within the entrance. She paused to look at the posting of the general plan of the exposition and saw that Devaux silk was to occupy the very place she would have chosen for herself. It gave Nicolas a definite advantage, and that in itself she found stimulating. Now any small victory she gained would count all the more. Even as she smiled to herself over this thought she saw him, and her heart lurched.

She felt weak. And yet how was this possible? She was nearly twenty-five, with four years of marriage behind her—certainly no longer a girl to be tossed from one emotional crisis to another. In a perverse way she resented loving Nicolas, while at the same time she welcomed coming alive. Love was a drug far more potent than anything doctors might prescribe.

She and Marcel were able to assemble the Roche display without gathering much attention, and then it was covered with soft cambric dust sheets to protect it and to keep it from view. There was a tacit understanding between exhibitors not to see rival stands until the day of the exposition, part of an old tradition of secrecy in the silk trade.

In the morning Yvonne was up early, ready to accompany Henri, Gabrielle and Émile to the exposition, instead of waiting to come later with Hélène. All three women had new outfits in the finest Roche silk. Gabrielle had chosen a jade color, and her dashing hat, in the latest military-influenced style, had a small rolled brim and a high crown trimmed with a plume placed upright in the front. Yvonne's velvet coat echoed the same influence in its braiding, and she preened a little in front of the looking glass in the hall before going out to the carriage in which she and Gabrielle and their husbands were to be driven to the exposition.

"Here we are," Émile said, leaning toward the window as the exhibition hall came into sight. In the busy entrance hall they were met by Marcel, who joined Gabrielle and Henri to go to the Roche silk stand, while Émile went to his own allotted place in the raw silk room. Yvonne began to saunter through the main hall, slowly studying everything that had already been unveiled from the lightweight dust sheets.

At the table adjacent to the Roche display, where orders would be taken, Henri arranged the inkpot, pens and order books as carefully as if moving pieces in a game of chess. Gabrielle went to tour the main hall. Now that the displays were unveiled, the whole place was transformed with fabrics of every texture and color. Jewellike colors blended with the metallic glints of lamé, and there was a whole range of pastels, all marvelously patterned in damask, velvet ciselé, chenille, satin, moiré and the output of many other special silk-weaving techniques.

When Gabrielle came to the Devaux display, she wanted to applaud, to laugh with praise, to exclaim her admiration. Almost as if there had been connivance between them, Nicolas was the only exhibitor other than herself to take a single color and show it in every variation. And dominating his stand was a spectacular swirl of sapphire damask on a satin ground, woven with the design of golden bees. It was a masterpiece, showing what could be achieved on a Jacquard loom.

Nicolas was writing at his table. Had he taken an order already? Then he turned his head abruptly and looked straight at her.

"It's good to see you, Gabrielle," he said, his eyes full of smiles. "How are you? Busy, of course."

"All the time. My congratulations on the Devaux display. It will be the sensation of the exposition."

He gave a shrug. "Do you realize that you and I are going to face severe criticism of our work? We are the only manufacturers here exhibiting work woven on the Jacquard loom."

"Maybe our work will persuade others to make the change."

"That's what I'm hoping. Monsieur Jacquard is going to put in an appearance today. Do you want to meet him?"

Her face shone. "Yes. I do. What a pleasure! I saw him demonstrate his loom."

"You were there, were you?"

"Yes, and I admired your rescue of Monsieur Jacquard."

He dismissed her praise with a sweep of his hand. "He is an old friend of my father's, and I served in the *chasseurs à cheval* with his son, Charles, who was killed at Cambrai. Because of false accusations, the Jacquards had to flee Lyons during the siege as we did. Their home was burned down. I'll bring him to you when he arrives. Incidentally, I haven't seen your display yet."

He went with her to a good vantage point. According to her instructions, Marcel waited until a minute before the public was to be admitted and had just removed the last dust sheet from the stand. Fellow exhibitors in the vicinity were already glancing toward it with surprise. Gabrielle watched Nicolas's reaction to her silks. His eyes deepened into a twinkle that told her she had won his full approval.

She had chosen *gris-de-lin*, a rich shade of violet, with gold eagles in flight, to hang in her exhibit as though in a throne room. To the forefront was a profusion of silks from deepest pansy to heliotrope and lilac, as if the eagles were flying above a turbulent sea flecked with silver and gold. The effect was handsome and dramatic.

He turned to her. "It's my turn to congratulate you." The amusement was still in his face, and she chuckled. The joke was their own. They saw the strange coincidence of their stands being the only two steeped in a dominant color as an affinity of thought. Neither knew that they were being observed by Émile, who had come across the hall with the intention of wishing his wife good luck. He watched them suspiciously. Knowing Gabrielle as he did, it seemed to him that her every little gesture proclaimed an exceptional interest in Devaux. Something the man said to her caused them to laugh together, and this increased Émile's resentment. As a handbell was rung to announce that the exposition was about to open, he saw his wife and Devaux part company, still smiling at each other, Gabrielle's face full of secrets. Émile turned away to return to his own trade site.

Gabrielle remained looking toward her display as Henri approached. "Well? What do you think of the opposition?"

"I think our most serious rival on the floor is Devaux."

Henri snorted. "You've only yourself to blame if Devaux takes orders away from us. You should have listened to me." He cast a contemptuous glance at the Roche display. Eagles! Customers wanted doves, or birds of paradise, he believed. The imperial eagle had no place in the average well-to-do man's home.

Contrary to Henri's gloomy expectations, the day proved to be an exceptionally good one. The dais by which he sat was surrounded by the first arrivals, a crush that continued without respite. Both the Roche and Devaux stands drew immediate interest because their silks had been woven on the Jacquard loom. And by choosing the imperial eagle, Gabrielle had caught the current pro-Bonaparte mood of the Grande Fabrique. Since Bonaparte now ruled half of Europe through his conquests, many old political symbols were being replaced by tributes to the emperor. On both the Devaux and the Roche stands were some marvelous examples of what could be hung in refurbished rooms of state.

Hélène came to see the Roche display in the afternoon. She was surprised but full of praise. "From what I can see, you and Monsieur Devaux have taken the world of the Grande Fabrique by storm," she said to Gabrielle. "I spoke to him on the way here. He presented Monsieur Jacquard to me. They're coming over to you shortly." Her attention was attracted by a movement in the crowd. "I think they're on their way now."

Nobody knew who started the clapping, but it was taken up on all sides, people moving to make a path for this man whose name had been passed from one person to another since his arrival at the exposition. Joseph Jacquard looked startled and shy, but as more and more people joined in the applause and the gathering around him increased, he began to smile, nodding his appreciation. His birthplace of Lyons—which had so strenuously rejected him—had taken him back into the fold at last.

DURING the days that followed, until the exposition closed, Gabrielle saw Nicolas many times, mostly at a distance. Whenever they did get a chance to speak, their words bore no relationship to the silent communication between them. She knew he was waiting for her, certain that the day would come when she would forget the bonds that held her. It gave danger and excitement to these encounters, but the aftermath was always sadness and a struggle to face again the reality of life.

On the last day of the exposition, when the flood of orders had ebbed, there was a sudden reappearance of Spanish buyers in Lyons. News had come that the emperor had made his brother, Joseph, King of Spain. Once more the imperial eagle in silk was in demand, this time for the throne room in Madrid.

One morning, after the exposition had closed and the first orders were being put into production, Gabrielle took time off to buy theater tickets. She was crossing the Place des Célestins on foot, the day being fine and dry, when unexpectedly someone held a bunch of crimson roses in front of her. She halted in surprise and laughed when Nicolas materialized. "Accept my tribute for brightening my day beyond measure."

She laughed again, taking the roses from him. "These are lovely. How kind and how gallant. You really surprised me."

"I could see you were deep in thought. I probably have the same expression when I'm wondering if all is going well at my mill. Where were you going just now?"

"To the Théâtre des Célestins." She indicated a building a few yards from where they stood. "I'm going to pick up tickets for tonight's performance. It's a play that Hélène wants to see, and I encourage her to go out as much as possible."

"Have you time to take coffee with me first?"

She hesitated only briefly, through the habit of always being wary in his presence. "I think so. That would be welcome."

They chose a café and sat at a table under a bower of foliage, dappled by sunlight and shade. A young girl sat by an upstairs window, playing a flute, and the notes were clear and sweet like a bird's song. They ordered coffee and it came almost at once. Since there was only one other customer, well out of earshot, they were able to talk freely.

"Will you and your sister-in-law be going unescorted to the play this evening?" Nicholas asked. "I could come with you."

She lowered her glance to the coffee steaming in the cup in front of her. "I'm afraid not. Henri and Yvonne will be with us."

"Ah." He sighed expressively. "Another time, perhaps."

"Perhaps," she said uncertainly.

"Gabrielle." His tone was soft. "Look at me."

Slowly she raised her head and met his loving gaze.

"You are the most beautiful woman I have ever known. All I want is to see you, to be with you." He leaned toward her as he spoke, reaching out his hand to take possession of hers and enfold it within his own. "I love you."

"That should never have been said," she protested shakily. Her heart was palpitating wildly.

"Do you love Émile Valmont?"

Her lustrous eyes were large with pain. "He loves me."

He increased his clasp on her fingers. "I repeat my question."

"I've given you my answer. It covers everything."

"Even divorce?"

It came as a shock to hear the word spoken aloud. Somehow she found the voice to reply to him. "Even divorce."

He caressed her hand then, the loving look in his eyes unshaken. "I want you forever, Gabrielle." Drawing her fingers up to his lips, he pressed a kiss against them. She was never to know if she might have spoken then of her love for him. A couple had been shown to a nearby table, and the moment was gone.

She picked up the roses, and he went with her to the entrance of the theater. There she selected one of her flowers and held it out to him. The simple, eloquent gesture said all she was unable to voice. They shared a smile as he took it, and he broke off the stem to slide it into a buttonhole in the lapel of his coat. Then she entered the foyer of the theater.

CHAPTER SIX

GABRIELLE suffered an unexpected setback. The order for imperial hangings, which she had hoped to gain from the Mobilier Impérial after her display at the exposition, went to the Devaux mill instead. She accepted the news in silence, while Henri ranted and raved over it until she could endure his tirade no longer.

"Be quiet, for mercy's sake, Henri!" she exclaimed fiercely. She was sitting at her desk, her hands clenched together in front of her. "There are other chances. We've yet to hear who is to make the campaign tent for the emperor."

Bonaparte wanted a tent lined with Lyons silk to use in the field that year of 1809, and in many ways this was the most coveted commission, since it was of a personal nature. All the major Lyons manufacturers had submitted designs. Marcel's incorporated a lion and a lamb, which surely symbolized the emperor's aim for the future, a peaceful Europe under the French flag.

"We have a good design," Henri answered, "but so long as you are sitting in that chair, we shall go on losing top commissions. The Grande Fabrique has no place for a woman. You must accept that you're a hindrance to the business."

She jerked up her head. "I won't give in to prejudice."

Henri's face was thunderous. "If we get the commission for the tent, I'll continue to back you. But if we lose it, I'll demand your resignation. I warn you that I'm not prepared to see Devaux skim away the cream from us for the rest of our days!" He turned away and left the room.

She was aware that she was trembling. There was nothing Henri could do to dislodge her, but there were other issues at stake. She saw every victory that Nicolas achieved as an undermining of her own emotional security. Unless she could be his equal in the silk world, how could she continue to find the strength to master her love for him and control her life? Their love was a torment with no release. She came close to a sense of panic, as if at last she had reached the quicksands. Packing up her work for the day, she left early to go home to Émile.

All the way from Lyons to the silk farm she made a silent plea to her husband. Help me, Émile. Please realize the danger our marriage is facing and help me. Nicolas is drawing me to him. I don't know how long I can fight my love for him.

Émile was not at home; she learned that he had gone unexpectedly on business to Avignon. She would have to wait to see him. All too often now their individual interests separated them. She spent the next morning in the flower garden gathering fresh flowers for the rooms. Finally she strolled through the woods, as if to gather the tranquillity of the surroundings into herself.

A FEW weeks later Henri Roche was preparing to go out in Lyons for the evening with Yvonne when a servant came to tell him that a prowler in the stable yard had been overcome by a couple of grooms. "Has he stolen anything?" Henri asked.

"No, sir. He swears he came to keep an assignation with a maidservant he had met, and mistook the address. He's in the scullery under guard now."

"Well, I'll take a look at this rogue."

It was rare for Henri to go belowstairs. Kitchen staff, whom he could not remember ever seeing before, stood amid scrubbed tables and gleaming copper pans to watch him go through to the scullery. There the intruder, a middle-aged ferret-faced fellow, was seated in a chair, his arms bound at the wrists.

"Well, well. So it's Monsieur Brouchier," Henri remarked, recognizing the intruder. "This is a surprise." He addressed the servant who had led him there. "Release him and bring him to my study. This is a matter I want to investigate myself."

In Henri's study, Brouchier accepted his invitation to be seated, thanking him for his release. "It was a nasty moment for me," he confessed. "I pride myself on never being nabbed."

Henri poured himself a glass of wine and sat down. "Ah, you're not out of the woods yet; I want to know what tricks you are up to.

Is my wife having me followed?" Years ago he had employed Brouchier himself to keep watch on a mistress of his.

Brouchier gave a rusty laugh, shaking his head. "Monsieur, I am a man of honor and can't betray my clients' names."

Henri pointed a finger at him from the hand that held the wineglass. "I can have you taken in for trespassing with intent to rob. You'll tell me everything. Speak!"

Brouchier shifted uncomfortably in his chair. "Émile Valmont, your brother-in-law, has engaged me to keep watch on his wife."

"What?" Henri sat forward, astonished. "Who's the man?"

The answer to his own question came to him even as Brouchier replied, "Nicolas Devaux."

"What evidence have you gathered?" he demanded hoarsely.

"Nothing of significance so far. They met some weeks back in the Place des Célestins. Since then there have been no meetings that I've discovered. As it happens, Devaux is among the guests at the dinner party the Valmonts and your sister-in-law are attending this evening. I was just about to follow their carriage."

Henri took a swig of wine and regarded his visitor grimly. "I'll not detain you any longer, but on one condition: anything you tell Monsieur Valmont you must also tell me."

Brouchier stood up. "I daresay that can be arranged, seeing that you're a former client, and one who was generous to me."

Henri took the hint. "You'll be rewarded." He swung his wineglass dismissively. "Now get out of here."

For a while Henri sat on alone in the room, thinking. It seemed he had an ally in Émile against Devaux, and he felt that they were gathering their forces for attack.

GABRIELLE had not known that Nicolas would be at the dinner party. She had barely been received by her host and hostess when she saw him coming across the room toward her. Her luxuriant hair caught bright tints from the candle glow, framing her lovely face to perfection. She was in a white silk gown with a décolletage bordered with gold embroidery, and she outshone every other woman present. When Nicolas reached her, he pressed the fingers of her hand lovingly.

"The gods are being good to me this evening."

She sighed in soft wonderment, completely captivated by his presence. "Who would have expected anyone in Lyons to invite a Devaux and a Roche to the same table?"

"It's only because our hostess knows nothing of local disputes."

"How fortunate for us," she whispered, thoroughly amused. Sharing their private joke, he led her into the gathering.

There were writers, artists and musicians present, as well as the prefect of the city. The conversation was mostly intellectual, but one disturbing piece of news from Paris was reported—that the emperor was considering a divorce from Joséphine. He wanted a son and heir, something she had been unable to give him.

At dinner Nicolas and Gabrielle were not seated together. He was on the opposite side of the table from her, distanced by candelabras and carnations in silver bowls, but the angle at which they were placed enabled him to view her without hindrance. Every time she glanced in his direction he met her gaze instantly, sending her silent messages that made his eyes glow as darkly as wine. His constant attention had its effect on her; she was assailed afresh by love and desire. Hélène, who was more of an observer than a conversationalist, hoped she was the only one noticing the interchange between them. Émile, at the far end of the table, did not seem to be.

During coffee, served in a salon paneled with ice-green silk, everybody was asked to take seats for the musical interlude. Nicolas reached Gabrielle in time to sit beside her. The music heightened her awareness of Nicolas's nearness, as if she were conscious of every breath he drew. When they rose to applaud, they did not disperse but remained facing each other.

"Meet me tomorrow," he implored quietly. "At the café in the Place des Célestins. There's so much more to be said."

She could not have refused him. They had to see each other again soon. "I will be there," she promised.

IN THE morning the news broke throughout Lyons that the Devaux mill had received the emperor's personal commission for the new campaign tent. For Gabrielle it was a shock on two counts. Once again Nicolas had gained on her through his own well-deserved success, and at the same time nothing symbolized the advance he had made on her emotionally more than his capturing this sought-after commission.

At the arranged time she arrived for their meeting at the Place des Célestins in a barouche driven by Gaston. Nicolas was already at a table, and he stood up to meet her, able to see by her face that once again a gulf had come between them.

"I can't stay," she said. "I just came to give you my warmest congratulations on your latest commission."

"Thank you. Please sit down for a few minutes."

If she sat there, she would be lost again. There was too much love in his eyes. "No, I must go. But there's one thing I want to ask you. Did you know last night that you had the commission?"

"I knew a week ago."

"Why didn't you tell me when you had the chance?"

"I love you, Gabrielle. I don't want to lose you, and yesterday evening we came so close that I wanted nothing to come between us. For myself I consider it a sad day for France that the emperor should need a campaign tent at the present time." He was referring to Austria's new declaration of war against France and to England's landing in Portugal to aid Spain in driving the French out of Portuguese territory. "I should have preferred to weave silken banners to celebrate peace throughout the empire."

"Perhaps your tent will play a part in securing that peace." She took a step away from him. "Adieu, Nicolas. I hope to see the tent when it is finished. I'm sure it will be a handsome sight."

She hurried back to the barouche, her face pale with distress.

All day Gabrielle expected Henri to arrive at the mill in a raging temper over the lost commission, but he failed to appear. Instead, he met her in the hall when she arrived home at the Rue Clémont. He appeared calm and in charge of himself, although there was a truculent set to his features. "You've heard, of course," he said to her.

She nodded. "It just shows me that Devaux silk still has the edge on Roche products. I intend to counteract that."

"Indeed? Come into the salon. Émile's here."

She was not unduly surprised. Over recent weeks Émile had taken to coming without notice to Lyons, sometimes to spend time with her, at others to accompany her home to the silk farm when it was the close of a working week. He turned from the window when she entered the salon. To him she always brought the sun into a room with her, but today he kissed her on the cheek with little warmth.

"Henri sent for me," Émile said. "The news of the lost commission this morning must have been a great disappointment to you."

"Henri sent for you?" She flashed a wary look from him to her brother's belligerent face. "In the world of business I have to take setbacks from time to time as do many others."

"But don't you think those setbacks are happening all too frequently now, Gabrielle?" he asked. "The time has come for you to ask yourself if you are fulfilling your late father's wishes. The world of the Grande Fabrique has set its face against you, and the dreams you cherish will never be fulfilled."

She was incredulous that her husband, who had suppressed his own wishes to give her his full support after the reading of her father's will, had chosen now to desert her. "Do you believe what you are saying, Émile?" she challenged fiercely.

"I do, my dear. I would not support your brother if I didn't think he was right. Dominique would never have wanted a Devaux to gain superiority over a Roche, and that is what has happened and will continue to happen unless you make Henri your deputy and retire from the public scene."

She was rendered speechless. In all their ups and downs he had never once withdrawn his support from her.

"I don't accept that I have failed. It's early yet—"

"Three years," Henri interrupted. "You've had three years."

She rounded on him. "That's nothing! I have a lifetime of silk still before me. I won't give up for you or anybody else."

Émile spoke quietly. "You may have no choice in a few months' time. It might be better to start the changeover now."

She was puzzled. "I don't understand."

Émile indicated with a brief lift of his head that Henri would clarify the remark. She saw the malevolent satisfaction stamped on her brother's face. "Yvonne is enceinte," he rasped. "If it is a boy, I shall have the legal right to contest our father's will and establish my own claim to the trust."

Gabrielle released a long sigh. "So that's it. I wish you a strong and healthy child, Henri, whether it be a boy or girl. As for the trust, Father willed it in faith to me and I'm going to prove that faith. In the meantime, everything is as it was before we had this discussion." She glanced in turn at both of them. "Now I'm going upstairs to change and get ready for dinner."

She went from the room with her head held high. It was not until she was out of sight that her whole body drooped as if all the strength had drained from her.

WHEN the Devaux tent for the emperor was finished, it would be shown at the *hôtel de ville*. Gabrielle received an invitation to the first viewing for the elite of the Grande Fabrique, and made a point of mentioning it to Émile.

"I'm most interested to see this tent," she said to him over breakfast one Sunday morning. "I want to see why the Devaux design won and mine did not."

He put down the cup of coffee he had been drinking and regarded her fondly. They had had a fine weekend together, and last night husband and wife had been together as they should. Let her see the tent and Devaux in the midst of a crowd of silk merchants, he thought. There was no danger in that. Brouchier had not come up with a single scrap of further evidence against her, and in his own mind he considered that the little flutter she had experienced was well and truly past.

"Would you like me to go with you?"

"Yes, if you would like to come," she answered readily.

That pleased him. Not the least hesitation there. "To be honest, I have other commitments here at the silk farm that day. You can tell me about it afterward."

As the days dwindled down to the time of the viewing, the dispassionate air she had tried to maintain toward the event dissolved without warning into a raging torrent of wanting to see Nicolas again. And so much had happened since she had last seen him! Not long before that Christmas of 1810 the emperor had divorced Joséphine, and rumors about a new bride were rife. As for the Grande Armée, that had been divided into two sections—one to defeat the Austrian threat once and for all and the other to surge forward in Spain in bloody conflict with the British, Spanish and Portuguese. Bad weather in Spain that year was adding to the misery of the troops on both sides of the conflict.

It was a bitter cold evening when Gaston drove Gabrielle to the *hôtel de ville*. Both were surprised to find no crush of carriages outside the building. "Are we early?" she asked him.

"No, madame. Right on time, as you wished."

It was a relief to get into the warm building. An attendant led her along a corridor into a domed hall, leaving her there. She found herself to be the sole spectator of the campaign tent.

Pegged out on a green carpet, as if it stood on grass, the tent was a large, pleasing oval. Woven in stripes of blue and white duck, the roof was embellished with scarlet embroidery and braided with black. Gabrielle slipped off her cloak and put it with her muff on a chair by the wall before approaching the tasseled ropes that formed a cordon around the tent. As she circled it she came to a gap. The entrance flaps of the tent were fastened back for access, and she went inside.

Lit by lanterns suspended from poles supporting the canopied ceiling, the interior was spacious and well proportioned. It housed an easily transportable camp bed, and chairs and tables, all foldable. One of two campaign chests, lined with red-and-white duck, was open. It held maps to demonstrate one of its uses. She was enthralled by the splendor of the silk hangings that lined the whole interior. The pattern of red-and-blue bouquets was simple and stylized against a pale gray ground, the effect as light and airy as a new morning.

Outside in the hall, the door opened and closed again as someone entered. Footsteps crossed the floor to become swallowed up on the green carpet. Her back was to the tent's entrance and she did not turn. Nicolas's voice addressed her. "What do you think of it?"

She closed her eyes briefly at the almost unbearable joy of

being near him again. "It's splendid. Just as I knew it would be."

A lantern threw his shadow in front of her as he came to stand by her side. "I've missed you, Gabrielle."

Unexpected tears filled her eyes and choked her throat. "I've missed you too," she admitted huskily.

He took her gently by the shoulders and turned her slowly to face him. Speech deserted them both at what they saw in each other's eyes. As his arms went about her ardently, she strained forward swiftly against him, savoring the perfection of the moment, kissing him from the depth of her heart.

When finally they drew breath, she felt a century had gone by. As if in a dream, she let her head sink onto his shoulder.

"My darling," he whispered. "I can hardly believe I have you in my arms."

Her voice was soft and barely audible. "I hadn't expected to find there would be no other visitors at this hour."

"I had to see you alone. It was a chance not to be missed." He took her hands into his. "Let's talk of your future and mine and how it would be to make a fresh start together, both of us to make amends for having let the other go."

"That was nearly six years ago," she said brokenly.

"Yet nothing has changed between us."

She knew it to be the truth. The love they shared had proved itself to be of unassailable strength. How could she go on resisting this man who held her whole heart? She drew up Nicolas's hands with her own and covered them with little kisses.

"I love you," she whispered. "I belong to you. I've fought against my feelings until I can't fight any longer."

"My darling, beautiful, wonderful Gabrielle," he whispered in return. "Now there are no more barriers between us."

Her face was full of longing. "I wish it were true. I'm not free to come to you of my own accord."

"When will you be?" He was impatient, desperate. "So much time has been lost. We need each other. I shall go to Émile—"

"No! You must not go to him!" She was adamant.

"Then how is this dilemma to be solved?"

"I don't know. At the moment I can only hope for a solution. All

I ask is that you allow me a little time. Then I'll come to you. Somehow I'll come to you."

He did not doubt her. The hope in her was infectious, and they smiled as if they were already free to be together. With his arm about her waist they left the tent together and went to the corridor. He helped her on with her fur cape, and they faced each other in parting. "When am I going to see you again?" he asked her.

"I can't say when. Don't come with me now and don't try to see me. That would only complicate matters. I must find my own way out of the maze to reach you. Good night, my darling."

Holding her cloak about her, she went from him to her carriage.

A LETTER from Brouchier was delivered to Henri at breakfast in his office. As he broke the seal he had little hope of anything of interest. Then, as he read that Gabrielle and Devaux had been alone behind a closed door at the *hôtel de ville*, he saw that the situation was beginning to move at last. This information was something to hold onto until his son was born. Then he could present a strong appeal in the courts. He locked the letter safely away in the desk that had been his father's.

To Émile, however, Brouchier went in person to deliver his report, riding out of Lyons at an early hour. When he arrived, he asked for Monsieur Valmont and was told he was at the silksheds. Following directions, he took a path through the trees and happened to spot his client coming out of one of the buildings.

Émile stiffened when he saw Brouchier. "You have something for me?" he asked.

"Yes, monsieur, what you've been waiting for." Brouchier took a sealed paper from his pocket and gave it to his client.

"Stay here." Émile took the report into his office and read it through. Then he unlocked a drawer where he kept money, slipped a certain amount into a moneybag and took it out to where the spy waited. He tossed the moneybag to him. "There you are. Your task is at an end. Get out. Never let me see you again."

Émile passed a shaking hand across his brow. He had planned what he should do if ever full confirmation of his fears came into his hands. Now he must put that plan into action.

WHEN GABRIELLE CAME HOME AT the week's end, Émile was in Paris. She had been fully prepared to put the whole matter of Nicolas before him, hoping he would show compassion toward her request for freedom. He had still not come home when she returned to Lyons, and it was to be another two weeks before she saw him again, for the following Friday Yvonne went into labor. Thirty-six hours later she gave birth to a daughter. The infant was weak, and lived only a few hours.

Henri did not go near Yvonne for two days. For him their loss meant that he must find some other means by which he could gain control of Roche silk. He refused to admit defeat. Brouchier should be retained, because there was always a possibility that, through Devaux, Gabrielle would fall. He sighed impatiently.

When Gabrielle, in Lyons, received a letter from Émile saying that he was home at the silk farm again, she felt completely weighed down. The tone of his letter was affectionate, expressing regret at having missed her. She had to talk to Nicolas before Émile arrived in Lyons. She was in the process of writing Nicolas a note at her office desk at the mill when the door opened without warning, and he was there. The rush of joy she always felt at the sight of him was immediately tempered by the anxiety in his face.

"What's happened?" she asked with trepidation.

Without reply he closed the door and came toward her, pulling her into his arms for several moments of wordless embrace. Then he looked down into her face as he broke the news.

"I have to go away, Gabrielle. I have to leave Lyons."

"Tell me why!"

"Something has happened that I never expected. I've been recalled to the colors. I've had orders to rejoin my old regiment of the *chasseurs à cheval.*"

"Oh, no!" She was aghast. Her arms tightened about his neck. "When did you hear? Perhaps there's been a mistake."

"There's no mistake. Less than an hour ago I received my papers telling me to report for duty. I depart tomorrow morning for the campaign in the Iberian Peninsula. That's why I had to see you without delay. Good can come out of this posting to Spain if you agree to go with me."

"Go with you?" she repeated unsurely.

"It is only a matter of time before you will be my wife. Don't you see? Émile would never try to hold you once you had left with me." He kissed her tragic face and tried to cheer her with an encouraging smile. "We can be married in Spain as soon as you are free. When the war is won, we shall return to Lyons together."

She thrust herself from him. There was not a vestige of color in her face. "It's too late, my love—my only love. I have to stay here and remain wife to Émile." Her voice faltered. She dreaded what she had to say next. Only recently had her private suspicions been confirmed. "I'm going to have his child."

He stepped back and stared at her, stunned. "Are you sure?"

She nodded helplessly. "There have been signs."

He drew her to him again. "You can still come with me to Spain," he insisted. "Nothing can come between you and me. I love you, and I'll love any child that is part of you."

Her heart was breaking in its own terrible anguish. "I would follow you anywhere if I were free," she said, "but in my present state I couldn't undertake such an expedition."

He took her chin in his hand. "Then after the baby is born—"

"No!" She jerked herself from him. "Don't you see? Can't you understand? Whatever chance we had to be together has gone!"

His anger flashed now, for this was a total rejection of all hope. "I want a promise from you that at some time you will at least visit me in Spain or wherever I might be sent afterward. I've desired you for too long to be denied some part of your life."

"You'd try to make me stay." Her voice deepened in despair.

"You have always withheld yourself from me!" he accused.

"Not through my own wish!" she retorted fiercely. "When Émile held me in his arms, do you suppose I didn't yearn for you? I told you in the emperor's tent that I would come to you when I was free. That still holds, except that I'm no longer able to see how or when, or if ever, it might be."

" 'Never' appears to be the appropriate word!" The hurt in his eyes was as stark as if he had been ripped apart inside. "This is beyond my belief. It would have been better for both of us if we had never met. Farewell now, Gabrielle."

Turning, he opened the office door and went out. She stood as if all power to move had gone from her, hearing and seeing nothing, only remembering the last words spoken to her by the man she would love until the end of her days.

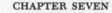

CHAPTER SEVEN

ÉMILE arrived in Lyons earlier than expected. Henri went to meet him in the hall. "Gabrielle is not home from the mill yet, Émile. Let me offer you some refreshment. A glass of wine?"

Émile declined with a dignified gesture. "Thank you, but no. I'll wait until Gabrielle is here. How is Yvonne?"

"She appreciated your letter of condolence. It was a great disappointment to us both that the infant did not survive. But come. There's no need for us to converse in the hall."

Talking together, the two men strolled into the gold salon, one of the smaller rooms in the house. "What has been happening in Lyons?" Émile asked. "It's four weeks since I've seen Gabrielle, and longer since I was here."

Henri's eyes gleamed with satisfaction. "Devaux has gone, for a start. Recalled to the colors. What do you think of that, eh?"

It seemed to Émile that his brother-in-law's tone bordered on the conspiratorial. "Indeed? Then the Devaux mill has closed?"

"Far from it. He left a manager in charge, a Parisian by the name of Michel Piat. A capable man, I've heard."

"Where has Devaux been posted? Do you know?"

"To the Iberian Peninsula. From all reports it's a difficult campaign. The Portuguese refused to obey the emperor's command to close their ports to British trade. We had to move in to take Lisbon and settle the matter. Our soldiers would have dealt with the Portuguese long ago if the British hadn't interfered."

"But Portugal was neutral," Émile said. "It had a right to decide what it wanted to do. The British will not be driven out easily."

Henri's expression changed slyly. "That suits you, doesn't it? You have your reasons, just as I have mine, for wanting Devaux in the emperor's army and out of the way."

Émile answered him with icy civility. "Why should I? The feud belongs to your family and is nothing to me. Devaux never purchased my raw silk, so I'll not miss his business."

"It was not his business I was referring to. I'm talking about Devaux's interest in Gabrielle—your wife and my sister."

"You have me at a loss," Émile bluffed coldly.

Henri's grin was malevolent. "Then why did you set Brouchier on to her comings and goings?"

Émile regarded his brother-in-law grimly. "He reported nothing incriminating. I dispensed with his services a while ago."

"So he told me. Brouchier is accurate and reliable; I retained him, mainly to keep an eye on Devaux. That's how I know that Devaux went to the mill to say farewell to Gabrielle a couple of days ago. It was a brief meeting. You have nothing to worry about. They won't be seeing each other again."

Émile's carapace of calm was shattered completely. An ungovernable rage possessed him and he lunged a blow at Henri's face and saw his brother-in-law collapse heavily on the floor. After a moment Henri propped himself up on an elbow to feel his jaw.

"You could have knocked my teeth out," he growled thickly. Wincing, he checked his mouth with an exploring finger. "I believe you've shaken the roots!"

"They'll settle down in a little while." Émile, dazed by his own action, went forward to assist him to his feet. But Henri furiously warded off his helping hand and got up by himself.

"Gabrielle is the one who deserves a beating. Your wife—"

"Get out!" Émile's temper had flared again, his hands balling into fists at his sides. Henri did not delay.

WHEN Gabrielle arrived home, a servant informed her that her husband awaited her in the gold salon. She found him gazing into the fire. At the sound of her entrance he glanced up and met her eyes piercingly in the large looking glass above the mantel. She thought he appeared strained.

"So you're home, then, my dear," he greeted her reflection. "I was impatient for your coming."

"How have you been since you returned from Paris?" she asked, coming to a standstill some distance from him.

He turned to face her. "I've been well. What of you?"

"I haven't been sleeping very well." She felt his sharp gaze following her every movement as she went to sit on a sofa. "Please sit down with me. I've something to tell you."

He studied her warily for a moment before he took the seat beside her. "What is it?"

She was looking down at her wedding ring, which she was twisting around her finger. Slowly she raised her head again, her gaze straightforward and direct. "We are going to have a child, Émile."

He stared at her, stunned by what she had said. His whole expression crumpled into jubilation. "My dearest wife!" Choked by emotion, he leaned over to kiss her ecstatically. He had no doubts that he had fathered the child within her, for the truth shone out of her. "When is it to be?"

"I've nearly six more months to go."

"We must get you home without delay." He was enthusiastic.

"No, Émile. The doctor insists I take no journeys of any kind."

"Do you imagine I would leave you here in Lyons, away from me, for the next six months?"

"It has to be."

His immediate pleasure over the forthcoming baby was spoiled by her opposition. "I suppose the same old reason is behind your determination to stay in Lyons as it has always been. Roche silk again, correct? You won't leave it?"

She noted that whenever he was out of humor he became tighter and neater, straighter and colder. She longed for the gentleness he could show toward her when so inclined.

"I liked going daily to the mill, but that will stop now. The office here has always been the main one."

"So the business is still to come before me! If you think I'll allow it to dominate our offspring, you're mistaken. After the birth you may stay in Lyons if you wish. The child shall be with me."

"Nothing shall take precedence over the baby as far as I'm concerned," she informed him strongly. "I've made arrangements accordingly. I'm sure you will recall Madame Hoinville, a customer of yours. I dealt with her during your illness. I recently offered her a post as my deputy at the mill."

"Did she accept?"

"Gladly. In fact she is already installed, and has begun to shoulder much of the work for me, and will continue to do so. I'm extremely pleased with her. I want our child to grow up with the devotion of both of us, and for that reason I shall come home to you in the country as soon as I have recovered from childbirth. Once the baby is weaned, I'm hoping I need travel only twice a week to Lyons. I promise you that we and our child will know family life together."

He was greatly mollified by her assurance. Relaxing, he raised another point. "It won't be easy for me to get to Lyons as your time advances. You know how busy I am from May onward, when the mulberry harvest is due and the silkworms are hatching."

"I realize that. I shall write to you and keep you informed about everything. What is the forecast for the harvest this year?"

"I haven't heard yet. My trees are in splendid condition."

"Good. I would have tried to get home earlier this evening if I had known you would be here. I was looking over patterns we'll exhibit at the Leipzig trade fair at Easter. Henri and Marcel are to represent me."

Behind his back Émile flexed the hand that had struck her brother. "The more I see of Henri, the less I like him. Maybe you were right after all to hold on to Maison Roche as you have done."

She was astounded by his words of support. "I can't tell you how much it means to me to hear you say so."

He rose from the sofa and drew her to her feet. "My dear, you have made me the happiest man in the world today." His arms encircled her. "If you need to remain in Lyons for the rest of your pregnancy, so be it. All I want is for you to be safely delivered of a healthy baby. You are everything to me, my dear. You and the baby that is to come. I pray we shall have a son."

She was touched by this show of tenderness. She was glad he

had remained in ignorance of her love for Nicolas and that she had caused him no suffering. It was her only comfort. Tears were never far from her since she and Nicolas had parted; they threatened to overwhelm her at the most unlikely moments.

Briefly she rested a hand on Émile's arm. "That is my hope too," she said to him.

IN APRIL in that year of 1810 there was a royal wedding. The emperor married Archduchess Marie-Louise of Austria. By the marriage the imperial seal was set firmly across that country, which was settling down at last after its final defeat at the Battle of Wagram. It was in France that unrest was brewing. The emperor had his enemies among his own countrymen, and the political undercurrents were having an increasingly bad effect on the financial state of the nation. Every aspect of business was being affected, and Gabrielle and other silk merchants in Lyons began to fear for their markets.

Émile came to the house on the Rue Clémont for Easter. The weather was unusually warm and sunny, the sky clear and blue. He arranged a boat trip on the river and a picnic beside it for Gabrielle. Hélène and her daughter, Juliette, joined them. The outing helped Gabrielle to stop wondering how Henri and Marcel were progressing at the trade fair in Leipzig, and it was a carefree day. Juliette's excitement over the whole event was infectious.

"Play hide-and-seek with me," she implored Émile when the picnic was over. She was greatly attached to Émile, who, unlike Henri, was kind to her.

"Very well," he agreed. "You and your *maman* shall hide first, and I will count to ten. Aunt Gabrielle will rest by the trees."

Hélène did not join the game for long, finding it somewhat hectic. As she returned across the grass, Gabrielle thought how young and pretty she looked with her cheeks flushed from exertion, and strands of hair awry. Not for the first time she wished her sister-in-law would dispense with her mourning black and let Jules rest. It was time for Hélène to let her heart heal.

"Ah, that's better," Hélène said thankfully, sinking down onto a corner of Gabrielle's rug. "Who would have thought it could be so warm at this time of year?"

"Yes. It is unusually warm."

After they had talked for a while, watching the glittering river flow past, Gabrielle tactfully broached the subject of Hélène's mourning. Hélène heard her out, looking down at a small wild-flower she had plucked from the grass. "When I feel the time is right, I shall put aside my black garments," she said finally.

Gabrielle understood. Hélène's mourning was her own private link with the man she still loved. It brought home to Gabrielle that she herself had no link at all with the living, breathing man who had gone from her own life.

When Henri returned from Leipzig, his conceit was enormous. Contrary to earlier fears, German customers had failed to be deterred by a tariff that had been imposed on imported goods, and vied with each other in placing their orders. Gabrielle was highly relieved. Although Henri claimed all the credit, Marcel informed her that her beautiful silks had virtually sold themselves.

Then, like a warning knell, at the beginning of May there was news from Naples. A freak frost had killed the silkworms there and damaged nearly all the mulberry trees. At the same time it began to rain throughout the whole of central and southern France.

In Lyons the gutters of the streets ran like rivers during the continuing downpours. Torrential rains kept the mulberry trees soaked and made harvesting impossible. Silkworms were hatching, and there was little to meet their voracious appetites. Before long the Rhone valley was flooded, and still it rained.

The clatter of a carriage arriving in haste took Gabrielle to her window one morning in time to see Émile leap out and run up the steps into the house. She hurried to meet him. One look at his haggard face as he removed his rain-spattered coat in the hall prepared her for bad tidings.

"The harvest is a total loss!" he exclaimed as soon as the door to the salon was closed after them. "The mulberry trees have been attacked by a blight."

"Oh, no," she breathed in dismay. Blight was a catastrophe dreaded by every silk farmer. The exceptionally bad weather must have created the right conditions for it to take hold. "What will you do? Could you ship in leaves from elsewhere?"

"You don't understand. The blight is developing everywhere." She sank onto a chair, stunned. "Are you sure?"

He nodded despairingly. "I saw the first warning signs yesterday. It's only a matter of a day or two before the news breaks that there'll be no mulberry harvest in France this year. I came to warn you. You must buy whatever raw silk you can lay your hands on."

Her mind was racing. The trust from Dominique would release the money she needed. She must summon her lawyers and a representative of her bank, disperse agents to buy on her behalf and, not least of all, send Hélène across the city on a special mission. "I'll act at once!"

Springing to her feet, she swayed and almost fell. Émile darted forward to catch her. "Not so fast! Remember your condition."

She took a deep breath. "I am remembering it. I'm also thinking of my weavers, their families and their unborn babies. You and I will not go hungry, but if I fail to secure the raw silk needed for weaving, they may starve."

The prospect haunted her as she began dispatching servants from her office with written messages, aided by Henri, who was moving more quickly under this threat of financial loss to Maison Roche than he had for a long time. The repercussions from the blight of the tree of gold would be devastating to the entire weaving community in Lyons. Although Maison Roche was in a position to weather the storm, not all the silk merchants would be so fortunate, and bankruptcies were inevitable. It was as if the lifeblood of Lyons were in danger of drying up.

At the first chance Gabrielle left her office to go in search of Hélène. She found her in the kitchen, supervising the arrangements for dinner. By the pantry door, out of earshot of anyone else, Gabrielle told her what had happened and explained what she wanted her to do.

Hélène, although curious, nodded briskly. "I'll leave now on foot. In that way I'll draw less notice to myself than by arriving at my destination in a Roche carriage."

"I thank you." Gabrielle embraced her. "You're the only one I could ask to do this for me. Now I must get back to my desk."

She returned to her office only minutes before her lawyers and a representative of her bank were announced. They arranged everything to her satisfaction. Letters of credit were drawn up for her agents, who would be going out of Lyons as soon as the papers were in their hands. Henri also received the necessary authority to buy raw silk. As the lawyers and the bank representative departed, he came downstairs ready to leave for Genoa.

"Good luck, Henri," Gabrielle said.

"Leave it to me," he replied complacently. "Father and I used to buy from this particular grower, and he won't have forgotten I was once a good customer."

He was driven away from the house, and in a short time Hélène was overtaken by his carriage. She thought it unlikely that her brother-in-law, sitting back in comfort, had sighted her. It was a strange task on which she had been sent, and she could not deny she felt timorous about it. If she had needed proof of Gabrielle's feelings for Nicolas Devaux, she had it now.

The clacking of the looms as she drew near the Devaux mill, to which she was bound, told her that Nicolas's absence had made no difference to the pace of work going on there. She chose to go to the street door of the house to make her call, and banged the heavy knocker. A maidservant answered.

"I want to see Monsieur Devaux's business manager, Monsieur Piat, at once. Please tell him it's an urgent matter."

"Yes, madame. Your name, please?"

"I will give it only to Monsieur Piat."

She had only a few minutes to wait until the man came through a door from a small courtyard. He was tallish, with light brown hair, his face thin and severe but not unkindly. His whole bearing was authoritative and purposeful. Hélène judged him to be about forty years old. As he approached her, she spoke firmly.

"I'm Hélène Roche, sister-in-law to Madame Gabrielle Valmont. I have to speak to you in complete confidence."

"Come this way, madame." He led her into a study and held a chair for her before seating himself. "Now what did you wish to speak to me about?"

"First of all, I want your word that Monsieur Devaux will never know that I was here today at my sister-in-law's request."

"My employer is now Captain Devaux of the *chasseurs à cheval*. Since I am entirely responsible for his interests while he is away, I can't give any such assurance until I know what it is you have to tell me."

She began nervously. "I came entirely with my sister-in-law's goodwill. She wanted me to give you warning that there will be little or no mulberry harvest this year. A terrible blight has taken hold everywhere. Madame Valmont doesn't want you to lose the chance of buying raw silk on Monsieur—er—Captain Devaux's behalf while there is still time. Please believe me and act now!"

He looked surprised at her words. "I don't disbelieve you. Fortunately, my employer was foresighted enough to cover any contingency during his indefinite absence. He bought all the raw silk he could before he left Lyons. I have a year's supply in hand."

Her sweet smile broke through. "I'm so glad to hear that."

He smiled too. "Please thank Madame Valmont for her concern."

Now Hélène leaned forward in appeal. "There's no reason for you to mention anything of this visit to Captain Devaux, is there? My sister-in-law was most insistent."

Michel Piat answered at once. "I'll say nothing."

Hélène was thankful that she had secured the promise Gabrielle wanted. She stood. "I mustn't take up any more of your time."

"It's been a pleasure to make your acquaintance." He moved to the door with her and reached in front to open it. "I've never met your husband, although I saw him at the Leipzig trade fair."

Her eyes went stark. "That must have been my brother-in-law you saw—Henri Roche. My husband died at Austerlitz."

It was then he realized that beneath the black cape, her dress, shoes and gloves were all in black for bereavement. "My condolences, madame," he said, regarding her in a new and compassionate light. "I lost my beloved wife, Elyanne, not long before I came to Lyons. I'm afraid that I unwittingly caused you some distress."

She felt a sudden empathy with this man who had been

through the same heart-tearing loss. "Please think no more about it. Do you have children, Monsieur Piat?"

"No, I haven't. Are you more fortunate?"

"I have a daughter, Juliette. She is five years old."

"A delightful age. She must be a great comfort to you."

"She is indeed. We have such fun together." She wanted to hear that his life was mending. "Have you settled down in Lyons? Do you like our city?"

"Very much. I'm still exploring. Do sit down again if you can spare the time. Are you Lyonese by birth?"

She told him about herself, and he in turn told her about his life in Paris and how he had worked there for Nicolas Devaux. This led to talk of his home and inevitably to his wife again. He spoke of how courageous she had been through her illness.

"Elyanne insisted I should never wear mourning for her. She wanted me to look to the future, not cling to the past. I need hardly say that doesn't mean I remember her less."

Hélène's brows drew together in a thoughtful little frown. "I don't suppose Jules would have wanted me to wear mourning for a long time. Yet it is a comfort to me."

"A shield, perhaps?"

He had startled her, and he saw it. It was something she had thought about herself, but this was the first time anyone had brought her face to face with the truth. In a cocoon of mourning she was isolated in her past love, safe from any fresh hurt. She spoke wonderingly. "Isn't it strange? I came here this morning to help you, and instead, I believe you have helped me."

"I prefer to think that we have helped each other."

The long look they exchanged seemed to come to both of them from far away. Once more she rose to leave, and she gave her hand in farewell, still bewildered that this meeting should have taken such an unexpected turn. "Adieu, Monsieur Piat. I wish you well."

"Adieu, Madame Roche. I hope we shall meet again soon."

As she turned homeward Hélène thought deeply over all that had been said. Back at the Rue Clémont, she gave Gabrielle the details of her trip to the Devaux mill, noticing how her cheeks

273

drew in when she learned that Nicolas had a year's supply of raw silk. It was obviously a tremendous relief to her.

Later, in her room, lying back on her bed, Gabrielle marveled that Nicolas should have shown such foresight in stocking his storerooms to cover any emergency. The financial outlay would have been tremendous, but he must have been certain of Monsieur Piat's ability to manage the business. She would like to meet the man. Hélène had spoken well of him.

IN THE morning the news broke. Only the Roche and Devaux houses remained detached from the turmoil throughout the city. Silk merchants bid against each other at a cutthroat level for whatever raw silk was still available. Many millowners foresaw closure and bankruptcy. The twenty-three days of rain without respite had brought as great a disaster to the Lyons silk industry as had the Revolution some seventeen years before. There was further consternation when a quantity of Italian raw silk disappeared without trace before leaving its country of origin. There seemed to be no end to the chain of calamities for Lyons.

Henri, however, returned from Genoa with three wagonloads of good raw silk for the Roche mill. He also returned full of smug satisfaction. He could have told his fellow Lyonese where the missing silk had gone. With the cooperation of his contacts in Genoa, it had been smuggled out, and the transaction had secretly lined his own pockets very generously.

As for Gabrielle, in addition to what Henri and her agents had managed to purchase, she had a good deal of surplus silk from Émile. She was grateful to him for letting her have it, when he could have sold it at exorbitant prices elsewhere. In all, she was confident of keeping her weavers at work throughout the difficult times ahead and of filling her orders from the Leipzig trade fair.

NEWS of all that had been happening in Lyons did not reach Nicolas until late summer. Very little mail from France reached the Iberian Peninsula, and he considered himself lucky that a letter from Michel Piat had finally come into his hands.

In blistering sun, his uniform jacket open and his neckcloth and shirt drenched with sweat, Nicolas sat beneath an orange tree. Eagerly he broke the seal and began to read the letter. It was the first communication he had received from his manager, and Piat had given a brief résumé of the points of interest.

As he read on, the tribulations of the Grande Fabrique seemed unimportant beside the horror of the war in which he was steeped. Only one line stood out from Piat's letter. "Madame Valmont has secured sufficient raw silk to see her looms through the dearth." Desire for Gabrielle shot through him as he remembered her in his arms under the canopy of Napoléon's tent.

He folded the letter slowly. At times he dreamed of Gabrielle. He loved her. That was the beginning and the end of it. The cruel fact was that he would probably never see her again.

"Captain Devaux! Your new mount is ready."

He looked up. Lost in thought, he had paid no attention to the sound of a horse being led toward him. Now he saw at once that the horse was a fine animal with an arched neck, an intelligent head and strong flanks. It was ready with his own saddle and saddlecloth, and Nicolas grinned as he pushed the letter inside his jacket and fastened its silver buttons.

He rose to his feet. This new horse was to bear the name Warrior, the same as that of his former mount, which had been shot from under him. He clapped Warrior's well-groomed neck.

"Well done, Sergeant," he said with satisfaction. He swung himself into the saddle and turned the horse into what had been the main dirt track through the hillside village where the brigade had bivouacked for the last couple of days. It was a poor place, as were most of the peasant villages, and not one of the hovels had escaped damage. The inhabitants had long since fled.

Nicolas glanced about him as he rode along at a leisurely pace. Smoke rose from army campfires, where scavenged fowl, wild birds and hunks of maggoty meat turned on spits over the flames. A strong smell of soap drifted from the laundry area, where soldiers' wives and other females among the followers of the camp were washing clothes. The army depended on the cooperation of a brave but motley collection of women to nurse the sick and wounded, and Nicolas held them in high regard. Their lot was entirely different from that of the officers' wives, who were kept far from danger zones and who enjoyed a pleasant social life in Madrid and Seville and other cities considered safe.

Riding on, Nicholas found it a relief to come into the shade of some fragrant orange trees toward the outskirts of the village. Everything was still and quiet away from the hubbub of the bivouac. The whole peninsula was a place where beauty and terror existed side by side. The magnificence of the brilliant landscapes never failed to please his eye, but in contrast to these vistas were the shell-wrecked cities and villages and the carnage of battlefields. The stench of death was commonplace; it was rare to breathe the pure scent of flowers without the loathsome and pervading taint.

At times Nicolas found it difficult to believe he had ever been the young hothead who had joined Bonaparte's army after he and his parents had fled Lyons. Then, he had had a reckless, dashing attitude toward soldiering, following a leader who exuded the promise of a great and glorious France. Now, his love for his country was as powerful as it had ever been, but this war had changed him in many ways. It was not a fight between soldiers. In this conflict innocent men, women and children were caught in the direct firing line, because the whole Spanish nation had risen up against those whom they regarded as foreign oppressors.

Bonaparte's claim that it had been necessary to invade Portugal to close the last European ports open to British trade no longer impressed Nicolas. He had come to see that it was a ploy by which the emperor intended to annex Spain. Although he accepted that Bonaparte's masterly government had restored France to greatness, he saw him now as a man intoxicated by power, ready to override the wishes of whole nations to further his empire. The principles of liberty and equality were being dragged through the mire by the very man who had once upheld them.

Nicolas kept his views to himself. To have voiced them would have brought his loyalty to the Tricolor into doubt, and that was unchanged. He would do whatever he had to do for his country in this campaign. If it brought about his death, so be it. Disillusioned, he rode back through the ruins of the village.

CHAPTER EIGHT

In Lyons, Gabrielle had developed backache that morning. By midafternoon Émile was notified via messenger that she had gone into labor. He set off at once for the city, full of trepidation now that her time had come.

He was not prepared for what the sight of her pain-filled eyes and her attempts at a smile did to him when he reached her bedside. Immediately he was overwhelmed by a sense of helplessness and inadequacy. There was nothing he could do to ease his wife's suffering. Somehow he managed a few encouraging words, and then Hélène tapped him on the arm.

"I think you'd better leave now," she said tactfully.

He was relieved, although he was at a loss as to how to spend the time. For a while he wandered aimlessly about the house, shuddering at the cries Gabrielle was unable to suppress. Then he went outside and followed the river, going over one bridge and returning by another. Once he stopped for wine at a café, and then dined at a restaurant. When he arrived back in the house, it was almost midnight. As he stepped into the hall a long, agonized moan came from the direction of Gabrielle's room.

"Dear God!" He was ashen. "It's not over yet."

"No, monsieur." The manservant took his hat and cane from him. "The doctor came two hours ago."

Cold with dread, Émile went into the blue salon to sit and wait. It was the longest night he had ever known. The sounds of Gabrielle's torment made him weep. Yet, to his shame, he slept.

A hand shook him. It was Hélène. "Émile! Wake up!"

He opened his eyes to see the room flooded with morning sunshine. He leaped to his feet in panic. "What has happened?"

Hélène, heavy-eyed with tiredness, was smiling at him. "You have a son. A beautiful boy with strong lungs. Gabrielle is exhausted, but she is going to recover quickly."

Émile was beyond words in his joy. Hélène laughed as he embraced her, lifting her off the ground in his exuberance. He set her back on her feet, then hurried to Gabrielle, taking the stairs two at a time. He reached the open doorway. Gabrielle lay white and drawn with her eyes closed in the freshly made bed, her hair brushed and shining. As Émile came into the room she turned her head and saw him. His expression was so joyous that she smiled, lifting a hand to hold it out to him. He rushed to the bedside to take it in both his own and press it to his lips.

"My dearest wife." His voice was choked, and there were tears on his cheeks. "If I had lost you—"

"Hush." She smoothed away his tears with her fingertips. "I'm here. I will always be here. Why not take a look at your son?"

He gazed into the crib at the scarlet-faced infant. "My cup of happiness is overflowing, my son," he said quietly.

Gabrielle, watching him, was thankful she had been instrumental in bringing him that happiness. Never had she been more grateful for the fact that he did not have the slightest suspicion that the love he yearned for had gone to another man. Through their newborn child, she had found a way in which to make up to Émile for her inability to give him her whole heart.

THEIR son was duly named André, after Émile's father. Hélène was a natural choice for godmother. On the day of the baptism she surprised everyone by appearing out of deep black for the first time, in a half-mourning shade of gray. Gabrielle, placing her son into her sister-in-law's arms, smiled in admiration.

"You look marvelous."

"It's in honor of your son. This is a time of new beginnings."

Gabrielle and Émile kissed her, then took Juliette by the hand to lead her out with them to the waiting carriages; Hélène and the rest of the christening party followed. Juliette kept looking back over her shoulder, enchanted by her mother's new appearance. It was as if the touch of a magic wand had transformed her.

True to her word, Gabrielle left the Rue Clémont for the country as soon as her doctor pronounced her fit to travel. The silk farm was not entirely at a standstill, because of the recovery of a cluster of mulberry trees that had escaped the worst of the blight. Second harvests did occur elsewhere, mostly in Italy, but hardly any of them came up for sale. Rumors were rife of their being shipped out to England, to the silk-weaving mills of Macclesfield. It was feared that the British might now take markets that would be difficult for the Lyonese to recapture.

As if Lyons had not suffered enough ill luck, another blow fell. The czar had decreed that luxury items of any kind were not to be imported into Russia, due to an urgent need to preserve currency. All over the city, silk merchants, including Gabrielle at her country retreat, received cancellation of the Russian orders that had been taken at Leipzig. Those who had risked everything to buy raw silk to fulfill these orders found themselves in deeper trouble.

By now Madame Hoinville had proved her excellence as a deputy. She made the journey twice a week to see Gabrielle and lay business matters before her, including new designs by Marcel for her approval. Altogether, Gabrielle was able to keep abreast of everything; she would have liked, however, to keep a closer eye on Henri, who merely corresponded with her.

Émile had never been more content. His son was thriving—a healthy, bonny-cheeked baby—and he had Gabrielle settled without restlessness under his roof, with nothing to threaten their lives together anymore. As a surprise, he had equipped an office for her next to his, and she had been delighted with it.

On the occasional visit Gabrielle made to Lyons in the first two months of the new year of 1811, she saw the miseries and suffering of those without work. It was many years since there had been so many beggars on the streets. Everywhere mills were closed and loom rooms stood silent. Her own mill and the few others still in operation were besieged daily by unemployed workers decimated by hunger and sickness.

Throughout the whole period Hélène distributed food, paid for out of her own pocket, to those with young children whom she knew to be in dire distress. Once, when the early spring weather was easing the cold away, Michel Piat caught up with her just as she left a house in the Croix-Rousse, not far from the Devaux mill.

"Madame Roche! What an unexpected pleasure. How are you?"

She turned her head, eyebrows raised in surprise. "Monsieur Piat. I'm very well and extremely thankful that this dreadful winter is at an end. Pray God we never see such suffering again."

"I agree. At least there are signs that the mulberry everywhere has recovered sufficiently to give a reasonable harvest."

"Yes, isn't it splendid. Are you still busy at the mill?"

"All the time. At the Devaux mill we had many German orders and far less from Russia. We felt the czar's decree less than most mills. How did your sister-in-law fare?"

"She lost a large number of Russian orders, but all her looms are operating at full pace."

"I'm glad to hear it." He paused. "I wonder if you would care to see the Devaux mill, now that you are so near?"

Hélène had made her last call of the day. "I'd be delighted."

He gave her a complete tour, for she had a natural feminine interest in the beauty of silk that made it close to her heart. She stopped by one loom where a particularly delicate design of wild roses was being woven into silk of dress weight—mist pink and green against a pale cream.

"That is quite the loveliest fabric I have seen for a long time," she raved. "You have a talented designer here."

"We think so."

After the tour they had coffee together in a charming salon with panels of green-and-white damask in a pattern of acanthus leaves. Michel told Hélène how Nicolas had restored the house upon his return to Lyons with some of the first silks to come from his Jacquard looms. Then Piat paused. He would have shielded any other woman from the ugly facts of war, but to Hélène he said, "I received a letter from Captain Devaux last week. At the time he wrote he was still in the winter cantonments. Now, as we have heard recently, the desperate fighting has resumed once more."

Her cheeks hollowed. "War is obscene, Monsieur Piat. I have never seen any glory in it. I understood my dear husband's passion for the army, his deep need to serve, and I shared totally his consuming love for France, just as I do today, but every time I watched him ride away, I knew that, even if I were lucky enough to have him home again, there would be many women less fortunate. My prayers are always for peace." She looked down quickly at the empty cup and saucer she held on her lap. "I'm talking too much. May I have some more coffee, do you think?"

He was even more impressed by her than he had been when she first came to warn him about the mulberry blight. He turned the conversation along other lines.

Two weeks later he sent her an invitation to dine. She accepted and enjoyed the evening, for Michel was an excellent host. Then on the first day of spring sunshine Hélène finally discarded her half mourning. A miniature of Jules remained by her bed, where it was the first thing she looked at every morning, but the rawness of grief had finally healed.

Her dressmaker had delivered a dozen new gowns, including three of Roche silk—one in Pompeian red, one in deep gold, and one in sapphire. She planned to wear the gold one when she attended a ball to be held to celebrate the birth of a son to Napoléon and his empress. The widespread national rejoicing had been marred somewhat by the recent news that Masséna, Napoléon's marshal, had been driven back out of Portugal. But the general feeling was that the tide would soon turn again, and that nothing should be allowed to spoil the Lyons ball, which was an expression of loyalty to the emperor.

It was to close with a fireworks display said to be the most elaborate ever staged. Émile and Gabrielle were coming to Lyons especially for the event, leaving their bouncing nine-month-old son in the care of a devoted nursemaid. Henri was making his own plans for the evening, which he would be attending with Yvonne. By arrangement, he had recently met Brouchier in a back-street café and given him instructions in low tones. A purse of gold was pushed surreptitiously across the table at which they sat, and there would be more when the spy's task was completed.

Nicolas Devaux's departure for the peninsula had not lessened Henri's resolve to wipe Devaux silk from the face of Lyons. What he had not expected was that the birth of an imperial heir would be instrumental in the timing of this final act of revenge. It was almost as if he and the emperor had been waiting the same number of years to achieve a special aim.

The evening of the ball was mild, fragrant with the scent of lilacs. Gabrielle, in a dress of copper silk, and Hélène, in her gown of gold, were visions of beauty and elegance as they entered the ballroom with Émile, their white-gloved escort. As the dancing began, Michel Piat came to bow to Hélène.

"My dance, I believe, Hélène."

She had promised him the first dance at their last meeting, when they had begun using each other's Christian names. There was firm guidance in Michel's capable hand as he took her fingers to lead her into the steps of the dance. Her feet felt curiously light. Suddenly it was almost as if she were waltzing on air.

For Gabrielle the highlight of the evening was meeting Nicolas's manager. The introductions took place when her sister-in-law and Michel Piat came in from the terrace. As it happened, Gabrielle's polonaise partner and Hélène were promised for the next dance together, and as they swept into a gavotte Gabrielle and Michel found themselves able to talk on their own. Inevitably, the topic was silk and the difficulties of the past winter. It brought Gabrielle to what she had wanted to ask from the first moment.

"I trust Captain Devaux has suffered no harm on campaign." She was conscious of holding her breath, of being on guard against giving herself away by crying out if she should hear he had been wounded.

"No harm that I know of" was the reply he gave her. He went on to tell her of the one communication he had received, although not in the detail he had given Hélène.

On the ballroom floor the gavotte had ended. When Gabrielle was claimed by a new partner, Michel stood by one of the balcony pillars and watched Hélène amid the twirling throng of dancers. He was content to wait until the supper dance, when he could take her hand again. On the terrace he had made his feelings known to her and told her of his prospects for the future. It had not been his intention to speak yet, but this evening there had been a special rapport between them. He had never thought he would find another woman he could truly love.

At the close of the evening, when everyone streamed out onto the terraces to view the fireworks over the river, Michel was with the Valmont party. The only person who made him feel unwelcome was Émile Valmont. The man was thoroughly distant.

"Oooo!" "Ahhh!" The sounds rose from the crowd as the fireworks soared into the air to burst into multicolored stars, lighting up the buildings and the upturned faces far below. Applause rippled out at the most spectacular displays. The sky was full of silver stars fading away when another kind of glow was to be seen in the direction of the Croix-Rousse.

"Fire! Look, there's a fire!"

Michel was immediately uneasy. He turned to Gabrielle.

"I came here on foot, madame. Might I have the loan of your carriage to get me to the fire? It may be nowhere near our mill, but I have to be sure."

"Of course. I'll take you to my servant Gaston. He will get you there in no time at all." She edged her way through the crowd, Michel and Hélène following her. The three of them hurried from the terrace and ran along the path that led to the courtyard.

"Gaston! Gaston!" Gabrielle called twice to make herself heard above the buzz of voices and the explosion of fireworks.

He heard her and broke away from the group with whom he had been watching the rise of flames into the night. "Madame?"

"Take Monsieur Piat to the Devaux mill as fast as you can."

"Yes, madame. It's been confirmed, has it?"

"What do you mean?"

"Somebody came riding by just now and said it looked as though it was the Devaux mill that was afire."

She was never sure why she got into the carriage with Michel. It was not a conscious decision, simply an instinct to try to do whatever she could for Nicolas's property. Hélène scrambled into the carriage with her, and they were tossed about as Gaston, his servant's uniform etched against the night, drove the horses at a gallop through the streets.

They had to alight at the head of the street, for a crowd had gathered. Michel groaned aloud at the sight that met them. The whole Devaux mill was ablaze, black smoke billowing over the rooftops. He plunged into the spectators to shoulder his way through. Like a bear, Gaston spread his arms out to envelop Gabrielle and Hélène, and they followed, half falling into the clearing.

An attempt was being made to save the Devaux residence as well as the tall houses at the far end of the mill. Several chains of buckets were being passed from both ends of the street to the nearest public water ducts. Gabrielle rushed forward to take a place in a chain reaching into Nicolas's house, which was already on fire, the upper floors having been ignited by sparks from the mill roof. Gaston gave a hand to those salvaging furniture, and Hélène helped drag to safety some of the lighter pieces. Michel had dashed through the house to try to get upstairs to save some of his possessions, but the smoke wrenched at his lungs and he fell back, choking. People were shouting to him to come out. He reached the hall in time to see through open doors the beginning of the destruction of the green and white salon as flames crept up from the floorboards and down from the ceiling.

He had just enough time to snatch up a package he had left behind earlier that day before Gaston's big hand descended on his shoulder to thrust him, dazed and coughing, through falling sparks and burning splinters into the street. There was a crackling in his hair, and Hélène hurled herself at him to smother the flames with her hands. He could hardly see her for the swelling of his red-rimmed eyes, but he threw his arms about her in the certain knowledge that she was his for the rest of his days.

Émile had not seen Gabrielle leave the terrace with Hélène and Michel and, unperturbed, continued to watch the fireworks. It was only when they ended that he learned of Gabrielle and Hélène's hasty departure with Piat and the reason for it. Something seemed to snap in his head, releasing all the blackness of mind and soul that he had begun to believe might have left him forever. With it came fury with Gabrielle. She had dared to go running off to Devaux's mill, deserting him?

He was shaking with temper as he hastened across the forecourt in search of a hackney. One came driving up quickly.

"Hurry!" he instructed the driver. "There's a fire in the Croix-Rousse. It may be the Devaux mill. Go as fast as you can."

He sat back in the stale-smelling interior and tried to drive away the thundering despair that had come upon him. All these months he had been harboring the illusion that he had at last won Gabrielle's love. His own happiness had prevented him from seeing that what he wanted most from her belonged to another man.

Lunging forward, he thumped a fist against the carriage wall behind the driver. "Faster! Do you hear me? Faster, I say!"

The hackney took him as far as possible. He leaped out, tossed the fare at the driver and ran forward to reach the crowd. He was at the south end of the fire, close to tall houses that had been ignited by the mill, which was clearly destined to be a total loss. He could see that Devaux's house was also completely ablaze. Suddenly, across the clearing, he saw Gabrielle.

She looked exhausted, standing beside Gaston at the forefront of the opposite crowd, gazing sadly up at Devaux's house as the fire consumed it. Her gown was torn and her face streaked with smoke grime, the gleam of her gold necklace an incongruous touch. He began to push his way through to the police line, shoving angrily at anyone who blocked him.

"Not so fast, monsieur. You can't go in front of those buildings."

Émile glared at the policeman. "Let me pass! My wife is over there!" He pointed across to Gabrielle, who caught the disturbance out of the corner of her eye. "She's waiting for me. Can't you see?" With that, he thrust himself forward, and began to run across the cleared area of the street, full of jealous rage.

Seeing him approach across the water-sloshed cobbles, a dark figure illumined by the glow of the flames, Gabrielle took a step forward. He saw, almost to his disbelief, that she looked relieved and happy to see him. She smiled, giving a little wave in order that he should not miss her whereabouts in the confusion.

Her smile went right to his heart, and his temper ebbed. Maybe he had made a mistake. Maybe it was not as he had feared. Then, abruptly, her expression changed, a look of terror stamping her face. She made a sharp move, as if to run to him, arms outstretched, but her coachman grabbed her back. Instinct told him what was happening. The fire fighters were scattering, running in total panic. There were screams and warning shouts mingled with a deafening roar and a rushing sound as the whole side of the mill began to bend and disintegrate into white-hot bricks and flaring wood and searing ashes. The cascading sparks were brighter than any fireworks display.

Gabrielle screamed as if she herself were dying. Gaston pressed her face into his shoulder and spared her the sight of Émile's instant but terrible death.

GABRIELLE bore her bereavement with dignity. The funeral took place in the village near the silk farm, where Émile was laid to rest in the little churchyard. Special prayers were included in the service for two other victims of the fire. Afterward family and friends went to the Valmont house for refreshments.

When everyone had gone, Gabrielle went to sit for a long while by her son, who was sleeping in his crib in the softly lit nursery. Her thoughts were full of Émile.

As for Henri, he did not appear to take long to throw off his sorrow and behave in his normal fashion again. Things were finally as he had always wanted them to be. After the fire there was no longer a Devaux loom left in Lyons.

Henri also had cause for relief in that Brouchier had not approached him for the rest of the fee for a job well done but had prudently decided to leave Lyons until all official inquiries about the fire were at an end.

The situation between Michel and Hélène had reached a distressing stalemate because of the fire. His prospects, which he had mapped out to her on the terrace during the ball, had vanished in the flames. Until he could be certain of his future once more, he felt himself to be in no position to propose marriage formally. She suffered her disappointment privately.

Michel seemed to be the only one unconvinced that the fireworks had ignited the mill. In the morning he had walked through the still smoking ruins. He saw that there had been some fire on the top floor, but that the flames had swept through the loom rooms in seconds. He remained suspicious, even though a burned-out rocket had been found on the cobbles in a neighboring street. Michel wrote a letter to Nicolas informing him of the fire, and the prefect of Lyons agreed to use his influence to get it sent with military dispatches to ensure its arrival.

Since Gabrielle no longer came to Lyons, Madame Hoinville resumed her visits to the country. Gabrielle seemed to have become thinner and paler every time they met, and Madame Hoinville found her inattentive to anything but the silk farm.

Gabrielle had taken on Michel to assist her, and she found him invaluable. The mulberry harvest was all that could be expected in view of the setback of the previous year, and there was no disease among the silkworms from the replacement cocoons that Émile had purchased at great cost. His finances had been left in a sorry state, and she could guess at the worries he had endured.

Hélène was becoming increasingly concerned about Gabrielle. It was as if, with Émile's death, she had succumbed to his domination as she had never done in his lifetime. The cause lay in the confession that had slipped out of her in the midst of her wild grief on the night of the fire. Hélène, holding her in comforting arms, had heard what she had already guessed.

"He was there because of me!" The tears had gushed from the beautiful eyes. "I saw his expression in those last seconds before he realized what was happening. There was only gladness in his face at the sight of me." Sobs overtook her again.

"Remember that," Hélène urged gently, rocking her as she would have rocked a child in distress. "Be comforted by it. Émile would never have blamed you for what happened."

It seemed that her advice had not been heeded. It was only when Gabrielle was with André, cradling him in her arms, caring for him and sometimes singing him a lullaby in a low, sweet voice, that she relaxed, letting the tautness of spirit go from her.

Two months to the day that Émile died, Gabrielle collapsed. She was in a silkshed when she folded onto the stone floor without a sound. Michel was the first to reach her, and he gathered her up to carry her along the path into the house. Hélène was sent for, and by the time she arrived, Dr. Jaunet had called.

"Why hasn't Madame Valmont been eating?" he demanded.

"I knew she had little appetite these days, but I thought it would right itself in time."

"In time! Good heavens, madame. Malnutrition is more than a decline in appetite. You shall get nourishment into her now, even if you have to spoon-feed her like a baby."

Hélène, experienced in nursing the sick, carried out her assignment efficiently, and soon Gabrielle was on the road to recovery. But contrary to Hélène's hopes, when Gabrielle did begin work on a full scale, it was again the silk farm that came first with her. Not once did she drive into Lyons to visit the mill or the design room. All her efforts were concentrated on raw silk.

Gradually various commitments made it necessary for Hélène to return to the Rue Clémont. "Why not come back to Lyons with me for a few days?" she suggested to Gabrielle: "You could catch up on business." They were sitting on the terrace in the balmy evening air, both André and Juliette asleep in bed.

Gabrielle brushed a tendril of hair away from her brow with a relaxed hand. "I should like to, but I'm too busy here."

"Have you considered selling the silk farm?"

There was a slight intake of breath from Gabrielle. "At the present time there are no buyers for struggling silk farms."

Hélène saw through her. "Am I to believe that it may be years before you return to the work you have always liked best?"

Gabrielle maintained her casual air. "Yes, that is how it is." Then, suddenly, her reserve broke and she sprang to her feet and went with a few swift steps to the edge of the terrace, standing to look out over the dark garden. "Why should I pretend with you? You are closer than any sister could have been. I hate it here."

Hélène was amazed. "Then why stay?"

"I must." Gabrielle continued to look away, clenching her hands together in front of her. "What you haven't realized is the effect that rejecting Nicolas's love has had on me. It was like a denial of life itself. To go back to Lyons would be to revive every association with the times he and I had together. Here, I am Émile's widow and Nicolas is far from me in the peninsula." Her voice shattered in her despair. "In Lyons he would be back in my heart." She bowed her head, covering her face with her hands.

Hélène hurried to her. "Forgive me. I didn't mean to probe. I have been thoughtless and unkind."

Gabrielle raised her head and took Hélène by the arms. "Never say that. You are incapable of unkindness. You had to know why I can't face seeing Lyons again. I'm thankful I've told you."

On the morning Hélène left with Juliette they were accompanied by Michel, who had business in the city. As Hélène settled her daughter back onto the seat she glanced across at him.

"In the letter you sent to Nicolas notifying him of the fire, did you mention that Émile Valmont had died?"

"No. I said there were three fatalities, but the whole of the letter was taken up with matters of insurance and so forth. I listed the casualties in a letter I sent later."

"Pray God he receives it," Hélène said almost to herself.

When Hélène arrived home at the Rue Clémont, she found that Henri and Yvonne had had their quarters in the house extravagantly refurbished; in addition they had annexed the grand salon, where important customers were received. Its walls had been redecorated with gleaming orange-red brocade woven with sunflowers.

"What do you think of it?" Henri asked with an expansive sweep of his arm as he led her into it.

Tired and dusty from the journey, Hélène frowned questioningly. "I thought Gabrielle had halted this kind of expense until the trade situation was better again."

"I'm in charge now. I make all the decisions now that my sister has chosen to bury herself in the country." Then he added, seeing that Hélène was about to stalk away, "Oh, there's something I have to say to you. In the future, would you keep your daughter from running all over the house? It disturbs Yvonne."

Hélène halted to stare at him in astonishment. "Juliette has never invaded the privacy of your apartments."

"No, but I'd be obliged if you would keep her in your own rooms whenever she is at home. You'll notice that a few changes have been made in your absence, quite apart from the alterations in this salon. It seemed foolish for Yvonne and me not to use the whole house when it's beginning to appear unlikely that Gabrielle will ever return here on a permanent basis. Yvonne has hired a new housekeeper and will settle the menus with her daily, so there's no longer any need for you to feel obliged to take part in running the household."

"I never thought of it as an obligation. I looked upon this house as my home from the day I came here as a bride."

"That may be, but you'll find things have changed."

Hélène angrily entered her own apartments to find that Yvonne had had several family pieces of furniture taken away. Closing the door after herself, Hélène was pensive. She had said long ago to Gabrielle that she would leave the Rue Clémont when she felt the right time had come, and Henri and Yvonne had now shown her they no longer wanted her under the same roof.

Unfortunately, it was not now convenient to leave. Michel's plans were still uncertain. He was applying for posts better suited to his ability than the silk farm; when he was relocated, she would marry him, and they would have their own home. In the meantime, she must put up with the situation.

The cooler days of autumn had come when Hélène received a message that Madame Hoinville wished to see her at the Roche mill. When the spinners arrived, one of them took charge of Juliette, leaving Hélène free to go into Madame Hoinville's office.

"Thank you for coming, Madame Roche," the woman greeted Hélène. "It was most urgent that I see you."

"You realize I have no connection with the business?"

"Of course. But you are close to Madame Valmont. I must ask that you do everything in your power to persuade her to return to Lyons. I believe she is being swindled in her absence."

Hélène was startled. "Please explain."

"Valuable orders, which should be coming into this mill, are being siphoned off elsewhere. Some faulty brocade was returned to this mill directly from a foreign customer. There was only a minuscule flaw, but it was consistent throughout a very expensive piece. I went to compare it with a pattern that had been made up with the same dyed yarns and supposedly on the same looms. I was able to see at once that it had not come from here, and yet it was a design exclusive to Maison Roche."

"Why don't you tell all this to Madame Valmont? You have only to show her the piece and the pattern. There is your proof."

Madame Hoinville sighed. "I'm unable to do that. The faulty piece was removed from its shelf without my knowledge."

"Do you know who took it?"

"I was told. There was no secrecy about the removal. Rejects are frequently sold off. If an enquiry should be made, I would expect to hear that the purchaser was a stranger who passed through Lyons and is now gone without a trace."

"This is an extremely grave matter. I must insist that you tell my sister-in-law everything you have told me."

"Madame, I cannot!" Madame Hoinville took a deep breath. "It is not for me to point a finger at her brother without positive proof. Yes, it was Monsieur Roche who removed the brocade."

Hélène drove out of Lyons to see Gabrielle the next day. Upon arrival she told her everything that Madame Hoinville had said. Although Gabrielle sat listening, her hands quiet in her lap, her gaze was directed sadly out the window. Afterward she turned her head to look at Hélène.

"How impossible it is to escape destiny. It seems I have to return to Lyons after all. I'll not have my son's birthright eroded through Henri's pilfering. I'll be ready to leave by this evening."

Hélène helped her to pack. It was noticeable that Gabrielle was taking no mourning garments with her. By evening, dust sheets covered all the furniture, valuables had been packed for transfer to the Rue Clémont and shutters were closed over the windows. An agent had been called in to arrange the sale of the silk farm, which Michel was to manage until it changed hands.

At the moment of departure Gabrielle was the last to leave the house to which she had come as a bride. She stood alone in the silent hall. "Farewell, dear Émile," she said softly. Then she turned and went out of the house, locking the door behind her.

When she arrived at the Rue Clémont with Hélène and André, it was to find that Henri and Yvonne were holding a musical soiree in the grand salon.

"Don't interrupt the festivities," she said to the servant who had admitted them. "Just make sure that all the baggage is unloaded quickly and inform the housekeeper of our arrival. You may bring a supper tray to my office. I shall be working there."

"Er—one moment, madame. Monsieur Roche moved from his office into yours several weeks ago."

"Indeed?" Gabrielle raised her eyebrows. "No matter. It is mine again now, and that is where you will find me."

A glance into Henri's old office showed that her possessions were stacked there as if in readiness for storage. As she opened the door into her own domain she saw that he had ensconced himself in a masterly fashion, with his large desk—which had once been their father's—his ornate silver inkstand with its inset sand shaker, and his leather chair. He had also had every one of his cupboard files brought in.

She set to work on the files at once, estimating that she had two hours before Henri learned she had returned. A supper tray was brought in. She nibbled at some of the food, hardly aware of what she was eating. Again and again the files revealed nothing in the least incriminating. Everything was in perfect order.

It was midnight when the company departed. Then, as she had expected, heavy footsteps came hurrying in the direction of the office, and Henri burst into the room. "What are you doing here?"

She gave him a direct look. "I'm back to stay, Henri."

"What about the silk farm?"

"That's to be sold. Whatever it brings will be most welcome at the present time. The coffers of Maison Roche are low."

He glared about the room. "All these files were locked. You had no right to go through any papers without asking me."

"Then it was careless of you to have left the keys in my office. You need have no fear that I looked at anything that did not deal with Roche silk, and for that I don't have to ask permission."

"Are you satisfied with what you've seen?" His whole stance was belligerent, and he looked as if he might strike her should she give anything but an affirmative answer.

She gestured toward what she had been reading. "Nobody could fault these ledgers. Everything is recorded meticulously."

"Since you are determined to work here," he said, "I'd like to get my desk and other possessions back into my old office right away. The file cupboards can stay here."

She collected the papers in front of her. "I think I will go to bed. The changeover of the furniture can wait until morning."

"No, it shall not." He jerked a chair aside, as if prepared to pull the desk out of the room unaided if need be. "Tomorrow I want to be able to begin work without hindrance."

As she left him he summoned servants to effect the move.

That night, while preparing for bed, Gabrielle thought about Henri. His blustering manner, his false bonhomie in difficult situations and his pompous airs had always made it impossible to think he might be capable of doing her or anybody else serious physical harm. But tonight something had made him desperate. His near panic at finding her there in the office was an indication that under this roof was evidence that would incriminate him.

Then something stirred in her memory. She pictured her father sitting at the desk that was now Henri's. Once in her childhood she had entered the office when her father was searching for a paper he had misplaced. He had not seen her enter. He had been annoyed when he looked up and saw her standing there, and had jumped up from his desk to hustle her out of the room and close the door again. Now she had a clue at last to the whereabouts of what she had been seeking since her return to the Rue Clémont.

At a run she went to Henri's office. The door was unlocked. Putting the lamp on the desk, she sat down in the chair and removed the small middle drawer. Then she reached into the aperture. After a few minutes of fumbling, she found the catch of a secret drawer and released it. The drawer slid forward into the lamplight, packed tight with papers.

She began to go through them with trembling hands. It did not take her long to discover that Henri had his own mill of the same name just outside Lyons, established not long after Maison Roche became hers. Ever since that day, he had stolen sections or entire orders from her, recording them in his files but not in the Maison Roche ledgers. It was impossible to estimate even roughly how many thousands of francs had been diverted from Maison Roche by her own brother.

Suddenly the door was flung open. Henri stood there in a dressing robe, his face congested with violent temper.

"You prying wretch!"

He lunged for her as she sprang up, seizing her by the throat and shaking her, the pressure of his hands choking her protests into gurgling sounds. He was enraged beyond control. Her arms flailed, and her fingers touched the heavy silver inkstand. She managed to grab it and swing it upward, sand and ink pouring from it down her arm and splashing over him until it crashed to the floor. Together they staggered about the room.

"Henri!" Yvonne's shriek of outrage came from the doorway.

He released Gabrielle, and she collapsed to the floor. Then he slumped down in a chair and began to sob. Gabrielle was aware of Yvonne's propping her forward to help her get her breath back. Then Hélène, who had been aroused by Henri's bellowing, rushed to the office to kneel by Gabrielle. Supporting her with an arm, she wiped her face with a handkerchief. There was ink on Gabrielle's hair and down her robe and nightgown, and the whole floor was gritty with sand. Next Hélène poured a small cognac from a decanter and held it to Gabrielle's lips. "Give a large measure to Henri," she instructed Yvonne.

Henri, still sobbing, emptied his glass at a gulp.

"What's all this about?" Yvonne now demanded shrilly.

He glanced at her with a hangdog air and looked away again. "Gabrielle has discovered I have a little sideline."

"You fool! You could have broken away from Maison Roche and started your own fabric house if you had wanted to do it."

He jerked himself out of the chair. "With your extravagant ways what other chance did I ever have?" he roared back. "Your debts have been a millstone around my neck for years!"

"So I'm to blame?" She wagged her head in mockery of him. "What of your gambling? You never were a winner! That's why your father never left you Maison Roche in the first place!"

He hit her with his fist. Then he went on hitting her, as if a second bout of madness had overtaken him. Yvonne screamed as he beat her down to the floor. Hélène left Gabrielle to try to intervene, but Henri thrust her from him, shouting, "Keep out of this!"

Then Gabrielle swayed to her feet to try to reach the bellpull to summon help, but before she could stretch out her hand to it, Henri stopped his onslaught as abruptly as he had begun. He stood over Yvonne, who lay whimpering on the floor.

"I've finished with you!" he bellowed. "You'll get out of my sight and out of this house tonight!"

He swung about and charged bull-like for the door, pulling it open. Gabrielle stepped in front of him and rested a hand on either side of the doorjamb to bar his way.

"It's you who must leave tonight, Henri. I always knew you were a bully and a coward, but I never thought you would go to the lengths I've just witnessed."

He did not attempt to throw her out of his way. "You can't turn me out of my home," he blustered. "I was born here."

"It was your home, and would have been to the end of your days if you hadn't chosen to do what you did. This is André's house now. I only hold it in trust for him, as I do Maison Roche, and nobody in the world is going to harm his interests, not even my own brother." She was sickened by him. "Now go, Henri. Both of you go and never come back to the Rue Clémont." Her arms dropped to her sides, and she leaned back against the wall to let him pass.

He stared at her, his lips drawing back over his teeth in a grimace of vengeance. "Damn you and your high-and-mighty ways. I always pitied Émile for having you for his wife. During the time when you and Devaux were meeting secretly, there was always a spy trailing you. It's my guess Émile went to his grave not knowing whether or not he had fathered your son!"

Gabrielle, already ashen from her ordeal at his hands, pressed herself against the wall as if to stay herself from falling. "Go, Henri," she repeated with colorless lips. "Go!"

With a self-congratulatory snort at what he had done to her, he strode from the office. Gabrielle looked wordlessly at Hélène, who had risen from attending to Yvonne to stand statuelike, struck into horrified immobility by the words of cruelty Henri had directed toward his own sister. Gabrielle opened her mouth twice in an attempt to speak, but her voice seemed to have gone in the shock of what had been disclosed.

CHAPTER NINE

GABRIELLE, elegant in her gown of tangerine silk, a gold brooch at her throat, received an important visitor in the grand salon. Monsieur Morard of the Mobilier Impérial, a distinguished-looking man with gray hair, came across the room to bow over her hand.

"I'm honored, Madame Valmont. I have been an admirer of Roche fabrics ever since I first saw your display at the Lyons exposition."

"I'm delighted to hear that. Won't you please sit down, Monsieur Morard, and allow me to offer you some refreshment."

When the preliminaries were over, he explained the nature of his visit. "The emperor has decided that the Palace of Versailles, which has been little used since the Revolution, when its fine rooms were destroyed, is to be completely refurbished. We of the Mobilier Impérial are interested in commissioning silks from you for several of the salons."

Gabrielle flushed with excitement at what was happening at last. Then, suddenly, her pleasure dimmed. "Am I to receive this commission because Maison Devaux is no longer in operation?"

"Not at all," the man hastened to assure her. "As there are many rooms in Versailles, we are also commissioning from other leading silk houses in Lyons. If the Maison Devaux had not been burned down, it would have received its share. The emperor wants to make this palace the most magnificent the world has ever seen."

"I shall be proud to take part in such an enterprise."

She then showed him a wide selection of exquisite designs, several incorporating the imperial bee. He picked out a number to put before the committee for a final selection.

"You should not have long to wait," he said as he was leaving.

As Monsieur Morard's carriage took him away, Gabrielle gave a laugh of sheer exuberance, then went in search of Hélène. The good news was in keeping with the whole atmosphere of the house now that Henri and Yvonne had gone.

Henri had left in the early hours of the morning after that terrible night. Yvonne was permitted to stay until her injuries were healed, but when a letter from Henri was delivered ten days later, she rose from her bed, packed her belongings, ordered a carriage and left the house.

Now, once again, Juliette played wherever she wished, and André toddled about after her whenever he could. She was like a sister to him, and Hélène was a second mother, always in charge until Gabrielle came home. It was Hélène who had made life bearable for Gabrielle after Henri's terrible disclosure.

"Never let your brother's evil words taint your memories of Émile," she had said the next day. "I remember Émile when André was born. I have never seen a man so happy. There was not the least doubt in his mind as to whether André was his child. He said to me more than once, 'I can see my father in my son.' "

Gabrielle felt very grateful for Hélène's reassurance. Now she opened the door into Hélène's salon with a flourish and found her writing at her escritoire. "Tra-la-la! It's happened! Roche silk is to hang at Versailles!"

Hélène put down her pen to clap her hands. "Congratulations! How wonderful!"

Gabrielle swept herself onto a sofa. She related all the details to Hélène and then said that her fears about gaining at Nicolas's expense had proved groundless. "That mattered to me more than anything," she confessed soberly.

"I'm sure it did."

She let her head drop onto the back of the sofa, her gaze far away. "I live for his return, Hélène. Being back in Lyons has done everything to me that I knew it would. Although the past is still with me, and always will be, I'm looking to the future, not only my own—with my longing for Nicolas—but my son's and that of Maison Roche."

"Have you written to Nicolas yet?"

"No. I do not dare. If I wrote, and received no reply, I would have no way of knowing if he had written to me or not. That would be more torment for me. When we see each other again, all will be well. I'm sure of it." Her face was suffused with hope and confidence. "I know Nicolas is going to come through the Peninsular War. I feel it in the marrow of my bones."

"I pray he does," Hélène said sincerely.

That same week the silk farm was sold at a higher price than Gabrielle had hoped to get. It seemed that she was on a crest that nothing could spoil. Michel returned to Lyons, and she offered him the post of manager of Maison Roche in Henri's place.

"I'm honored," he said enthusiastically. "I have served one great silk house in Lyons, and now I am to serve another."

He went without delay to tell Hélène of his new appointment. She rose excitedly to give both hands into his outstretched clasp.

"That's splendid news!" she exclaimed.

"It means we can look to the future now." He kissed her gently. "We can set a marriage date as soon as we find a house."

"Let us live here in this house for a while before we get our own home," she said. "It is a help to Gabrielle to know that André is in my charge when she is busy, and when the orders come in from the Mobilier Impérial, you and she will not have a minute to spare." Smiling lovingly at him, she linked her fingers behind his neck. "In any case, I don't want to wait for house buying before we marry. Let it be soon."

"Tomorrow?" he teased.

"The day after," she said, not teasing.

There was a civil ceremony, followed by a religious marriage at the Church of St.-Nizier. Only a few close friends were present, and the bride wore a gown of Devaux silk. Michel had rescued the length from a package in the midst of the fire. It was the cream silk with the pale pink roses that she had admired on her visit to the Devaux looms, and he had had a piece put aside for her. To Gabrielle the beautiful, shimmering gown was like a banner being flown for a silk house that would rise again.

The bride and groom left for a honeymoon in the fishing village of Antibes, on the Mediterranean coast. During their absence Gabrielle heard from the Mobilier Impérial. She was commissioned to produce the fabrics for eight rooms at Versailles, including a study for the emperor himself. This marvelous commission encompassed wall hangings, draperies and upholstery fabrics. Alone in her office, Gabrielle twirled around with the letter like a very young girl. Her looms would gleam with woofs and warps of imperial colors, and glitter with silver and gold *filé* and *frisé*, to bring Maison Roche to the notice of the world.

By the time Michel and Hélène returned, she was already getting samples of dyes together. Michel took up his work as effortlessly as if he had been with Maison Roche for years. When he was at the mill one morning, a letter was brought to him. After reading it, he returned to the Rue Clémont, where he went in search of his wife. After she had read the letter, he said, "I thought it best that you be the one to break the news to Gabrielle."

She nodded sadly. "I'll do it now."

Hélène went to the design room, where Gabrielle sat perched on a high stool beside Marcel. She waited until Gabrielle, catching sight of the letter in her hand, came toward her, able to tell by her expression that it was a serious matter.

"Let's go to the blue salon," Hélène said, turning.

"Wait!" Gabrielle put out a restraining hand, her voice low and hoarse with dread. "Is Nicolas dead?"

Hélène was dismayed by the query. "No! Neither is he wounded." She put an arm about Gabrielle's waist.

"It's still bad news, isn't it?"

"I'm afraid so." Hélène's expression was sympathetic. "Michel heard from Nicolas today. One thing is certain. Although Michel's letter about the fire got through, the later one, telling of your widowhood, never reached him."

"How do you know that?"

"Two reasons. The first is that in the last paragraph Nicolas sends his compliments to Monsieur and Madame Valmont."

Gabrielle's face did not change. "And the second reason?"

"He has put the site of Maison Devaux up for sale, and written that he never intends to return to Lyons."

"That's impossible! I don't know how to believe this." Gabrielle put her fingertips to her temples. "If peace should be restored tomorrow, there would be nothing to stop him from going anywhere in the world, and I might never find him."

Hélène briskly dismissed this statement. "The campaign in the peninsula is far from over, which gives us the time we need. Somehow we must find a way to get a message through to him."

"The time for letters and messages and waiting is over. Would you look after André for me if I go away? I could never leave him with anyone else."

"You don't have to ask me. I love taking care of him. You know that." Hélène's brows drew together. "But where are you going?"

There was an eager determination in Gabrielle's expression. "To Nicolas! I promised him once that if ever I was free, I would go to him. That time has come."

"You can't! No woman can travel alone into a field of war."

"I'll not be alone. Gaston will come with me, I know. He's an old war-horse himself, and I'm sure he'll leap at the chance." She began to outline a plan. "I should be able to get to Ciudad Rodrigo by Christmas. There'll be no fighting at that time. The troops on both sides will be in their winter cantonments. I should be able to have at least a week or two with Nicolas before turning homeward again." There was a sudden swim of tears in her eyes that she could not keep back. "The hardest thing for me to bear will be my separation from André. He will miss me as I shall miss him."

"Then please don't go." Hélène's voice shook. "I beg you."

"I have to. I realize now that this is why destiny brought me back to Lyons. I'm being given a last chance to share my life with the man I love."

Hélène could not say anything more after that to dissuade her.

As GABRIELLE had expected, Gaston did not hesitate when she put her request to him. Without asking why, he simply wanted to know how soon she wished to start.

"As soon as possible," she replied.

"Allow me two days, madame, to select horses and put together supplies."

His first step was to make inquiries about any departure of reinforcements from the local barracks. He learned that a baggage train would be moving out under military escort at dawn the next morning. It was bound for Salamanca, which was on the same route as Ciudad Rodrigo. They would not have many miles to go after that, and all within range of French protection.

After notifying Gabrielle to be ready sooner than expected, Gaston worked the rest of the day and into the night. She had given him the money to pay for everything. Swiftly he ticked off the items: spyglass, canteens for water, horseshoes, hammer and nails, kettle, cooking pot, tinderbox, knife and hatchet, storable food. There was also feed for the horses, his musket, a bludgeon, pistols and ammunition as well as blankets and extra clothing.

Shortly before dawn he and Gabrielle rode away down the Rue Clémont, a packhorse in their wake. Her last action before embracing her sister-in-law had been to kiss her sleeping son.

Gabrielle had chosen to travel in a warm, comfortable and thoroughly unfashionable riding habit cut straight around the hem, with leggings beneath. Her black hat was flat and brimmed, and over her shoulders hung a cape that was virtually rainproof. Gaston, also practically clad, wore a goatskin jacket, thick breeches, a cloak, and a well-worn rust-red felt hat pulled down to his ears. They could easily be mistaken for a farming couple.

At the barracks, Gaston reined to wait, and Gabrielle followed suit. Soon officers on horseback, soldiers on foot and wagons loaded with ammunition and other supplies emerged from the archway and went past with a clatter of hoofs and a rumble of wheels over the cobbles. Gabrielle and Gaston fell in with wives and others following, behind the rear guard. As the sky lightened, the whole convoy passed across the wide and spacious Place Bellecour. On the slopes of the city rising beyond, the first rays of the wintry sun touched the tips of the tallest spires.

Contrary to Gabrielle's hopes, she was not to be in Ciudad Rodrigo by Christmas. As the days passed she wondered if she had ever lived any existence other than jogging along in the saddle behind creaking wheels and thudding feet. The suburbs of Salamanca were reached in the first week of the new year of 1812. While the baggage train went on toward the center of the city, she and Gaston continued on alone.

They came within sight of Ciudad Rodrigo on the evening of

January 12. Gabrielle wanted to ride on to reach the fortress city, but darkness was falling and Gaston did not want to risk the dangers of travel in the dark. In the middle of the night Gabrielle heard a clink of metal. Gaston had heard it too. Throwing off his blanket, he knelt on one knee, listening intently. Then he heard it again. Weaponry. He thrust one of the pistols he always kept by him into Gabrielle's hands.

"I'm going to scout around to find out what is happening."

He slipped between the trees. It was a moonless but starry night. Coming to a place where the land sloped down, he saw a whole sea of men making their way toward a hill where a few lights twinkled on the top. He guessed the lights came from a redoubt, part of the defenses of Ciudad Rodrigo, and these were not guerrillas he was observing. These were British soldiers! They were going against all the traditions of warfare in breaking out of winter cantonments early in January to make a surprise attack on his unsuspecting countrymen. There was nothing he could do to warn the redoubt, but he had to find a way to get Gabrielle away from here and out of danger.

When he came back to her, she refused to consider going home. "I haven't come all this way to turn back now! Ciudad Rodrigo is only a few miles from here. I don't care about Wellington or the rest of the British. I'm getting to Nicolas, whatever happens."

"That's what I thought you'd say," he commented phlegmatically. "Now you'd better get to sleep. The enemy won't stray in this direction. They've something else to do."

He slept as soundly as she did, both of them finally overcome by the exertion of their journeying. They awoke at dawn and were starting their day when the attack on the redoubt began. She paused as the staccato gunfire sounded in the distance.

"Let's hope the redoubt holds," she said fervently.

It was approximately twenty minutes later when silence descended again. By then they were riding through the trees to where they could look through Gaston's spyglass toward the hill in the expanding daylight. The surprise attack had been successful. Scarlet jackets were streaming like ants through a gateway.

"The next target will be Ciudad Rodrigo," Gaston stated grimly.

"All of my experience tells me to keep you away from there."

"Just try!" She flicked her whip against her horse's rump and went galloping off down the slope, her cape billowing. He followed, leading the packhorse. Everything depended on whether he and Gabrielle could reach the city before the British.

Keeping a safe distance from the enemy, they rode on and skirted the heavily surrounded gates of the fortress city. There were gaps in the assembled encirclement of men and horses, and one of these was where the river Agueda formed a natural barrier. Through his spyglass Gaston could see there was a French outpost placed to defend a bridge that he and Gabrielle should be able to reach. Borrowing a white kerchief from her, he tied it to his musket and held it high as they rode forward, urging their tired horses to a canter to cover ground as quickly as possible. When they were within hailing distance, they were ordered to halt and declare themselves.

"Gaston Garcin and Madame Valmont on an important mission to Captain Devaux of the *chasseurs à cheval*."

"Pass, friends."

Gaston gave Gabrielle a wink as they rode across the bridge into the outskirts of the city. French defenses were set up everywhere, the cannon muzzles gleaming above empty pigpens and by closed wineshops. They had ridden only a short way when the British assault broke forth in a tumultuous burst of artillery fire. The French cannons leaped in reply. Gaston urged his horse into a gallop, and Gabrielle followed closely behind.

When they were near the wide-open city gates, a sentry shouted to them, "Stand clear! The cavalry is coming."

Gaston reached over and seized the bridle of Gabrielle's mount, and hauled the horse onto the verge of the road. In a burst of color and a jingling of harness a squadron of the *chasseurs à cheval*, two hundred and fifty strong, came out of the gates at a gallop, sabers drawn. They wore their hussarlike fur hats, green and red plumes swaying back, and their fur-lined pelisses hung from their left shoulders and flew out behind them. Gabrielle, who had been staring wide-eyed from the second they appeared, sighted Nicolas and screamed out his name.

"Nicolas! I'm here!"

He neither saw her nor heard her cry, and galloped by within a few feet of her. Seeing him again, it was as if her whole soul had flown to him. When the last horseman had gone past, she turned her mount to follow him, but again Gaston seized her bridle.

"No, you don't. That's no place for you."

Her face was pale and strained. "Then I'll wait for him here."

"You'll not do that either. We'll go into the city, where you can eat and rest and be refreshed for his return. He'll be back." When she remained as she was, still staring down the road at the disappearing chasseurs, he leaned over to tug at her sleeve. "Remember what you once told me? You said you were sure Captain Devaux would come through this campaign."

She turned her staring eyes on him, her mouth tremulous. "Then why do I feel so afraid for him now? Everything seems to be slipping out of control."

"It's only because you've seen a battlefield for the first time and that has unnerved you. Nothing else has changed. You and he are the same as before. Come along now." She obeyed him finally.

They rode to a nearby hostelry, where Gaston secured a room and stabled the horses. The room was small, with dirty straw on the bed and no bed linen. He removed the dirty straw, washed the bedstead and let it dry for the blanket he would spread on it.

"You'll be better off on this, even if the wooden slats are hard," he said to Gabrielle.

She turned from the window, where she had been looking out. "It's getting dark," she said, her thoughts away from the room.

"The maid I summoned will be bringing up a jug of hot water for the bowl any minute. I'm afraid that was the best I could do."

Wrenching her thoughts back to him, she came forward to give him a smile of gratitude. "Forgive me for being distracted. I appreciate everything you've done to bring me here safely." Her voice faltered. "Shouldn't Nicolas be back by now?"

"I'll go to the gates and make inquiries."

Once in the street, he made his way to the gates. The bombardment was still in force, which was a cause for concern.

"No news yet" was the answer, which did not surprise him. While waiting, he went into a shop and bought a pair of men's breeches that he judged would fit Gabrielle should an emergency arise. With his spare coat on her and her hat pulled down, she would pass for a boy well enough. He had just paid when a shout came from the gates. He hurried out with his purchase.

Soldiers were clearing the street, shoving people back with brutal haste. "Make room! The army is coming in! The whole defense line is falling back! Get back there!"

Gaston drew into the shelter of a doorway to watch the mass exodus from the battlefield. Through the gateway came a torrent of men, horses and gun carriages. A number of chasseurs rode in, some wounded still in their saddles. As far as Gaston could see, Devaux was not among them. He set off to find out what he could.

For Gabrielle the hours of waiting were endless. Each time there was a step on the stairs, she had looked out and been disappointed. Finally it was Gaston coming up the stairs.

"Is Nicolas back?" she cried.

He paused to look up at her. She looked as fresh and beautiful as a spring morning, her hair newly washed and entwined with a narrow pink ribbon. She had prepared herself for her lover, and Gaston had to shatter her hopes. He cleared his throat.

"Captain Devaux has been taken prisoner. He will be shipped to England and kept there until the emperor makes a truce with King George the Third's government. The war is over for him."

Gabrielle cried out, overwhelmed with despair.

FOR two days the fortress artillery kept up a roaring barrage against the British, the acrid smoke from the guns drifting down over the city. But by the third morning the British had entrenched themselves dangerously near, and their artillery began to have greater effect. Buildings were badly damaged by shells and round shot; fires broke out, adding to the hazards.

On the fourth day of the siege the enemy blasted two breaches in the fortress walls. The next evening hundreds of British burst through, shouting their vengeance, fighting like madmen and impossible to stem. Stabbing with bayonets, firing muskets point-blank and lobbing grenades into buildings as they came, the redcoats began to sweep through the streets like a scarlet river.

It took them two hours to take the city, and even then the killing went on, the frenzied victors striking down anyone in their path. Gaston, who had left Gabrielle from time to time to fire his musket at a defense post, was on his way back to her now. He hastened through dark passageways that threaded between and behind buildings and relieved two dead French soldiers of their coats and waistcoats.

He found Gabrielle pressed against the wall of her room, watching the carousing in the streets through the window. At the sight of him she sprang forward, her features gaunt with fear.

"You're back! I was so afraid. They've been dragging out the women! Even old women and young girls." She pressed the back of her hand to her quivering mouth. He did not pause to answer her but threw the military clothes to her.

"Put these on!" He darted to his saddlebag and pulled out the breeches he had bought for her. "These too! And hurry!" Turning his back, he yanked off his goatskin jacket and thrust an arm into the sleeve of the other uniform. It felt soggy. Swinging around, he saw that Gabrielle was holding the clothing and staring at her left palm, seeing it was wet with blood. He had to break through her shock, and he bellowed at her, "Put it on! If you don't, it'll be your blood and mine next. The redcoats are on a rampage. There's a bloodbath taking place in this city tonight!"

She pulled herself together and nodded. "I'll put it on."

He turned his back again and continued talking. "Our only chance of getting out of this mess alive is to be in uniform. It will take the British officers time to restore order. In the meantime, they'll be doing their best to save lives by taking prisoners and herding them into a place where they can ensure protection. My guess is that it will be the main barracks. Are you ready?"

"Yes."

Gaston looked at her. She had buttoned the breeches at the knees and tucked them into her boots. The waistcoat was loose enough to disguise her figure, and the blue cutaway coat would pass on her, although blood darkened it all down the right side.

"Get that hat on," he ordered. "Whatever happens, leave ev-

erything to me. If a British officer should question you, be too
dazed to reply. That's normal with the drummerboys, and you look
young enough in those clothes to be one of them. Now let's go."

They crept from the building. Gabrielle had to hold on to his
coattails in some places where the passage became a tunnel and
everything was pitch-black. Every time there was an opening into
the street, she glimpsed bodies slumped and sprawled in death.
Women's screams echoed and reechoed against the stone walls.
Gaston brought her to the east wall of the barracks and left her
there while he scouted ahead. In minutes he was back.

"The barracks yard is full of captured French soldiers. We'll
wait until more are brought in, then we'll fall in with them. You'll
not let the British officers know you're a woman until discipline
is restored, and then it will be safe for us to leave the city and start
for home. I've only to show them my game leg to prove that I'm
no longer a regular soldier, so they won't keep me a prisoner."

In that second Gabrielle made her resolve. She would remain a
prisoner of war and be shipped to England. Then she would
reveal her identity and be set free to find Nicolas. Suddenly hope
was high in her again. A new phase of her life was about to begin.

CHAPTER TEN

IT HAD not been Gabrielle's intention to
have Gaston accompany her into captivity.
When he failed to sway her from going
ahead with her plan, he stated he would
come with her. She was aghast.

"No! I beg you. Don't come with me.
You must get the horses and go back to
France. I would not have a minute's
peace if you should risk permanent in-
carceration because of me." She had
enough to bear in adjusting to an extended
separation from her child without this further harassment.

"I made a promise that I'd see you safely back to Lyons,"
Gaston said. "You can't ask me to go against that vow. I may not be a

gentleman born, but I have a soldier's pride in keeping my word."

They were marched out of the city that afternoon, a long column of blue-coated Frenchmen with one disguised Frenchwoman and a redcoat escort. Before long they were out in the countryside with the whole of the battle area left behind. Gaston's game leg had been troubling him before the march, and by the time they reached Oporto, the port of embarkation, he could barely hobble along, and was forced to lean heavily on Gabrielle for support.

On board ship, the men were packed together, with no room to lie down, and as they were below water level, the only light came from lanterns swinging and flickering overhead. For Gaston it was particularly difficult, because he had to sit with his leg stretched out before him, and it was frequently knocked or kicked accidentally.

Gabrielle had decided she must wait twenty-four hours before revealing the truth to the authorities, for she could not risk being set ashore if the ship put back into port for any reason. After a night filled with sounds of groaning and retching and snoring, sailors appeared with bread and cheese and several tankards of drinking water. At eleven o'clock the ship's surgeon, Dr. Rogers, a hawkish-looking man immaculately dressed in a blue-and-white naval uniform, came to attend the ill and the wounded.

"Now's your chance," Gaston muttered to her. "Good luck."

They exchanged an encouraging clasp of hands before she left her place to reach the companionway and wait by it for the surgeon. As he came to remount the steps she spoke to him.

"Doctor! I am a woman and should not be here."

He narrowed his eyes at her. "Follow me," he said in French.

In his cabin, she gave him her name as she took off the hat she had worn night and day. He invited her to sit down and asked whether she was a soldier's wife.

"No. Neither am I a camp follower."

"I did not think you were, Madame Valmont. I have spent some time in France, and your voice tells me you're a woman of some position. My guess is that you are following a lover. Am I right?"

"You are," she admitted.

"What is the name of the prisoner of war you are following?"

"Captain Nicolas Devaux of the *chasseurs à cheval*. Might he be on this ship? He was taken into captivity before me."

"There are none of that regiment on this ship. I did hear that a number of chasseurs boarded the warship in the harbor a few days ago, bound for Portsmouth. How far have you come?"

"From Lyons." She told him the whole story of the journey, leaving out only the personal details that had caused her to set out in the first place. Lastly she mentioned Gaston's game leg.

"If your companion is in such pain," the doctor asked, "why was I not informed as soon as he came aboard?"

"He wouldn't allow it. He said it would only lead to questions as to why he, a soldier invalided out of the army, should be here. It was for my sake that he did not take the risk."

The doctor sat back in his chair, putting the fingertips of both hands together, and looked grave. "Your friend is in an exceptionally awkward position. He has marched with the French army, wearing a uniform, and is a prisoner of war. He could face the charge of being a spy and thus suffer the death penalty."

"Gaston is no spy!" She reeled as she stood up. "Let me go down to his deck again to tell him what is happening."

The surgeon was fierce. "You seem to forget you are an enemy noncombatant and will come under the rules. I shall arrange for some hot water to be brought here, and you will wash yourself from head to toe, because there must be no risk of infection brought to the upper decks. There are two officers' wives on board, one English and the other Portuguese, and I am sure they will be charitable enough to find some suitable garments for you. Discard your uniform, such as it is, and when you are ready, you will report for registration to the officer in command."

With that he left. Alone in the cabin, Gabrielle was frustrated that Gaston would be facing either years of imprisonment or charges of spying—depending on the surgeon's diagnosis. If only she could have had a chance to prepare him for what was in the wind.

Two sailors brought the hot water, and she bathed herself thoroughly to ensure that the last traces of travel and imprisonment had gone from her body. Then she put on the clothes provided. The donors had been generous. Fine undergarments and a green woolen gown were accompanied by a thick woolen shawl.

Registration was completed quickly, and after it was over, she was escorted to a tiny cabin, where the two wives lay on narrow bunks, one above the other, both recovering from seasickness. A sailor showed her how to set up a hammock almost at floor level, and then Gabrielle introduced herself and thanked the women for the clothes.

The Englishwoman glared at her. "I do not speak French!" she said in English, turning her back rudely. There was a different reception from the very young Portuguese woman on the top bunk, who propped herself on one elbow and regarded Gabrielle with magnificent long-lashed eyes. She had rich black hair that tumbled down about her shoulders, and she seemed no more than sixteen years of age.

"I'm Isabella Harding, and it's Mrs. Moncrieffe in the bunk below. I sent you the clothes." She spoke in fluent French, and reached out a hand to Gabrielle. "Please help me down the ladder. I'm nervous about falling and"—her voice dropped to a whisper—"that creature will do nothing to help me. You see, her husband is a colonel and mine is only a lieutenant. She thinks she should have the cabin to herself."

Once on the floor, the young woman sat on a wooden traveling chest set against the wall. Gabrielle saw she was pregnant.

"What made you decide to have your baby in England?" she asked as she took a seat beside her on the chest.

"My dear Edward is on his way with the Duke of Wellington to Badajoz, and he wanted me to have our baby at his home in the county of Berkshire. My own home was destroyed, and all my family killed, during the French invasion of Portugal. I escaped only because I was visiting friends in Lisbon, where I met my English husband."

Gabrielle gave a little shake of her head, moved by what she had heard. "You have suffered much through the actions of my country, and yet you sent me the clothes."

"It is men that make wars. Never women. We are innocent of their crimes." Without warning, a sob choked her, and the tears gushed up to spill into trickles down her face. She fumbled for a handkerchief. "Forgive me. My grief still overtakes me at times. I miss my mother more than ever now."

"I'm sure your husband's family will receive you kindly."

"Will they? I wish I could be sure." Isabella blinked away her tears. "How do you expect to fare in England?"

"I don't know. It never occurred to me that I would be treated as a noncombatant taken in battle." She told Isabella about her search for Nicolas and how close she had come to a reunion, only to lose him again. Isabella listened to it all eagerly.

That night the ship hit a great storm in the Bay of Biscay. In her hammock, Gabrielle fared better than the two women in the bunks, for they constantly slithered from side to side, Isabella frequently crying out in fear. Gabrielle, who had folded blankets on either side of Isabella's bunk as padding to prevent her from knocking herself against the wooden guardrail, occasionally left her hammock to hold the girl's hand and comfort her. In the morning Dr. Rogers came to see how Isabella was. He beckoned Gabrielle to follow him out of the cabin afterward.

"She is more advanced than she thought, and may go into labor at any time. Would you know how to help with a delivery?"

"I attended the births of both my sisters-in-law's babies, and I have a son of my own."

"Then I shall count on you when the hour comes."

"Yes, of course. What of Gaston?" she inquired anxiously.

"I've seen him. My diagnosis is that it is an old wound aggravated by recent active service. He is a prisoner of war."

She stared after him as he walked away. He had believed her account and thus had chosen to spare Gaston the charge of spying. It was a merciful act; yet it condemned Gaston to a terrible future. Somehow she would have to work for his release and her own.

The storm lasted another two days. As the wind began to ease, Isabella gave a cry that was different from her cry of fear. Gabrielle went at once to the surgeon's cabin to notify him that the labor had begun. Isabella was carried to his cabin on a litter by two sailors and placed in his bunk. He gave Gabrielle one of his aprons, and she tied it about her before rolling up her sleeves.

313

"It will be several hours yet," the doctor said to her. "Do what you can to comfort Mrs. Harding. She's frightened and nervous. I shall look in now and again until it is nearer the time."

Gabrielle sat by the bunk and did all she could to help Isabella through the labor, bathing her forehead, talking soothingly to her and offering her hand.

At dawn, when the sea lapped yellow and gold, Isabella gave birth to a daughter, and when the infant was placed in her arms, she sighed with happiness. "I shall name her Luisa, after my mother." It was both pain and pleasure for Gabrielle to hold and bathe the baby, for memories of André tugged relentlessly at her.

It was not until the ship was sailing up the Thames that Isabella began to worry again about the meeting with her husband's parents. By the time the ship docked in London, she was panic-stricken. A knock came on the door then, and a sailor stood there.

"Mrs. Harding. A lady and gentleman are waiting for you at dockside. Shall I take your baggage now?"

Isabella threw her arms about Gabrielle. "I'll never forget your kindness to me."

"Now don't worry. Everyone will love you and Luisa."

"And you'll find your Nicolas. I know you will."

Gabrielle carried the baby at Isabella's side for as far as she was allowed to go. When a guard moved his hand in warning, Isabella, white-lipped with anxiety, took Luisa into her arms. Then she disappeared out onto the deck.

As Gabrielle returned to the cabin Mrs. Moncrieffe came out and swept past her without a word of farewell.

A customs officer now came to take charge of Gabrielle. He told her his name was Woodbury and that he and his wife were to be her custodians until such time as she should be granted parole. She collected her bundle, which contained two more dresses that Isabella had given her, and followed the man to the deck. The fresh air and the bright daylight dazzled her after the gloom of the cabin. The Thames was busy with ships, and there was a forest of masts at dockside for as far as the eye could see. She had hoped she might catch a glimpse of Gaston, but the customs officer shepherded her away before the disembarkation of the prisoners began.

Farther on she saw a line of warships that housed many thousands of prisoners of war. The sight struck a chill into her, sharper than the crisp February day. Everything from the rigging to the figureheads had been stripped away from the vessels, which had been tarred a dismal black. Each had a gallery built around it for patrolling guards.

The Woodburys' home was near the customs house. It was small, neat and clean. Mrs. Woodbury, a plain, well-meaning little woman, appeared nervous at having a Frenchwoman of some style under her roof. But when Gabrielle smiled and greeted her in English, as she had been taught by Isabella, the ice was broken. Even Mr. Woodbury's strict countenance showed satisfaction when Gabrielle produced a gold piece for her keep; she guessed they had been expecting to give her bed and board on a meager allowance paid to them by the authorities.

Every evening a young warehouse apprentice, Oliver Burns, gave Gabrielle English lessons, as she had requested. During the day she studied. She was not allowed to go beyond the garden gate, but would lean over it to gaze down the cobbled street toward the river. Through Oliver she learned that the prisoners from her ship were lodged in the hulks along these wharves. She asked him if he would try to find out where Gaston was.

Letters she wrote requesting parole went unacknowledged. As March warmed into spring, and April daffodils gave way to lilacs, she developed a growing command of the English language. By now she knew which hulk Gaston was housed in, and Oliver had managed to get a note to him. A reply came back on a scrap of paper. "Am well, but troubled by my leg. We will meet at the prisoners' market when you get your parole. Gaston."

One afternoon at the end of June a government agent came to see Gabrielle. He had the news she had long awaited. "You have been considered for parole, Mrs. Valmont."

"At last!" She breathed with relief. "I wrote many letters of appeal."

"Perhaps they went to the wrong department. Your name only came to my notice after a gentleman asked about you."

She was puzzled. "What was his name?"

"I can't recall. It was some weeks ago. As far as I knew, you were not in my district, or I should have given him your address."

"Did he leave an address?"

"No. Now let us get down to business. I shall first read you the conditions of your parole."

She listened, nodded and duly signed the declaration that she would abide by all that was set down there. He then paid her the first allowance due to her, explaining that noncombatants in British hands were paid on the same scale as army and navy lieutenants. She was glad of the money, for the funds she had brought from Lyons were very low now.

"I should like to apply for a change of address," she said. "I want to go to Portsmouth. I have reason to believe that someone I know was bound for that harbor. I'd like to meet him again."

The agent gave a nod. "I've no objection. I'll give you a written permit, but be sure to report with it and your new address to the government agent in Portsmouth on the day you arrive. Now I'll bid you good day." On his way out of the house he paused and looked back at her. "I believe I recall the gentleman's name that eluded me. Harding. Yes, that was it."

As she closed the door after him, she smiled to herself. It must have been Isabella's father-in-law. Dear Isabella. It was a comfort to Gabrielle to know that she had a friend in England. And an even greater comfort was the knowledge that reunion with Nicolas had come one step nearer.

HAVING bade a tearful good-bye to Gaston and taken the stage to Portsmouth, Gabrielle began a search of that city that went on for weeks and stretched into months. In December she was no nearer finding Nicolas than she had been when she first landed. She could think of no other path to follow. It was as if she were in a black abyss with no outlet. Her longing for her son, which was ever with her, added to her deep despair.

It was close to Christmas when she returned late one afternoon to the Dolphin Tavern, her present address, from a walk. A visitor was waiting to see her. He was a distinguished-looking man, with wavy brown hair graying at the temples and a clever, sharply honed face with keen and alert blue eyes; his mouth, severe in repose, was charming in a smile. He addressed her in the hallway.

"Good day to you, Madame Valmont. I know you from Isabella's description. I am Andrew Harding, at your service."

"Mr. Harding!" The sadness that had been lodged in her eyes was lifted at this surprise appearance of her friend's father-in-law. "I can hardly believe this is happening. How is Isabella? Oh, there's so much I want to ask."

"I've ordered dinner and wine to be served to us in the private dining room, where we can talk undisturbed."

At the table, he told her that Isabella had become increasingly worried about not hearing from her, convinced that some calamity had occurred. Whereas the girl might have settled down happily enough, for she had been warmly welcomed by the Hardings, her anxiety about Gabrielle had added to her homesickness. "I was certain that sooner or later you would come to light," Mr. Harding said, "and when I investigated again, more recently, I was given your address here in Portsmouth."

"You speak as if you have access to government records."

"I do. I am a member of Parliament for the Berkshire borough of Twyford."

"I had no idea. But then," Gabrielle added, sharing a smile with him, "Isabella talked of little else except her baby for most of our voyage together."

"That brings me to the other reason I wanted to find you. My wife and I would like to do something for you in return for your part in bringing our grandchild safely into the world. I must tell you that I know your whole story, related to me by Isabella. I can only suppose by my finding you here on your own that you have failed to trace Captain Devaux."

"That is correct." Her breath was suddenly tight in her chest.

"I shall find him for you," he said with assurance. He could see she was momentarily beyond speech, her eyes full. She hid her face in her hands until she had recovered, then raised her head again.

"I can never thank you enough, Mr. Harding."

"There is no need for thanks. I regret having to ask you to exercise patience for a little longer after all you have been through, but the list of captives is immense, close to one hundred and twenty thousand."

"You said you had heard my story from Isabella. Then you will also know of the part that my servant, Gaston, played in it, surrendering his freedom to protect me. He is in one of those hulks on the Thames. Is there any chance of his being moved to a better place? More important, is parole ever granted to the men in exceptional cases?"

"Men have been repatriated for special reasons. His case interests me. My solution rests with an invitation that my wife and I hope you will accept, which is to stay with us at our home in Twyford until I can send you in one of my own carriages to Captain Devaux. It will give Isabella the greatest happiness to have your company again, and we want to do all we can for you. As for your servant, I can get him released if you will guarantee he is to be trusted and will not attempt to escape."

Gabrielle was overjoyed. "I can guarantee that."

"Then I'll arrange everything. We'll leave for London in the morning." He took up his wineglass. "Now a toast. To reunions!"

"To reunions," she echoed, her face radiant.

THE journey to London took them to the houses of Parliament, where Mr. Harding's clerks secured the papers for Gaston and for her. Then, on the wharf, he told her to wait in the carriage while he went aboard one of the hulks. She watched in suspense for Gaston to appear. When finally there was some activity, she saw to her dismay that Gaston was being carried off the hulk on a canvas litter borne by two soldiers, Mr. Harding following behind. She leaped from the carriage and rushed across to the gangway. Gaston's face broke into a smile at the sight of her, but she was staring horrified at the bloody bandages about a stump. His game leg had been cut off above the knee.

"What have they done to you?" she exclaimed frantically.

"All life was going from my toes, and the condition would have worsened. Have you found Captain Devaux yet?"

"Not yet, but very soon, Mr. Harding says."

"Good. We're having a bit of luck at last, aren't we?" He smiled again. "I'm going to be nimble and without pain once I get the peg leg that the gentleman has promised me."

"Oh, Gaston." She was between laughter and tears. "You are indestructible."

He was carried to the home of the Woodburys, Gabrielle's former custodians. Between them, Gabrielle and Mrs. Woodbury bathed him clean of all traces of his prison life, put him in one of Mr. Woodbury's nightshirts and made him comfortable against some pillows. Mr. Harding arranged payment with Mrs. Woodbury for care of the patient, and left a purse of money for new clothes with Gaston. When Gabrielle kissed him on the cheek in farewell until they should meet again, he held her by the arm.

"Getting out of that hulk has made this the best day of my life so far. Yours is soon to come."

THE Harding country home was of ivy-laced plum-colored brick, and the graceful windows were enhanced by dressings of cream stone. Isabella's face appeared at one of them as Mrs. Harding came out to welcome Gabrielle. Moments later Isabella raced down the staircase with a shriek of delight and hugged Gabrielle with such exuberance in the entrance hall that she was almost swept off her feet. Still in the same whirl, Isabella flung her arms about Mr. Harding.

"Thank you for finding her, dear father-in-law!"

It amused Gabrielle that this rather staid English couple should regard their flyaway daughter-in-law with such enchantment. Since Edward was their only son, she could guess how Isabella and the baby were filling a gap in their lives until he returned. Luisa, now ten months old, was a bonny, fair infant with big long-lashed eyes like her mother's.

Christmas was the happiest that Gabrielle had known for years. There were carols to sing and hot punch to drink, and she tasted mince pie and plum pudding for the first time. She was able to relax completely and enjoy herself, all the while carried along by the knowledge that Nicolas was only just beyond her reach.

Two days after the holiday festivities were over, Mr. Harding opened a letter at the breakfast table, read it through and then smiled at Gabrielle. "We have what we have been waiting for. Captain Devaux is lodging at Holly House, Paradise Lane, in Macclesfield, and is employed as manager at the Barnett silk mill there."

It was Isabella who gave a jubilant outburst. Gabrielle sat silent and thankful. She was on the brink of her great day.

In a Harding carriage she journeyed to Macclesfield, staying overnight on the way. In the early afternoon of the next day the carriage drew up in the forecourt of Holly House. She rang the shiny brass bellpull, and a maidservant came to the door.

"Is Captain Devaux at home?" she inquired.

"No, ma'am. He's always at the mill at this hour."

"Thank you. I shall go there."

The maidservant closed the door and turned back in the direction of the kitchen. As she did so a fragile young woman named Jessica came down the stairs. She looked over the balustrade at the maid as she passed below. "Who was that at the door?"

"A foreign lady asking for Mr. Devaux," the maid answered. "I told her he was at the mill." The green baize door to the kitchen swung shut behind her. On the stairs Jessica stood with a hand pressed against her chest, as if trying to still the suddenly frightened drumming of her heart.

Gabrielle soon arrived at the mill. It was as if her feet were not touching the ground in her excitement. When she entered the hallway, the clatter of the looms made everything warm and familiar. It seemed as though there had been no time between this day and the last time she had seen Nicolas.

She reached the door that had his name on it. Lifting her cape hood from her head, she opened the door swiftly and just as swiftly closed it behind her, leaning against it. Nicolas was sitting at a large desk going through some designs and did not look up, although he held out a hand in her direction as if he was expecting her to be a clerk with papers for him. "You did those quickly, Briggs," he commented.

She was glad of those few seconds in which to gaze at him in profile, to absorb the sight of him into herself. He, mystified at getting no response, glanced up and saw her there. Never would she have believed that love could show itself so instantly in a man's face, filling his wondering eyes and his whole being.

"Gabrielle!" He was out of his chair and had her in his arms before she could take another breath. They kissed, wildly embracing, starved for each other. "What are you doing in England?" he gasped exultantly, and then kissed her again before she could answer him. Lips and caressing hands blended together in the mutual expression of their love and long-denied passion.

But then the door opened, and as their lips drew apart a horrified hiss cut through the air like the swish of a sword's blade.

"There is someone here you must meet, Gabrielle," Nicolas said to her in a low, sad voice.

She gazed questioningly at him, then turned within the circle of his arms. She saw a pale young woman, with soft fair hair thoroughly windblown, leaning as if for support against the jamb of the open door. Gabrielle glanced back at Nicolas. "Yes?"

His embrace tightened still more about her. "This is Jessica. She is my wife. We were married on Christmas Eve."

Gabrielle stared for a long moment at this woman as inwardly she screamed in an anguish too profound to be borne. She tilted forward in a dead faint, but Nicolas swept her up in his arms before she could fall. Jessica straightened herself in the doorway, shuddering from shock.

"Send her back wherever she came from," she said, beseeching Nicolas in a high-pitched voice. Then she sped back in the direction of home. Her lungs tore on every gasping breath in an effort that had been forbidden her since a childhood illness, but she did not stop until she could lose herself in tears in the privacy beyond her bedroom door.

At the mill, Gabrielle soon returned to consciousness. Nicolas sat massaging her wrists as she lay on the leather-upholstered bench in his office.

"How do you feel?" He peered anxiously into her face.

She avoided his eyes. "I'll be all right in a moment or two."

"How did you manage to get across the Channel?"

"It's too long a tale to tell. I came because I promised you once that if ever I was free, I would come to you."

"Are you saying Émile is dead?" he demanded incredulously.

"On the night Maison Devaux burned down, he was one of the three victims."

"So long ago! I never knew!"

She met his tormented gaze then. "I realize that now."

"Oh, Gabrielle." He caught up her hand and pressed the palm to his lips. "I've never stopped loving you."

She was glad he made no excuses about his marriage. She understood he had made Jessica his wife simply because he had never expected to see her—Gabrielle—again. It was all she could do not to caress his face once more, to touch his lips.

"I must go." She stood up, and found that her head had cleared. Mercifully, her heart was still numb. "We have come to the end of all that has been between us. I wish you well with my whole heart, as I have always done. This meeting mustn't be prolonged, for your sake and for mine. Farewell, Nicolas!"

He seized her wrist as she reached the door, bringing her to a standstill. She did not look back at him, her whole straight-backed stance a rejection of any last attempt at persuasion, and he released his hold. His final words followed her as she went. "You are my life and always will be."

THE numbness stayed with Gabrielle all the way back to Twyford. Once there, she concluded that she should return to France and take up her life again. But despite this decision, war conditions forced her to accept the Hardings' compassionate hospitality for an extended period. As soon as Gaston was well enough, he too was invited to stay in their household, and was in his element when allowed to care for the Thoroughbred horses in the stables.

Finally developments on the other side of the Channel began to make Gabrielle's plans a possibility again. Bonaparte's empire was beginning to disintegrate. The czar had now allied his country with Britain, Prussia, Sweden and Austria. As a result, the remnants of the Grande Armée had not only been forced to retreat from Russia but were being driven across Europe. In the west

Wellington was advancing toward the Pyrenees, the last barrier before reaching French soil.

In October 1813 Napoléon was soundly beaten by the allied forces in the Battle of the Nations, near Leipzig. A few weeks later Mr. Harding arranged for Gabrielle, Gaston and seven other noncombatants to be escorted under armed guard down to Dover, where they were put on a fishing smack.

The sails flapped and filled in the fresh wind. Gabrielle, looking back at the white cliffs, was saying farewell to Nicolas and to love itself. There would never be anyone else for her. When the cliffs finally melted into the sea, she turned toward France, the wind tugging at her hair. She was going home. Home to Lyons and her son. Home to Maison Roche and her looms. After her long absence the blood stirred in her veins once more.

CHAPTER ELEVEN

 GABRIELLE took down the silk portrait of Napoléon from the wall of her office in the Rue Clémont and regarded it with mixed feelings. It should have come down at the time of his abdication the previous April, or when he had gone into exile on the island of Elba. Yet, somehow, all the main events of her life had been bound up with the actions of this extraordinary man. Through his attack on Austria she had lost a brother, and Gaston had come to Lyons. The imperial invasion of Portugal and Spain had taken Nicolas away from her forever.

But the emperor had done what he believed right for France, and had given it laws and reforms that would endure. Moreover, he had helped Lyons to become once again the greatest silk center the world had ever known. It was her personal regret that her marvelous Roche silks, commissioned for Versailles, had gone into storage and might never be hung in that great palace. An imperial era had passed, and with it all its splendor.

Sadly she placed the silk portrait in tissue paper and put it in a drawer with other rare samples that belonged to the history of Maison Roche. Her decision to remove it today had come with the news that five days ago, on March 1, 1815, the emperor, having escaped from Elba, landed in the south of France. He was raising a new army to advance on Paris and drive King Louis XVIII from his throne.

Having seen war for herself on the peninsula, Gabrielle wanted no more of it for France. Good relations had been restored with Britain and the rest of Europe. Even Wellington had said that France had no enemies—it was only that Bonaparte had to be deposed. Her country needed peace now, not more bloodshed. Because she could not condone the emperor's return, she was shutting the drawer on a visage that belonged only to the past.

"Maman!"

She turned as André came running through the office door toward her. A boisterous four-year-old, he had just come home from a walk with his nursemaid and, as always, had sought her out immediately. Laughing and stooping to sweep him up in her arms, she swung him around before hugging him to her, his round cheek cool against hers from the March wind.

"Have you had a splendid time? Did you meet Aunt Hélène? She bought you a candy stick? *Là!* What a lucky boy you are!"

Gabrielle let him spend as much time as she could with Hélène and Michel in the home they had bought a few months before the birth of their twins, a son and a daughter. His initial shyness after her return home to Lyons had been painful to bear, but gradually a normal relationship was restored between them. If she had to be away on business, he was content to stay with the Piats. A trip was in the offing now, and Gabrielle decided this was as good a time as any to prepare him.

"Next week, André, I have to go to visit a large country estate where Roche silks are being hung. As you know, Maison Roche is fast becoming the silk house that people consult when they want an entire residence refurbished, and I always view the finishing stages to make sure every detail is perfect."

He understood. Some of his happiest moments were spent at

the mill with his *maman*. He loved the colors and the patterns of the silks, and the smell of the place. "When can I come with you to see the silks hung?" It was his usual question.

"When you're older," she promised, as she had before. "You will be in charge of everything when you're a grown man."

While she was preparing for her journey, news and further details of Bonaparte's swift approach swept in. All along his route veterans of the Grande Armée were rallying to him with shouts and cheers of welcome. The old magic was still there, undiminished by months of exile, and he was rekindling France one more.

The day before Gabrielle was due to leave, she took André to the Piats' house. On the way their barouche was brought to a halt by a surging crowd. Bonaparte was entering Lyons, and the Lyonese were going wild. André, excited by the noisy cheering, the waving of the Tricolor and the lusty singing of "The Marseillaise," bounced up and down on the seat. Gabrielle opened the window and held him to it as Bonaparte came into sight above the heads of the crowd. He rode proudly, clad in his gray campaign coat and black bicorne hat. Gabrielle felt herself gripped again by the mesmerizing personality of this warrior-leader.

"Now you have seen the emperor," she said to André. "Whatever else he's done, remember he did more for Lyons—and for France—than any other Frenchman who has ever lived."

Celebrations were still going on when she left the city the next day. She missed Gaston's presence whenever she was being driven anywhere. He had left her employ and gone south to the coast. "Every old war-horse dreams of peaceful pastures," he had said. "That time has come for me, madame."

She did not let him go empty-handed. He had a good horse, a new suit of clothes and a banker's draft to give him a moderate income until the end of his days. It was a long time before she heard from him. Then it was to let her know that he had settled in the peaceful little village of Cannes, where he was looking after the horses of a retired colonel. She hoped he had found contentment.

The great country mansion in which her silks had been installed was only a few miles from Limoges. She stayed for over four weeks, until the very last of the upholstered pieces had been delivered, making sure that all her silks had been used to perfection. While there, she heard that the emperor had received a tumultuous welcome in Paris after King Louis's hasty departure for Belgium. Throughout the Tuileries the white lily of the Bourbons had been stripped away from hangings and carpets to reveal the imperial bee once more. It seemed as if her silks for Versailles would soon be taken out of storage after all, but what was the cost in lives going to be this time? Already the newssheets were proclaiming the emperor had three hundred thousand loyal Frenchmen under arms, and hundreds more were volunteering.

The news was bad when Gabrielle arrived back in Lyons. British and Prussian troops were massing in Belgium, and the armies of the Austrians and the czar were gathering in force farther to the east. France was again surrounded by enemies.

It was too late in the evening to fetch André home when she arrived there. She would collect him in the morning. After she had bathed and changed, her maid brought her a letter in the blue salon, where she was having a light supper.

"I think you should see this, madame. A gentleman came six or seven times in as many days in the hope of your having returned. Yesterday he left this letter with the request that it should be given to you immediately upon your arrival."

The handwriting almost made her heart stop. It was from Nicolas. She drew in a deep breath before ripping it open.

> Jessica died of consumption six weeks ago. Her courage, as well as her devotion to me, will remain in my memory always. I have returned to France to find you again in the hope that there might be some time left for us to spend together after the task still left for me to do.

"Oh, my love!" Gabrielle breathed, reading on.

> I had never thought I should come back to the land of my birth. But the end of hostilities between France and Britain released me from the code of honor which had kept me to British shores, and I have come back to Lyons and rejoined my regiment of the chasseurs. I have a heartfelt belief that every Frenchman is

needed at this time. I will not see France defeated as the world intends it now. If you have any love left for me, allow me to see you once more before I leave Lyons.

She ran from the room, calling to her maid as she went. "My cloak! Quick!. At once!" It came, and she threw it about her shoulders, rushing from the house and across the square. She knew the address on the letter. Her shadow flew in and out of circles of light cast by the overhanging streetlamps. A few minutes later she arrived breathless at the door of the house and hammered on the knocker. The door was opened by an army servant.

"Is Captain Devaux here? I'm Madame Valmont," she said.

"He's out, madame, but I had orders to fetch him immediately if you should call at any time of the day or night."

He showed her into Nicolas's apartments on an upper floor and left her there. Regaining her breath, she loosened her cloak and let it drop across a chair. She went to the window, where she watched and waited until a hired calash approached at a gallop, and she saw Nicolas in uniform fling himself out of it and into the house. He came bounding up the stairs. The door was thrown wide and there he was, as if their separation had never been.

Once again they were looking at each other as they had done long ago when a wedding carriage and a funeral-cortege coach had clashed wheels and brought them into each other's lives. This time they were alone. This time the hour was theirs at last.

"Nicolas," she breathed, holding out her arms and swaying toward him. "Show me this is no dream."

"My own Gabrielle!" He rushed to her and held her to him, kissing her. Tears of happiness trickled from under her closed lids, and she buried her fingers in his hair, as if she might die should he lift his head and take his lips from hers.

Lifting her up in his arms, he kicked open the door that led into the bedchamber and carried her through. The bed, large and wide and downy with pillows, awaited them. It was loving such as she had never experienced.

As he lay beside her, she slowly trailed her fingers down the back of his neck and kissed his forehead lovingly.

"I love you," he murmured, as if he had not said the same words already, more times than either of them could remember. "Marry me. In the morning. Before noon."

Abruptly the truth dawned on her. "You're going away soon."

"Tomorrow. Before evening."

"Where are you going? Do you know?"

He propped himself up on his elbows. "The emperor has already led an advance across the border into Belgium. The Prussians have massed at Ligny, and it is said that Wellington is moving troops to a place called Quatre Bras. When these armies are defeated, we march into Brussels." His face relaxed into a smile. "Will you meet me there, my love?"

"I'll do more than that," she replied fervently. "I'll travel with you. This time I'll be with the officers' wives. I'm not going to lose sight of you as I did at Ciudad Rodrigo."

Then she told him the whole story. He resolved that somehow he would live through whatever lay ahead and make it up to her, in the years to come, for all she had been through.

EARLY the next morning they went together to see the priest at a little church nearby. It was arranged that the marriage should take place at eleven thirty, after a short civil ceremony at the *hôtel de ville*. While Nicolas went to check on final orders for departure at the barracks, Gabrielle went home to pack and write notes to Hélène and André, with explanations to cover her hasty departure. She flew into the house and was halfway up the stairs when she heard the well-remembered thump of a wooden leg coming from the direction of the kitchen. She spun around to race down again. "Gaston! Of all people."

He looked extremely spruce, with a stout cane, a green brass-buttoned coat, and a gold pin in his neat cravat. There was no mistaking his exuberance at seeing her.

"Madame! I've been trying to find out where you were."

"About to be married! I've found Nicolas again. At last we are to be together. Wish me joy, Gaston! Come and be witness to our wedding. Nobody belongs there more than you."

He gave her a shrewd look, with something close to a twinkle in it. "I'm wed myself now. My Jeanne is a lively creature, full of spirit, and we've a child on the way."

"I'm so glad to hear that. Have you brought her with you?"

"No. I left her safely in Cannes. She is linenmaid in the colonel's house where we both reside, and soon we're to have a cottage to ourselves."

"That's marvelous news. Why are you here, then? Don't tell me you followed the emperor from Cannes?"

"I did indeed. All the way to Paris." Gaston had witnessed touching demonstrations of loyalty en route and cheered with the rest when whole battalions with their officers had joined the swift march toward Paris. Then, once the capital had been reached and the emperor again installed in the Tuileries, Gaston had begun the journey homeward. And that was how he had arrived at the house in the Rue Clémont.

"Come with me to the *hôtel de ville* and then to the church," Gabrielle urged him now. "I have no time to spare. Today Nicolas leaves Lyons for Belgium, and this time I'm going too. I'll never be parted from him again."

Gaston gave one of his deep chuckles. "Then it seems I couldn't have arrived at a better time. What hour do we depart?"

She raised her eyebrows at him in astonishment. "You would accompany me to war again?"

"It will be like old times, and I've a mind to see the emperor win a great victory once more. What do you say?"

"I shall be glad, my good friend. So very glad."

In the church with its shining altar the bride and groom exchanged wedding vows. When the ceremony was over and the priest's blessing received, Nicolas and Gabrielle had to part on the church steps. He held her lovingly and kissed her. Then he clapped a hand on Gaston's shoulder. "Look after my wife for me as you guarded her once before."

"I shall do that, Captain. You may depend on it." It was an easy promise for Gaston to make. Now that he was with Gabrielle again, his own wife was all but forgotten—not out of heartlessness, for he loved Jeanne, but because his protective loyalty toward Gabrielle had been rekindled and was as strong as ever.

The squadron left the city two hours later, preceded by the regimental band playing a stirring tune. Behind the chasseurs came the wagons, the spare horses and the usual collection of women and children. Gabrielle and Gaston brought up the rear.

During the ride from Lyons to the Belgian border, the squadron bivouacked at nightfall outside villages. Gabrielle would take lodgings in an inn or farmhouse, and Nicolas came to her there. They spent the hours together, the past still too much with them and the future uncertain. They lived for these hours they still shared.

On the seventeenth of June, on Belgian soil, Gabrielle saw Nicolas's squadron join forces with the emperor. Napoléon's successful army had captured Charleroi and won a battle at Ligny, putting the Prussians to flight and forcing the British to retreat. Torrential rain descended on everyone, but nothing could dampen the high spirits of the troops. Tomorrow would come a great battle with the British near the village of Waterloo.

That night the accommodation that Gabrielle secured was in a peasant family's cottage. Overhead the unrelenting rain continued to drum on the roof, but she and Nicolas were aware only of each other in the deep warmth of the feather bed.

"Since I found you again I have known the happiest hours of my life," Nicolas said to her as she lay against his shoulder within the circle of his arm. "If I should not come back—"

"Don't!" She pressed her fingertips against his lips.

Gently he took her wrist and drew her fingers away. "I only want to say it is my hope that we shall have a child from these hours of loving, because then I shall live on for you, no matter what the outcome may be in the field tomorrow."

He left her at daybreak. She was sleeping and did not feel him go from the bed. Closing the door quietly behind him, he went down the stairs and out into the dawn light. It had stopped raining on this Sunday morning, and the air was sweet and balmy. His army servant was waiting with his mount, and he swung himself into the saddle. As he turned his horse he saw that Gaston was waiting by the gate. The fellow saluted him as he rode through.

"Good luck, Captain."

Acknowledging the salute, Nicolas cantered away.

331

GABRIELLE WOKE TO THE SOUNDS of a commotion in the yard outside. She had been alone for more than an hour. Slipping on a robe, she went to the window and looked out. The family of the cottage were departing, their possessions bundled up in the back of a donkey cart. Others were also on the move, getting out of range while there was still time. Meeting them from the opposite direction were all kinds of military traffic, from ammunition wagons to riders on army business.

Gabrielle watched the passing cavalcade as she washed and dressed. When she came downstairs, she found Gaston making coffee in the fire-blackened camp kettle he had brought along.

"I can hear 'The Marseillaise,'" she said, listening intently.

"The emperor will be reviewing the troops. It's customary before a great battle."

She went to sit down on a bench at a rough table, where he had set out a breakfast for her. She had little appetite that morning, but she ate doggedly, needing to take nourishment to sustain her through what she had planned for the hours ahead.

"What time do you think the fighting will begin?" she asked, tapping an egg with a spoon to crack it open.

"My guess is not for two or three hours yet." Gaston had seated himself opposite her. "It's no use trying to do battle until the ground has had a chance to dry out. In its present state horses and men would slither about in the mud and fall in all directions, while the guns would be completely bogged down. The emperor will strike when the time is right, never fear."

"I'm not sitting around here for hours twiddling my thumbs," she stated emphatically. "I'm going to one of the field hospitals to offer my assistance."

"You'll need a strong stomach," Gaston warned.

But her face was set grimly, and he could not argue with her.

They covered the distance on foot to where the field hospitals had been set up, the traditional black flag flying above them to denote the site to friend and foe alike. The tents had been erected at the edge of woods within reasonable access to the battlefield.

The surgeons were passing the time until they should be needed, sitting about in camp chairs, talking together, reading and dozing.

Within the tents, operating tables had been set up, the surgical instruments glinting on side tables. Outside, there were innumerable barrels of wine ranged on trestles, the opiate and strengthener for those about to face surgery. The orderlies were organizing some of the women accompanying the army to open bundles of clean linen for the binding up of wounds.

Gabrielle looked toward the valley where the battle would be fought. It lay framed to her view by the foliage of trees on either side of a gap in the woods. Away to her left she could see her countrymen waiting.

Another two hours of steadily mounting tension went by before the drums began to roll, sounding the call to arms. The surgeons began to move, discarding jackets and donning their leather aprons. Orderlies snapped shut the camp chairs and took them out of the way. One gave Gabrielle a thick canvas apron, such as the other women were wearing, and she tied it on. Gaston had the task of helping with the wounded outside as they arrived, making sure that the most seriously injured had priority.

At exactly half an hour before noon the French cannons opened fire with a barrage of earthshaking force. Gabrielle wondered how the British could withstand such a terrible bombardment. Thick clouds of smoke from the cannonade drifted across the treetops and over the black flag.

The first casualties to come through the gap in the woods were soldiers hit by stray rounds shot from enemy guns. Distressed, Gabrielle watched them carried into the tents. Then one of the surgeons hailed her. "Madame Devaux! Prepare for bandaging!"

"I'm coming, Major Arnoul!"

She grabbed a basket of clean linen and took her place at an operating table. It was her initiation. She saw it all—the orderlies tipping wine into the mouths of the groaning men on the tables, the flowing blood, the holding down of patients as the saws rasped through bones that could never be made whole again. When the time came for her to pad and bandage her first patient, she and an orderly worked together.

The French cannonade stopped as abruptly as it had begun, giving way to the drumming of the soldiers' rapid steps. On her way to replenish her linen basket, Gabrielle paused to look down through the gap in the woods toward the valley. Wide columns of French infantry were advancing shoulder to shoulder, with at least one hundred and fifty men in each straight rank, flanked by cavalry. From that distance they looked like toy soldiers set rigidly in their formations, as if on a parade ground. She hurried on to carry out her task.

When the opposing forces met, the noise of the battle resounded in musket and rifle fire, shouts and yells, the booming of British cannon and the screams of men and horses alike, as the killing went on. The river of wounded began to flow in through the woods.

Gabrielle, sighting a chasseur with a slashed arm, hurried across to ask him if he knew Nicolas and if he had seen him. He nodded, holding his arm to ease the pain, his face chalk white.

"He had three horses shot from under him. Each time, he grabbed a riderless one in the field and remounted. Don't worry, madame. He was very much alive when I saw him last."

As the day went on, a picture of the battle emerged. The British had suffered heavy losses and were pressed back into a defensive position; the French were at a strong advantage. By late afternoon Gabrielle had lost all sense of time. She was soaked in blood. One of the women told her that a massive French cavalry charge had thundered down the valley and over the British ridge. The battle was almost won. She nodded and uttered a silent prayer for Nicolas as she continued to bind a bayonet wound.

More good news came. The defenses of the British had been diminished. Wellington's hours were numbered. Everyone was waiting for the emperor to deliver the final blow.

The sun was beginning to set. Gabrielle looked up once after that as an orderly appeared in the entrance of the tent and shouted, "The emperor has sent in the Garde Impérial!"

The cream of the whole army! The emperor's chosen men! Now they would wipe out everything in their path.

Lanterns were lit in the tent to aid the fading daylight. Outside, the wounded waiting for treatment covered almost every inch of ground. Through the gap in the woods the torrent of casualties was increasing all the time. Cries for water were constant, and

Gaston had joined the women as they went from man to man putting cups to parched lips.

All these wounded could count themselves fortunate, for lying in the valley were thousands of their comrades similarly wounded who could not be reached in the fighting. Some struggled weakly to find a place out of the fray. Nicolas was among them.

He had no clear recollection of being wounded. Vague images came into his mind between bouts of unconsciousness. Everything was muddled and confused. His lifeblood was flowing out of his wounds and his strength was ebbing as he lay face down amid the muddy carnage of men and horses.

Beneath Nicolas the earth began to tremble again, coinciding with one of the brief lucid spells that still came periodically. Another cavalry charge was on the way. Was it two or three times he had been ridden over where he lay? To add to his wounds, the thundering hoofs had crushed his right hand and snapped his arm like a twig. Now the cavalry were coming again.

With effort he opened his eyes. The sky had become the rich orange of sunset. In its splendid light the horsemen were coming at full pelt, and in their wake thousands of running foot soldiers, the brass cap plates on their bearskins flashing the sun's late brilliance as they came. Recognition dawned. It was the Garde Impérial, finally thrown in to smash those seemingly impenetrable British lines and take the glory of the day. Yet what was amiss that his pain-wearied brain was unable to define?

The charge swept over him with crashing hoofs and pounding boots before he slipped into the sanctuary of oblivion once more. When his mind cleared, he realized that it had not been an advance that had passed over him but a retreat. An ignominious rout. The Garde Impérial had broken and fled before some final strategic attack of Wellington's that, in spite of all odds, had won the day. Cheering echoed from the British ridge.

A great yell of rage and disappointment welled up in his throat, giving him the superhuman strength to rise up with it, a swaying, half-broken figure in the sunset's blood-red glow.

"No!" he bellowed, crazed beyond reason. *"Vive la France!"*
He staggered forward, then fell down, motionless.

THE EVENING DARKENED AND the stars came out. Nicolas opened his eyes and saw garlands of red and blue flowers glowing about him in the pale moonlight, under and around him like a rich tumbled carpet. It was the silk his looms had woven for the emperor's tent, which now lay on the ground, knocked over and trampled into the mud by a fleeing army. He and Gabrielle had declared their love in the midst of these garlands. Now this Devaux silk was to be his shroud.

He closed his eyes slowly, feeling his strength go. He thought he heard her voice and spoke her name. Gabrielle.

In the surgeons' tents the work went on. The lights were attracting moths, which caused fluttering shadows to dance here and there. Gabrielle, finished with one patient, turned for the next and saw Gaston standing in the tent's entrance. The expression on his drawn face confirmed her fears.

Wordlessly she removed her apron and went toward him.

"I have had reports from five different sources," he told her huskily. "Captain Devaux is dead. In the midst of one of the great cavalry charges he was badly wounded protecting the standard, and although he handed it over and went on toward the British lines, he fell almost at once from the musket fire."

She nodded starkly to show she had grasped all she had heard.

She turned over her duties to another, and with Gaston she left the tent and walked down through the paths between the wounded, into the woods and to the peasants' cottage. He sat her down in a kitchen chair and fetched a bowl of water. Then he washed the smudges of dried blood from her face and bathed her hands.

"Now," he said, raising her up from the chair, "go and change while I get a fire going. The evening is turning chill."

She paused at the foot of the stairs. "I want to find his body and take him home to Lyons. He will not be buried in foreign soil."

Experience had taught him to know when her mind was made up. While she changed her garments upstairs, he checked the pair of pistols in his belt and made sure he had plenty of ammunition. He knew what a battlefield was like when darkness fell and looters from the local peasantry moved in.

When she came downstairs, she was simply and warmly

dressed, a shawl about her shoulders. He had found a couple of lanterns and lit them. She took one from him, and together they went out into the darkness. They harnessed one of their horses to a light farm cart from the peasants' barn and drove to the place where earlier that day the vast spread of men had been waiting to move into their battle lines. It was deserted now, the earth churned up by thousands of feet. Their horse became alarmed, scenting death, as they went on. By some trees Gaston brought the horse to a halt and fastened it securely before he and Gabrielle set off with the lanterns on their search.

The dead of both sides lay everywhere, and the lanterns' glow passed over many awful sights. Most heartrending to Gabrielle were the pleas of the wounded for water. Gaston had had the foresight to bring four full canteens with him, and he and Gabrielle paused to give drinks to French and British alike. Some of the wounded clutched at her skirts, begging, for fear of looters, not to be left. Whenever possible Gaston salvaged a pistol from a dead soldier nearby to leave the wounded some protection.

There were plenty of looters in the darkness. They moved about easily, being familiar with the terrain, and scuttled away like rats when Gaston, enraged, roared at them.

The search for Nicolas went on for hours. The canteens were empty, and there was nothing left to give as they went on shining their lanterns, hoping for the sight of a chasseur's green jacket. It was dawn when the rising sun picked out a gleam of flowered gray silk with a familiar figure in dark green sprawled across it. A cry burst from Gabrielle's throat as she sighted Nicolas.

"There!"

She ran to him, stumbling and dodging and leaping over obstacles. Flinging herself down on her knees beside him, her tears coming at last, she drew his head gently into her lap and bent over him, rocking in her grief. "My darling. My love. My life." Then under her fingertips she felt a faint pulse beating in his neck. "Merciful God!" she breathed incredulously. "He is alive!"

Gaston thumped down on the knee of his good leg and reached inside Nicolas's jacket to feel his heartbeat. "Only just," he said heavily, forewarning her.

She thrust her face forward. "I'm going to keep him alive!"

"Let's make a litter of this silk, then, and carry him to the cart."

With his knife he cut the amount needed. Since Nicolas was already on the roughly shaped rectangle, they had only to turn him gently onto his back to ensure that he would be as comfortable as possible. Then began the arduous task of hauling him. They struggled and stumbled along. Getting him into the cart was eased by Gaston's rounding up two looters at pistol point to help in the lifting, after which he made them run ahead of the horse to be at hand at the cottage to bear the wounded man upstairs.

When that was done, he had booted them off the premises and returned to the upper room where Nicolas lay, with eyes closed, on the bed. Gabrielle was cutting away his uniform. "I'll fetch one of the surgeons from the field hospital," Gaston said.

"No! We can do better in the circumstances. Get me some wine and hot water, and bring me my saddlebag. I've some clean linen in it. After that, build up the fire. He must be kept warm."

He obeyed her without question. Then together they set the

patient's broken arm and fingers with splints. She gouged grape-shot out of his flesh with a spoon and stitched the lips of a saber slash together. When she had done all she could, she dripped warm wine over the wounds, a process that was to continue for days. Nicolas was highly feverish, his thirst insatiable, and his delirious mumblings were frequently broken by screams of pain. Gabrielle showed no emotion, and never slumped or showed a sign of fatigue, sleeping and eating only when it was Gaston's turn to keep vigil.

Downstairs, the peasants had returned home and were resent-ful at finding one of the defeated French still under their roof—until Gabrielle changed their attitude with a handsome payment.

Gradually Nicolas's fever began to subside. The day came when recognition dawned in his sunken eyes and he knew the face of the woman by his bed.

"I thought you were here," he whispered.

"Yes, my darling." She kissed his forehead, choked with emo-tion. "It won't be long now before we'll be able to go home."

It still took a number of weeks. As soon as it was safe to move him, they traveled as far as a small town just inside the French border, where Gaston found comfortable accommodations. After a further period of convalescence, during which Nicolas was able to walk again without support, it was decided that they could now cover the last lap. It was then that Gaston said good-bye, first to Nicolas and then to Gabrielle on her own.

"You have Captain Devaux now," he said to her. "I don't suppose you'll ever need me to escort you anywhere again, but remember, if you do, I'll come at once."

Her eyes were full. "I'll never forget you, my friend. May God go with you."

He mounted his horse and waved to her as he rode away.

Not long after Gaston's departure Gabrielle and Nicolas came back to Lyons by way of Fourvière. It had been her suggestion that they should see the city again from her favorite place. Even though she was joyfully impatient to see her little son once more, she stopped the carriage at the spot she had always liked best, alighting first to run forward and look out eagerly at the view.

"Look! How clear everything is today. See those ripples in the wake of that boat down there on the Saône."

Nicolas had followed more slowly to reach her side. Pain was still with him, and it would be for months to come. But he had survived and could look forward to the years ahead with the woman he loved. She was going to continue to produce Maison Roche silk until André was of an age to take over, while he would build up Maison Devaux from scratch. They would be business rivals, lovers and partners. Their marriage would never be dull, and if recent signs proved to be right, it would be fruitful too.

"It's a fine sight," he agreed, putting his arm around her. Pointing with his cane across the river, he indicated a large plot of land that was up for sale. "That would make a good site for Maison Devaux down there on the quayside."

"I agree. But there's still the question of where our new home should be." They had decided between them that the Rue Clémont house should be closed up until André was of age. They themselves would build a new residence.

He smiled broadly, turning her to him. "I think that was settled a long time ago when you told me of marking out a place here on these slopes with a piece of Roman pottery."

"So you have always remembered that." She was deeply moved, putting her hand lovingly against his face, and he covered it with his own.

Then together they looked out again toward the mellow vista of roofs and glinting spires and lush treetops and gleaming water that would be theirs for the rest of their lives. She drew it into herself as though it were the air she breathed. Lyons. Her beloved city.

The inspiration for *Tree of Gold* came to historical novelist Rosalind Laker during a trip to New York City several years ago. One of Napoleon Bonaparte's campaign tents was on exhibit with other early nineteenth-century silks from Lyons.

Rosalind Laker

"The tent was lined with exquisite silk patterned with red-and-blue garlands," says Miss Laker, "and immediately I thought of the rivalry for the commission to weave that silk. From that single idea came this book."

Relentlessly curious, the author tracked down her story by traveling first to Lyons, where a number of silk mills still operate. "I saw marvelous examples of Lyons silk there. Next I visited Fontainebleau to see the empress Josephine's own choice of silk hangings for her salons, and then Versailles and other palaces." Miss Laker also watched the weavers at work in the Paradise Mill Working Silk Museum, in Macclesfield, in her native England, and even made a trip to the Lullingstone silk farm, in Kent, where the silk was spun for Princess Diana's famous wedding dress.

Perhaps the most interesting sidelight to the story of Lyons silk is the evolution of the Jacquard loom. "The whole mechanism was most extraordinary," Miss Laker explains, "because its possibilities didn't end with silk. The punched cards that chose the individual threads for weaving led to the punched cards used in computer systems." An American named Herman Hollerith utilized Jacquard's principle for his tabulating machine, and the company he founded in 1896 later expanded and became known as IBM.

Rosalind Laker has written more than twenty novels, five of which have appeared in Condensed Books. *This Shining Land* was a recent favorite.

There's a killer out there.
And Joanne is next on the list. . . .

THE
DEEP
END

A condensation of the novel by
Joy Fielding

Illustrated by Dennis Luzak

Today is the day. Paul has come
to take the girls to camp. In a few
moments Joanne will be completely alone.
No children. And no husband, for
Paul has left her, rented his own apartment
while he decides the fate of their marriage.

Now the house is still. Except . . . except
for the insistent ringing of the telephone.
Joanne does not answer it. She knows
who is calling. There is a killer on the other end
of that phone. Someone who has murdered
before and intends to murder again.
Someone who has chosen *her* as victim.

It all started two months before this
heartbreaking day. Two months ago, when
Joanne was still happy. . . .

PART ONE

Chapter 1

THE phone is ringing.

Joanne Hunter stares at it from her seat at the kitchen table. She makes no move to answer it, already knowing who it is and what he will say. She has heard it before, has no desire to hear it again.

The phone continues to ring. Joanne closes her eyes, trying to conjure up images of happier times.

"Mom."

Joanne hears her younger daughter's voice and smiles toward the girl in the doorway.

"Mom," her daughter repeats. "The phone's ringing. Should I answer it?"

"No," Joanne tells her.

"It might be Daddy."

"Lulu, please . . ." But it is too late. Lulu's hand is already on the white wall phone, lifting the receiver to her ear.

"Hello? Hello?" She makes a face. "Is someone there?"

"Lulu, hang up," her mother instructs sharply, then instantly softens her tone. "Hang up, sweetie."

Joanne smiles at her daughter, named Lana on her birth certificate but called Lulu by everyone. The child has the remarkable ability to look both younger and older than her eleven years.

"Why would someone call if they're not going to say anything?" The child pouts.

"I don't know," Joanne says. "Maybe it was a wrong number. Are you ready to go?" she asks, changing the subject.

"I hate this dumb uniform," Lulu announces, looking down at herself. "Why couldn't they pick something pretty?"

Joanne checks her daughter's sturdy frame. Lulu is built more like her husband, Paul, whereas Robin, her older daughter, is built like herself. Joanne thinks the dark green shorts and lemon-yellow T-shirt are, in fact, flattering to Lulu's fair complexion and long, light brown hair. "Camp uniforms are always yucky," she tells the child. "Is Robin ready?" Lulu nods. "Is she still angry?"

"She's always angry."

Joanne laughs, wishing it were not true.

"What time is Daddy picking us up?"

Joanne checks her watch. "Soon," she realizes aloud. "I'd better get ready."

"Why?" Lulu asks. "Are you coming with us?"

"No." They had decided that it would be better if only Paul drove the girls to the camp bus. "I just thought I'd change. . . ."

"What for?"

Joanne runs a nervous hand down the length of her orange shirt and white shorts. She looks at her bare feet. Her two big toenails are a deep purple from playing tennis in shoes half a size too small. She thinks of slipping on some sandals but decides against it. If Paul notices her toes, it will give them something to talk about. It has been several weeks since they have talked about anything but the children.

The doorbell rings. Joanne's hand flies skittishly to her hair. Perhaps she could quickly pull a brush through her hair and change into the turquoise sundress that Paul has always liked.

It's too late. Lulu is at the front door. Her hand on the doorknob, she turns back to her mother. "You look fine, Mom," Lulu reassures her. She pulls the door open.

The stranger who greets them is Joanne's husband of almost twenty years. Paul Hunter is of average height and build, though Joanne notices new muscles under his blue short-sleeved shirt, undoubtedly the result of his recently implemented weight-lifting regimen. She thinks in that instant that she prefers his arms the way she has always known them—on the thin side. She has always had difficulty adjusting to change. This is probably one of the things that drove Paul away.

"Hello, Joanne," he says warmly, his arm around Lulu. "You look well."

Joanne tries to speak but is unable to find her voice. She feels her knees go weak, is afraid that she is about to fall or burst into tears. She doesn't want to do this. It will make Paul uncomfortable, and that is the last thing she wants. Above all else, she is still hoping that he will decide to come back. After all, nothing has been decided yet. It's been only two months. He is still "thinking things through." She is still in limbo.

"How have you been?" he asks.

"Fine," Joanne lies, knowing that he will believe her because this is what he wants to believe.

"What happened to your toes?" he asks.

"Mom's been playing tennis in shoes that were too tight," Lulu answers for her.

"They look very sore," Paul observes.

"Actually," Joanne says, "they don't hurt. They did before they turned purple, but now I guess they're kind of numb."

Paul checks his watch. "We should get going pretty soon," he says, his voice casual. "Where's Robin?"

"I'll get her." Lulu disappears up the stairs, leaving her parents to walk their invisible tightrope without the safety net her presence provides.

"Would you like a cup of coffee?" Joanne asks as she follows Paul into the large, bright kitchen.

"I'd better not." He walks directly to the sliding glass door that makes up the kitchen's south wall and stares into the backyard. "Quite a mess," he comments.

"You get used to it," Joanne tells him.

The mess to which he refers is a large, empty, concrete-lined, boomerang-shaped hole that was supposed to have been their new swimming pool. Designed by Paul, it was intended to be their "summer cottage without the traffic," as the man from Rogers Pools described it only days before his company went belly-up.

"I'm doing all I can to get things moving again," Paul tells her.

"I'm sure you are." Joanne smiles to convince him that she understands he is not at fault. "And I don't swim, anyway."

He turns from the glass door. "How's your grandfather?"

"The same."

"And Eve?"

"The same." They laugh.

"Any more phone calls?" he continues after a slight pause.

"No," she lies, recognizing that to say otherwise would only make him edgy. He would then be forced to repeat what he has already told her: that everyone gets crank calls; that if she is really worried, she should call her friend Eve's husband, Brian. He's a police sergeant and lives right next door. Paul has also told her, as gently as he could, that he feels she is exaggerating, that it is her way of trying to keep him tied to her, making him feel responsible for her when he has abdicated that responsibility, at least temporarily. He has not suggested, as Eve has, that the calls might be a product of her imagination, her way of dealing with her present situation.

The girls are waiting for them at the foot of the stairs. "Got everything?" their father asks.

Joanne stares hard at her daughters, looking for hints of the children they once were. Lulu has changed the least since infancy, she thinks. Her enormous brown eyes—a gift from her father—are still the focal point of her face.

At age fifteen, Robin is different, although she has her father's upturned nose and square-set jaw. Her legs are too long and her body too short. In another year or so, Joanne thinks, Robin will be beautiful. Surprisingly, however, and unlike Joanne's at her daughter's age, Robin's looks are very *in*. She dresses accordingly. Even now, she has obliterated the bland statement of her camp uniform by defiantly lacing a shocking-pink chiffon scarf through her short, overpermed hair. Her eyes—hazel like her mother's—stare resolutely at the floor.

"I'll wait in the car," Paul tells them, stepping outside.

Joanne smiles, feeling her heart beginning to pound. This is the first time that she will be completely on her own. For the summer, there will be no one but herself to look after.

"Don't worry, Mom," Lulu begins before Joanne has a chance to speak. "I know the speech by heart. I'll be careful; I'll write every week; I won't forget to eat. Did I leave anything out?"

"How about having a good time?" Joanne asks.

"I'll have a good time," Lulu agrees, and throws her arms around her mother's neck. "Will you be all right?"

"Me?" Joanne asks, smoothing a few stray hairs out of Lulu's eyes. "I'll have a ball."

"Promise?"

"I promise."

"Things have a way of working out," Lulu intones, so seriously that Joanne has to cover her mouth to hide a budding smile.

"Who told you that?"

"You do," Lulu informs her. "All the time."

Joanne's smile spreads beyond her fingers into the corners of her eyes. "You mean you actually listen to what I say? No wonder you're so smart." Joanne kisses Lulu as much as the child will allow, then watches her run down the stairs to Paul. Robin is immediately at the door. "Will you at least *try* to enjoy yourself?" Joanne asks.

"Sure. I'll have a ball," Robin mimics pointedly.

"I think you'll see that we made the right decision. We all need time to cool off and think things through."

"Sure," Robin grunts.

"Can I kiss you good-bye?" Joanne interprets Robin's silent shrug as a go-ahead, enveloping the girl in her arms and kissing her cheek. "Take care of yourself," she calls after her older daughter, watching her run down the stairs.

Paul looks back toward the house. "I'll call you." He waves to his wife before getting into his car and driving away.

THE phone is ringing as Joanne steps back into the house. She ignores it as she proceeds past it through the kitchen and out onto the back porch. She walks down the newly constructed steps that lead to the pool. Slowly, the phone still ringing behind her, she lowers herself onto one of the rose-colored slabs of flagstone that surround the concrete-lined hole and dangles her feet into what was supposed to have been the pool's deep end. It's hard to feel too sorry for a woman with a swimming pool, she thinks, looking up at the house next door and catching sight of her best friend, Eve, staring down at her from the bedroom window.

Joanne raises her hand and waves, but the shadowy figure in the window suddenly backs away. She brings her hand up to her eyes to shield them from the sun, but Eve is no longer there, and Joanne wonders if in fact she ever was. Lately her mind has been playing tricks. . . .

"I'm not saying that someone isn't phoning you," she remembers Eve saying.

"What *are* you trying to say?" she had replied.

"Sometimes the mind plays tricks."

"Did you talk to Brian?"

"Of course." Eve was suddenly defensive. "You asked me to, didn't you? He says you should just hang up on the guy."

"I'm not even sure it *is* a man! It's such a strange voice. I don't know if it's young or old, male or female."

"Well, of course it's a man," Eve stated flatly. "Women don't make obscene phone calls to other women."

"These are more than just obscene calls. He says he's going to kill me. He says I'm next. Why are you looking at me like that?"

"I was just wondering whether the phone calls started before or after Paul left."

Now Joanne is wondering the same thing, trying very hard to assign some order to the events of the last several weeks. She knows only that everything in her life has been turned upside down. Familiar objects have fallen away from her, and there is nothing for her to grab on to, no arms to pull her to safety.

She pulls herself to her feet, aware that in the house the phone has stopped ringing. She walks to the shallow end of the aborted pool and climbs into it. Maybe I am crazy, she thinks.

Joanne Hunter watches the world recede as she progresses into the deep end of the empty concrete hole. Sitting with her knees drawn up against her chest, she hears the kitchen phone ring again. It's just you and me now, he is telling her with the persistent ring. Joanne nods her head in silent acknowledgment of the unstated fact and tries to conjure up images of happier times.

As JOANNE recalls, the phone had been ringing just before Eve arrived at her front door almost two months earlier. "Hello?" Joanne had said into the receiver. She shrugged her shoulders and replaced the receiver as Eve came inside. "Kids," Joanne pronounced.

"You ready?" Eve asked.

"I just have to find my racket." Joanne opened the closet in the front hall. "I think I buried it back here somewhere."

"Well, hurry up. I understand that the new pro is delicious, and I wouldn't want to miss a minute of our lesson."

"I don't know why I let you talk me into these things."

"Because you've always let me talk you into everything. It's part of your charm." Eve looked toward the kitchen door. "The pool seems to be coming along. I keep tabs from my bedroom window."

"Well, the man said ten days to two weeks, so it looks like they may finish on schedule. Found it," Joanne said, retrieving her racket from the closet. "I'll just tell the men I'm leaving."

"Hurry. We'll be late."

"You're always in such a hurry." Joanne laughed.

"And you're always so slow," Eve countered. "That's why we've been friends for so long. If we were both like me, we'd blow each other up."

It was true, Joanne thought as they drove to Fresh Meadows Country Club. They had met in seventh grade, at the age of twelve. Even then Eve had been something of a standout, a tall, gangly redhead with an infectious giggle and a commanding tone to her voice. Mutt and Jeff, Joanne's mother used to tease. If Eve asked you to jump off the Brooklyn Bridge, would you do it?

Probably, Joanne realized.

They arrived at the clubhouse, deposited their handbags in their lockers, and headed directly for the courts.

"Hello," a muscular blond young man said. "I'm Steve Henry, the new tennis pro."

"There really is a god," Eve whispered as she and Joanne took up their positions in front of the net.

AN HOUR later, as they entered the women's locker room, Eve nudged Joanne. "So what do you think?"

"Seems like a good instructor."

"That's not exactly what I was talking about," Eve informed her friend, with a mischievous twinkle.

"I don't look at men that way," Joanne told her.

"Well, he was sure looking at you," Eve teased.

"Looking at my rotten backhand, you mean. If I hear the words 'follow through' one more time, I'll scream."

"Why do you always put yourself down?" Eve demanded, her voice suddenly serious.

"I just have a realistic understanding of my own limitations."

"There's nothing wrong with you that a little self-confidence and maybe a few blond streaks wouldn't fix."

Embarrassed, Joanne ran a hand through her light brown hair. "And losing five pounds, and getting my teeth straightened."

"Talk to Karen Palmer. Her husband's a dentist."

"Talk to her yourself. She's right behind you."

"Hi," a woman greeted them. "Did you hear about the latest grisly Great Neck killing?"

"Third one this year," Eve elaborated. "I thought we all moved to Long Island to be safe."

"That poor woman. Strangled, then hacked to pieces!" Karen Palmer further embellished. "Can you imagine the terror she must have felt—"

"Do we have to talk about this?" Joanne interrupted.

"She's no fun." Eve smiled at the obviously deflated Karen Palmer. "She never lets you talk about any of the good stuff."

Karen shrugged. "Did you just have a lesson?" she asked, seeking safer ground.

"The tennis pro is after Joanne." Eve laughed, removing her purse from her locker and slamming the door shut.

"Oh, I'd follow through on that one if I were you," Karen advised with obvious relish.

"You are crazy," Joanne admonished them playfully as she and Eve left the clubhouse and walked toward the parking lot.

"Excuse me, Mrs. Hunter," a masculine voice called from across the lot. Joanne looked up to see the tennis pro running toward them.

"You left these on the court," he said as he reached the women, producing from his back pocket a set of keys dangling on a chain.

"Oh, thank you. I'm forever leaving those things somewhere." Joanne felt a blush spread across her cheeks as she took her house keys from his hand.

"See you next week." He smiled and was gone.

"Mrs. Hunter is red all over." Eve laughed.

"You really enjoy embarrassing me, don't you?" Joanne asked good-naturedly.

"Yeah, I do," Eve admitted, and both women laughed.

AT HOME half an hour later, Joanne stepped out of the shower and heard the phone ring. "Blast," she muttered, throwing a towel around her wet body and running toward the bedside phone. "Hello?" There was no response. She returned the receiver to its cradle in disgust. "Good-bye," she said, catching a glimpse of one of the workers in the backyard as he passed under her window. Immediately Joanne ducked beneath the windowsill. Had he seen her? No, she thought, crawling back toward the bathroom on her hands and knees. She could see him, but he couldn't see her.

The idea of being watched gave Joanne a momentary shudder. She reached the bathroom, checked to make sure the blinds were closed, and only then stood up.

Joanne felt herself being drawn toward the mirror, her fingers reaching up to smooth out the small lines around her eyes. Her eyes reflected the passage of the years. They were more knowing, less trustful. How long had it been since someone had stared into

353

them and told her how beautiful she was? A long time, she thought.

Lately Paul had seemed preoccupied, distracted. She had assumed it was a temporary malaise. All couples went through periods of decreased ardor. When his work load lessened, she reasoned, his interest in her would pick up.

Suddenly the phone rang again.

She moved quickly to answer it, careful not to walk too close to the window. "Hello?" As before, there was no response. She waited a second, then dropped the receiver back onto its cradle. "Go bother someone else," she admonished it.

"Hello? Is anybody home?" a masculine voice called as Joanne heard her front door open and shut.

"Paul?" Startled, Joanne quickly retrieved a robe from her walk-in closet and wrapped it around her before her husband appeared in the doorway. "What are you doing home in the middle of the afternoon? Are you feeling all right?"

He didn't look well, she thought, kissing him gently on the cheek. "I wanted to talk to Mr. Rogers," he said, looking out the window. "Has he been around today?"

"Just the workers. Although he might have been here—I was gone for a few hours, at the club. A new instructor. He seems to feel that I have a certain natural ability, but I don't know. It's been so long since I played. . . ." What was she rattling on about? Why was she so nervous?

She looked at her husband's back as he stared out the window. There was something about his stance, the visible tension in his shoulders, that made her uncomfortable. He turned toward her, and she didn't like the expression on his face.

"What is it?" she asked. "Is something wrong? Something the matter with the pool?"

He shook his head. "No, it's not the pool. It's me." There was a long, uncomfortable pause. "I have to talk to you," he said finally.

Joanne sank into the blue, well-stuffed chair at the foot of their bed. She didn't know what he was going to say. She knew only that she wasn't going to like it.

Chapter 2

LATER that evening, after her husband had packed some things and left to spend the night in a hotel, Joanne sat on her big, empty bed and reran the scene in her mind. She had said nothing, nothing at all, as her husband told her he intended to leave home. She had simply sat there and listened as he tried to explain himself, tripping over his confusion, apologizing, trying to force some sense into his words. She hadn't opened her mouth, hadn't moved except to swipe at unwanted tears. She had just listened. In the end she had remained in their room while Paul had repeated his intention to leave home to Lulu and Robin. When they had reacted later, after he had gone, their anger had been directed at her, not at the man who had left, just as she had known it would be.

It's not my fault, she had wanted to tell them, but she didn't, feeling somehow that it was.

That night, feeling smothered by the empty space beside her in the bed, Joanne went to stand by the window. She looked in the direction of Eve's house next door. The lights surrounding Eve's patio were bright and accusing. Pulling the curtains closed, Joanne picked up the telephone and dialed, hanging up when Eve failed to answer after eight rings. She remembered that Eve and Brian were out late, attending some police function.

Lulu was asleep, or at least she had pretended to be when Joanne had looked in on her earlier. Robin was at a party.

Moving like an automaton, Joanne crawled back under the covers of the king-size bed she and Paul had purchased shortly after moving to this house some twelve years ago from their older, smaller home in Roslyn. Up the ladder of success, she thought, feeling her life reduced to an unpleasant statistic.

Her parents had lied to her. She would grow up, their smiles had silently promised, and she would have control over her actions, her fate. She would be secure in a world that was fixed and permanent. And for a while they had been right. She had grown up essentially as planned, had married, and had borne children of her own.

355

Hearing a key turn in the lock, aware of Robin's footsteps on the stairs, Joanne fell asleep with the memory of the smell of her mother's perfume.

In her dream she saw the sun shining as she walked toward the small white cottage ahead. She was perhaps five years old. Her brother, two years her junior, was taking his afternoon nap. She could hear her mother and grandmother in the kitchen preparing supper for when their men returned from the city, as they did every Friday afternoon during the two months of summer that the family gathered at this cottage in the country. Joanne skipped toward the front door, projecting ahead an hour or two, when the car would pull into the driveway and first her grandfather—a huge, robust man—and then her father, smaller but with a hearty laugh, would appear. Her father would kiss her before disappearing inside, but her grandfather would linger, scooping her up into his arms and twirling her around. When you're older, I'll teach you how to play gin rummy, he would tell her. And each week Joanne would wonder if she was older yet. She reached the front door of the cottage, hearing her mother's high, girlish giggle ringing inside.

The phone was ringing. Joanne groped for it in a daze, her eyes unwilling to open. "Hello," she said, not sure for the moment who she was, only that she was no longer a little girl.

There was no one there. Not even silence, she realized slowly, coming fully awake. A dial tone only. She lay back down, her heart thumping wildly. Joanne spent the rest of the night trapped between sleep and wakefulness, wondering whether the ring that woke her had been the telephone or her mother's laughter.

THE girls were still asleep when Joanne left the house the next morning and crossed from her front lawn over to Eve's. She was tired; her eyes were swollen from a combination of tears and lack of sleep.

She mounted the steps to Eve's front door and knocked. No one answered. She knocked again, then rang the bell. She needed to talk to Eve. Eve would make her laugh, or at least they could cry together. Where was she? Why wasn't she answering the door?

Eve's husband, Brian, appeared just as Joanne was about to give up and go back home. A tall man projecting a strong, imposing image, Brian Stanley had surprisingly gentle eyes. The perfect policeman's face, Joanne thought as he ushered her inside. He was smiling but preoccupied. "You talk some sense into her," he said, indicating that his wife was in the kitchen.

Joanne found Eve at her kitchen table, nursing a cup of coffee. "What's up?" Joanne asked, realizing that her friend was still in her bathrobe and that her usually perfect hair was uncombed.

"Nothing," Eve told her, making no effort to disguise her annoyance. "It's a lot of fuss over nothing."

"Sure it's nothing," Eve's mother chided, appearing out of nowhere to stick a thermometer into her daughter's reluctant mouth.

"Hello, Mrs. Cameron," Joanne said, wondering what Eve's mother was doing here. "What's going on?"

"What's going on," the woman repeated, "is that my daughter collapsed last night and had to be rushed to the hospital."

"What!"

Eve whipped the thermometer out of her mouth. "I did not collapse. I am perfectly fine."

"Put that back in your mouth," her mother instructed. Eve looked imploringly toward the ceiling but did as she was told. "You didn't have pains last night and have to leave the party? Brian didn't take you to the emergency room at North Shore Hospital? He didn't call me first thing this morning and ask me to come look after you?" her mother asked.

"I had a few pains," Eve corrected, once again removing the thermometer, "and everyone overreacted."

"What kind of pains?" Joanne asked, temporarily forgetting her own problems.

"Just a few small pains in my chest. I've been having them for a few weeks."

"Just a few small pains," her mother repeated. "Pains so bad that she couldn't stand up."

"I just wish somebody would tell me what is going on here," Joanne implored, remembering countless such scenes she had witnessed between these two throughout her girlhood.

"Look, ladies, I have to go. I'm late already." Brian was exasperated. "The facts are that Eve started experiencing some pains in her chest at around midnight, so I took her to the hospital."

"Where they gave me some tests and decided that everything was all right," Eve stated.

"Where they gave her an EKG," Brian continued, "and recommended that she have further tests later in the week."

"For what?" Joanne asked, concerned.

"Ulcer, gallbladder, that sort of thing," Brian answered. "But she's refusing to go."

"It was a little indigestion. I am not going to put myself through a battery of unpleasant tests just so some doctor can get some much needed experience at my expense. I saw all I ever want to see of hospitals six months ago, thank you very much."

"Talk some sense into her," Brian repeated. "I have to go." He kissed his wife reassuringly on the top of her head, a gesture that brought the threat of tears to Joanne's eyes. Before they could form, she turned and quickly swiped at her face with her hand. Now was obviously not the time to announce Paul's sudden departure.

The three women listened in silence as Brian closed the door behind him. When Eve opened her mouth to speak, her mother automatically thrust the thermometer back into it.

Eve angrily hurled the thermometer to the floor and watched it break. Then she said gently, "Mother, please go home." Her voice had become a sudden gasp of pain.

"What's the matter?" Joanne and Mrs. Cameron asked together.

"It's all right now. The pain's gone. It wasn't that bad." Eve sat back in her chair. "Don't worry."

"Maybe you should see the doctor," Joanne urged, trying to sound casual. "What can it hurt to have a few more tests?"

Eve's eyes moved from her mother to her closest friend.

"All right," she agreed after a lengthy pause.

Mrs. Cameron turned her attention to Joanne. "How are your daughters?" she asked, abruptly changing the subject and almost managing to sound interested.

"They're good kids." Joanne smiled. "Like Eve."

Eve laughed. Her mother did not. "Sure, stick together like you two always have. But am I wrong to be concerned because my daughter was rushed to the hospital?"

"Mrs. Cameron," Joanne began. "If it'll make you feel any better, I'll take Eve to the doctor myself." She turned back to Eve. "When's your appointment?"

"Friday." She winked. "Morning. So we don't miss our tennis lesson."

"Tennis," her mother scoffed. "It's too soon after the miscarriage to be playing tennis."

"Oh, let's not start that again," Eve pleaded. "The miscarriage was six months ago."

"You work too hard. You take too many classes. You do too much."

"I'm a teacher, Mother."

"A professor," her mother corrected, looking at Joanne to check that the distinction was not lost. "A psychologist."

"A psychology professor, okay? I don't work too hard. I have Fridays off. I'm taking a few extra courses at night—"

"What do you need more courses for? You're forty years old. You need children, not Ph.D.s."

"I don't want to talk about this," Eve said, banging a fist on the table. "You are making me crazy, Mother."

"Sure, blame the mother for everything. Tell me, Joanne," Mrs. Cameron continued, again trying to change the subject. "How's your grandfather?"

"He's okay. I'm going to visit him this afternoon."

"Now, you see?" Eve's mother asked. "This is a responsible girl. Nobody has to remind her to show respect for her elders."

Joanne rolled her eyes in her friend's direction, and Eve stuck out her tongue in return.

"Sure, make a joke," Eve's mother said. "I'm going to watch television. Call if you need anything. Nice seeing you, Joanne."

"She hasn't changed a bit," Joanne marveled as the woman disappeared into another room. "You should be used to her by now."

"Some things you never get used to," Eve said, and Joanne

knew instantly that that would be true of Paul's departure. "You look tired," Eve observed suddenly.

"Some idiot phoned in the middle of the night and hung up," Joanne told her. "Eve—"

"You don't think these pains really could have anything to do with the miscarriage, do you?" Eve interrupted, looking very fragile. "Maybe they left something in there after they cleaned me out."

"I'm positive they didn't," Joanne assured her. "You'd be dead by now if they had," she added, and both women laughed.

"Thanks." Eve smiled. "You always did know how to cheer me up."

BAYCREST Nursing Home was located on South Drive, a block and a half from Great Neck Hospital. It was an old brick structure that had survived several renovations without any noticeable change to its appearance. The corridors still looked as sad and abandoned as most of the residents who walked them, Joanne thought as she moved toward her grandfather's room at the end of the hall.

She could hear the commotion even before a nurse appeared in the doorway. "I don't believe that man!" the nurse exclaimed as she struggled to calm herself. "Oh, not your granddaddy, honey," she said, recognizing Joanne and smiling. "Your granddaddy is no trouble at all. Sleeps like a baby, and he looks so cute in his little hat."

"Is Mr. Hensley giving you problems?" Joanne asked. Sam Hensley was notorious among the nurses. He had been shuffled around the various floors ever since his arrival six months ago.

"I went in to ask whether he needed help, and he threw the bedpan at me. Fortunately, it was empty! Honestly, I don't know what happens to some people when they get old—" The woman stopped abruptly. "I don't mean any disrespect, Mrs. Hunter," she stammered. "Your granddaddy is such a sweet little man."

"My grandfather doesn't know where he is most of the time," Joanne said, thinking how strange it sounded to hear her once massive grandfather described as sweet and little.

He had started shrinking, she recalled, in the year following the death of his wife of almost sixty years. He had begun spinning his cocoon soon after he checked himself into the home five years ago, and he had sealed himself inside it around the same time that Joanne's mother had discovered a lump in her left breast. He had never asked why his daughter's visits became less frequent, and when she had succumbed to the disease three years ago, Joanne and her brother had decided not to tell him. Instead, she had stepped in to fill the vacant hole, visiting him every week, less from a sense of duty than because he provided her with her only tangible link to the past.

This was the man who had sat with her on rainy afternoons at the summer cottage and patiently explained the intricacies of gin rummy, who had boiled her perfect five-minute eggs each weekend morning, watching while she ate them, talking to her animatedly about his week in the city, always exuberant and bursting with life.

"Linda?" her grandfather asked as Joanne approached his bedside and took his hand in hers.

"Yes, Pa," Joanne answered. "I'm here." When was the last time he called me by my rightful name? she wondered. It's Joanne, she wanted to tell him, but he was already snoring, and she was left wondering whether she would ever get used to being called by her mother's name.

"Amazing how they can just drop off like that," a voice said from somewhere beside her. Joanne looked over at the other bed, where old Sam Hensley was sleeping. "A minute ago," the woman standing at the foot of that bed continued, "my father was a raving lunatic. He threw a bedpan at the nurse! I don't know what I'm going to do if they kick him off this floor. This is the third home I've had to move him to. I'm going out for a cigarette." She spun around, and for the first time since Joanne had entered the room she was aware that the woman's son was also present, tilting his straight-backed wooden chair against the wall, his head resting against his right shoulder, his eyes closed. "Can you believe this?" the woman demanded. "If either one of these sleeping beauties wakes up, tell them I'm out in the lounge."

Joanne watched the woman leave, trying to connect a name to her curious combination of defeated face and defiant strut. They had been introduced about a month ago when the woman's father had been transferred to this room. Marg something-or-other, Joanne recalled. Crosby, she remembered with some satisfaction. Marg Crosby and her son, Alan, a boy of about eighteen.

"Linda," her grandfather murmured.

"Yes, Pa," Joanne answered, almost by rote. "I'm here."

Again the old man fell quiet. Where are you? Joanne asked him silently. Where do you go? Her eyes moved across his pale, thin face. His expansive forehead was completely hidden by the baseball cap perched atop his head, a gift from her on his eighty-fifth birthday, ten years ago.

"Paul's left me, Grampa," she whispered. "He doesn't want to be married anymore. I don't know what I'm going to do." She cried softly as the old man opened his eyes and stared directly into hers, as if he understood exactly what she had said.

"Do you work here, dear?" he asked.

Old Sam Hensley suddenly bolted upright in his bed and burst into song. *"It's a long way to Tipperary,"* he bellowed.

Beside him young Alan Crosby almost fell off his chair with the sudden sound. "Granddad," he whispered, jumping to his feet and looking nervously toward the door. "Sh . . ."

"Sh yourself if you don't like it," the old man shot back loudly, returning to his song.

"It's his military period." Alan smiled meekly at Joanne as his mother and the nurse ran back into the room.

"Oh, for heaven's sake, Dad!" Marg Crosby barked as the nurse tried to push Sam Hensley gently back against the pillow.

"Get away from me," he shouted at the woman.

"Why don't you just let him sing?" the Crosby boy asked, leaning back against the wall, trying to suppress a smile.

"Oh, Alan!" his mother exclaimed impatiently. "Don't you start."

"Linda," a frightened voice cried. "What's all the commotion?"

"It's all right, Pa," Joanne whispered. "I'm here."

Chapter 3

THE phone woke her up at not quite seven o'clock the next morning. "Hello," Joanne said groggily. "Hello? Who is this?"

There was no reply.

Joanne dropped the receiver back onto its cradle. "Kids again," she muttered. She pulled the blankets up over her head, trying to block out the early morning light. But as soon as she buried her nose into the soft down pillow she smelled traces of Paul, his absence filtering up through her nostrils.

Her eyes drifted open. Paul was inside her head now, and he would stay there no matter what she did or where she went. This new day would produce only fresh regrets for which she could berate herself. If only she hadn't done this; if only she *had* done that. If only Paul would come back, she would be more *this* way, less that.

She had fallen into bed at one a.m. She was still awake to hear the front door open at just past three, to listen as Robin sneaked past her mother's bedroom, then closed the door to her own room softly behind her. Joanne decided to wait until the morning to confront her daughter, who had never been this late before.

It must have been five a.m. before Joanne had finally succumbed to sleep. Two whole hours, she thought now, trying to will herself several more.

She was still trying to force herself back to sleep half an hour later when the phone rang again. "Hello," she whispered. There was no response. "Hello? Hello? Is someone there? Why are you doing this?" she pleaded, about to hang up when she heard something. "Did you say something?" she asked, returning the phone to her ear.

There was a brief pause. Then, "Mrs. Hunter?"

"Yes?" Joanne tried to place the raspy sound, but while there was a quality to it that was vaguely familiar, she was unable to determine who it was. Certainly no one she knew well. "Who is this?" she asked.

"Have you read *The New York Times* this morning, Mrs. Hunter?

There's something in it that concerns you. Page thirteen of the first section." The voice was curiously ageless, sexless.

"Who is this?"

The line went dead in her hands.

"Hello?" Joanne sat motionless in bed for several minutes, listening to her heart thumping. Whose voice had she heard, and why the intrigue? What could there possibly be on page 13 of the paper that would concern her?

Pulling her arms through the sleeves of her housecoat, Joanne walked quickly down the stairs to the front door. She wasn't even sure the *Times* would be there this early.

It was, she found, lifting the heavy Sunday paper and carrying it into the kitchen, where she dropped it onto the heavy pine-wood table. She flipped quickly to page 13 and took a cursory glance down the columns. There was something about a union dispute, a report of a rooming-house fire, and some further details about the woman who had been hacked to pieces in her home in Saddle Rock Estates. Joanne shrugged and closed the paper. What had the caller wanted her to see? She ferreted out the entertainment section, deciding that maybe she'd take the girls into Manhattan later in the week to see a Broadway play.

At that moment Lulu shuffled sleepily into the kitchen in her pajamas and slippers. "It's raining," she announced.

"Maybe it won't last," Joanne replied hopefully. "What do you want for breakfast?"

"French toast?" Lulu asked, plopping into one of the chairs. Her mother cracked some eggs into a bowl.

"Did you sleep well?" Joanne asked. Lulu only shrugged, leafing absently through the paper. "I thought maybe we could see a play this week," Joanne offered.

"That would be nice," Lulu agreed, a smile creeping into her half-closed eyes. She peered into the backyard. "When are they going to be finished out there?"

"Soon, I hope." Joanne flipped two slices of soggy bread into the frying pan.

"Will Daddy come to the play with us?"

Joanne's hand began to tremble. "I thought it was something

just the three of us could do. You know, kind of a girls' night out."

"Why did Daddy leave?" the child asked abruptly.

Joanne aimed another piece of bread toward the pan, but it missed and landed on the counter. She picked the slice up again, watching as it came apart against the prongs of the fork. "I'm not sure," she said, trying to keep her voice steady. "Didn't he tell you?"

"He said he needed time alone, to think things through. What things? Why can't he think at home?" Lulu asked accusingly.

"I don't know, sweetie," Joanne told her, flipping the browned toast onto a plate and bringing it to her daughter. "Those are questions you'll have to ask your dad."

She watched as Lulu scooped a glob of butter onto each piece of toast before drowning her plate in syrup. "Good?" Joanne asked as Lulu began stuffing the pieces into her mouth with almost manic determination, careful to avoid her mother's eyes.

"Is it because of me?" the child asked finally, unable any longer to keep the tears away. "Because I'm not doing very well in school?"

"Oh, no, sweetheart," Joanne rushed to assure her. "Daddy's leaving has nothing to do with you. Besides, you're doing fine in school. There's nothing wrong with your marks."

"They're not as good as Robin's."

"Robin is a different type of student. She can memorize anything you put in front of her. You just have different ways of showing how smart you are."

Lulu sulked, apparently unimpressed, then left the room.

The phone rang as Joanne was rinsing off Lulu's plate. "Hello," she answered warily, glancing toward *The New York Times*.

"You'll never guess who's going to be a movie star!" came the excited exclamation from California on the other end of the line.

"Warren!" Joanne shouted, barely recognizing her brother's voice. "What are you talking about?"

"They want to make your baby brother a star. Steven Spielberg, no less. Wait—Gloria will tell you all about it."

"Gloria, what's happened to Warren?" Joanne said, laughing, when her brother's wife came on the phone.

"It's true," Gloria announced. "I slave in show business for years and where do I get? Your brother delivers some star's baby and gets introduced to Steven Spielberg, who takes one look at Warren's blue eyes and decides to give him a small part in his new picture. They shoot early this fall."

In the background Joanne could hear high-pitched yelling. "What's that?"

"The girls are fighting, as usual," Gloria told her. "It never stops. How's everything on the east coast?"

"Everything's fine here," Joanne lied. Why upset her brother and his wife? What could they do from three thousand miles away?

"I'll let you talk to your brother," Gloria was saying.

Joanne and Warren spent the next fifteen minutes in conversation, Warren filling his sister in on the more important events of the past week, Joanne leaving them out.

"You're sure everything's all right?" her brother asked as the conversation wound to a close.

"What could be wrong?" Joanne asked in return.

"Keep smiling," he told her before he hung up.

Robin was standing in the doorway. "Uncle Warren?" she asked, coming into the room.

Joanne nodded. "He sends his love." Robin yawned loudly and flopped into a chair. "I'm surprised you're up this early. You were out very late last night." She watched her daughter's shoulders stiffen. "After three, wasn't it?"

"I didn't notice the time."

"Well, I did, and I don't want you coming in that late again," Joanne stated simply. "Is that clear?"

Robin nodded.

"Who did you go to the party with?" Joanne continued gently.

"Scott."

"Who's Scott?"

"Just a guy." Robin regarded her mother shyly. "He's real nice."

"I'd like to meet him. The next time you go out with him, why don't you bring him around to say hello?"

"Sure," Robin agreed quickly.

"Is he in your class?"

"No," Robin said, aware her mother was waiting for further elaboration. "He doesn't go to school."

"He doesn't go to school? What *does* he do?"

"He plays guitar in a rock group." Robin shifted uneasily.

"How old is he?"

Robin shrugged. "Nineteen. Maybe twenty."

"That's too old for you," Joanne stated flatly.

"Mo-ther!"

Joanne bit down on her lower lip. "Where did you meet this Scott?"

"A party at somebody's house maybe a month ago."

"You're very vague."

"Look, I said I'd bring him around the next time I saw him."

Joanne stared hard at the wood grain of the kitchen table. "Would you like some breakfast?" she asked finally.

Robin shook her head. "I promised I'd help Lulu study for her history test."

Joanne watched wordlessly as Robin departed.

The phone rang just as a loud fight between the sisters erupted upstairs. "Girls, please," Joanne shouted as she reached for the phone. "Hello," she said.

"Mrs. Hunter . . ."

Joanne recognized the strange voice immediately. "Yes?" she asked, afraid though she wasn't sure why.

"Did you read page thirteen of the paper?"

"Yes, I did," she replied. "But I think you've made a mistake, or you've got the wrong Mrs. Hunter."

"You're next," the voice said simply, and was gone.

"Hello? Hello?" Joanne repeated. "Really, I think you've made a mistake." She hung up the phone, her eyes returning to the paper. Slowly the strange voice, like an invisible magnet, pulled her back across the room until her fingers were brushing against the rough edges of the newspaper. Nervously she flipped through the pages until she found page 13. With growing uneasiness she retraced the columns, her eyes finally coming to rest on the story of the housewife who had been murdered in her home in nearby Saddle Rock Estates. Without warning Joanne felt an invisible presence standing beside her, bending close to whisper in her ear.

"You're next," it said.

"For heaven's sake, why didn't you tell me?" Eve Stanley was pacing back and forth across Joanne's living room.

"I tried last weekend," Joanne said softly. "But you weren't feeling very well, and your mother was there. The rest of the week kind of got away from me."

"Yeah. Well, I can understand that," Eve admitted. "Actually, Brian mentioned that he hadn't seen Paul's car all week. I didn't even notice—I've been so busy with my aches and pains. Anyway," she continued, "when I came home this afternoon, I saw Lulu sitting outside. She didn't look very happy."

"She failed her history test."

"I asked her if Paul was out of town, and she told me the news. Needless to say, I almost fainted dead away."

"I'm sorry. I should have called. I'm not functioning well lately."

"And no wonder. I can't believe Paul would do such a thing. May he rot in hell."

Joanne smiled. "I knew you'd cheer me up."

"What exactly did he have to say?"

"He said he wasn't happy." Joanne laughed, trying hard to keep the laugh from becoming the sob it was aching to be.

"He has no right to be happy. I hope he gets a toothache every time he smiles. Do you think he has somebody else?"

Joanne shook her head. "He says no. He says he's never been unfaithful to me."

"Do you believe him?"

"I always have."

"You believe everyone," Eve stated flatly.

"Do *you* think he has someone else?" Joanne asked.

"No," Eve replied truthfully.

369

"I think he just stopped loving me," Joanne said simply.

"People don't just stop loving other people for no reason. It *has* to be something more specific."

"I know. . . . I'm sure it was all my fault."

"Hold on a minute," Eve insisted. "Who said so?"

"Obviously it was. Why else would he have left? I didn't do *anything* right."

"In twenty years you didn't do anything right? What about Robin? What about Lulu? You have two beautiful daughters—"

"I have two beautiful *obnoxious* daughters," Joanne corrected. "I mean, I love them more than anything else in the world, but I don't know what happens to girls when they get to a certain age. Were we like that?"

"According to my mother, I still am." Eve shook her head. "Maybe it's a good thing I had that miscarriage," she continued matter-of-factly. "She's always wished on me a daughter like the one I was. That's the only reason she wants grandchildren, you know. Anyway, we are not talking about my mother. We are talking about you, about how you haven't done anything right in twenty years and probably your whole life." Joanne tried to smile but failed. "Is there anyone on earth who makes better pies and cakes than you do?"

"That doesn't count."

"What do you mean, it doesn't count?"

"I've been baking a lot of pies and cakes this week, and thinking about how I've spent the last twenty years. Eve, I'm an anachronism. Everything I was brought up to be has gone out of style."

"Being a loyal wife is out of style? Being a good mother is out of style? Being a terrific friend doesn't count anymore? Says who? Show me who says it, and I'll beat him up right now." Eve paused. "Anyway, I better not say anything else, because if I do, and you and Paul get back together—which you will—you'll hate me, and I'll have lost my only friend in the world."

"You'll never lose me." Joanne smiled. "You're the one constant in my life. I can't imagine not being friends."

"I love you," Eve said simply.

"I love you too," Joanne replied, embracing her friend. "What time is your doctor's appointment tomorrow?"

"Oh, forget it. You don't have to take me."

"Don't be silly. Why should you go alone? Besides, if I stay home, I'll just bake more of those dumb pies and cakes."

"Okay, you talked me into it. It's at nine thirty." Eve caught her reflection in a mirror on the wall. "Look at me! I look awful." She rubbed the skin around her eyebrows, so that it produced small white flakes. "I'm falling apart."

"It's called dry skin," Joanne told her.

Eve laughed. "I don't know—I always used to have oily skin."

"The joys of middle age."

"I suppose. I'd better go. I have a million papers to mark."

"Eve." Joanne's voice stopped her friend. "What do you know about that woman murdered in Saddle Rock Estates?"

Eve shrugged. "Not much," she said. "Just what I read in the papers. She was raped and beaten and strangled and stabbed. Anything that he could do to her, he did. According to Brian, it's the third one this year by the same guy. Why?"

Joanne told her about the phone call. "He says I'm next."

Much to Joanne's surprise, Eve burst out laughing. "I'm sorry," she said quickly. "Really, I didn't mean to laugh. It's just that you look so worried."

"Well, I *am* worried. Paul's gone and—"

"And some crazy tells you you're next on his list. Guys who get their kicks on the phone don't do anything in person. But if it'll make you feel better, I'll tell Brian about it. Okay?"

"I'd appreciate it," Joanne said.

"You don't have to appreciate it." Eve smiled. "Just don't worry about it. You have enough to worry about right now," she said, opening the front door. "And don't forget about our tennis lesson tomorrow afternoon."

Joanne waved. "Meet you in the driveway at nine."

"YOU'LL just have to study harder," Joanne was saying only minutes later as Lulu helped herself to a second piece of freshly baked cake. "That's enough. We're eating supper in an hour."

"Why'd you make it if we're not supposed to eat it?" Lulu shoved some moist lemon cake into her mouth.

"I made it for dessert."

"So I'll have some for dessert too."

Joanne decided against pursuing the subject. "Maybe we could work out some sort of system that would help you remember the dates for history. I always remembered the date of the Battle of New Orleans because there was a song about it. '*In 1814, we took a little trip . . .*' " she began, then stopped. "Well, I don't remember all the words, but I always remembered the date."

"Life isn't *Sesame Street*, Mother," Lulu reminded her, finishing off the piece of cake.

An eleven-year-old is telling me about life, Joanne thought.

There was a knock on the sliding glass door. Joanne turned to find one of the workers from the pool—a tall, skinny, dark-haired man—smiling at her from the other side of the glass. She rose slowly from her seat and slid the door open.

"We're finished for today," the man informed her. "I was wondering if I could use your phone."

Joanne backed out of the way to let him in. As she pulled the door shut behind him she noticed that his shoes were caked with damp earth, which he was now scattering carelessly across the kitchen floor. "It's on the wall," she replied, pointing to the white phone.

"Thank you," he said, smiling at Lulu. When he turned toward the wall to dial, Lulu made a face in her mother's direction. The man suddenly swiveled around again. "Got me on hold," he muttered, and Joanne nodded. "Your husband home?" he asked.

Joanne shook her head. "Do you need to speak to him?"

"Nothing that can't wait." His attention was redirected to the phone. "Hello? . . . Yes, can I—" He snickered impatiently. "Got me on hold again."

"Dad phoned," Lulu said softly, newly reminded.

"When?" Joanne felt her hands start to shake. "Why didn't you call me?"

"You were in the bathroom. And I didn't call you, because he didn't ask to speak to you. Just to me."

Joanne felt the saliva stick in her throat. "What did he want?"

"Me to spend the weekend with him in the city. I said okay."

"Don't you think you should have checked with me?"

"No. He's my father. I can see him if I want to."

"Nobody said you couldn't see him."

The man at the phone cleared his voice, as if to remind them he was there, and then shifted back toward the wall, speaking in a whisper. Joanne lowered her own voice accordingly.

"What about Robin?" she asked.

"Robin has a date Saturday night."

"Okay." Joanne gave in. "You can spend the weekend with your father. Just make sure he has you back early on Sunday night."

"Excuse me," the man broke in. "I'm finished. Thank you." He moved away from the wall and stepped outside.

Joanne closed the door and snapped the lock shut after him.

"He gives me the creeps," Lulu whispered, watching him laugh with one of the other workmen by the deep end of the pool.

"Why?" Joanne asked. "He seems nice enough."

"I don't like the way he stares at people. He drills holes in you like he's working on one of those pieces of stone."

"You've been watching too much television," Joanne said.

Chapter 4

"So how'd it go?"

"Please, let's just get out of here. Then we'll talk."

Joanne had to walk quickly to catch up to her friend, who was already half a corridor ahead. Eve pushed open a heavy door and started toward the main entrance of the hospital. "I'm starving," she announced.

"Are you going to tell me what they did to you in there or not?" Joanne asked again as the two women emerged into the drizzle outside.

"Oh, no, it's still raining."

"Where do you feel like eating?" Joanne asked.

"Let's go to The Ultimate. It's always nice, and it's close."

When they were seated, Eve ordered a bottle of white wine to go with their Caesar salads.

"What did the doctor say?" Joanne asked as Eve filled their glasses.

"Nothing that any normal human being can understand. They speak the language of the gods they think they are." Eve took a stab at her salad. "Aren't you going to try the wine?"

"I don't think I should. You know how dizzy wine makes me. Especially in the afternoon."

"Come on, don't be so timid," Eve admonished. "Wine at lunch isn't so decadent. We're liberated now, you know."

Joanne sighed and took a healthy sip. "So," she said. "Do you or don't you have ulcers or gallstones?"

"After strapping me on this dumb table and turning me virtually on my head, the doctor said he couldn't see a thing wrong on the X rays. The results of the blood tests will be a while."

"Why'd they do blood tests?"

"Why do they do anything? It gives them an enormous sense of power."

"So what happens now?"

"Life goes on. We finish our lunch, then play some tennis."

"It's raining," Joanne reminded her. "We'll have to skip the lesson."

"Then we sit here and drink," Eve replied.

But in the end they decided to go to a movie.

"I don't believe I let you talk me into seeing this film," Joanne said, giggling, as they took their places in the theater.

"Film is too good a word"—Eve laughed—"for what we are about to see." She grabbed a handful of popcorn from a box in Joanne's lap and watched as half spilled onto the floor.

"Thanks a lot," Joanne told her. "I thought you said you never ate popcorn."

"I thought you said you never go to horror movies."

The two women dissolved into giggles as the theater was plunged into total darkness and the curtains parted.

Joanne was aware of a slight movement nearby. She swiveled

around as a young man carrying a motorcycle helmet seated himself directly behind them, despite the fact that most of the other chairs in the theater were vacant. He seemed to be smiling as he lowered the helmet to his lap. Joanne turned and whispered to Eve, "Let's move."

"Why? I'm comfortable."

"There's this funny guy sitting behind us. I don't like the looks of him."

Eve turned to stare. "He looks okay to me," she whispered.

"Why does he have to sit so close?"

"Why don't you stop worrying and watch the picture?" Eve chided. "This is going to be great," she promised as a pretty young ingenue with blond hair ran in obvious terror across the screen. Joanne watched the helpless girl fall straight into the arms of a deformed madman with a knife, who wrenched the girl's head back violently and proceeded to slit her throat. Blood dripped from her neck and gathered in pools at the bottom of the screen, only to rise again seconds later in the form of undulating capital letters: SWAMP MONSTER OF DOOM.

Joanne felt her stomach turn. What was she doing here, she pondered, in the middle of a Friday afternoon, in the middle of a life that was disintegrating, watching a gore-filled horror flick? Wasn't it enough that her husband had walked out on her, and some lunatic with a phone fetish was threatening her?

"Are you crying?" Eve asked suddenly.

"I don't think so," Joanne replied.

"Why is your head down? Why aren't you watching the movie?"

Joanne lifted her head just in time to see another young woman, this one with a long, angular face, moving across the screen. A phone rang and the girl went to answer it, unaware of the danger lurking just out of camera range. The camera followed her into a kitchen, where she picked up the phone. "Hello," she said, eyes wide, voice soft, and then repeated the word when she received no answer.

Joanne squirmed uneasily in her seat, glancing over at her friend, whose eyes were riveted to the screen. Why had Eve brought her here?

"Don't be so nervous," Eve reassured her.

"Hello?" the girl on the screen repeated.

"Mrs. Hunter," a voice whispered menacingly in Joanne's car.

"What?" Joanne gasped, feeling the warm breath on the back of her neck and jumping from her seat as she spun around.

There was no one there. Even the boy with the motorcycle helmet had disappeared.

"What are you doing?" Eve cried. "You scared me to death!"

"I thought I heard someone call my name. Mrs. Hunter."

"I know what your name is," Eve replied testily. "And no, I didn't hear anybody call you. Now I have to go to the bathroom."

She stood up. Joanne turned to watch her leave and caught sight of a young man sitting alone at the rear of the theater. The boy with the helmet? she wondered, straining her eyes through the darkness for a better look. But the young man raised his hand to his face, and Joanne could discern nothing. She turned back to the screen.

She sat for a moment, then stole another surreptitious look around the dark theater. The boy in the last row was gone. Had he been there at all? Eve bounced down into the seat beside her, and they watched the remainder of the movie in uneasy silence.

"At least it's stopped raining," Eve said as they emerged from the theater and walked toward Joanne's car.

"I don't see why they make films like that." Joanne sighed.

"Because people like you and me pay good money for them," Eve told her as they headed for the maroon Chevrolet parked at the end of the street.

"What's that on my windshield?" Joanne said.

"Darn—a ticket!" They drew nearer to the car. "No, it's a piece of newspaper. Looks like the wind blew it across your windshield." Eve reached the car before Joanne and pulled the piece of newspaper free and tossed it onto the road. "Too bad about that rooming-house fire," she said matter-of-factly as she and Joanne climbed into their respective seats.

"What are you talking about? What rooming-house fire?" Joanne asked as she pulled the car away from the curb.

"It happened last week, I guess," Eve said. "I don't know. I noticed a headline about it on that paper I took off your windshield."

Joanne slammed down hard on the brakes, thrusting both women forward despite their seat belts.

"What are you doing?" Eve exclaimed.

"That newspaper," Joanne demanded. "Where is it?"

"I threw it away. Why? What are you doing?"

But Joanne had opened her door. She ran around to the other side of the car and scooped up the newspaper from the curbside.

Most of the page had been torn away. Still, it was unmistakable. Last Sunday's *New York Times*. Page 13.

"It could be a coincidence," Eve was repeating as they waited in Joanne's living room for Paul to arrive.

"You keep saying that. Do you really believe it?"

"I don't know."

"Could you try Brian again?"

"I've already left two messages," Eve told her.

"Well, maybe I should try someone else at headquarters."

"You don't think you should wait till Paul gets here?"

"Who knows when that will be? You know the traffic on a Friday afternoon," Joanne said as the two women walked into the kitchen. "Paul didn't sound very happy about having to drive out here. He's taking Lulu for the weekend tomorrow, and this means he has to make an extra trip."

"Tough," Eve said simply. "Some crazy threatens the mother of his children, I think the least he can do is drive out here and give you some support. Are you going to ring the police?"

"I don't know the number."

"Let me do it," Eve said, going over to the phone. "Sit down. You look like you're going to faint." Joanne lowered herself into one of the kitchen chairs. Her eyes watched Eve, who smiled as if to reassure her that everything would be all right.

"Hello. . . . Yes. This is Joanne Hunter," Eve said. "I live at 163 Laurel Drive. I'd like to report some threatening phone calls I've been getting. Who am I speaking to, please?" Joanne leaned back in her chair in admiration. She would never have thought to ask for the man's name. "Sergeant Ein," Eve repeated, then wrote the name down on a piece of paper. "Yes. . . . I've been getting these calls lately. They started—" She looked at Joanne.

Joanne shrugged. "He spoke to me for the first time last Sunday, but I've been getting weird calls for a few weeks now, maybe more," she whispered quickly.

"Yes, I'm still here. I've been getting them for a few weeks now," Eve said. "Some guy"—Joanne lifted her palms into the air to indicate doubt—"at least I *think* it's a guy," Eve corrected, "has been calling at all hours. And then on Sunday he threatened me. . . . What exactly did he say?" she repeated.

"He says I'm next," Joanne whispered.

"Well, when he called last Sunday," Eve embellished, "he told me to look at page thirteen of *The New York Times*"—Joanne nodded approval—"and I saw that article about the woman who was murdered in Saddle Rock Estates, which is just near here. And then he called back and told me that I'm next." There was a pause. "No, he didn't come right out and say he was going to kill me, but today I found a piece of newspaper on my car windshield, and it was the same page thirteen of the *Times*. So this guy is obviously following me, and I'm afraid . . . I realize that, but . . . Well, I hate to do that. Isn't there anything else you can do?" There was a long pause. "Yes, I understand. Thank you very much." She hung up the phone in obvious disgust.

"What did he say?"

"That 'You're next' isn't exactly the worst threat he's ever heard, and have I any idea how many phone calls the police have received from women convinced they're the Suburban Strangler's—that's what they're calling him—next victim? He said that if they had to investigate every crank call, they wouldn't have time for anything else. So he advises me—or rather, he advises you—to change your phone number, because there's nothing that he can do unless the guy actually makes a move."

"At which point I could well be dead."

"Come on, cheer up. Brian wouldn't let anything happen to you. That's one of the benefits of living next door to a cop."

"What did the policeman say when you told him about the newspaper on the windshield?"

Eve shrugged. "Not much. Basically, they have to wait for this kook to make a move. Which he won't," she added quickly. "What about installing a burglar alarm?"

"That's a good idea," Joanne agreed. "It would make me feel a lot safer. I'll ask Paul when he gets here."

"Why don't you just tell him?"

"I'll ask him," Joanne repeated as the doorbell rang.

"I'll get it," Eve volunteered, walking to the front door.

Joanne hoped that Eve would excuse herself and leave, but after greeting Paul Eve followed him into the kitchen and stood watching them carefully and obviously going nowhere.

Joanne felt a dull ache at the sight of him. He looked so handsome, so concerned.

"You've called the police?" he asked, directly to the point.

"Eve just spoke to them. They say there's nothing they can do unless the guy actually makes a move."

"Where's this piece of paper?"

"It's in the living room," Eve said, leading the way.

Paul quickly looked over the newsprint. "There's nothing here about a murder."

"That part is missing," Joanne explained, feeling a sudden hollowness in her chest.

"There isn't even a page number," Paul continued, a slight impatience creeping into his voice.

"It's page thirteen," Joanne told him. "I know because I read every article on that page several times."

"Joanne, don't you think that's a little farfetched?"

"I don't know," she said, sinking into a chair. Was it?

"Look," Paul continued. "Some crackpot calls and scares you half to death. It's only natural you'd be spooked, especially now that I'm not—" He broke off, looking toward Eve.

"I'd better go," Eve said quickly. "Nice seeing you, Paul. Don't forget to tell him about the alarm, Joanne," she added before she left.

"What alarm?" Paul asked.

"Eve thought it might be a good idea to put in a burglar alarm."

"Fine, if it would make you feel better."

"What do I do?" Joanne asked, feeling foolish.

"I'll arrange it," he said, "and call you Monday."

"Thank you." They stood in the living room awkwardly. "Would you like to sit down? I could make some coffee. . . ."

"No, thank you," he responded quickly. "I have to get back to the city. Where are the girls?"

"At a track meet."

"How have they been?"

"They miss their father."

"I know," Paul said softly. "I miss them too. It's very quiet without them."

"Lulu's looking forward to tomorrow," Joanne said. "Can't wait to see her dad's new apartment."

"It's not much," Paul explained. "It's very cramped, very impersonal. Did Lulu give you my phone number?"

"Yes."

"If you need anything, don't hesitate to call."

"I won't." There was an awkward pause. "Have you had time to think things through yet?" she asked finally.

Paul looked across the room. "Not really. I've been so busy with the move, trying to get organized. It's only been a week."

"You look well."

"Thank you."

"I must look awful."

"You look fine. A little tired, maybe. Those phone calls haven't helped your sleep, I'm sure."

"I was scared."

"Try not to worry about it," he said. "Just hang up the next time the jerk calls."

Joanne stared at him. "I miss you," she said simply.

"Joanne, don't."

"I don't think I can manage without you."

"You can. You're strong."

"I don't want to."

"You have to." There was silence. "I'm sorry. I didn't mean

to sound harsh. You know I'm always here if you need me."

"I need you."

"You can't come running to me every time you have a little problem. It isn't good for you, and it isn't good for me."

"This isn't just a little problem."

"Joanne, if I were home, you wouldn't give this matter a second thought."

"But you're not home."

"No," he said, the softness of his voice undercutting the harshness of his words. "And this isn't going to bring me home either. Joanne, if our marriage has any hope of surviving, you have to give me this chance to be by myself. You can't keep finding excuses to bring me back here."

Joanne said nothing. Had she been overreacting?

"I have to go now. I have clients waiting."

Joanne nodded, following her husband to the front door.

"I didn't mean to sound so cold—"

The phone rang.

"Do you want me to wait?" he asked.

"Yes!" Joanne ran to the kitchen and picked up the phone. "Hello?"

"Mrs. Hunter."

Joanne froze at the sound of the familiar voice, her eyes frantically summoning Paul. He walked quickly toward her and took the phone.

"Hello," Paul said forcefully. "Who is this?" Joanne waited. "Who?" she heard him ask. "Oh, yes. . . . Yes, she's right here. I'm sorry, she must have misunderstood." He handed the phone back to Joanne. What was going on? "I have to go," he said quietly. "Tell Lulu I'll pick her up at ten o'clock tomorrow morning."

"Hello?" Joanne asked, hearing the front door close.

"Mrs. Hunter?" the voice said again, this time more of a question. "It's Steve Henry, the tennis pro. Are you there?"

"Yes," she whispered, recalling the look that had passed across Paul's eyes moments earlier. The phone call had only confirmed his suspicions. "I'm sorry, I didn't recognize your voice."

He laughed. "No reason that you should. I thought you might

like to arrange for another lesson to make up for the one you missed today. I have some free time over the weekend."

"No, that's impossible."

"All right," he said quickly. "I guess we'll just leave your lesson until next Friday."

"That's fine." She hung up without further comment.

How could she have made such a dumb mistake? Especially when Paul was there. But when she picked up the receiver, the caller had said "Mrs. Hunter" in that same way.

The phone rang again. Joanne reached over automatically, thinking that it was probably Eve.

"Mrs. Hunter," the voice said before Joanne had a chance to say hello. "Did you get my message, Mrs. Hunter?"

This time there could be no mistake.

"What message?" Joanne asked, knowing the answer. She sank slowly to the floor beneath her feet, her breathing almost still.

"The one I left on your car, Mrs. Hunter. You couldn't miss it. I left it right across your windshield, where you'd be sure to find it. Did you enjoy the movie, Mrs. Hunter?"

"Listen," Joanne pleaded. "I think you better stop this little joke right now. My husband doesn't think it's very funny."

"Your husband's gone, Mrs. Hunter," the voice informed her casually. "In fact, he's gone for good. Isn't that so? And I know how lonely women get when their husbands aren't around to take care of them, and I intend to see that you don't have that problem. Yes, ma'am. Before I kill you, I'm going to show you a good time."

Joanne let the receiver drop, hearing it hit the wall with a sharp crack. She remained in this position, her back against the wall, her knees drawn up to her chest, with the phone buzzing an insistent signal beside her, until her daughters burst into the house demanding to know what was for dinner.

THE two men from Ace Alarms Incorporated arrived the following Thursday morning to begin installation of the new alarm system.

"I guess I should show you around," Joanne told them. They were both brown-haired and muscular, divided by perhaps a

generation. Possibly father and son, Joanne thought, remembering how disappointed Paul had been when their second child had not been a son. Maybe if she had given him a son . . .

Stop this, she scolded herself, smiling at the men. Masking a growing uneasiness, she tried to recall exactly what Paul had told her to do when he had telephoned to inform her of the arrangements he had made.

"Your husband didn't think it was necessary to install wires around all the windows," the senior of the two men—Harry, he'd said his name was—told her as she led the way into the kitchen. "Just the ones downstairs. And around the front door and the sliding glass doors, right?" Harry knelt at the base of the sliding kitchen door, examining its construction.

"That's right," Joanne answered, hearing her suddenly high-pitched voice. The men followed her into the hall. "You saw the front door," she squeaked. Why was she so nervous? These men were here to help her.

"When we came in," Harry said.

"Yes, of course." She led them to the family room.

"We'll replace the outside locks," Harry told her. "The ones you've got are strictly Mickey Mouse. It's a wonder you haven't been broken into already."

Through a glass door Joanne caught a glimpse of the dark-haired, skinny worker who Lulu said gave her the creeps. He was staring at her from the side of the pool, but quickly looked away as their eyes met.

"We'll put Charley bars in the tracks of these sliding doors," Harry continued. "And a dead bolt on the front one. That won't keep anyone out, but it'll make it harder to get in. Most crooks don't like to work that hard. Where's your fuse box?"

Joanne led the men down to the furnace room, where the large metal fuse box was located. "Can I get you a cup of coffee?" she offered as they set about examining the assorted fuses.

"That would be real nice," Harry agreed. "Leon, how about you?" Leon nodded but said nothing. "Cream and sugar for me. Black for my brother."

So they were brothers, Joanne thought, returning to the kitchen to prepare the coffee. There was quite an age difference, she calculated, her mind conjuring up a history for the two men: the father had left Harry's mother for a younger woman when Harry was a boy, and started a new family. Leon was the result.

Joanne watched as the coffee dripped slowly into the glass pot of the coffee machine. If Paul were to remarry in the next year, she further calculated, and if he started another family, well then in less than two years Robin and Lulu could have a new baby brother. . . .

There was a knock on the sliding door. Joanne swung toward it as if she had been struck. The dark-haired, skinny worker was smiling at her from the other side of the glass. I need to use your phone, he mouthed.

Joanne walked hesitantly to the door and pulled it open. The man, in his late twenties or early thirties, stepped in immediately.

"Thank you." He smiled, his eyes seeming to take in each detail as he ambled across the room and picked up the phone, leaving another trail of dirt across the floor. He dialed the appropriate numbers. "Got a new number, huh?" He indicated the new number printed in the center of the phone.

Joanne nodded, trying not to listen to his conversation as she noisily retrieved the sugar from its shelf, uncomfortably aware that his voice carried familiar traces of a slight rasp.

Her eyes locked on the back of his head at the same instant that he turned away from the wall, so they found themselves staring directly at each other. Casually he replaced the receiver, and almost provocatively relaxed his posture, making no effort to leave. "Your husband home?" he asked.

"He's at work," Joanne answered, realizing he had probably overheard part of her conversation with Lulu the previous week and had already figured the situation out for himself.

There was a sudden knock on the front door. Joanne jumped. "Busy day," the man said, his lips twisting into a smirk. Joanne squirmed uneasily. She wanted to move, but couldn't. The man's smirk broadened into a grin. "Aren't you going to answer it?"

Don't be silly, Joanne silently admonished herself. Just because the man looks creepy, that doesn't mean he *is* creepy. How many times had she warned her daughters that bad people didn't always look bad, that appearances could be deceiving? And many people's voices were vaguely raspy. It didn't mean anything. She was letting her imagination run away with her. She went to the front door and opened it.

"Mrs. Hunter," the short, pear-shaped man before her said.

"Mr. Rogers," Joanne greeted him in return, recognizing the man who owned and operated Rogers Pools.

"I was wondering if you could move the truck in your driveway. My men need to get in and start pouring the concrete."

"Oh, yes." Joanne raced into the hall to the top of the basement stairs. "Harry . . . Leon . . . could one of you move your truck?"

Leon took the stairs two at a time, saying nothing as he skipped down the front steps and headed toward the driveway.

Mr. Rogers walked past Joanne into the kitchen, taking it for granted that he had been invited inside. "How do you like the pool?" he asked, staring out the glass door at the backyard.

"Well, it's kind of a mess," Joanne said meekly, relieved to see that the creepy man was gone from her kitchen, though she noticed his trail of muddy footprints. She saw her purse on the floor beside the phone. Had it been lying on its side that way when she ran to answer the door, or had it been moved?

"It'll be beautiful. You'll see. You'll love it."

"When do you think it'll be finished?" Joanne ventured.

"Another few days, tops. It depends on the weather. We'll get the concrete in today. After that, it's just finishing touches."

"Seems like there's quite a bit of work left."

"Not once the concrete's in. Which, by the way, means another payment. Could you have a check ready for me by the end of the day? Just give it to Rick there."

"Rick?" Joanne glanced over at the pool, half expecting to see the skinny worker who had been inside her home.

But Mr. Rogers pointed at another man with dark hair. "That's Rick," he said. "Just give him the check."

Mr. Rogers handed her an invoice. "See you later," he told her as he and Leon passed each other at the front door.

"Your coffee's ready," Joanne called after Leon, but he continued down the stairs to the furnace room as if he hadn't heard. Why doesn't that Leon ever speak? she wondered, returning to the kitchen, pouring coffee into mugs.

She felt her hands shake and the coffee slosh about in the mugs. She lowered them to the counter. It seemed that every man she encountered might be the mysterious caller. A man who, everyone assured her, was just a harmless crackpot. Someone who hadn't even phoned in the few days since she'd had the number changed.

"Okay," Harry said, appearing behind her without warning.

"Oh!" Joanne gasped, spinning around and almost knocking over one of the mugs.

"Careful," Harry cautioned, taking both mugs and setting them down on the table. "We're ready to start now," he informed her, and Joanne realized that Leon had also quietly entered the room and had been observing her.

"How long will it take?" she asked.

"A couple of days. We got a lot to do."

"What exactly?" Joanne asked.

"Don't you worry about it," the man said. "I'll explain how everything works once we get it installed. You decided yet where you want the intercom?"

"The intercom?" Now that she heard the word, Joanne vaguely remembered Paul saying something about . . .

"Your husband told us to install an intercom system. The house is already wired for one. You gotta have a main terminal. Most people like it in the kitchen." He looked around the room. "There, beside the phone. That's probably the best place for it."

"All right," Joanne said.

"Good. Then let's get to work," Harry announced. Quickly Leon followed his brother out of the room.

The rest of the day had the feel of an out-of-focus photograph, the house full of men scurrying about like mice. At various intervals a shrill bell would sound. "We're testing the system," Harry informed her. Rick came to the door to collect the check promptly at five o'clock, just as Harry was asking Joanne what combination of numbers she had selected for the alarm.

"Numbers?" Joanne said, again aware Leon was watching her.

"You're supposed to pick four numbers, Mrs. Hunter," Harry said. "Whatever combination you want." He led her to the small box they had installed just inside the front door. It contained a series of push buttons like the face of a telephone. "Whenever you're going to leave the house, you push the four numbers. A green light will go on. Then you have thirty seconds to get out and close the door behind you. The same thing when you come back. You come inside, and you have thirty seconds to press the numbers to turn the system off. The green light will go out. If you don't, the alarm goes off. Understand?"

Joanne nodded.

"So pick four numbers."

"Any numbers?"

"Whatever numbers your little heart desires."

Leon suppressed a chuckle, disguising it as a cough.

"When was the start of the Civil War?" Joanne asked, her mind unable to focus.

"I beg your pardon?" Harry asked. "The Civil War?" He looked toward his brother.

"Eighteen sixty-one," Leon said evenly.

A perfectly nice voice, Joanne thought. "Can I use that?"

"You can use the start of the Boer War if you want," Harry told her. "One eight six one it is."

"My younger daughter is weak in history, in remembering dates. Maybe this will help her," Joanne confided, but the two men were already halfway down the stairs.

Joanne turned back toward the kitchen. The skinny, creepy workman was standing in the doorway. "I knocked on the kitchen door," he explained. "Guess you didn't hear me. Is your husband home yet?" Joanne shook her head. "He said that he wanted to talk to me before we went ahead with the tile."

"I'll call him," Joanne said, walking past him into the kitchen.

She thought, as she listened to the man talking quietly to Paul over the phone moments later, that his voice had lost any trace of the raspiness she had heard in it earlier. In fact, there was nothing especially creepy about the way he looked either.

The man replaced the receiver and faced Joanne. "Thank you." He smiled, his eyes burrowing into hers as if he knew something she didn't. All her misgivings instantly returned. Had he been into her purse earlier? How long had he been standing in the doorway? Had he heard the numbers she and Harry had discussed for the alarm? She couldn't take a chance that he had. She'd have to change the combination.

"Harry," Joanne called down the stairs seconds after the worker had departed and she had securely fastened the lock on the sliding glass door behind him.

"Yes, Mrs. Hunter?" Harry's voice echoed with benign impatience, as if he already knew what she was about to say.

"When was the start of the Boer War?" She heard Leon break into unrestrained laughter. He thinks I'm an idiot, she thought.

Chapter 5

"You have a strong natural backhand, Mrs. Hunter," Steve Henry was explaining enthusiastically. "You just have to be more aggressive. Lean into the ball more. Here, like this." He positioned himself behind her to guide her right arm. "That's right. Back foot firmly on the ground. You're doing very well, Mrs. Hunter. Just relax. You're supposed to be having a good time."

Joanne smiled, stealing a glance at her watch. She was tired, her legs ached, and she was perspiring into her new white tennis dress. Can't he see that I'm an old lady? she wondered.

"Follow through, Mrs. Hunter," the voice across the net urged. "Follow through."

What is he talking about? Joanne asked herself, swinging wildly at the ball and then lobbing the next one high into the air. Tennis lessons were Eve's idea. Why does she get to stay home sick, while I have to run around this dumb court chasing balls? Don't you realize that I have more important things to do? Joanne shouted wordlessly at the young man on the far side of the court. Like waiting for my daughters to come home from school. Like waiting for my husband to make up his mind! She slammed the next ball straight into the net.

"Follow through, Mrs. Hunter," Steve Henry called out, his body sweeping forward to underline his words.

She swung ferociously now at an oncoming ball, missed it entirely, and landed hard on her behind.

Steve Henry was instantly at her side. "Are you all right?" His voice was solicitous as his arms reached under hers to help her up. "Well, you followed through all right." He smiled. "But you took your eye off the ball."

"I'll never get the hang of it," she told him.

He laughed. "Want to rest a few minutes?"

"I think I've had it for today," Joanne said. "I'm too old for this."

"Too old? You have the best legs of any woman at this club." The remark was casual, yet Joanne felt her face flush. "Sorry, I didn't mean to offend you," he covered quickly, though his smile remained.

"You didn't," she told him, turning to walk off the court.

"How old *are* you?" he asked, following alongside.

Joanne took a deep breath and let it out slowly. "Forty-one."

"You look ten years younger."

"That's not young enough, I'm afraid."

"For whom? Afraid of what?"

Joanne bit her bottom lip. Was he coming on to her? She dismissed the unsettling idea. He was just a natural flirt.

"Your husband's a lucky man," Steve Henry said as he opened the door to the court and stepped back to let her pass through. "See you next week."

THAT evening Scott Peterson finally appeared at the front door for a date with Robin. Joanne thought that he was a distinct anticlimax. He was as lean as a sharpened pencil and not very tall, with short, dark blond hair. His face, while thin and pale, wasn't any more emaciated than the currently acceptable social norm.

"Scott, this is my mother," she heard Robin say.

"Hi," Joanne and the boy said together.

Scott Peterson looked through Joanne as if she were invisible, the way young people often look at their elders.

"Ahem," came a loud coughing noise from the stairs. Lulu stood twirling her long brown hair between nervous fingers.

"This is my sister, Lulu," Robin said.

"Lana is my real name," came the immediate correction.

"I kind of like Lulu," Scott said, smiling. "Little Lulu and the Lunettes. Great name for a group."

Lulu said nothing, her face frozen in admiration.

"We'd better go," Robin announced, putting a preemptive hand across Scott's arm.

"I'll have her home by one, Mrs. Hunter," Scott assured Joanne. "Nice meeting you. You too, Lana."

"Lulu," the child said quickly.

"You liked him?" Joanne asked her younger daughter after the front door closed.

"He's neat," Lulu said, floating through the hall. "Robin doesn't deserve him."

IT WAS late when Joanne undressed for bed. She opened the middle drawer of her dresser, and as she searched wearily for her nightgown her hand stumbled across an old T-shirt of Paul's that lay at the rear of the drawer. She pulled it out and put it on, feeling it hug her body loosely, reassuringly.

Joanne climbed into the king-size bed, struck anew at how empty it felt these days. She drifted in and out of sleep until she heard Robin come home at ten minutes to one. Only then did she give in to her fatigue, quickly falling into a deep, dreamless sleep.

The phone rang.

Joanne sat up and grabbed the receiver before she knew what she was doing. "Hello," she whispered, the thumping of her heart sounding louder than her voice.

"Mrs. Hunter," the voice teased. "Did you think I wouldn't find out your new number?" An unpleasant chill ran down the length of Joanne's spine.

"Stop bothering me," Joanne replied, glancing at the luminous face of the bedside clock and seeing it was four a.m.

"Your new locks won't keep me out." Joanne felt her hand begin to tremble. "Sweet dreams, Mrs. Hunter."

Joanne jumped from her bed and raced down the stairs. Moving like a woman possessed, she checked all the locks on the main floor. Everything was secure. She returned to the front hall, glaring at the buttons of the alarm system on the wall. There was a way of turning on the system while you were in the house without setting off the alarm, she remembered, trying desperately to recall what Harry had told her. There was another button she could push. Her eyes darted frantically across the small box. "The bottom button," she said aloud, hearing Harry's voice gently against her ear. The one without a number. Simply press it, and the alarm would be set. It would go off if someone subsequently opened one of the doors or downstairs windows. Slowly Joanne's trembling finger moved toward the button. She pressed down, watching the small green light flicker on. Holding her breath, she waited for the unwanted shriek of the alarm. But none came. I did it right, she sighed. At least now we'll have some warning if he tries to break in.

"You should have seen us," Joanne was saying. "Robin didn't know the alarm was set, and she woke up early and opened the front door to get the paper, and the alarm went off—you had to hear those sirens—and she started screaming, and Lulu and I were blasted out of our beds, and of course we started screaming, and naturally I couldn't remember how to turn the thing off, so it rang for over half an hour, and *finally* the police came, and I had to explain everything, and needless to say they weren't thrilled."

"Mom," Robin said wearily. "He doesn't hear you."

"He hears me," Joanne replied stubbornly. "Don't you, Pa?" Joanne stared into her grandfather's soft blue eyes. "Anyway, I had to call Paul and ask him how to shut the alarm off, and the alarm people had to explain the whole thing to me again. And now Paul is mad at me and the police are mad at me and Robin is mad at me—"

"Who said I was mad?" Robin demanded angrily.

"Anyway," Joanne continued, trying to laugh, "at least we know the alarm works."

"And I'll never forget the date of the start of the Boer War,"

Lulu piped up from beside the window. Joanne smiled, grateful that at least one of her children was trying to take a congenial part in the conversation. She glanced at the other side of the room, where old Sam Hensley sat berating his daughter and grandson, then back at her grandfather, who lay still under a mountain of covers.

"Mom," Robin whined. "Can't we go now?"

"No, we can't," Joanne said sharply. She immediately softened her voice. "Look, you don't come here very often. It's not going to kill you to sit still for a few minutes."

"He doesn't know who I am," Robin protested.

"You don't know that."

"Linda . . ." the weak voice called out, the old face all but swallowed up by the stiff white sheets.

"Yes, Pa. I'm here," she replied automatically.

"Who are all these people?" His eyes were unable to focus on anyone in particular, though his voice was instinctively wary.

"These are my daughters, Pa," Joanne said proudly. "You remember Robin and Lulu." She reached out her hands in their direction, drawing them to her. "You probably don't recognize them, they've gotten so big. This is Robin"—Robin smiled meekly, afraid to get too close—"and this is Lulu, my baby."

"Mom!" Lulu protested. "Hi, Grampa," she whispered, not sure how she should address this man she barely knew.

The room was suddenly silent. Joanne looked over at the other bed and saw old Sam Hensley propped up by several pillows, his visitors gone, his eyes clouded with tears. "Mr. Hensley," Joanne said softly, crossing to the other bed. "Are you all right?"

Sam Hensley said nothing. But as he stared at Joanne his hawklike features underwent a subtle metamorphosis, curiosity becoming indifference, indifference disappearing into animosity, animosity swallowed whole by a hatred so intense that Joanne actually felt herself stumbling backward, as if she had been physically pushed away. Large bony hands reached up toward her, as if eager to encircle her throat, and a low wail began to fill the room.

"Wow, he's worse than the alarm," Robin exclaimed nervously.

"What did you say to him, Mom?" Lulu demanded.

"I just asked him if he was all right."

The low wail continued building in intensity as Sam Hensley lay motionless in his bed, his eyes wide open and fierce. In the next instant the room was filled with nurses. Joanne saw the flash of a syringe. She looked over at her grandfather. His eyes were closed; he was completely unaware of the commotion that raged around him.

"Let's go, Mom," Robin whispered, pulling on Joanne's arm.

Joanne nodded wordlessly and led her daughters out of the room. They walked silently down the corridor, catching sight of Sam Hensley's daughter and grandson in the visitors' lounge, across from the elevators. Marg Crosby was smoking a cigarette while her son stared at the television set. Joanne approached the woman and explained what had happened.

Marg Crosby shrugged. "It's happened before," she said, getting to her feet. "You coming, Alan?" she called to her son, whose eyes remained riveted on the TV. "Alan?" she repeated.

He turned in his mother's direction, as if surprised she was there, but his eyes quickly continued past her, past Joanne, to somewhere behind them, a small smile gradually creeping into the corners of his mouth. Both Joanne and Marg Crosby turned around, only to find Robin, her eyes shyly downcast, with the same small smile on her overglossed lips.

"Down, Rover." Mrs. Crosby chuckled knowingly, and Joanne thought, as she had the previous night with regard to Robin's friend Scott, He doesn't even see me.

"Time to go home," Joanne stated, maneuvering her daughters in the direction of the elevator.

"Ma'am?" a voice called after her. The boy came to an abrupt halt several paces behind her. "Are these yours?" he asked, referring to a set of keys in his outstretched palm.

Joanne immediately recognized the key chain as her own. She felt the sudden weight of the keys as the boy dropped them into her hand. "Where did I leave them this time?" she asked.

"On a table in the visitors' lounge," Alan Crosby said, and smiled again just past her to where Robin stood waiting.

"I REALLY DON'T FEEL ANY older than they are," Joanne was telling Eve, who sat at her kitchen table drinking a large glass of milk and clutching nervously at her blue terry-cloth robe. "I look at Robin and Lulu, and I can feel what they're thinking—that we're worlds apart—and I want to tell them that we're not."

"You expect youth to understand what it's like to grow old?" Eve chortled. "As far as they're concerned, growing up means falling apart, and as far as I'm concerned, they're absolutely right."

Joanne laughed, though she was concerned about her friend's depressed state. Eve had always taken great pains to look, if not spectacular, at least dramatic. The only thing dramatic about the woman sitting at the table at this moment was the fact that she was drinking milk, something she hadn't done in years. It disturbed Joanne, threatened her already shaky frame of reference, to see her friend, always the stronger of the two, so overwhelmed by her discomfort. She prayed the doctors would discover what Eve's problem was and fix it quickly. Aloud she asked, "When's your next doctor's appointment?"

"Tuesday morning at the cardiologist. Friday morning at the gynecologist. You don't have to go with me."

"Of course I'll go with you." There was a moment's silence. "Maybe you could convince Brian to take you to a movie, get your mind off everything."

"I can't sit up straight for that long. Besides, when was the last time you saw Brian?"

"He's still working overtime?"

"The man loves his work. What can I tell you?" Eve suddenly caved forward, sucking in her breath.

"Eve? Are you having more pains?"

"Let's call it a spasm," Eve whispered, straightening her back and trying to smile.

"Let's play some cards," Joanne said quickly, looking toward the shelf where Eve usually kept such miscellaneous items. "Come on. We'll play gin rummy." Joanne found a deck of cards and slid them from their package, feeling a rush of childhood exhilaration pushing through her fingers.

"I can never beat you at gin." Eve grimaced.

"Too late. I'm already shuffling. Ten cards. . . ."

"You dealt. That means I go first," Eve said after Joanne had lowered the deck to the table. Eve looked at the upturned queen of diamonds. "I don't need that," she said, her lips a pout.

"Neither do I," Joanne agreed.

"Then I pick," Eve said triumphantly, and pulled the first card from the top of the deck. "Don't need that one either." She tossed the unwanted card on top of the queen.

They played a few turns without speaking.

"Has Brian said anything recently about—" Joanne broke off.

"About what?" Eve looked up from her hand.

"About the guy who murdered those women," Joanne muttered, trying to sound casual, as if the thought were unimportant.

"Your secret admirer?"

"Thanks."

"Sorry, didn't mean to upset you." Eve laughed and threw off the jack of spades. "No, nothing new. Did you tell the police about last night's phone call?"

Joanne nodded. "They said there was nothing they could do. I told them that he knew my new phone number, and about my new locks. They said to change my phone number again and keep turning on my alarm every night. But to please remember to turn it off the next time *before* we use the doors." She smiled. "Gin," she added, laying down her cards, trying to disguise the trembling in her hands.

"You caught me with a mittful." Eve laid down her cards. "Don't look so scared, Joanne. It's just some dumb kid playing a sick prank. Come on, deal." Joanne reshuffled the cards and dealt. "It's probably one of Lulu's or Robin's friends. You know how dumb teenagers are."

"I don't think any of the girls' friends are that dumb." Joanne picked up a five of clubs and threw off the queen of spades.

"It could be anybody," Eve said. "Does he sound like anybody you know?"

"That's the problem. He sounds like everybody I know."

"Wait a minute—what's that card? I'll take it." Eve pulled the card from the top of the discard pile and smugly tucked it into her hand. "Are you going to change your phone number again?" she asked.

"I don't know," Joanne admitted. "It's such a nuisance. Think of all the people I'd have to call again. And whoever it is will probably find out the new number this time too."

"Or he'll get tired, and that'll be the end of it. Unless that's not what you want."

"What do you mean?"

"Nothing," Eve stated, tossing her head. "Play a card."

Joanne threw off a king of diamonds, which Eve appropriated, discarding a three of clubs. "That's gin," Joanne said, nervously laying down her cards, puzzling over Eve's earlier remark.

"I give up. Your granddaddy taught you too well. I'd better stick to solitaire." Eve took the deck and began laying out cards flat across the table. "At least this way I can cheat."

"People who cheat at solitaire are insecure," Joanne said, smiling as she recalled her grandfather's words.

"You know I'm a sore loser. Give me victory or give me death," Eve declared, then doubled over in pain, sending the cards flying and spilling what was left of the milk.

"I'll get it." Joanne grabbed a dishcloth from the sink and quickly mopped up the spilled milk. "Are you all right? Maybe I should take you to the hospital."

Eve waved away the suggestion with an impatient hand. "It's okay. I'm sure I'll survive till Tuesday morning."

"Why don't you go lie down for a while?"

Eve agreed to the suggestion with surprisingly little argument. They made their way upstairs, and Joanne pulled down the covers of Eve's large four-poster bed and watched her crawl under the blankets. "Can I get you anything before I go?"

Eve opened one eye. "There's a *People* magazine somewhere," she said. "You can just lay it on the bed."

Joanne looked around but saw nothing. "You have a new cleaning lady or something? I've never seen this place so neat."

"My mother's been 'fixing,' " Eve said. "But maybe Brian took it. Look in his office."

It was always a strange experience being in Eve's house, Joanne thought as she walked along the hallway to the front of the house. Everything was the reverse of what it was in her own home, a disconcerting mirror image. Brian's office, located to the right of the hallway, was the larger of the two front rooms. In her own home the larger of the two rooms was located on the left and was occupied by Robin. Joanne took a brief glimpse around the study, curious but reluctant to snoop. There were lots of papers, a police manual, and a few books, but no *People* magazine.

She approached the room across the hall and stood in the doorway. It was the room that Eve and Brian had been reserving for a nursery. Six months ago it had been a pink-and-white dream, decorated for the hoped-for little girl who was due at the beginning of May. After years of frustration a baby had finally been expected, her name selected, the appropriate merchandise assembled. Now the room lay empty. Joanne was about to turn away when she saw the *People* magazine lying on the floor by the curtainless windows. Quickly she tiptoed across the pale pink carpet to retrieve it. What was the magazine doing in here? Did Eve come here to brood? If so, it was time to do something else with the room, Joanne thought, deciding she would mention it to Eve. But when she approached her room, she saw that Eve was already asleep, and so she laid the magazine at the foot of the bed and silently left the house.

Chapter 6

JOANNE stood half naked in the middle of her walk-in closet with a frown on her face and a pile of discarded clothes on the floor around her bare feet. There was simply nothing in here that she wanted to wear. Everything that her hands touched felt foreign and unfamiliar, as if each item had been purchased by someone else.

She reached over and grabbed an outfit, a white linen number some saleslady had cajoled her into buying. It was unquestionably the most stylish thing she owned, but the linen wrinkled too fast, and even though the saleslady had assured her that it was supposed to look wrinkled—that was the look—Joanne had always been uncomfortable with wrinkles. It was bad enough that she felt uncomfortable; she didn't want to *look* uncomfortable. She wanted to look beautiful. She wanted Paul to take one look at her and throw his arms around her and tell her how sorry he was, and if she would just forgive him please and take him back, he'd spend the rest of his life making it up to her—and all that in front of Robin's math teacher, Mr. Avery, who would smile and say that he was sure the problems he was experiencing with Robin would straighten themselves out now in time for exams. Her cutting his classes and failing his tests would stop as suddenly as it all began a few weeks ago.

Joanne dropped the white linen dress to the floor and felt a tear fall the length of her cheek. That would never happen, she thought. It would never happen, because she had nothing to wear. She would meet Paul in Mr. Avery's office an hour from now, and she would be wearing the same old clothes as the woman he had left, and Paul would look at her and smile—her dowdiness reinforcing his decision to leave—and they would sit side by side without touching, concerned parents still, if nothing else, and listen to whatever Mr. Avery had to say. And then they would go out for lunch and they would try to determine the best way to deal with Robin's problems in a civilized fashion.

The phone rang.

Joanne stood in the closet and stared in the direction of the telephone without moving. He knew she was in here, she thought. Somehow he could see into this small, windowless room. She held her breath lest the sound of her breathing betray her, until the phone stopped ringing. Then she resumed riffling through her closet, finally selecting a turquoise sundress that had at least a spark of youth about it.

Makeup, she thought suddenly. She needed a little makeup. She hurried to the bathroom, flung open her medicine cabinet, and pulled out the expensive tubes that Eve had once persuaded her to buy. Paul had told her repeatedly that he disliked artificiality of any sort. Still, a little makeup couldn't hurt. She rubbed a hint of color into her cheeks, decided it wasn't enough, then

rubbed in some more. Reaching for her mascara, she began rolling the curved applicator upward in slow, careful gestures.

The phone rang. At the sudden sound her hand jerked roughly
into her eye, her eyelashes blinking furiously at the unexpected
sharp pain. Joanne pressed her hand to her right eye to stop the
harsh stinging, and when she looked at herself seconds later, she
saw that she had smeared the mascara all over the side of her face.
"Terrific," she said out loud. The phone was still ringing. "Look
at what you made me do. It's not enough you're going to kill me,
you have to ruin my makeup!" She stomped angrily over to the
phone and jerked the receiver off its cradle. "Hello," she barked,
bracing her body for the strange rasp.

"Joanne?"

"Warren?" She was momentarily disoriented. Why was her
brother calling her? It was barely seven a.m. in California.
"What's the matter? Is everyone okay?"

"Everyone's fine on this end," he responded curtly. "You're
the one I'm calling about."

"Me?"

"Joanne, why didn't you tell me?"

It took her a moment to guess what Warren was talking about.
"You mean about me and Paul?" she asked.

"Among other things. Why didn't you tell me?"

"I didn't want to upset you. I was hoping it would all be
worked out by now," she explained.

"But it's not."

"No," she admitted. "At least not yet. But I'm having lunch
with Paul today and—"

"I spoke to Paul yesterday."

"You did? What did he say?"

"Well, you can imagine what kind of idiot I felt like," Warren
began. "I phone your number only to be told it's been disconnected, so I call Paul's office and I ask what's going on, and there
is this awkward silence, and he says finally, 'You mean Joanne
hasn't told you?' And I say, 'Told me what?' And so he tells me."

"What?"

"What?" he repeated. "That the two of you have separated.

That he has his own apartment in the city. That you were getting some obscene phone calls. Joanne, are you all right?"

"Of course I'm all right," she said. "Paul just needs time to—to think things through. He's confused, that's all."

"Would you like some company? Gloria could fly over for a few days."

"No. I'm fine, really."

"Gloria wants to say a few words to you."

"Hello, Joanne. How are you holding out?"

Joanne told her that she was fine. She didn't tell her that she was convinced she was to be the Suburban Strangler's next victim. She said she was fine, because she knew that was what Gloria wanted to hear.

"Well, that's good. I know it's your life," Gloria continued, "but don't take it too seriously. You know what I mean?"

"I THOUGHT we were going to have lunch," Joanne was saying.

"I know, and I'm sorry," Paul explained, a slight edge in his voice. "I tried to call you this morning when this thing came up, but nobody answered." Joanne saw herself standing in her closet, the phone ringing shrilly from the bedside table. "I'm really sorry, Joanne. There was nothing I could do. This is an important client, and when he suggests lunch, it's more than a casual suggestion." Joanne looked toward the floor. "But I do have time for a quick coffee," he said, his voice softening.

"Where?" Joanne asked, her eyes skimming the empty high school corridor.

"There's a cafeteria, isn't there?"

"Here? In the school?"

"What better place to discuss Robin's problems?"

You had to admire his skill, Joanne thought as he guided her toward the cafeteria. In one simple sentence he had said everything: they were here to discuss their daughter's problems, not their own; he was prepared to go no further.

"Here we are," Paul said, opening the door and letting her pass through. "What would you like?" He grabbed a tray from the stack and slid it along the steel bars toward the cash register.

"Just coffee," Joanne said.

Paul led the way to a table by a window. He removed their mugs from the stained orange tray and slid the tray over to the adjoining table. "So, what did you think of what Avery had to say?" he asked.

"I think he's very concerned about Robin."

"You don't think he's overreacting?"

Not everyone is overreacting these days, Joanne wanted to tell him, but said instead, "I don't think so."

"I just meant that it's June, for Pete's sake, school's almost over, and he admitted that Robin was sure to pass."

"He's concerned about next year, her attitude. . . ."

"She'll be fine by the fall."

"Will she? Why?" Joanne was startled by her question. "Will things be any different in the fall?" she pressed.

"Joanne . . ."

"Sorry," she said quickly. "I just don't think we can afford to be too cavalier about this."

"Nobody's being cavalier. There's no question we'll have to talk to Robin, make her understand that she can't afford to start the next year the same way she finished this one, that skipping classes is unacceptable behavior."

"When are *we* going to tell her all this?"

Paul said nothing, taking a long sip of his coffee. "I'll speak to her on the weekend," he said finally, pointedly checking his watch.

"Paul, we need to talk." Joanne hated the tremble in her voice.

"We *are* talking," he said, deliberately missing the point.

"I miss you," she whispered.

Paul looked from side to side with obvious discomfort. "This isn't the place."

"What is? You keep saying you'll call, but you never do. I was hoping we could talk at lunch."

"Joanne, I haven't had enough time," he told her, as he had told her once before. "I'm just starting to get used to being on my own." He lifted his eyes from the table to stare directly into hers, his voice low now. "You have to get used to it too."

"I don't want to get used to it," she told him, surprised at her own assertiveness.

"You have to," he repeated. "You have to stop calling me at the office over every little problem."

"This wasn't a little problem. Mr. Avery—"

"I'm talking about things like the gas bill."

"There was a mistake on the invoice."

"I'm talking about *Sports Illustrated*."

"I didn't know if you wanted to renew your subscription."

"You could have made the choice."

"I didn't want to make the wrong one!" She promptly burst into tears. "I'm sorry," she sobbed softly, grabbing a paper napkin and blowing her nose. "I didn't mean to cry."

"No," he said gently, reaching across the table and taking her hand in his. "I'm the one who's sorry. I shouldn't have said anything. I knew this wasn't the time or place."

"Are my eyes smeared?" she asked as he withdrew his hand.

"No." Paul's eyes were soft, his voice tender. "You look lovely. You know I've always liked that dress."

Joanne smiled. "I love you," she said, not looking at him, her lips quivering despite all efforts to control them.

"I love you too," he said simply.

"Then what are we doing?"

He shook his head. "I don't know," he admitted.

"Come home."

He looked toward the door to the cafeteria as a young couple bounded in. "I can't," he said.

"MRS. Hunter," a voice called to her from across the lobby of the country club.

Joanne swung around abruptly.

"Sorry, I didn't mean to startle you," Steve Henry said, crossing toward her.

"Did I leave something on the court?" Joanne asked.

"No." He laughed. "I had a cancellation, so I was wondering if you'd like to join me for coffee. We could talk about how much your game has improved over the last couple of weeks."

403

"I don't think so. I'm running kind of late."

"Sure," he said easily, walking beside her toward the door. "You were hitting some nice shots there," he continued. "I sent you all over the court, and you were getting all of them."

"And sending them right into the net."

"You're still not following through all the way," he agreed. "But, I don't know, I sensed a new aggressiveness out there this afternoon." Joanne laughed despite herself. "There. You know what I'm talking about, don't you?"

"Look at my toes," she wailed, not sure what else to say, looking down at the toenails poking out from her sandals. "They look like they're about to fall off."

"You probably will lose the nails," he told her matter-of-factly. "Your shoes must be too small. They're fine for walking, but to play tennis you need shoes half a size larger. What's happening is, your toes keep jamming into the top of your sneakers."

"They're such a lovely shade." She smiled as they reached the front door.

"Like your eyes," he told her.

Oh, Joanne thought. We're not talking about tennis.

"YES, so then what did you say?"

"What do you mean, what did I say? I didn't say anything."

"Joanne." Eve exclaimed impatiently. "The man was obviously making a pitch. He tells you your toenails are lovely like your eyes—" Both women suddenly burst out laughing. "The point is that he's obviously interested."

"In me?"

"Why not in you?" Eve demanded. The two women were standing in Eve's kitchen, looking over her Saturday night dinner. "Loosen up a bit, put a few blond streaks in your hair, and you're a very beautiful woman."

"I think all the X rays you've had have affected your brain," Joanne told her friend playfully.

"You're the one who's crazy if you don't take advantage of what Steve Henry is offering you."

"I can't," she said. "I'm a married woman."

There was a long pause before Eve spoke. "You think Paul is telling everybody he's a married man and sitting home nights?"

"What do you mean?" Almost before the question was out, Joanne was sorry she had asked it.

"Look, I'm not saying that he has anything serious going, and I don't know anything for sure," Eve backtracked. "But a few people have seen him around."

"With whom?" The question was pushed out of her throat by the sudden rapid beating of her heart.

"Some girl. Judy somebody-or-other. Nobody anybody knows." Eve shrugged. "A blonde, naturally."

"Young?"

"Mid to late twenties."

Joanne braced herself against Eve's kitchen counter.

"Listen," Eve said quickly. "I did not tell you about this Judy to upset you. I told you about her to get you moving. Steve Henry is a certifiable hunk. Think about it, Joanne. That's all I'm asking."

"What's going on in there?" a masculine voice called from the dining room. "I thought we were going to have some dinner."

"Coming," Eve called. She began organizing the meal she had prepared. "Brian's in a rotten mood," she informed Joanne as they left the kitchen, their hands loaded with various delicacies. "Try not to talk about his work, okay?"

Joanne nodded. She doubted she'd be able to say anything at all to Brian with the lump that was blocking her throat.

"So how are the girls?" Brian asked her as he helped himself to food.

"They're fine," Joanne replied automatically. "Well, actually, Robin is driving me nuts, because she's convinced she's going to pass her final exams without having to do any work. And Lulu's driving me nuts, about failing history. That exam is Monday, and the only date she can remember is the Boer War."

Brian laughed. "Why the Boer War?"

"Oh, it's the combination for our burglar alarm system."

"I understand you had another false alarm this morning," Brian said, helping himself to salad.

Joanne nodded. "After telling the kids a million times to make sure the alarm is off before they open the door, guess who forgot to do that? Oh, well." She smiled sadly. "It gave me something to tell my grandfather."

"How is he?" Eve asked.

"Not good." Joanne set her fork down. "He's starting to look a little gray around the edges."

"You keep the alarm on even when you're in the house?" Brian asked, returning to the original conversation.

Joanne nodded. "I feel safer since the phone calls."

"What phone calls?" Brian asked.

A sudden loud noise—Eve's fork cracking against the side of her plate as it fell from her hand—transferred the focus of attention to her end of the table. She jumped to her feet clumsily, knocking over her wineglass, spilling what was left of the expensive burgundy into her salad. "Oh!" she exclaimed. "I seem to be having a sharp pain."

"Where?" Joanne asked, immediately at Eve's side.

"The usual places. My heart, my lungs, my stomach." She gasped, trying to laugh. "Look at this tablecloth!" Joanne glanced down at the bloodlike stain that was shaping itself around Eve's plate.

"It's all right. I'll wash it out," Joanne offered. "Maybe you should go upstairs and lie down."

Eve glared at her husband, who sat impassively across the table, not moving. "Okay," she agreed.

"I'll help you."

"No, I can manage. I'll be down soon. You finish eating," Eve said, and disappeared up the steps.

Joanne was clearing away the dishes when Brian interrupted her. "Sit down," he told her with an unmistakable authority.

Joanne reluctantly returned to her seat and stared coldly at Eve's husband.

"You think I'm pretty coldhearted, don't you?" he said.

"That's an essentially accurate description." Joanne was surprised at her own directness.

"You don't know the whole story, Joanne," he told her simply, his deep-set eyes revealing nothing.

"I may not know the whole story," Joanne admitted, "but I do know Eve. This is not a woman who gets hysterical about aches and pains. She's always been very much in control. Even after she lost the baby, she just picked herself up and carried on with her life."

"You didn't think that was just a little bit strange?"

His question caught Joanne off guard. "What do you mean?"

"A woman tries for seven years to have a child and she finally conceives at the age of forty, loses the baby, and goes right on with her life as if nothing had happened. Doesn't shed a tear. Joanne, *I* cried!"

"Eve was never one to show her emotions in public."

"I'm not the public. I'm her husband!" Brian realized he had raised his voice and took a deep breath, looking toward the stairs.

"Then why aren't you helping her?"

"I'm trying. She won't accept the kind of help I'm offering."

"Which is?"

"I want her to see a psychiatrist. I've spoken to all the doctors she's seen. Some more than once. They all say the same thing: that there is nothing physically wrong with Eve, that the tests indicate nothing out of the ordinary. Joanne, nobody falls apart all over their whole body. Eve has pains everywhere. Take her to one doctor, it's pains in her chest. Take her to another, they're in her groin. Her stomach isn't working properly, she complains; her weight's down, her temperature is up. She's obsessed."

"She's in pain!"

"I don't doubt that." He looked around the room helplessly. "I spoke to the police psychiatrist. I asked her what she thought."

"And?"

"She said that it sounded to her like a fairly typical case of depression brought on by the miscarriage, the same thing that the other doctors have concluded. She said that I shouldn't cater to Eve's illness, because I'd only be reinforcing it; that I should suggest strongly that Eve talk to someone on a professional basis. But, of course, Eve won't hear of it. She's already seen half the specialists in New York; she has appointments with the other half. She'll see all those doctors, why won't she see a psychiatrist?

I mean, if you were in horrendous pain, wouldn't you do everything you could to get rid of it, even if it meant talking to a shrink?" Joanne stared into his eyes but said nothing. "I'm sorry. I didn't mean to dump all this on you."

"Eve is my closest friend. I want to help her if I can."

"Then convince her to see a psychiatrist," Brian urged. "Sorry, there I go again. You obviously have enough to worry about right now. What was that about some phone calls you've been getting?"

The sudden switch in gears took Joanne by surprise. "What?"

"Before Eve had her attack, you were saying something about feeling safer with the alarm on since the phone calls."

"Yes. Didn't Eve tell you about the calls?"

"The only thing that Eve and I have discussed over the past few months are her assorted aches and pains."

Joanne told him about the series of phone calls, the threats, the newspaper left on her windshield, the fact that she had changed her number and still the calls continued. "Eve never mentioned any of this?" she asked again, suddenly feeling queasy.

He shook his head. "Would you like a drink?" he offered, moving to the liquor cabinet.

"No, thank you." She watched while he poured himself a healthy snifter of brandy. "Paul thinks I'm overreacting," she said. "So does Eve."

Brian laughed out loud, taking a sip of his drink. "Eve's a fine one to talk about overreacting. But she's probably right about there not being anything to worry about. Loonies like the Suburban Strangler bring all the other nuts out of the woodwork. We must have seen a thousand guys who've confessed to the killings."

"I'm not even sure it *is* a guy," Joanne heard herself reply.

Brian regarded her with a subtle yet unmistakable interest. "What makes you say that?"

"Some quality in the voice. Neither here nor there. Although," she added, trying to laugh, "the Suburban Strangler could hardly be a woman."

"You know something we don't?" he asked.

"You're saying that the killer could be a woman?"

"It's a very remote possibility, I grant you. But who knows?

Anything's possible. Besides, whoever's phoning you isn't necessarily the killer. It's probably just some sickie who's gone off the deep end and could very possibly be a woman."

"Eve says women don't make obscene calls to other women."

"Eve says a lot of things," Brian replied cryptically. "Look, try not to worry. I'll talk to my lieutenant about it, see if we can't get someone to drive by your house on a regular basis. And, of course, I'll keep an eye out."

"Thank you," Joanne said gratefully as he walked her to the door. "Tell Eve that I'll call her tomorrow."

"Will do," he said, watching her as she cut across his lawn to her own and ran up her front steps.

She waved good-bye, fishing in her purse for her keys. "Where are they?" she muttered out loud, unable to find them. "Darn it, I must have left them at Eve's." She glanced over to where Brian had been standing, but he'd already retreated inside his house and closed the door. She debated running back. "Oh, forget it. I'll get them tomorrow." She rang her doorbell and waited, her eyes looking back at Eve's house, catching sight of a quick movement in the window of the smaller front bedroom. "Come on, Lulu, where are you?"

A loud voice suddenly blasted into the darkness. "Who is it?"

"Wow!" Joanne cried, realizing that the voice was Lulu's and that it was coming from the small box next to the doorbell, part of the new intercom system. "It's Mommy," she answered, her heart pounding wildly.

"Where's your key?" the child asked as she pulled open the door and backed away, her eyes resolutely downcast. Joanne had only to look at her to know that something was wrong.

"What's the matter?" Joanne asked immediately.

Lulu shook her head, turning away. "Nothing," she mumbled.

Joanne reached out and touched her daughter's shoulder, slowly spinning the reluctant girl around and lifting her chin with gentle fingers. "Tell me," she said. "What is it? What happened?"

Lulu opened her mouth as if she were about to speak, then said nothing.

"Lulu, something's wrong. I could see it the minute I walked in

the door. Did you have a fight with Robin before she went out?"
Lulu shook her head vehemently. Too vehemently, Joanne
thought. "What happened, Lulu?" she asked again.

"I don't want to tell you."

"That's obvious. It's also obvious that it has something to do
with Robin." Lulu raised her head, opening her mouth to protest,
then quickly lowered it again, saying nothing. "Does whatever
happened have anything to do with Scott Peterson?"

"No," the girl said, a touch too adamantly. "Yes," she whispered.
Joanne saw her daughter's eyes fill with tears. "Lulu, tell me."

"Robin and Scott were smoking marijuana," Lulu said quietly.
Joanne felt her body go numb. "What happened?"

"Scott came to pick her up a few minutes after you left. Robin
was still getting ready. You know how long she takes. Well, Scott
said he'd go up and hurry her along. He went into her room, and I
was trying to study, but they were making so much noise. Robin
was giggling like crazy. I went in there to tell them to please keep
it down. I knocked first, but they didn't hear me. So I opened the
door, and there they were . . . passing this joint back and forth."

"Then what did they do?"

"They offered me a drag. Robin looked kind of scared. I think
she was afraid that I might tell you, but that if I smoked some too,
then I wouldn't."

It all came clearly into focus: Robin's change in attitude toward
schoolwork, the poor grades, the absences from class. The classic
signs of involvement with drugs Joanne kept hearing about from
friends with regard to their teenagers. But not mine, Joanne had
always thought. "And then?" she asked.

"Nothing. I said no, I didn't want any, and I went back to my
room. A few minutes later Robin came in and told me not to tell
you, that you've been upset enough since Dad left. That's why I
was so worried. I didn't know what to do."

"You did the right thing," Joanne assured her, smoothing a few
stray hairs from Lulu's tearstained face.

"What are you going to do?" the child asked sheepishly.

"I'm not sure. I'll have to speak to your father about it." Joanne
looked at her watch. It was almost eleven o'clock. Was it too late

to call him? "You go to sleep, sweetie. It's late." She kissed her daughter's cheek, slightly sticky from her tears, and watched her run up the stairs.

Joanne went to her room and sat on the bed. Her hand rested on the phone for ten minutes. Would she be waking Paul up? Would he even be home? Would he be impatient, tell her that this was precisely what he meant when he said she should be handling things herself?

She pulled the phone off its carriage and dialed Paul's number. Let him be furious, she thought. The phone rang once and then was quickly picked up, as if he were expecting her call.

"Hello," a strange voice answered. A woman's voice.

For an instant Joanne said nothing, convinced she must have the wrong number. She was about to hang up when the woman spoke again. "Did you want to speak to Paul?"

Joanne felt sick to her stomach. "Is he there?"

"Well, he is." The girl giggled. "But he can't come to the phone at the moment. Can I take a message?"

"Is this Judy?"

"Yes, it is." The voice sounded pleased to be recognized.

Joanne let the receiver drop gently into its cradle. "No!" she suddenly shouted, grabbing Paul's pillow off the bed and hurling it across the room before dropping on her knees to the floor, swaying her body back and forth, bursting into outraged sobs.

The phone rang.

Joanne jumped to her feet. It must be Paul. Judy had told him about the strange phone call, and he had concluded that it could only be her. He would be angry. Well, so what, she thought, bringing the phone to her ear.

"Mrs. Hunter," the voice teased. "You've been a naughty girl, haven't you, Mrs. Hunter? Playing around with your best friend's husband." The words held Joanne in an instant state of paralysis. "You're going to have to be punished, Mrs. Hunter," the voice continued gleefully. "I'm going to have to punish you."

"Go to hell!" Joanne shrieked, and slammed the receiver down so hard that it bounced and she was forced to slam it down a second time.

411

"Mom?" a frightened voice asked. Joanne spun around to see her younger daughter in the doorway watching her, eyes like saucers. "What's the matter? What are you doing?"

"I had an obscene call," Joanne answered quickly, her voice husky, her breathing rapid. "Didn't you hear the phone ring?" she asked, seeing the look of surprise that crossed Lulu's face.

Lulu shook her head. "I only heard you yelling."

Joanne stood still for a minute, letting this statement sink in. "Sorry, I didn't mean to wake you up." She escorted her puzzled daughter back to her room. "Go back to sleep, sweetie."

"Is Robin home yet?"

"Not yet."

"I thought at first you were yelling at her," Lulu explained. "It's so strange to hear you yell," she whispered.

Joanne went downstairs to wait for Robin to return home.

"TELL him to come in," Joanne said evenly as Robin was about to close the front door.

"You better come in," she heard Robin whisper to the young man behind her.

Scott Peterson shuffled inside and smiled innocently at Joanne. "Close the door," Joanne told him. "Maybe we should go into the living room," she suggested, and the silent couple reluctantly followed her inside. Joanne flipped on the light. "You can sit down if you like," she indicated, but no one moved. "I think you both know what this is about."

"The little tattletale." Robin sneered.

"Don't start blaming Lulu for this," Joanne cautioned.

"It wasn't anything—" Robin protested.

"And don't tell me it wasn't anything," her mother countered, her voice rising. What was she supposed to say next? She cleared her throat. "I don't want to argue with you," she said, her voice steady once again. "As far as I'm concerned, there's nothing to argue about. I think I have a pretty clear picture of what happened. You can dispute me if anything I say is substantially wrong." That sounded fair, she decided, looking from her daughter to Scott Peterson, whose eyes were burning holes right through her. She wasn't invisible now, she thought. "Lulu said that you were in your room earlier this evening smoking . . . a joint . . . and that you offered her some."

"She had no business coming into my room," Robin objected.

"I beg your pardon!" Joanne exclaimed. "You don't think she had any business coming into your room? She knocked, didn't she? Listen to me now—"

"Mom!"

"Mrs. Hunter, it's really not all that big a deal."

"You shut up," Joanne shouted at Robin's boyfriend. "I'll decide what's a big deal around here. How dare you bring dope into this house! How dare you offer it to my children!"

"Robin's not exactly a child, Mrs. Hunter. Nobody forced anything on her. She didn't have to take it."

"No," Joanne said with sudden icy calmness, "and neither do I. Get out of this house," she continued, her voice level rising steadily. "And don't you ever try to see my daughter again, or I'll have you arrested. Do you understand me?"

"Mom!"

"Get out of my house," Joanne raged.

"Gladly." The boy sneered, pushing past her, his bony shoulder catching the corner of hers. He opened the front door and walked out into the street without looking back.

"What have you done?" Robin shrieked. "You had no right to talk to him like that."

"Please don't tell me what my rights are."

"Now he'll tell everyone I'm a kid!"

"That's what you are. And not a very bright one at that. How could you be so stupid?" Joanne demanded.

"This is all Lulu's fault."

"This is all *your* fault."

"She didn't have to tell you."

"Really? What choice did you leave her? You didn't have to smoke right under her nose. Were you looking to get caught?"

For once Robin was silent. "So what happens now?" she asked after a long pause.

Joanne shrugged. "I'll have to talk to your father."

"Why?"

"Because he's your father, and he has the right to know," Joanne answered simply. "In the meantime, until I can speak to him, you're grounded."

Robin said nothing, her body fidgeting nervously.

"Do you understand?"

"Yes," Robin said. "Can I go to bed now?"

"Go to bed," Joanne agreed, and waited for her daughter to reach her bedroom. Then she walked to the front door, double-locked it, and pressed the bottom button of the alarm.

PART TWO

Chapter 7

THAT all seems so long ago now. Since then Mr. Rogers has gone bankrupt, leaving this ugly gash in the backyard. The girls have just left for camp. And Paul has not come home.

The phone is still ringing as Joanne picks herself up from the deep end of her empty pool and heads back inside the house. With the girls at camp, she is completely alone for the first time in her life. She glances at the phone. It's just you and me now, he is telling her. When the phone stops ringing, the house is completely still, as quiet as it has ever felt. Before, she'd been alone a few hours, perhaps, never more than a day. She shuffles into the living room and plops down on the large, comfortable sofa.

Joanne wonders how the girls will like camp this summer, how Robin, in particular, will get along. She wonders whether the decision to send Robin to camp was the right one. Visitors' day is in four weeks; she will have some idea then of the correctness of their choice. *If* I'm still around, she thinks.

The phone begins ringing again. Joanne jumps, as she does every time she hears the once welcome sound. She has changed her number a second time and yet he has found her. There was a brief seven-day respite—one week when she felt her body relaxing, her fears subsiding—and then the calls started again, angrier and nastier than before. Do you think you can escape me so

414

easily? he demands. Change your number as often as you please, he taunts her. I'll find you.

Joanne returns to the kitchen, standing in front of the phone until it stops its shrill cry. Then she picks up the receiver and dials Eve's number. Eve answers immediately, as if she has been expecting Joanne to call.

"How are you?" Joanne asks.

"The usual," Eve answers. "Did the girls get off okay?"

"Paul drove them to the bus this morning. They're probably halfway to camp by now. I just hope we're doing the right thing."

"Sure you are," Eve says quickly. "A few months in the country, all that fresh air. . . ."

"Do you feel like going for a walk? I need to get out of the house."

"Are you kidding? I couldn't get as far as the corner."

"Come on," Joanne pleads. "It'll do you good. I'll meet you outside in five minutes." She hangs up before Eve can say no.

"So what tests are scheduled for this week?" Joanne and Eve are circling their block for the third time. They have already discussed the weather forecast—continuing sunny skies—and the current state of Joanne's toenails—continuing purple—which leads to talk of tennis, which leads to talk of Steve Henry, which leads to Joanne's abrupt change of subject.

"You're avoiding the issue," Eve tells her.

"There's nothing to say," Joanne answers. "What's the point of tennis lessons when I have nobody to play with? When you get better, we'll start the lessons together again. What's the big deal?"

"Steve Henry's the big deal. And he's yours for the taking."

"I don't want him."

Eve stops dead in her tracks. "Why not, for heaven's sake?"

"I love Paul," Joanne whispers. "And I don't love Steve Henry."

"Nobody's asking you to love the man."

"Can we please talk about something else?"

Eve is silent as they continue walking.

"You haven't told me what tests you're scheduled for this week." Joanne notices that Eve's pace has slackened.

"Tuesday," Eve replies, "is a series of tests at St. Francis Cardiac Hospital. And Thursday is an appointment with a dermatologist in Roslyn. Dr. Ronald Gold, I think his name is."

"Why a dermatologist?"

Eve stops, rolling back the hair from her face with the back of her hand. "Joanne, look at this."

"Look at what?"

"This flaking! Everything in my body is drying up."

"It's a very exotic condition," Joanne tells her. "It's called middle age."

"Look, Joanne," Eve pleads. "Maybe I am acting a little peculiar. But something is happening to my body, and nobody can tell me what it is. I know what's normal for me and what isn't."

"Take it easy, " Joanne advises, her arm encircling her friend's waist. "Somebody's going to figure all this out soon enough. I promise." Eve smiles, her body relaxing against Joanne's arm. "You said you're seeing a Dr. Ronald Gold?"

"On Thursday. Why?"

"We went to school with a boy named Ronald Gold, remember?" Eve shakes her head. "I wonder if he's the same one."

"He must have been short if I don't remember him," Eve quips. They are back in front of Eve's home. "I think I'd better go inside now."

"More pains?"

"Same ones. It feels like . . . like someone is tightening a belt around my ribs. I can't explain it. The more I try, the crazier it sounds. Brian wants me to see a psychiatrist."

"Maybe that's not such a bad idea," Joanne says, catching the look of animosity in Eve's eyes. "Just to help you deal with it."

"I don't want to deal with it," Eve informs her. "I want to get rid of it." She looks toward her house. "Look, sorry. I didn't mean to snap at you. Believe me, if I thought I needed a psychiatrist, I would be the first person to go to one. Just stick with me, huh? Be my friend. Please."

"I am your friend."

"I know," Eve agrees. "Going to visit your grandfather this afternoon?"

Joanne nods. "Right now."

"Give the old guy a kiss from me."

WHEN Joanne walks through her front door several hours later, the phone is ringing. "Enough!" she states emphatically, marching toward it, watching it ring, not picking it up. Has he been following her? Is it a coincidence that he is calling at the precise moment she has walked into the house?

Joanne picks up the receiver on the fifth ring. "Why are you doing this?" she says instead of hello.

There is a pause. Then, "Joanne?" the voice asks.

"Paul!" Joanne tries to laugh, she's so glad to hear his voice.

"Joanne, are you still getting those calls?" he asks.

"No," she says quickly. "Just someone pestering me about some theater subscription."

He accepts the lie easily. "That's good. I called you earlier—you were out."

"I went for a walk. Then I went to see my grandfather. Did the girls get off okay?"

"Everything proceeded on schedule. Smooth as a whistle."

"Did Robin say anything?"

"Just good-bye. It was all I could do to keep from shaking her."

"That would have gone over big with the other parents."

"You'd be surprised." He laughs. "I got the feeling I wasn't the only father entertaining such thoughts." Joanne can feel him smiling. He says nothing, but she senses a reluctance on his part to terminate the conversation. "They're really growing up!" he finally exclaims, a sense of wonder in his words. "You remember what it was like on the first day of camp?"

"I never went," she reminds him. "We had the cottage."

"Oh, yeah, that's right. Do you think the girls missed something by our not having a cottage?"

"The girls have always enjoyed camp," she tells him, wondering where this is headed.

"They better enjoy it, for what it's costing," he says. "It's like

417

going to a resort for two months. Not like when I went. We slept in sleeping bags in tents."

"You did not. I've seen the photographs of you at camp, of your beautiful log cabins, and I remember your mother's same complaints about what it cost to send you."

He laughs loudly and easily. "I guess you're right."

There is another long pause. "Paul?" Joanne asks, breaking the silence, then lapsing back into it.

"Yes?"

"Do I have any life insurance?" she asks, the question catching her by surprise probably as much as it does him.

"No," he answers. "But *I* have plenty. Why?"

"I think I should have some."

"Sure," he agrees quickly. "If you'd like. I could make an appointment for you with Fred Normandy."

"Thank you. I guess I should let you go now."

"Joanne?"

"Yes?"

Silence. Then, almost tentatively, "Are you busy tonight?"

SHE is more nervous than at any moment in her entire life. She has been getting ready for two hours. She has soaked herself raw in the bathtub, washed her hair, set it, then combed it out, only to reset it again and wet it yet a third time. She is still trying to decide what to do with it as she checks her reflection in the bathroom mirror. "What is that?" she asks suddenly, her nose pressing against the glass of the mirror. "It can't be a pimple!" Now she knows how Robin feels when pimples appear just minutes before a scheduled date. "I can't believe I have a pimple."

She is still muttering the same thing when the doorbell rings half an hour later.

"I LIKE your hair."

"You're kidding."

They are sitting by the window of a lovely, romantic restaurant overlooking the Atlantic Ocean. The room is dimly lit; the ocean crashes rhythmically against the rocks below them.

"No, really, I think it's great. It has a kind of . . . I don't know . . . carefree abandon to it like that."

Joanne laughs. "That's me, carefree and abandoned."

There is silence as the full weight of what she has just said hits her. "I didn't mean to say that."

"That's okay," Paul is saying, and Joanne realizes he is on the verge of laughing. "Actually, it was a pretty funny remark." His voice is suddenly serious. "One I deserve, at any rate."

Joanne says nothing. What is he leading up to? I'm sorry? Forgive me? If you let me come home, I'll spend the rest of my life making things up to you?

"I'm not ready to come home yet," he says instead. "I had to say that now because I don't want to mislead you."

"I understand."

"I love you, Joanne."

"I love you too." Please don't cry, she tells herself. The man is telling you he loves you. Don't spoil it by crying.

"I need more time," he continues. "There's so much on my mind right now."

"You mean at work?"

He nods. "I can't seem to get out from under."

"In what way?"

"I'm not sure I can explain it. It's not the work load. I can handle the work load. It's just that I'm so *tired* all the time. No matter how much sleep I get, it doesn't seem to make a difference."

"Have you seen a doctor?"

"I had Phillips do a complete check. Basically I'm in pretty good shape for a man my age. I should exercise more, he told me, so I've started working out a bit."

"I noticed."

He checks his arms, now hidden under the light blue jacket he is wearing. "What do you think?" he asks shyly.

Joanne shrugs and giggles, feeling like a silly schoolgirl. "You once told me that you could never develop muscles," she tells him, watching his smile grow.

"What? What are you talking about?"

"You once told me that the reason your arms were so thin was because when you were a boy, you broke them, and as a result they never developed the way most boys' arms do."

"I didn't tell you that," he protests, the smile in his eyes betraying his words.

"Yes you did."

"Well, I did break my arms a couple of times, but that doesn't have anything to do with muscles." He takes a sip of his coffee. "I told you that, did I?"

"It was one of the things that made me fall in love with you," Joanne says quietly, not sure whether she has gone too far. He seems interested, even flattered, by the unexpected admission. "You were always so sure of everything you did. And you were so handsome. . . . *Are*," she corrects, then returns immediately to the more comfortable past. "But you had no muscles, and I thought that was strange. Most boys your age had *some* kind of muscles, and one day you told me about falling and breaking your arms, and you suddenly seemed so vulnerable that I started to fall in love with you." She smiles widely. "And now you're telling me that it wasn't true!" Their eyes fasten on each other, each seeing a reflection of their youth in the other's eyes. Joanne quickly looks down into her coffee.

"So I was always sure of myself, was I?" he asks.

"Always."

"Pretty obnoxious, I guess."

"I liked it. I was always the opposite."

"You never gave yourself enough credit. You still don't."

"That's what Eve's always telling me."

Paul finishes his coffee and signals to the waiter for a refill.

"What are you thinking about?" Joanne ventures, catching a look of fleeting bewilderment in his eyes.

"That I used to think I'd be the new Clarence Darrow," he admits with a laugh.

"And you've discovered you're not?"

He shakes his head. "Not even close."

"Is that such a bad thing?" Joanne asks. "You're a good lawyer."

"I'm an excellent lawyer," he corrects her, managing not to sound boastful.

"Then what's the problem?"

"I don't know." He seems to be searching the room for the right words, then returns his gaze to Joanne. "Let's talk about something else. This can't be very interesting for you."

"But it is," Joanne tells him truthfully. "It's something we never talked about before, and I think it's important."

"I never liked bringing my work home with me."

"Your work, no. But how you feel about it is important to me."

Paul releases a deep breath. "We're having problems with a couple of the partners. They don't like the way the firm is being run. They want to get rid of McNamara."

"Why?"

"They say he's being too easy on some of the less successful partners."

"Is he?"

"Maybe. Look, we're talking about a major Wall Street law firm. You want to be successful, you have to produce. Of course it's high pressure."

"Are you starting to feel that pressure?"

"I *thrive* on that pressure. At least I used to." He laughs. "I guess this is what they refer to as a typical mid-life crisis. How come our parents never had mid-life crises?"

"They didn't know they were supposed to," Joanne says, and they both laugh. She is aware that she has said two things tonight that have made her husband laugh. She also realizes that it is the first time they have laughed together in a very long while.

"Do you remember the first time you took me to a Broadway play?" she asks, not sure what has put this thought into her head. "I'd always wanted to go on one of those horse and buggy rides through Central Park, and I was going on about it after the play until you finally offered to take me on one. I will never forget looking over at you halfway into that ride and seeing the tears in your eyes and thinking, My gosh, he's so sensitive, so romantic—"

"So allergic," he interjects.

"And you ended up spending the rest of the weekend in bed. Why didn't you tell me you were allergic to horses?"

"I didn't want to spoil it for you."

"But then your mother bawled me out, told me I should take better care of you."

"She should have told you to run away as fast as you could."

"Too late. I was already in love."

"With my allergies and skinny arms," he says. "And I always assumed it was my fine mind and good looks."

"Funny, the things we fall in love with," Joanne states as Paul signals to the waiter that they are ready to leave.

"I DON'T think I should come in," he says at the doorway to their house. Joanne nods, though she has been just about to ask otherwise. "Not that I don't want to," he adds quickly. "It's just that I don't think it would be a good idea."

"I agree," Joanne whispers softly.

"First night alone," he comments as she fumbles in her purse for her keys.

"I have to get used to it sometime, I guess. I'm a big girl now." She triumphantly produces her set of keys.

"New key chain?"

"I lost my other set," she tells him, fitting the key into the lock. "Can you imagine? I have all the locks changed, and then I go and lose the stupid keys. I thought I left them at Eve's, but she swears I didn't." She pushes open the door and moves quickly to the alarm box, pressing down the appropriate buttons. "I'm nervous every time I do that," she tells him.

"You do it very well." He smiles. Joanne stares at him expectantly from the other side of the doorway. Is it all right to kiss on your first date when the date in question is your husband of twenty years? "I had a lovely evening, Joanne," he says, and Joanne can see that he means it.

"So did I."

"I'd like to do it again," he tells her, and Joanne is about to ask when, but stops herself. "I'll call you." He leans forward to kiss her lightly on the cheek.

I love you, she mouths silently after him as she watches him climb into his car and pull away from the curb.

Once up in her bedroom, Joanne feels good about the future for the first time in months. Paul will come home, she tells herself. It's just a question of time, and she will give him as much time as he needs. In return, he has given her hope.

Chapter 8

"You're late," Eve's mother tells her as Joanne steps inside the front door of Eve's house.

Joanne checks her watch. "Just five minutes," she says, determined not to feel guilty. "Where's Eve?"

"I sent her back upstairs to lie down." Her mother calls up the stairs. "Eve, your friend finally got here."

"Really, Mother!" Eve exclaims from the landing above. She walks down the steps. "Don't you think you're being just a touch heavy-handed?"

"Sure, stick up for each other," her mother says as Joanne and Eve exchange knowing glances. "And don't give me those smiles that you think I can't see," she further admonishes as the two women walk out the front door.

"How long is she staying this time?" Joanne asks. She backs the car out of the driveway.

"I think until I either get better or pass on." The two women laugh as Joanne pulls the car onto the street.

"How does Brian feel about having her around all the time?" Joanne asks.

"I think he's relieved," Eve says. "He doesn't have to feel guilty about never being home himself. And when he does come home, there's always a hot meal waiting for him. I wouldn't be surprised if, after I die, he marries my mother."

"You're not going to die."

"That's what everybody keeps telling me."

"But you don't believe them?" Joanne says, thinking she would like to talk about something else. It seems that all she and Eve talk about lately is the state of Eve's health. "Do you have life insurance?" Joanne asks her suddenly.

"What makes you ask that?"

"I took out a policy."

"You did? Why?"

"I thought it was a good idea. If something happened to me . . ."

"Nothing's going to happen to you," Eve says, dismissing this possibility. Joanne has noticed that Eve doesn't like to discuss the phone calls she has still been getting. Eve begins to fidget, and her voice takes on an unpleasant edge. Joanne decides not to tell Eve that she has included in her new insurance policy a clause for double indemnity.

"So," Eve says, changing the topic, "you really think this Dr. Ronald Gold is the guy we went to school with?"

"I'll be with you as soon as I can," the dermatologist is saying as he comes out of his office into the crowded waiting room. He is about five feet seven inches tall, with a full head of reddish blond hair and an engaging smile. There is no question he is the same Ronald Gold they went to school with. Joanne watches as he fumbles with the appointment calendar on the cluttered desk; she recalls similar gestures with his chemistry notebook. He hasn't aged a day, Joanne thinks, wondering whether he will feel the same way about her should he ever get the time to notice her presence.

"I apologize for the chaos," he says, obviously searching for a pen. "I know I put it down here somewhere." Joanne sees a silver pen peeking out from underneath a stack of papers but feels it is not her place to point it out. "My receptionist quit last week," he announces to no one in particular. "I called an agency to send me a temporary, but she never showed up." He looks up from the table sheepishly. "Anybody here have a pen they can lend me?"

Joanne moves to the desk, extricates the lost silver pen from under its paper mountain, and hands it to the boy who used to crack his knuckles behind her in chemistry class.

"You want a job?" he asks. Then, "Do I know you?"

"We went to school together. Joanne Mossman— Well, that is, it was Mossman. Now it's Hunter." Is it? she wonders.

His smile grows until it stretches to his ears. "Well, Joanne Mossman!" he exclaims. "I wouldn't have recognized you. You look so much better now than you did as a kid." Joanne laughs. "I'm serious. You were always pretty, but you were always a little uptight. You know what I mean? You look a lot looser now." Joanne is aware she is blushing. "Hey, you still blush. I like that too." He puts his arm around her waist and motions with his other arm for the attention of the rest of the room. "Everybody, this is little Joanne Mossman. What's your married name again?"

"Hunter."

"Little Joanne Hunter. Same husband you started out with?" Joanne nods, not sure what else to do. He studies her face. "What's this? A pimple?" His expert fingers move across her face. "Nothing serious," he says. "We'll take care of it."

"I'm not here to see you," Joanne says quickly. "I'm here with a friend." She points to Eve, who is sitting in a chair against the wall, a disgruntled expression on her lips.

"Is that little Evie Pringle?" Dr. Ronald Gold asks as Eve stands up, towering a good three inches above him. "Still together, you two, huh?"

"It's Eve Stanley now," Eve tells him. "We had an appointment twenty minutes ago."

If he is aware of the intended sarcasm, he ignores it. "Yeah, well, I'm sorry about the delay." The phone rings and he reaches over and grabs it. "For you," he says to Joanne. Her eyes widen. "Just kidding," he says quickly, catching the look of concern. "Yes, this is Dr. Gold," he says into the phone. "Certainly I can see you, Mrs. Gottlieb. Drop by this afternoon." He hangs up and looks at Eve. "I'll be with you as fast as I can," he tells her, then turns back to Joanne. "And after your friend, I want to take a look at you."

"So when did you start getting these?" he is asking as Joanne lies on the examining table. Her face is cold after the cleansing treatment the doctor has applied. Ronald Gold's fingers press down hard on her chin.

"Just in the last month," Joanne tells him. "I couldn't believe it. Women my age aren't supposed to get pimples."

"Show me where it's written that women your age—*our*

425

age—aren't supposed to get pimples. I have lots of women coming in here in their forties, even their fifties."

"Great. Something to look forward to."

"Tell me, what have you been doing to your skin lately?"

"What do you mean?"

"Anything different?"

"I've been using a new moisturizer that Eve recommended."

"Eve's a dermatologist?"

"No, but she said I should start taking better care of my skin."

"You still do everything Eve tells you? Just like the old days?"

Joanne smiles. "Well, it's just that I never did anything with my skin before."

"Doesn't that tell you something?" He backs away. "Those fancy creams have been plugging up your pores, giving you pimples. Stop using them."

"And do what?"

"And wash your face once a day—once—at night, that's all you need. With a mild soap. I'll give you some vitamin A lotion to apply before you go to bed. If you're going to wear makeup, use one with a water base, and use a powder blush, not a cream. Cream clogs the pores. And stop listening to your friend Eve. What's her problem, anyway?" he asks in the same breath.

"We were hoping you'd tell us."

"I'm a skin doctor. That's for the outside of the head, not the inside."

"You're saying it's an emotional problem?"

He shrugs. "Psychiatry is the dumping ground of the medical profession. A doctor can't find something physical, he assumes it's emotional. There's nothing wrong with Eve's skin. It's a little dry, that's all. More than that I can't tell you." He studies Joanne's face. "That should do it," he says. "So, you want a job?" Joanne laughs, then realizes he is serious. "You found my pen, you can do anything. Go ahead—name your price."

"Are you really serious about this?"

"Do I look like a man who's joking? I look like a man in desperate need of a good receptionist."

"What would I have to do?"

"Answer the phone, greet the multitudes, keep my appointments straight, laugh at my jokes."

"Can I think about it?" Joanne asks, surprising herself. What is there to think about? I can't seriously be considering working for this man. Why not? she asks herself.

"Sure. Think about it and call me Monday. Not that I'm trying to pressure you, you understand." He smiles.

"Why do you want *me* to work for you?"

"Why not you?" he asks. "Something wrong with you?" His gray-blue eyes are clear and warm. "I like you," he says simply. "You remind me of my youth. Hey, I read this somewhere. You want to know what's the really scary thing about middle age?" She nods. "It's waking up one morning," he tells her, "and realizing that your high school class is running the country."

"I DON'T know how I let you talk me into this."

"Hey, that's *my* line."

"The last thing I feel like seeing is some glitzy Broadway musical." Eve pouts, staring out the car window at the early evening sky.

"They say it's wonderful," Joanne tells her.

"Who's this 'they'? The good doctor again?"

Joanne forces a smile. "As a matter of fact, yes," she answers, hoping to avoid an argument. Every time she and Eve get on the topic of Joanne's new boss, they invariably begin to bicker. "Look, if this is really such an ordeal for you, I'll turn the car around. . . ."

"Now? We're almost there. Who said anything about wanting to go home? Jeez, you're so touchy!"

Joanne feels her shoulders relax. "I'll be fine. Highway driving always makes me a little nervous," she lies.

"You don't think this job might be too much for you?" Eve asks.

"How do you mean?"

"Well, you know, you're not used to working. I mean, you haven't worked outside of the home ever, have you?" Joanne shakes her head. "And suddenly you're working all day every day. You're bound to be tired."

"I'm not tired."

"You look tired."

"I do?" Joanne finds herself glancing at her reflection in the rearview mirror. If anything, she is looking and feeling much better than she has in months. "I feel pretty good," she says. "I love the job."

"How can you love a job that has you staring into faces full of zits every day?"

Joanne tries to laugh, but the resulting sound is more of a grunt. "Ron couldn't be a nicer person to work for."

"So you keep saying. Do you think you'll keep working after the girls get home from camp?"

"I don't think so," she says. "I only agreed to take the job for the summer. By then Ron will have found a receptionist, and maybe Paul and I—" She breaks off in mid-sentence. It has been two weeks since she last saw her husband.

"Maybe Paul and you . . . ?"

"Who knows?" Joanne shrugs, not wanting to pursue the subject of a possible reconciliation. There are increasingly few subjects she feels comfortable discussing with her oldest and closest friend. The conversation lapses into silence for the rest of the trip.

They have to park six blocks away from the theater and must run to make the eight-o'clock curtain. The crowd is moving slowly inside as Joanne and Eve arrive and stand under the marquee, breathless and laughing.

From inside the theater a persistent bell is calling them to their seats. "I guess we should go in," Eve says. "Isn't that Paul?" she asks suddenly.

"What? Where?"

"He just went in. At least I think it was Paul. I only saw his profile. It might have been someone else."

Joanne feels her heart starting to thump wildly. She wonders how she looks and tries to catch her reflection in the glass doors. Eve said she looked tired. Does she? Her skin is clear once again, but her hair is a mess from running the six blocks to the theater. She hands her ticket to the usher and is immediately guided along the back wall toward the appropriate aisle.

They find their seats and sit down, Eve craning her long, elegant neck to get a view of who is sitting where. "I can't see him," she says, obviously referring to Paul, then stretches to look behind her.

"It probably wasn't him," Joanne says, knowing instinctively that it was. "Paul was never big on plays."

"I couldn't see who he was with," Eve states as the lights go down and the orchestra starts up.

The music is loud, the beat thumping and vibrant. The audience seems to sway collectively in the darkness, anticipation mounting. Joanne sees the curtains part, a set that instantly dazzles, costumes that startle and almost take one's breath away; she hears voices rising in clear, joyful confidence. Yet all she hears, sees, and thinks is, I couldn't see who he was with.

Of course, if Paul is here, he is here with someone. Please let it be a client. Maybe a friend. Let it be a male friend. More likely a date. Possibly little Judy whatever-the-rest-of-her-name-is.

I couldn't see who he was with.

Joanne focuses hard on the spectacularly lit stage, now bathed in bright swatches of color. In the center is a man cloaked all in black; he is singing to three women dressed in multicolored layers of chiffon, their hair dyed to match these layers. Suddenly the lights go blue, then deep indigo, the women seeming to disappear into their surroundings, their faces reemerging as gold-and-silver masks. Joanne feels disoriented, at loose ends. She glances at Eve. Her face reflects the same silver and gold, her hair the icy blue of the stage lights. Her eyes are black and empty.

I couldn't see who he was with.

Suddenly the bodies of the women return and the stage is a bright, pulsating lemon-yellow, the man in black disappearing into what seems to be a great glob of blinding sunlight. Joanne closes her eyes against its persistent glare. Fighting her growing anxiety, she focuses her attention on the stage, on the women, now clothed in iridescent layers of light.

The curtain suddenly goes down on the first act. The house lights come up. The theater bursts into a prolonged period of applause. "I can't believe it went so fast," Joanne hears herself say, aware that her mind was elsewhere for much of the time.

"Let's go outside to stretch our legs," Eve suggests.

"I'd rather stay put," Joanne says.

"Let's go outside," Eve repeats. The discussion is closed.

On the way up the aisle, Joanne hears words like "innovative" and "original," "breathtaking" and "wonderful." They reach the lobby, Joanne's eyes resolutely downcast. "There he is," Eve says immediately. Joanne looks up. Paul is standing by himself alongside the dark red wall. Eve raises her arm to wave, catching Paul's eye and signaling for him to come over. "Here he comes," she adds.

Joanne takes a deep breath, feeling vaguely sick to her stomach. She reluctantly turns in Paul's direction.

He is wearing a gray suit and a maroon tie, and though he is smiling, he looks uncomfortable. "Hello, Joanne," he says softly. "How are you, Eve?"

Joanne nods as Eve replies, "Dying slowly."

"You look fine," he tells her, and Eve grunts.

"How are you?" he asks, turning back to Joanne.

"Good," she replies, realizing that she means it. "I have a job."

"A job? What kind of job?" He is surprised, interested.

"I'm . . . sort of a receptionist, for a skin doctor . . . for the summer. Till the girls get back from camp."

"Sounds great."

"I'm enjoying it a lot," she tells him.

There is a moment's silence. "I've been meaning to call you," he says awkwardly. "I thought that maybe we could drive out to the camp together on visitors' day. That is, if you haven't already made other plans."

"I'd like that," she agrees. "I think the girls would too."

"Have you heard from them?"

"Not yet. You?"

"Not a line. Typical, I guess." He looks around. Why does he seem so uncomfortable? "Great show," he enthuses. "Don't you agree?"

Joanne is about to respond when she is interrupted by the appearance of a young, attractive—if overly made-up—blonde who has materialized from out of nowhere to take a firm grip on Paul's arm.

Paul smiles in her direction; Eve smiles in her direction; Joanne smiles in her direction. The young blonde smiles back. They are all standing in the middle of the lobby smiling at one another. Joanne feels her knees go weak. She wonders whether Paul will introduce them when suddenly the bell begins calling them back into the theater. Saved by the bell, Joanne thinks.

"I'll call you," Paul says quietly, leading the young blonde away without introductions. Hasn't he told little Judy how much he dislikes artificiality? Hasn't he cautioned her about overapplying the blusher?

"Are you all right?" Eve asks as the lobby slowly empties of people. "Do you want to leave?"

Joanne nods. If she tries to speak, she will break down. Stupid, stupid! she berates herself as Eve guides her outside.

"Look," Eve tells her on the drive back to Long Island. "Let's not blow this thing out of proportion, okay? You saw your husband out with another woman. That's bound to be a bit upsetting."

"A *bit* upsetting?"

"I'm only trying to tell you not to let it get to you."

"Why not?" Joanne demands, pulling the car over to the side of the road and slamming down on the brakes. "Why shouldn't I let it get to me? I love my husband. I'm desperately hoping we'll get back together. Why shouldn't I go to pieces when I see him out with another woman? Why is everything that happens to me so inconsequential and everything that happens to you so important? Why is my pain somehow less valid than yours?"

"Joanne, let's not get silly here. Your life is not at stake."

"Neither is yours!"

"Oh, really? You know that, do you?"

Joanne takes a deep breath. Somehow, she thinks, the conversation always reverts to Eve. "Yes," she says emphatically. "Yes, I do. Eve, how many doctors have you seen? Thirty? Forty? How many do you need to tell you that there is nothing wrong?"

"Don't you dare tell me there's nothing wrong with me! I have pains all over my body!"

431

"Precisely, Eve. Nobody falls apart over their entire body. Sure, you had a miscarriage, you lost a lot of blood. Your whole system has been upset. But whatever happened to you isn't fatal—"

"How do you know that?"

"Eve, nobody thinks you're going to die but you. Would it hurt so much to see a psychiatrist?"

"I am in *physical* pain!"

"Yes, but physical pain can have an emotional source. Nobody can tell the difference."

"Joanne, I am not the one who's having a mental breakdown. I'm not the one who's imagining weird phone calls."

Joanne takes several seconds to let the words sink in. "I wondered when you were going to get around to that," she says.

"I'm not the one whose husband left her after twenty years and feels she has to make up crazy stories to get attention."

Joanne asks quietly, "Is that what you think I've been doing?"

Eve suddenly brings her hands to her face and bursts into tears. A second later she flings her head back in an angry gasp, swallowing the cry, stuffing it back inside.

"Let it out," Joanne urges softly, her own anger vanishing. "There's so much rage in there, Eve. Let some of it out."

Eve leans back against her seat. She looks at Joanne. "Why argue with me? You know I always go for the jugular."

"You never have with me before."

"You've never fought back before."

"Maybe the phone calls *are* all in my mind," Joanne admits after a long silence, during which neither friend looks at the other. "I really don't know anymore. Tell you what," she says, laughing despite herself. "I'll see a psychiatrist if you'll see one. We can drive together to our appointments. Make a night of it. Go to dinner and a movie. How does that sound?"

Eve does not laugh or even smile. "I don't need a psychiatrist."

THE phone is ringing.

"Dr. Gold's office," Joanne chirps into the receiver. "I'm sorry, Dr. Gold is all booked up for the next two months. The earliest

appointment I can give you would be September twenty-first. . . .
Yes, I'll try. In the meantime, I'll put you down for the twenty-first
of September at two fifteen. May I have your name, please? . . .
Marsha Fisher. And your phone number? . . . Yes, okay. I'll call
you sooner if anything opens up." Joanne replaces the receiver
just as Ronald Gold comes out of his office, followed by a girl of
fourteen with tears in her eyes. "Sorry I hurt you, darling," he is
saying. "You forgive me?" The girl smiles through her tears.
"Give Andrea another appointment for six weeks from now.

"She'll be fine, Mrs. Armstrong," he says to the anxious woman
who has risen from her chair and now stands protectively beside
her daughter. "What can I tell you? Puberty. The pits! We all live
through it." He points to Joanne. "We went to school together,"
he says. "Her skin was a mess, you wouldn't have believed. In
fact, she was my inspiration to get into this line of work. Now look
how beautifully she turned out. That's one reason I hired her.
How you doing?" he asks, winking at Joanne.

"Renee Wheeler called. She has some sort of boil."

"Yuck, boils, I hate 'em!" Ronald Gold exclaims, and young
Andrea Armstrong bursts out laughing.

"Who's next?" the doctor asks.

"Susan Dotson," Joanne informs him.

"Susan Dotson, my favorite!" the doctor exclaims as a snarling,
overweight teenager walks past him. "She's crazy about me," he
whispers, and follows the girl into one of the small examining
rooms off the main reception area.

"Is he always like that?" Mrs. Armstrong asks.

"Always," Joanne answers as the phone rings again. "Dr.
Gold's office. . . . Hi, Eve. How was the test? . . . Oh, that sounds
awful. Did it make you gag? . . . What did the doctor say? . . .
Again? Why put yourself through it again if he doesn't think it's
necessary? . . . Well, no, of course you have to do what you think
is best. . . . Okay, I'll speak to you later." She hangs up and begins
idly rearranging the papers on her desk. It has been a quiet week,
she reflects. Her brother, Warren, called Sunday to see how she
was doing. Paul phoned that same afternoon. He was friendly and
warm, making no mention of having seen her at the theater. He

also said nothing about seeing her again before visitors' day at camp. This morning she received three letters from Lulu, but she has yet to hear anything from Robin. Perhaps Paul has received a letter; perhaps she could call him. . . .

She puts her hand on the telephone, mentally rehearsing her opening lines, about to lift the receiver when it rings. "Hello. Dr. Gold's office," she says quickly.

"Mrs. Hunter . . ."

"My God!" She should hang up, Joanne thinks, but her hand is paralyzed.

"You're looking good these days, Mrs. Hunter," says the raspy voice.

"How did you find me?" she whispers.

"Oh, you're easy to trace, Mrs. Hunter. The easiest one yet."

"Leave me alone." With a hand she blocks her mouth.

"I have been leaving you alone. I just didn't want you to think that I'd lost interest in you . . . like your husband has. Hasn't he found himself another love?"

Joanne slams the receiver back into its cradle and riffles through the pages of her appointment calendar, realizing that her hands are shaking. How has he found her? "No," she whispers. "I will not jump every time the phone rings. I will not."

"Talking to yourself again?" Ron Gold asks, emerging from his examining room behind Susan Dotson. "Make another appointment for Susan in eight weeks. My mother always used to talk to herself," he continues. "She used to say that whenever she wanted to talk to an intelligent person . . . You know the rest."

Joanne laughs agreement.

"Who's next?"

"Mrs. Pepplar."

"Mrs. Pepplar? My favorite!" A tall dark-haired woman of around fifty rises from her chair. "Right this way, Mrs. Pepplar."

Joanne hands Susan Dotson her new appointment card as Ron Gold and Mrs. Pepplar disappear down the narrow hallway. "See you in eight weeks," Joanne says to the girl, who pockets the appointment card and exits. The room seems strangely quiet, although it is still filled with people.

Joanne opens her purse and finds the letters that Lulu has written. She takes the last one out and reads it through quickly again.

Hi, Mom. Camp's great. The food stinks. Weather is great. SEND FOOD! Robin seems to be having a good time, although we don't communicate much. See you on visitors' day. Much love. SEND FOOD!!!

Love,
Lulu

P.S. How are you? Love to Dad.

Love to Dad, Joanne reads again, picking up the phone, pressing down quickly on the appropriate numbers before she can change her mind. "Paul, it's Joanne," she says when he comes on the line.

"How are you?" He sounds glad to hear from her. "I was going to call you today."

"Yes?"

"I had a letter from Lulu," he tells her.

"I had one too. Actually, I had three. They all came at once."

"She seems to be enjoying herself—except for the food."

"Yes." Joanne smiles. "She wrote the same thing to me." There is a pause.

"Are you at work?" he asks finally.

"Yes. It's been very busy all day."

"Here too. I should go. . . ."

"Paul?"

"Yes?"

Joanne hesitates. "Would you like to come for dinner this weekend? Either Friday or Saturday night."

Even before she is finished, Joanne can feel the discomfort on the other end of the line. "I'm sorry, I can't," he tells her quietly. "I'm going out of town for the weekend."

"Oh." Alone? I bet you aren't going alone.

"But the following Sunday, visitors' day at camp . . ."

"Sure, that's fine."

"I'll call you."

Chapter 9

JOANNE pulls her car into a vacant spot in the parking lot of Fresh Meadows Country Club. She gets out of the car and proceeds around the clubhouse to the tennis courts. It is almost six o'clock in the evening. Will he still be here? she wonders. She walks behind the wire fence past a court where four women are wildly fumbling with the ball. None of the players is any good. They are laughing and having a good time, not bothering to keep score.

He is watching her from the next court, his eyes following her as she walks behind the wire fence. The basket of bright green balls rests at his feet as he picks up one and hits it across the net at the young man he is coaching. "That's it," he calls out. "Keep your eye on the ball." He acknowledges her presence: I'll be with you in a minute, he tells her, without saying a word.

She sits down on a nearby bench and lets her eyes drift haphazardly from court to court, her mind a bright green tennis ball bouncing back and forth between now and earlier this afternoon. She hears Paul's voice—I'm going out of town for the weekend. She hears the phone ring. Dr. Gold's office. Mrs. Hunter. How did you find me? Oh, you're easy to trace. How did you find me? I'm going out of town for the weekend. Mrs. Hunter. Mrs. Hunter.

"Mrs. Hunter?"

"What?"

"Sorry," Steve Henry is saying, his tanned body blocking out the sun. "I didn't mean to startle you."

Joanne jumps up. "Am I interrupting your lesson?" she asks.

"It's over. I have a couple of minutes. I'm assuming it's me you want to see." It is as much a question as a statement.

"I have a job," she tells him. "That's why I haven't been around, why I had to cancel the last few lessons."

"I'm here until nine o'clock in the evening," he tells her, smiling. "Do you want to make an appointment for more lessons?" Joanne says nothing. "Mrs. Hunter?"

"Please call me Joanne," she tells him. "I was wondering if you'd like to come for dinner this weekend," she continues quickly. "Either Friday or Saturday night, if you're free then."

"I'd love to," he answers. "Saturday would be great."

She nods. Whatever possessed her to invite this man for dinner? Because my husband said he was busy, a little voice answers, and because there's some lunatic out there who's not going to give me a whole lot more time on this earth. "What?" she almost shouts, realizing he has spoken.

"I asked you what time you'd like me?"

"Eight o'clock? Or are you still giving lessons then?"

"Not on Saturdays. Eight o'clock is fine." She turns away, not sure what else to do. "Joanne," he calls after her. "Your new job must agree with you. You look terrific."

Joanne Hunter smiles, and drives back to her home thinking that she must be crazy after all.

"I'M EARLY," he says as she opens the front door and steps back to let him enter the well-lit hallway.

"Come in," Joanne tells him, forcing the words out.

Steve Henry stands smiling before her, his blond hair brushed away from his forehead. He looks relaxed in white pants and a pink shirt. "Brought you something," he says, displaying a bottle of wine. "I didn't know if you preferred red or white, but I thought that white was the safer choice."

"That's lovely. Thank you." Joanne takes the bottle, not quite sure what to do with it, what to do with him.

"Would you like to sit down?" she hears herself ask, and motions toward the living room.

"You have a lovely home," he says, moving easily inside and—ironically, she thinks—settling into the cream-colored swivel chair that is Paul's favorite.

Joanne remains in the hallway, not sure whether to follow him into the living room or take the wine into the kitchen. "Did you have any trouble finding the house?" she asks, deciding to put the wine in the fridge.

"No. I've been here before," he answers as she disappears into the kitchen.

"You have?" Joanne stands rooted to the tile floor.

"Well, not here exactly. My parents have friends who live over on Chestnut. Can I help you with anything?"

"No, not a thing. I'll be right there." She doesn't move.

"I love your art," he is saying. "When did you start collecting?"

Joanne has no idea what he is talking about. What art? Her mind is a blank. At this moment she has absolutely no idea what her living room even looks like. She can see nothing on the walls.

"Joanne?"

"Sorry. What did you ask me?" She has to go into the living room—she can't spend all night in the kitchen. Still, maybe if she stands here long enough, he'll take the hint and leave. She should never have invited him over in the first place.

"I asked you about your art," he is saying from the kitchen doorway. "How long have you been collecting?" he repeats.

"We started a few years back," she tells him, unconsciously switching to the plural pronoun.

"I like your taste." He takes several steps into the kitchen.

"It's Paul's taste, mostly," she explains, and he stops. "Dinner's not quite ready. Would you like a drink?"

"Yes," he says. "Scotch and water, please."

"Scotch and water." Is there any Scotch? she wonders.

"If you don't have any . . ."

"I think we do." She hurries past him into the dining room, to the buffet, where Paul keeps the liquor. This has always been Paul's department—she has never been much of a drinker. Down on her knees, she riffles through the various bottles in the cabinet.

"Here," he says as he bends over her to extricate the correct bottle. "All I need now is a glass." Joanne moves to the breakfront and gets a suitable glass. "And a smile," he tells her as she places the glass in his outstretched hand. She finds herself staring into his eyes, her mouth trying to form the requested shape. "That's better," he says. "I think that's the first time you've really looked at me since I walked in the door."

Joanne immediately looks away.

"No, don't do that. Look at me," he instructs her. Reluctantly her eyes return to his. "You look lovely," he is saying. "I've been wanting to tell you that since I arrived, but we always seemed to

438

be in different rooms." She finds that she is smiling in spite of herself. "You've done something different to your hair."

Joanne's hand lifts automatically to her head. "I had a few streaks put in it," she tells him, feeling self-conscious. "Too much? I told him to just put in a few."

"It's beautiful. Just the right amount. I like it."

"Thank you." Joanne blushes.

"Why are you so nervous?" he asks.

Joanne wants to laugh away the question. Instead she replies, "You make me nervous."

"I do? Why?"

"I don't know why. You just do." She abruptly turns and walks back into the kitchen. He is right behind her. As he mixes his drink she notices that he is smiling.

"You think I'm going to pounce?" he asks.

"Are you?"

"I don't know. Do you want me to?"

"I don't know."

"Why did you ask me for dinner?"

"I'm sorry, I must seem like a real idiot to you!" Joanne exclaims, not sure whether to laugh or cry. "I mean, I'm forty-one and I'm acting younger than most of the girls I'm sure you date."

"I don't date girls," he corrects. "I date women."

"What does that mean?"

He laughs. "It means that I think most women don't get really interesting until they reach thirty."

"And men? When do they get interesting?"

"You'll have to tell me."

Joanne's head moves restlessly from side to side. "This was a mistake," she says finally. "I should never have asked you here."

"Do you want me to leave?"

"No," Joanne whispers after a pause, realizing it is true. "I want you to stay." She tries to laugh. "I spent all day cooking."

"All day?"

"Well, almost all day. I took a few hours off this afternoon to visit my grandfather." Steve Henry looks interested. "He's ninety-five years old," she continues, not sure why except that it feels good to take the focus off herself. "He lives in a nursing home."

He nods and takes a sip of his drink.

"I visit him every Saturday," Joanne continues, reassured by the sound of her own voice. "Most of the time he doesn't know who I am. He thinks I'm my mother—she died three years ago. Anyway, I visit him every Saturday afternoon. Everybody thinks that must be very hard on me, but the fact is that I enjoy it. I tell him everything; it makes me feel better."

Why is she going on like this? What does Steve Henry care about her grandfather? "Are your grandparents still alive?" she asks.

"Both sets." He smiles.

"You're lucky."

"Yes, I am. We're a very close family."

"You've never been married?" Why is she asking that? Why is she bringing the conversation back to this room?

He shakes his head. "Came close once, but we were too young. How old were you when you got married?"

"Twenty-one," she says. "I guess that was pretty young, but it just seemed right." She stops abruptly. "Why am I telling you this? You can't be interested. . . ."

"Why can't I be? Things that interest you interest me."

"Why?"

"Because *you* interest me."

"Why?"

"Why not?"

Joanne pauses, trying to organize her thoughts into something vaguely coherent. "For one thing, I'm far older than you. I know that you think that women don't get interesting until they hit thirty," she continues quickly, "but the fact remains that I was a teenager while you were still in diapers."

He laughs. "I'm out of diapers now."

"What do you want from me?" she asks.

"Dinner?" he ventures shyly.

"THAT's the best lemon meringue pie I've ever tasted," Steve Henry is telling her as he finishes his second piece and pushes his plate toward the center of the long rectangular oak table.

Joanne smiles, grateful that the dinner is over and that it has been a success. Steve Henry is sitting at her right elbow. He has said all the right things, made none of the wrong moves. They have discussed tennis, her toes, and the state of world politics. He has been pleasant and attentive. Why then does she so desperately wish that he would leave?

"How about a liqueur?" he asks, pushing his chair back and moving to the liquor cabinet, obviously in no hurry to rush out.

Joanne hesitates. She has always found the taste of liqueur too sweet. "Maybe just a bit of Benedictine," she ventures.

"A bit of Benedictine it is."

In the next moment they are toasting each other with delicate glasses of amber liquid. "To tonight," he says.

Joanne nods without speaking and takes a tiny sip from her glass. The thick syrup warms her immediately. "It's good," she has to admit, savoring it.

"Tell me about your husband," Steve Henry says, surprising her. She feels the small glass almost tumble out of her hand.

"What can I say?" she asks, careful not to look at him. "He's a lawyer, very smart, very successful."

"Very successful, maybe. Not very smart."

"What do you mean?"

"If he had any brains, I wouldn't be here."

"I wish you wouldn't say things like that."

"Why?"

"Because they make me uncomfortable," she tells him, taking another sip of her Benedictine, feeling her throat warm.

"Why should compliments make you uncomfortable?"

"Because they're too facile," she says strongly. "I'm sorry. I don't mean to be unpleasant, but I've never been good at this."

"At what?"

"At . . . this! The games. Dating. I wasn't very good at it twenty years ago, and I'm worse now."

He laughs. "Is that why you have every light in the house on?"

It is her turn to laugh. "Subtlety was never my strong suit."

"Tell me about you. Describe yourself in three words."

"Oh, come on."

"No, I'm serious. Indulge me. Three words."

She rests her head in the palm of her left hand, positioning her face away from his penetrating eyes. "Scared," she whispers finally. "Confused." She lets out a deep breath. "Lonely. How's that for an uplifting appraisal?" Her eyes return reluctantly to his.

"Lousy," he says, and suddenly he is kissing her, his lips softly pressing against hers. "Now how do you feel?" he asks.

"Scared," she replies evenly. "Confused." She laughs. "Not quite so lonely."

He leans to his left to kiss her again.

Immediately she brings her glass to her lips. "I don't think I'm ready for this."

"Ready for what?"

"For whatever this is leading up to."

"Which is?"

"Can we talk about something else?" Joanne pleads, standing up and starting to clear away the dishes.

"Sure. We can talk about anything you'd like. Here, let me help you." He picks up his empty plate.

"I'll do that," she tells him.

"Let me help you," he repeats.

"Oh, put the damn dish down!" she shouts, then buries her face in her hands.

Suddenly he is beside her and his arms are around her, his mouth buried against her hair. "Let me help you," he says again, his lips finding hers, pressing tightly against them.

"You don't understand," she tries to tell him.

"I do understand."

"I'm afraid . . ."

"I know." His hands delicately caress her arms as he draws them around his narrow waist. "You're beautiful," he mutters, kissing her neck.

Suddenly she is pulling away from him, covering her eyes with her hands, her arms blocking her body. "Sorry," she apologizes, but her arms refuse to budge from their protective position.

He stops abruptly. His tone is curious. "What's the matter?"

She shakes her head. "There's nothing the matter."

"You sound angry."

"I'm not angry."

"If you're not angry, then put your arms back around me."

Her arms drop to her sides. "I can't. I'm sorry. I wanted to. I thought I could."

"Maybe you thought you could," he corrects her, "but you certainly don't want to."

"It's not your fault. It's not you."

"Who else is it?" he demands. "Who else is here?"

"Too many ghosts," she replies helplessly, after a pause. She takes a hesitant step away from him. "Are *you* angry?" she asks.

"Yes," he tells her truthfully. "But I'll get over it."

"It really has nothing to do with you."

"So you've said. What exactly does that mean?"

"That I love my husband," she says quietly. "It may be stupid and old-fashioned, but something inside me is telling me that there's still hope for Paul and me, and that if I give in to . . . this, then I'm somehow giving up on us. I don't know if I'm making any sense."

"I'm a tennis pro," he says. "What do I know of sense?"

She smiles. "I like you."

"I like you too." They laugh.

"I'll show myself out," he says.

Joanne watches as he walks through the doorway. She hears the front door open and close, listens to his footsteps on the steps, listens as the house lapses into silence. She lowers her face into her hands and pulls at the sides of her hair in frustration.

The phone rings.

"No!" she yells. "I can't take it anymore."

Joanne runs into the kitchen and glares at the telephone. "Come and get me already," she cries. "Just stop playing with me!" He is hiding out there, has been hiding out there all evening waiting for Steve Henry to leave. He is out there now—right this minute.

She yanks the receiver from its hook. She says nothing, only waits.

443

"Joanne?"

"Eve?" Joanne feels the tears springing to her eyes.

"What took you so long to answer the phone? What's going on there? Where did Steve Henry go?"

"I couldn't get to it," Joanne replies, answering Eve's questions one at a time. "Nothing's going on. He went home."

"What do you mean, he went home? What happened?"

"Nothing happened, Eve."

"Please don't tell me that, Joanne. You'll ruin my night. What do you mean, nothing happened?"

Joanne shrugs, grateful for the sound of Eve's voice, though she is reluctant to go into details.

"He made his pitch," Joanne says. "I said no."

"You said no? Are you crazy? I can't believe that you actually let that magnificent hunk get away. I said to myself as I saw his car pull out, She can't be letting him leave. Maybe he's going out for some cigarettes. Maybe he forgot his toothbrush and he's going home to get it."

"What were you doing watching my house?" Joanne asks.

"I happened to look out my window and saw his car pulling away."

"Why aren't you asleep?"

"I'm too nervous about that CAT scan on Monday."

"Well, try not to think about it. Why don't you come by the office after it's over, and we'll have lunch together."

"I can't."

"Why not?"

"I just can't. Look, I'll speak to you tomorrow."

Joanne stares at the receiver as the line goes dead.

WHAT am I doing here? Joanne wonders as the outside air brushes against her bare legs. She is standing in her backyard by the deep end of her empty, aborted swimming pool, staring through the darkness at what looks like a giant open grave. My grave, she thinks, for when he comes for me.

There is something in her right hand. Joanne lifts her arm into the air. The tennis racket slices silently through the night sky.

Follow through, she hears Steve Henry say. "Forget it!" she calls into the stillness, letting her arm fall to her side.

Why is she standing in the middle of her backyard in the middle of the night, clutching her tennis racket in her right hand? Why couldn't she sleep?

"You're an idiot," she whispers, wincing as she recalls her little speech to Steve Henry. "I can't give up hope," she hears herself say. What hope? she wonders. The hope that your husband will come back? Your husband is going forward, not coming back. He's away for the weekend, out for the duration. You can bet that he isn't worrying about you.

Lifting the tennis racket, Joanne hurls it with all her strength into the deep end of the empty pool. It crashes against the concrete side and bounces several times along the bottom before finally spinning to a lonely stop. She has no more use for tennis rackets. Standing alone in the darkness, Joanne thinks that this empty concrete hole is the perfect symbol for her life.

It is several minutes before she is aware of other sounds, a crackling of branches, a subtle rustling of grass. She turns quickly but sees nothing.

So he has come, she thinks, feeling her heart beginning to race. He has been waiting for just this opportunity, and now she has handed it to him. She pictures the headlines in the paper, wonders where the police will discover her body, tries to imagine her final seconds of life.

"Mrs. Hunter." The voice wafts eerily through the stillness.

Joanne gasps, closing her eyes against the sound of the recognizable rasp. "What do you want from me?"

"You know what I want," the voice replies.

Where is he? Joanne wonders, trying to figure out from which direction the sound is coming. Somewhere to her left she hears a movement, feels someone walking toward her.

"Mrs. Hunter," the voice calls from almost at her side.

Joanne spins around to see a tall figure emerging from the blackness. Gradually she discerns the familiar outline of a long, angular face framed by hair that falls in even waves. "Eve!" she cries as the figure comes fully into view.

Eve's laugh is a shriek. "You should see your face!" she hoots.

"What are you doing?" Joanne screams.

Eve is nearly hysterical with laughter. "You should have heard your voice. 'What do you want from me?' " she mimics. "I love it! You were wonderful."

"What are you doing here?" Joanne repeats as she almost collapses, sobbing. "You scared me half to death."

"Oh, come on," Eve retorts, managing to sound like the injured party. "Where's your sense of humor? I was looking out my window and I saw you here. I thought you might like company."

"Are you crazy?" Joanne can see Eve clearly now. She sees the smile on Eve's face turn sour, her expression freeze. "Why should you try to scare me like that?"

"I didn't think you'd take it so seriously," Eve replies. "I forgot how obsessed you are about all this."

"Obsessed?"

"Yes, obsessed. You should hear yourself sometimes. You sound positively Looney Tunes." Her voice slips back to its eerie rasp. "Mrs. Hunter. I'm coming to get you, Mrs. Hunter. . . ."

"Stop it!"

"Look, Joanne, I'm sorry I scared you. I really didn't think you'd turn it into such a big deal."

"Eve," Joanne begins, her voice rising with each successive word. "Get out of here before I push you into the damn pool."

A masculine voice cuts through the darkness. "What's going on down there?"

Both women turn toward the sound, looking up. Joanne recognizes Brian's voice, is grateful for it.

"Joanne, are you all right? Is that Eve with you?"

"We're fine," Eve answers for her.

"What are you doing? It's after midnight. Is something wrong?"

"Everything's fine," Eve says wearily. "Stop yelling before you wake up the whole neighborhood. I'll be right up." She turns to Joanne. "You're not angry, are you?" she asks plaintively.

"Yes, I'm angry," Joanne responds.

Eve's eyebrows arch and her jaw stiffens. She says nothing as she spins around and vanishes into the night.

Chapter 10

"ARE you tired?" Paul is asking.

Joanne leans back and closes her eyes against the bright morning sunlight, realizing it has been a long time since she has occupied the passenger seat of her husband's car. It feels good, she thinks, glancing over at him. "A little," she confesses. "I didn't sleep much last night. I guess I'm a bit nervous."

"Don't be," he tells her. "Everything will be fine."

Joanne smiles, trying to look reassured. Will the girls be glad to see her? She pictures Lulu running full throttle toward the car, sees Robin linger behind in the shadows.

"It's hard to believe the summer's half over," Paul is saying.

Joanne nods. Time goes by quickly when you're having fun, she thinks, checking her watch. It is almost eight o'clock. Barring any unforeseen accidents, they should reach Camp Danbee in two hours. Will Robin be waiting at the gate to greet them?

She has had one brief letter from Robin in the past month.

Dear Mom,
How are you? I am fine. The weather is good. I am participating in all the sports. The counselors are okay; the food is not. Your new job sounds interesting.

Robin

At least it was something, Joanne supposes, studying the scenery along the highway. How green everything is, how beautiful in the early morning sunlight, although the weatherman on the car radio is gloomily predicting rain for later in the afternoon.

"Did you see your grandfather yesterday?" Paul asks.

Joanne nods. "He slept the whole time."

"And Eve? How is she?"

Joanne feels her body tense. "I haven't spoken to her all week," she tells him. "We've both been busy."

"Your job keeping you occupied?"

"Never a dull moment," she comments wryly, thinking how wonderful Paul looks. His face is deeply tanned against the open neck of his white shirt. His legs look lean and muscular beneath white shorts. "Are you still working out every day?" she asks.

A brief chuckle escapes his lips. "Not quite every day," he admits sheepishly. "I was pretty good for a few weeks, but I don't know. I just can't seem to get into it the way these younger guys can. That stuff hurts! Not that I've dropped it completely, but my enthusiasm is definitely on the wane." He smiles. "Besides, my arms will never develop fully anyway. All those accidents as a kid." He looks over at her slyly and they both laugh. "You look wonderful," he says. "What have you done to yourself?"

"I put some streaks in my hair."

He shakes his head. "It's more than that."

"I lost a few pounds. I've been running around a lot lately."

She feels his eyes on her legs. "And the tennis lessons?"

"I've stopped those." She clears her throat nervously. "Too hard on the toes," she tells him, her eyes watching his as they travel the length of her bare legs to the tips of her sandaled feet. "I think the nails are about ready to fall off."

He winces. "And then what happens?"

"Ron says there are probably new ones under there already."

"Ron?"

"The doctor I work for. I told you. We went to school together."

Paul shrugs, his eyes returning to the road ahead, but not before Joanne has caught a strange expression in them. "Have I ever met him?" he asks.

"I don't think so."

"The name sounds familiar. What does he look like?"

Joanne has to suppress a smile. Is Paul jealous? "He's not too tall," she begins. "He has reddish blond hair. He looks the same as he did twenty-five years ago."

"Married?"

"Yes."

"You still planning to stop work at the end of the summer?"

"Yes," Joanne replies after a pause.

"You don't sound sure."

"Ron doesn't want me to leave. He says he'll be lost without me." She laughs. "I think he's right."

"So you're thinking of staying on?"

Joanne ponders the question. "No, not really," she says finally.

They drift into silence, the remainder of the journey passing with only a minimum of words between them, the music on the radio providing a soothing backdrop for their individual reveries.

Can it be that Paul is jealous? she wonders again. Probably not jealous, but certainly curious. The thought that there could be another man in her life is something that had obviously not occurred to him. He had been sure that she would remain available until he decided their fate, confident that he had all the time in the world. Now he is not so sure.

He looks at her and smiles warmly. Surprisingly, she is the first to turn away, laying her head against the headrest, gradually allowing her heavy lids to close. Something is happening here, she feels, though she is not sure what it is.

When she opens her eyes, their car is off the main highway, traveling slowly down a different road.

"We're almost there," he tells her. "How was your sleep?"

"Terrific," she says, amazed she dropped off so easily. "What time is it?" They are joining a line of cars at the camp gates.

"Just after ten. We're right on time."

"Do you see them?" she asks, looking through the crowd of campers gathered just inside the gate.

"Not yet."

Paul maneuvers the car to the designated parking area inside the camp grounds. Joanne looks eagerly around for a glimpse of her daughters, her previous anxieties returning full force. What will the day be like? What will the drive home be like? Will they ever be a real family again?

The car comes to a stop and Paul pulls the keys out of the ignition. Deliberately he reaches over and takes her hand in his. "It'll be all right," he tells her softly, reading her thoughts. Then quietly he adds, "I love you, Joanne."

Joanne's heart lurches. The lushness of the surrounding scenery vanishes; the noisy crowd grows silent. She is aware only of Paul, of the touch of his fingers, the sound of his voice.

"Mom!" Joanne turns to see Lulu banging on the car window.

"Sweetie!" She opens the door and encircles her daughter in her arms. "Let me look at you. You've grown a foot since you left." Joanne pushes the hair out of her daughter's eyes. "And your big, beautiful eyes have gotten bigger!"

"It just looks that way because the rest of me is wasting away," Lulu says. "Did you bring food?"

"Yes, we brought food." Paul laughs, joining them. "You look terrific. Are you having a good time?"

"It's great. One kid in the cabin is a pain, but everybody else is great." She throws her arms around their waists, pulling them toward each other with surprising force. "I missed you both."

"Where's Robin?" Paul asks, a question Joanne has avoided.

"She's at the waterfront," Lulu tells them. "In the sailing exhibition. I'm supposed to take you if you want to see it."

"Of course we do," Joanne says, her arm around her daughter. "What about the food?"

"We'll get it later," Paul tells her, moving to Lulu's other side. They proceed to the waterfront, arms tightly interlocked. Joanne feels happy, confident, even peaceful. Something has changed between her and Paul. They will be a family again, she thinks, as a panorama of white sails greets their smiling eyes.

"SO THEN I go—just trying to be nice—I go, 'Do you know you have your sweatshirt on inside out?' And she goes, real snooty, 'Of course I know it's inside out. It's supposed to be inside out. That's how everybody at Brown wears them,' like *she* goes to Brown University. And I go, 'Oh, really? Tell me about it.' "

Joanne is listening to Lulu but watching Robin. The family is sitting on a large red-and-blue quilt that once belonged to Joanne's mother, eating the barbecued hamburgers and drinking the soft drinks that are the regular staples of the camp's annual visitors' day picnic. Lulu has been chattering nonstop since they sat down; Robin has volunteered almost no information since their polite but reserved greeting at the waterfront.

"Anybody for another hamburger?" Paul asks.

"Me!" Lulu shouts immediately.

"Anybody else?"

"No, thanks," Joanne tells him. Robin shakes her head.

"Mustard and relish and a pickle on mine," Lulu orders quickly as her father stands up. "And a tomato," she adds.

"Maybe you'd better come with me, Lulu," Paul says, his eyes on Joanne as Lulu grabs hold of his outstretched hand.

He's giving us this time alone together, Joanne understands. She looks at Robin, who looks back at her expectantly. Clearly, Joanne thinks, she is waiting for me to say something.

"So," she begins. "Are you having a good time?"

"It's all right." Robin shrugs.

"We were very impressed with your sailing."

Robin acknowledges the compliment wordlessly.

"What are the boys at Mackanac like this year?" Joanne asks, hoping that this is a safe enough topic.

Robin looks into her lap. "There's one guy who's kind of cute."

Joanne says nothing.

"His name's Ron," her daughter continues.

"Oh? The same as my boss."

Something almost approaching a smile appears on Robin's lips, then disappears. "How's your job?" she asks.

"Great," Joanne replies enthusiastically.

Robin stares off in the direction of the waterfront. "How are things between you and Dad?" she asks quietly.

"Better," Joanne answers.

Robin brushes an imaginary bug off the quilt. "Camp is good," she says softly, nodding her head, looking back toward the water, careful to avoid her mother's eyes. "It was good that I came. You were right," she adds. "Not just about camp . . ."

Should I take her in my arms? Joanne wonders, wanting to. I'm afraid to do that, afraid to overstep my bounds. She reaches over and takes Robin's hand in her own. Robin doesn't pull away.

"So, what do you think?" Paul asks after they have bidden their daughters a tearful good-bye.

Joanne dries her eyes and smiles. "I think it went well."

"So do I. Robin seems to have come around."

"She told me that she was determined not to have a good time, but that everyone was so nice to her and there was so much to do, she couldn't help herself. Plus I think meeting that boy, Ron, had something to do with her change of mood."

"I never quite understood the point of having an all-girls camp if you're going to have an all-boys camp right beside it," Paul says, turning on the windshield wipers.

"It was nice that the rain held off."

"It's going to be rough driving home, though," he tells her. "We're heading into a real storm."

"Are you hungry?" she asks him minutes later, the rain now pounding against the windows.

"Not really," Paul answers. "I ate three hamburgers at lunch."

"I was thinking that maybe we could stop at one of these lodges along the way for something to eat and wait until the rain lets up a bit." She looks over at Paul, aware that he is staring at her. She feels her body starting to tremble. "We could have dinner . . . or something," she adds, her voice breaking.

He pulls the car into the parking lot of the next motel. "Or something," he says.

This is what she has been imagining these past few months. He is everywhere around her, touching her, loving her and telling her that he needs her. They have been here in this room, with its tacky purple bedspread, for several hours. The rain has stopped, but if Paul has noticed, he has ignored it.

At first she was nervous, but soon he was whispering how beautiful she was, and his hands were reassuring and familiar, and they had forgotten nothing of what they had learned over the course of twenty years. Techniques of the heart, she thinks. Something Steve Henry couldn't understand. And soon any embarrassment or fears she might have had passed, and she was lost in the act of love as she had been raised to believe it should be. And she thought that this was the best time in all their years together.

And now they are lying in each other's arms. Joanne feels her body slowly relax, though she knows sleep will be impossible. But it doesn't matter. They are sharing the same bed. And when he wakes up, she will be beside him.

"DO YOU HAVE A NINE-O'CLOCK appointment?" Joanne asks as he pulls into their driveway the next morning. It is almost nine already, and he has to drive all the way back to the city.

"No. I told them on Friday not to expect me until after ten."

She feels a stab of anxiety. Had he known then, on Friday, what would happen between them? Had he been so sure? She dismisses the uncomfortable thought. He obviously planned that they would reconcile this weekend; this is what he means. Why, then, does she feel so unsettled? Why has she felt this way since he pulled himself out of bed this morning and hurriedly showered and dressed, saying little on the drive back, smiling guiltily in her direction only when he could no longer avoid her gaze?

Paul walks her to the door, carrying the bags of unneeded items the girls have sent home. He rests the bags on the doorstep.

"Do you have time for some coffee?" Joanne asks. Should she ask him now when he plans to move back in?

"I'd better not. I still have to change, shave," he tells her.

"Will I see you tonight?" she ventures.

"Joanne . . ."

"What's happening here, Paul?" she asks when she can no longer bear the suspense.

"I hoped you'd understand about last night," he begins.

"Understand what? I understand that we made love, that you told me that you loved me. . . ."

"I do love you."

"What else is there to understand?"

"That it doesn't change anything," he is saying, and Joanne finds that she is backing into the doorway, trying to get away from his words. "Maybe I shouldn't have let last night happen," he continues, "but I wanted it to happen. And face it, Joanne, you wanted it to happen."

"What are you trying to tell me?"

"That what happened last night doesn't change anything," he repeats. "That I'm not ready to come home."

"Last night . . ."

"Doesn't change anything."

Joanne fishes wildly in her purse. "I can't find my keys."

"I didn't mean to mislead you."

"Then why didn't you tell me these things *before* we made love?" She flings her purse to the ground. "I can't find my keys." She buries her face in her hands.

"Joanne . . ."

"Just leave me alone."

"I can't leave you outside on the steps, crying."

"Then find my keys and I'll cry inside."

"Joanne . . ."

"Find my keys!" she screams.

Paul scoops up Joanne's purse and riffles through it. Seconds later he finds the house keys and holds them out to her. "I see you found your old set," he comments absently.

Joanne grabs them from his hand, glancing at the keys she thought she misplaced weeks ago. She fumbles at the lock, finally making the proper connection, and the door falls open. She stands in the doorway, unable to move.

"Don't you have to shut the alarm off?" he asks.

Joanne moves like an automaton to the alarm box as Paul lifts the bags inside. "I'm sorry, Joanne," he offers. "I'll call you."

Joanne says nothing. She waits until his car pulls away before stretching back with her foot and kicking the front door closed.

HE IS sleeping when Joanne enters the room.

Joanne stares at the old face, the baseball cap atop the egg-shaped head from which escape long gray-white hairs. This has always felt right. Grandfathers should have white hair, she decides. How comforting our stereotypes are, she thinks, sitting down beside the sleeping old man. How much more pleasant than reality.

She is not used to Mondays. For the past three years she has visited this room every Saturday, when the halls are busy with family members paying their weekly respects. She didn't realize how still everything became during the week. Like her grandfather, most of the elderly residents are asleep, though it is not yet one o'clock. She has come on her lunch hour. Ron told her to take the rest of the day off, to take all the time she needed.

He had only to take one look to know that she had been crying. Talk to me, he said, leading her out of the crowded reception area and into an empty examining room. She broke down and told him everything that had happened between herself and Paul. He took her in his arms and held her. Take the rest of the day off, he urged. I can manage. And they had both laughed. All right, he quickly amended, I *can't* manage—take a long lunch. Take as long as you need.

But she couldn't eat lunch, couldn't stop the endless stream of tears. And so she got into her car and drove until she saw the familiar institution.

And now she is here, sitting beside an old man who has given her a wealth of memories, but who no longer remembers who she is. She isn't sure herself who she is, she realizes, looking around the room. She glances over at Sam Hensley, thinking how exposed he appears without the combined presence of his daughter and grandson. She is used to sharing her space with them.

Her grandfather's eyes flicker open. As he looks at her the many lines that fill his ancient face crease upward into a series of small smiles. "Joanne?"

"Grampa!" The tears, which Joanne has been barely managing to keep in check, return. "You know me?"

He looks puzzled, straining to sit up.

"Here, I'll help you." She moves to prop up his pillow.

"I think there's something at the foot of the bed that you can turn," he says clearly.

Joanne is instantly at the foot of the bed, cranking the handle to raise the bed so that her grandfather can comfortably assume a sitting position. The baseball cap falls into his lap. He grabs it and once more places it on top of his head, his eyes merry, twinkling.

"Who's going to take the series this year?" He smiles, then looks at her intently. "Why are you crying?"

"Because I'm happy," she tells him. "I'm so glad to see you."

"You should come more often. Your mother comes every week."

"I know. I'm sorry. I'll try to. . . ."

"You've gotten so grown up." Joanne laughs, wiping more tears from her face. "How old are you now?" he asks.

"Forty-one," Joanne answers.

"Forty-one?" He shakes his head. "That must make your mother . . . what?" .

"Sixty-seven," Joanne says quickly.

"Sixty-seven! My little Linda is sixty-seven. I can't believe it. How's your husband?" The questions come rapid-fire now, as if he knows he has only a short time to get them all in.

"Fine," Joanne responds automatically. "He's good."

"And your children? You have how many?"

"Two."

"Two. Forgive me—I sometimes forget."

"Robin and Lulu. Lana, really, but we call her Lulu."

"Little Lulu. I remember." He closes his eyes, and Joanne fears for an instant that she has lost him, but when he opens them again, they are still focused, almost mischievous. "Do you have time to play a few hands of gin?" he asks.

Joanne gasps loudly with delight.

"Is everything all right in here?" comes a voice from the doorway. "Oh, hello, Mrs. Hunter," the nurse continues, recognizing her. "Didn't expect to see you today. Your granddaddy okay?"

"Do you have any playing cards?" Joanne asks quickly.

"Playing cards?"

"You know, for gin rummy. Cards," Joanne repeats.

"I think your granddaddy has some in his drawer," the nurse says after a second's thought. "I remember seeing them somewhere."

"They're here!" Joanne exclaims triumphantly, pulling out an old deck of well-worn cards. "I found them."

The nurse is gone before Joanne has finished dealing the cards onto the stiff gray-white sheets. Her hands shaking, she arranges her cards in proper order, too excited to concentrate. All she can think about is that she is actually playing cards with her grandfather. And suddenly she is ten years old again, and they are sitting at the round table in the living room of her grandparents' cottage, listening to the sound of the rain outside.

"You taking that card?" her grandfather is asking impatiently.

Joanne realizes that she has been staring at the two of hearts for several seconds. "No," she says, deciding too late that she should have picked it up. Her grandfather quickly tucks the two of hearts into his hand and discards a seven of diamonds. Joanne checks her hand carefully to make sure she has no use for this card before she draws one from the deck. It is the ten of spades, which she takes, putting it between the eight and the jack of the same suit. She needs the nine.

Her grandfather's eyes narrow in concentration. He draws a card from the deck and quickly discards it, watching as Joanne does the same, grabbing the card that she has thrown out, watching as she picks up his discard. Joanne looks at her hand. She is only one card away from gin—the nine of spades. She debates throwing away a needed card, eager to prolong the game.

"Gin!" her grandfather suddenly exclaims, proudly displaying his cards. Joanne stares at him. "You thought I was going to give you this one?" he asks slyly, turning over the nine of spades.

"I don't believe it," Joanne states incredulously. Then, eagerly, "Think you can do it again?"

"I'll try," he ventures.

The results of the next hand are the same as the first. "Gin!" he cries with a child's delight. The third and fourth hands proceed in almost identical fashion, though these take longer to play. Each is punctuated by the same satisfied yelp. "Gin!" her grandfather exclaims, though his voice is starting to fade.

"One more hand, Grampa?" Joanne asks.

"Deal the cards," he tells her softly.

"We can stop now if you want to rest for a while."

"Deal the cards," he says again.

Joanne gives them each ten cards and quickly sorts hers out, noticing that her grandfather doesn't bother.

"The four of clubs, Grampa," she tells him, looking up from the exposed card. "Do you want it?" He shakes his head. "Then I'll take it." She smiles, refusing to acknowledge that he no longer sees the cards. She throws off an eight of hearts. "An eight, Grampa. Do you want the eight?" He shakes his head. "Well, then, pick a card," she proceeds stubbornly.

She stares at him. The smiling eyes vanish, close in sleep as his neck stretches back against his pillow. "Grampa," she cries, and his eyes snap open before closing once again. "Please don't leave me, Grampa. Please don't go. I need you!"

Her trembling hands reach out and gather the cards together, dropping some on the floor, scooping them up, forcing them inside the worn box. She stands at the foot of his bed for several seconds before turning the crank to lower the bed to its original position. Then she returns to her grandfather's side, taking his arm in her hand, surprised at how light it feels.

"Please wake up, Grampa," she pleads, knowing he will not. "I'm so lost. I don't know what to do anymore. I lied to you. You asked me how Paul is and I said he was fine. Well, he is fine. . . . It's just that he's gone. I told you before that he left me. But I always felt that he'd come back. I love him so much, Grampa. He's been my life for twenty years. Now he wants a different life, and I don't know what to do. Everything is falling apart. I'm losing my children—they're growing up. They're growing away from me. And Eve . . . You remember Eve?"

Joanne searches her grandfather's face for a flicker of recognition, but finds none. She continues. "Well, something is happening to Eve, Grampa. She's acting very peculiar. I can't explain it. She's been my best friend for thirty years, and all of a sudden I don't know who she is—I don't trust her anymore. I'm afraid of her!" Joanne pauses, startled by her admission, letting this thought sink in. "I've been getting these phone calls, Grampa. Scary, sick phone calls. A voice threatening to kill me. I can't believe any of the things that have been happening to me these past few months. I'm so confused. I don't know what to do. Please help me, Grampa."

Slowly her grandfather's eyes open. "Would you like to trade places?" he asks gently.

Joanne collapses into the chair beside his bed, his words echoing in her ear. His hand reaches out to hers, bringing her fingers to his dry lips.

The room is suddenly filled with sound. *"It's a long way to Tipperary!"* Sam Hensley is bellowing loudly.

"Linda?" her grandfather asks, startled by the sudden noise. *"It's a long way to go. . . ."*

459

"Linda?"

Joanne stands up, bends forward, and kisses her grandfather's cheek. "No, Grampa," she whispers as his eyes close in sleep. "It's Joanne."

As SHE pulls the car into her driveway Joanne thinks she sees Eve staring down at her from the window of the small bedroom at the front of Eve's house. Joanne climbs out of her car, checking her watch. It is after five o'clock. She has been driving all afternoon, her head an echo chamber of spoken words and unspoken thoughts. Now she wants only to take a bath and get into bed, yet something is pulling her toward Eve's house.

As she crosses her front lawn she again looks to the window of the small bedroom, the room Eve had been saving for the baby that never arrived, but the window is empty. Is Eve on her way down the stairs to answer the door?

Joanne knocks, then rings the bell. No one comes, though she can hear voices arguing. "Eve," she calls. "Are you all right?"

The door opens and Eve's mother stands before her. "Eve doesn't want to see you," she says simply.

Joanne has trouble digesting this information. "Why not?"

"She says she's tired of having to defend herself to everyone, that if you were really her friend, she wouldn't have to."

"I *am* her friend."

"I know that. And deep down, I think she knows it too, but—"

"I'm too tired to argue, Mrs. Cameron. I'm going home. Tell Eve I was here and . . . tell her that I love her."

Joanne runs down the steps and cuts across the lawn to her front door. She turns the key in the lock, opens the door, and stretches out her hand to shut off the alarm. It isn't on.

Joanne takes an involuntary step backward. The green light isn't on. Can it be that she has forgotten to set the alarm?

Her mind returns to the morning. She was upset when she left the house. She was thinking about Paul's latest abandonment. It is entirely possible that she forgot to set the alarm. Stupid! she thinks, deciding she'd better check the doors and windows to make sure they are secure. It's possible that someone might have tried to get in. Despite Brian's earlier assurances that he would have someone watch the house, she has never seen any police cars patrolling the area.

She proceeds cautiously into her kitchen to the sliding glass door. The lock is securely fastened. Joanne feels herself relax, thinks she is being silly, but feels her feet leading her into the living room and then the dining room. Nothing has been tampered with. Almost reluctantly she moves to the family room, where she quickly checks out that sliding glass door. It too is securely fastened. No one has been here.

The bedrooms are the same—still, empty, all the windows locked. Joanne collapses on her bed. Maybe she won't bother with a bath. Maybe she'll just crawl under the covers and try to sleep.

The phone rings just as she is starting to doze.

Joanne picks it up on its first ring. "Hello, Eve?"

"Bad girl," the voice chides her. "Tramp!"

Joanne slams the receiver into the cradle and buries her head in her hands. In the next instant she is racing down the stairs to the kitchen, rummaging through her address book, finding Brian's phone number at work. Her hands shaking, she dials.

"Sergeant Brian Stanley, please," she says to the policeman who answers the phone.

"He's not here right now. Can I help you?"

"Who is this?"

"Lieutenant Fox here. Can I help you?"

"This is Joanne Hunter, Lieutenant Fox. I live next door to Brian Stanley."

"Yes?" He is waiting for her to continue.

"I've been getting threatening phone calls, and Sergeant Stanley said he was going to speak to you about having a patrol car keep an eye on my house. I haven't seen any police cars, and I just got another call and I know it's probably nothing to worry about, but I just wondered when was the last time the police—"

"Slow down a minute, please. You say that Sergeant Stanley asked me to have a patrol car keep an eye on your house?"

"Well, he said he was going to, but that was a while ago. . . ."

Her voice drifts to a stop. "He never mentioned it to you?" she asks, already knowing the answer.

"What was your name again?" the lieutenant is asking as Joanne replaces the receiver.

Chapter 11

"THIS is delicious, Joanne. Thank you."

Brian Stanley, looking five pounds slimmer and ten years older than the last time Joanne was here, smiles at her from across his kitchen table. He is finishing the last of a fresh raspberry pie that Joanne has prepared this afternoon and brought over.

"Just what you need," Eve says coolly. "Cholesterol."

"I used whole wheat flour in the crust," Joanne tells them. "And only half the sugar the recipe calls for. . . ."

"Aren't you the considerate one?" Eve asks sarcastically.

"Cut it out, Eve," Brian says flatly.

"Oh, the big, tough cop act. I love it. Don't you, Joanne?"

Joanne stares at her friend, scarcely recognizing the woman she has known and loved for most of her life. Like Brian, Eve has lost weight, and the angular features, once so attractive, are now pointed and severe. The red hair and the green eyes have lost their former, natural vitality. Eve looks as harsh and as mean as she sounds. The trusted friend has become a stranger.

"Did you have any more tests this week?" Joanne asks, forcing the words out of her mouth.

"Did I have any more tests this week?" Eve repeats cruelly. "What do you care? You're too busy these days with your own doctor to worry about me."

"I called several times this week. Your mother said you didn't want to speak to me."

"Why should I? All I ever hear from you is that I'm crazy."

"I never said you were crazy."

"You say it every time you open your mouth," Eve states, then bursts into tears. "Lord, I hate this!" She struggles to regain her composure.

"Cry, Eve," Joanne urges. "Let it out. It's good for you."

"How do you know what's good for me?" Eve demands. "Why do you want to watch me break down? Do you enjoy it?"

"Of course not. It hurts me to see you like this. I only want to help you." Joanne's hand reaches out to her friend; she rests her fingers gently on Eve's arm.

"Do you know what Brian did, Joanne?" Eve asks, her voice suddenly that of a child. "He sent my mother away. Yesterday. He made her go home."

"The woman was falling apart," Brian starts to explain.

"*I'm* the one who's falling apart!"

Joanne shakes her head. "I don't know what to tell you—"

"Tell her that if she goes to enough doctors, she's bound to find a few who are willing to tell her what she wants to hear," Brian states flatly, rising from the table. "A surgeon likes to operate. That's what he's there for! You have a pain in your groin, fine. We'll give you a hysterectomy. You're experiencing a shortness of breath? Well, who needs two lungs anyway?"

"Shut up, Brian," Eve orders. "You're being a fool."

"Eve, take it easy," Joanne cautions.

"Why did you come here?" Eve demands suddenly. "Isn't Saturday your day to visit your grandfather?"

"I was there this afternoon." Joanne lowers her head. "He was asleep. He didn't wake up."

"That's what I'm so afraid of," Eve whispers. "I'm afraid that if I close my eyes and go to sleep, I'll never wake up again."

"Of course you'll wake up."

"I don't want to die, Joanne."

"You're not going to die."

"Then what's the matter with me? Why can't anybody tell me what's the matter with me?"

"Because nothing's the matter, damn it!" Brian shouts.

"Brian . . ." Joanne begins.

"No, Joanne. Stop coddling her. She manipulates you, her mother, me, everybody who cares about her."

"You don't care about me!" Eve screams.

"Shut up!" Brian rages, advancing toward his wife, his fists clenched. The next instant is a blur: Brian's fist unclenching, his open hand extending into the air, catching the side of Eve's face, her red hair spilling across her cheek, her body tottering off the side of her chair into Joanne's arms.

"Brian, stop it!" Joanne screams, struggling to steady Eve's chair so that it doesn't fall over, her eyes registering fear and disbelief at the violence she has witnessed.

Brian's hands remain poised in midair. He sways back and forth unsteadily. For an instant Joanne wonders if he is going to faint, but he only looks around him questioningly before wordlessly fleeing the room.

Joanne turns back to her friend.

Eve is staring at her with undisguised hatred. "Go home," she says.

JOANNE is in her kitchen when she hears the knock on the door. She has been sitting at the wooden table for almost an hour, not moving, witnessing the same scene over and over in her mind.

The persistent knocking continues, followed by a ringing of the bell. Joanne forces herself out of the chair and over to the intercom. "Who is it?" she asks.

"It's Brian Stanley, Joanne," comes the response.

She starts reluctantly toward the door. What does he want? What is there left to say? She stops. Why hasn't he spoken to Lieutenant Fox as he said he would? She opens the door.

Brian's large bulk fills the doorframe. "Can I come in?"

Joanne backs in to let him enter. He closes the door and follows her into the kitchen.

"Sit down," she offers. "Do you want some coffee?"

He takes a seat, shaking his head. "I'll be up all night as it is." He stares out the sliding glass door into the darkness. "I never hit a woman before," he says finally. "I didn't mean to hit her, Joanne. I don't know what happened. I just went blank." He lowers his head into his hands. "I *do* know I can't stand much more of this. I'm pretty close to cracking myself these days."

Joanne stands still, not speaking. Not knowing what to say.

"Maybe I should do what Eve says," Brian continues. "She wants me to leave. Maybe I should."

"You can't go. What would Eve do? How would she manage?"

Brian looks up, and she is startled by the look of hopelessness in his eyes. "Maybe I will have a cup of coffee, if you don't mind," he tells her. Joanne moves to the coffee machine, hoping that her face doesn't register the anger she feels toward him.

"Why didn't you ask your Lieutenant Fox to have a patrol car watch my house?" she demands suddenly, surprising them both.

"Joanne, what are you talking about? I did ask him."

"No you didn't. I've spoken to your Lieutenant Fox. He didn't know what I was talking about."

There is a long pause. "I couldn't," he finally admits.

"Why not?"

"Because I'm afraid," Brian mumbles, turning away from her.

The word is not one Joanne is expecting. "Afraid? Of what?"

There is another long pause. "Afraid that Eve might be the one who's been phoning you," he confesses.

Joanne says nothing. His words are only an echo of her own thoughts, after all. Until all the ramifications sink in. "You're not saying that you think that Eve might be the Suburban Strangler, are you?" she whispers incredulously.

He shakes his head vigorously. "No! But then I don't think that whoever's been phoning you is the killer. I don't think one thing has anything to do with the other." He smiles at Joanne sadly. "What can I say? I'm sorry, Joanne."

The phone rings.

"Do you want me to listen in?" Brian offers. "I'd recognize Eve's voice no matter how hard she tried to disguise it. You must have a phone in your bedroom," he continues, already on his way up. "Give me a minute before you answer it. Let it ring three more times. Pick it up after the third ring from now."

The ringing continues as Joanne hears Brian's footsteps overhead. At the end of the third ring she slowly reaches over and picks up the receiver, listening dully as the voice on the other end makes its terse announcement.

Brian hurries downstairs to her side. "I'm sorry, Joanne."

"It had to happen sooner or later," Joanne tells him. "He was ninety-five."

JOANNE LOOKS AROUND THE ROOM at the small collection of mourners. Counting herself, there are six people present. Her brother, Warren, and his wife, Gloria, are now sitting on either side of her. Directly behind her is her boss, Ron, and near him, Eve's mother. Across the aisle, on the other side of the small chapel, sits Paul. Eve is not here, being too sick; nor is Brian, being too busy. Joanne's daughters are not here either. There was no point in making the girls return from camp, she decided.

"It's so hard to believe he's really dead," Warren says, staring up at the coffin at the front of the chapel. "He was always such a strong man. I don't know if you remember him, Gloria. . . ."

"How could I forget him?" Gloria's husky voice fills the small room. "He was master of ceremonies at our wedding. I think he'd had a few drinks. He kept calling me Glynis."

"He always liked the name Glynis," Warren remarks, and suddenly both Warren and Joanne are laughing.

"Sounds like *my* grandfather," Ron Gold interjects, leaning forward to rest his elbows on the back of their bench. "He was quite senile by the time I got married. As my future wife and I were approaching the judge, my grandfather, who was sitting in the front row, yelled out, 'Who is that nice-looking young couple?' " He joins in the laughter.

Joanne's eyes steal over in Paul's direction. He sits alone, his posture indicative of an internal debate about whether to stay where he is or to join the rest of the small group. For an instant Joanne is tempted to make the decision for him, to walk over and lead him back to the others. Then she decides against it. The man has legs of his own. They have led him to exactly where he wants to be. Her eyes return to the front of the chapel.

The ceremony is brief. A psalm is recited; a few necessary words are spoken. It is over.

"I won't go to the cemetery," Eve's mother is saying.

"It was so thoughtful of you to come here," Joanne tells her.

Gloria touches Joanne's arm. "Are you ready?" she whispers.

"I'd like a few minutes alone with my grandfather," Joanne says, looking toward the coffin.

"We'll be outside," Warren tells her. Joanne watches as her

brother and his wife disappear up the aisle behind Paul and Ron, who exchange curt nods.

Slowly Joanne advances toward the front of the chapel.

Her grandfather's body lies inside the open plain pine box, dressed in a dark blue suit, the eyes closed, the cheeks slightly rouged. Joanne reaches into her purse and pulls out his crumpled baseball cap. "You've got to take a hat with you." She smiles, laying it gently on top of her grandfather's hands.

"That's better," she says, feeling her grandfather agree. She bends forward and kisses the kind old face. "I love you, Grampa," she whispers for the last time.

"I just wish we didn't have to rush off so quickly," Warren is saying as Gloria clears the kitchen table of dishes. They are all at Joanne's, drinking coffee and eating rhubarb pie.

"Don't be silly," Joanne tells her brother. "Of course you have to get back. You don't have to apologize."

"Why don't you come with us?" Gloria asks.

"I can't," Joanne answers quickly. "The girls will be home from camp soon. And I have a job." Joanne glances at Ron Gold, who looks instantly relieved.

"I'm lost without her, I swear." Ron laughs. "I mean, I'd like to be noble and all that, but I really need her."

Paul glares at the doctor. "I was under the impression that Joanne was leaving at the end of the month anyway," he says.

"I've decided to stay on," Joanne tells him, clearly catching him by surprise. She looks at her watch. "Warren, shouldn't you be leaving for the airport pretty soon?"

"I'd be happy to drive you there," Paul volunteers.

"All right," Warren agrees, glancing at his sister.

The small group proceeds to the front door. "Say hello to Eve for me," Warren says. "Tell her that I'm sorry I missed her, and that I hope she feels better soon."

"I will."

There is a pause during which no one seems sure of what to do with hands and feet. "Take care of yourself," Warren finally says, drawing his sister into his arms. "Call if you need anything. . . ."

She smiles as she pulls back. "I'll call."

"Good-bye, Joanne," Gloria says, hugging her sister-in-law.

Paul glances around the small hallway impatiently. "Ready?" he inquires, opening the front door. "Are you leaving now?" he asks Ron Gold casually as Warren and Gloria step outside.

"I think I'll stay around awhile and keep Joanne company."

Paul nods, the beginnings of a smile freezing on his lips. He looks at Joanne. "I think we should talk," he tells her.

"I think that's a good idea."

"Maybe I could drop over tonight."

"That would be fine."

He stands awkwardly in the doorway. "What time is good?"

Should I ask him for dinner? Joanne wonders, then decides that she doesn't feel like making dinner. "Eight thirty."

"See you then." Paul takes a final look at Ron Gold before following Warren and Gloria down the front steps.

"Your brother's a nice guy," Ron says. "I don't remember him from school at all."

"He was a few years behind us."

"I must say you surprised me today."

"How do you mean?"

"I thought you'd fall apart."

"How many times can you fall apart?" she asks. "Eventually you have to start to pull yourself together. Let's say I've started."

"I'm glad. Paul's dropping by later won't upset you?"

"It probably will," Joanne admits.

"Think you're up to coming back to work tomorrow?"

"Face it," Joanne deadpans. "Without me, you can't function."

"I knew that the minute you found my pen."

PAUL steps nervously into the front hall at just after eight thirty that night. "How are you?" he asks, following her into the living room, where Joanne quickly sits down in the swivel chair Paul has always staked out for himself. Has she done so deliberately? she wonders as Paul tries to make himself comfortable on the sofa. "The place looks good," he comments.

Joanne nods. "Would you like a drink?"

468

Paul is immediately on his feet. "Yes, as a matter of fact. Can I get you something?"

"No, thank you." She notices a certain hesitancy in his gait. He is aware of a subtle change here, and though everything looks the same, he has been thrown slightly off balance and feels unsure of where things are.

She hears him pouring himself a drink, feels his hesitation at the doorway before he reenters the room.

"It was nice to see Warren again," he says, sitting down and taking a sip from his glass.

"He looks good," Joanne agrees.

"It's too bad they had to rush off so quickly."

"Well, I'm a big girl now," Joanne says. "And I have a job."

Paul stares at his glass. "You're sure that it's a good idea, your continuing to work?"

"I'm very sure," she answers simply.

"It'll be difficult to hold a full-time job and run a household."

"So we'll eat out more, order in more, and the girls will have to learn to help out. I think it'll be good for them. I think it'll be good for me," she adds, her voice strong.

Paul finishes his drink. "You've changed," he says.

"You didn't leave me much choice."

Her answer clearly upsets him. "There's no need for you to work, Joanne. You know I'll support you."

"It's not the money," she says, then backtracks. "Well, no, that's not entirely true. I like earning my own money. It gives me some independence. I'm not saying that I don't expect you to contribute. My salary is no great shakes, and I have a house to look after. You have two daughters to support."

"You're talking as if I'm never coming back," he says quietly.

"Are you?" Joanne asks directly.

"I asked you to give me time."

"I've given you time," she says coolly. "Time's up."

"I don't understand. A week ago—"

"A week ago my husband and I made love, and I thought everything was all right again. I woke up to find nothing had changed, and as long as I'm prepared to put up with it, nothing will."

469

"Has Ron Gold had something to do with this sudden epiphany?" Pauls asks pointedly.

Joanne almost laughs at his choice of words. "Ron Gold is a lovely, generous man who gave me back a little of what I'd lost over the years, what I'd given away—my self-respect. For that, I will always love him and be grateful. But we're not having an affair, if that's what you're implying."

"Then why the sudden deadline? Why the rush?"

"It's been almost four months, Paul," she informs him. "I can't waste any more time waiting for you to decide. I have my own life to get on with. My grandfather told me that." Paul looks confused. "I went to see him after we came home from camp. I was very upset. I was complaining about all the awful things that were happening to me, when he suddenly opened his eyes and asked me if I'd like to change places. I realized that I didn't want to change places with a dying old man. I'm young—or at least I'm not old—and there's still lots that I want to do." She takes a deep breath. "I love you very much, Paul. I want you to come home. But I'm not prepared to wait anymore for you to come to your senses and see that I am worth a truckload of little Judys."

A look of surprise passes across Paul's face.

"And if you haven't discovered that for yourself by now, that's your problem. Not mine. Not anymore." She swallows hard. "The girls come home in about two weeks. We're either a family by then or we're not. I'll wait till then before calling a lawyer."

"Joanne . . ."

"I don't want to see you again, Paul," Joanne says steadily, "unless it's the sight of you pulling your suitcases up the front steps." She walks to the door. "Please go."

A LOUD knocking wakes her up just before seven the following morning. Confused, Joanne reaches for the alarm clock, which suddenly goes off in her hands. "Darn!" she exclaims, jolted instantly awake. Realizing someone is at the front door, she proceeds to the intercom on the bedroom wall. "Hello?" she asks, sleep still clinging to her voice. "Is someone there?"

There is no reply.

Joanne stands absolutely still in front of the intercom. She understands that the knocking was not part of any dream. She knows that there is someone downstairs, waiting for her.

With deliberate slowness she proceeds to her closet and throws on a robe. Her feet are bare against the carpet of the stairs. She reaches the front hallway, pressing her body against the heavy oak door to stare through the small peephole. She sees nothing. Carefully she reaches over to shut off the alarm, her fingers drawing back abruptly when she realizes that the alarm light is not on.

She has forgotten—again. "Way to go, Joanne!" she exclaims loudly, pulling open the front door.

It is lying at her feet beside the morning paper, large and black and eerily appropriate.

Joanne bends down and gingerly scoops the funeral wreath into her arms. She brings it into the house, slowly extricating the white envelope that has been wedged between the branches. She tears it open and pulls out the note inside. Across it is scrawled one word in large black letters: SOON.

Chapter 12

JOANNE is putting her house in order.

It is Saturday night. She has spent the day going from room to room, straightening up, deodorizing, reorganizing. For the last several hours she has been going through her daughters' rooms, throwing out papers they no longer need, sorting through their closets to see which clothes are too small or too worn-out to be used again. She is only trying to make things easier for them when they return from camp next week. It will be difficult enough to come home to the news that their mother is gone. Not that she intends to go anywhere without a fight.

Everything is in order now. The house is clean. There are fresh fall clothes hanging in the closets. The freezer is stacked with food. She is ready for September, though she is not sure that she will be around to enjoy it. Instinctively she understands that her tormentor will strike this week. Before her daughters come home.

Before neighbors who are away for the summer begin filtering back.

Joanne crosses the upstairs hall, heading directly for the bedside phone. Balancing herself on the edge of the king-size bed, she picks the receiver off its cradle and dials.

Surprisingly, Paul answers the phone on the first ring. "I was just thinking about you," he says.

When he doesn't elaborate, Joanne speaks. "I wanted to make sure about next week," she begins crisply. "That you'll pick the girls up at the bus station."

"A week today," he confirms. "One o'clock."

"You won't forget?" she presses.

"Joanne, is everything all right?"

"Everything's fine," she tells him. "I just wanted to make sure. Paul . . ." She stops. How can she tell him to take good care of the girls should something happen to her?

"Yes?"

"Don't be late," she says. "You know how upset they get when they're kept waiting." She says good-bye before he has the chance to ask anything more.

She has just made her way downstairs to the kitchen when the phone rings.

"Hello?" she says, picking it up.

The voice on the other end of the line is bordering on hysteria. "Joanne," it manages to spit out. "It's Eve's mother."

"Mrs. Cameron," Joanne says, concerned. "What's the matter? Has something happened to Eve?"

The words that follow proceed in short, staccato bursts, making them difficult for Joanne to follow.

"I don't know. I called to check on her and she started shouting, calling me names, screaming that I'm a witch, that I ruined her life, that she wishes I were dead."

"Mrs. Cameron, please try to calm down. I'm sure Eve doesn't mean those things. You *know* she doesn't mean them."

"I don't know anything anymore," the older woman sobs. "You had to hear her, Joanne. It didn't even sound like her."

"What can I do?" Joanne asks helplessly.

"Go to her, Joanne," Eve's mother tells her. "She's all alone. I told her that I'd come back, but she said she'd kill me if I tried to come near her. You're right next door. She'd never hurt you. Please make sure she's all right."

Joanne stares out the sliding glass door into the darkness. "Okay," she says after a slight pause. She is not sure she is up to Eve right now.

"Call me back," Eve's mother instructs.

Joanne hangs up and walks to the sliding glass door. She stands staring out at the night with no conscious plan in her mind. Slowly she unfastens both locks and slides the door open, the warm night air pulling her onto the porch.

She stares into the dark open pit that is most of her backyard. A perfect night for a swim, she thinks, making her way down the porch steps. She pictures herself gliding gracefully across the pool. If she survives the summer, she might even resume her tennis, she thinks, approaching the edge of the pool and searching for the tennis racket she threw away, unable to locate it.

It's quiet. She hears only the familiar shuffling of leaves in the trees. She feels peaceful, even serene.

The sound of the phone ringing jolts Joanne abruptly back to the present. She pivots toward the sound, catching sight of Eve glaring down at her from her bedroom window next door.

Joanne runs quickly back up the stairs and inside, leaving the sliding door open behind her. "Hello?" she says into the phone.

"Did you speak to Eve?" the voice asks.

"I'm going to now, Mrs. Cameron. I'll call you later," Joanne states flatly, and hangs up. Then she dials the appropriate numbers, hearing Eve's phone ring six times before it is picked up. There is no sound on the other end.

"Eve?" Joanne asks. "Are you there?"

The voice that responds is remote, as if the call were long-distance. "What do you want?" it asks.

"I want to know what's going on," Joanne replies. "Your mother called. She was very upset."

"Just like the old days," the voice cackles.

"Are you alone?"

"Just me and my pains." Eve laughs, sounding like herself for the first time in the conversation. "Want to join us?"

"Do you *want* me to come over?" Joanne asks in return.

"I'm dying, Joanne," Eve suddenly cries.

"You're not dying."

"Yes I am!" Eve screams. "I'm dying and I can't get anybody to believe me."

"I'll come over."

"Hurry."

"I'm coming now." Joanne races toward the front door, almost forgetting her house keys, returns to the kitchen to fish them out of her purse, then, returning to the front door, is suddenly aware that she has left the sliding glass door in the kitchen open. She hurries back to lock it.

The phone rings as she is scurrying past it. Her hand shoots out automatically to pick it up.

"I'm leaving right now," Joanne promises quickly.

"Mrs. Hunter . . ." the voice begins, and Joanne feels her heart stop. "Did you like my flowers, Mrs. Hunter?"

Joanne squeezes the keys in her hand, feels them digging into her palm.

"I was sorry to hear about your grandfather," the voice continues. "Still, I bet you're glad. One less obligation to meet. Gives you more time to have fun."

"Who are you?" Joanne asks steadily.

"Well, now, if I told you that, it would spoil the surprise. And we wouldn't want to do that, would we? Especially since I'll be there so soon, and you'll be able to see for yourself. I'm coming for you, Mrs. Hunter."

"You're crazy."

The voice loses its teasing tone. "And you're dead." There is a second's pause before the soft lilt returns. "I'm coming for you, Linda," it repeats, capturing its former rhythm.

"Wait a minute. My name's not— You have the wrong—"

But the line has gone dead. Racing toward the front door, her keys firmly in her hand, she sets the alarm and rushes out of the house.

JOANNE CUTS ACROSS THE TWO front lawns, stealing a hurried glance down the street. There is a phone booth at the corner. From this distance, in the dark, it is impossible to make out whether or not someone is inside it.

I'm coming for you, Linda.

Just my luck, she thinks sardonically, running up Eve's front steps and knocking loudly at the door. I'm not the woman he really wants. The story of my life, she decides.

No one answers her knock.

"Eve!" she calls, pressing down on the bell and then knocking again. "Eve, it's me, Joanne. Let me in."

"I can't answer the door, Joanne," she hears faintly from inside the house.

"Why not?"

"I'll die if I answer the door."

And I'll die if you don't, Joanne thinks. "Eve, for God's sake, open the door!" she screams, and immediately the front door falls open. Joanne pushes her way roughly inside and slams it behind her. "What is this nonsense about dying if you answer the door?" she demands angrily.

"I'm so scared," Eve whines.

Joanne stares at her friend. Her hair is pinned back erratically from her gaunt face. Her cotton housecoat is stained.

"Of what?"

"I don't want to die, Joanne. Help me."

"Listen to me, Eve," Joanne begins as she puts her arms around Eve's shoulders. "You probably won't like what I'm going to say."

"Say it," Eve urges, surprisingly docile.

"You're having a nervous breakdown," Joanne tells her as gently as she can. "You're *not* dying."

"But I'm in pain! I know you don't even believe me about the pain."

"I do believe you."

"But you think that my mind is creating it."

"Yes," Joanne says frankly. "But let's say there is a physical source to your pain that all the doctors have missed. Eve, thousands of people suffer from chronic pain that doctors are unable to diagnose or treat. Ultimately these people have to make a choice. They can either make the pain the center of their lives, or they can ignore it, *get on* with their lives."

"That's very easy for you to say."

"No," Joanne argues. "It isn't. Because I've been going through the same sort of thing for the past few months."

"What are you talking about?"

Joanne hesitates. "The phone calls," she says finally.

It takes Eve a moment to understand Joanne's reference. "The phone calls," she repeats with disdain. "You're convinced you're the strangler's next victim, and *I'm* the one who's crazy?"

"All right," Joanne concedes. "Maybe I am crazy too. I don't know anymore. I think I'm getting these phone calls from someone who says he's going to kill me. He called me tonight, before I came over. He says he's coming soon."

Eve laughs out loud.

"The point is," Joanne continues, "that this has been going on for months now, and nobody believes me. I've done everything I can. I've informed the police, I've changed my phone number twice, I've installed an alarm system. So now I have a choice. I can either lock myself up in my house forever, or I can make the most of what's left of my life." She searches Eve's eyes for a glimmer of understanding. "I don't want to die," Joanne admits. "But certain things are beyond my control, and I guess part of being an adult is learning to accept that."

"Our situations aren't comparable," Eve informs her.

"I think they are."

"Who cares what you think?" Eve demands angrily, suddenly pushing past Joanne and running up the stairs.

"Eve!"

"Go home, Joanne."

"Let me help you," Joanne urges, following Eve up the stairs and into Brian's office. "What happened in here?"

Joanne stares in bafflement at the once tidy room, which now bears all the earmarks of a bungled burglary attempt. Books lie scattered across the floor; the chair behind the desk has been overturned. "What happened in here?" Joanne repeats in a whisper.

"Hurricane Eve," Eve tells her, and smiles, her hand reaching over and swiping at the few papers that are still clinging to the top of Brian's desk, sending them scattering to the floor.

"But why?"

"He said he was going to have me committed." Eve sneers, sitting down in the center of the mess. "They have no idea who it is, you know," she adds cryptically.

"Who? What are you talking about?" Joanne is already on her knees, gathering papers.

"The Suburban Strangler," Eve whispers, her voice a singsong. "They're completely stumped. I've been doing some reading. They say it could even be a woman." Her voice has an eerie, nasty undertone. "It could even be me." Eve smiles, obviously enjoying herself.

"Don't talk nonsense," Joanne says curtly.

"Why couldn't it be me?"

"Because I know you. Because I know that you couldn't hurt anyone except—" Joanne breaks off.

"What?" Eve asks quickly. "You stopped. Finish what you were going to say."

"You couldn't hurt anyone except yourself." Joanne lets the papers slide back onto the floor. "Eve, you had a miscarriage," she says quietly. "Something was wrong that was beyond your control. How long are you going to punish yourself for it?"

"For as long as you continue practicing psychiatry without a license," Eve quips humorlessly.

"Eve, do you understand what I'm trying to say? It wasn't your *fault* that you had a miscarriage."

"I know that."

"Do you?"

When Eve speaks, her voice is a low moan. "Any idiot can have a baby, Joanne. Why couldn't I?"

"Our mothers had it easier," Joanne whispers as Eve begins to sob. "They had rules to follow, roles to play. They . . . My God!"

"What's the matter?" Eve asks through her tears.

"Our mothers . . ."

"What about them?"

"My mother's name was Linda."

"Joanne, are you all right?"

Joanne is suddenly on her feet. "He called me Linda. It wasn't a mistake. He thinks that's my name. And why wouldn't he? It's the only name he ever heard my grandfather call me."

"What are you talking about?"

"It all makes sense. Where he got his information, how he knew everything. He was there listening to me pour my guts out every Saturday afternoon. Eve, I know who it is!"

"Joanne, you're scaring me."

"I have to use your phone." Joanne moves toward the desk.

"You can't use it!" Eve shrieks suddenly.

"Eve, I have to call the police."

"No! I know what you really want to do. You want to call the hospital. Brian put you up to this."

"No, Eve, I swear—"

"I want you to get out of here!"

"Eve, I know who's been threatening me. It's that boy from the nursing home. I have to call the police."

"No!" Eve is at Joanne's side, ripping the phone from her hands and hurling it across the room. "Get out of here," she shouts. "Get out of here before I kill you myself!"

"Eve, please—"

"Get out of here."

"Call Brian," Joanne begs, fleeing Eve's fists and rushing to the office door. "Please, tell him I know who's been phoning me, that I know who the killer is. Tell him to call me. . . ."

"Get out!" Eve scoops up a book from the floor. Joanne sees it hurtling toward her, but is unable to duck in time to escape the impact of the blow as it crashes into her back. Tears stinging her eyes, she races down the stairs, Eve still screaming behind her. Joanne reaches the door and escapes into the night.

Seconds later she is at her own front door, fumbling in her jeans for her keys. She hears something at her shoulder and spins quickly around. There is nothing there. Calm down, she says to herself. Your keys are here somewhere. They have to be here. Finally she locates them in her back pocket. "Thank goodness," she mutters, turning the key and pushing the door open, moving in one fluid motion to the alarm.

The alarm light is not on.

"Oh, no, not again," she moans. "How could I be so stupid?" She reaches over and presses the button that activates the system. Taking a deep breath, she heads for the phone. She dials 911.

After three rings the phone is answered. "Hello," Joanne starts. "I'd like a policeman—"

"You have reached police emergency," a voice begins.

"Yes, I'd like a—"

"This is a recording. All our lines are busy at present."

"Oh, no."

"If you need assistance, please hold on. Someone will take your call as soon as possible. If you wish a police car to come to your house, leave your name and address after the tone."

Joanne waits for the tone. Then, "Joanne Hunter," she says clearly, and gives her full address. "Please hurry," she adds, deciding to stay on the line in case someone human answers her cry for help.

Thirty minutes later she hears a car pull up in front of the house. She waits for the familiar sound of footsteps on the walk outside, for a loud knocking at the door, but she hears nothing except the unending stream of recorded music coming from the telephone receiver in her hand.

She transfers the phone from one hand to the other, her joints stiff from the strain of holding the phone against her ear. Slowly she raises her head, her eyes falling absently across the sliding glass door.

She sees him standing in the darkness, his face pressed against the glass, peering inside. Before she has time to think, to recognize the police uniform, she is screaming wildly.

At the same moment there is a loud banging at the front door. Joanne hangs up the phone and runs to the door. "Who is it?"

"Police," the voice curtly informs her. "We received a report of an emergency at this address."

"Yes, I phoned!" Joanne exclaims, about to open the door, remembering that the alarm is on, pressing the button to turn it off. The young, slender policeman looks nervously around.

"What's the problem?" he asks, moving into the kitchen. "May I?" He gestures toward his partner outside the sliding door.

Joanne watches him unlatch the side lock. "There's one at the bottom too," she informs him. In the next second his partner is standing beside him.

"I'm Officer Whitaker," the first policeman says. "And this is Officer Statler. What is the problem?"

"I know who the Suburban Strangler is," she announces, trying to ignore the look of skepticism that passes between the two men.

"This is police emergency, ma'am," Whitaker reminds her.

"And this *is* a police emergency," Joanne states vehemently.

"I see. Is this strangler here with you now?"

Joanne shakes her head. "No, but he called earlier. He said that he was coming."

"Nice of him to let you know," Officer Statler remarks, suppressing a grin.

"Listen, I am not some crackpot," Joanne tells them.

"Okay, okay," Officer Whitaker says, checking his notes for her name. "You reported a police emergency, Mrs. Hunter. Why don't you tell us what you think you know, and we'll do our best to follow up on it as soon as we can."

"As soon as you can? What does that mean?"

"Tell us what you think you know," he states again, and Joanne tries not to bridle at the implicit condescension of his words.

"He's been calling me for months," she says, "telling me that I'm next. . . ."

"You've reported these calls to the police?"

Joanne nods. "I didn't know who it was. The voice sounded familiar, but it was a very strange voice. Now I realize that he was mimicking his grandfather's voice—not exactly, of course, but that rasp that old people sometimes get."

"I'm not following."

"You see, every Saturday I visit my grandfather at a nursing home—or I did until he died about ten days ago—and every

Saturday this boy was there, visiting his grandfather. He was always with his mother, and usually it would look like he was sleeping, but I guess he was only pretending to be asleep. He was really listening. Listening to everything that I was telling my grandfather. That's how he knew that the girls would be away at camp, that my husband had left me—"

"You're divorced?" Officer Statler interrupts.

"Separated," Joanne tells him. "Anyway, it was only after Sam Hensley was transferred to my grandfather's room that I started getting the phone calls."

"Sam Hensley?" Officer Whitaker asks.

"Sam Hensley is the boy's grandfather. You see, everything falls into place. How he got my phone number, how he knew when I changed it. Our phone number was kept at my grandfather's bedside."

"The boy's name is Hensley?" Officer Statler asks.

"The old man's name is Hensley," Joanne corrects. "The boy's name is something different." She sees the image of the young man before her, but his features are blurred. She never really noticed what he looked like.

His mother is the easier of the two to remember. She has a voice that sticks in the memory. Alan, Joanne hears the woman call, summoning the reluctant boy away from the television in the visitors' lounge. "Alan," Joanne repeats aloud. "Alan something. . . . Alan Crosby!" she exclaims triumphantly. "That's it. Alan Crosby. He's about eighteen or nineteen. That's all I can remember about him."

"Thank you. We'll check this out," Officer Whitaker tells her.

"When?" Joanne demands.

"We'll get started on it right away," he says. "It's Saturday night, but we'll do what we can."

Joanne nods.

"Try not to worry, Mrs. Hunter," Officer Statler says as they go to the front door. "We picked up some guy last night we're pretty sure is our strangler, but if it'll help you sleep any easier, we'll drive by the house as often as we can tonight."

"I'd appreciate that."

Joanne shuts the door after them, double-locks it, and reactivates the alarm. "So," she says aloud. "It appears I'm safe after all." She flips off the hall light and makes her way up the stairs to her bedroom.

Chapter 13

JOANNE is exhausted. It has been a long day and a longer night. But the nightmare is almost over, she thinks as she undresses, tossing her clothes across the chair at the foot of her bed.

Sliding her bare feet across the thick carpet, she enters her bathroom and begins filling the tub. Her body is sore; her muscles ache. A hot bath will soothe her, help her sleep tonight.

Thoughts of Eve, of the police, of Alan Crosby crowd into her head. She doesn't want to think, she decides, pushing the thoughts rudely back out.

Joanne steps into the bathtub and shuts off the water. It is very hot. Perhaps a touch too hot, she tells herself as she lowers her body. She closes her eyes, stretching out her arms and legs. I could fall asleep right now, she thinks. Just drift off.

She hears a noise, feels her body instantly tense. Sitting up, Joanne waits to hear the noise again. But there is nothing, and after a few minutes she relaxes back against the white porcelain of the tub. The alarm is on; the Suburban Strangler has probably been identified; the police are keeping an eye on the house. The nightmare is over. Almost, she hears a little voice whisper. Don't close your eyes. Don't fall asleep.

She closes her eyes despite the silent admonition, but it is already too late. She is no longer alone in the tub. Eve has joined her, and the two officers, and Alan Crosby. They are crowding her out. Joanne opens her eyes and grabs the bar of soap, quickly sudsing herself and then rinsing the soap off and stepping out onto the floor.

Back in her room, Joanne pulls on an oversize T-shirt and is getting into bed when something makes her turn. Almost against her will, she finds that she is tiptoeing across the upstairs hall, peeking first into Robin's room and then Lulu's.

Passing by the top of the stairs, she decides to make a final check on the alarm. She remembers having turned it on after the police left, but she wants to be sure.

In the downstairs hall, the green light shines brightly from the small box on the wall, telling her that the alarm is on. She is safe. Proceeding next into her dining room, she stares out the front window at the street, is further reassured when she sees a police car drive by, slowing down to take a good look at her house.

Joanne is tired, so tired that her head is beginning to throb. She goes upstairs. Climbing between the bedsheets, she immediately lets her eyes shut. Don't close your eyes, the little voice warns. Don't fall asleep. "Go away," she tells it impatiently, falling asleep almost before her head reaches the pillow.

JOANNE is playing cards with her grandfather.

He is winning, which does not surprise her. What does surprise her is the number of people who are gathered inside his room at the Baycrest Nursing Home to watch them play. Her mother's eyes watch her from beneath Eve's startling red hair. Lulu's arms reach out to her from Robin's shoulders. Her father's full-throated laugh emanates from Paul's open mouth.

Go away, she tells them silently. I can't concentrate when you're so busy moving around. Stay still or go away. Instead, the strange audience remains; the cards disappear. She finds herself in a soundproof booth. Her grandfather, an aging master of ceremonies, is asking her a question. But the sound in the booth is faulty. How can she answer the question when she can't hear it?

We're rooting for you, her mother enunciates clearly, though Joanne cannot hear the words. She nods, but she is worried. She doesn't want to disappoint her mother. All her friends are here; she doesn't want to let them down.

You can't disappoint us, her father says clearly, and then the sound is gone. We love you, he mouths silently.

We should go now, Eve says. Let you concentrate.

I love you, Paul tells her.

And then they are gone. She is alone. The sound in the booth crackles ominously, as if the booth has been electrified.

Are you . . . your question? her grandfather asks, his voice fading in and out.

I can't hear you. Joanne gesticulates wildly.

When is . . . date . . . start of . . . ?

I'm sorry, I can't hear you. I don't know the question.

Joanne feels the stirrings of panic in her chest, knows that her glass booth has become an airless prison. She wants to get out. But she must answer the question correctly before they will release her. She is in a room full of strangers, whose faces blend into their surroundings. Her breath catching in her throat, she sees that she is in a room full of Alan Crosbys.

The glass booth is not a prison, she realizes in sudden desperation as she watches it disappear. It is what has been keeping her alive. Now she stands unprotected in a room full of killers.

What is the date of the start of the Boer War? their collective voices taunt her, their bodies drawing closer.

I don't know, Joanne pleads.

Sure you do, the voices insist. Just ask Lulu. She told us she'd never forget it.

What are you talking about?

"Linda . . ."

We were there when you told your grandfather.

"Linda . . ."

We know the combination to your alarm.

Suddenly Eve's voice pierces through the others. I'm dying, Joanne, she cries. Help me!

I'll be right there, Joanne calls to her, pushing through the tight circle of Alan Crosbys into her front hall. She pauses for an instant to press the numbers on her alarm system before racing out the door.

I turned on the alarm. . . .

I turned it on when I left to go over to Eve's, but it was off when I came back.

"Linda . . ."

I turned it on. Someone turned it off.

He's in the house. He's been here all along.

Joanne bolts upright in bed, her eyes open wide in terror.

"Linda . . ."

The voice fills the room.

"Linda . . ."

Joanne's eyes move to the intercom on her bedroom wall. She is not asleep; she is wide awake. The voice she has been hearing is not part of any dream. The voice is real. It is part of her nightmare. And it is real.

Alan Crosby is in the house.

"Wake up, Linda," the voice sings eerily, like a child. "I'm coming to get you."

Joanne feels her hands start to tremble, her body start to shake. She feels sick to her stomach. Where is he? What room is he speaking from? Where can she hide? Where can she run?

"Linda . . . I know you're awake now. I can feel it. I can feel your fear. I'm coming."

He must have taken her keys from her purse and returned them after he'd had copies made. Why hadn't she thought to put it all together?

"Ready or not, Linda, here I come."

Joanne looks around wildly as total silence suddenly surrounds her. The voice is gone. The house is completely still except for the sound of her own shallow breathing. Somewhere in the house he is moving. He is coming for her.

Joanne scrambles to her feet. She grabs at the phone and tears at the three digits that will connect her to police emergency.

"You have reached police emergency," the familiar taped message informs her. "This is a recording. All our lines are busy—"

Joanne hears a click. A different voice comes on the line. "Can I help you, Linda?" it asks, less human than the tape. Joanne drops the receiver, too terrified to move.

I can lock myself in the bathroom, she thinks, then immediately decides against it. A simple bobby pin is all it takes to open the lock. Her only hope is to get outside the house.

Perhaps the police are circling the block. She checks the time. It is after two o'clock. Are they still out there? Where is Alan Crosby? Still by the phone in the kitchen, or has he sneaked upstairs?

She continues holding her breath, listening for the slightest sound, hearing nothing. She looks frantically around the bedroom. What can she use to defend herself? A hanger? A shoe?

Her eyes return to the phone. Well, why not? she thinks, pulling the cord from the wall, brandishing the phone in front of her.

Slowly she moves toward her bedroom door.

Her eyes stare down the upstairs hallway through the darkness, seeing nothing. Is he hiding in Lulu's room? In Robin's? Was he there, under a bed, when she checked their rooms earlier? Joanne inches down the stairs. She is on the last step. If she can only get to the front door . . .

She sees the movement before she hears the sound, hears his piercing scream before she hears her own, feels his hands reaching for her throat. In a panic she drops the phone she has been carrying to defend herself, feeling its weight crash close beside her, hearing another sharp cry, this time of pain, escape his mouth, feeling his hands retreat. Everything is happening so fast that she is halfway out the door before she realizes that she has dropped the phone on his foot.

And then she is outside, screaming again, racing down her front steps.

She sees Eve peering at her from the window of her small bedroom. "Eve!" she cries, running across the grass toward the house next door, watching as Eve disappears from view. "Open the door!" She stops midway between the two houses, waiting for Eve to open her door, turning her head to catch Alan Crosby smiling sickly at her from beneath the front-porch light. He is holding something in his hand. As she watches, a long silver blade snaps menacingly into view.

Move! her inner voice commands, and instantly she obeys, her bare feet carrying her through the lane between the two houses into her backyard. Now what? she screams silently, staring into the empty pool. My grave, she thinks, racing toward the shallow end and tripping down the three steps into the empty pool.

There is no moon and few stars. Maybe he won't see me. Maybe he won't see the hole. Maybe he'll fall in and break his neck!

Sure, she thinks immediately, hearing the loud pounding of her heart against her chest. As if he hasn't carefully gone over every inch of my backyard. Of the whole house! Why hasn't the alarm rung? Because he turned it off, of course.

Her fingers tracing the sides of the pool, Joanne creeps toward the deep end. She hears him. He is moving across the flagstones. Joanne lowers her chin into her chest, trying to muffle the sound of her breathing. She feels the concrete, rough against the backs of her bare legs.

"Linda . . ."

The voice twists through the darkness like a snake through grass. He is somewhere across from where she is crouching. It is possible that he hasn't seen her. Perhaps he is hoping that his voice will frighten her into betraying her hiding place. It is important that she stay very still.

"Linda . . ." the voice calls again, this time closer.

Where are the police? Officers Whitaker and Statler? They said they'd keep an eye on her house. But that was hours ago. They're probably in bed by now, long since sound asleep.

There is a slight movement above her head, which Joanne realizes a second too late is a hand moving toward her. Instantly her hair is scooped into a tight ball, the force of his arm lifting her to her feet. She twists her head back to see a knife flashing through the air. A horrifying shriek escapes her lungs as the knife slices across the top of her hair.

"Cowboys and Indians!" the boy whoops as Joanne trips over her feet to the other side of the pool's deep end.

"Leave me alone," she yells.

"I'm not finished with you yet." He waits to see which way she will move.

"The police will be here."

"Not unless they're mind readers," he says confidently. "Come on, I want to show you that good time I promised you."

Joanne starts inching along the side of the pool back toward the shallow end, toward the steps.

He moves with her. "That's a girl," he says. "Come to Papa."

She watches in horror as Alan Crosby leaps easily into the

shallow end after her, opening and closing his knife blade.

In a mad scramble Joanne dashes toward the steps, feeling something slam against her shins, causing her to lose her balance. She stumbles, feeling her body crumple. Her fingers curl into the strings of her tennis racket as her hand reflexively reaches out to block her fall. She scoops up the racket and scrambles up the steps. Hostile hands behind her grab hold of her T-shirt.

She struggles to free herself, but the boy's grip on her T-shirt is solid. Again she hears the ominous click of the switchblade.

"You promised me a good time," she suddenly snaps, catching them both by surprise with the vehemence in her voice. "I am *not* having a good time!"

What am I talking about? Joanne wonders, feeling his grip relax and taking advantage of the confusion of the moment to propel herself out of his reach.

She tries to run away from the poolside, but he is only inches behind her. Once more she feels him at her back, hears the knife swishing through the space between them. The blade slices through her T-shirt. "No!" she cries defiantly, her left hand joining her right on the handle of her tennis racket. Watching herself as she spins around, Joanne Hunter bends her knees, her back foot planted firmly on the ground, and, starting low, swings the racket full force, up and through.

Chapter 14

JOANNE hears the car pull up as she is finishing her morning coffee. Putting down her cup, she waits for the doorbell to ring. She shoots the intercom a nasty look, walks briskly to the door, and peers through the peephole.

"Hi," she says, pulling open the door.

"Hi," he says in return, and husband and wife stare awkwardly at each other. "Can I come in?"

Joanne says nothing, simply moves aside so Paul can enter.

"I tried to reach you," he says wearily. "As soon as I heard what happened, I called. . . . I came over. Eve's mother finally told me that you'd gone to California."

"I needed a few days away," Joanne explains. "I'm sorry. I should have phoned you. I wasn't thinking too clearly. Everything happened so fast." She looks around distractedly. "It's not every day I almost kill someone," she says quietly.

"Couldn't have happened to a nicer guy. That's quite a swing you've got," Paul jokes. "I understand that he broke his arm and leg when he fell into the pool. I guess it was a good thing that it wasn't filled, after all."

"Things have a way of working out." Joanne smiles.

Paul sits down at the kitchen table in what was traditionally his seat. Joanne pulls out the chair across from him and wonders why he is here. The girls' bus is due in from camp in less than an hour.

"I feel so guilty," he says at last.

Joanne shrugs, saying nothing. What is there to say?

"I should have been here," he continues, unprompted. "None of this would have happened if I'd been here."

"That's not so," Joanne tells him. "Those women that the Suburban Strangler murdered had husbands around to protect them. They died anyway; I didn't. Maybe the fact that I had only myself to depend on is what saved my life. I don't know. Anyway, it's over now, and I'm okay."

Paul looks at Joanne with more than a trace of surprise. "You shouldn't have had to go through it," he says quietly.

"No, I shouldn't have," Joanne agrees. Her head pivots toward the pool. She sees the darkness, feels the knife slice through her T-shirt, hears the swoosh of her tennis racket as it crashes against the boy's head, watches as he plummets into the concrete hole. "I'd like to sell the house," she announces evenly.

"I can understand that," Paul tells her.

She is grateful that he doesn't feel the need for a discussion. "Find something without a pool," she adds.

"Agreed," he says easily. "How was California?"

Joanne laughs. "Actually, it was kind of quiet."

"How's your brother?"

"Good. He's trying to convince me to move there."

"Are you considering it?" Paul asks, his shoulders arching stiffly, though his voice remains steady.

"Not really. It would mean uprooting the girls, putting them into new schools. Besides, I have my job."

"Still planning to keep working?"

"Yes."

Paul's shoulders relax. "I think that's a good idea."

"I thought I'd take the girls with me to the office sometime soon," Joanne tells him. "Show them where I work."

"I think they'd enjoy that."

"I think it's important that they see their mother as more than a doormat with a welcome sign across her back."

"I'm sure that's not how they see you."

"How could they see me any other way?" Joanne asks. "I submerged myself in everybody else's expectations, and I disappeared. I'm not blaming you," she adds quickly. "It wasn't your fault. You didn't do it to me. I did it. Somewhere along the way, I forgot how to be me. I don't blame you for leaving, I really don't. How can you live with a shadow?"

"I wasn't any great shakes myself."

"Well, at least you were honest."

"Honest, nothing!" Paul exclaims. "I was self-indulgent and stupid. I mean, what did I think I was going to get out there? Adventure? Youth?" He laughs bitterly. "There's nothing sadder than a middle-aged man trying to find his lost youth. So what if I'm not Clarence Darrow? I'm still a damn good lawyer. And I've finally discovered there's really nothing else I want to be."

He stares at her, waiting for her to speak, but Joanne says nothing, simply returning his steady gaze.

He is the first to break away, looking toward the doorway. "How's Eve?" he asks, seeking safer ground.

"She's in the hospital. She agreed to let Brian take her. I think what happened that night finally shook a little sense into her. She's the one who called the police, you know, got hold of Brian, made sure they finally got here."

"Some summer."

"It hasn't exactly been a summer I'd care to repeat," Joanne admits, running a hand across her head. "He gave me a punk haircut." She laughs. "Think the girls will like it?"

"Why don't you ask them when we pick them up?" he suggests.

"I don't think that would be a good idea," Joanne answers slowly, finding the words difficult to speak.

"Why not?" Paul asks.

"Because I think that if they see us together, they'll get their hopes up, and then we'd have to let them down again."

"Would we?"

Joanne stares at her husband. "What are you trying to say?"

There is a slight pause. "That I'd like to come home," he says.

"Why?"

The question is startling in its simplicity. "Because I love you," he answers. "Because I realized in the four months that I've been gone that there's nothing out there—"

"There's everything out there," Joanne interrupts quietly.

Paul smiles sadly.

Joanne stares out the sliding glass door. "So much has happened. So much has changed. I've changed."

"I like the changes."

"That's the problem." Joanne turns back to confront him. "I won't always have a psychotic killer around to bring out the best in me!"

They are suddenly both laughing.

"We should get going," Joanne says finally.

"There's something I have to do first," Paul tells her, walking steadily to the front door. Following behind him, Joanne watches as he heads down the front stairs to his car, quickly extricating two suitcases from the back seat.

Smiling confidently, Joanne watches as her husband of twenty years pulls his suitcases up the front steps.

Fans of the television show *Gunsmoke* might remember Joy Fielding as the mute pioneer girl who regains her voice, thanks to Marshal Dillon, in one memorable episode. That was about the extent of Miss Fielding's acting career in Hollywood, shortly after she graduated from college in 1966. "The directors kept telling me my looks were 'very special,' which basically meant I was unemployable," she says. "I wound up working in a lot of banks to support myself."

Joy Fielding

But while trying her hand in Hollywood, Miss Fielding was sending long, heartfelt letters to her mother in Toronto, Canada, the author's birthplace. And her mother was sending letters back urging her daughter to come home. In time she took that advice and returned to pursue her first professional love—writing.

Joy Fielding honed her storytelling skills on television scripts, eventually selling several to the Canadian Broadcasting Corporation. She then turned to novels, and *The Deep End* is her seventh book. Its contrast between domestic life and sudden, stark terror is one of the author's favorite themes.

"Things aren't always what they seem," Miss Fielding explains. "You never really know what's going on in a life, or where the danger lies. I also wanted to express my concerns about middle age. All those things came together in the character of Joanne."

Joy Fielding is married to a Toronto lawyer and has two small daughters. This is the first year both girls have been at school all day, leaving the author free to write for uninterrupted hours. How does being a best-selling author affect family life? "Actually," she says, "if you want to stay at home with your children, writing is the best profession."

Cry Wild

A condensation of the novel by
R. D. LAWRENCE

Illustrated by Ken Laager

In the remote forests of northern Canada a wolf cub named Silverfeet is born. As the seasons pass, he grows to maturity, learning of the pleasures and dangers of his wilderness world. Then, one hot July, a fire rages through the forest, driving Silverfeet and his pack far to the south—to country inhabited by man. There, an even deadlier danger lies in store, for a trapper sees in the wolf a rare opportunity for his own financial gain. . . .

A gripping novel that sheds new light on one of nature's most misunderstood animals.

APPOINTMENT CARD

IDENTIFICATION NO.

(10)

NAME AND ADDRESS OF VA STATION

VETERAN'S NAME AND ADDRESS

Rosati, David

(9989)

NOTE: An appointment has been made for you as indicated. If you unable to keep this appointment, please call the number listed here at least 24 hours before the date and time specified.

TELEPHONE NO.

EXTENSION NO.

DATE	TIME	SERVICE	INITIALS
10/30	11:00	~~(scratched out)~~	
11/5	11:00	Wound care	
11/12	11:00		

VA FORM
DEC 1990 **2502**

SHOW THIS CARD TO RECEPTIONIST
WHEN REPORTING AND LEAVING

Change
Dressings
Every 3 days

1

GRAYNESS enveloped the land. Writhing clouds—leaden, and tortured by swellings of moisture—hovered threateningly over the evergreen forest. On winter-sered earth a covering of hard snow shone dull white, creating a mood of chill foreboding that matched the frowning sky.

It was afternoon. The gloom was a heavy thing that shrouded spruce and balsam, opaquing their green and forming dense, shapeless shadows within the private places of their branch coverings. No bird trilled gladness on this day. No squirrel called. Instead, there was silence and cold and the white threat of snow clouds awaiting their time to burst.

On a flat table of land grew a mature balsam, a mighty tree of thick girth and spreading, brittle limbs that shaded its plot of earth and deprived other green life of the right to grow there. Within the conical spread of the balsam's lower limbs was a cavern of space, a natural tent that surrounded the leathery trunk.

Inside this shelter lay a she-wolf, curled nose to tail in fitful slumber. She was thin, this huntress of the forest, and aging, and her gray hair was matted and in places rubbed down to short bristles, exposing patches of dark skin. Her meager flanks rose and fell in time with her lethargic breathing. Now and again a whimper escaped through her black nostrils, for she was dreaming of the hunt and of sleek, lazy days when meat was plentiful and her belly round.

The wolf had not eaten for three days, and four previous days of hunger had sapped the coil-spring energy from her lithe body. Her meal three days ago had not been much: a thin portion of hare, which she had stolen from a spitting bobcat. The wolf had smelled the kill and the killer from half a mile away. Normally she would have changed course, leaving the cat to enjoy its spoils, but this was famine time in the forest, and her gnawing vitals had driven her toward the food.

In a small clearing ringed by spruce trees the tomcat was devouring fresh meat. It was noon and late for a kill, but hunger drove hunters away from instinctive habits.

The wolf paused on the edge of the clearing, left forefoot arrested in the act of setting pad to snow crust. Her broad head with its long, sensitive muzzle was held high; the black nose, dry and cracked, siphoned the aroma of newly dead hare and the musky odor of angry cat. The wolf's black-lined lips curled, revealing the long, gleaming canines that flanked the white chisels of her cutting teeth. A savage noise leaped from her throat.

The cat stopped eating. A hastily gulped mouthful rippled down his throat, and with an answering growl, short and piercing, he attempted to drive the wolf away. But she needed the remains of the hare, and she advanced, teeth bared, eyes fixed on the enemy.

Instinct warned the wolf to avoid the chunky carnivore that stood, back arched, just paces away. But hunger drove her onward. She moved closer and snarled more loudly.

The arch formed by the spine of the bobcat became more pronounced. The round head dropped closer to the ground; short, tufted ears flattened against the skull. Now the right foreleg was raised, and the claws of the cat's big paw showed black beneath the fur and the flesh of the pads. Closer came the wolf.

The cat's growls increased in pitch and tempo, and a hissing, spitting sound came from the opened mouth. The yellow eyes were slitted, and there was great fury in the gaze. Closer yet came the wolf.

Now the cat moved. Holding his humpbacked pose, he backed away from the hare, walking cautiously on stiff legs, wailing his banshee rage but giving ground. Closer came the wolf.

The cat broke. A last, earsplitting wail of frustrated fury erupted from his throat and seemed to hang over the clearing even after the snub-tailed cat had disappeared into the underbrush.

The wolf gazed an instant at the place where the cat had vanished; then she turned to the hare. Its remains were soon gone. The portion had been small, but this feeding promised yet one more respite from death.

Three more days of hunger came. In her white world the wolf searched without finding, while her last stores of strength left her. She loped slowly, stopping to hunt among the branches of the evergreens for signs of grouse. But there seemed to be no life in the wilderness, and at last she sought shelter under the great balsam fir and curled her miseries around herself and slept.

This was December, a lean month made wicked by the stab of frosts that nightly drove temperatures down to forty degrees below zero. The wolf had met this kind of month before, and she had met too the months that preceded it—when scarlet leaves were plucked early from their branches; when the birds pointed south and the berries withered on their stalks; and when the snowshoe hare changed his coat from brown to white four weeks before his time, then seemed to disappear off the face of the frozen earth. And the wolf knew that when the snowshoe hare goes, famine is near, for the big hare is life to the forest hunters.

So, before the famine began, the wolf had led her pack toward the south, away from the knifing cold. And her pack followed, content, as usual, to let her show the way. Had she not always led well and found meat? Seven wolves made up the pack: her mate, a big, rawboned dog two years younger than she; a two-year-old male who had somehow become unattached and had joined the pack rather than wander alone through the forest; and the four pups that had been born to her last May and were now half grown. She had led them south that autumn, to a domain she had never before visited. And that was her mistake.

They had broken out of the forest early one morning in late

November and saw before them a land still green, a new kind of land, of few trees and much grass. And grazing on the grass was a flock of sheep, a new kind of animal to her.

The wolf was unsure at first. She stopped, sat and tested the wind. The odor of the creatures in the clearing was strong, almost acrid in its intensity. Her alert senses told her that the slow-moving things before her would be easy to kill. These were stupid creatures, or why did they continue to pull at the grass in the presence of her pack? There was no sign of alarm among the sheep. No noticeable leader, no nervous, restless buck to stop his grazing and look around, ears straining for signs of danger. The wolf wondered why, and something within her cried a warning.

Not so her mate. The big dog looked at the she-wolf, his manner urging her to rise from her haunches and lead the pack in the hunt. But when she remained sitting, undecided, he waited no more. Only some seventy yards separated the wolves from their quarry, and the dog was not disposed to caution. An excited yelp left his throat as he flung his body into a fast lope.

The others followed him—all except the leader. She stayed where she was, watching the pack converge on the flock, which even then showed no alarm. The adult male wolf was the first to strike. A ewe lifted her head, and now there was panic in the sheep eyes. But too late did she bleat fear and begin to run. The wolf charged her, knocking her down with his massive weight, and before the sheep's kicking legs moved twice through the air his fangs sank into her throat and the life was torn from her.

The sight of the kill and the smell of the blood drove the other wolves to frenzy. They slew nine sheep as the rest of the flock was scattered over the meadow, their bleats of panic creating bedlam in the stillness.

The wolves settled to their feast, but still the leader sat on the edge of the clearing. She quivered with hunger and an almost irresistible urge for the meat that lay waiting on the grass. But another emotion had gripped her, something stronger than her desire for food. This was fear—stark and vivid and primordial. And it held her back.

She was still there when the men came and the guns exploded

and her pack rolled in agony beside the mutilated sheep. All except the two-year-old wolf. He ran, dodging the bullets and the men who raced after him in a roaring, rattling machine, and he led them away from the leader.

She slunk back into the forest and turned toward the north woods, in her ears the clamor of the men and their machine. The wolf galloped now, setting her long legs to a fast pace and attaining a speed of twenty-five miles an hour. She ran thus for more than an hour, then slowed to the mile-consuming lope that she could maintain for many hours, running straight north. Twice a white-tailed deer fled from her path, and once a silver fox sprang up almost from under her pads; yet despite her hunger she ran on, concerned only with finding the sanctuary of the deep woods.

When the wolf at last stopped, it was not yet dark, but long shadows filled the bushland. Where the wolf now stood, flanks heaving, mouth agape, was heavy forest, wild and tangled, clustered with jack pine and tamarack and birch. She sought a hidden place in which to restore herself after her great run. A downed pine, interlaced with creeper and brush, offered her shelter and concealment, and she crawled under it, circling three times in the age-old ritual of smoothing the chosen bedding place.

In torpid slumber the biting in her empty vitals fled. Snow came that night, a light sprinkling of white that coated the forest, but she slept unaware until the coming of a sickly dawn.

As THE morning brightened, the she-wolf awoke and stood, shaking the snow from her body and stretching the stiffness from her muscles. Head held high, she smelled the air: the scent of cold, the aroma of the pines. Suddenly there was the strong smell of grouse, a subtle, hunger-reviving odor that instantly alerted her hunting senses.

The wolf stood tall and still, sniffing, separating the one odor from the rest, probing for its source. It came from the northeast and told her many things. There was distance yet between her and the grouse; and there were several birds, three perhaps, judging by the subtle differences in each aroma. The wolf set out, letting her nostrils guide her, carefully seeking the cover of pine and brush. Slowly she advanced toward her quarry, noting with each step the increased flavor of its smell.

The scent led her through heavy forest, up a slight incline and down into a shallow valley. Here the odor was strong. The wolf stopped; her nose probed, discovering that there were now four slightly different smells, which told her that there were four grouse in the valley.

The wolf crouched low. She set out again, bellying her way down the slope, keeping her dark body hidden behind whatever cover she could find. Some time ticked by, and then the wolf knew that she must stop and find her quarry with her eyes. The smell now was so strong that one of the birds must be within leaping distance. Her body blended with the forest floor in almost lifeless immobility; her eyes searched with painstaking purpose, scanning every twig, every mound of snow, every shadow and log. Thus she discovered the grouse.

It was a cockbird, brown and sturdy and plump, and it sat in the lee of a young pine. It faced away from the wolf, engrossed in the antics of three hens, which, out of sight of the wolf, were scratching at the snow, seeking frost-nipped cranberries that had fallen from a high bush. The wolf inched forward, first stretching her body to its full, then moving slowly, silently, until the powerful springing muscles were coiled and the feet and legs braced and quivering beneath bunched haunches.

The wolf's stalk was soundless, yet something, perhaps the deeply rooted instinct of self-preservation, alerted the grouse. He sat higher and whistled softly. The hens took up the warning sound and began pacing, their necks held forward, low to the ground, their stubby tails stiff, their crests erect. The cock rose and imitated his mates. Still peeping, hoping that their call would cause the danger to show itself, they high-stepped through the underbrush, and all the birds were revealed to the waiting wolf. She could restrain herself no longer. As she leaped for the cockbird, the grouse exploded in all directions, their stubby wings beating a drumroll as they rose from the ground.

The wolf touched ground and launched herself again, this time jumping mightily, her mouth reaching for the swiftly winging shape of the cockbird. The flashing teeth found flesh and closed upon it. The wolf's feet touched the snow anew, and the grouse hung limp in her jaws, dead. The she-wolf settled to her kill.

Afterward she slept, and life melted from the forest that housed her, for the smell of death clung to the wolf. The beasts and birds sought sanctuary elsewhere; they sensed that the wolf, made harmless by slumber, would soon awake and hunt again, for one grouse, though plump, is not enough to sate a wolf.

And when the wolf did awaken, she raised herself and pointed to the sky, and her long, tremulous howl floated free. The despair in her voice sailed away. In her mind was the remembrance of the day before, of the terror of man. There was remembrance also of her pack, and there was loneliness. She needed her own kind around her, and she was driven to seek solace in new company.

The wolf rose to all fours and stretched her body, scenting the forest for new prey. But there was nothing; and so she moved from her bedding ground and geared her legs to a steady lope, the hunting pace fast enough to carry her away from this now empty forest, but slow enough to allow time for her nose and her ears and her eyes to search for prey. Four days later she stole the hare from the bobcat.

For three more days the wolf pressed ever north and west, seeking the dense wilderness; and during this time not once did she sense another living creature. Now she stopped. A glance at her surroundings was enough to tell her that she was still alone, and she whined a little before she allowed her head to hang, mouth agape, while her labored lungs pumped and pumped again.

It was early afternoon, and there hung over the wilderness the certainty of snow. The wolf knew it, and she sought shelter, ignoring her hunger and her weakness. She pushed her body into motion again, this time pumping her legs faster as she fled through the forest. She ran for another half hour and then stopped, for her quick eyes had spotted the tall balsam.

Within this matted sanctuary she smoothed her bed and curled her body and closed her eyes in sleep. And the wind came and the hovering clouds burst and the flakes of white fell upon the wilderness and shrouded the wolf in her bower.

ALL AFTERNOON THE SNOW FELL, drifting in open places, packing into the brush and into the branches of the trees. Only the howl of the wind could be heard, for even the movement of the tree branches went unnoticed before the storm's wrath. And then, suddenly, the wind stilled. Now there was silence—the intense, cold silence of a storm-freed northern wilderness.

The clouds were spent. They trundled about the sky, and as they slipped away, strong light began to reach the bushland, and the treetops became tinted with the glow of the setting sun.

Under the balsam, the she-wolf slept on. The red of sunset was gradually replaced by the blue of twilight, which in turn ran before the advancing dark. The forest was a ghostly place of outlines, and the opaque bulk of trees and brush blended into vague, gargantuan shapes. Time passed. Stars shone, each sparkling with the shine of living fire.

The sleeping wolf twitched to wakefulness and shrugged the covering of snow from her body. She rose and stretched; then she sat on her haunches, ears upright, nostrils testing for scent, eyes scanning the forest. She shook herself again and stepped away from the balsam. The snow reached to her chest, so she had to bound to travel through it, and in her state of weakness this called for almost more strength than she could muster. But the wolf refused to die. On she went, a slow, labored progress. Often she stopped for breath, and often she paused to scan the forest in the hope of discovering prey.

In this manner the night faded and a paleness arose in the sky. The snow grew harder, for the forest was more open, and it furnished footing for the big feet of the wolf. But now and then she would break through the snow crust, and great effort was required to scramble out and regain the surface. Afterward she would sit and rest, mouth open, thin flanks pulsing with the fast rhythm of her gasping breath. Death came a little closer to the wolf that morning.

Then she smelled food, and at once she changed. The listless eyes glinted; she was a huntress again. The creature was a porcupine; the wolf knew this by its smell. Another time she would have passed by this bristly beast, but today she had no choice.

She must face those deadly sharp quills if she was to survive.

The porcupine was only yards in front of the wolf, vainly trying to reach the sanctuary of a tall balsam. The wolf snarled low but clear, and the quilled pig stopped its struggle with the snow. Now it would remain at bay; it knew that it could not outdistance the wolf, that its only hope of survival lay in its sharp defenses.

The porcupine hunched, a dark figure atop the hard-packed snow. Plentiful among its long winter hairs were the pale yellow quills with black needle tips, each one erect. The stubby tail, where the heavier quills were, was already sweeping back and forth; the small round head was buried between the stiff forelegs; the shoe-button eyes were alert, watching the enemy's advance.

Now the wolf was within feet of the porcupine. She tried to outflank her prey, and at once the porcupine swiveled on its front legs, keeping its menacing tail before the wolf. She turned, moving in; again the porcupine swiveled and the wolf backed off. The two settled to their deadly battle.

They were like duelists, feinting, dodging, the wolf seeking to reach the porcupine's defenseless head, the porcupine intent always on presenting its formidable tail to the enemy. If the wolf should once be able to grasp the round, quill-free nose, the porcupine would die; if the porcupine could but smash its bristling tail into the wolf's face, the wolf would most likely die. The prize for each combatant was life.

One hour passed. The wolf was tiring, and her elusive quarry seemed as fresh as ever. Twice the armored tail of the porcupine brushed the wolf's muzzle, and she retreated to wipe at the soreness with a paw; the quills were not firmly embedded and they came away, leaving droplets of crimson and a sting of fire. It seemed that the fight had reached an impasse, but the weakened wolf would not give up. Instead, she redoubled her charges, increased her speed; and now the porcupine's actions were not as sure, its turns not as swift.

Suddenly the wolf leaped right over the crouching porcupine. But instead of hurtling into the deep snow, she twisted in midair and landed just inches from the coveted place; in another instant her flashing jaws had secured a good grip on the porcupine's head. Now she started moving backward, dragging the thrashing porcupine and tightening her grip on the head. The porcupine fought, but the wolf kept pulling back, back. . . .

At last it was over. The powerful jaws of the wolf did their work, and the porcupine died.

The wolf relaxed her hold and moved back a step. She examined her right forefoot, which showed the ivory yellow of three quills firmly embedded between two toes. Lowering her gleaming teeth to her paw, she pulled out the quills one at a time, gripping each firmly with her cutting teeth.

Half an hour later some fifteen pounds of fresh meat and bone filled the wolf's shriveled belly, and the time of want, the specter of death, the tired, aching body, were but vague memories. The wolf licked herself clean and then sought a place to sleep. Tonight she would travel again, refreshed, strong.

2

THERE was stillness, and moonlight, and a thousand shadows and as many reflections, for the forest in this place was broken by the oblong of a wilderness lake. And there was snow, sparkling in the moonlight like a scattering of sequins.

It was February, a bitter month to some animals of the northland, a time of snow crusts that cut sharp hoofs with their knife-edges. A time of great cold, of hunger, and of death. Yet also a time of life, for many forest creatures breed during this month.

It was such a month for the wolf. She sat this night on an outcrop of granite, her eyes fixed on the snowbound lake. Now and then she whined, for she was made restless by the mating urge. Wolves are sociable creatures and she had been alone all winter. The wolf raised her broad head, pointed her muzzle at the sky and cried her anguish to the night. Her call was deep and throaty, a clear sound, long and low, yet it carried far: *a-woo* . . . *a-woo* . . . *a-woo* . . . *wooooooo.*

For perhaps one minute there was silence, then an answer reached her. It was faint, for it had traveled across more than a mile of forest. She raised her head and launched her call anew.

More silence, again an answer, and this time it was stronger. Now the wolf rose and bounded into the forest, heading west to intercept the male who had answered her call. She knew he would be running east to meet her.

Both animals were silent now. Each had located the other; there was no more need to howl. Instinct drove them unerringly toward their trysting place.

The wolf smiled as she ran. Her eyes softened; her lips were parted wide, revealing her gleaming teeth. There was friendship and eagerness in the eyes. This was the wolf smile, a physical sign denoting happiness as clearly as the widest human grin. She ran on, seemingly oblivious of all, yet vibrantly alive to the sights and sounds of the forest.

It was a place of almost pure darkness now. Countless spruce trees conspired to shut out the moonlight. In this place the white-tailed deer found shelter from winter storms; and here too wolves sought the deer, while ruffed grouse and spruce grouse flew in explosive bursts among the tightly packed tree trunks. Red squirrels lived in the trees, their woven nests anchored securely to high branches. The gray jays called often with their many voices of mimicry, and sought to steal the seeds that the squirrels husbanded.

In this sanctuary, the wolf met her mate.

He was a young male seeking to breed this season for the first time. He was brash and eager and had much to learn. He measured three feet at the shoulder, and he was beautiful. His sleek coat was charcoal black, lightly laced with gray. He ran with careless abandon—grinning, his ears forward, his neck outstretched, his handsome tail trailing like a black plume.

The she-wolf and the male heard each other's movements while still separated by a quarter of a mile of forest. Minutes later they saw each other, and both stopped. The male whined and advanced a few steps, his head held to one side, his nostrils busy with the new scent. The she-wolf held her head high, her ears flattened, the smile on her mouth tinged with warning. She wanted time to inspect this youngster. The dog advanced a few more steps, and when he stopped, he bowed, sliding his forelegs along the snow. His whine of excitement was higher; his body quivered with emotion. He bounded sideways suddenly, chased his tail for three revolutions, then bowed again as the she-wolf moved forward, stopped and copied his antics. In this ancient ritual of greeting, their wariness was now replaced by open affection.

They stood shoulder to shoulder, still as statues. One moment, two, then the she-wolf moved. Swiftly she nipped the male's shoulder, rose on her hind legs and leaped over him to go racing through the trees. He gave chase, and the snow flew as they ran madly. As quickly as she moved, she stopped and turned to face the oncoming male. He stopped half a length away. Both bowed, the she-wolf to the right, the male to the left, and the she-wolf nipped him again, but it was a coy invitation. Again they stood side by side but facing opposite directions, tails wagging rapidly. The dog lowered his head and scented her. And she turned toward the dog, quiescent.

Then occurred the ritual of creation, as natural as the wilderness, as ancient as the beginning of time.

MARCH replaced February, and there were nights of intense cold and high, screaming winds. The wilderness creatures sought shelter within the embrace of tangled spruces and balsams. There they lay quietly in their beds of snow, the solitary ones huddled in tight balls, the companionable ones seeking warmth from each other's bodies.

In a dense patch of balsams the she-wolf and her mate had scooped a den within the bower of a downed tree. Each slept, curled nose to tail, empty of belly but content. This storm had lasted three days and there had been no food during that time, but the two healthy wolves were unconcerned. Their range held abundant game, and the two knew that they would satisfy their hunger with a change in the weather.

New life was already stirring inside the female. Soft jerking movements pulsed her sides when the unborn litter became restless. And each time they wriggled she felt content, the hardships of winter blotted out by the comfort of the young inside her.

Around the two, the wind was losing some of its power—the

trees trembled less, the loose snow drifted more freely. In the east a vague glow showed fleetingly above the treetops. Slowly the wild north wind tired, blew less fiercely and at last was still. Now nothing moved. The land was as a thing dead, a contoured map of white and dark in the intense stillness of predawn.

The wolves stirred in unison. They uncurled stiffly, breaking the caked layer of snow that cloaked their bodies. They rose and shook, and showers of white flew from them. The male licked the she-wolf's muzzle; it was a caress, a love greeting. She bowed and pranced a little, her eyes alive with excitement. Her mate whined and dived at her, and the two flayed through the snow in play. But as quickly as their game began it stopped and the two stood immobile. Then the she-wolf walked slowly south, leading her mate on the hunt. Gone now was the playfulness.

Before them the forest was a place of fading black, gripped by the quiet of this new day. Both animals moved with a long-legged lope that appeared slow yet covered ground at a goodly speed. The she-wolf led, and carried her head high, and her nostrils constantly tested the air. For fifteen minutes they continued, their big pads supporting them easily on the frozen snow crust.

Suddenly the she-wolf stopped, and instantly her mate emulated her. Both wolves probed the air, their ears pricked. Then the she-wolf turned east, toward the glow of the sun. She galloped, her mate following, the snow flying behind their kicking feet.

Somewhere ahead, not far, there were at least three deer. And as the wolves ran, their keen senses detected sudden movement, and they knew that their own scent and the noise of their passage had alarmed their prey. The hunters threw their great bodies into a powerful gallop that could be sustained for hours.

The chase led through thick forest. The she-wolf turned her head and looked full at her mate. The dog understood her signal. He changed course, leaving her to run at the heels of the quarry while he pointed northeast, redoubling his stride and quickly disappearing into the forest. The she-wolf barked, a high-pitched yelping sound, which she repeated often to panic the fleeing deer.

She gradually changed direction, angling southeast, herding the quarry toward her mate, who was by now almost ready to intercept the animals. The deer began to swing slightly to the north, unaware of the trap that had been laid. The she-wolf yelped louder and ran faster, driving the deer harder, crowding more panic into their minds.

So the chase continued, the fleeing deer wearing down their strength as they plunged through the deep snow. The sun rose, and daylight aided the hunters. Now and then the female caught sight of a kicking hoof or a waving white tail. Now too she could see the carmine of blood staining the snow of the trail, evidence that the ice crusts were taking their toll on the deer.

More than an hour passed. For the last thirty minutes the male had been sitting atop a small knoll, waiting for the quarry. He had followed his mate's progress attentively and knew that she was succeeding in her intent. It was only a question of time, so he waited patiently. Then, suddenly, he tensed with excitement and rose to all fours. The quarry was close, very close. He moved forward to intercept, fresh from his rest. The hunt was his now.

The male wolf and the deer sighted each other simultaneously. The wolf bunched his tough body for the final effort; the deer— three of them—turned away in frantic haste. The wolf was a flashing ball of black fury. One of the deer was slower than the rest. Yard by yard the wolf gained, encouraged by the excited yelps of his mate, who, though lagging, was still in the chase. The leading deer sped on; the slow one stumbled once, righted herself and tried to outdistance the bared fangs that were only yards from her kicking legs. But relentlessly the wolf closed the gap, and now he was running beside the deer. His speeding legs moved just a little faster, and suddenly he lunged. The impact of his weight sent the doe crashing to the snow. In an instant the wolf was upon her, and the deer died quickly.

The hunters fed greedily and in silence, quickly chewing the meat. When the meal was over, they sat upright and washed their faces and chests.

The she-wolf yawned, a huge gape that ended in a sudden whine. The male wagged his tail at her and watched as she rose to go tumbling in the snow. She seemed young again, a yearling pup, as she rolled over and over, long legs kicking at the air. Her eyes beckoned her mate to share this snow bath. Soon he did. Afterward they shook the powdery white from themselves and trotted away, seeking a new den in which to pass the day.

Almost before the forest had hidden the wolves' shapes, two gray jays plummeted from the top of a spruce to the scene of the kill. They had been waiting for the king beasts to be done with their meal and their frolic. Now they came to peck at the carcass, jaunty and hungry, their dark beady eyes alert, making sure that some other hunter did not come along to make a meal out of *them*.

Suddenly the jays squawked in unison and sped upward, landing on the same branch that they had so recently left. They scolded the newcomer, a vixen fox who stepped lightly over a small dead spruce and sauntered toward the remains. Her nostrils had picked up the tantalizing scent from almost a quarter of a mile away. She had arrived while the wolves were eating, and had waited upwind. She had watched them finish their meal and begin to play, and she felt reassurance then, for she knew, as all wild creatures know, that when wolves have sated their hunger they will rarely attack again. The vixen was dainty as she crouched at the deer, her coat a chestnut glow in the sunlight.

Ten minutes later, while the fox was still eating, the gray jays flew down again. Like her, they knew that they were safe now. Five chickadees came also, perky little gymnasts of the forest, and the vixen let them be, for there was plenty for all. She was content, even though alone, because she, like the she-wolf, had young in her belly. Yet deep within her was a vague sadness, which caused her to turn her head frequently and scan the forest behind her, as though in expectation. She was unconsciously looking for her mate, the dead father of her unborn kits. The dog fox had stepped into a trap. It had fastened on his right hind leg and held him in agonizing frenzy while the vixen, powerless to help, had fled, her instincts telling her to take the unborn to safety.

This is perhaps the prime rule of the wilderness: the individual is expendable, but the species must be carefully guarded. Thus, the dog fox died (a trapper would get three dollars for his fur); but the pregnant vixen lived and would bear his young, so his kind would continue.

And now she was eating, and when she was done, she would seek sanctuary for the night. Later, when the snows began to melt, she would look for a den in which to birth her kits.

IT WAS a morning of clean skies and warming sun. Little streams of crystalline water made music as they tumbled from high places and sought to soak into the partly frozen earth. High in the blue above the forest, a wedge of Canada geese eased north, the high-pitched calling of the birds clearly audible below. The wilderness was quickly changing to the time of new life, for March was spent and April was vigorous.

The wolves watched the forest from a place midway up the slope of a sandy knoll. The early sun found reflection in their yellow eyes and danced gleaming on the white of their teeth. Visages that were ferocious during the hunt were now smiling and relaxed. The eyes were bright, alert; the mouths were open, the black lips parted in wolfish grins, the whole combining to belie the devilish reputation that these great beasts have acquired.

The she-wolf yawned. Her mate turned and nudged her with his muzzle, then licked her face. She caressed his muzzle with her pink, moist tongue before she allowed her body to sprawl full length on the sun-warmed grass. The male sat up straight upon his haunches, ears forward, his gaze fixed on some point in the forest. The she-wolf slept, snoring slightly.

The two had found this place a short time before. The female had approved of the location: it afforded a commanding view of the forest, and digging was easy in the sandy loam. At once she had set about remodeling this disused fox burrow for the raising of their litter. Now the male was free to roam at will, sometimes hunting, often just exploring, etching upon his mind the places where hare were plentiful, the watering stops of the deer, the small meadows where the mice lived, the beaver houses, the muskrat lodges. He sometimes ranged far, into new country, and on such occasions he might be gone for two or three days, while his mate worked on her burrow and now and then went on short hunting trips of her own.

The male was always solicitous and gentle with his mate. He

never came home without bringing her meat from a kill. At times he might carry home a groundhog. The she-wolf would eat this while he watched her, and after she had finished she would lick her chops clean and nuzzle into his thick neck, burying her nose in his heavy mane.

When the she-wolf grew big with her young, she became testy, snarling at her mate if he showed curiosity over her burrow. It was to be her domain until the pups were whelped and at least two or three weeks old. The male was patient with her moods and conscientious in his work as a provider. His mate did not go hungry now that her time was near, and if occasionally he felt impatience, if he found himself sometimes longing for her romping companionship, he did not show his feelings.

3

WHEN Silverfeet was pushed from his mother's womb onto the bare earth floor of the wolf den, the sun of late April was rimming the western horizon. One spear of rosy red light found its way into the burrow. It tinged the inner gloom with a suffused glow that revealed shapes of four little wolves and the bulk of their fierce mother.

Silverfeet whimpered, not understanding the newness that surrounded him. He was blind and wet, but he found comfort in the soft, moist tongue that glided smoothly over his short puppy hair. And there was promise in the sweet smell of milk that already trickled from his mother's dugs.

The she-wolf lay on her side, her body curled around her litter, and her heart was full of great love for her young. She nuzzled them gently, pushing them to the comfort of her nipples. One at a time the little wolves glued their blind faces to her, first a light gray female, then a black female, then a stubby, brindled male pup, and finally Silverfeet, the last born but the biggest of the four. As the young nursed, the mother lay placid, her shaggy head hanging over her offspring, her yellow eyes etched in shiny relief by the dying sunlight of the day.

Outside, the father stood guard. He had not left his post for two hours, even when a squirrel scrambled down a nearby tree and sat just above his head, churring and squeaking spite at the great hunter below. He merely raised his eyes once and stared at the cheeky mite, who immediately scuttled higher up the tree. The big wolf was ready to kill any creature that threatened the safety of his mate and her young.

A MILE south of the wolf den the red vixen had also given birth. There were seven kits in the rock cave that she had found at the base of a low escarpment. They were ten days old when Silverfeet came into the world.

They were alone in the cave next morning, for the vixen had gone hunting. She had not eaten meat for three days and the suckling young had taken strength from her body. She was hungry, but she made herself travel with caution, appeasing the urgings of her belly with an occasional mouthful of spring grass.

As the vixen prowled, the world into which her cubs had been born awoke to newness and life. It was a big, busy world—a place of great trees, of bushes and grasses, of flowers and rocks and water. The wolf pups and the fox kits would have to study them as actively as children in a schoolroom but with more pressing need, for few mistakes are tolerated by the wilderness, and those who are slow to master the lessons of life die quickly.

Suddenly the vixen had a scent strong and sweet in her nose. She stopped, her red body flattened, her ears pricked forward and her nose twitching. Somewhere ahead, hidden behind a rise in the land, was a groundhog. She moved forward with renewed stealth, and as she neared the hillock the grizzled torpedo shape of her quarry scampered over the rise.

The surprise was mutual. Both animals stopped instantly. The groundhog realized his danger and turned to escape, but the vixen flashed forward and closed her fangs on the groundhog's short neck, clamping down hard and shaking at the same time. Both animals lost their footing and rolled down the hillock, the groundhog emitting strangled squeaks of fear. Suddenly it was over; the groundhog was dead.

The fox settled to eat. Presently she picked up the ground-

hog's remains and turned toward her den, taking it to her cubs.

Halfway there she froze, then pushed her supple form beneath a deadfall spruce. She had heard and scented the male wolf as he hunted. The wolf passed some distance from the fox, but she remained immobile until she was sure he was gone.

THE she-wolf licked her pups while they fed lustily with little grunts of pleasure.

In size and in looks, the pups resembled the young of a large domestic dog. Though their heads and faces were wolfish, their bodies were not. The long legs, handsome brush and big feet of the wolf had not yet developed.

After a while the she-wolf pricked her ears forward, then rose quickly and stood by the den mouth. Her mate was coming home; she could hear him, and by the slowness of his coming she knew he was carrying fresh meat. When he emerged from the forest, her nose told her that he'd brought deer, even before her eyes saw the haunch clamped between his jaws.

The she-wolf drooled, her front legs spread wide, her hind-quarters raised slightly, so that she appeared to be bowing. Her tail wagged and she whined; the sound was both a greeting and a reflection of her hunger. Her mate trotted toward her, eyes smiling, tail wagging, every move showing the pride of the hunter bringing home food after a hard chase.

The male deposited the deer meat in front of his mate, who bent her head to smell it, then lifted her head again to lick the male affectionately. Then she ate.

The male, meantime, was sated; and he was tired. He sprawled by the den opening, his ears cocked toward the feeble sounds of his offspring. The little wolves were crawling aimlessly around the nesting chamber, now and then chewing at each other's ears in the habit of many young animals.

In the sky, the sun bathed the forest with new light and warmth; in his tree overlooking the den sat the peaceful, sleepy-eyed squirrel. On this April day around the den there was beauty, there was savagery, there was wilderness, there was love, there was young life. A butterfly floated down and landed on one of the scraps left by the she-wolf. A bird settled on a shrub and sang, the echoes of its melodious voice adding gladness to the scene.

The male wolf yawned, stretching wide his cavernous mouth. His mate looked at him; he smiled. Then she arose and bellied her way into the den to lie with her pups. The four cubs suckled until, one by one, they fell asleep.

Silverfeet was the last to finish—he was always the last. He seemed always to be hungry, but perhaps that was because he was the most active—exploring, crawling, poking into this corner or that. Several times already his mother had had to drag him back from the den entrance. But today Silverfeet was lazy, and after taking his fill, he found his favorite spot between the she-wolf's thighs. There, with his blunt little head hanging over one of her legs, he snored gently.

SILVERFEET was eleven days old when his eyes began to open. The cubs were alone in the den that afternoon, for the she-wolf had gone on a hunt with her mate, forced by hunger to leave the young ones. Wolves hunt together in packs, for survival. The male and his mate, before the coming of the pups, had made an efficient, if small, hunting unit, but the male alone could not hope to provide enough big game for the cubs. So the two had paired again and gone to hunt, leaving the cubs unguarded.

Silverfeet and his brother and sisters made small dog noises as they huddled together. Silverfeet had one of his black sister's ears clamped firmly in his mouth, and he was sucking it, comforting himself as a human baby might do with his thumb. At first, when the gummy lids of his right eye separated just a crack, exposing the eye to the sunlight that slanted into the den, panic seized him, and he tried to bury his head beneath the squirming bodies of the others. Then his second eyelid parted a little, chasing away more darkness. Fear was overcome by curiosity. Silverfeet withdrew his head from the bundle of living fur and blinked owlishly toward the cave mouth. The strong light hurt his eyes and he turned away, but slowly the pain of the light became less and less, until at last it left him altogether. For the first time he could see, though dimly.

That afternoon all the pups gained their vision. Until then they had been guided by their ears and by their noses. Now they discerned each other for the first time, and they recognized the smells and sounds of the den with their eyes. And if it frightened them at first, it held new promise.

The four rose to unsteady legs and peered at one another. They were small and feeble, and their muscles would not coordinate properly, but the light drew them. Silverfeet was the first to make for it—slowly, wobbling, but determined to reach the daylight that beckoned. The others followed. All of them inched toward the outside on their short, rubbery legs, ignorant of the dangers lurking there.

Finally they were at the den entrance. Silverfeet stopped abruptly, dazzled by the sun. The others huddled around him, small, scared and excited. Silverfeet's chubby little body was toppled forward by the combined weight of the others. He rolled a little way outside, then scrambled slowly to his feet. He moved two steps forward, paused and peered back at the others to see what they were doing. The small gray female was moving, following Silverfeet; the black female was sprawled flat on her belly; the brindled little male was still framed by the darkness of the burrow, but he too was beginning to follow.

At last the four cubs were outside. They again huddled together, fear beginning to crowd their senses. They were so small and so unsure, and this new green world was so big. Silverfeet felt the urge to return to the safe dimness of the den, but he did not know which way to go. Instead of retracing his steps, he moved farther away from it. His siblings came after him, a ragged little group that traveled inches at a time. Some instinct warned Silverfeet that he was going in the wrong direction. Perhaps the smell of the den became weaker; perhaps fear sharpened his senses. He stopped and the others stopped. They sat undecided.

The squirrel that lived near the den had been watching the young wolves. Squatting lazily on his nesting branch, he suddenly sat upright and riveted his gaze on a thicket of scrubland a quarter of a mile from the den. His keen ears had caught a heavy sound coming from the brush area, and suddenly he chittered his alarm cry. He churred for perhaps half a minute, then bolted up the tree and disappeared into his hole. The cubs heard the squirrel's noise, but they did not know it signaled danger.

Silverfeet had succeeded now in pointing himself in the right direction. Wobbling, he was slowly making his way toward the den mouth. His sisters were following, but his brother had lost his bearings and was wandering farther away.

From the direction of the scrub patch a piglike grunt disturbed the stillness of the afternoon. On its heels came the crackling of brush, and the shaggy bulk of a black bear emerged into view. He paused now and then to snuffle at something on the ground. Once he stopped at a dead log; with two slow smashes of his powerful forepaws he tore it to pieces and stooped to lick up the ants from within the rotting wood. When he had lapped up the last scurrying ant, he ambled up the hill. Suddenly he stopped. The scent of the wolf den had penetrated his nostrils. He knew that smell and he knew that he could expect to find some young; these would be delicate mouthfuls for the still winter-hungry bear. But he knew also the savagery of timber wolves when protecting their young, and so he paused, working his nostrils and flicking his ears, trying to locate the adults.

A few yards farther on he smelled the cubs. He squinted, trying with his poor vision to locate their whereabouts, at the same time deciding that the parent wolves were not nearby. He quickened his steps, and the scent of the pups guided him toward the feebly moving shape of the brindled male.

Returning home from a successful deer hunt, the parent wolves had picked up the bear's scent. Now they raced toward the den in their fastest gallop, jumping deadfalls and smashing through brush to get to their pups ahead of the marauding bear.

They burst out of the forest just as the black bear seized the brindled cub. The bear stood on all fours, facing the den entrance and eyeing the remaining pups. The little male was entirely hidden within his great jaws. He bit down, and the life was crushed from the brindled body. At this moment two furious, savage things unleashed themselves on the bear.

With flashing fangs the wolves smashed into him from either side. The female seized the animal's left hind leg; the male sank his teeth into the hairy right flank. The bear whirled, shaking off both wolves. He dropped the body of the pup. The wolves attacked again, their growls of rage mingled with the bear's roar of surprise. The bear rushed the male, trying to clasp him in his strong arms and crush him to death. The she-wolf struck him hard in the shoulder, knocking him off his feet. The male wolf hit again and slashed a furrow in one of the bear's ears.

The bear was nimble. Quickly he regained his balance and charged the she-wolf. She retreated, and the male bore in from the other side. Slowly the two wolves were easing the bear away from the cubs. The fight was fierce, and the noise of it filled the forest with fear. The three remaining pups, meanwhile, lay as though frozen.

The bear was trying to gallop away, but each time he was met by one of the charging wolves. Again and again they bit him. Step by step, yard by yard, they drew him away from the den, until at last they were down the slope and close to the brush out of which the intruder had come. The male wolf had a wound on his right shoulder, where one of the bear's claws had raked him. The bear was bleeding from several superficial bites, but his matted hair made him almost impervious to the fangs of the wolves.

The wolves paused, and the bear took advantage of the moment to wheel and charge into the heavy brush. The male pursued him. The she-wolf hesitated, the mother instinct conquering her desire for vengeance. She climbed the slope to her pups.

She went first to the three, and smelled them and licked them, noting that they were unharmed. She turned to the dead cub then, licked it all over and nuzzled it as though urging it to move. Then she whined and licked her baby again. Carefully she opened her mouth and picked up the small body. She entered the den and deposited the dead pup there. In a moment she was back outside, and one by one she carried her other pups to safety. She lay down with them, and Silverfeet and his sisters suckled from her. The dead pup lay on his back near her front paws; she nuzzled him and pushed him toward her dugs.

The male wolf had no desire now to attack the bear, but he kept chasing him, pushing him out of the wolves' territory. They ran in this fashion for about two miles. At last the male stopped. The bear kept traveling, grotesquely agile, looking like a moving black ball as he disappeared over a hilltop. The male listened a few moments, and when he could hear the bear no more, he turned and raced for home.

When the male arrived back at the den, his mate greeted him at the entrance. She whined and licked at the blood on his shoulder, cleaning the wound. He caressed her muzzle with his tongue. They stood silent for a time, until the she-wolf whined again. They both felt a great uneasiness, for their den had been discovered, their pups attacked. They would have to move.

In the she-wolf's memory was a place that she had inspected before she had found her present home. This first location was a hollow under the bell-like root of a fallen balsam tree that had at one time served as a fox den. To this place she would eventually move her young, but not tonight.

She left her mate at the den mouth, entered the cave and again lay with her pups. The dog, tired after his fight, flopped down in front of the burrow. His senses remained on edge, and for some time he sniffed the wind. Eventually, when no disturbing scent came to him, he let his head slump on one of his paws, closed his eyes and slept.

Inside, the mother wolf was licking the body of her dead pup. Silverfeet and his sisters had nursed and were sleeping, curled up against her belly fur. She had the dead cub between her forepaws and was nuzzling it and moving it from one side to the other. An occasional soft whimper told of her distress.

Outside, the sun was sinking. The animals and birds of the forest were strangely silent. The fury of the fight had cast a spell on the area—a spell that would last until a new day came to break it.

NEXT morning the other creatures had recovered from the death of the previous day. But not the wolves. Both adults were still uneasy, especially the she-wolf. Twice the male went to enter the den chamber. Each time he was driven away by his mate, her savage growls a warning, for during her time of distress she made no distinctions. She was there to guard her young— even against her mate.

The male accepted her anger. As yet the tiny brood awoke in him little more than an instinct of protection. But his den had been ravaged; this kind of memory lasts in the wilderness.

The male ambled away to the scene of yesterday's deer kill. There he fed, and when he had finished, he carried a partly gnawed haunch to the den. Outside the den mouth he whined once and dropped the meat, then retreated a few steps. Presently the she-wolf emerged, looked her mate full in the eyes, picked up the meat and disappeared into the burrow. The dog curled into a ball, his coloring blending into the shade cast by the squirrel's tree. The sun of early May was benign, and it warmed the wolf, filling him with a pleasant drowsiness. Soon he slept.

Morning gave way to midday. Inside the den the she-wolf awoke from her own sleep and yawned, then turned to her pups, who were cuddled to each other in a lupine bundle. She licked them and nosed them a little, but the young wolves were sleepy and did not respond. The mother tarried over her young for a moment before walking slowly to the entrance of the den. She looked outside at her sleeping mate; instantly his eyes opened wide. The male got up and moved closer to the den. Sitting by her, he too yawned and then stretched, and afterward nibbled gently at his mate's shoulder.

The female turned and reentered the den, and when she came out again, she carried Silverfeet, the small pup almost entirely hidden in her mouth. She had decided to move to new quarters. The male wolf would stay and guard the remaining pups while she carried the first to the new place.

In a little while the female was back, and this time when she emerged from the den, she carried the black pup. One by one the pups were taken to their new home, the male joining his mate on the last trip. Inside the abandoned den the body of the dead pup was left behind.

4

SCALY-BARKED jack pine dominated both sides of the wide ravine in which the wolves had made their new quarters, but in the ravine itself, cedars and balsams jostled for growing room, darkening the forest with their wide skirts. Here and there was an open, wet place holding a few shaggy alders and willows. Three-foot-tall fiddlehead ferns were everywhere, and beneath these, tiny forest creatures scurried fearfully in pursuit of their living.

The ancient root under which the she-wolf had fashioned a new home for her young belonged to a long-dead balsam that had been smashed out of the earth by a wild autumn wind. Its interlaced rootlets stretched their bony fingers upward, some still clutching clumps of dried earth. The once massive trunk was rotten and eroded by tunneling mice, insects and squirrels. All these, since the wolves had come, had either left the area or fallen prey to the fangs of the pups, who were now eight weeks old and full of boundless energy.

It was late June. The days were long and warm, and the nights pleasantly fresh and cool. But mosquitoes and blackflies were in full season, and the young wolves showed signs of bites on their noses and within their ears. With the stoic endurance of all wild creatures, the pups withstood the constant attacks of their tormentors, brushing them away with a paw, or twitching an ear or a muscle to shake off an unusually persistent pest.

The parent wolves left the pups alone often, now that they were old enough and fleet enough to escape the few dangers of the forest. There was need for meat to feed the family, for the female was weaning the pups. Occasionally she would allow them to nurse, but more and more she discouraged them, leaving them behind while she went with her mate on hunting trips.

Silverfeet now weighed seventeen pounds and was starting to look like a wolf. He had the outlines of his parents: the sharp, arrow-shaped ears, the slanted, amber-yellow eyes, the broad forehead and the long muzzle. He was a beautiful, lithe wild thing, young and playful, a healthy whelp who must always be on the move. He managed more often now to catch small creatures: mice, young hares, even insects.

Silverfeet's coat was dark gray, almost charcoal, peppered with lighter guard hairs, which gave him a grizzled look and set off his silver-white legs and feet. His black sister was considerably smaller but just as lively. She shone a glossy ebony in the sunlight, and the white splash on her chest was startling. Her eyes were as active and vigilant as her brother's and as full of mischief. But the small, light gray female was ailing. She was always the last to eat. Increasingly she lay down and refused to join her brother and sister in their joyful romps, her yellow eyes dull, her flanks pinched, her hair dry and brittle.

There are always more young born than the forest can sustain; and always some of these young are doomed. This is the way that nature keeps balance. Deadly bacteria called *Listeria* coursed through the little gray female's bloodstream, weakening her and making her feel more keenly the effects of the bloodsucking flies. Inertia, lack of appetite, and the disease within her would soon cause her death; but for now, the small female wolf slept languidly in the shade.

ONE MORNING EARLY, WHEN Silverfeet was exploring a small clearing some little distance from the den, the buzzing of powerful insect wings attracted his attention. His keen eyes, aided by his magnificent sense of hearing, soon located the flier, a giant, two-inch-long water bug winging its way from its customary pond in search of a mate. The big bug landed in a clump of grass a few yards away. The young wolf bounded over to it, reached down with open mouth and picked it up. Instantly he let it go and brushed at his lips with a paw, trying to appease the hurt that the water bug's stinger had inflicted. Silverfeet was nonplussed, but only for a moment. He pounced again, smashing with a powerful paw at the heavy brown body. He again opened his mouth and seized the insect, his sharp teeth piercing the chitinous armor. But its taste was unpleasant and he spat it out.

Silverfeet regarded his prey, cocking his head first to one side, then to the other. Eventually he decided that what could not be eaten should certainly be rolled on, especially when it tasted so bitter. He dropped on his side and rolled over and over on the insect, smearing his body with its tangy smell. His actions were instinctive, the unconscious need of the predator to mask his own scent with the odors of other things.

Now Silverfeet spotted movement in the grass ahead. He trotted to it and nosed a snake into the open. The harmless garter snake coiled and struck at its tormentor. Again and again the small serrated teeth of the reptile fastened feebly on the young wolf's nose, but Silverfeet just shook his head and the snake flew off, to be pounced on again. The game lasted several minutes and would have gone on longer had the black female not joined her brother. Between the two, each competing for the prize, the snake escaped, slithering under a small pile of rocks.

Next Silverfeet decided that a wrestling match with his sister would divert him. He eyed her speculatively for a moment, then charged, striking her roughly and bowling her off her feet. They rolled over and over, slashing playfully at each other with their razor teeth. Once Silverfeet clamped his teeth on one of his sister's ears; she squealed her pain, and the snarl that ended her cry contained anger. When Silverfeet let go, bounded to his feet and charged again, she was ready for him. She sprang right over him, and his rush ended in a tumble. The exercise and experience of infighting that the young wolves were now gaining would help them when they were adults exposing themselves to the dangers of the hunt.

As abruptly as the wrestling bout had started, it ended. Silverfeet had once more spotted movement nearby. This time it was a fat, slow-hopping bullfrog returning to its breeding pond. Silverfeet pounced. But with growing caution he did not immediately attempt to seize the frog. Instead, he lowered his head and sniffed. Just at this moment the frog jumped, catching Silverfeet by surprise. He ducked and jumped back.

This was Silverfeet's first frog. He was intrigued by this new creature that did not scurry fearfully away but only jumped just as it was about to be nudged. Silverfeet watched the frog for a few moments. It sat still. The pup advanced stiff-legged; the frog did not move. Silverfeet entered into what appeared to be a new and exciting game. He darted forward. Hop—the creature was two feet away. Yelping with excitement, Silverfeet chased it, and this time his nose touched the bullfrog's back. The contact furnished a nerve-tingling shock, and the young wolf sprang away. This strange hopping thing was not only cold, it was actually wet. Repeatedly he nudged the frog with his nose, not quite daring to open his mouth and take it.

After a time he began to get bored, and looked for his sister. When he saw her high-stepping through long grass with tail erect and ears forward, he abandoned the frog and raced toward her, eager to hunt for the mice that he knew she had scented.

The two pranced through the grass, the smell of the rodents strong in their nostrils. Silverfeet pounced once, twice. His paw felt something warm and wriggling, and he pressed down. Then he withdrew his foot and lowered his muzzle all in one smooth action, and when he lifted his head, the tail of a mouse protruded from his jaws. At once his sister went for him, but he turned his back on her and swallowed the morsel whole. The small black pup soon found a mouse of her own and ate it. And now they could hear the call of the parent wolves.

At once both cubs tensed, their bodies quivering with excitement, their noses testing the wind. The calls were repeated. The pups lifted their heads and replied, their young voices thin and querulous, contrasting with the deep, throaty tones of the adults. Now silence. The pups waited a moment; then Silverfeet bounded forward, his sister close behind, and the two pups raced wildly and happily through the forest.

Behind them in the den, the gray pup whined, but did not move.

The parent wolves had killed a deer, a white-tailed buck, and had already fed on the haunches. When the two young wolves met their parents, they became frantic at the sight and smell of meat. But the adults kept their hold on the food in spite of the jumping, whining pups, and ran on toward the den, unwilling to drop the meat until all three pups had a chance at it.

When they reached the old root, the she-wolf allowed Silverfeet to wrench a partly eaten leg from her mouth. He dragged it away to a clump of balsams, and his black sister copied his actions. But the small gray female made no move to capture her share. The mother went to her and whined and caressed the whelp with her tongue, licking her all over, nudging her with her nose. Yet the gray pup did not respond. She was dying; and by morning her stiffened body lay alone under the root.

JULY came furnace hot, its turgid breath seeming to banish every cloud from the sky. The days were humid and still; the nights were alive with the droning of mosquitoes. That year it was a month of almost volcanic fever that scorched the earth, dried the sap in trees, emptied the beaver ponds and sucked life's moisture out of streams and rivers.

The animals of the wilderness sensed the danger of this time and were restless and nervous. Some, the lesser ones, were forever ready to escape, their bodies gripped by taut nerves that would propel them into instant, frantic action. Others, like the wolves, were uneasy, but found value in this month, for its heat had sapped the energy from many creatures and the hunting was good.

It was dawn during the fourth week of the month—a still, hot daybreak alive with the scream of mosquitoes. The sun had inched over the eastern trees, a molten rind of orange with rays of lavender, yellow and red. The scene was beautiful—deadly beautiful. Even the wolves, as they sat on a rocky knoll and surveyed their world, felt the threat that lingered over this day.

Four miles distant, the wind fanned a thin black finger that lanced evilly at the sky. The she-wolf stared at it for a time, then whined. There was fear in her voice. She knew the meaning of that skeletal black wraith: fire had come to the wilderness.

The four wolves stood up and watched the streamer of smoke. They saw it become blacker, spread from a finger to a column, from a column to a mushroom and from a mushroom into a long, ragged wall that began to advance rapidly in their direction.

Soon the orange of flame was visible. Now and then quick explosions sent red sparks high into the air. The fire gained momentum, veering directly toward the place where the wolves stood. Its roar was ominous and thundering.

The wolves howled their terror. The she-wolf broke. Taking one last look at the charging wall of flame, she tucked her tail deep between her legs and turned her face to the rising sun. She ran, and her pack ran with her.

As they fled they were flanked by other forest dwellers. The vixen fox, her cubs at her heels, ran near the pack. Snowshoe hare bounded madly ahead, uncaring about the wolves. Four white-tailed deer passed within yards of the hunters, never even glancing at their greatest enemies. The creatures of the wild were not at war today. All forest life had a common goal: to escape the roaring, galloping inferno.

The smoke was with them, pungent and dark. The wolves redoubled their speed. So did the other animals. Some died running, so full of panic that they crashed into tree trunks. Food was forgotten; all things were—except fear.

The fire roared like some mighty wounded beast. From its maw came ash and sparks that were fanned forward by the heat, to fall, hungry, on other parts of the forest. The staccato crack of splitting wood added percussion to the terror; ignited birch trees, flaring

like Roman candles, lent fury to the kaleidoscopic hell that had been unleashed upon the wilderness.

In the path of the flames sat an owl. It was confused; fear had robbed it of direction. The big gray bird rocked on its branch, attempted to see through the thickening smoke, and hesitated. At last it took flight, but it was too late. The air had become searing hot. The owl's feathers shriveled, curled and blackened, and the bird plunged into the fire.

A she-bear tried to coax her twin cubs to hurry. The young ones had been scorched, and they kept stopping to drag their round rumps over the hot ground, in an effort to appease the sting of their burns. The mother grunted at them, ran ahead a short way, then turned and retraced her steps. Motivated by fear, she growled threateningly and cuffed one cub vigorously with a huge forepaw. The cub screamed. Then she cuffed her second cub and

it too screamed. But nothing could hurry these terror-stricken babies. The she-bear stopped, at a loss. Alone she could save herself, but death was inevitable if she stayed with her cubs. She chose to stay and, powerless, reacted to the fire in the only way that she knew. She roared her fear and anger, and charged into it. She died quickly. Moments later the relentless flames passed over the seared bodies of her cubs.

The fire reached the edge of a small beaver pond, consuming all its vegetation before the flames were split by the water and coursed on, surrounding the pond. In the water many beasts had taken refuge, some swimming in frantic aimlessness, others huddling on the beaver lodge. They all died, even the beavers inside their home. The pond was small; the fire had boiled its water, scalding to death those it could not incinerate.

Ahead of the fire ran the wolf pack, swiftly, panic dominating their instincts. They fled south, unheeding where their pumping legs were taking them. And almost as swiftly roared the fire.

Its heat had already touched the wolves. They began to slow as their lungs choked on the hot air and smoke and fine ash.

Then, blessedly, came a swift river.

The she-wolf led her pack into the current. Downstream they went, struggling for life against this new threat yet feeling the coolness of the waters, unafraid of this rushing, twisting watercourse that carried them away from the merciless fire.

THE two men squatted beside a patch of damp, muddy ground, scrutinizing it intently. One, middle-aged, seamed of face and casual in dress, was slowly wiping mud from a hand obviously at home with farm chores; the other—younger, leaner, wearing hip-clinging jeans and a checkered shirt—was still probing with a bony finger at something etched in the mud. He turned to the farmer.

"Yeah . . . they're wolf tracks. Fresh, too." He stabbed again at the mud. "I'd say two old ones an' two cubs."

The older man stood up and rocked on his heels, scratching his thinning hair. "What're you goin' to do?"

The other was silent for a moment. His fingers were absently caressing the pad marks so clearly defined in the mud. There was a distant look in his eyes, which were directed to the woods at the far end of the farmer's clearing. "Could use strychnine. Sure would love to trap them pups alive, though."

The farmer frowned, and when he spoke his voice was harsh. "What would you want to livetrap them varmints fer? Kill 'em, that's what you're paid fer. Next thing, they'll be into my sheep."

The trapper shook his head slowly. "The fire put those critters down here. The way I see it, they're already heading back north."

"What about my sheep, though? Suppose they kill some of 'em?"

"Listen," the trapper said, rising from the ground. "I can get a hundred bucks for each one of those pups, alive. Dead, I just get a few bucks. Besides, I'm sure they're heading outa here."

"Well, they better be, is all!" The farmer spoke angrily.

"Tell you what. I'll keep an eye on your sheep for the next

week or so. If I see wolf tracks around your place, I'll put out poison. Okay?"

The other nodded grudgingly, and the two turned away.

AGAINST her will the she-wolf had been driven by the forest fire into man country. She was uneasy.

When the four exhausted animals had climbed out of the river at a point where the watercourse made a wide turn and slowed its violent flow, there had been only one thought in her mind: they were safe from the fire.

From where she and her pack stood dripping on the riverbank she could still see the pall of smoke that darkened the northwestern sky, but instinct told her that the inferno was not coming in her direction. So she stood on the grassy bank, head down, mouth agape, sucking great gulps of pure air into her smoke-sore lungs. She was exhausted and battered, even bleeding in several places where driftwood had gouged her on the downriver ride. So too stood her mauled mate and their pups.

As usual the pack waited for the she-wolf to make the decisions, for she was the most experienced. And to her keen nose, the scent of man, an enemy even more dreaded than fire, was strong. So she looked to the shelter of the forest, perhaps a quarter of a mile away, on the other side of a lush green field.

She led. The others came in single file. Their steps were slow, for pads were raw and muscles were stiff, but luck had been with them that day. They had lived, while many others had perished. If their luck held for just a little longer—long enough to allow them to cross the open field and fade into the forest before the eyes of man could see them—all might yet go well.

5

Two months had passed since the fire had driven the wolves into man country. The she-wolf had kept her pack hidden in the wilderness that fringed this small settlement area. She always led them after wild game, remembering the slaughter she had witnessed when her first pack had attacked man's strange, docile creatures. So the farmer lost none of his sheep. He had forgotten about the wolves.

Not so the trapper. He had spent weeks following their progress, had been near them now and then, and had listened as the pack spoke during the full moon. Now he began to plan.

THE scarlet maples brushed bold color onto the canvas of early autumn. September had been gentle and fresh, an insect-free time that filled the two young wolves with joyous excitement. They had learned to hunt, and took pride in helping their parents chase after deer. Often they ventured alone to stalk groundhogs or hare, which afforded them much sport and heightened their predatory instincts.

The cubs, almost six months old now, were half grown. They were lithe, beautiful in an ungainly way, and powerful. The needlelike milk teeth were falling out and being replaced by the strong, gleaming white teeth of adulthood. The pups' coats held the glistening sheen of healthy life, the outer guard hairs long, the silken underfur already thickening in preparation for the oncoming freeze.

Autumn was their testing time, and they seemed to know it. During the final weeks of this season Silverfeet and his sister had to pass their last trials, like students their final exams. But in this classroom, failure meant death, and sensing this, the pups flung themselves wholeheartedly into the business of living.

Early one afternoon the pups awoke, stretched, yawned, and looked to see what their parents were doing. The adult wolves dozed, content to let the pups amuse themselves alone. The pack had brought down a deer the night before and had fed well. The older wolves wanted to enjoy the contentment of a full belly and the pleasure of a lazy day. Not so the pups. They were too full of energy to continue their sleep.

The two young wolves began to play, snarling in mock anger. The game took them away from the shelter of the balsams and down a short slope into a small clearing. Here the two paused, panting; then they were at it again, running and jumping and snapping, their mock growls loud in the afternoon stillness.

Suddenly Silverfeet raised his head and sniffed at a new scent that had just reached him. In a moment he was off, his prancing gait telling the other pup that he was on to prey. She streaked after him. Silverfeet ran faster, his nostrils guiding him unerringly toward a creature that the pups had not met before. Silverfeet had smelled a skunk.

The black-and-white cat-size creature was foraging for insects, carrion or anything else that was edible. He waddled slowly, secure in his awareness of the noxious scent that the twin glands under his tail were capable of discharging.

Startled by the sudden appearance of the two wolves, the skunk stopped, flinging his bushy tail into an upright position and peering shortsightedly at the brash beings who dared to invade his world.

A small creature that did not immediately try to escape them puzzled the wolves. They stopped their wild charge. Silverfeet whined, then yapped excitedly. The quarry remained motionless.

Still puzzled, the young wolves held back. The skunk stamped his front feet. His warning was lost on the inexperienced stalkers. They did not know that this stamping preceded the release of the skunk's powerful, choking spray.

Even as they watched, still hesitating, the black-and-white beast bent his body so his head and tail faced his tormentors. Then the skunk waited, ready.

Silverfeet whined again and made a sudden rush toward the skunk, mouth open and ears stiffly erect, the glint of hunting excitement filling his eyes. His sister copied his actions.

The skunk fired his salvo. Instantly the forward movement of both wolves was arrested, as though a solid wall had come between them and the skunk. They uttered shrill cries of anguish and surprise. Pawing at their muzzles and at their eyes, they began rolling frantically on the ground, trying to suck air into their lungs but receiving, instead, further doses of the oily spray that still surrounded them. As they struggled with this new and horrible enemy, the skunk turned and ambled on its way.

The powerful musk smell reached the adult wolves just as they were rising to investigate the disturbance. They flopped down on the ground again, knowing that their young were not in danger and that they had learned yet another wilderness lesson.

By this time Silverfeet and his sister had recovered slightly from the shock and the power of the fumes. They moved away from where the musk was strongest and rolled over the ground, pushing their faces against the soft mulch that covered the forest floor. Silverfeet and his sister would never forget this experience.

FULL in the cloudless sky, a pale yellow moon beamed soft light on the wilderness. Against the moonlight the velvet dark glowed with the twinkling of a million stars, and now and then could be heard the whistle of fast-beating wings and the muffled voices of geese made restless by the migration urge.

On a bare outcrop of rock the four wolves sat still as statues. They were hungry and would soon hunt, but for the moment they were listening to the night. They squatted on their haunches, heads held high, eyes ahead, ears erect.

Half a mile from the wolves was a small lake, one of those marsh-bordered water holes that dot the northern bushland. In its center, surrounded by cattails, rose a mound of sticks and mud and decaying vegetation. Below, within the darkness of his lodge, an old beaver was grooming himself. Painstakingly he was combing his belly fur, squatting like a ball upon his own tail, one back foot raised and cupped so that its long claws could pass through the hairs of his coat time and time again.

Last winter his mate and young had shared the lodge with him, until one by one they had fallen to the steel snares set in the ice by the man who was now intent on trapping the wolves. The beaver had not mated again. He was too old. Instinctively he knew his time was growing short, and he spent most of it within the safety of his lodge, going out only at night on short feeding forays.

Now he finished combing his fur, then slid his tail out from under him and moved toward one of the two holes that gave him entry and exit to the lodge. Clumsily he pushed himself into the aperture and entered the water.

For perhaps ten feet he paddled under the surface; then he steered upward with his broad tail. As his head broke the surface he snorted softly. He began swimming toward a canal that had been built long ago by beavers, to provide safe access to a heavy stand of poplars on the south side of the pond. Five yards from the canal mouth he paused and circled the area quietly, seeking to detect the presence of enemies. At last he was satisfied. He swam up the canal to a muddy landing place. Here he searched the dark forest again before waddling up the short slope toward a small tree that he had felled earlier that night. He began to feed, stripping the tender bark from the young topmost branches, standing on his back legs and using his tail as a prop.

On their rock the four wolves stirred. The male looked at his mate with a quick flick of the yellow eyes. In unison they rose and one by one bounded down—quick, sleek shadows in the night. The she-wolf pulled into the lead, her mate just a step behind, the pups running in the rear. Once Silverfeet went to take the lead, but he was quelled by a swift look from his father. He knew the discipline of the hunt. He knew also that this was not the time for playfulness. Silently the pack ran.

Soon the wolves reached the beaver pond and the leader slowed. She had scented the beaver. She turned and led the pack in a circle that would bring it downwind of the quarry. Then she slowed again and stopped. She looked at Silverfeet, who sat impatiently beside her. The young wolf rose and went on alone. The she-wolf looked at her daughter, and the young female knew she must remain. This was Silverfeet's hunt. But the she-wolf did not fully trust her inexperienced son. She led the pack in another circle, to intercept the beaver should Silverfeet miss it.

In the moon-splashed forest Silverfeet padded softly. His mother need not have feared. The young wolf knew that this was his test; he sensed that after this kill he would occupy a position of maturity in the pack. Deeply he inhaled the beaver scent.

Silverfeet stopped. Only some fifteen yards separated him from the beaver. A horned owl hooted nearby, and the wolf allowed his eyes to swivel once toward the sound; then he fixed his gaze on the spot where his nose and ears told him the beaver must be. He moved forward, his body tense, his powerful muscles quivering. With infinite care he placed each broad pad softly upon the ground, avoiding dry leaves and brittle sticks that might crack or rustle and warn the beaver. He stopped again, gathering his haunches for the leap. Then he launched himself.

As quickly as he could the beaver twisted his body away from the tree, aiming toward the canal. But he was too late.

The wolf landed lightly after his initial leap, bunched his legs and thrust himself into space once more, coming down just two feet short of the fleeing beaver. In an instant his reaching muzzle found the beaver's wet back, and his fangs bit deep.

The beaver screamed, and Silverfeet braced himself against the frantic struggles of his quarry as it tried to escape the killing grip. The wolf shook his head savagely to the right and opened his jaws as the beaver fell sideways, exposing the underside of his neck. Swiftly then Silverfeet bit into the beaver's throat.

When the rest of the pack arrived, Silverfeet dropped his victim, straddled it and growled a warning to the others that this was his kill.

The parent wolves and the black female stood quietly for a time around Silverfeet. Then the she-wolf reached down past her son's bared fangs and dragged the beaver away from him. She dropped it, looked up at her son and then lay down beside the kill and began to eat. Seconds later the four wolves settled to the meal, and if Silverfeet growled now, his voice held no threat. Rather there was a note of pride in it.

Perhaps it was the success of his kill, or maybe it was the Indian-summer night. Whatever it was, Silverfeet suddenly rose to his feet and wailed his long, melancholy cry. The ululating song galvanized the others, and the forest night was filled with the deep baying of the wolves. Howl after howl sailed over the trees into space, and when it was over, the forest was a place of quiet. Even the very wind had stilled its journey. Then the bark of a fox rang out, and the heart of the wilderness beat again.

IN HIS camp a mile south of the beaver pond the trapper heard the wolf howls. He was lying in the warmth of his sleeping bag, idly watching his smoking fire. At once he sat up, looking toward the northwest. A smile fixed itself on his thin lips.

He had been ranging that section of the forest for four days, looking for fresh signs of the wolves. During supper that night he had been ready to abandon his quest; he was beginning to believe the pack had left the area. Tonight he realized that they had headed farther north than he had thought.

Settling himself back in his bed, he decided to set out after them at daylight. He would first have to return home and load the live trap onto his old truck, but he reasoned that the wolves would rendezvous during the daylight hours. This would give him enough time to reach that part of the forest where he guessed they would be sheltering.

With these thoughts he finally slept.

SILVERFEET's beaver had been but poor fare for the four wolves, so, unaware of man, the wolf pack trotted northward in search of deer. They had caught the scent of the animal shortly after they had stopped howling. They ran abreast, strung out in a line, and traveled thus for ten minutes. Before long they heard the rustling noises of deer, directly ahead, and just past a deep swamp they downed a thrashing body.

For an hour they fed. Then they bedded down for the night in a thick tangle of deadfall and gnarled cedars.

Dawn found them asleep. By full daylight, the sun was a flaming ball hovering over the forest; the day held promise of autumnal warmth. The wolves were content. They woke occasionally, stretched, yawned, changed position and went back to sleep. Today the big hunters were at rest.

6

THE wolves awoke to the crashing of thunder. Heralded by a flashing spear of light that split the air, it roared its sullen anger. For a heartbeat the night forest was illuminated whitely; then the dark became intense while the sound rumbled away.

There were three more flashes of lightning, three drumrolls of thunder; the rain fell in torrents, soaking the earth and the trees and the animals of the wilderness. This storm was the spearhead of winter. Gone was the softness of Indian summer. Full autumn had come, bringing with it cold rains.

Above the forest floor the leaves were torn from their branchlets and whirled into the vortex of the squall. Now and then some rotting branch would snap, the crash of its tumble scarcely audible above the wailing of the wind and hammering of the rain.

The wolf pack lay curled within the tangle of cedars, noses tucked into flanks and covered by their tails. They lay quietly, seemingly asleep yet feeling the wet that soaked their bodies. But there was no fear in them. This was nature's might; it had been experienced many times before by the adults. So the pack rested, sometimes sleeping, then waking to lie unmoving. And toward dawn the rain stopped and the wind lost its violence.

The wolves, grateful for the respite, remained curled in their beds and slept for yet another day. They were still full of meat and would remain here until more time passed and they felt the need for more food.

A MILE to the north the trapper was busy as the rain let up. He had arrived in the area the night before, during the height of the storm, and had waited in his truck for the downpour to cease. He was glad of the wet; it would wash off any vestiges of his scent clinging to the heavy-mesh wire cage that sat in the vehicle's cargo well. The trapper had loaded the cage last night, slipping a cased rabbit skin over each hand while he arranged the trap mechanism. He had been careful to place it on top of the deer hide that he had spread in the back of the truck.

The man was a professional. He knew the keen sense of smell of the animals on which he preyed. And wolves, he knew, were the most suspicious of all wild creatures. Leave just a faint trace of human smell, and they would avoid the trap.

When the rain stopped, he set six snares in hare runways, hoping he would catch at least one for use as bait and to further mask his own scent on the trap. He guessed that the wolves would stay in concealment during the remainder of this day. He thought he had plenty of time to catch a hare or two, unload and bait the trap, and place it in position before dusk, when he would have to leave the area. With these thoughts, he curled up as best he could on the uncomfortable seat and tipped his wide-brimmed hat over his eyes. In five minutes he was asleep.

IN THE bush, life began to stir. Birds twittered as they searched for food; red squirrels raced through the trees, now and then pausing in their quest for seeds and berries, to chatter spitefully.

On the beaten trail where the trapper had set his snares, a buck hare was hopping silently, making his way to a patch of grass. Always his long ears were swiveling, searching out each sound, testing for signs of an enemy. His life depended on his hearing and on his long legs, which could propel him away from danger in bounds of fifteen feet and more. But the threat that faced him now he had never encountered. It lay circular, cold and silent in his path—a cruel, strong wire waiting to choke the life out of him.

The hare stopped. He nibbled at a tender young fern, his jaw moving from side to side. The uneaten portion of the plant protruded from his mouth and slowly disappeared inside it. In a moment the fern was gone, and the hare moved forward again.

At first he did not notice the noose. Its light touch was like the caress of a grass stem. But as he continued forward it tightened about his neck. He jerked his head to one side, trying to free himself, but the steel wire only tightened more. In an instant, panic filled the hare's mind.

With stiffened legs he jumped. The noose brought him crashing to the ground, tightening its hold still more. Again and again the hare sought to escape, and he screamed, a shrill, piercing cry that echoed like some banshee wail through the morning forest. The voices of the day were stilled, as though shocked into silence.

The wolves too heard the cry of the hare. They opened their eyes, listened, then went back to sleep.

The hare lay on his side, struggling but silent. At last, mercifully, his heart gave out and he was still.

THE man in the truck awoke, recognizing the scream. He yawned, rubbed his face with callused, dirty hands and smiled. Reaching for a thermos of coffee, he unscrewed its plastic cup and poured out some of the brew. When he had finished it, he stepped out of the truck.

An hour later the man had unloaded his trap, baited it with the hare's brown body and was back at the truck. He stopped beside the vehicle, his woodsman's eyes sweeping the forest; then he climbed in behind the wheel, started the engine and reversed his way out of the area, content to let time have its way.

It was November, the last full month of autumn. The air was made crisp by the previous night's rain. The hour was late evening. There was a yellow moon peering coldly from a sky illuminated by the aurora, and stars were studding a cloudless firmament.

Silverfeet was the first to stir, sitting up and yawning, and one by one the others followed his lead. He looked at the moon and wailed, and before the echo of his solo had stilled over the forest the others pointed their faces up and vented their emotions. A great gray owl joined them, its deep hoots blending into the song of the pack. Then there was silence.

One by one, led by the she-wolf, the hunters rose quietly and drilled their lean bodies into a steady lope, moving with lithe grace. They ran in a straight line for some time, heading directly for the place where the man had set his trap. But then the leader increased her speed, and she turned east.

However, Silverfeet had grown restless. He left the others and trotted slowly through the forest, stopping frequently to listen and to smell. He was rambling aimlessly, not really hunting, just curious, content to be alone on this quiet foray.

As he passed through an open glade the early morning sun picked out the shine of his coat and the sleek, powerful grace of his young body. It highlighted the fluid, stealthy ease of his movements. Then he was gone, into the shadows of the trees.

He stopped under a tall pine and tested the smells of the forest. A faint, tantalizing odor had reached him. Nostrils quivering, he moved away at a gallop, his keen nose leading him on.

For five minutes he ran, then he stopped suddenly; a second scent had reached him.

Silverfeet sat down. He was puzzled. The first scent he recognized as hare. It told him the hare was dead. But the other odor he had never come across before. While he was not afraid, inbred caution held him back. He could not identify the thing that was making the strange odor. It was not strong, but it was clearly noticeable and it came from the place where the hare was.

A blend of inexperience and curiosity made him move ahead restlessly, shutting his mind to the warnings of his nature. Soon he sensed that the object was near, and again he stopped. Standing with one forepaw raised, he listened for danger sounds. Only the known noises of the forest came to him as he sniffed the scents once more and strove to penetrate the foliage that separated him from the mysterious object. He stood poised for perhaps one minute; then he walked through the undergrowth. He was about to emerge from it when his eyes sighted the object. Instantly he froze. The cage stood deceptively quiet, seemingly innocent. The two-inch wire mesh allowed Silverfeet to see the body of the hare lying on the floor of the trap.

Silverfeet was alarmed, but he was still curious. His eyes were fixed unblinkingly on the cage, alert for the slightest sign of danger. For five minutes he stood staring and listening and smelling. Nothing happened, and slowly the feeling of alarm left him.

He came out of concealment, stopped, stared again and moved forward. Step by step, cautiously.

Now he was but inches from the side of the trap, and temptation prickled his taste buds. He inhaled the hare's odor and reached forward. His nose touched lightly against the cold wires of the trap, and in a flash he leaped back and prepared to run.

Reassured by the inanimate character of the trap, he advanced once more, this time moving more resolutely. Deliberately he touched the mesh with his nose, and he did not shy away. He pressed against the side of the trap, like a child who flattens his nose against the window of a candy store. The drool ran from his mouth; in his mind he could already taste the hare. He pushed harder at the wire, and when he could not part it as he would have done a bush, he sat on his haunches and puzzled over his problem. He rose and began to walk around the trap, easing along its length, his head always turned so he could watch the hare. After making almost a full circuit, he came to the entrance.

Silverfeet stopped, tense. First he thrust his head into the square opening and held it there. When nothing happened, he took a tentative step with his right front leg, and paused. Nothing. He brought his left front leg forward, shuffling his hind legs so that his head and shoulders were inside the trap.

He stopped and waited. There were no threatening signs. Then he could stand it no more. Quickly he ran forward, intending to grab his quarry and escape, because he still did not fully trust this strange thing.

As his eager teeth grasped the coveted hare, there was a sharp, metallic click, followed by a loud crash.

Silverfeet had released the hare as soon as the first sound impinged on his mind. But it was too late. Even as he was turning, his body a blur of speed, the sliding door had clanged shut. He slammed jarringly against the heavy mesh.

Stunned by the jolt, he sprawled back, legs kicking in the air. Already, blind fear had taken hold of him, and with it came the instinctive curling back of his lips and the baring of his fangs. A low growl came from his throat. He snarled and snapped, and flung himself at the relentless mesh again and again.

He bit at the wire, gashing his lips and gums, so that blood flowed. He snapped, growled and whined, smashing his body into the unyielding steel prison. The lithe, beautiful wild creature, the hunting dog to which creation had given such powers of endurance and intellect, had in a trice disintegrated. And in its place was a mindless thing, frantic, malevolent, tortured.

THE pack was calling. Long and mournful, their voices rose and fell as the three remaining wolves sought to bring back the one who had wandered away. The she-wolf and the male and their black daughter called and called again, but no answering howl reached them.

It was early evening. The sun had slipped out of the sky, seemingly chased by gray clouds drifting in from the northwest. Ahead of the clouds had come the chill of early winter and a kaleidoscope of sullen colors that forecast an autumnal storm. The fat, tumbling clouds were edged with rose and mauve, while here and there feeble fingers of sunlight played gently against them. On the forest floor a blue gloom made wraiths of the wolves as they traveled silently through the evening.

The she-wolf was leading, her mate and her daughter trailing, as she went toward the place where the trap had been set. Fear filled her mind. Instinct told her that Silverfeet would have answered the calls of the pack had he been able to do so. She knew that something had happened to him, but still she plodded on, unwilling to turn her back on her son.

She stopped and howled again. At once the male and the pup raised their muzzles and the three wailed to the wilderness. No reply came. The pack moved again, and presently it reached the place where the trap had been, but was no longer.

The lingering scents of man, wolf, hare and steel confused and frightened the wolves. Suddenly the black pup bolted, streaking north, followed by the she-wolf and her mate. The wolves fled as though pursued by demons, all thoughts of Silverfeet banished now from their minds; the smell of man spurred them away.

SILVERFEET was many miles away from where he had been trapped, his steel prison bouncing in the back of the hunter's truck. The cruel buffeting of the cage and the sight and smell of man had combined to intensify his terror.

The captive bore little resemblance to the healthy wolf of but a few hours ago. Blood flowed from the cuts on his lips and gums. His front paws were torn and bloody, their claws ripped off during his futile battle with the steel cage. As he lay crumpled in the bottom of the trap, his hair, which earlier that day had reflected the sunlight, was dull and matted, worn away in places by his frantic struggles to escape.

He had been savagely fighting the cage when the man had come earlier that evening. Lost in fear and wild combat, the wolf had realized the man's presence only when his captor was standing a few paces away, a satisfied smile on his lips.

For an instant the wolf and the man stared at each other, and in that instant an undying hatred was born. The wolf stilled his frantic scrambling and crouched on the cage floor, his yellow eyes meeting the look of his captor with such a blaze of fury that the man shifted uneasily.

The man felt fear, even though the wolf was held by the cage. And because the captive, despite his helplessness, had been able to make the man uneasy, the trapper became ashamed of his emotions and he conjured up hate for the wolf.

Avoiding the fury that glared from those eyes, the man muttered to himself, hesitated, then looked around for a stick. He found a dead pine branch with a jagged point. Keeping his distance, he pushed the thin pointed end through the mesh to poke cruelly at the wolf's face.

Silverfeet backed away, retreating against the far wall of the cage only to swing back fast and snap at the object that seemed to be an extension of the hated being who stood leering outside the cage. From his throat emerged a deep, savage growl. There was a flash of bloodied fangs. The stick snapped and the man, unnerved, jumped back, letting go of the pine branch.

The man cursed loudly. His voice mingled fear and hate. Again the beast had humiliated him. It was unforgivable that a caged wolf could instill such fear in man, he thought. Ashamed, the man darted forward, picked up the stick and smashed again and again at the cage, cursing the wolf. And when he stopped, the stick in his hand broken short, he was sweating with rage.

No such complications existed in the mind of the wolf. He knew fear—rank, bitter-tasting panic. And he knew hatred—wild, blazing hatred for the man, for his cruel voice. But he stayed crouched, alert for another attack, and he kept his eyes glued to his captor.

7

THE memory of those fearful moments when he was face to face with his enemy still lingered in the wolf's mind, mingling with the new terror that came with each jolt as the cage bumped and bounced in the truck bed.

But nature was beginning to aid Silverfeet, dulling his mind, triggering the mysterious reactions that come, sooner or later, to the wild thing that finds itself suddenly caged. He lay huddled on the floor of the trap, his body flaccid, except when it was seized by the quivering that accompanies shock. Now and then he licked his bloody lips. Eventually he lay spent, his eyes closed, his breathing slow. He lay like that for almost two hours, and then the truck squealed to a halt, throwing him violently against the cage.

Silverfeet backed to the center of the trap, eyes open again. The sound of the truck door opening caused him to bunch his muscles for a spring, and he waited as the trapper approached.

Wolf and man stared at each other again. Once more the hate in the yellow eyes of the wolf caused the man to flinch involuntarily. For perhaps ten seconds they stood thus: the man with one hand on the tailgate, the trapped wolf crouching, his gaze fixed upon the man's face. Then the trapper laughed, seeking to cover his fear. With an air of bravado he unhooked the tailgate and let the

heavy metal drop with a resounding clang; to his surprise, Silverfeet did not jump at the sudden noise.

From the truck box the trapper took the two iron hooks with which he had lifted the cage into the truck. He fastened one on each side of the cage, steeling himself against any possible lunge by the wolf when his hands came near the wire.

Silverfeet had risen, his eyes moving from side to side, all his attention centered on the hooks and on the man's hands. By now he knew that his tormentor was safe while he stood on the other side of the wire barrier.

The wolf wasted no more energy in futile charges. With the patience that all wild things can muster, he waited, biding his time, still hoping to get free. He no longer had any fear of the man, only hatred. The wolf's fear was of his imprisonment—the mesh walls of his cage, the noises it made as it was dragged toward the end of the truck.

Soon half the cage was overhanging the dropped tailgate. It balanced there for a moment while the trapper made sure that the catches held the sliding door securely. With a thin-lipped grin twisting his face the trapper deftly released both hooks simultaneously and let the cage fall to the ground.

The toppling cage propelled Silverfeet upside down against its roof. As the wolf scrambled madly to keep his balance, the cage landed with a crash. His head hit the wire and his body somersaulted, so that for an instant his entire weight pressed down on his neck. The force with which his head struck the cage stunned the wolf; he felt pain through a dim haze. The cage settled on its side and was still, and Silverfeet lay panting, helpless.

"That'll teach you, varmint!" the man said loudly as he again fastened the hooks in the mesh and began dragging the trap toward his ramshackle clapboard house.

Bringing the cage to a stop beside the door of the house, the man released the hooks and gazed speculatively at his captive. He nodded to himself, having arrived at a decision. He returned to the truck, closed the tailgate and went back to the house.

As he passed the cage he gave it a kick that sent it rocking again, and he laughed loudly as Silverfeet sought frantically to retain his footing. With his hand on the knob of the house door, the trapper turned for one more look at the wolf.

"Mebbe a night in that cage'll cool you off, varmint," he said. And he turned and entered the house.

THE man's name was Morgan. He had a first name, but few people knew it. To his face his neighbors referred to him as Morg; behind his back they called him other names. Though farmers and ranchers who lost stock to coyotes and foxes paid him to get rid of the raiders, he was not a man who inspired liking. Because his living depended upon the killing of animals, he had become coarse and unfeeling. A hare strangled in a trap represented merely food and a few cents for the pelt. A beaver was a big prize; it offered dollars in exchange for the tedious task of skinning, and the added reward of musk scent, which he used to attract other creatures to his traps.

So Morgan lived alone in a frame house steeped with the smells of decay, skins tacked to his walls to dry. He followed his trapline and he killed and he skinned. He followed the only trade he knew, and felt scorn for the men who would pay him to be their executioner because they would not willingly undertake the job themselves.

That night he lit his fire, cooked his supper and stretched out on his bed without a thought for the trapped wolf that lay suffering outside his door. And Morgan slept, snoring loudly.

SILVERFEET was awake, listening to the noises inside the house. His nose sensed many odors, some familiar, others strange and frightening. One smell dominated all—the smell of his captor, an odious, sickening aroma.

To the wolf, time seemed endless. He was hungry, he was dirty and cramped, and his body hurt. And so, like his mother when she had faced starvation alone, Silverfeet sought solace in sleep. He sank down, curled himself into a tight ball, closed his eyes and slipped into a sleep that was more coma than slumber.

The moon came up. It hung full, round and lemon yellow in the sky, bathing with its light the semiconscious wolf. It seemed to be comforting him, telling him that it could offer a link with his pack, for its rays penetrated the entire forest.

As the night grew older the moon weakened, and one by one the stars paled. Silverfeet remained curled up. His nose was buried in his flank, his breathing lethargic. He was a creature lost, despondent, distraught, the spirit of the wild in him destroyed.

That was how Morgan found him when he emerged from his house later that morning. The man opened his door, yawned, and scratched his shirt-clad torso. He looked at the cage. His black eyebrows rose in surprise; then he frowned. He was disturbed by the wolf's apathy, by the absence of that ferocious spirit of the previous day. But he felt no pity. His concern was for the profit that he hoped to realize from the live animal. Slowly he approached the cage. He stopped, bent to look more carefully at the wolf and straightened again, still frowning.

Tentatively Morgan kicked the cage, a soft nudging kick that merely rocked it slightly. Silverfeet moved his head a little and opened his dull eyes. Beyond that, nothing. Morgan cursed, then retraced his steps to the house. Presently he emerged carrying a small piece of raw meat. Carefully, using a stick, he poked this through the mesh and let it fall a few inches from Silverfeet's nose. The wolf ignored it. He closed his eyes again and thrust his head deeper into his flank. Again Morgan cursed.

His problem was simple. If the wolf died, he would get nothing for his efforts. Silverfeet's coat, dry and matted and bare in patches, would yield little on the fur market. And no zoo would pay for the live wolf in its present state. Morgan pondered, standing by the cage and watching the captive.

Finally he decided. He would keep the wolf in larger quarters until it either recovered or died. But where to house it? He had no suitable pen, and construction of a proper enclosure would take time and money. Then he remembered the old henhouse. It was built of logs and had a metal roof and one small window. This would do, if he nailed wire mesh over the glass and cut a small, square hole in the bottom of the door, through which he could put in meat and water. With that he went to work, and an hour later he finished the job.

Going back to the cage, he found that Silverfeet had not moved. This pleased him now, for it would be easier to put the wolf into the henhouse if it remained docile.

With the hooks he dragged the cage to the henhouse, opened the door of the building and lifted the cage over the low step, making sure that the sliding door of the cage faced the door of the new prison. Then he solved the problem of releasing the wolf without being attacked or allowing it to escape. With a brace and bit he drilled a small hole near the top of the henhouse door. Next he found a brass cuphook and screwed this into the roof of the building immediately above the door of the cage. He found some twine, threaded it through the hole he had drilled, passed it through the hook in the roof and then tied it to the top of the sliding door of the trap. He released the door's catches.

Silverfeet watched with little interest. Morgan looked at the wolf for a moment, then went out of the building and firmly closed the door, securing it with a stout catch.

He grasped the string and pulled, and the sliding door of the cage eased upward. When it was fully opened, Morgan tied the string to a nail and stooped to look through the hole that he had cut in the henhouse door. A smile creased his lips. Silverfeet was showing more interest. He had lifted his head and was eyeing the opened door of his cage. Morgan left, going to the house for water and some more meat.

When he returned, Silverfeet was standing with his head outside the cage's opening. With a stick Morgan pushed the meat and the pan of water just inside the small trapdoor; then he left.

The henhouse was small, twelve feet square. Though its log walls were solid, they were badly chinked with lime mortar, and through the cracks a few rays of light and a little fresh air reached the gloomy interior. The one small window, grimed and covered now with wire, served only to admit a little diffused light. The floor was concrete, but it was covered with old litter.

Silverfeet remained standing inside the wire cage for half an hour after Morgan went away. He wanted to leave the confines of the trap but was suspicious of this new place; his instincts forced him to check every nook and cranny. As his mind began to

549

function more normally he became conscious of hunger, and particularly of thirst. His nose told him that food and water stood near the door. Confidence slowly returned to him now that he was alone, and at last he stepped onto the henhouse floor.

This small action further awakened his dulled mind, and as he became accustomed to the sights and smells of the place he relaxed a little. Slowly most of his keen intellect returned, and the urge for self-preservation began to course through him once again.

He walked stiff-legged toward the door and the container of water, but when he detected the odor of his enemy, he curled his lips in a silent threat. He stood bristling before the metal pan, debating whether or not to charge at it. In the end his intellect won out. He realized that, though connected with the man, the waterpot offered no threat. He went to it and drank thirstily.

The meat attracted him and he put his nose to it, but again he encountered Morgan's smell. He walked away from it.

He prowled now, exploring every inch of his new prison. Instinct urged him to escape, and he forced his injured feet to endure the pain of walking. Once he tried to scratch at the small trapdoor, but he whimpered when his raw toes encountered the rough wood. An hour later he gave up and slumped despairingly in the darkest corner of the henhouse, lying on his side, licking his lacerated front paws. Then he slept. And he had a dream.

Freedom came to his sleeping mind. Once more he was with the pack, running a deer. The chase was hot. The snow was deep and crusted, and the prey was floundering. The sleeping wolf whined his eagerness as in his dream he spurted alongside his quarry and readied himself for the lunge that would cause the deer to break stride and fall. In his sleep Silverfeet's legs were moving, twitching at first, then pumping intermittently. It was this that woke him.

At first he could not understand his surroundings, and he quickly rose to his feet. Memory returned. With it came the terror of captivity and hate for the man, and he vented his feelings in the only way he knew. He raised his head and howled his sadness.

Morgan heard the sound and was pleased. If the wolf could

howl, there could be little wrong with him. He went to the hen-house, unfastened the trapdoor and bent to peer inside.

Without warning, a snapping fury thrust at him. Such was the speed of the wolf's attack that the sharp canines laid open to the bone the index finger on Morgan's left hand. Morgan cursed and slammed the trapdoor shut and backed away from the henhouse, fear pumping his heart. He clutched at his mutilated finger and ran for the house. There he dressed and bandaged his wound, his face pale, his mouth contorted by rage.

As the pain in his finger fanned his hate, Morgan suddenly became aware of his predicament. He could not get at the wolf without shooting it, and shooting it would bring him no profit. When Silverfeet recovered, he would have to be returned to the cage for shipment to the zoo. He had not stopped to think about this when he had turned the wolf loose in the henhouse. He could not simply open the door of the henhouse and seize the wolf, that was obvious.

Morgan cursed the wolf again. He was beginning to wish that he had not captured it alive. Had he set out poison, he thought, he might have seized two or three wolves and their prime hides. As it was, the pack had left the area, and here he was with a live wolf on his hands.

Morgan found a bottle of whiskey and a glass and poured himself a stiff drink. Nursing his finger, he sipped the whiskey and thought about his problem.

IN THE henhouse Silverfeet paced back and forth with renewed vigor. Once more his eyes glowed with a fierce, wild light. Once again his keen brain was fully alive. Urged by hunger, he had eaten the meat that Morgan had left.

He stopped suddenly, facing the window. He backed as far away from it as his confinement would allow. He crouched an instant, then launched himself forward, hitting the wire screen with such force that it was pushed outward and his stiff paws smashed the glass.

He recovered his balance in midair and landed lightly on the floor. He paused to lick his right paw; the glass had inflicted a cut.

Morgan, who had heard the smashing of the glass, appeared outside the window just as Silverfeet launched himself again.

The wolf was already in midair when he saw the man. His growl was low but charged with hate. The man saw the fearsome gaping mouth of the wolf coming straight for him, the blood that Silverfeet had licked from his paw staining his jaws crimson. He was horrified.

Morgan ducked in sudden panic, expecting the furious wolf to land on top of him. The wire held, though it creaked in protest and bulged out a little more. Pieces of shattered glass fell on Morgan, and one of them cut his neck slightly, so that blood flowed. Silverfeet charged at the wire again, still growling.

But Morgan was no longer there. He was running for the house, continually glancing over his shoulder, his face ashen. He slammed the door of his house when he reached it, as though fearing the wolf would come charging after him.

Silverfeet hit the wire once more. Again it bulged, and two small gaps appeared between the window frame and the wire. Had the wolf charged two or three times more, he would have found his freedom. But he stopped. The man had gone and Silverfeet's front paws throbbed, the cut from the glass bleeding profusely. The wolf lay down and licked his hurts.

In the house, Morgan had recovered somewhat. He held a loaded rifle; he also held a hammer and had thrust some nails into his mouth. Carefully he opened the door and peered out, the rifle ready. But outside, there was no danger.

Walking softly, Morgan went around to the back of his house. There he found a square of plywood large enough to fit over the window. He thrust the hammer into his back pocket and gripped the wood clumsily with his bandaged left hand. Holding the gun in his right, he walked toward the henhouse. He knew that the wire over the window could not withstand many more of the animal's lunges. He hoped he was still in time.

Slowly he approached the henhouse. Silverfeet heard him coming and stood up. Morgan stepped carefully to a corner of the building, and there he paused. All was quiet. Leaning the rifle against the henhouse, he put both hands to the plywood, and holding it before him like a shield, he ran to the window and slapped the wood against it, pressing it there with his weight. Instantly the wolf charged and almost knocked the wood out of Morgan's grasp. But it held.

Knowing that the wolf would leap again, Morgan quickly slipped a nail out of his mouth and grabbed the hammer from his back pocket. Pushing against the wood with his left hand, he started the nail home with three strong blows. At this moment Silverfeet charged and the plywood bounced under Morgan's hand; but again it held, and the man finished driving the first nail.

By the time Silverfeet jumped at the window again, Morgan had banged home his second nail. Quickly he put nails all around the wood, then went in search of larger nails and two pieces of two-by-four lumber. These he fastened against the plywood, feeling sure that the wolf would not be able to escape.

Silverfeet charged again, but this time the solid wooden barrier threw him backward and he crashed heavily to the concrete floor, hurting his spine. Whimpering, he limped to a corner.

Once more his mind saved him, taking him into the twilight zone that borders on coma, and he lay down and stayed thus for two days, ignoring the man when he came with meat and water. And Morgan worried again.

On the second day, thirst drove Silverfeet to seek water. Painfully he uncurled himself and stood up. He was so weak that he could hardly keep his balance. He hobbled across his dark prison toward the waterpot and drank, finishing all it contained. With his nose he pushed at a piece of half-rotten meat, but he spurned it, walked back to his corner and set about trying to ease his sore body.

He licked his wounds and then rose again, the pangs of hunger forcing him to go back to the fetid beef. Silverfeet gulped it down. Then he nuzzled the waterpot again, but it was empty. So he lay down in his corner and slept. It was a true sleep this time, the kind of refreshing sleep that would allow his body to regain some of its lost strength.

The next morning Morgan was elated to find the meat gone and the waterpot empty. He fished out the pot gingerly with a stick and took it back to the house. There he replenished the water, and from the carcass of a deer that he had killed the previous day he cut off a portion of meat. Back at the henhouse he opened the trapdoor and retreated a step, waiting for the wolf to charge. But by now Silverfeet knew that the opening of the trapdoor meant food and drink, so he held back, some instinct telling him that if he were ever to escape he must first build himself up again.

When the door closed, Silverfeet went to the food. He ate and then he drank, and although the meal was meager, it gave him strength. But his newfound energy increased his longing to be free again, to run wild, to find his pack. Since he could not have these things, he lay down to sleep, to seek forgetfulness.

One day followed another. The wolf ate his ration of meat and drank his pan of water. Never was there enough meat to round his belly nor enough water to slake his thirst. Once every morning Morgan opened the trapdoor, threw in the meat, hooked out the waterpot, replenished it and pushed it back in with a pole. He was very careful to keep his hands out of reach of the wolf's fangs.

At the end of ten days Silverfeet's injuries were almost fully healed and he had regained some of his strength. But he was thin, and his coat was still dull and brittle and rubbed away in places. Though he walked more surely, he still favored his front paws, the nails of which had not yet grown back.

Daily Morgan peered through the trapdoor to note the wolf's condition, and every time his face came level with Silverfeet's eyes, the wolf's savage growl made him straighten hurriedly. Then, at the end of two weeks, Morgan came with another man. The two stood outside the henhouse talking. Silverfeet had been curled up in his corner. He arose and padded over to the trapdoor, standing before it, head down, teeth bared.

"He's not in bad shape now," Morgan was saying. "A bit thin, but he'll do, especially after a few weeks in a proper cage."

"Well . . . a hundred dollars is high for a wolf," the second man said. He was of medium height, and fair. He spoke softly.

Morgan frowned and scratched his head. "Listen, you don't know the trouble I had with that varmint. Even got my finger bit, right down to the bone. He's worth a hundred."

"No, not to me, he isn't. Tell you what. I'll give you seventy bucks, and that's it. And not till after I've seen him."

Morgan wanted the money, but now, perversely, he did not really want to sell the wolf. Silverfeet had become a symbol of power. He still feared the wolf, but unconsciously he was glorying in his hate for him, in keeping him a helpless prisoner. Greed and hate jostled each other in his mind. But greed won.

"Okay," he said finally. "You can have him for seventy, an' damn the varmint. He's caused me enough trouble already."

The zoo man carried a flashlight. He had it ready as he squatted to see into the henhouse. He told Morgan to open the trapdoor.

"Watch yourself," Morgan warned. "That wolf's a killer!"

He opened the trapdoor. Instantly Silverfeet's muzzle thrust itself through the square, growling and snapping. Both men jumped back. There was fury in Morgan's eyes as he picked up the stick that he used to push the water into the cage. He jabbed at Silverfeet's face, but the wolf ducked.

"No need for that," the zoo man growled.

He bent down again and shone the light into the henhouse. He could see Silverfeet standing defiantly in the center of the floor, facing the trapdoor. After a few minutes the man rose.

"Okay. I'll take him for seventy dollars. But how do you figure to get him out of there without losing an arm?"

"I already thought of that. I made me a catching pole, with a noose at the end. I figure to open the trapdoor like I did just now, wait for the varmint to come, and slip the noose over his head. It's wire, an' the pole's oak. Both will hold him. When he's played out, I can shove him back in the trapping cage."

"If you don't choke him to death," the other man replied. "Tell you what, you get him caged and bring him to my place alive and in good shape, and you get the money. Okay?"

Morgan nodded and closed the trapdoor with the tip of his boot. "Pay for the gas?" he asked.

"Yeah, I'll give you an extra five."

They shook hands, and the zoo man left. Morgan stood contemplating the door of the henhouse, and there was pleasure in his eyes at the prospect of half strangling the wolf.

8

MORGAN rose early the next morning in anticipation of his battle with Silverfeet. After breakfast he donned a heavy bush coat and thick leather gloves, and went outside to fetch the crude catching pole he had made. He examined it carefully. It consisted of eight-foot oak stock some two inches thick at the butt and tapering to an inch at the end. Along its length he had fastened heavy metal eyelets. Through these ran a wire. This formed a running noose at the end, which the man could tighten or slacken by adjusting his hold on the wire. Once it was around the animal's neck, it could be held just tight enough to control the beast without killing it, if the operator was careful.

Morgan wanted revenge. And he was afraid. He was determined to choke the wolf until it became unconscious; then he would open the henhouse door and drag Silverfeet by the neck to the cage he had placed outside the henhouse. Morgan tested the noose once again. It worked smoothly.

The man walked slowly toward the henhouse. He lingered over the short journey, hating the wolf for creating his fear. Then he stood three paces away. He knew that Silverfeet had heard him, knew it as surely as if he could see the wolf standing, ready to charge. Inwardly Morgan quaked. He forced himself to think of the seventy dollars, goading himself into action.

He had thought out his moves a thousand times already. Quietly he slipped the catch on the trapdoor free, then eased the door open. He stood back. Nothing happened. Morgan moved forward again and slowly lowered his left hand, as though to reach inside the henhouse. In an instant Silverfeet's muzzle and those fearful teeth appeared in the opening. Morgan thrust the noose at the wolf's head. When Silverfeet saw and felt the wire he bit at it, and Morgan was able to slip the noose over his head and pull it tight.

Bedlam erupted inside the henhouse. A fierce growl ended in a strangled gasp as the wicked noose contracted, but the wolf thrashed and pulled wildly, contorting his body with such fury that twice he almost had his neck broken.

Morgan, pale and fearful, could only try to hold on to the pole. Once the wolf's mad struggles almost pulled it out of his hands. But slowly the man and his pole and his choking noose began to win, as Silverfeet's writhing body lost power.

The wolf panicked as never before. His breath was a grating torture; his throat, bruised by the noose, felt on fire; his stomach convulsed and grayness filled his eyes. He fell on his side and tried feebly to rise. At last he was still. His breath came slow and rasping. Then even this sound sank to a pathetic whisper.

Morgan was smiling broadly. Fear had left him. The wolf was at his mercy and he enjoyed his moment of triumph. He wanted to savor this victory. He kept the noose pulled tight.

But presently Morgan began to worry. Had he killed the wolf? He slackened the noose a bit and waited. A weak gasp followed. He loosened the wire still further and by bending low was able to see that Silverfeet's chest was moving slightly.

Now was the time. Again tightening the noose, Morgan lifted the catch on the henhouse door and opened it some six inches, maintaining his grip on the pole but allowing it to slide through the trapdoor. He peered inside. Silverfeet lay stretched out, but Morgan saw that he was not quite dead.

The man opened the door wide now, shifting his grip on the pole from his left hand to his right. When the pole was free of the trapdoor, he was ready to drag the nearly dead wolf to the cage, which he had placed near the henhouse the previous night. The sliding door was up, in position to slam down as soon as he released the noose from the animal's neck.

Again Morgan relaxed the noose just enough to allow a little air to enter the wolf's lungs. Silverfeet remained unmoving, but his body responded to the oxygen. The black that had filled his brain turned to gray. The wolf became semiconscious, but he was too weak to move.

Morgan began dragging Silverfeet. The noose tightened and again cut off the air, but when the wolf's body flopped onto the ground, the noose slackened slightly and more precious oxygen entered the struggling lungs.

Silverfeet was heavy. Morgan knew that he had to be careful

not to break the wolf's neck. He eased the limp body slowly toward the cage, pausing often enough to allow the animal to breathe. Soon he had Silverfeet beside the entrance. This was the moment Morgan dreaded most. To get the wolf into the cage, he had to let go of the pole and put the wolf in with his hands.

He hesitated, his mind full of dread. His hesitation allowed Silverfeet more air, and somewhere in the wolf's dulled brain the instinct of life responded.

Morgan dropped the pole, grasped Silverfeet's back legs and swiveled him around. Quickly he went to the wolf's shoulders and pushed him into the trap, hindquarters first, until only his head protruded from the cage. Morgan again took the pole in his hand and tried to shove the wolf far enough inside to allow the drop gate to close. Now! Swiftly he bent down to loosen the noose. It slipped off Silverfeet's neck and Morgan started to rise, reaching for the trip that would lower the gate.

At that instant the wolf's eyes opened. With horror Morgan met the baleful yellow gaze. He stood transfixed for perhaps five seconds.

Five fleeting, precious moments of time turned the balance. Without the murderous noose around his neck Silverfeet was able to draw great gulps of air. Drunkenly he rolled over from his side to his chest. The trap could not close against him. His head and part of his shoulders were outside the door.

Morgan's face became ashen. He knew with a dreadful certainty that the wolf was going to get away; he knew with terror that Silverfeet intended to even the score. Fear bit deep into Morgan, robbed him of reason. He might have saved himself by taking immediate action. But he stood as though frozen.

Yet for the wolf, time was an ally. Silverfeet let his body rest, drinking air as a thirsty man sucks up water. The indomitable vigor of the timber wolf struggled against great odds, and it won.

Silverfeet heaved his body upright and began moving forward, his teeth bared. Morgan drew breath and began to back away.

It happened then. Silverfeet, using every scrap of strength in his tortured body, launched himself at Morgan.

The wolf's front paws hit Morgan square in the chest. Man and wolf crashed to the ground and became as one swiftly thrashing body. Morgan screamed, and the vengeful teeth closed on his throat. The contest was short.

Mercifully, Morgan lay still. And the wolf slumped over the body of his enemy.

HALF an hour later Silverfeet staggered upright and hung his head. The wolf had been too weak to move away after the struggle, and his instincts had told him to lie still. Now he trembled, and he labored for breath that did not want to pass by the torture in his throat. In his mouth the blood of his foe tasted bitter.

Silverfeet was hungry, but he could not linger in this place of awful memory. He began to move, slowly, clumsily. The open air was clean and sweet. And he was free.

He walked northward, mysterious urgings guiding him toward the boreal forests that were his heritage. He wanted to run, to unleash his body into the lithe, mile-eating lope that had once been his, but he could not. He was a half-dead creature sustained only by will. For an hour he walked through scrubland that held scant cover. Twice he saw farm buildings in the distance and he skulked by them. Once a dog barked at him but dared not leave the safety of his porch to chase a wolf.

At last, exhausted, he crawled under the thorny shelter of a dwarf juniper bush. Its small, sharp needles forced their way under his coat and scratched his skin, but it was the only cover that he could find, and he could not go on. He closed his eyes and sleep came to him. Overhead the weak sunshine pierced the last shreds of morning mist, highlighting the tracks that Silverfeet had left on the muddy ground.

IT WAS late afternoon, and the zoo man had become impatient with Morgan, who had promised to deliver the wolf by noon that day. The trapper's failure had brought the zoo man to Morgan's isolated house. He sounded his car horn as he got out from behind the steering wheel, and began walking toward the ramshackle dwelling. Then he saw Morgan's outstretched body. He knew at once what had happened. He forced himself to go near the body and reach down and place a hand over the still heart. He was pale when he rose and ran for his car. He turned the machine around and raced out of the yard. He drove fast all the way to town, and there he reported his finding to the police.

FOR five hours Silverfeet remained curled under the juniper, gripped by the deep sleep of exhaustion. It was near evening when he awoke. The light was failing, and the clouds hung gray over the countryside. Rain would soon come. The wolf lay unmoving for some moments. Something had penetrated his sleep and had alerted his trigger-taut instincts.

He listened, his ears upright and swiveling, and gradually a sound that would have defied human hearing caused him to scramble from under the bush and stand statue stiff, head raised, scanning the far distance. In another moment he forced his stiff body into a fast lope to the north. The faint sound continued to pursue him. He knew it for what it was: the sound made by the thing that had carried him to the trapper's house.

But Silverfeet did not know that the machine contained three men armed with rifles. Still he ran, knowing that man's presence meant fear and danger. He had learned his lesson. He would never forget it.

The country was flat and there was scant cover; the three men in a four-wheel-drive vehicle were gaining on Silverfeet, even though they had to stop often to check his tracks. To them it was of no importance that the wolf had responded in the only way he knew to the hatred implanted in him by the man. A wolf had killed a man and this could not be tolerated. In the sky a government helicopter was guided by the men in the car, who had signaled the pilot by radio. Only the coming darkness offered hope to the exhausted wolf.

His lope had dwindled to little more than a walk. He was weak, his body hurt and his front feet were bleeding. Once he stopped in the gloom and saw over his shoulder the twin lights of the pursuing machine. He gulped air painfully, for his swollen throat restricted his breathing, but he forced himself to run faster, ignoring his pain.

At first he did not separate the sound of the automobile from the roar of the helicopter. Then he directed his gaze to the sky and he saw it, like a strange bird, coming fast.

He was lucky. The low cloud cover and the lateness of the day helped his body blend into the color and contours of the earth. The two men in the helicopter did not see him, though they were a mere hundred feet from the ground. The roar of the rotors and the sudden swooshing sound immediately over him caused Silverfeet to swing off his northerly course, ducking wildly toward the west. And luck again helped him.

He had almost reached the shelter of a willow break that bordered a small stream when the pilot sighted him. In another instant the helicopter swept over him again, but this time the passenger was leaning out of the plastic bubble, a loaded shotgun in his hand.

Silverfeet dodged just as the gunner squeezed the triggers, firing both barrels. Had the wolf swerved a second later the end would have come. As it was, only one pellet hit Silverfeet, raking his ribs and opening a shallow furrow in his skin.

The burning pain of the wound, the bark of the gun and the din of the helicopter's engines drove the wolf to extremes of which he would otherwise not have been capable. Instinct made him run a zigzag course to the willows no more than fifty yards away.

As the helicopter turned to come in for the kill, Silverfeet thrust his body into the tangle of riverbank growth. The shadows were deeper there, and the wolf disappeared from sight. The helicopter pilot radioed his information and said he was turning back. It was getting too dark for the aircraft.

Silverfeet crouched trembling in the center of the willow thicket. He licked his wound and noted the retreat of the flying thing. But almost at the same moment he heard the approaching Jeep. He moved deeper into his shelter of brush. He was spent. If man was to find him, it would be in this place. The wolf crouched low and waited, all his senses keyed to the nearing danger.

Light flashed into the thicket as the vehicle slowed, then stopped. Voices reached Silverfeet, and he bared his fangs.

"We should've brought the dogs," said one man.

"Yeah. I don't fancy going in there to look for him. Can't see a thing, and that animal's a killer," another man replied.

The third man was the one who had found Morgan's body, the zoo man. He felt a coldness deep inside him. "There's no way that you'll get me in that place. If that beast is holed up in there, he could grab any one of us fast and the others couldn't shoot. No, I'm for letting it go tonight. We'll come out in the morning with the dogs and see if we can pick up his trail again," he said.

For a time the men stood by their Jeep discussing the matter. At last they climbed into their vehicle and left.

When the sound of the engine had faded, Silverfeet left his hiding place and again headed north. After an hour, full darkness came, aiding the fugitive in his slow, stealthy passage between two large farms. Had he been stronger, he would have circled them, but tonight he could not afford the time and energy. So he skulked from scrubby bush to boulder, seeming to slide along the ground, to disappear totally in the hollows of the earth.

He was almost past the first house when the barking of a dog disturbed the quiet. Silverfeet forced himself to go faster. He was about to enter an area of scattered evergreens when he realized that the barking was nearer. The dog was giving chase—foolishly, for he was alone.

Silverfeet knew he could not outdistance the dog, so he backed into the shelter of a balsam tree whose lower branches swept almost to the ground. Here the wolf waited, his back protected, his fangs ready to meet whatever was coming.

The dog was but ten paces from the wolf when a whistle pierced the air and a man's voice called him. But the whistle and the call alone would not have stopped the dog. It was a hidden instinct, an ancient warning that made him halt, probe the scent of the stranger, then quickly turn for home. In another instant he was racing back to the house, his tail tucked between his legs. Silverfeet came out of hiding and continued slowly on his way.

The wolf's suffering had become intense. He felt himself driven onward, although his every impulse told him to stop, to sleep, to recuperate and to find prey. He needed food desperately. But he continued on, always heading north, forever seeking cover. He would not give in. He simply limped on, panting, aching, bleeding. He was indomitable, every fiber denying defeat, every hidden strength being summoned.

He struggled on for several more hours, passing three other farms without raising an alarm, and gradually he neared a treed region that offered better cover than the open fields and marshy bushlands over which he had passed. Toward dawn he reached the trees, and luck was with him. He had stumbled upon a low-lying wooded section of land that had been abandoned for years. Storms had furnished many places of shelter where trees had crashed and formed an almost impassable labyrinth of junglelike decay. Silverfeet eased his failing body toward the largest tangle. His tracks became indistinct in the marshy land, and his scent was diluted by the strong odors of rotting vegetation.

Before him lay a large dead elm. Under the overhang of its bell-like root system, nature had eroded a perfect refuge. Stopping only long enough to quench his thirst from a pool of stagnant water, Silverfeet crawled under the roots. He curled himself into a ball of misery, and within seconds he was asleep.

HE WAS awakened by the baying of hounds during late afternoon of the next day. He stayed in his shelter, his senses slowly returning. He listened. The hounds were close, perhaps half a mile south, but Silverfeet's keen ears could not detect man.

He rose and went to quench his thirst again. Although his body was stiff and sore, the long sleep had restored some of his lost energy. After drinking, he faced the clamor of the dogs, deciding on the course that he should follow. He felt stronger, though he knew that he could not outrun the pack. So he crawled back under the root, wedging himself tightly into the small space so that only his head and shoulders were vulnerable to attack. Then, resting his head on his paws, he waited.

More than a mile south, the three men who had pursued him yesterday stopped their vehicle and were preparing to follow their dogs on foot. Each carried a gun. To the west and east, similar groups of men with dogs were scouring the country. The entire neighborhood had been alerted, and all men living in the area were eager to join in the hunt. All of them wanted the life of the wolf.

The group closest to Silverfeet's hiding place paused on the edge of the wooded marsh, listening to the bugle calls of their dogs. They knew by the hounds' voices that the scent was fresh, but faced by the barrier of downed timber and spongy moss, they hesitated, remaining on high ground.

The zoo man turned to his two companions. "That's pretty tough country in there," he said.

"Yeah," one of them replied. "I hope the dogs will flush him out. Don't fancy wading in through that mess."

The third man lifted his rifle, pumped a shell into its chamber and fired a shot high over the trees. "Mebbe if we take potshots, he'll break cover," he said.

The other two nodded, and one at a time they too fired their rifles into the woods.

Silverfeet stayed where he was. He knew the dogs had lost his scent by the way they had scattered. Two had gone beyond his hiding place; the third, a grizzled veteran, was still circling about, snuffling at the ground with determination.

Suddenly this hound's voice became deeper and more urgent. He had struck the trail and he ran on it, the fever of the hunt making him reckless. Ten minutes later he found Silverfeet. He stopped just outside the root overhang and called in earnest. He was answered immediately by the other dogs, who were by then almost half a mile away.

The dog and the wolf stared at one another, the hound noisy in his bugling, the wolf silent, deadly, his fangs ready. Suddenly Silverfeet hurled himself at the dog.

His rush was so swift that the hound was unable to dodge it. In an instant Silverfeet's fangs had fastened over the dog's jugular vein. Moments later, without even a yelp, the hound lay dead.

He left the dead hound and went out to meet the second dog, who was approaching from the northwest. He ignored the third dog, who was more distant and coming from the east. The wolf's fighting instincts were so aroused that he no longer felt his wounds or the effect of his long fast.

The hound advertised his presence with his loud voice. The wolf walked wraithlike to meet him, moving slowly and purposefully. Soon only forty yards separated the two, but they could not see each other through the denseness of the woods. The wolf crouched behind a tangle of fallen trees and waited. When the dog rushed by, Silverfeet leaped on him and closed his fangs on the back of his neck. The hound yelped in fear and pain. For a few moments both animals struggled, growling. Silverfeet released his hold just as the hound overbalanced. The dog rolled and started to rise, but the wolf came in quickly for the kill.

The men knew what had happened when they heard the dog cry out. So did the third hound. He had reached the body of the pack leader and he stopped beside it, raising his voice loudly, calling to the men. The hunters cursed and began to scramble frantically through the tangled growth. But by then Silverfeet was running north, putting distance between himself and his pursuers.

The hunt ended then. The men knew that with only one dog they could not hope to bring the wolf to bay. They knew also that they were facing a formidable creature, for this was an animal tortured by suffering, fear and hate.

9

THE young muskrat walked in a humped and ungainly fashion, looking for a place in which to den. He was one of the many creatures who every year are turned out of their birthplaces and forced to seek living quarters in other parts of the wild. This one had wandered far in his quest. He had inspected bank dens along the northern length of the creek on which he was born, only to be repulsed ferociously by their occupants. He had stopped often in marshes and beaver ponds to check the muskrat lodges there, but he had found these places occupied too.

When Silverfeet saw him, he was crossing an open meadow, heading for another marsh. The muskrat was so anxious to find sanctuary before the snow fell that he had become careless.

The wolf cut him off. But the other animal had courage. He stood on his back legs and squealed and gnashed his teeth, jumping for Silverfeet every time he went in for the kill. Had the wolf been healthy, the battle would have been over in seconds, but Silverfeet's movements were slow and clumsy. Twice the rat's chisel teeth fastened on the wolf's muzzle; twice Silverfeet shook his head, sending the rat flying several feet. Silverfeet waited until the agile rodent became tired from its furious exertions. Then his jaws found it, and it died.

Silverfeet ate his prize slowly. When he had finished, he licked himself clean, crossed the meadow and disappeared among the evergreens that crowned the top of a ridge. He was exhausted, and his only thought now was to find a secure sleeping place.

After a time he bedded under a newly fallen spruce, bellying his way under the thick cluster of green branches to a place that afforded perfect concealment. He slept all that night and the next day, and when he awoke at sundown he looked different.

He was still lean and his wounds were raw, but the meal of muskrat and the long sleep had worked wonders. No longer did he carry his tail between his legs; he did not flinch when he sucked air into his lungs. Instead, he carried his brush high and held his head up, and his ears were constantly alert for prey.

It was late afternoon when Silverfeet killed again. This time a snowshoe hare was his victim, but only by luck. The hare had been resting under a downed tree, and the wind had favored the wolf. The animal was so startled when it noticed the wolf a few paces away that it leaped too hurriedly, hurtling headlong into a tree. Before it could recover, Silverfeet was on it. Again he ate and felt a surge of new strength.

At sundown he took the prize away from a fox that had killed another hare. This time, when he had finished eating, he felt almost satisfied.

A week passed. The wolf was in better condition, but he still went hungry. He was too slow for most game.

He continued to head north, putting more miles between himself and civilization every day. The going was slow, because he was forced to hunt almost constantly. Day after day he edged toward the big country of spruce and pine and tamarack, lonely for the sight and sound of his kind.

Twice he made detours to avoid isolated farms. During the second detour he saw a man moving about the farmyard, and the great hate that he still carried with him welled up and brought a snarl to his lips. But he kept traveling, ever alert for prey though seldom getting anything more substantial than a hare.

When he awoke from a long sleep during the eighth night, he found himself in a new world. Snow had fallen steadily all night and lay five inches deep in the open places of the forest. For the first time in his short life, Silverfeet felt the chill of winter against a coat that was still bare where it had rubbed against the cage. The snow offered only one blessing to the animal: he could eat it and quench his thirst without having to go in search of water.

He stood and shook the snow from his body and he shivered. Above, a shining crescent moon hung in the blue-black sky. He felt alone and melancholy. He howled, but his wail elicited no reply. Again and again he howled before he stretched and started trotting north, for the northland beckoned, and the wolf was anxious to find his home range. Night was his time, and if he ran well, he might reach true wilderness by morning. He set out at a good lope, moving with greater ease than he had done since his escape. Around him the night glowed and the sounds of dark were trusted companions to the running wolf. By dawn he had reached muskeg country. This was wilderness. Here, he knew, he would find other wolves. The journey had been long, but he had survived. At last he was free.

IT WAS late December. Deep winter had come, bringing cold and snows and biting winds. But life persisted in the brittle grip of freeze-up.

Under the heavy snow mice scurried through tunnels as they journeyed from feeding haunts to nest chambers, reasonably secure from the hunters of night. By day, red squirrels ransacked the forest, alert for overlooked pinecones.

In the sheltered places of the forest, where the evergreens mantled the floor with their spreading branches, the snow was less deep and was crisscrossed with tracks. Weasel, fox, wolverine; deer, squirrel, grouse—all had left their marks.

The trees stood in serried clusters, their branches weighted with snow. In these trees were the northland birds. The gray jays could spy food no matter how cunningly concealed. The little fluffed-up chickadees, with their bright faces and black caps, called their names as they bustled about in the evergreens, searching for insect eggs. The nuthatches, with thin, black beaks and hoarse, nasal voices, walked upside down on trunk or branch as easily as they walked upright.

This vastness of forest and river and lake was Silverfeet's kingdom, but right now it was a lonely one. Night after night he launched his wild, sad cry, always hoping to receive an answer.

The wolf had finally regained his strength. His old hurts were fully healed. His coat was prime; the long, shining guard hairs and thick, silken underfur insulated his body.

There were times when the hunting was bad, when it seemed that luck had deserted him, but hungry nights and days are normal to a wolf. He could endure them now that he had recovered from the depredations of Morgan and his neighbors. And then he would strike and gorge, and his body would store energy, building itself up for the next time of failure. This was his natural life, the way of the wild, and he understood it.

His loneliness was something else. Deep social instincts drove him to run with a pack, where each shared in feast and in famine, in hardship and in ease, where companionship made endurable the coldest night. He still remembered his own pack: his mother, his father and his small black sister. And at these times he thought of the one who had parted him from them, and the hate grew in him like an ulcer. He vented it on prey, tearing, growling and snapping at his victims long after he had killed them.

Normally Silverfeet, like all wild creatures, would not have known the meaning of hate. He would have killed fiercely but dispassionately when hunger drove him to the hunting trail; he would have braved the rivalry of his own kind during mating season. But whatever violence came his way would not have been inflicted because of hatred or vengeance.

The hate that had been aroused in him by Morgan would linger until the wilderness, in its compassion, restored him fully.

As a sphere of orange sun dispelled the shadows of predawn, Silverfeet crept from his den under a downed spruce only two hours after he had curled up for sleep. He had hunted well last night, cornering an ailing deer in a deep snowdrift and effecting a quick kill. He had gorged and then settled in for what usually would have been a long sleep. But restlessness woke him, and he stood and stretched his powerful frame.

He sat then and howled, waited a moment and howled again. When no answer came, he trotted from the shelter and turned north. He kept loping all through that day, forced to obey the urge that drove him on. And so he ran until night and fatigue stopped him. Then, finding a shelter, he curled his body nose to tail, closed his eyes and slept.

All that night he remained a tight ball of breathing fur, but when the sun tipped the trees, he set out north again, his head and nose pointing down. In this way he ran for an hour.

Suddenly he stopped. He had reached a place of numerous tracks, and his nose told him that these had been made by a pack of wolves. Into his eyes came a gleam of joy; his tail wagged for the first time in weeks. He sniffed at the paw prints, inhaling the smell of wolf; then, ecstatically, he began to roll in the snow, his eyes half lidded in joy. At last, after one great kick at the air with all four paws, he bounded to his feet and, nose to the trail, ran swiftly after the pack.

Half an hour later he found the wolves resting within the bower of a tight ring of spruces. He stopped before he saw them, and let their odors penetrate his mind. And from within the trees the resting pack scented Silverfeet.

At first the six wolves merely lifted their heads and pricked up their ears. Then the pack leader, a brindled male, rose and stood facing the place where he knew Silverfeet waited. The five other wolves rose also. They watched their leader and one by one lifted their hackles as he had done and stood silent and stiff, waiting for the stranger to show himself. This was a ritual as old as time itself; it said clearly that this pack judged strangers cautiously and with mixed feelings.

When Silverfeet stepped softly into view, the pack was tense, showing that it was ready to attack if the leader so decided. This is the way of the wolves. A stranger of their own kind may or may not be accepted, depending on the mood of the pack and of the stranger. And although Silverfeet had never before encountered such a situation, his instincts told him that he must use caution; that, eager though he was to become a part of this pack, he must obey the ancient ritual.

He strode slowly toward the others, his movements showing submission to the will of the pack. But his tail wagged eagerly, and his lips peeled back in a lupine smile. After a few yards he stopped, wagged his tail more vigorously and whined, the noise both a greeting and an appeal.

Some members of the pack began to relax; one twitched his tail in a half wag. But the big leader retained his aggressive posture. He took a step toward Silverfeet, stopped and growled. Immediately the rest of the pack stiffened again. Silverfeet advanced another three steps, still wagging his tail, whining now and then.

Perhaps a faint scent of man still adhered to Silverfeet, or perhaps his size and obvious power threatened the big brindled male. Whatever the reason, the leader was not disposed to allow him to join the pack. The leader growled again, and this seemed to signal the pack into action. The wolves moved forward and surrounded Silverfeet, who bowed a greeting. This too was customary. Even when a pack was prepared to accept a newcomer, it first tested him. And again, Silverfeet knew this instinctively.

Suddenly the leader charged Silverfeet, hitting him with his right shoulder and knocking him down, then snapping at one of Silverfeet's flailing legs. This started the other pack members, who at first offered only token aggression, their bites hard enough to hurt, though not enough to draw blood. But not the pack leader. He bit Silverfeet's rump, drawing blood. The sight and smell of the wound put frenzy into the rest of the pack, and Silverfeet, startled by the pain of the bite, found himself rolling and dodging under their feet as he tried to avoid the snapping, flashing teeth that sought him from all directions.

Silverfeet knew now that unless he escaped, he would be killed. He heaved himself upright and fled, racing swiftly into the spruces.

The wolves did not follow. They had rejected the newcomer; that was all that pack law required.

Silverfeet ran through the forest, and loneliness returned. An hour after his encounter with the wolves he stopped, sat down and cried his anguish. He licked his injuries, which were not severe; the worst was where the pack leader had sunk his teeth into his rump. After a time he moved on. He was hungry, so he walked with stealth, scenting constantly and stopping often to listen. By late afternoon he had killed four snowshoe hare, and his hunger was appeased. He settled for the night.

THREE days later Silverfeet was still traveling north through a land heavy with timber and rich in game, a forest of stately beauty.

The young wolf had eaten well since his brush with the pack. But his longing for companionship seldom left him. He howled often, and while maintaining a northerly direction, he systematically quartered the forest, forever searching for another wolf pack. Occasionally he found old tracks and eagerly followed them, only to stop and howl despondently when the tracks ended, covered by fresh snow.

One night he uncurled himself from his bedding place and looked up at the fullness of a sparkling moon. He sat and contemplated the shining disk and he howled, a long, deep, mournful baying that rang through the trees and over the lakes. As he ended his song, he hung his head, drew breath and began to point moonward again to vent his feelings a second time. Just at this point a chorus of answering howls came to him out of the night.

Silverfeet became transformed. His ears pricked forward; then he lifted his broad head and sang in full voice, a new note replacing the nostalgia that had been in his howl for so long. For a time he and the pack called to each other; then Silverfeet ran toward the sound of their calls. Soon he was on the edge of their rendezvous. The howls had stopped; the pack had scented him, and now they waited quietly for the stranger to show himself. Silverfeet hesitated, to assure the wolves that he came in friendship, not wishing to startle them by a sudden appearance.

Presently he moved toward the place where the pack was sitting, stepping as he had done before, slowly but with determination, not attempting to conceal the sound of his arrival. In a moment he saw eight wolves sitting in a semicircle. The ritual began anew. Silverfeet stopped, wagged his tail and bowed submission. He stood upright, tail still wagging, then advanced again and repeated his greeting. The pack waited.

In another moment they rose as a unit and advanced, surrounding him. The leader was a female; she walked up to Silverfeet and extended her nose to him. For a fraction of time the nine wolves stood poised in the moonglow.

Suddenly the leader pushed Silverfeet, signaling the ritual attack. He was snapped at and rolled over, but he offered no resistance. He knew by their actions, by their bloodless bites, that this pack would accept him.

One by one the wolves lost interest in testing the stranger and wandered off under the trees. Silverfeet had come back to his own. Five minutes later the pack was at rest, and Silverfeet lay with them, close to a young female about his own age. In his eyes shone contentment. He curled up and sighed his happiness.

Two years had passed since Silverfeet had killed Morgan and escaped into the northland. In that time he had grown to full stature, inheriting the size and power of his father. He had been taught anew by his companions the laws of the wolf hierarchy, and he had obeyed them. He had accepted his place, low in caste, until his size, strength and self-confidence asserted themselves and he climbed the social ladder. Eventually, he attained such respect that he now led the pack.

He and the young female by whose side he had stretched out that day had become companions immediately, but the two did not mate until the following winter, when Silverfeet was almost two years old. And that spring Silverfeet had fathered three pups.

The pups, he discovered, belonged as much to the pack as they did to their parents; often one or another of the pack wolves fed the growing pups after a successful hunt. At first Silverfeet kept a wary eye on his companions, but as he saw the affection all of them showed for his young he relaxed, and later he helped to look after other pups as well as his own.

It had been a good year for the pack. Game was plentiful, and all the pups thrived. Some of the young wolves of breeding age left the pack to seek mates, so it did not grow beyond the point of efficiency. And this too was the law of the wild, which dictated that through death or migration each pack should multiply only to a size where there would be food for all.

The warm sun of late June felt good on his back. Silverfeet lolled, taking his ease this afternoon after the previous night's hunt, in which he and his pack had killed a bull moose. He lay on a knoll near the den, and there was pleasure in the eyes that settled, every so often, on the five pups nursing at the female's side. Around him some of the adult pack members reclined also; it was a soft, balmy day of contentment for Silverfeet.

The sky was clear, and the air by its very softness instilled a sense of peace and well-being in the pack. A small bird sang, invisible in a bush. Somewhere, high in a tree, a red squirrel chattered. A stand of aspens rustled their heart-shaped leaves, and above them sounded the huskier sighs of the pines.

Silverfeet rolled onto his chest and yawned. He grinned. And suddenly, lying there, he aimed his head at the sky and vented his pleasure in a series of musical calls. At once all the wolves joined him, some sitting, others standing. Their voices rose and fell in a spontaneous concert, prompted by a whim of joy.

The pleasing melody drifted over the forest and was done. Silverfeet yawned again and rolled onto his side, resting his head upon one big paw.

Once, years before, he had cried anguish. Today he cried wild.

"The single most potent force in my life," says Canadian naturalist and wildlife writer R. D. Lawrence, "is my consuming interest in living things, from mouse to man." Indeed, Lawrence has been exploring nature and writing about it ever since he was a child growing up in the coastal city of Vigo, Spain, where his English father worked as a journalist.

After stints as a reporter and editor in London and in Winnipeg, Canada, the author served in the British army during World War II. He then returned to the place of his heart—the wilderness—and wrote more than fifteen books on the subject, including the memoir *The North Runner*, a Condensed Books selection in 1979. *Cry Wild*, his first novel, is based on some of his extraordinary experiences in the northern Ontario forests.

R. D. Lawrence

Lawrence relates one particularly harrowing event he faced while homesteading alone as a young man. "I was working deep in the woods when suddenly I found myself surrounded by eight large timber wolves, all of which howl-barked as they circled me, twenty feet away. Terrified, I stood with my back to a tree, clutching an axe, sure that I was going to be torn to pieces.

"Eventually I forced myself to break out of the circle. To my amazement, the wolves allowed me to leave in peace. When I returned later, the wolves had gone, but they had left behind the remains of a fresh kill. I realized then that I had unwittingly interrupted them as they fed. Yet instead of attacking me, they had cleverly conspired to scare me away.

"That day I lost my deep fear of wolves," Lawrence says. "Since then my admiration and liking for them has grown steadily."

The author lives in Norland, Ontario, with his wife, Sharon.

ACKNOWLEDGMENTS

Page 8: map by George Buctel.

Pages 179, 197, 211, 223, 237, 252, 264, 277, 297, 309, 323: fabric renderings by Steven Schindler.

Page 362, line 21; page 459, lines 34–35, 37: from the song "It's a Long, Long Way to Tipperary" by Jack Judge and Harry Williams, copyright © 1912 by B. Feldman & Co., London. Copyright renewed, Chappell & Co., Inc. All rights reserved. Used by permission.

Page 372, lines 8–9: from the song "The Battle of New Orleans," copyright © 1957 by Jimmy Driftwood, published by Warden Music Company, Inc.